CUP

(Second Edition)

Rachael K. Kasper & Robert E. Wills

Welcome to England in the 1920s

This was the decade they called, 'Roaring'. Cars were called motors, modern music was jazzy and upbeat, cinema theatres played silent films. In 1927, a new cinematic wonder emerged with synchronised sound with the picture. Hemlines rose to scandalous heights and dancing in clubs was a youthful indulgence. Modern appliances made life easier with Hoovers, electric washing machines, and electrical kitchen appliances. Central heating systems began to take the chill away from the dampness of an English winter. The telephone was a new and accessible way to communicate whilst more traditional styles of communications remained as etiquette dictated. Your news came to you in a daily or weekly newspapers or by radio which was called 'the wireless'. People were either struggling to conform to past social standards or struggling to flee from previous rules of conformity.

Amid the noise and bustle of the 'Roaring Twenties', midway through the decade, a subtle thunder rolled throughout England. The aristocracy and class system was dying. Old families with old money were no longer able to compete with a steadily growing middle class. Their fortunes dwindled quickly as they fought to sustain themselves in the face of ever-increasing costs of running a massive estate. Women were working outside of the home, either by choice or by necessity. Education was increasingly available to even the lowliest citizens and was compulsory for children.

Complicating matters, the economy came to a crossroad. Without work, some people were forced to travel to ply their trades or had to leave kith and kin to seek jobs in larger cities and towns. Although it was against the law, children did work long hours in squalid factories to help support their families. The cushion of finding employment as a servant to an aristocratic family was wearing thin. Whilst the rich were struggling to stay rich, the poor became even more desperate in their bid to survive. The most stable employment were occupations that remain so, even into the modern age. Medical professionals, officers of the peace, shop-keepers, and grocers have always been necessary components of a community. The middle class had come to stay.

Family units were traditional and often multi-generational. People who were considered upper-middle class at the time could have afforded household staff, but on a far more modest scale than the aristocracy. It would not be unusual for a such a family structure to include a father who owned his own business, a mother who stayed at home, and children who were strictly brought up to conform to society's rules with the help of a trusted nanny who was frequently the provider of a child's earliest education. Charitable works, planning entertainments, and maintaining correspondence through the post, would fall to the adult women in the home. A housekeeper and, possibly, a cook would shoulder the less desirable tasks. Parents who travelled on holiday with their children brought their nanny to care for them if the adults wished to pursue leisurely amusements where the presence of children would not be permitted or desired.

Laws regarding all of these changes in society needed to change, as well. Those changes attempted to keep pace with new attitudes and reassessments of resources. There were evolving laws regarding families, transactions, education, business, and many other issues having a direct impact on a changing society. Surprisingly, this legal evolution failed to address things we take for granted today, such as working conditions and quality control in manufacturing. The legal process was and is in a constantly evolving state.

Health care was as good as one could afford, although an increasing number of hospitals were exclusively dedicated to the treatment of the poor. Physicians came to a patient's own bedside if they were ill. Babies were born in hospitals in ever increasing numbers because the medical circle began to treat pregnancy and childbirth in the same way they managed illnesses. Midwives were required to have an education and training as a nurse if they were to assist at a birth by the demands of the medical establishment. This led to the extinction of the sort of midwife you would call upon because you trusted her for having delivered dozens of babies, not because her credentials were in order. Even with these medical advances, many women chose to bear their children at home.

What you have just read have a common thread. Humanity. Regardless of technology, cultural milieu, education, or location, people are and always have been people. Understanding a story is enhanced by an appreciation of the background, improving it with colour and life. Such a history transports you into the story as an integral part of it, not just as a casual and voyeuristic observer. With this, we close our greeting and open our invitation for you to join us on a journey that begins...

In England, 1925

Dear Mum,

If you don't have anything to do right now, you might wish to take a moment and hear about this unusual situation that happened in our town. It seems that a young woman turned up at the home of a couple nearby. Turns out, mum, that she cannot hear, speak, read or write. Even sadder, she had signs of terrible abuse. These days, as you know, times are trying here. This poor young woman must have been living in abject poverty since she wore only ragged clothing when she appeared. I feel for these souls who need so much and have so little.

At any rate, the family, the Thorpe's, are good people. Mrs Thorpe instantly refused to allow this young lady to leave the house until they were able to find out who she was and where the abuses came from. It hasn't been easy for them, and they've had to develop hand gestures to try to communicate with her. Rather smart, I'd say.

She is a very sweet, shy young lady but has such a fearful way about her. She also seems very curious, as if everything 'round her is new. I would guess she might be between nineteen to early twenties in age. If I know you, Mum, you would just want to tuck her in your pocket, help her, and keep her safe. The affection and care that I've seen from the Thorpe family towards her is like no other generosity I've witnessed before. I just hope they can help her in the way she needs. I think of the situation often, and it weighs heavily on me, at times. Since I'm involved in a way, through my work, I'm not at liberty to speak of this to just anyone, and you've always given my tales a good listen.

Again, mum, if you have the time, read this and tell me what you think. It will take you on a journey. Tell dad I said hello and will see you both in a fortnight.

Love always,

Harrison

Chapter One
Petworth, West Sussex, England.
26 December 1925

She trudges along the road. Icy daggers of wind threaten to tear away her ragged garments. Its cruel talons punish her for venturing out so poorly clad against the elements. She draws her arms up over her chest, fists clenched in front of her neck. Shivering, her gaze is drawn upwards to the streetlamp's light, partially obscured by the steady snowfall. Stopping in front of a house, she stares at it. Coming three paces closer, she peers at windows full of sheer lace, illuminated from within. Shivering again, she walks to the door, glances from side to side then fixes her sight on a shiny brass door knocker, the wind whipping matted hair against her face.

John is not at home. Johanna, all of eighteen months old, is asleep in her cot, tended by their housekeeper and nanny, Sarah Brown, who has also turned in for the night. Anna Thorpe teas tea, heavy with milk, and selects a few biscuits from their tin, arranging a tray for herself. The nagging whisper hearkening a message of something happening, and soon, follows her from the kitchen to the sitting room. It is a shadow that cannot tap her on the shoulder and reveal itself, yet hints of an inner instinct she has learnt to trust. She sets the tray of tea and biscuits on a side table and settles into her favourite chair with a small bit of comfort awaiting in the form of a book. Rupert, their faithful dog, a Jack Russell terrier, watches her with his comical head-tilt, turns 'round several times and plops down next to her chair. Anna smiles down at him, scratching his ears before turning her attention to the novel in her lap. Crackling sounds from the fireplace and fairy lights from the Christmas tree are just distracting enough to divert her fragile concentration from the story, causing the words to melt into squiggly lines. Sighing, Anna closes her book and reaches for her teacup. The porcelain chases the chill from her hands as she takes a long throat-warming sip, and looks out the window, feeling lonely without John. Wind rattles the panes of glass next to her, sending a shiver up her spine as if she hears icy fingernails on a white chalkboard. One tug draws her shawl from the chair back to her shoulders and two thuds mark the landing of shoes on carpet. Anna tugs the shawl about her shoulders and

1

tucks her feet underneath her skirt. Not having spilt a drop of tea, she takes another chill-chasing sip.

Still at the haberdashery shop he owns, the most reputable shop of its kind in the county, able to boast the local elite and gentry as his clientele, John Thorpe rings his wife, Anna. The device rings several times. The familiar click of the receiver brings a smile to his lips, anticipating the sound of Anna's voice. She sounds startled as if she had been deep in concentration. Her favourite book, no doubt.

"Anna, I will need to stay later than usual. Lord Ashton wishes to speak with me about something specific for a state occasion in London. It shouldn't take long since I know his tastes and measurements, but he was insistent on speaking with me immediately. This must be a momentous occasion. He's on his way, now."

Her sigh tells him she is unhappy that he will be late. A cheerful voice, though, tells him not to worry and to take his time since everything at home is as it should be. This is the Eve after Christmas and Anna would rather have him at home. Both of them sense an unspoken unease of late which has unsettled the household in subtle ways. He appreciates her efforts to seem cheerful and patient, even when he knows otherwise and does the best he can to set her mind to rest.

"Sweet one, I miss you, and I love you. He's here, so I'd best go. 'Till then."

He rings off and opens the door to greet his wealthiest and longest-standing patron.

Hanging up the receiver, she looks at the device for a moment, almost hoping it would ring again and it would be John. Shaking her head, she reaches down to stroke Rupert, her constant shadow. Anna walks out of the kitchen and back to her chair in the sitting room and sits down, taking her cup of tea to warm her hands. Staring into the flames heating the room from the fireplace, she feels a small peace struggling its way into her spirit. Imagining the flames take on dancing shapes, she shakes her head, wondering if she is more fatigued than she thought.

"Yes, Rupert, we'll go to bed after John comes home and has had a proper supper."

She stares into the fire, allowing its heat to penetrate into her bones. Rupert comes to attention and barks, running halfway to the front door and stops, staring at it. The odd feeling in Anna's chest causes her heart to beat faster. She places her teacup down, gets up, and hurries to the door. Unnoticed, the thump of her book landing on the floor and the swish of her shawl landing next to it leave evidence of anxious haste. She opens the door and steps back, beholding an unfortunate thing, wearing no coat. Only tattered clothing stands between this girl and frostbite who jumps back a little, almost falling from the steps. Her face is filled with fear, eyes and mouth wide open, her arms clutched about herself. It would be impossible for Anna's heart to harden against her. The girl's eyes dart a glance into the house, then back to Anna, making unmistakable gestures showing the poor waif is hungry. Anna considers as she takes in her thin, grubby form, she might be too frightened to speak.

"Come in, come in. Yes, you must be famished. I'll get you something to eat."

She waits for the girl to enter, but she stands, shivering, and staring into the house. Leaving the door open, Anna hopes the warmth will entice her to come indoors. Walking into the kitchen, Anna gathers cheese, bread, and smoked meat in a tea cloth and ties the corners together, nice and snug. She hurries back to where the lass waits, standing on the top step, and hands her the bundle with a compassionate smile and a nod. Contrary to Anna's social experience, the girl just takes the food, looks down, makes her way down the steps, and begins to walk away. Closing the door, Anna shakes her head as she walks back to the kitchen, trying to put her finger on what does not seem right. What is glaringly wrong is the fact that this lass is out where neither man nor beast should be on a night like this. She must rectify this and persuade the girl to come back.

Berating herself for grossly lacking in hospitality, she dashes out of the kitchen and into the night, forgetting her coat in her haste to find the girl. Waving her hand, she calls after the girl.

"Miss...Miss? Come back..."

The girl does not turn 'round or acknowledge the urgent invitation to return. Anna stops, watching the girl trudge away with her shoulders hunched and head bowed down. She runs along the walkway, catches up to the lass, pats her arm to attract her attention, wondering if, perhaps, the wind had made the sound of her voice fly away.

"Miss?"

The girl springs aside at Anna's touch, looking down at her arm, and drops the parcel of food to the ground. She kneels, looking up at Anna with wide eyes and a flinching manner as she scrambles to gather the food and wrap it up as quickly as she can. She finally stands, returning the food to Anna, recoiling with a visible shiver. The poor girl's breath comes out, sharp puffs of fear in the frosty air, punctuated by falling snowflakes. Anna cannot fathom why the girl would show such terror in this situation. She looks at this hungry, cold, and destitute lass, and to prove that her generosity is not a cruel joke, as the girl holds out the parcel of food.

"No, this is for you, but please come back with me. It's too miserable for you to be out here. I'll give you a hot meal and sort a place for you to stay the night."

Finding it odd the girl just continues to stare at her with a steady but wary gaze, Anna holds out her hand to the girl and gestures for her to follow, hoping she is not too afraid to accept kindness. They watch each other for a few moments more, then the girl nods and lowers her gaze as she allows Anna to lead her back to the house. Once inside, with the door shut against the elements, Anna smiles at her unexpected visitor. Details of her appearance emerge for the first time in Anna's perception. She guesses her age to be, perhaps, eighteen? Twenty? As thin as she is, it is hard to estimate, but given the form underneath the tattered rags, she is not a child. Even Rupert is curious as he sits by the sitting room door, watching their guest with a tilt of his head one way, then the other. She motions for the girl to follow her to the kitchen where she takes some leftovers from the cold box and begins to prepare a warm meal for the girl. Anna observes her out of the corner of her eye, their visitor backed into a corner like a frightened animal. As the food warms on the cooker, Anna watches the girl look 'round the room, her arms crossed in front of herself, shaking, her breathing laboured, and licking her cracked lips. Her gaze settles upon Anna, and she smiles at the lass.

"My name is Anna. What's your name?"

Anna waits a few moments, waiting for an answer and is perplexed with her single response of staring with occasional blinking. With a sudden and gut-wrenching epiphany, the silence becomes dense like smoke from food smouldering in an overheated pan. What if the girl is too terrified to speak? What if she cannot hear? What if... Digesting the possibilities and allowing her practical nature to take the reins, Anna sets her mind to draw a bath for the girl so she will be warm enough to enjoy a hot meal. Perhaps, this shall inspire the girl's trust in her intentions. Nourishment and bathing are both, apparently long overdue. Turning the burner down on the cooker where the stew pot is heating, she turns to the lass and smiles. She grapples with the problem of communicating bathing if the girl cannot, as she suspects, hear. She hopes she is wrong about the girl's ability to hear, and the girl is just too afraid to reply. Pointing to the loo just down the hallway, Anna pantomimes scrubbing her arm, then flares out her skirt a little, as she speaks what her gestures mean.

"I'd like to draw a bath for you so you can wash and I'll fetch a dress and clean under things for you to wear."

The girl continues to stare at Anna who nods at the girl, holding out her hand in a small motion to follow her, noting her cautious stance has not changed. Slowly, the girl follows her, lingering back several paces, furtively glancing side to side and behind her as they walk. Arriving at the loo, their guest watches Anna fill the tub with warm water. She takes clean towels, puts them on a chair next to the tub, drapes a flannel over the spigot, and lays fragrant soap on the ledge made for that purpose. Anna points to the girl and points to the tub filled with warm water. She points to herself and points to the door, hoping the girl understands she will give her privacy.

"I'll leave you to your bath, dear, and I'll find something clean for you to wear."

She leaves her in the loo and noting she and the girl are of a similar size, one of her old dresses will do, and the underthings should fit. She hurries to the kitchen to stir the stew, then rushes upstairs to the bedroom, hating that she has no name for her except 'the girl'. She riffles through the armoire and bureau to find something cosy and modest. She spots a warm nightdress, dressing gown, and house shoes she has not worn in ages. Gathering everything, she walks back downstairs. She has set herself to a mission that this lass should have some comfort even if it is for one night.

She makes her way to the loo where she knocks, purely from habit. She walks in to lay the clean clothing on the chair near the tub. She glances at the girl, stops with shock, and her stomach leaps into her throat at the sight of her back. It is bruised, with dried blood on red, raised marks from what might have been a belt, gauging by the width of the welts. Her arms show scarring, and there are marks of fingers on her arm. A grip firm enough to leave bruises must have been a brutish grip. The most heartbreaking of all, the telling marks snaking their way to her side from the front, showing she brought a child into this world. Anna stifles a horrified gasp with her hand covering her mouth, unable to comprehend such cruelty to an innocent soul. Without a doubt, this timid girl could never have done anything to warrant such treatment. Anna walks out of the loo and closes the door, leaning against it, feeling physically ill as she tries to compose herself and piece together in her mind what may have transpired.

She makes her way back to the kitchen and checks the food

warming on the cooker, her hand shaking as she stirs the pot's contents. Putting the tea water on to heat, she tries to take her mind off their guest's plight by believing they should treat the girl as they would any other guest in their midst, with kindness and respect. Rupert, a calming presence at her feet, is looking up at her with his tail wagging. The sight of his apparent glee at the prospect of a treat gives Anna a little smile. With the food ready to eat, she turns off the heat and covers the pot with its lid to keep it warm. The teapot's whistling announces the water's readiness to make tea. She gets plates and cups and utensils out, hoping John will return soon enough to have a hot plate of food with them.

Hearing the loo door open and close, she is glad their second loo, and spare bedroom are near each other on the main floor. She is sure the girl would feel nervous at the prospect of having to wander about a strange house, and this gives her a small area with which to become familiar. Anna smiles, anticipating her reaction to having a hot meal and wearing clean clothing. She sets a place for her at the table and realises she should have come into the kitchen by now. She walks out of the kitchen, looks down the little hallway where the loo and spare bedroom are, but the girl is absent, and Rupert is not by her side. The familiar thump-thump-thump of Rupert's tail leads Anna into the sitting room. The girl stares, almost transfixed, at their Christmas tree with its ornaments and fairy lights. Raising an eyebrow, Anna considers the remote possibility that this is the first time the girl has ever experienced anything of its kind. She shakes her head at the old clothing the girl has put back on. Ruined clothing, for now, is the least essential matter at hand. Still unsure whether she can hear, yet sure of her fear and the reaction to being startled, Anna approaches from a direction where she is visible to the girl. Anna stands still for a moment, waiting for her to become aware of her presence. She observes the girl inching closer to the tree, seemingly fascinated by it. Anna can relate to someone losing themselves in its twinkling lights, sparkling ornaments, and the wonder of its scent. Her reverie is interrupted by the girl staring at her, pointing to the tree. Anna smiles, the only option at hand since an explanation would be impossible if the girl cannot hear.

She points at the big growing thing, to the base of the big growing thing, and holds her left hand curled 'round her right-hand fist. She pushes her right hand up and extends her fingers, tilting her head to the side.

Watching her hand gestures, Anna is now convinced she is unable to hear. The girl is compelled to use hand gestures as her way of communicating, which further explains her silence. Anna mentally replays the gestures and concludes she might be asking if the tree grows up from the floor. If this is the case, it is no wonder that this seems baffling. Not knowing the gestures to explain, Anna crouches down and lifts the lower branches. Now, the stand filled with water in which the tree sits is visible. Coming closer, warily looking at Anna, the girl crouches down, reaching in to dip her fingers into the water. She brings her wet fingers to her nose, sniffing them, no doubt detecting the scent of pine. She stands, stares at the tree, shrugs her shoulders, and shakes her head.

This might be a good time to show her the clothing she chose for her. The food will remain warm, and she can enjoy a hot meal once she is dressed. Gesturing to the lass to accompany her, Anna leads the way to the loo where she ducks in to retrieve the clothing and back out to the hallway where the girl waits. Anna smiles as she motions for her to follow into the spare bedroom. In case John should come home, Anna closes the door most of the way for privacy. She lays the clothing on the bed, in the order in which it should be donned. Pointing to her, Anna points to each garment in turn and points to the girl, again, attempting to say that these garments belong to her, now. The girl looks at the clothing on the bed, reaches out to touch the dress, then pulls her hand back as if the dress was aflame. Looking at her with wide eyes and an expression of fear as if she might be reprimanded, Anna smiles, the only reassuring message she is able to convey. Once again, Anna points to herself, points to the clothing, then points to the girl to impress upon her that the dress is a gift. Reasonably, she deserves privacy to change. Anna points to herself and points next door to the loo where she intends to tidy away towels and such. The girl's scrutiny is palpable as she leaves the room and, again, closes the door most of the way.

Entering the loo, Anna observes what she had not noticed before when she came in to retrieve the clothing. The girl had wiped the tub dry, folded the towel and flannel, leaving them draped over the side of the tub and placed the soaps in the washbasin. Astonished, Anna shakes her head and retraces her steps to offer their guest assistance if necessary. Knocking on the door before entering, Anna is reminded how such a small habit can be so useless with someone who is unable to hear. She slowly walks in, watching her, careful to make an obvious approach. The girl is unaware of Anna's presence as she touches the flowered fabric, tracing the petals with her fingertip. Anna is hopeful the girl finds the dress pleasing. She looks up from the dress to see Anna.

She looks at the lady, points to the dress, points to the lady, points to herself, and tilts her head to the side.

Replaying the gestures in her head, Anna remains ignorant of what she is attempting to say, so deflecting the awkward moment is her only option. She points to a full-length looking glass and motions the girl to come closer so she will view herself dressed in something far removed from the rags that hung from her body when she arrived. This is the part Anna always found most enjoyable and most frightening in her work as a seamstress. That moment when a client could experience their new frock and either loves it or hate it. More often than not, they were delighted with the elegant outcome of her talents. This is no different, to her, in fact, it is amplified because she knows nothing of this girl's preferences, style, or anything else, for that matter. Holding her breath, she watches the girl walk over to the looking glass, stepping back almost in surprise at her reflection, then move close enough to reach out and touch it, staring at herself. Anna's heart drops as the girl looks down at her dress, smoothing the skirt, shakes her head with tears rolling down her cheeks, then begins to unbutton the dress to take it off.

Not knowing why she is reacting in this manner, Anna still believes that this dress is preferable to the pitiful rags she had worn upon arrival. She places her hand tentatively on the girl's arm to gain her attention. The girl stops what she is doing, looks down at her arm as she wipes her tears with the back of her hand, then looks up at Anna. A smile warms Anna's face as she nods, points to herself, points to the dress, and points to the lass to tell her yes, the dress is a gift. Looking up at Anna, almost to confirm what Anna communicated, she buttons each button and stands with her hands folded in front of herself, looking at the floor. Anna waves to attract her attention and motions to the girl to follow. She leads her to the kitchen where the hot tea and food await. Taking a plate, Anna ladles a generous amount of stew over a piece of bread, hands it to her, and makes a motion with her hand towards the table.

Looking at the plate of food, her eyes wide, she takes the plate and views about the room. She hurries out of the kitchen and into a corner of the sitting room where she crouches down, eating voraciously with her fingers. Rupert, always present where there is food, sits next to her, watching. More than a little surprised at the girl's behaviour, Anna returns to the kitchen to fetch a glass of milk to wash down her supper. The girl looks at her empty plate as if she does not know what to do with it. She looks 'round the room, an expression of fear returning to her beautiful face. Returning to the corner where the girl sits, Anna smiles, crouches down to her eye level, and holds out her hand to take the plate, exchanging it for the glass of milk. In her head, Anna wonders if this is how she was treated. She is so thin, so famished, and behaves as though someone would snatch the food away if she did not hide and hurry to eat it. Anna waits whilst the girl drinks the milk, then Anna gets up to return the glass and plate to the kitchen. Anna's visitor remains in the corner with Rupert who has made himself cosy in the girl's arms, having found a new friend.

Hearing John come in, Anna pops her head out of the kitchen, looking down the hall towards the front door.

"John, I'm in here, and I have supper ready for you. You're just in time. I'm glad you're home."

John walks into the kitchen with a smile, having his priorities in order; he first stops to kiss Anna, his happiness expressed in his embrace.

"I'm happy as well. Lord Ashton had an exhaustive list of what he needs, mostly written by Lady Ashton, but we'll finish the lot for him before this event. It might mean a trip to London, but I shouldn't be gone overnight."

Hesitating, Anna tries to reason a way to explain the girl's presence in their house. She pauses, takes a deep breath, speaking with urgency as she goes on, and watches John's expression to gauge his reaction.

"I'm glad you won't be gone that long. John, we, ummm...we have a guest. A young woman was wandering about in the cold and came here begging for food. I couldn't turn her out into the night. She was so hungry and cold. And, it's snowing."

His visage transforms into one of concern by the set of his jaw, and he looks at Anna with a seriousness rarely seen on his face.

"A guest? Is this wise, Anna? What do we know about her? What's her name? Who is she? How do you know she doesn't have a place to go, a family waiting for her?"

Anna sighs, bracing herself for an uncomfortable explanation, unable to exorcise the memory of the girl's visible injuries from her mind.

"I've a feeling she's run away from somewhere or...someone. I drew a bath for her...she was, I hate to say, filthy and her clothing was little more than rags. When I went into the loo to bring her clean clothing, I saw her back and arms. She's been sorely abused with bruises and, I think, whip marks. She was mistrustful of me at first, but I believe she has come 'round to the idea that I'm not going to hurt her. She's also unable to hear, and she hasn't uttered a word. At first, I thought she might be too frightened to speak, but now, I don't believe so, as she uses hand gestures to communicate. John, I gave her something to eat, and she acted as though someone would grab it away from her. I don't know her story, but it can't be a happy one."

Looking at John with pleading eyes, she knows, under a practical façade, beats the heart of a compassionate man. A wave of relief washes over her as he nods his head in reluctant agreement.

"No, you're right. It's horrible for someone to treat anyone in that way. You did the right thing. We'll sort this out in the morning. Where is she now? Perhaps introductions are in order? I'd like to let her know, somehow, she's welcome to stay the night."

Anna points to the sitting room.

"She's in there, still sitting on the floor in the corner where she ate her food. She was holding Rupert, the last I saw of her. Let me go in first since she seems to understand I mean her no harm. I don't know what she'll be like with other people. When she first saw me...the terror..."

Shaking her head, she leads John to the sitting room where he remains at a respectful distance in the doorway. He watches the lass holding Rupert, rocking him back and forth, the dog accepting her attention and licking her cheek now and then. Anna approaches her, crouches down, and touches her arm. John has to agree that she cannot hear since she looks down at her arm before looking up at Anna. He smiles as Anna points to him. She looks up at him, and her reaction to him is instantaneous and shocking. Her eyes open wide, a clear expression of pure terror etched on her face. Her mouth is wide open as if trying to scream, her breathing heavy and gasping, every part of her shaking, tears flowing down her cheeks. She holds Rupert closer to her with one arm as she tries to push herself further back into the corner, and extends her arm, palm facing outward in a defensive posture, one taken by a person expecting something horrible to happen to them at any moment. John backs up into the hallway, wondering what to make of this.

"Anna, something is terribly wrong. I'll wait in the kitchen whilst you try to calm her."

Anna nods, as shocked as John is by the girl's reaction. She slowly approaches the hysterical girl who is now on her knees, watches the tears coursing down her cheeks and wonders what kind of hell she has endured, causing her to react this way to John. Has she never been shown love or kindness? Anna reaches out to touch the girl's arm, stroking it to calm her. Inching closer so she can slip a comforting arm 'round her shoulders, she keeps the girl's injuries uppermost in her mind. She speaks softly, the way she would talk to Johanna if her baby girl were upset.

"Shhh...it's all right...no one is going to hurt you...shhhh..."

Still breathing heavily, she looks down at her arm and up at the lady. She wipes her tears away with her hand and looks towards the kitchen. She looks up at the lady and shakes her head.

Wondering why she is so afraid of John, a thought passes through her head. Is it possible she may fear all men, considering she's never set eyes on John before and her extreme reaction? With a mother's instinct to soothe and protect, Anna strokes the girl's hair for a few moments, gives what she hopes is a reassuring smile, pats her arm, scratches Rupert's ears, then gets up to talk to John in the kitchen.

She watches the lady walk away; her breathing becoming heavier, again, as her eyes fill with wetness. The dog licks her face, and she holds him even closer, the water from her eyes running down, and her body shaking.

Walking into the kitchen, Anna's expression matches John's.

"I didn't expect that, but it shows she's most likely afraid of anyone she doesn't know. I'm even gladder, now, I didn't allow her to just walk away."

She walks back to the doorway of the sitting room and peeks in, motioning for John to come. There sits the girl, holding Rupert, weeping silently from the depths of her soul. John comes to the doorway, careful to keep himself hidden. His heart fills with compassion.

"Anna, I don't know what to say. How do we begin to reach her? She cannot hear us, and she isn't speaking. I don't know how we can help her, and it breaks my heart. Why don't I stay in here with my supper whilst you tend to her? We'll figure something out in the morning."

Grateful for her husband's understanding of the situation as it appears, Anna nods and walks back into the sitting room to crouch down near the girl who seems calmer as she looks up at her. Anna pulls out her handkerchief and hands it to her to wipe away her tears. She waits for her to notice it and the girl finally looks up at her who pantomimes the purpose of the little cloth. Anna watches her finish wiping her eyes, softly pats her arm, and smiles, as the girl looks down at her arm before looking up. Anna takes note of this, and it might be the best way to attract her attention as well as approaching from an angle where she can see who is coming to prevent unnecessary panic. Pointing to her, Anna gestures in the general direction of the spare bedroom puts her hands together and lays her head on them as if they were a pillow, hoping she will understand she is welcome to spend the night. Although it will take a bit of getting used to, this staring the girl does, since her only response is a barely perceptible nod that may indicate understanding and agreement.

Standing up, Anna motions for her to follow as Rupert hops off the girl's lap standing close, like a furry guardian angel. Anna leads the way, noticing her glances 'round her as they leave the sitting room, most likely looking for signs of John. They enter the spare bedroom, and Anna turns down the blankets on the bed, fluffing the pillow and smiles at Rupert as he hops up on the bed. She holds up the nightdress to the girl and points to her, hoping she will know the nightdress is hers as well. Nodding, not knowing what else to do, Anna backs out of the room, leaving the door ajar just a tiny bit just in case Rupert wants to come and go as he pleases. Returning to John in the kitchen, Anna sits down at the table with him as he finishes his supper. John, still shaken by the girl's response, is unaccustomed to anyone reacting as though he would do them grave harm. Anna places her hand on John's arm and squeezes it.

"I'm sure it's not you...It's my guess she's most likely afraid of anyone. She may have calmed down, though, and Rupert has taken a liking to her. Tonight, she can sleep safely in a warm bed. I hope she's not too afraid to sleep, but I imagine that kind of fright would exhaust anyone."

John nods as he gets up to rinse off his plate in the sink and pour a cup of tea for him and Anna, returning to his place at the table. He serves Anna her tea and sits.

"Yes, we've much to consider. We don't even know her name and, apparently, she has no way to tell us. I feel horrid for frightening her so. I've been sitting here shaking my head, and I wonder how anyone could...it's Inconceivable and we may never know exactly what has happened to her. I am glad, though, that she came here. Who knows what might have become of her if you hadn't taken her in."

They sit in silence, drinking their tea, their minds struggling to arrange the evening's events into some kind of order. Finally, their tea finished, there is nothing left but to consider retiring for the night.

"Anna, do you reckon she'll be all right down here with us upstairs for the night?"

Anna nods, gets up to put their cups and saucers in the sink and gives everything another rinse. Sarah can do them when breakfast is finished in the morning. She smiles at John, takes his hand, and walks with him out of the kitchen, through the sitting room to the staircase. John gestures that Anna should lead the way upstairs where the two of them peek in on their daughter, Johanna, sleeping in her lovely cot, her fingers in her mouth. They smile at each other before leaving the nursery to make their way to their bedroom, closing the door, ready to welcome their favourite houseguest, Morpheus.

The girl, fully clothed, finally sits up to look 'round her, having lain in bed staring up at the ceiling whilst stroking the dog. Standing, she walks to the door, peeks out, and walks down the hallway. She looks into the kitchen, and over her shoulder towards the sitting room. Entering, she peers 'round and spots some bread and cheese on a plate. Making a little pouch by pulling her skirt up slightly and holding it with one hand, she tucks the food inside of it. Walking back out into the small hallway, she looks 'round her, then reaches down to stroke the dog following on her heels. She walks into the sitting room, and her eyes open wide as she walks over to the tree. Darkness fills the room except for the fairy lights, and she stands, staring at them, inhaling deeply. Looking 'round her, she tilts her head to the side, walks over to the sofa, runs her hand over the wood, and pushes against the cushions. She looks 'round the room before returning to the bedroom where she was invited to sleep. She watches the dog follow her in before she closes the door. Taking the bread and cheese out from the pouch she had made with her skirt, she tucks the food under the bed. She looks up at the dog hopping up on the mattress, pawing at the covers. She sits on the edge of the bed, stroking the quilt with her hand, and slips under the blankets, touching the fabric again before she settles herself into the warmth. With her head resting on the new pillow and Rupert nestled against her, she turns to her side and lays there staring at the wall.

.

Chapter Two
27 December 1925

A new day in the Thorpe household passes as normally as it can, with each member adjusting to the idea of an unknown girl has been welcomed into their midst. John and Anna talked into the wee hours of the morning, debating what to do about the poor lass. Finally, they set upon a course of action, or to be more correct, inaction, which has the girl's best interests held uppermost. They would harbour her in safety and secrecy as best they could, given her state when she arrived. The thought of notifying authorities was unthinkable as they might, with the best intentions, send the girl back to the hell from which she had undoubtedly emerged. As a result, keeping her a secret would be difficult, but they know who amongst their friends could be trusted. John and Anna agree that both of them, convinced they have done the right thing, would shoulder whatever consequences should arise from this decision.

Keeping a watchful and protective eye on the girl proves to be easy for Anna. She sits by the fireplace holding Rupert who laps up the attention. Now and then, she looks 'round her and slides herself closer to the Christmas tree, inhaling deeply as she stares up at it. She looks about her before touching an ornament, as if this might be some forbidden act. Anna wonders what the girl thinks since the only clue is observation. Anna walks into the kitchen with Johanna on her hip, bouncing her and tickling her as they go. The teakettle is filled and set to heat whilst cups come out of the cupboard. Anna points to each item, saying its name, and laughing as her sweet baby girl looks in wonder and laughs merrily. Perhaps the young lass would like some tea if she has never had tea before now. Anna wonders just how much of the world the girl has never experienced. Earlier, Sarah had come to her, relating that upon tidying up the girl's room, she found bread and cheese hidden under the bed. The previous evening, Anna remembered how eager she was to eat as quickly as possible. She must have been starved, as spare as she appears which makes the idea of her hoarding food understandable. Anna shakes her head, again, wondering how anyone could be so cruel to another.

Raising an eyebrow at the sound of the door to the garden open, she turns off the cooker and proceeds to investigate. No, John cannot be back from the shop already, could he? The door is ajar, and a quick peek into the sitting room shows that the girl is not there, either. She had not walked past the kitchen to the spare bedroom, so Anna calls Sarah to come to fetch Johanna. Sarah, who seems to be everywhere at once, comes straight away, without question, taking Johanna in her arms and smiling at the little miss.

"Mind my little love for a whilst, would you? I need to see what's afoot with our girl."

"Yes, Ma'am, I'll look after her. I do hope nothing's amiss."

Sarah steps back with an expression of curious concern on her face as she watches as Anna shrugs on her parka and walks outside, closing the door to the garden behind her. Sarah hopes Rupert is with her, as he has been her shadow since she set foot in the door, and the loyal dog would indeed protect her. Holding Johanna and humming softly, she resumes her duties as best she can with her young charge in her arms.

Looking about the garden she finds the girl sitting on the special bench John crafted. Smiling, Anna slowly walks over to her, shaking her head slightly that she has no coat. She takes off her own wrap and comes 'round to stand in front of the girl, gently leaning down to pat her arm for attention. The girl starts slightly as she looks down at her arm, then up at Anna. Anna's heart fills with sadness as the lass cringes away from her, looks down, and makes hand gestures, Anna cannot even begin to sort out. Rupert puts his front paws in the girl's lap and nuzzles her arm. Anna puts the coat 'round the girl's shoulders, hoping she will accept it as a sign of good will, as she still looks rather discomfited. The girl shakes her head, tries to push it back, but Anna smiles and pats the girl's arm as the only way she knows to convey the idea that it is necessary for these winter temperatures. She looks up at Anna, nods, and wipes a tear from her cheek. She reaches down to stroke the dog, picks him up and holds him close in her lap. After a little whilst, Rupert is eager to get down and run. The girl watches him cavorting about and without looking at Anna, she tries to communicate again to her.

She points to herself and places a fist on her chest. Then, she points to her eyes and points 'round where they are. She points to the dog, makes her fingers run on the palm of her other hand, then gestures 'round them. Tears falling anew, she looks up at the lady and moves her hands held palms together from her chest out to the lady.

Replaying the gestures in her mind and making her best effort to figure out what they might mean, she guesses that the girl is referring to Rupert. Oh! Anna wonders if she is curious about the outside and followed Rupert when he dashed out, as he usually does. She looks at the girl with an outpouring of sympathy, as apparently, she must think she had committed some error, worthy of punishment. Anna pats the girl's hands as she smiles and nods, hoping she will understand that everything is all right. They sit quietly together, Anna beginning to shiver from the cold but resolved to stifle the outward signs of her chill. Determined, Anna will stay with the girl for as long as necessary.

Keeping in mind the girl's anxiousness about being in too close proximity to another person, Anna follows her gaze to two unique stones. The girl gets up and crouches down in front of the rocks, running her fingers over them, touching their unusual interiors. They are geodes, one with a mother-of-pearl opalescence shining out from it, and the other filled with crystals in every shade of blue imaginable. She looks up at Anna, points to the stones and tilts her head to the side. Anna concludes the girl is wondering why such unusual rocks are in the garden. How to explain them? The first, a memorial marker for their daughter who did not have a chance to be born, dying as a result of a motor accident before it was time to bring her into the world as nature intended. The second is a memorial marker for their son who was born too soon and died in her arms. Sighing, all she can think of to gesture, by way of explanation, is to point at the stones, point to herself and cradle her arms as if holding a baby, then finally trace her finger down her cheek from her eye to mark the course of a tear. The girl had to have noticed the presence of only one child in their family, so she hopes the girl understands that these other two children did not survive.

She looks at the lady, looks at the lady's belly, and points to the rocks. Silently, she begins to weep. She looks up to the sky, her upheld hand moving across the heavens. Looking back at the lady, she places her hand on her own stomach, draws her finger down from her eye, and pushes her hands quickly outward from her belly, flinging her arms open wide. Shaking her head, she gets off the sitting thing, kneels on the ground, her finger moving in the hard dirt and cold white. Stopping with heavy breaths, her head lowered, she crumbles to the ground silently weeping, pounding the earth with her fist. Pulling herself up, she beats harder with both fists, her teeth held tightly together, then looks up into the sky, shaking her head.

Anna kneels down beside her. Even though she is confused by the girl's gestures and what they might mean, she does feel sure the girl has also suffered the loss of a child and feels the grief deeply. Tentatively, she places her hand on the girl's back and rubs softly in a circular motion, praying that this closeness does not frighten her. It is only right for two mothers who feel the heartache of their children's deaths should at least share their mutual affliction. They are able to object in unison to such overwhelming unfairness that defies comprehension. Even though the girl is unable to hear her, she murmurs comforting words as Rupert trots over to nuzzle the girl's face and lick her salty tears.

"Shhh...They're not here with us, but they're in our hearts always...shhh...oh how I wish..."

Coming home a little earlier than usual from the shop, concern has simmered in the back of John's mind all day for what might be transpiring at home. He removes his anorak and hat, greeted at the door by Sarah who is holding Johanna. With a smile, he takes his daughter in his arms and kisses her forehead, causing his little princess to reach up and pat his face.

"Daddy is here, little one. Did you miss me? I missed you. Where's your Mamma?"

He looks to Sarah for the answer, glances about and the house echoes silence at the presence of neither Anna nor the girl.

"Sir, Ma'am is outside with the young lass and Rupert. I don't know what's happened, but they've been out there some time, now, and the last I looked, Ma'am wasn't wearing a coat."

"Thank you, Sarah. I'll take one out to her."

He holds the baby close, tickling her cheek lightly and kisses Johanna one more time before handing her over to Sarah who takes the child in her arms and carries her so she can watch her father. He reaches over to retrieve another coat for Anna from the wardrobe, drapes it over his arm, and walks to the door to the garden, turning to smile and wave at his baby girl. A quick glance out of the door's window shows the girl and Anna kneeling on the ground. Appearances lead him to believe that Anna might be comforting her, and if so, he can only imagine what might have brought about the need for Anna's peaceful manner. Walking outside, he closes the door quietly behind him, his mind divided between not wanting to disturb them and feeling the need to know what is happening. Rupert runs over to John, wagging his tail enthusiastically, barking, and his front paws extended with his head down, ready to play. With a chuckle, John reaches down to scratch Rupert's ears.

"Not right now, boy, later on, maybe we'll have a bit of sport."

Hearing the door and John's voice, Anna smiles sadly at him. She stiffly gets up, thanks to the bitter cold seeping into her bones from the frozen ground. She is glad he has come home. Already, Anna has much to narrate about their girl, as Anna has come to think of her. With startling swiftness, she feels the girl behind her, clutching the back of her dress. She looks back at the girl, seeing wide eyes in a fear-filled face peering 'round her at John.

"John, she truly is afraid of men, I think. She hasn't reacted this way to Sarah, although our girl keeps her distance."

She thinks a moment, trying to decide how best to communicate that John is a good man. She turns to face the girl, and in doing so, the girl's fingers relax their hold from the back of her dress. Keeping herself between the girl and John, Anna points to herself and points back to John. She pats the girl's arm reassuringly with a small smile and nod. She turns to John as she slowly walks closer to him.

"Perhaps if she watches our affection, she'll understand I trust you, and you're a good man. I hope."

"Yes, I agree. Showing her might be best. I'll put the wrap 'round your shoulders as well so she can know I'm kind to you."

Holding the wrap in one hand by the collar, John opens his arms as he smiles at Anna, drawing her into a warm embrace made even warmer by the application of a sensible parka 'round her shivering shoulders. He rubs Anna's back through the jacket, feeling her shiver against his warmth. A kiss on her cheek silently tells her what words could never convey. Startled by the slam of the door, they glance about them, the girl nowhere in sight. John shakes his head.

"Come, Anna, let's get you inside and warm with tea by the fire. I don't know what to make of her reaction. Could it be that she's never seen a man and woman show affection?"

John opens the door for Anna and suggests she wear her coat until the tea is ready. He nearly trips over Rupert who is impatient to be the first one into the house. Once Anna is inside, John decides that fuel for the fireplace is a good idea, so he fetches wood from the pile. Returning to the warmth indoors, he glances about as he makes his way to the sitting room, his arms laden with food for a hungry fire. John prepares himself for a hasty retreat should there be an unexpected encounter with the girl, unwilling to frighten her further. The everyday task of stacking the wood on the hearth is finished in a jiffy. The whistle of the teakettle engages his attention and lures him into the kitchen. Her coat now draped over a chair, Anna pours tea into three cups.

"Tea will warm you, Anna. I'm sure the girl could use tea as much as you can."

"Yes, I heard a noise in the bedroom, and I thought it might be good to bring it to her. As upset as she was outside, I thought giving her a little time to compose herself before I intrude would be a welcome respite. John, later, I'll tell you more, but I think she tried to tell me she lost a baby."

Anna places two cups of tea on a little tray with a small jug of milk and a bowl of sugar. Down the corridor to the spare bedroom, she passes, realising it is time Sarah cooked supper, and it must also be time for Johanna's bath, but Sarah will have to manage it all for the time being. Her immediate focus is the girl who must be as frigid to the core as she is. Anna knocks on the door out of habit to the spare bedroom and enters. The girl is sitting on the bed, her arms wrapped 'round herself, crying as she rocks back and forth. Anna sets the tea tray on the bureau and approaches the girl. Kneeling in front and slightly to one side of her, Anna places her hand on the girl's arm, not wishing to startle her in her state of wretchedness. The girl looks at her arm and then at her, eyes wide, breathing heavily, trying to blink back tears.

She puts her hands together and moves them from her chest towards the lady.

Nodding in acknowledgement of the girl's heartfelt and apologetic gesture, she wishes she could tell her that there is nothing to forgive. Anna takes the girl's hands in her own. She hopes the girl can evolve an understanding of the compassion this family holds as a principal virtue, forgiveness being the cornerstone. The girl gets up and walks over to a dressing gown lying across a chair, leaving Anna still kneeling by the bed.

She removes the long piece from the garment, points to the lady, and points to herself, then, points to the sleeping thing.

Still kneeling, curiously and almost with dread, Anna watches as she walks back to the bed. The girl's breath comes faster and with more effort as the girl's eyes widen. She begins to whip the bed with the belt over and over, more quickly, the frenzied intensity growing with each blow. With an alarming spasm, she arches her back, reaching behind her, and then collapses next to the bed. The girl's shoulders heave with inconsolable yet silent sobs. Her shaking hands fill themselves with the fabric of the quilt, pulling at it in her distress. Unwilling to believe her eyes, Anna fights her own impending tears. She struggles to fathom the cruelty that has left such sadistic marks, not just on this girl's flesh, but on her soul, as well. These wounds are as fresh in her mind as they are on her body. With a will of its own, her hand reaches out to stroke the girl's arm, her whole being striving to communicate solicitude.

The return to calm seems like a hopeless wait for the sun to come back after a violent storm. The girl's breath still comes in gulping pants, their eyes meeting in a tearful understanding, both of them wiping the evidence of weeping away on convenient sleeves.

She places her hand on her own heart and puts her shaking hand over the lady's heart and nods.

Nodding and covering the girl's small hand with her own, and she is sure that her racing heartbeat must be infinitely more sedate than that of the girl. She manages to show a small smile, hoping this sweet child understands she is safe here and no one will cause her harm. She prays that the girl knows, now she is free to express whatever she wishes without fear of rebuke or humiliation. Anna's inner being fills with a protective maternal instinct towards her. She realises it had been planted there as a seed from the first moment, and with time, grows stronger. Anna watches her get up, finally, and sit in the chair nearby, just staring at her.

The tea she had first brought in must be cold by now. Getting up from her place on the floor, she holds up a finger to say she will be right back and hurries out of the bedroom and into the kitchen to retrieve more hot tea for them. Taking only a moment, she kisses John's cheek and Johanna's head as they sit eating the supper Sarah prepared. A brief moment of explanation of needing to tend to their girl will have to suffice for now. Returning to the girl's room, having brought two fresh cups as well, Anna holds up a finger with a smile and pours them each a cup of tea. She fixes her own tea to her preference and takes a tiny sip to show the girl that this is scalding hot and sipping it slowly is best. Setting down her cup, Anna hands the girl one and pantomimes drinking with a smiling nod.

Anna watches with anticipation as the girl looks into the cup, holds it carefully to her nose as she closes her eyes. The girl opens her eyes and looks at her, and Anna smiles with a nod, taking another sip of her own tea. The girl takes a small sip and sits up straight, looking at her with wide eyes. Watching her with growing affection, Anna muses to herself that their young guest is lovely. The girl drinks the tea as quickly as the heat will allow and hands the cup back to Anna when finished. Pleased that the girl apparently enjoyed the tea, she pantomimes pouring more into the cup and points to the girl, asking if she would like more. She is even more pleased when the girl nods her head.

Anna pours her another cup of tea, then turns to the bed and finds it lacks adequate blankets for such a cold night. The darkness grows deeper outside as does the numbness creeping in like a thief to steal any warmth it can find throughout the house. The bureau nearby obediently yields its treasure of a quilt that Anna fluffs across the bed in a sweeping flick. She watches the girl set down the now empty teacup and walk over to the bed, almost reverently touching the pieced-together flower basket with its patchwork blooms. She is at a loss to understand the meaning behind the girl's gesture of holding up a finger and then placing her other hand on it with fingers spread, so she just smiles and nods. With everything, the girl has expressed, physically and emotionally, Anna discerns she must be exhausted. She places her hands together and rests her head on them as if on a pillow to ask the girl if she is tired and would like to go to bed.

Nodding, she puts her hands together, rests her head on them, and looks at the lady. She holds up one finger, points to herself, draws an X in her hand, shakes her head, and pantomimes eating.

Once more unable to grasp what the girl is trying to say, Anna hopes she is right in gathering the general idea that the poor dear might be too exhausted to eat. Anna nods at her and turns to leave, affording the girl some privacy to ready herself for bed. She feels a pulling on her sleeve and turns to see the girl breathing anxiously, pointing to the dressing gown and nightdress. Anna smiles and points to the items and points to the girl to affirm; they are as much hers as the other garments are. She turns to leave once again when she feels another tug at her sleeve. The girl's eyes are wide as Anna points to the chair with her head tilted to the side, in what seems to be a request for Anna to sit. She does so, unwilling to refuse any reasonable request the girl may have. The girl turns 'round and begins to undress, Anna's eyes avert, as modest decorum requires. She gives the girl respectful privacy as she would for any woman trying on a garment in the dressing room. Anna's attention returns to the girl when she walks over to the looking glass and looks at the scarring, bruises, and welts on her back.

Holding the sleeping dress up to cover herself, she turns with tear-

filled eyes, points to herself, points to her reflection, points to herself, and draws an X in her hand as she shakes her head.

Desperately wishing she had a speedy understanding of what the girl means and feeling wholly inadequate for the task, she at least owes the girl honesty. She shrugs her shoulders and shakes her head, pleading ignorance of the girl's communication.

Her head is slightly leaning to the side, and she nods. She points to the lady, then to her mouth. She touches her sleeping dress cover and points to the lady. Breathing heavier, she points to the lady, then clasps her hands then points to herself. She looks at the lady.

Even more confused, now, Anna has no choice but to repeat the shoulder-shrug and headshake, hoping the girl is not frustrated by her ignorance. The girl moves closer to Anna with huge and pleading eyes.

Tilting her head to the side, she points to the lady, places her hand on her own heart, and points to herself.

Feeling utterly stupid and berating herself harshly for not understanding, Anna's heart goes out to the girl, so isolated in silence. The mental clouds part, no longer obscuring the clear message the girl is trying to communicate. The painful radiance of truth flashes deep into her spirit as she realises that all the girl wants is to be loved. Not only does the girl want to be loved, like any living being desires, but the girl also wants to be cherished by HER. Her own hand shaking, she decides to risk her heart. She points to herself, places her hand over her heart, and points to the girl with a deep peace settling into her soul.

Her hands shaking, she points to the lady, places her hand over her heart and points to herself.

Anna watches the girl's face crumble into silent sobs and is astonished to see the girl open her arms slowly. In reply, she opens her arms, tears streaming down her own face. How could Anna refuse to allow the girl to come to her? She stands, finally able to gather the girl into her arms. Anna holds her like a precious and long-lost daughter, surprised at the strength with which the girl clings to her, seemingly unwilling to let go. Through the haze of emotion, Anna wonders if anyone has ever held her like this? Has she never known a mother's love? Has anyone ever treated her with kindness? She holds the girl to her, softly stroking her thick hair, gently stroking her back, mindful of any physical pain the girl might feel. Anna allows herself to love this dear, sweet, nameless girl. Swaying as she does with Johanna, Anna holds her. Eventually, the girl's tears subside, shaking eases, and breathing returns to a normal rhythm.

She swallows hard and steps back. She looks at the lady. She points to the lady and holds her hands upwards, opening and closing her hands, then points to herself. Looks at the lady again and nods.

She smiles at the girl, so lovely even with such a sombre expression, and nods in reply. Anna is grateful for the chance to show her the truth that she deserves affection and acceptance. The girl's gestures might indicate something from heaven, and whatever it is, it makes the girl smile, and that is more than adequate.

She reaches out and takes the lady's hand, tilting her head against the lady's hand. She closes her eyes. She lets go of the lady's hand and looks at the lady's eyes. She points to herself and puts her hand on her heart, then points to the lady.

Anna watches the girl turn aside, lift the blankets, and slip into the bed. It must be more comfortable than anything she has known recently. She smiles as the girl settles herself. The girl points to herself, places her hand over her heart, and points to Anna once more, smiles, then nestles under the blankets with Rupert emerging from under the bed to hop up and take his self-designated post for the night. With a soft chuckle at what a sweet pair they make, Anna leaves the room, the door cracked just a little bit if Rupert needs to come and go.

She lingers in the hallway, leaning against the wall for a few minutes, acutely aware of the quiet in the house. Sarah must be in bed now, as Johanna will be as well. Her thoughts return to the exchanges between herself and the girl, her heart still warmed. She hugs herself to keep the feeling alive, imagining with hope that a glimpse of trust has reached the girl. She closes her eyes to sear this memory into her mind and heart, something rare and unique she has never experienced before. Smiling, Anna takes a deep breath, hoping that John might still be awake so she can share this with him, perhaps, late into the night

Chapter Three
29 December 1925

Whilst Sarah is upstairs putting Johanna down for an afternoon nap, John helps Anna wash dishes after their leisurely Saturday lunch. Drying a plate, he cannot resist walking out of the kitchen to peer into the sitting room. The girl sits on the floor by the fireplace, cuddling Rupert. John returns to put the plate away and takes another one to dry.

"I do wish we knew what goes on in her head. At least she is not hiding in her room. I reckon that is progress of sorts. The girl seems to trust you, Anna, and for that, I am glad. Oh, I also thought perhaps we need to take down the tree soon. Having the house burn down wouldn't end the holidays on a festive note."

Placing the last plate in the drying rack, Anna nods as she twists the excess water from the tea towel.

"Yes, we'll take any progress we can get. The girl has taken a curious interest in Johanna, as well. You are right; the tree needs to come down. Perhaps in a day or two. Maybe the girl would like to help."

John walks back out of the kitchen and over to the doorway of the sitting room, peeking in to see what the girl is doing now. The girl is just sitting, staring into the fireplace and looks up at the Christmas tree occasionally. He fervently hopes the girl is relatively healthy. Their friend, Clara, is coming and should be able to assess the girl's health. He expects good food and safety will be the best thing for her. Going back to the kitchen, he leans on the counter to speak confidentially, even though the girl would not be able to hear them.

"She does seem to like the tree. You did tell Clara what we are dealing with, did you not? I wish communication were easier, but I reckon we'll have to work with what we have."

"I explained everything to Clara, including the nightmares. She will have to assess things for herself. She said she would arrive after lunch, which should be any time, now."

Standing at the door to the Thorpe house, Clara Dewhurst pauses and takes a deep breath. She clutches the handle of her medical kit a little more tightly than necessary. This might be the most challenging case she has ever seen. Mrs Dewhurst is a nurse, a matron at the hospital, and a parish nurse who makes rounds with Father Willington. She sifts through her memory for anything she might rely on. None of her training or experience has prepared her for what Anna described to her by telephone. She briskly knocks on the door, hoping the girl is not too fearful to cooperate. At the sound of Mrs Dewhurst's rapping, John covers the distance between the kitchen and front door, answering it. Greeting Clara, he takes her parka and hat, then shows her into the kitchen where Anna is just wiping her hands on her pinny.

Anna hurries to her old chum, embracing her.

"Clara, I'm so glad you agreed to come."

"Of course, Anna, I am always happy to help. You said this would be a challenge, and you know me. Challenge continuously turns up for me like a bad penny."

Clara chuckles and puts her bag on the kitchen table, getting to the point without pretence or delay.

"Have we a plan and where shall we do this? Somewhere private would be best, I think."

"Yes, John should probably go upstairs once we go into the girl's room, and he'll do his best to remain out of sight. We can't take a chance she'll become agitated."

"Yes, excellent. Where is the girl, now?"

"She is in the sitting room. Clara, she will be nervous to see a stranger. If you don't mind staying back a little whilst I try to explain…you."

Nodding, Clara picks up her bag and pats John's arm. Feeling as ready as she will ever be, she follows Anna into the sitting room to meet the girl who has piqued her curiosity. Clara stays by the door where she remains visible. A pleasant smile on her face, she hopes the girl will perceive her as non-threatening. She takes notice of Anna approaching the girl and crouching down to the girl's level. Clara chuckles to herself how she learnt this technique when she was training as a nurse. Here, without formal training, Anna displays an intuitive approach that accomplishes a peaceful interaction. Anna touches the girl's arm gently. It is no wonder the girl has come to trust Anna. The girl looks down at her arm, then up at Anna.

Anna meets the girl's gaze with a smile and the girl nods. The girl points to a shiny ornament on the Christmas tree, then nods again at Anna. In reply, Anna points to a similar decoration on the tree. The girl nods and pulls Rupert closer, cuddling him. Taking a deep breath, Anna points to Clara as she also draws attention to her own smile. Her goal is to make it understood that Clara is a good person and welcome in their home. Trying to remember how to say Clara came to see the girl, she hesitates a moment. Anna points to Clara, again, then points to her own eyes, and points to the girl. Noticing Clara, Rupert wriggles free of the girl's arms. He shakes his body from nose to tail and trots over to her. Laughing at Rupert's antics, she places her medical kit on the floor and scoops him up in her arms, cuddling him and scratching his ears.

"What a good boy you are! I'm happy to see you too, Rupert! Have you been taking good care of your new friend? I think you have!"

She sets him back on the floor with another scratch to his ears and strokes the little fellow along his back.

Looking at Clara, the girl's eyes grow large. She scrambles to stand and finds the nearest corner. Arms crossed over her chest, her breathing becomes more burdensome, and she begins to tremble. Her eyes dart back and forth between Anna and Clara as she shakes her head. Rupert turns to look at his new friend and trots over to her, sitting down, leaning against the girl's legs. Anna sighs, thinking this might prove more difficult than she had anticipated. She slowly approaches the girl and thinks about how to explain what Clara does. Hitting upon a solution that she hopes the girl will understand, Anna pantomimes hurting her finger. Anna shakes her hand and brings her finger to her lips as if soothing it. Then, she points to Clara and mimes wrapping the finger. Finally, she pats her hand with a smile to indicate thanks to Clara, the finger is mended.

Clara and Anna turn to look at each other in dismay as the girl quickly moves 'round the perimeter of the room glancing at them both. Clara stands aside. Anna assumes the girl will retreat to the relative security of her room, and this expectation proves true. They hear the girl's bedroom door slam shut. Rupert dashes after her, scratching at the door and whining for entry.

"Oh dear. The girl is afraid of everything, isn't she? No wonder she has frightening nightmares. Anna, this may be more complicated than I had thought. You know her better than I do. What do you suggest we do next?"

"Let me think. Perhaps if I try to get through to Ellen in private, we might have a chance. If we can't persuade her to tolerate a brief examination, then we will have to accept that. Hmmm. Have you a tin of antiseptic I might borrow?"

Nodding, Clara sets her bag on a nearby chair and finds the item in question. She hands it to Anna, having a reasonable idea what Anna might do with it. Anna tucks the tin in her pocket and motions for Clara to follow. From a discreet distance, Clara watches Anna open the door to the room that has become a private refuge for the girl. Anna enters the room slowly, leaving Clara in the hallway. Rupert dashes in, past Anna, straight to the girl.

Quietly, Clara positions herself in the hallway so she can watch Anna. Perhaps she can gain some insight into how she can interact with her most effectively.

Anna's heart sinks to see the girl sitting on the floor in the corner, rocking back and forth, and holding a pillow. Crouching down, she hopes to attract the girl's attention without touching her. Rupert's wiggling presence brings the girl's attention to Anna in moments. Rallying a small smile, Anna points to herself as the girl looks up at her. Then she places her hand on her heart, finally pointing to the girl. The gestures expressing Anna's growing love for the girl.

She looks up at the lady, blinking her eyes. Pointing to herself, she lays her hand on her heart and points to the lady. She points to where the strange lady is and points to her own eyes, then to herself. She shakes her head.

Anna understands the girl does not want Clara to look at her. She pulls the tin out of her pocket and shows it to the girl. Opening it, Anna takes a little on her fingers and rubs it on her arm where she had an almost-healed scratch. She points to the scratch and then to the salve, hoping the girl will grasp the idea that the antiseptic shall help it heal. Hearing Clara at the door, she turns and points to Clara. Placing her hand on her heart, she points to Clara and then points to the tin, trying to communicate that Clara is the one who gave it to her because Clara is a good lady. The confused expression on the girl's face tells Anna that her efforts at communication are falling flat. The girl's gaze returns to Clara with an intensity that both Anna and Clara find palpable in the silence. Clara takes a couple of steps into the room, puts her bag on the floor, and softly speaks.

"Anna, may I try? The worst that can happen is she sends me on my way."

"Of course, please do."

Anna scoots aside so Clara will be visible to the girl. Clara smiles at the girl and uses the gestures she had seen Anna and the girl use. She puts her hand over her heart as Anna had done. Clara points to her own eyes and points to Anna and the girl, telling the girl by her gestures that she has come to visit both of them. In doing so, she extends a gesture of friendship. Diligent training as a nurse and years of experience renders Clara unwilling to let the girl's scrutiny unnerve her. Rupert takes this opportunity to lick the girl's face before he trots over to Clara in a bid for more attention. Grinning at the affectionate dog, Clara reaches down to scratch his ears and strokes him, hoping the girl might trust an animal's judgement of character over that of a person.

The girl looks at Clara and then looks at Anna. Shrugging her shoulders, she continues glancing at Clara with narrowed eyes. Setting the pillow aside, she stands up, clutching Anna's arm, following Anna's lead to stand.

"Clara, if you examine me first, she might realise you won't hurt me."

"Yes, even if I can manage to see her back and the injuries you described, I'll be satisfied."

Clara removes a stethoscope from her bag, waiting for Anna to unbutton her dress for the faux examination. Anna sits on the bed, pulling her dress aside in a modest fashion. Placing the earpieces in her ears, Clara slips the stethoscope under the fabric and listens, watching the girl. A touch of uncertainty clouds the girl's features as she tilts her head, sitting on the bed next to Anna, still holding tightly to Anna's arm. When Clara has finished, she removes the stethoscope and takes the earpieces out of her ears. Keeping it in her hands, Clara nods to Anna with a smile to show all is well. Nodding, Anna opens the salve, lowers her dress, exposing only her back, and hands the tin to the girl, pointing to her own back and then pantomiming the application of the oily preparation.

Still appearing wary, the girl brings the container to her nose, sniffing its contents. She touches the mixture with her fingers, feeling its texture. Wrinkling her nose, she takes some on her fingers and haltingly applies it to Anna's back. Once the task is accomplished, Anna smiles and nods as she buttons up her dress. She pats the girl's hand and takes the tin from her. Now, the anxious moment has come. Anna points to Clara who is standing there with a kind expression on her face. Anna points to the stethoscope in Clara's hands and then points to the girl. She tilts her head to the side as if to ask the girl if she would allow Clara to evaluate her in the same fashion.

Rupert jumps up on the bed and walks over to Anna, sniffing her back and wrinkling his nose in much the same way the girl had done. Clara stifles a chuckle at Rupert as she waits for the girl to make her decision. She wonders for a moment if the girl has ever had the opportunity to make decisions for herself. Indeed, the girl is able to communicate and seems to be in her right mind. She watches the girl look at Rupert, relaxes her grip on Anna's arm, and then look up at her with a wary expression as she slowly nods assent. Slowly, Clara moves closer, holding out the stethoscope for the girl to touch if she wishes.

The girl reaches out a finger to touch the stethoscope and then draws her hand back, looking up at Clara. The girl unbuttons her dress as Anna had done. Clara smiles at the girl. She places the stethoscope in her ears and puts the bell over the girl's heart, pleased to hear a normal rhythm. Next, she reaches 'round to position the bell on the girl's back, careful to not cause discomfort to the injuries already present. Clara hears clear and healthy lung sounds. As she removes the stethoscope, Clara examines the girl's back and shakes her head. She stands up straight and steps aside, smiling at the girl, hoping she feels her approval.

"Anna, you weren't exaggerating in the least. Those are brutal contusions and abrasions, some still open. My first concern would be an infection. She needs the antiseptic on her back until they heal. The wounds to her soul, though, are out of my league."

"I agree, Clara. I don't know how anyone would ever do such a thing to her."

Looking at the girl, Anna points to the tin and points to the girl's back. She pantomimes applying the ointment. The girl looks down at the container, then back up to Anna. Slowly she nods her head, turning her back towards Anna, with a brief glance at Clara. Gently, Anna applies the foul-smelling preparation to the girl's back. When finished, she pats the girl's shoulder and helps her tug her dress back up to cover herself again. Anna turns to Clara and heaves a sigh of relief.

"If it took this much effort to get a peek at her back and apply some medicinal ointment, I believe we are well within our rights to judge this examination successful, don't you think?"

"Goodness, Anna, I'm just happy we were able to do this much. Can you manage to apply the antiseptic twice a day?"

"Oh yes, but I believe she is under the impression that I need it, too. Have you any more of this? We may be using a fair amount of it until her wounds heal."

Anna pats the girl's hand with a smile. She gestures to herself and Clara, then points to the door to let the girl know that the two of them would leave and not pester her any longer. The girl nods, sitting back on her bed, taking a pillow into her arms. Rupert noses his way under the pillow to be closer to her, and the girl sets it aside in favour of the dog's company.

The women walk into the kitchen where Clara sets her bag on the table. She opens it and withdraws several more tins of the healing salve.

"Here you go, Anna. After we had spoken on the telephone, I thought you might need a good supply, and I was right."

"Thank you. I'll let you know either way if her back heals or gets worse."

"Please do, and let me know how she's doing in general. I think it's good for her to have some control, as we've done, by giving her choices and the chance to refuse something. I cannot help but wonder if that has been denied her and for how long. Keep giving her choices, Anna, safe ones. It's important to and for her. I'm going to discuss her with Dr Harper, as well."

"Thank you, Clara, and I will keep you apprised of her progress. Let me show you out. I am so grateful you could come. I didn't know who else to ring."

Anna leads Clara to the entry hall where the two good friends embrace. Clara dons her anorak and laughs when Anna hands her the gloves she is desperately fishing for in her pockets.

"Give John and Johanna my love, and greet Sarah for me. It's a shame I can't stay, but, another time."

Walking out the door and turning back, Clara gives a cheery wave as she departs. Anna closes the door and makes her way upstairs to tell John how their girl withstood Clara's visit. She finds John and Johanna in the nursery. John is in the midst of entertaining their daughter with a most engaging tale of horses, princes, castles, and a breath-taking princess. Chuckling, she remarks to herself that Daddy's lap is Johanna's favourite place to be. She smiles with a nod to Sarah who is gathering things for Johanna's bath after supper.

"When you're finished, Sarah, Mrs Dewhurst has gone, and you may have the kitchen to yourself to prepare supper. I promise we won't disturb you."

Sarah smiles, nods, and hastens away to put Johanna's things in the loo. Quickly returning to the nursery, she pokes her head just inside the doorway.

"Ma'am, will the girl be joining us at supper or shall I make a plate for her separate, as I've done before?"

"A separate plate will be all right, Sarah. I will take it to her once we have finished eating. She seems to feel comfortable with this routine so we will accommodate her as long as it is necessary. Thank you for asking, though."

With a nod, she bustles her way to the kitchen, plans for the meal filling her head. Sarah fails to notice the swish of a floral skirt disappearing into the room where the girl spends most of her time. Sarah also fails to detect, as she busily prepares this and that, a small, new-sharpened chef's knife has gone missing from the drawer.

Chapter Four
8 January 1926

A fortnight after the girl's arrival is marked by a beautiful morning that reaches through the windows. John readies himself for his daily duties at the shop and watches Anna, who looks to be more energetic these days. With a smile, he gives his suit jacket sleeves one last tug as Anna flits about their bedroom gathering dresses and undergarments.

"Anna, you have yourself set on a task, haven't you?"

"As a matter of fact, John, I do. What do you think of the name 'Ellen' for our girl?"

John raises an eyebrow as Anna stops what she is doing to look him square in the eye. He wonders where he was when the topic changed.

"Ellen? Well, I reckon that might be a nice enough name. What made you think of it?"

"Well, I was dreaming last night, and in the dream, I saw a pretty cross-stitch sampler with the name Ellen worked into it, but not yet finished. I don't know if it means anything or not, but honestly, she deserves a name."

Nodding his assent, he takes the garments from Anna's arm and lays them across the bed. Smiling down at her, he brushes a stray strand of hair away from her forehead before he pulls her close in his arms and kisses her for a moment longer than usual.

"Mrs Thorpe, Ellen is a beautiful name for our girl, and I believe you look exceptionally fetching this morning."

Chuckling, she pats his chest, straightening an imaginary wrinkle out of his tie, and gives him her most charming smile.

"Thank you, Mr Thorpe. I think you have excellent taste."

With a wink back at John, Anna gathers the garments in her arms and proceeds downstairs towards the kitchen where she drapes the clothing over the first chair she finds. She hears John at the front door putting on his parka, so she trots out to give him one last kiss to send him on his way with luck. Anna lingers at the doorway, waiting and watching until he drives away. Closing the door against the chill, she hurries back to the kitchen's warmth.

"Sarah, breakfast was fantastic, as always, for all of us. Now, I think I will bring Ellen some new things to wear."

"Thank you, Ma'am. I'm happy you and Sir enjoyed it, and I hope you're right that the girl is pleased with her meals. Little Miss seemed to tuck into her porridge. Wait...Ma'am...Ellen?"

"Forgive me, Sarah. John and I feel it's only decent for the girl to have a name. She deserves one. Further, she should have more than just one dress to wear. Ellen is her name, these are her new dresses, and Johanna is going to help me deliver them."

With a gentle chuckle and a wink to a slightly bewildered Sarah, she picks up Johanna and positions the toddler firmly on her hip. With her free hand, she slips the stack of garments from the back of the chair onto her arm. Years spent as a dressmaker have given her an extra pair of hands when she needs them. Humming a little tune made up in her head causes Johanna to erupt in soft laughter and a bright smile, giving Anna the impression that Johanna rather likes the little ditty.

"Here we are sweet one. Let's see how Ellen likes her new dresses."

Carefully turning the door handle, she nudges the door open further with her toe. Rupert dashes out of the room towards the kitchen. A sparkle catches Anna's eye first thing. Looking closer, she sees an ornament from the Christmas tree. The gold and pink ball is lovely and what a smart idea to hang it in the window like so, catching the light in such a merry way. She looks at Ellen with a quizzical smile. Ellen notices Anna standing there, and she looks at what has drawn Anna's attention. Ellen bows her head, walking over to the bed to sit down and folds her hands on her lap. Anna sees a stray tear trace a path down her cheek. She lays the dresses on the bed and sets Johanna on the floor out of mischief's way. Sitting next to her on the bed, she pats Ellen's arm to get her attention. Ellen looks down at her arm, then up, her eyes filled with more tears.

She looks at the lady. She points to herself and points to the shiny. She shakes her head as she points to herself and draws an X in the palm of her hand. Placing her palms together, she moves them from her chest towards the lady.

Gathering from the girl's, no, Ellen's, gestures, Anna understands she feels sorry for taking the ornament. Patting Ellen's hand, she shakes her head with a smile. There is nothing wrong with wanting to make her room pretty. Anna holds up one finger. She points to Ellen, points to her own eyes, and points to Johanna. Anna gets up and goes to the door, turning again to Ellen as she holds up one finger to say she will be right back. She hurries to the sitting room and finds a similar ornament on the Christmas tree. Holding the prise in her hands, Rupert comes running past her in the hallway. He tries to stop but slides on the polished wood floor. Anna cringes as the silly dog crashes into the loo door. She shakes her head and mutters something about John's dog before she returns to Ellen's room and presents the silver and pink sphere to Ellen with a triumphant smile.

She looks at the lady and the shiny. She looks at the lady again. She points to herself and tilts her head to the side.

Anna is confident that Ellen will understand in just a moment. She walks over to the second window in the bedroom and hangs it in the same way Ellen had attached the first one. Rupert runs into the room and stops long enough to lick Johanna's face before hopping up on the bed. He sits, ears perked, watching his mistress and his new friend. Anna walks 'round to Johanna and picks her up, showing Johanna the pretties in the windows.

"See, sweetheart? Ellen had a superb idea! Isn't that pretty?"

Johanna's squeal of delight and attempts to reach for the ornaments from across the room confirm that decorating the windows in such a way is a capital notion and should be tucked away for future reference. Turning her attention to Ellen, she sees her standing, looking at the ornaments, and wiping away her tears. Seizing the moment, Anna reaches down to pat the clothing on the bed. She points to herself, Johanna, and then points to the clothes. She points to Ellen, hoping her meaning is clear, that these garments are for her.

She looks at the lady and points at the shinies. She points to the clothing. She points to the lady and places her hand over her heart. She points to herself and shrugs and tilts her head.

Anna's heart breaks that Ellen would ask why someone would love her. She points to herself, places her hand over her heart, and points to Ellen. She does not know what to say, beyond that. How do you answer such a question with anything other than 'I love you'?

Slowly moving in a maternal rhythm with Johanna on her hip, she watches Ellen bow her head again, as if ashamed. She watches as Ellen holds up one finger, then opens the bureau drawer and takes out a knife. She walks to the bed and lays it down. Surprised to see a knife from her kitchen in Ellen's possession, Anna is alarmed that Ellen might feel it necessary to have such a thing in her possession. Instinctively, she holds Johanna a bit closer but remains calm as she waits for some kind of explanation. She watches Ellen return to the open bureau drawer and reach in. Her hand cups 'round some small object. Ellen brings it closer to Anna and opens her hand.

Anna gasps as she takes the delicately carved hummingbird from the nest of Ellen's hand. She can hardly believe her eyes. As she admires Ellen's extraordinary talent, tears begin to blur the intricate details. Ellen sits in the chair nearby and hangs her head, her hands folded in her lap. Anna cannot help but compare Ellen's posture to that of a child waiting for inevitable punishment. She reaches down to pat Ellen's arm for attention. Ellen looks down at her arm, then up to Anna. Anna points to herself, places her hand over her heart, and points to the hummingbird figure. Again, Anna points to herself, puts her hand over her heart, but this time points to Ellen.

She watches the lady and nods. She points to the shinies and the clothing. She points to the lady. She places her hand over her heart and points to herself. She points to herself, places her hand over her heart, and points to the lady. She points to herself, points to the thing, then points to the lady.

Anna smiles and nods as she brings the little carving to her lips, kissing it. She hopes Ellen will understand how much this means to her. She could give Ellen everything under the sun, and it would not mean a fig compared to this precious gift made by Ellen's loving hands. The hummingbird tucked safely into Anna's pocket, she opens her free arm, inviting Ellen to come. Silently crying, Ellen nods. She gets up and allows herself to experience a mother's love. They hold each other, Anna rubbing Ellen's back and Ellen holding Anna tightly. Johanna, sensing things only a baby could, leans her head against both of them.

Time passes, only a brief span that seems to stretch endlessly. Leaning back from their embrace, both of them wiping away tears, Anna sees Ellen smile a tiny smile fluttering at the corners of her mouth. This is the first time she has seen even a hint of a smile, and she can truly appreciate the lovely face that hides an even more beautiful soul. Anna's heart melts with happiness. Reluctant to break away from the moment, she steps back and pats the dresses on the bed, gesturing that Ellen should choose one of them to put on. She points to the dress Ellen is wearing and pantomimes washing as best she can and then pats an empty spot on the bed. Anna looks at the knife lying on the bed. She picks it up and puts it back in the bureau drawer. As she closes the drawer, she looks at Ellen and smiles.

Bouncing Johanna on her hip, Anna leaves Ellen to change. She walks into the kitchen with the intention of making a list of things Ellen needs. She spies an empty spot in the china cabinet, next to her hummingbird tea set. Treading lightly over to the cupboard, Anna takes from her pocket the carved hummingbird Ellen made for her. Holding it in her hand, she allows Johanna to touch it for only a moment. She places it next to the other hummingbird treasures and closes the cabinet's curved glass door. Satisfied that Ellen's gift has found a proper place, Anna returns to the kitchen to carry out the task at hand. As she muses, she puts the tea water on to heat. Happily, Anna snuggles and kisses her daughter. She sits the baby on a blanket that lies on the floor and gives her little girl a pink bunny toy.

"Now, there's my sweetheart. Mamma is right here watching whilst you play."

A cup from the cupboard, some cream, and sugar find their way to the counter to wait for that first splash of hot tea. Anna finds a pencil and paper for her thoughts. The list in Anna's head comes faster than she can write it and she mutters to herself in a good-humoured fit of pique.

"Wait, hold on, I've not finished making my tea, but you want to jump out of the pencil and onto the paper before I'm ready. Hang on a moment, would you?"

She considers making Ellen a few things, but she does not know her preferences for colour, style, or anything else. The teakettle whistles and she finishes making her tea just the way she likes it. Settling herself at the table, she thinks it best to watch what Ellen chooses to wear off the peg before buying or making her anything else. 'Unmentionables' are a necessity, regardless of what dress covers them. So, focused on the task at hand, she does not sense Ellen's entrance. She stands with her hands clasped together at her waist, staring at Anna. Catching a glimpse of a blue dress, Anna looks up at her with a smile.

Anna's stomach bleats like a cantankerous old goat, and she looks up at the clock on the wall. Well, that solves the mystery of why her stomach is making such indelicate noises. She looks up at Ellen and gestures for her to sit at the table with her. She pantomimes eating and points to herself, Johanna, and then to Ellen. Anna tilts her head to the side as Ellen does, to form these gestures into a question, as she has seen Ellen do. She sits at the table and looks 'round her in the kitchen.

She looks at Anna, nodding. Excited at Ellen's willingness to eat at the table, she nearly hops up out of her chair and finds sandwiches in the cool box. On laundry days, Sarah always makes the loveliest sandwiches and a little something special for Johanna. Anna puts the sandwiches on plates, fills another cup with tea, and serves them at the table. Anna lifts Johanna to sit in her high chair and pulls the chair up close to give Johanna bits of her sandwich. Rupert is at the ready, stationed aside Johanna's high chair, prepared to make the ultimate sacrifice to keep the kitchen floor clean.

Settling back into her chair, Anna breaks off bits of sandwich for Johanna that, today, is a little soldier and his horse. She chuckles at Sarah's delight in making any little thing amusing for Johanna. Who would have thought to use biscuit cutters to slice a child's sandwich into a playful shape? Cheese rolled into small cannonballs, and a soft biscuit shaped like a flower. Her excited little girl is becoming more adept at feeding herself. Johanna looks down at poor Rupert, sitting there, hoping for a crust. With Mamma shaking her head, Johanna laughs and reaches down to give Rupert a soggy piece of her sandwich. Rupert's tail wags his gratitude as he gently takes it from those tiny fingers and swallows it whole. Anna watches Ellen look about the room as she eats her sandwich. She finds it fascinating how Ellen scrutinises everything. Then, she will try to emulate what she has observed. Anna surmises that Ellen's inability to hear or speak must be a terribly inconvenient pair of obstacles hiding a quick mind and curious intellect.

With a satisfying end to their light lunch, Anna places Johanna back on her play blanket and then turns to the cooker to make more tea. Ellen stands and begins to pick up dishes carefully, taking one tiny scrap and feeding it to an eager Rupert who lays down next to the baby on her blanket. Anna cannot help but laugh at Rupert's patience as Johanna lays on him, covers his furry face with kisses, and pats him with all the affection a child can display at her age. Anna is pleasantly surprised to see Ellen bringing dishes to the sink. Ellen even left the teacups on the table. Their bright girl knows already that delicate items are the last things to go in to be washed. She pats Ellen's arm to draw her attention. Once Ellen has looked down at her own arm and then up to Anna, she proceeds to gesture her thanks for clearing the table.

She looks at the lady and nods. She points to the table and points to the washing place. She pantomimes washing the eating things. She points to herself, places her hand over her heart, and points to the lady.

38

Anna smiles at Ellen, nodding acknowledgement that Ellen's desire to help comes from love. Not wanting Ellen to think she is ungrateful, Anna holds up a finger. She puts a bit of soap in with the dishes and fills the sink with hot water. She holds her hand over it with a nod, trying to say they will just soak for now. Gently placing her hand on Ellen's arm, she points to herself, puts her hand over her heart, and points to Ellen to underscore her appreciation of Ellen's desire to help motivated by a need to love and be loved. Anna motions for Ellen to return with her to the table where they can enjoy their tea together. Teacups are filled, once more, and Anna looks again at the list she is making. She checks off each item. Winter-weight stockings. Undergarments. A sweater would be desirable and adds that to the list. Ellen scoots herself closer to sit next to Anna.

Staring at the squiggly lines the lady makes with the stick thing, she tilts her head to the side as she taps the lady's shoulder. She points to the stick thing and points to the squiggly lines. She leans her head to one side, shrugging her shoulders.

Anna watches Ellen's hand movements. Slowly, Ellen's gestures take on a profound meaning. Ellen is illiterate. Why did she not think to consider writing as a means of communication? Anna figuratively kicks herself and feels wholly dense. The struggle begins to find a way to explain writing. Tearing off her list, she sets it aside, pulls the cup of tea close, and points to it. Holding the pencil up, she writes clearly on the fresh paper, 'CUP'. She points to the word on the paper and then to the physical object. Looking at Ellen, she hopes to see a glimmer of understanding. Ellen holds out her hand and points to the pencil, her head is still tilted quizzically. Anna puts the pencil in Ellen's hand and smiles as she watches Ellen, possibly for the first time, handle a writing instrument. Ellen gives the pencil back to Anna and shrugs her shoulders. Not only do objects have words associated with them, but people also do, too. Anna points to herself and writes 'ANNA' on the paper. She shows it to Ellen and points to her name and then points to herself. Ellen slowly nods. Ellen points at Rupert and tilts her head to the side. With growing excitement, Anna writes 'DOG' on the paper and points to Rupert who is sound asleep. He has become the adoring pillow for Johanna who has joined him in an impromptu nap. Ellen points to Johanna and points to the paper where Anna gleefully writes 'BABY' on the paper.
Ellen takes the paper, looking at the words and looking back to what

each word represents.

Ellen sits for a moment, staring at the paper in her hands. With a trembling hand, she points to herself and points to the paper with her head tilted to the side as if to ask whether she has a word of her own. At every turn, some new thing about Ellen breaks Anna's heart. The paradox is that the brokenness of Anna's heart allows it to fill to overflowing with maternal affection. Ellen does not know she has a name. Ellen might not have a name for all they know, but she has one, now. Anna takes the paper, writes 'ELLEN' on it, and then points to Ellen in answer. Ellen stares at the words, tears forming in her eyes, dropping softly on the paper. She holds out her hand for the pencil, which Anna eagerly gives her. Holding the pencil awkwardly, Ellen tries to copy the words Anna had written. As Ellen tries to write, in a surprisingly legible fashion one might add, Ellen points to what she thinks she remembers each word represents. Anna watches in amazement and views Ellen's efforts as a courageous triumph! In her excitement, she fails to notice that Ellen is pointing to Johanna after having written 'DOG', pointing to Rupert after writing 'ANNA', and pointing to the teacup after writing 'ELLEN', pointing to herself after writing 'CUP'.

Ellen looks up at Anna with her head tilted to the side. She points to Anna and points to the paper. Ellen points to herself, places her hand over her heart, and points to Anna and then gives Anna the pencil, seeming to ask that Anna write down the words 'I love you'. Willing to do anything her sweet girl asks of her, Anna gladly writes out the words on the paper, followed by their corresponding and profound gestures. Anna's heart goes out to Ellen as she watches her hold the paper with a tear or two rolling down her cheeks. Slowly, Ellen gets up from the table and holds the papers close to her. She leaves the kitchen, and in a moment, Anna hears the door to Ellen's room click shut.

Rupert awakens and shifts himself out from under the still-sleeping Johanna. He trots out of the kitchen and down the hall to Ellen's room, scratching and whining softly to get in. Anna casts a protective eye on her daughter and is assured that she is safely asleep. She goes to Rupert's aid and opens the door just enough for Rupert to nose his way into Ellen's room. With a smile, she returns to the kitchen to wash the dishes that have been soaking in the dishwater. Finished, Anna wipes her hands on the tea towel and hangs it up to dry. She stops to admire her beautiful baby girl before she scoops Johanna up in her arms to carry her upstairs. Unwilling to let an opportunity to cuddle her daughter pass her by, she sits with Johanna in the rocking chair. Humming softly to Johanna, she reaches for a blanket from the cot to warm them both.

Sarah walks into the nursery carrying Johanna's freshly laundered things and proceeds to put them away. She smiles at mother and baby rocking together and then sobers, speaking softly.

"Ma'am, whilst I was doing laundry and gathering and whatnot, I found something in the girl's room. I mean Ellen's room. A knife, Ma'am. From the kitchen. I left it there, not sure what to do. I thought you should know."

"The knife can stay in Ellen's room for as long as she'd like to use it, Sarah. She is using it to carve things. If you look in the china cabinet next time you walk past it, you will see a sweet little hummingbird she carved for me. She means to do no harm with it. Thank you for telling me, though. It was thoughtless of me to forget."

"Yes, Ma'am. I am much relieved to hear it, and I will look at the little bird. Hidden talents, so it seems. If I may say, Ma'am, at first, I was not sure about having a strange girl in the house, but now, I rather think she belongs here. She fits, if that makes sense, Ma'am. I don't understand her gestures, but I believe she knows that and just nods at me when I smile and shake my head. I feel sorry I can't understand her, but her hand motions don't make sense to me."

"It's all right, Sarah. She is a bright and gifted young woman, and she understands, I'm sure, that not everyone will be able to comprehend her. I have trouble, too, at times. Consider it like this. She speaks a foreign language. She is not able to learn our language, but we are trying to learn how to speak hers. We must all be patient with her and with ourselves."

Sarah nods and retreats to her own thoughts. As she puts things away, she thinks how lucky the girl, Ellen, was to come here of all places. She finishes in the nursery, which was the last of her laundry duties.

"Ma'am, would you like me to get out the boxes for the ornaments on the tree? You'd talked about taking it down before it becomes a hazard with fire and all."

"Oh yes, what a splendid idea. We may not get to it today, but perhaps tomorrow. We will at least have the boxes ready. Thank you, Sarah. You can put them in the corner of the dining room out of the way until we're ready."

With a slight nod and a smile, she leaves the nursery to fetch storage boxes for Christmas ornaments and decorations. Some of them have an underlying history, some have been in their families for generations, and some are just pretty ones that Ma'am liked. Sarah's mind wanders to Ellen. She almost behaves as if she had never seen a

Christmas tree. So many things, it appears, that the girl has never seen. It is almost as if, along with her strange language, she comes from a foreign place that none of them could imagine. Shaking her head, she returns to her task, chiding herself for entertaining such a silly idea. Coming from a foreign place! The girl appeared in rags begging for food. She is English, no doubt, but more likely, that distant place is not so much a place as it is a situation. Sagely, she nods her head as she carries out her duties so she can move on to fixing the family's supper.

John finally returns and is happy to enter the warmth of their house. He feels the heat from the fireplace, and he looks forwards to a cup of tea whilst he warms his toes. Taking off his coat and hat, John remembers the treat he brought. He takes out the little package from his pocket and tucks it into his suit pocket with a satisfied pat and a smile. The familiar scent of Sarah's cooking tickles his nose, and he looks into the sitting room to see if anyone is about. Seeing neither Anna nor Ellen, John starts to walk into the kitchen to see if Sarah will allow him to snitch a preview of supper. Suddenly, he stops, seeing Ellen in the hallway staring at him just outside her door. He smiles and backs away from her slowly, folding his hands in front of him as he has seen her do. In this way, John hopes to convey that he is not going to harm her. Surprisingly, Ellen does not flee or cower. He sees her look about nervously, but she remains where she is. The papers she holds in her hand arouse a bit of curiosity, but he knows better than to inquire.

She looks at the man and tilts her head to the side. She taps two fingers on her chest and shrugs her shoulders.

John has not the first inkling what Ellen might be trying to say, but it seems she is asking something. He shakes his head and shrugs, unable to understand Ellen's question. As John struggles to deduce what Ellen might be trying to ask, he hears Anna and Johanna come down the stairs and into the sitting room. Breathing a sigh of relief that his 'translator' is en route to rescue him, he calls out to Anna.

"Anna, sweetheart, I'm home, and I need your translation skills."

Smiling at the sound of John's voice and chuckling at his request, she makes her way to the entry with Johanna in her arms. She winks at John and stands on her tiptoes to kiss him.

"Someone just knew Daddy would be home soon, so she insisted we come down to see. Isn't that right, little one? Yes! He's home, and I'm sure he missed us as much as we missed him."

Johanna wiggles and squeals as she reaches for her Daddy. John gathers his daughter in his arms and covers her face with kisses to make her laugh. Pausing, he winks at Anna with a chuckle.

"Yes, I missed you, and I'm happy to see you, my angel. And, you, too, Anna. Now, I believe Ellen was trying to say something to me, and I have no idea what she wanted to tell me or ask, rather. I caught the head tilt and the shrug, but that's all I could make out."

Nodding, she walks over to Ellen and is surprised Ellen has been just watching the three of them together. She tilts her head to the side to ask Ellen what she might want to say.

She points to herself and places her fist on her chest. She points to her eyes and points to the lady. She points to the man and shrugs.

"Oh...John, I guess she was looking for me, and you either didn't know where I was or didn't understand her."

"Yes. All the above."

Anna gives John an amused look and turns to Ellen with a tilt of her head. She points to Ellen, points to her own eyes and then points to herself to find out why Ellen wanted to see her.

She points to herself, places her fist on her chest and stops. She holds up the papers and points to the lady's squiggly lines. She points to one of the squiggly line things and points to herself. She points to the lady and taps two fingers on her chest.

Anna's eyes mist over as Ellen's meaning grows clearer with a little thought and she turns to John who remains at a respectful distance with an adoring Johanna in his arms.

"John, she was curious, earlier, about me writing things. I wrote some words on the paper and pointed to what the words were like baby, cup, my name, dog. She even wrote on her own, and it was copying what I wrote, but she tried."

"So...she's illiterate as well...why didn't we think...oh, Anna. Bless her. I'm proud of her for wanting to learn and doing so well on her first attempt, though. Can you ask her what the tapping of two fingers on her chest means? That was a gesture I hadn't seen before."

Anna turns to Ellen and tilts her head to the side. She taps two fingers on her chest and shrugs. Ellen looks at John, then back to Anna. She holds up the papers and points to the word 'ANNA' and points to Anna. She taps two fingers on her chest and points to Anna, in her way, saying she has given Anna her own name in her silent language. Anna is deeply touched that Ellen has chosen to give her a name. She opens her arms to Ellen, to thank her for such a special gift. After a brief embrace, Ellen pulls away to point at John. She taps three fingers on her chest and nods her head.

"Oh, John, she's given us each a gift. My name in her language is two fingers tapped on the chest. Your name is three fingers tapped on the chest. John, we have names!"

"Well, that is an honour and cause for celebration. Oh, does she know what her name is?"

Anna takes the papers from Ellen's hands, holding them up in one hand. She points to Ellen and points to the papers. Once, again, she points to Ellen with her head tilted to the side, hoping she will be able to point to her name as written on the paper. Hopeful, she watches Ellen nod as she points to the word 'CUP' and then looks at her and John with a serious but tentatively proud expression on her face. Not wanting to spoil Ellen's perceived moment of triumph, John and Anna smile at one another, as it is clear she believes her name is CUP. They just nod proudly, glad for any bit of progress that helps Ellen feel happy. There is time enough for learning more, and she will come to see that her name is not Cup. Now, it is time to celebrate small victories.

Chapter Five
9 January 1926

Crackling and popping sounds emanate from the fireplace's warmth. 'Tis after supper and Johanna is upstairs for her evening bath and story time with Sarah. John and Anna smothered their darling baby with kisses and cuddles before she was whisked away. All the whilst, Ellen sat near the Christmas tree watching. Anna clears an area off the table in front of the sofa for the ornament boxes.

"Well, John, I hate to see it come down, but it is time."

John looks at the tree, still twinkling merrily as it had the first night they had put it up. He chuckles at the memory of Rupert's help during the ordeal.

"I'll get the boxes from the dining room. Anna, I still laugh when I remember how your dog helped decorate."

Laughing, Anna raises an eyebrow at John's comment.

"Excuse me, Mr Thorpe, but I believe it was YOUR dog who thought stringing ribbon throughout the house was a good idea."

John shakes his head with a chuckle as he walks to the dining room and returns carrying the boxes, a grin on his face as he recalls the mayhem.

"I can't help it if the poor fellow got his tooth stuck in the ribbon and tore through the house trying to get it off. You have to give him credit for participation."

"John, if points for participation are what you would like him to have, then Rupert shall be awarded his points. He is still your dog, though."

Anna laughs and shakes her head, returning to her task. She arranges the boxes on the table and sofa, lids off, ready to receive their treasures for another year. She begins removing the ornaments that have special sentimental meaning, first. She holds the straw angel Granny made for their son's first Christmas, that he never lived to see. Anna touches it tenderly, letting the kindness of this gift warm her memory. It will always be a reminder of their little boy. The next ornament she takes down is also from Granny. This one is a rose pressed between two ovals of glass in memory of the baby girl who never had a chance to be born.

Pangs of grief are long gone, and all that remains are the thoughts of what might have been. They are but faint sighs echoing in Anna's heart. She wraps the ornaments, including Johanna's little angel and Rupert's decorated stick, adorned with a festive red ribbon. She places them in their box and turns to talk to John.

"John, are you going to help or would you rather...."

His response is a gentle snore, from where he sits. Rupert is sprawled across John's lap, and he seems to be dreaming with little 'woofs' and the occasional twitch of a paw. Anna shakes her head and chuckles to herself. It does not matter. John deserves to relax after a nice supper. For a moment, she looks at her husband of fifteen years. Anna is without a doubt that he and their daughter are the greatest gifts life could ever have offered her. With mixed feelings, she moves forwards with the annual task. It is never as exciting to put the decorations away as it is to festoon the house with merriment before Christmas. Life's pace in their household has allowed the New Year to come and go without notice.

Ellen comes 'round the tree to see what Anna is doing. Taking the small box of special ornaments in her hands, Ellen opens it. She touches each ornament. Ellen takes out a shell ornament and runs her finger over the ridges. Holding it up, she taps Anna on the shoulder and tilts her head to the side. Anna looks at Ellen, then the ornament. It occurs to her that it is possible Ellen has never seen a shell, much less the ocean. They must make it a point to take Ellen to their seaside cottage in the summer. Anna smiles and nods, wishing she knew how to say the word 'pretty' in Ellen's language of gestures.

Ellen stands back to watch what Anna is doing with the tree and ornaments. Anna takes one ornament after another off the tree and places them one by one into the box. When the box is full, she puts the cover on and sets it aside. Out comes the next empty box ready to be filled. She is glad John took down the star a couple of days ago. It would have been much too high for her to reach. Anna continues her task, lost in memories attached to each shiny bauble.

Ellen opens the boxes as soon as Anna fills them and then she hangs the ornaments back on the opposite side of the tree, out of Anna's view. Her eyes grow wide as the tree is filled, again, with the dazzle of glistening shapes. She even hangs some of them linked together as space on the branches is depleted. As quickly as Anna fills a box and sets it aside, Ellen empties it.

Anna fills the last one, intending to put it with the others. To her consternation, she sees the previously filled boxes are open and empty.

Puzzled, Anna could swear she had filled at least two boxes with ornaments. She pushes the branches aside. A few more are found hidden deeper within the boughs, but where are the rest? Anna looks at Rupert asleep on John's lap, eliminating John's dog as a culprit. Sarah and Johanna are upstairs. She wonders if she has gone daft as she scratches her head.

Finally peeking 'round to the other side of the tree, she grins and begins to chuckle and then laugh aloud. The other side of the tree is exceedingly festive with Ellen's enthusiastic re-decorating. She sees a plethora of ornaments that would make the tree fall over, were they any heavier. Anna shakes her head and is unsure of how to communicate that the tree must come down and the ornaments cleared away. Explaining why would be the most complicated part. She smiles at Ellen, unable to fault her for wanting the merry decorations to stay right where they are. In fact, she applauds Ellen's stealth and speed in keeping up with her. As fast as Anna took down the decorations, Ellen put them back up. Anna begins to remove the trimmings and place them in their boxes.

Frowning at Anna, Ellen persists in replacing the baubles on the tree. Just as quickly, Anna removes them and tucks them into their boxes. Back and forth, Anna only realises her dilemma again after the third go-round. She shakes her head, wondering how she will ever get this done with Ellen's help. Anna pats Ellen's arm and waits for Ellen to look down at her arm and then up to meet Anna's eyes. Anna points to the decorations on the tree. She points to the boxes, nodding her head firmly but kindly. She hopes Ellen understands she cannot take 'no' for an answer. The tree must come down, and the decorations put away.

A somewhat dejected look on her face, Ellen takes a blue ornament and sits on the sofa, watching Anna. She holds it in her hand and pulls her skirt up a bit. She holds the ornament next to the fabric of her dress for a moment. Ellen finally reaches over to place it in the box with the rest of the tree's embellishments. She looks down at her hands folded in her lap, only looking up now and then to see the tree denuded of its splendour. Having awakened, Rupert leaps off John's lap and trots over to his friend. Hopping up on the sofa, he nuzzles himself under Ellen's arm and leans against her, seeming to sense her disappointment.

Anna carries the full boxes to a corner of the dining room where they can remain until John or Sarah puts them away. On the morrow, Sarah will finish removing the last traces of Christmas from the house. Returning to the sitting room, she sees Ellen still sitting on the sofa, staring at the denuded tree. Anna walks over to sit next to her and pats her arm. She sympathises with the feeling one has when something special needs to go away. Ellen most likely does not know they will have another tree next year. Assuming Ellen stays with them. Giving Rupert his essential ear scratches, Anna turns her attention to John who is still sleeping in his chair. She frowns at what must be a terribly uncomfortable position.

Anna's soft voice and her kiss to his forehead bring John to a sleepy awareness. She whispers in his ear.

"I love you, sweet one."

"Mm...I love you too, sweetheart."

He opens his eyes and smiles at Anna, reaching up to caress her face. Her precious visage is the first happiness he sees in the morning and the last joy he sees before he falls asleep.

"Did you need help with the tree? I apologise, I must have dozed off."

"You did doze off rather soundly, Mr Thorpe. The tree is empty, ornaments are in their boxes, and I'll help you carry the tree outside if you like."

"Did Ellen help?"

"Oh yes, she was a great help. Later, I will tell you how much of a sweet help she was. She seems disappointed that the tree is empty. She will be even more disappointed and confused when we take it outside. I just have no way to explain this to her."

Uncomfortable, he repositions himself in the chair and stretches. He remembers the treat he brought for his girls.

"Anna, I have just the thing to cure disappointment."

John reaches into his jacket pocket and withdraws something wrapped in paper. Immediately Anna's eyes light up with the scent of chocolate wafting towards her nose.

"John, I wonder if Ellen has ever had chocolate. I have an idea that might help her thaw towards you a bit more."

Anna hurries to the kitchen and returns with a small plate in her hand.

"John, put the chocolate on here whilst I get Ellen's attention."

John places the sweets on the plate. He holds the plate so Ellen will know that this treat is from him. Anna walks over to Ellen and sits next to her. She pats Ellen's arm and waits for her to look down at her arm and then back up. With a hopeful smile, Anna points to John holding the plate. John smiles and holds it up. Anna walks over to John and breaks off a piece of the chocolate. She sniffs it and then closes her eyes with a blissful smile as she savours the scent. Anna takes a tiny nibble followed by a smile and an enthusiastic nod. As Ellen watches, Anna hopes Ellen will understand that the delicacy she is eating is delicious. She breaks off a small bit and offers it to Ellen who takes it in her hand. Sniffing it, she looks back up at Anna. Anna nods, encouraging Ellen to taste it.

Still staring at Anna, Ellen takes a minuscule taste. Her eyes grow wide, and she takes another bite. Obviously enjoying her first taste of chocolate, Ellen pops the rest of the piece in her mouth.

She nods her head and pats her hands together.

Anna and John can only assume that patting hands together must mean 'good'. Pleased that Ellen likes the chocolate, John and Anna smile at one another. They are glad for another bit of success in making Ellen happy. Ellen takes another piece of chocolate from the plate and stuffs the whole chunk into her mouth. Still chewing the chocolate, Ellen picks up the plate and leaves the sitting room. Shortly after, John and Anna hear the door to Ellen's room close. Rupert dashes down the hallway after her. Another cringe-worthy moment comes as they hear the familiar crash of Rupert, unable to stop on the slick floor.

"John, your dog has to be the dearest bumble I've ever seen."

"MY dog? I thought he was your dog?"

They laugh as Anna sits on John's lap and kisses his cheek.

"Thank you for the chocolate, John. It was delicious, and Ellen has a new favourite treat, it seems."

"Yes, I believe you're right. I am sure your chances of having any more chocolate off that plate are remote. I never did get a piece."

"Aww, I am sorry, John. Next time, snitch a bite first when nobody is looking."

Through their gentle laughter, a solemn figure stands in the doorway. Ellen holds her hands clasped tightly in front of her. She wears a dressing gown covering a modest nightdress. Ellen watches John and Anna until John notices her standing there.

"Anna, I believe someone might want your attention. Go see to Ellen, and I'll take care of the tree and sort lights and doors."

One last kiss between them and Anna turns her attention to Ellen. Tilting her head to the side, Anna asks Ellen to share whatever is on her mind.

She looks at the man and turns away from him and looks at the lady. She points to herself and pulls her arms up, crossing them over her chest. She points to the lady and points to herself. Pointing towards the place where she sleeps, she puts her hands together and rests her head on them.

Anna understands Ellen is afraid and wants her to be with her whilst she falls asleep. Perhaps Ellen is fearful of having a nightmare. Ellen has gestured that she sleeps poorly at times and holds her arms up in the gesture meaning 'afraid'. A few nights ago, Anna heard a noise in Ellen's room. Upon investigation, found Ellen dissolved in uncontrollable sobbing.

"John, I think she's afraid to go to sleep without someone with her. I shouldn't be long."

She walks with Ellen back to her room where Rupert is waiting on the bed. Anna turns down the covers and fluffs the pillows. She tries to show Ellen she cares about her in big things and in small things. Patting the bed, Anna smiles at Ellen. Nodding, Ellen slides between the sheets. Anna pulls the blankets up to cover Ellen in the cosiest way possible. She sits on the edge of the bed and reaches out to stroke Ellen's hair in the same way she strokes Johanna's hair to lull her daughter to sleep.

Ellen stares at Anna, her eyes closing and then opening wide as if fighting the urge to sleep. Anna gives Ellen a reassuring smile. She points to herself, places her hand over her heart, and points to Ellen to make sure she knows she is loved.

She points to herself, puts her hand over her heart, then points to the lady, and nods. She reaches over to the side table to pick up the papers and points to the three squiggly lines the lady wrote.

Anna is touched that Ellen remembered the words 'I love you' on the paper. Anna smiles as Ellen places the paper back on the night table, takes Anna's hand, and puts it back on her head as a silent request to continue stroking her hair. Maternal warmth filling her, she fulfils Ellen's request. In a short time, Ellen yawns and her eyes flutter closed. A deep sigh escapes Ellen's lips as her body relaxes. Anna continues stroking Ellen's hair for a whilst longer until she is satisfied that Ellen is asleep. Not wanting to disturb her, Anna gets up and moves towards the door, taking one last look back at her girl.

She sees Ellen's face become tense, her leg jerking under the blanket. Ellen's breath comes faster and heavier, beads of sweat glisten on her forehead. Before Anna can return to her bedside, Ellen begins thrashing about. Rupert dashes under the bed to hide. Alarmed, she realises that Ellen is asleep. In an attempt to calm Ellen and gently awaken her, she sits on the side of the bed. Murmuring soothing words Ellen cannot hear, she rubs Ellen's arm. To Anna's horror, Ellen erupts into a sitting position, still asleep. Ellen's eyes are wide open and filled with terror, her mouth open in a silent scream. Ellen's hands flail at something unseen, and she begins hitting her own head. Anna undertakes the monumental task of preventing Ellen from harming herself. She shakes her head violently in what appears to be a refusal to whatever is attacking her in the nightmare. She tries to move away from whatever is tormenting her, pushing Anna away. The blankets are too tangled, preventing Ellen's escape. Anna reaches down to unfetter Ellen's limbs from the bedclothes. Ellen bolts out of bed and cowers into a corner. Rushing to Ellen's side, Anna kneels beside her, hoping she will return to the present from this hellish dream.

Ellen gradually comes to herself, and her eyes spark with awareness. They dart 'round the room as if she struggles to remember where she is. She looks at Anna, for a moment, confusion spread across her face. Finally, with a glimmer of recognition, she lunges into Anna's arms, her body wracked with sobs. Holding her, she rocks Ellen in the same way she would soothe Johanna. She resumes stroking Ellen's hair and rubs her back in small circles. Time passes unnoticed until Ellen is calm to the point of tearful hiccups. Taking her handkerchief out of her pocket, Anna wipes away Ellen's tears.

She bows her head, looking down at her hands. She wipes wetness from her eyes on her sleeve then looks back up at the lady. She moves her hands, palms together towards the lady. She points to herself and draws an X in her hand.

Shaking her head, Anna takes Ellen's hands in her own. She engages Ellen's gaze and points to her. Anna pats her hands together to tell Ellen there is no need to make an apology, nor is she bad in any way. After what Ellen must have endured, it is no wonder she has nightmares. Anna has never seen such a violent night terror, and it has left her shaken. She is determined to mother her girl through these. Neglecting to assist Ellen during these times of panic would be unforgivable, and she chides herself for not realising this need sooner.

Ellen calms further, nodding that she is ready to try to sleep again. Anna takes her hand and helps her back to bed, straightening the blankets. Ellen lies back down and stares at Anna. She takes Anna's hand and places it on her head for Anna to stroke her hair again. She clasps Anna's other hand and just holds it close to her. She strokes Ellen's hair and gives her hand a reassuring squeeze. The storm seems to have passed for now. For Anna, it appears to take a long time for Ellen to relax and close her eyes. She turns on her side, facing Anna, still clutching Anna's hand. Finally, exhaustion claims Ellen. She stays with Ellen, reluctant to leave her. When Anna is confident there will be no more nightmares, for now, she stands and gently extricates her hand from Ellen's grasp. A soft pat on Rupert's head is his reward for remaining with Ellen.

Anna leaves Ellen's door ajar, making her way in the familiar darkness through the house. She goes upstairs to Johanna's nursery. Walking over to her sleeping daughter, she leans down to kiss her forehead, brushing a blonde curl aside. A whispered wish for sweet dreams and a caress to the baby's cheek are her good night blessings to her little love.

Through the darkness, she arrives at the bedroom she and John share. She opens the door and watches her dear husband as he sleeps. He has been completely unaware of the tribulations downstairs. She will share this with him soon enough. She changes for bed and slips under the quilt beside him. The violence of Ellen's nightmare lingers with Anna, and she is still upset by it. Draping her arm over John, she nestles against his warmth. Her mind races and refuses to allow sleep to encroach on the disturbing images lingering in her mind. She repeatedly comes back to the question, what happened to Ellen that would induce such horrific terrors? She wishes she could tell John of this unsettling event, but has no heart to wake him. She takes a bit of comfort from John's presence as she feels the warmth of his hand resting on her arm as she whispers.

"I love you, John."

Chapter Six
10 January 1926

Wind whistles 'round the house with talk of a cold snap coming in the next day or so. Chill has crept into every corner since the New Year. He has to admit that Anna's insistence that they install a central heating system was a splendid idea. With the birth of Johanna, having a warm house is a boon. Still, there is nothing as pleasant as a fireplace. Splitting wood is a healthy exercise, even though a local farmer who owns what he calls a 'tree farm' delivers it in large pieces. In Petworth, the town fathers would most likely frown at the loss of their picturesque trees falling to the ground as firewood.

John stops to catch his breath and tug his hat further down on his head. He raises the collar of his parka against the icy fingers of wind trying to tickle his neck. The wool garment he wears was another brilliant idea of Anna's. She found a large anorak that could have fit two of him inside of it. Anna and Sarah washed and soaked it in the hottest water possible, and dried it in front of the fire to shrink it. He had been dubious at first, but it shrank to his approximate size. With a bit of careful tailoring, it fits John as if it had been made for him. It might be the warmest parka he has ever owned, and with today's wind, he is glad for it.

Rupert watches his master, eagerly waiting for the next bit of bark or small branch to fly from his master's hand so he can fetch it. John notices the dog's readiness for more sport, so he throws a little bit of kindling. Rupert takes off like a shot to retrieve the makeshift plaything.

"Go get it, boy! That's the ticket! Bring it back, there's a good fellow!"

Rupert proudly trots back to his master with the kindling and drops it at John's feet. Laughing, John strokes him and tosses the wood into the pail where it belongs.

"You must be frozen by now, my friend. Let's get you inside to warm up a bit."

He walks with Rupert to the garden door and opens it just enough to let the dog inside. Closing the door, John returns to the stacks to separate the freshly cut wood from that which is already dry. John claps his gloved hands together to warm them. He stoops to pick up the larger scraps of wood and tosses them under the bushes after the kindling bucket is full. He returns the axe to the shed and retrieves the rake to finish cleaning up. With deft strokes of the rake, the debris is under the shrubbery. He places the rake back in the shed and latches the door upon leaving. It will not do to have the wind whip the door open as it did last winter. John is not keen to replace door hinges again this year.

Gathering an armload of wood to carry inside, he notices their neighbours and frowns. Jane and Lewis Adderley must be walking home from the market. Mrs Adderley, a widow, is one of the most disagreeable individuals John has ever met. Her son, Lewis, is equally irksome and has been a mischief-maker since birth. John hopes they do not notice him and just continue on their way. Even a superficial conversation with Jane Adderley turns into a fishing expedition. She wants to know everything about everyone. If one desires scuttlebutt, one only has to pay a visit to Mrs Adderley. She will relate her version of 'news' with glee, whether it is true or not.

Hearing the door open and close, he turns to see Ellen walking at a cautious distance from him, without a coat. Her eyes look at him and back down at the ground. He wonders if she is looking for some wood to carve now that she has his old carving toolset to use. John waves at Ellen as best he can with the wood in his arms. He points to a stack of wood that would be suitable for carving. He nods with a smile and walks to the door. Anna will be pleased to know Ellen seems to be feeling more at comfortable and free to move about the house and garden as she pleases. No doubt, the high shrubbery 'round their property gives a sense of privacy and safety. He fumbles with the door handle, and it finally succumbs to his efforts, as it swings inward. Ducking inside, John kicks the door shut with his foot and hurries to put the wood away so he can fetch Ellen a proper wrap.

Shivering, Ellen looks 'round the garden after she sees John go indoors. Each corner and every bush come under scrutiny. She picks up the odd piece of wood here and there, filling her arms like a bouquet of something yet to manifest beauty.

Mrs Adderley slaps her son's arm to stop him as she sees a strange young woman in Mr and Mrs Thorpe's garden.

"Well, look at that, why don't you. Looks like the Thorpe family has a guest. A cousin mayhap? Lewis, look smart. We're going to introduce ourselves."

Giving his mother a sullen eyeball, he stubs out his cigarette on the ground beneath his foot. The lanky young man then dutifully follows his mother. He adjusts the shopping baskets hanging from his arms, chunters to himself, and looks about to see if anyone notices them. Lewis snickers to himself and wonders what this girl will think of his mother. Jane Adderley has the reputation of a shrew on a good day. He cannot bring himself to disagree, even if he is her grudgingly devoted son. With almost a cringe of embarrassment at his mother's audacity, he lags behind to watch. His mother, true to form, marches up behind the girl.

"Excuse me; I'm Jane Adderley, a neighbour to your cousin. The Thorpe's are your relation, aren't they?"

Ellen does not respond in any way to this intrusion, her back to the overly assertive woman. Not pleased with the perceived slight, Mrs Adderley grows instantly cross. She walks closer and taps the girl on the shoulder.

"Young lady? I am speaking to you. It's rather uncouth to ignore a guest."

Lewis rolls his eyes at the word 'guest' and his mother's over-inflated sense of importance. His disparaging thoughts regarding his mother are interrupted by the girl's reaction to his mother's so-called introduction. Ellen jumps away and turns towards the source of this sudden encroachment. Her eyes widen, and her face contorts in fear as she backs away, her sticks falling to the ground.

Ellen puts her arms 'round herself and in a panic, looks 'round her. She looks at the house as she continues to back away from the stranger who now stands between her and safety. Unable to see the tree root behind her, Ellen trips, falling backwards. She scrambles backing up towards the bushes, not taking her eyes off the woman.

"Good Lord, what's wrong with you? Cat got your tongue? For heaven's sakes, I'm not going to bite you. You're none too graceful, either, are you? Maybe Mrs Thorpe will teach you some proper deportment."

Rupert joins John as he comes out of the house to bring Ellen an anorak and John sees the disruption caused by Mrs Adderley and her son. Rupert senses that these two humans are not welcome and runs to Ellen, putting his front paws on her shoulder. Ellen's terror-filled face is enough to goad John forwards. He rushes to Ellen as he shrugs off his coat and, drapes it over her shoulders. He gives her a nod and smile, hoping to reassure her. Turned so only Ellen can see, he makes subtle gestures. He points to himself, points to the two interlopers, and with his palm towards Ellen, he urges her to stay where she is and allow him to handle the situation. John turns to the odious woman blocking Ellen's escape, his jaw, now, set in controlled fury; he moves to stand between Ellen and Mrs Adderley. John casts a sharp glance at Lewis who immediately begins to slink away.

"MRS Adderley. What makes you think you can walk into my garden and strike up a conversation with whomever you please? I suggest you take your leave before you wish you'd thought of the idea yourself."

John closes the distance between himself and the woman as she begins to back away.

"I'll have you know that I was just being a good neighbour in trying to introduce myself to this, this, girl. I don't know what sort of relation she is, but you'd best teach her some manners."

A haughty toss of the head punctuates the end of Mrs Adderley's aborted tirade. She turns away with haste, trotting over to Lewis. She grabs her son's sleeve and drags him after her.

"Come along, Lewis, don't be lollygagging. We do not need to tolerate inhospitable people. Come along with you!"

Lewis looks back at the girl and Mr Thorpe as his mother drags him away.

"Mum, there's something wrong with that girl."

"Ha! I would say there is. She is addled or dim-witted. Or, I would wager, just rude like so many people are in this miserable town. I do NOT understand why people aren't sociable with us, Lewis. We try to be good neighbours. We try to help. We go to church. They're all hypocrites, that's what they are, Lewis, every one of 'em. You and I might as well be the only honest people left in Petworth since your father perished from that Spanish flu. Spaniards! Them's what brought it over here, you know. You can't trust foreigners. Like that girl back there. I'm convinced she isn't English. Couldn't speak a word of it."

Lewis tries to manage the shopping baskets that seem to grow heavier by the minute. He finds the tugging of his incessantly chattering mother most annoying. Mentally cursing his burden and gloved clumsiness, he takes longer than he would like to light his cigarette. With his upper limbs so occupied, he lets it dangle from his lips, letting the ashes fall where they may. Lewis knows better than to contradict his mother, but he saw the girl's face. She was afraid, genuinely afraid. That's what's wrong with her. She is right and honestly frightened. A wry chuckle threatens to rise in his throat as he muses to himself. If the girl is frightened of his mother, she must not be too simple-minded.

In John's haste to oust the mother and son, his hat and gloves lay on the ground where they had fallen from his pocket. His heart goes out to Ellen, still quaking with fear at the encounter with Mrs Adderley and her son. Of all the people to meet, why did it have to be them? John scolds himself for not watching her from the window, for not hurrying, for leaving her alone out here for even a moment. Seeing the wood Ellen had gathered, he stoops down to pick it up for her. John collects the firewood into a neat pile when a jagged sliver slices into his hand, causing him to bleed rather profusely. He puts his injured hand to his mouth, trying to stem the bleeding as he turns towards Ellen. John sees her staring at him, not moving from the spot where she sits. He wishes he could reassure her.

Thinking it might be best to retreat indoors and let Ellen come in on her own, John gives Ellen a smile that he hopes gives her a measure of reassurance. He points to himself and to the house. He then turns and walks back into the house, then watches through the door's window. His desire to protect Ellen overrides his need to disengage this blasted sliver from his hand. Soon, John sees Ellen stand. She pulls the parka tight 'round her and then stoops to pick up the wood she had collected. Satisfied that she will be indoors shortly, he walks to the loo to tend this insult to his hand. John nods as he hears the garden door open and close. Rupert's paws pad down the hallway followed by soft footsteps.

He squints with the tweezer, digging at the sliver, only causing the wound to bleed even more. John mutters things he would never let Anna hear until the fragment finally gives way. Mercurochrome is applied after a liberal washing with soap that stings like the devil. Last, he fumbles with a bandage. He holds out his hand to estimate the severity of Anna's inevitable scolding at his failure to ask for help with rendering first aid. John's attention turns from his hand to Ellen's reflection in the looking glass, as she stands in the doorway behind him. Slowly, he turns to see Ellen staring at him, holding his hat and gloves. He meets her steady gaze as she reaches out to give them to him. John takes them from her, grateful that she brought them in.

She points to the man, points to her hand, draws a line on it, and points to the man's hand. She tilts her head to the side and pats her hands together.

John smiles and nods as he holds up his bandaged hand. He is touched that Ellen would ask if he is all right. He expects her to walk away, but he is surprised that she does not. She looks down at her hands folded in front of her. All he can do is wait.

She looks up at the man, points to him, places one fist on the palm of her other hand, points to herself, and nods.

57

Confused by the new hand gesture, he can only smile and nod. He recalls his mother smiling and nodding as her hearing faded. He watches Ellen walk away and must admit, even though Ellen is the one who is deaf, the hearing folk in this house are the ones who cannot always hear what Ellen tries to communicate.

John cleans up what Anna would consider 'carnage' in the loo and finally removes his anorak. He strides down the hallway to the kitchen. Anna is not there, as he had hoped, but Sarah bustles about and doting on Johanna. John assumes she must be upstairs in her sewing room, working on a new frock for a customer. He follows his instincts and finds her there. For a moment, John stands, watching her work. Leaning against the door jamb, his arms crossed, he waits for Anna to notice him.

"Oh! John, I did not see you standing there. This is a treat."

Anna gets up and walks over to John, kissing his cheek.

"Your nose is warm, Mr Thorpe. I thought you were going to cut firewood?"

Chuckling, John leans down to kiss Anna's nose.

"Your nose is warm, too, Mrs Thorpe. Actually, I wanted to speak with you about something that's happened."

The smile vanishing from Anna's face, she steps back a pace.

"What is it, John? What has happened? Your hand..."

John guides Anna to a chair and he pulls one up to sit in front of her. Taking her small hands in his, he sighs.

"My hand is fine. Now, I don't want to alarm you..."

"John, when you say that, I become terribly alarmed. Tell me."

"Whilst I was bringing in firewood, Mrs Adderley and her son stopped here. Apparently, Jane tried to introduce herself to Ellen. Let's just say, it didn't go well."

Anna rises from her seat and begins pacing, one hand on her forehead, and the other hand on her hip.

"Oh no. Of all the people to see Ellen. Was Mrs Adderley rude? Never mind. Of course, she was. I hope she doesn't go spreading this 'round. This is the last thing we need."

John gets up and walks close to Anna, gently taking her by the shoulders to turn her to face him. He touches her cheek with his forefinger and looks into her eyes.

"Anna, we will deal with whatever happens. We will manage it together. We will protect Ellen. She has already become part of our family. You are like a mother to her, and she is even beginning to tolerate me. I am not saying we shouldn't worry because we do need to be concerned. I'm just suggesting we not cross bridges that aren't there."

Out of the corner of her eye, Anna sees movement in the garden outside. It is Ellen.

"John, Ellen is back outside. Let's hurry and check on her."

Nodding, John sprints down the stairs with Anna close behind. John goes to the window at the garden door whilst Anna tries to watch from the kitchen, ignoring Sarah and Johanna who stare at her. Looking about, he sees no one else in the garden. Ellen is gathering pine branches from one of the larger shrubs that are dying anyway. As Ellen comes back towards the house with her greenery, John ducks into the kitchen where Anna is waiting.

"What is she doing, John? I could not see from the window. Is she all right?"

"She's fine, Anna, I have no idea what she's doing, though. I know she never does anything without a purpose, but this baffles me. We'll find out, I guess."

They hear the garden door open and close followed by the familiar small footsteps coming down the hall. John and Anna look out of the kitchen doorway to see Ellen disappear into the sitting room. Looking at each other with baffled curiosity, they walk to the sitting room door.

"Oh, John...look."

Anna takes hold of John's shirtsleeve and points. There is Ellen, on her knees with the ash bucket in front of her. She pushes the ends of the pine branches firmly into the ashes until the bucket is full. Sitting back on her heels, Ellen tilts her head to the side. Then she leans forwards to move the bucket, approximating the same spot that held the Christmas tree.

"She misses the Christmas tree, bless her. John, I've tried to explain the Christmas tree to her, but my gestures seem meaningless."

"I think you're right. Ellen pulled the tree back inside twice after I took it out. I feel the same way about communicating with her. Earlier, she made a gesture I had never seen before, and I felt like my deaf mother. She'd just smile and nod as people talked, and all I could do was smile and nod at Ellen."

Looking up at John with a spark of excitement, she bounces a bit on the balls of her feet.

"John, I've an idea. Do you remember those potted pine trees we saw at the market when we found our Christmas tree? Do you know if those are still there? Can we get one for Ellen? She can have her own tree wherever she'd like to put it, and it'll be alive, she can tend it, she can decorate it if she likes..."

Laughing, John holds up his hands.

"Slow down, Anna. Yes, I believe those little trees are still for sale. Yes, we can get one for her. In fact, why don't we take her with us so she can pick one out herself."

Anna's enthusiasm wanes at the thought of taking Ellen anywhere, especially out in public. Who knows who might see Ellen?

"Are you sure taking Ellen out to the market is a good idea? After what happened today, I'm not so sure."

"Not to worry, sweet one. I will ask the fellow who sells them if we can come when the market is closed. No one will be there, and we will have the place to ourselves. I'll gladly pay extra for him to accommodate us in this."

Anna brightens and kisses John's cheek.

"I hope this will make Ellen happy. Well, let us see how well I can explain this to her. Wish me luck."

John kisses Anna's forehead for luck and chuckles as Anna takes a deep breath before she turns and walks over to Ellen. He watches from the doorway as Anna kneels down next to her and begins 'talking' with hand gestures. The smell of Sarah's cooking and Johanna's happy babbling lures him back to the kitchen where he intends to give his daughter proper notice and attention. As John walks the few paces from one room to the next, he smiles and knows if anyone can explain something to Ellen, it is Anna.

Chapter Seven
4 February 1926

Wondering what Ellen's reaction to taking a ride in the motor will be, Anna ponders a way to explain it. This new venture might cause Ellen a bit of worry. No doubt, she has seen John drive away and come back in the motor. Soon, she and John will take Ellen to the nursery to pick out her own potted evergreen. Anna has even picked out the smallest ornaments and ribbon for Ellen to adorn her little tree.

Anna scoops up Johanna in her arms and covers her cheeks with kisses. Johanna laughs and snuggles close to her Mamma. The baby has been keeping her company, content on her blanket in the sewing room. Anna looks for Sarah through the bedrooms upstairs. She finds her in the nursery gathering things to give Johanna a bath after supper.

"There you go, little one. Sarah will tend you. Mamma and Daddy must take our Ellen out for something special! Be a good girl for Sarah."

Sarah takes the baby and bounces her lightly on her hip, tickling the plump little cheek.

"Ma'am, shall I save supper for you, Sir, and Miss Cup?"
Anna chuckles at the nickname Sarah has given Ellen ever since she pointed to the paper with words written on it, thinking her name was 'Cup'.

"I believe sandwiches and some soup will be enough for us. Thank you for remembering. I'd completely forgotten about our supper."

"Yes, Ma'am, I'll be happy to make that for you."

Anna hurries out of the nursery and downstairs as she hears John walking into the house. Seeing John always makes her smile. She goes to him and greets him with a happy kiss.

"Well, you're in a good mood, Anna. It's nice to come home to such a kiss."

Anna winks at John and pats his chest as she grins up at him with a soft chuckle.

"I always greet you at the door like that, John. Is something awry with your memory?"

"Not at all, sweet one. I must say, though, I like reminders that you're happy to see me."

"Is everything arranged for this evening? I've not told Ellen yet just so she's not disappointed if we have to wait. I wish we could take Johanna, but it is too cold and too late. Oh! And Sarah said she'd leave us soup and sandwiches to eat when we return."

John laughs, putting his hands up, almost in a gesture of surrender.

"Slow down, love! All is arranged so you may go and tell Ellen about our plans. After all of that in one breath, I am going to have a cup of tea. I need time to sort out what you've said."

John gathers Anna into his arms for another kiss and then caresses her cheek.

"Off with you, then, and good luck."

With an excited smile, Anna turns to walk down the hallway. She peeks into each room as she makes her way to Ellen's room. Stopping in the doorway, Anna smiles. She gave Ellen curtains in pink and green from which to choose. Ellen is fussing with the pink curtains, adding a warm and feminine touch to her room that had been missing, before. She takes note of Ellen's preference of pink over the green. Anna thought Ellen might wait for help to put them up, but this explains Ellen's time spent going from room to room, looking at the window curtains. She had figured it out and decided to proceed on her own.

Ellen has even set aside some lovely pictures to hang up in her room as well. Anna had stored the paintings in the attic since they were not to their taste. Now they have a purpose. Framed flowers and landscape are not surprising selections for Ellen to make. She chuckles as she pictures in her mind, Ellen hunting for John's hammer and nails to hang the pictures. No doubt in her mind rears its head that Ellen could accomplish it. Anna reflects that Ellen seems to enjoy making decisions and wonders if she has ever had the option of doing so. Making choices is an essential part of life. It seems only right that Ellen should be encouraged in this way, as Clara advised.

Entering Ellen's room, Anna is careful so Ellen will notice her without becoming startled. Rupert is laying on the bed, supervising the sprucing-up process. She admires the cheery transformation of what had been a rather drab room. The dog scoots on the bed over to Anna to ask for his usual dose of affection. With a chuckle, Anna scratches behind his ears and rubs his chest as Rupert rolls over to his back. Noticing Anna, Ellen looks up and smiles. She points to the curtains and pictures with what Anna surmises is a proud expression on her face. Anna nods with a smile as she pats her hands together, saying that Ellen's efforts are excellent.

Anna's thoughts turn to the challenge of communicating that they will go for a ride in the motor on a happy errand. She finally settles on a set of gestures that she hopes will be understandable. Anna points to Ellen, points to herself, then taps three fingers on her chest and pantomimes driving a motor. She repeats the same gestures and moves her hands in the gesture that she remembers Ellen using for 'tree'. She holds her hands a small distance apart to show that the tree will be small. All this is Anna's struggle to say that the three of them will go for a ride in the motor to get a little tree for Ellen.

Her eyes grow wide, and she points to herself, points to the lady, and taps three fingers on her chest. She holds her fists in front of her, moving them slightly as the lady had done, tilting her head to the side. She points to herself and pushes her hand up through the other as she extends her fingers and points to herself with her head tilted to the side.

Ellen's understanding brings Anna comfort. Her relief turns to dismay as Ellen draws her arms up and crosses them in front of her with her fists clenched, shaking her head. Anna pats her hands together and nods her head with a smile to try to say everything will be all right. She points to herself and to Ellen and holds her forefingers upright next to each other to try to convince Ellen that they will stay together. Another wave of relief fills Anna as Ellen relaxes her arms and nods. She motions for Ellen to follow her.

They walk down the hall towards the front door where John is waiting for them. He hands Anna the wrap for Ellen, and she helps her put it on. John, in turn, assists Anna to don hers. John holds the door open for his two ladies and briskly walks to the motor to keep the door open for Anna.

"John, Ellen was a bit nervous earlier so I should sit in the back with her, so she feels more secure."

"Of course, that is a good idea."

"I'm glad you arranged this, John. We don't want to see Mrs Adderley and that son of hers."

"If we should encounter them, I will deal with that situation. You can count on that, Anna."

John nods, a firm set to his jaw as Anna mentions the names of the last two people he would want to see. Opening the rear motor door, Anna enters first and slides over behind the drivers' side. Ellen stares at Anna for a moment, then she looks at the motor and runs her hand over the smooth metal. She gets in and slides as close as she can next to Anna. Anna takes Ellen's hand and gives it a squeeze. John closes the door and walks 'round to take his place behind the wheel. The engine roars to life and begins taking them to the nursery. Anna watches Ellen intently as she stares out the windows. She looks at Anna now and then, pointing to things as they proceed towards their destination. They see houses and cottages, trees, shops, and more trees. At a turning, they drive down a short road and come to the nursery. John parks the motor and turns to Anna and Ellen.

"Well, here we are. This is going to be fun."

He steps out of the motor and opens the rear passenger door for Anna and Ellen. Anna exits and turns to hold out her hand to Ellen. She stares 'round this new place as she takes Anna's hand and steps out. She stands close to Anna, clutching her sleeve.

"If you'll follow me, ladies, the owner told me where to find what we are looking for."

John leads the way through the greenhouse doors and the maze of tables. Ellen's eyes open wide as the array of colours and scents displayed on the tables in the midst of winter dazzle her senses. Anna smiles at Ellen's wonderment, as she seems to savour every colour and smell. Ellen stares 'round the greenhouse, reaching out to touch a leaf or a petal as they walk past. Halfway through the greenhouse, Anna is delighted to see a familiar figure. Granny is helping at the greenhouse by watering plants, plucking dead leaves, and talking to each plant. Granny became a widow after her husband was killed during the battle of Neuve Chapelle in The Great War. The couple never had children. As a result, she launched her own personal campaign against her grief and regret. She became 'Granny' to every child in town. She was the first to help when there was a need of any kind. She always had an ample supply of milk and biscuits for children who stopped by to say hello. Granny's generous hands and a heart full of compassion have made the poorest people in the community less miserable and have brought smiles to the faces of the lonely, and infirm.

Anna is always chirpy to see Granny. She waves, hoping to attract the good-natured woman. She knows that Granny is irrefutably trustworthy since she will see Ellen but not tell a soul. Granny sees them, waves and bustles over to them with a happy smile.

"How are you my dears? I am so glad to see you. And who might this pretty young lady be?"

"This is Ellen. At least that is what we've named her. Perhaps if you stop by the house for tea, I can explain more, later. It's best to not say too much. We'd like to keep Ellen's presence with us as quiet as we are able."

"Ever the prudent Anna Thorpe. Yes, of course, and I won't breathe a word, even if I've no idea, yet, what tale you'll tell me. I would be happy to come, and I daresay John wouldn't protest at some biscuits coming with me."

Granny laughs as she winks at Anna. Anna shakes her head with a grin.

"No, he wouldn't refuse biscuits no matter who made them. I do hope you'll come soon."

"Yes, my dear, I will. I'll ring you up to put the kettle on."

Ellen stares at them with her hands folded in front of herself as the two women bid their goodbyes. Anna turns to Ellen and points to John who is a little distance from them, talking to the owner. Ellen tugs at Anna's sleeve and shakes her head. Wondering what might be the matter, she stops to give Ellen her full attention.

She points to the lady and points in the direction the kind lady had gone. She puts her hand up near her mouth and pantomimes talking. She points to herself and looks down as she shakes her head.

Her enthusiasm fades as she realises that Ellen feels isolated when she sees people talking. Of course, Ellen would suffer such feelings. How would it be to not hear or speak? Ellen watches others do what she cannot do, without explanation. She imagines that it would make a person feel more like a piece of furniture and less like a human being. Anna places her hands together, holds them near her chest, and moves them towards Ellen to ask her forgiveness. She points to herself, points outside, and places her fingers by her mouth and pantomimes talking. She points to Ellen, points to her own ears, and draws an X on the palm of her hand. Anna apologises for leaving Ellen out of a conversation that she cannot hear. She feels remiss in showing Ellen such a lack of respect. As Ellen nods what in a way that may be considered forgiveness, Anna promises herself and Ellen that she will translate conversations from now on. She nods and takes Ellen's hand, pointing to John.

Together, they walk towards John who is already paying for the tree. With a smile and a grand flourish, he gestures towards the dozen or more potted evergreens.

"Here they are! One lucky tree is going home with us."

Anna smiles at John. She is excited at the prospect of watching Ellen choose which tree will be hers. She turns to Ellen to explain. Anna points to Ellen, points to a potted evergreen and shrugs, tilting her head.

65

She repeats this several times. Anna points to Ellen and pantomimes carrying one and points to the motor in hopes that Ellen will understand that she may pick out one that she likes.

She stares at the lady and stares at the man. She tilts her head to the side, points at the living things, puts her hand up, pushes the other hand up behind the first hand and extending her fingers like branches, and points to herself.

Anna nods with a smile, encouraging Ellen to pick out any tree she wishes to have. Pointing to herself and John, she considers a moment how to say 'gift'. She places her fist on her chest, extends her arm outward as she opens her hand towards Ellen to explain that this tree is a gift from her and John. She is glad when Ellen nods her head and leans down to touch each plant. Patting the soil in the pots, she finally points to the one she wants. Anna smiles and pats her hands together to tell Ellen that she has picked out a fine one. Looking at John, she gestures as she speaks. Pointing to John, Anna follows by pantomiming carrying the tree to the motor.

"John, did you pay for this already?"

"Yes, I did, and a little extra for staying open so late for us. Shall we go, then?"

"That's good. Supper awaits, and I am starving! Would you mind taking this to the motor? It's better that I hold Ellen's hand."

"I'm hungry, too, and I'm sure our girl is peckish by now. You're right, Anna, this is all new to her, so it's best to keep her close and feeling safe."

John expresses his thanks to the owner again with a nod and a wave. He picks up the evergreen and carries it to the motor, not realising that Ellen has tugged on Anna's sleeve. Anna looks at Ellen, tilting her head to the side. Ellen pulls Anna back towards the potted trees and points to them. She points to Anna, gesturing that Anna should have a little plant as well. Anna nods and picks out the tree that she thinks will be most suitable. Anna calls out to the owner as she pulls money out of her handbag.

"My daughter wants me to have a tree, also, so I'll leave the money right here if you don't mind."

The owner waves his understanding of the situation. Wondering where Anna and Ellen are, John walks back to the greenhouse looking for them.

"There you are. I thought you two were right behind me."

"Well, Ellen thought I should have a little greenery too, so I picked one out and paid for it. Would you mind...?"

Anna points to the pot, and John feigns a groan as he hefts the planter into his arms.

"This time, we're going home, right?"

"Yes, John, this time, we're going home unless our Cup thinks you need one."

Laughing and shaking his head at Anna's teasing, John walks towards the motor again. The second tree is deposited on the floor in the back where Anna and Ellen will sit. He gestures to Anna and Ellen to get in, pantomiming to Ellen that she should hold the trees steady. Smiling at Ellen's nod, he closes the door of the motor. The motor hums along under John's expert control. Ellen turns to Anna, tapping her on the shoulder. She stares at Anna for a moment.

She points to herself, puts her fist on her chest, points to the other living thing, extends her arm as she opens her hand, and points to the lady.

Touched, Anna smiles at Ellen and nods her head in gratitude. She leans down to smell the freshness of a miniature tree that is bursting with life. For the second time, Ellen has wanted to do something nice for her. Anna realises that without thinking, she had called Ellen 'my daughter'. The thought makes her happy, yet it makes her nervous. A series of 'what ifs' wander through her head. Anna pushes them away with a determination that only a parent could know. With her free hand, she takes Ellen's, noticing that she is barely able to keep her eyes open. Ellen finally leans her head against the window and falls asleep.

Warm lights shine from the windows of cottages and houses as they move homeward. Anna is eager to be in the comfort of their kitchen with a supper of sandwiches and hot soup waiting for them. A turning and another bend of the road bring them to a stop; the glow of welcome is an irresistible lure from the chilly evening. Anna slips her hand away from Ellen who remains asleep. She gets out of the motor to allow John access to the plants.

"If you carry these inside, I'll wake Ellen. She'll want supper and her own bed."

"Yes, I imagine you're right. Whilst you're out here with Ellen, I'll start heating the soup and make some tea."

John kisses Anna's forehead before picking up both trees in his arms. He immediately regrets their weight. Without complaint, he carries them to the house, up the stairs, fumbles with the door, and goes inside with them. Before John can close the door, Rupert dashes out and tears 'round the corner of the house. He closes the door and shakes his head, muttering something about Anna's dog. He places one evergreen in the sitting room and carries the second tree to Ellen's room. For a moment, John stops to admire how Ellen has made the room her own. With a smile, sets the tree down on a chair in the corner of the room and walks out to the hall. He leaves the door ajar and heads to the kitchen with thoughts of a warm supper uppermost in his mind.

Still, in the motor, Anna strokes Ellen's arm and speaks out of habit.

"Sweetheart, we're here...honey, wake up...we're home..."

Ellen's body unexpectedly jerks with a startled panic. Anna sighs with a silent 'Oh no, not again' disquiet. Ellen's arms spread out in protection and cowers down into her seat, shaking. Anna slides close, letting Ellen see her there with her. She continues to try rubbing Ellen's arm in a lulling manner. She sits where Ellen can see her when she opens her eyes. Ellen's face twists as though in pain and she opens her mouth as if screaming without sound. Sitting up suddenly, she opens her eyes, looks 'round, and breathes in gasps. Ellen turns to look at Anna and begins to cry. Anna envelops her in her arms, rocking her and rubbing her back. Once, again, Anna shakes her head at the horrible treatment that might be the root of Ellen's terrors, seeping into her dreams. Anna's imagination is the only conception she has of such things. A maternal protectiveness grows within Anna. She promises to always and forever protect her daughters. Shoulders still heaving with sobs, Ellen clings to Anna.

She leans up from the lady, points to herself, and makes an X in her hand.

Ellen bends back down and rests her head in Anna's lap, her arms 'round her. She tries to stop crying with muffled hiccups as she wipes her tears away on her sleeve. Anna seeks Ellen's attention by tapping her shoulder, waiting for Ellen to look up at her. She takes Ellen's hand and makes an X on her palm and makes the motion of wiping it away, flinging it far from Ellen. Anna tries to convey that Ellen is not bad, that thoughts of anything terrible must fly far away. She holds Ellen, rubbing her back until she senses that Ellen begins to catch her breath. Her breathing slows, and she swallows deeply as she sits up, wiping her tear-stained face with her hands.

She looks at the lady. She holds the palms of her hands together and moves them towards the lady, then lowers her hands and looks down at them.

Anna smiles at Ellen and reaches out to wipe away a stray tear with her thumb. She gently lifts Ellen's chin with her forefinger to look into her eyes. She smiles and nods, pats Ellen's hands and points to the door of the house and Ellen turns to look, nodding. She gets out of the motor waits for Anna, her arms up against her chest with her fists under her chin. As Anna also exits the auto, she closes the door after them. She puts her arm 'round Ellen's shoulders and together, they walk up the stairs to the door. Anna opens it to allow Ellen first entry, hoping the familiar sights and smells of their house will further calm her. Before Anna can secure the door against the tentacles of cold that seek entry, Rupert slips into the house, running towards Ellen's room. Reaching out to rub Ellen's back, Anna holds out her hand in an offer to help with removing her parka. Ellen shakes her head and slowly walks to her room, still wearing it. Anna frowns, shaking her head at what an abomination these nightly torments are to Ellen. She doffs her parka, hangs it up, and walks to the kitchen. Anna pokes her head in to tell John how Ellen awakened in the motor, and how she needs to tend to Ellen, as she is still frightened. John nods, wondering when and if the savage dreams will ever end for their sweet girl.

With her parka still on, Ellen lays down on top of her bed and curls up in a foetal position, closing her eyes. Rupert jumps up on the bed and curls up next to his friend, his eyes wide open, ears up and alert. Anna tentatively walks into Ellen's room and makes her way to the bed. Taking one side of the quilt, she pulls it over Ellen to cover her and sits on the edge of the bed, stroking her hair. Anna waits for Ellen to give her some sort of sign to stay or go. She would stay all night if it helped Ellen feel safer.

She opens her eyes, looking up at the lady. She points to herself, puts her hand over her heart, and points to the lady from under the blanket.

Smiling, her heart warms and at the same time breaks for Ellen with the morbid fear that emanates from her. She points to herself, covers her own heart with her hand and points to Ellen to say, 'I love you'. Weary, Ellen sits up, sliding her arms out of her parka. She tries to take off her dress whilst sitting up in bed. Anna helps her with her dress and encourages her to stand up to change for bed. She hands Ellen a warm nightdress, and as Ellen puts that on, Anna turns down the covers, then fluffs the pillow. Ellen looks at her pillow and crawls into bed. She looks up into Anna's eyes, reaching out to hold onto one of Anna's fingers as she slowly drifts back to sleep.

Anna sits by her side, rubbing the knuckle of Ellen's hand with her thumb and strokes her hair with her free hand. She hopes that someday, somehow, this broken young woman's dreams will be happy ones.

Chapter Eight
20 February 1926

Sitting on the floor in her room, Ellen spent most of the morning decorating her little tree. Now, it was after lunch, and she had refused Sarah's offer of a mid-day meal. She stays in her room, continuing her endeavours, with Rupert lying on the bed, watching her every move. Ellen places a tiny ornament on the tree and frowns. Then she moves it and ties a red ribbon where the bauble had been. Leaning back, she looks at the tree with another frown. She rearranges the ornaments and decorations again. Finally, her project is complete. Ellen stands; steps back a few paces, and smiles. Looking 'round the room, she sees a flat surface upon which she can place her potted tree. She moves the table into a shaft of sunlight streaming through the window. Walking over, she adjusts the curtains to allow more sunshine to fall upon the small table. As she walks over to the potted tree and lifts it, her face contorts with the effort, her tongue sticking out of the corner of her mouth. Hefting the load in her arms, Ellen places it on the table. She turns the pot and adjusts a few adornments that went askew. Stepping back, she looks at the living tree, tilts her head, and nods. She touches the dirt in the pot and nods.

She turns and walks 'round the bed to the looking glass. Smoothing her green linen dress, she brushes off a bit of dirt that clings to the fabric. Ellen stares at herself as she had stared at herself earlier. Before donning her modest dress and a sweater this morning, she had seen the scarring on her back, arms, and legs. A single tear rolled down her face, now, as before.

She lowers her head, points to herself and draws an X in the palm of her hand.

She shakes her head and dashes the tear away with a handkerchief Anna had tucked into her pocket. Rupert hops off the bed and leans against his friend's leg, looking up at her. Ellen looks down at him and tries to smile as she strokes his head. Looking towards the door, she smells something coming from the kitchen. This smell is much different from the breakfast and lunch Anna or Sarah brought her.

She wanders into the kitchen with Rupert following close behind. Ellen stands in the doorway with her hands clasped in front of herself and stares at Anna removing a pan of biscuits from the cooker. Ellen had never been in the kitchen when anything came out of the cooker. Anna notices Ellen standing in the doorway staring at her, smiles at Ellen and places the pan of biscuits on a cooling rack. They are a delicate golden brown, baked to perfection. She takes the next baking sheet and slides it into the cooker quickly, careful not to burn her hand. She stands and motions for Ellen to come in, pointing to the bowl containing some of the ingredients for a batch of different biscuits. Anna tilts her head to the side, points to Ellen, places one fist on the palm of her other hand, and points to herself. In Ellen's language of gestures, Anna asks Ellen if she would like to help since it might provide a new source of enjoyment for her. Rupert remains in the doorway, looking from his friend to his mistress and back. He wags his tail and sniffs the air, with an expectant look on his furry face.

Ellen nods, walking into the kitchen and over to the table where there is a large bowl. She looks inside the container, leaning down to sniff the mixture. Anna ran out of time between mixing the new batch of biscuits and minding those in the cooker. She wonders how Granny ever manages to bake and knit and do all the other things she does in the community, all at once, it seems.

Anna enjoys sewing which is her formal occupation. She helps a client design a garment, choose a flattering fabric and fit the frock to its new owner. She toils at her passion daily, sewing formal gowns for aristocratic Ladies or fashionable dresses for upper and middle-class women, such as herself. Anna even sews simple dresses, donating them to the needy. Yes, she enjoys sewing, but it wears on her if she pursues her trade for too long at a time. Baking is Anna's rare escape from this repetitious profession.

Anna takes a pinafore, rather, a pinny, from the peg on the wall, holds it up, points to Ellen, and points to her own pinny. Ellen nods, takes the pinny, and puts it on, fumbling with the ties in the back. Stepping over to Ellen, Anna helps her tie it. Ellen smooths the bright yellow fabric of the pinny over her green dress as she looks down at it, and, following Anna's example, pushes her sleeves up to her elbows. Patting Ellen's arm, Anna waits for Ellen to look down at her arm, then up at her. She points to a large bag on the counter that says FLOUR and nods to Ellen with a tilt of her head, and points to the table, asking Ellen to bring the flour over to the table.

Walking over to the counter with a nod, Ellen lifts the bag of flour, which everyone knows, is more substantial than it looks. Everyone, except Ellen. The bag slips from her grasp, landing on the floor with a dull thud, a soft cloud of white floating through the room. Anna turns to look and rushes over to pick up the bag that still contains some of its contents. In her haste, she slips in the loose flour and lands on the floor, her sit-upon withstanding the worst of the impact. With an expression of panic, Ellen backs into the nearest corner of the room. Accidents happen, and Anna finds such things amusing if there is no harm done. Ellen's face pales beneath the flour that covers her. Her breathing becomes more rapid, and her eyes grow wide as she stands and walks over to Anna, extending her shaking hand to help her rise to her feet. She also slips in the flour, landing next to Anna. She watches Ellen's face turn from a deathly pallor to a reddish hue with tears tracking through the powder and down her sweet girl's face. Ellen shifts to kneel in front of Anna.

She places her hands together against her chest and moves them towards the lady.

Anna shakes her head and pats her hands together, telling Ellen that there is nothing to forgive and all is well. She decides to distract Ellen from her fear of punishment with a bit of frolic. With a playful smile on her face, Anna picks up a bit of flour in her hand and blows it towards Ellen. Anna's face is full of good humour, and her eyes twinkle with jollity. Relieved, she watches Ellen relax a little and stare at her for a moment, tilting her head. Ellen picks up a handful of flour, her hand still shaking, and blows it towards Anna. The powder in the air is puffy like the snow falling outside. Ellen begins to smile, watching Anna laugh. She is happy to see a smile on Ellen's face and slaps her hands into the flour, Ellen following suit. More flour rises into the air, causing them both to sneeze violently. Rupert barks and wags his tail as he watches them from the doorway, a confused tilt to his head. Anna laughs even harder. Ellen's face appears happier, now, and this pleases Anna. For a speck of time, Anna considers whether Ellen has ever had a chance to play and enjoy fun just for the sake of frivolity.

Soon, their mirth subsides, and Anna points to the mess of flour and pantomimes cleaning. Ellen nods and carefully gets up. She extends her hand to Anna, assisting her to her feet. Anna points to Ellen's dress, points to Ellen's room, and pantomimes putting on a clean frock. Ellen nods and walks to her room, Rupert following his friend. Anna looks at the clock and hurries to snatch the biscuits from certain doom. With a sigh of relief, they are the same delicate golden colour as the previous biscuits. She places the next pan into the cooker and sweeps up the flour. She wets a cloth, wiping away the last traces from the floor.

With deliberate care, Anna walks down the hall to the sitting room, and she tries not to get flour on anything. Seeing John, she chuckles. He is sound asleep on the sofa, his favourite Saturday pastime, oblivious to the hilarity that came from the kitchen. He would have joined right in, and Anna knows he will be sorry that he missed their fun when he hears of it. Anna takes the stairs up to their bedroom on the second floor to change her clothes. Whilst Anna is upstairs, Ellen comes out of her room, wearing the flowered dress she seems to favour most. She walks with Rupert down the hallway and peeks into the kitchen, dining room, and the sitting room. She stares at John sleeping, and Rupert begins to wag his tail, moving towards his master. Ellen reaches down to stop Rupert, and he looks up at his friend. He obeys her, sits, and continues to wag his tail.

She tilts her head to the side, taps two fingers on her chest, and shrugs her shoulders.

John continues to snore at a manly volume. The newspaper he had been reading slipped to a heap on the floor an hour ago. As she turns to walk out of the sitting room, Anna comes down the stairs. Out the corner of her eye, she sees Anna and motions for her to come. Nodding, Anna follows Ellen out of the sitting room and down the hallway, where they stop at the doorway to her bedroom.

She points to herself, places a fist on her chest, points to the lady, points to her own eyes, and points to her room.

Anna nods and wonders what Ellen wants to show her. She enters the room, nearly tripping over an eager Rupert who scoots under the bed, out from the other side and leaps up on the bed. He wags his tail and shakes himself from nose to tail. Ellen motions for Anna to come further into the room and points to the little tree. Anna smiles at Ellen and delight at her efforts fill Anna's heart. She points to the tree and pats her hands together to tell Ellen that she did well. Many ornaments remain in the box, and Ellen picks one up. She gives it to Anna and points to the tree. Anna is happy that Ellen seems to want to include her in decorating it. She looks for a spot that just begs for a bauble. Anna finds such a place and hangs her ornament. She looks at Ellen and tilts her head to the side, seeking Ellen's approval.

She nods and points to the lady and pats her hands together.

Anna smiles and claps her hands together with glee, happy that Ellen approves. Ellen hands Anna another ornament, and then a ribbon. Finally, with plenty of decorations still unused, Anna holds up her finger with wide eyes and a grin. She takes the box of ornaments and motions for Ellen to follow her.

The two of them make their way to the sitting room, not far from where John enjoys his nap. Rupert wags his tail and peers 'round their legs at his master. Anna holds up a finger and gives Ellen the box of ornaments. She takes one and sneaks up to the still-sleeping John. She hangs the decoration from a button on his shirt and tiptoes back to Ellen who waits with her eyes open wide.

She shakes her head, gives the shinies back to the lady, taps three fingers on her chest, pounds her fist on her open palm repeatedly, and points to the lady.

Anna shakes her head and smiles, denying that John would ever beat either of them. Anna's smile grows, and she holds up the box and takes another ornament. She points to Ellen, then points to John, encouraging Ellen to take part in the prank. Ellen's eyes still wide, she makes a step back and shakes her head.

She pulls her arms up over her chest with her fists clenched and shakes her head. She points to the man, pounds her fist on her hand several times, and points to herself and the lady.

Anna shakes her head. She understands that Ellen might have good reason to assume John would react badly to having baubles placed on him. She tries to impart that John will not beat them for engaging in a jolly caper. She lays the box on a nearby table, holds up one finger, and winks at Ellen. Anna pads to the sofa and fastens another ornament to a belt loop on John's trousers. Quietly sneaking back to Ellen, she takes another ornament from the box and holds it up. She nods at Ellen to let her know that this is all in good fun. Anna points to John and draws a smile on her face to assure her that John will enjoy this. Slowly Ellen takes the ornament in her hand and takes a step forwards. She begins to shake her head and steps back, giving the ornament back to Anna. Of course, she is frightened. Men terrify Ellen even though she has warmed to John a little bit. Ellen does not know John's personality as well as she does, of course, so she would not know what to expect if he awakened suddenly. Anna nods towards Ellen in an understanding fashion. She takes the ornament over to John and with enviable stealth, she fastens it to another button on his shirt. Coming back to Ellen, she sees that Ellen is holding an ornament.

She points to herself, hangs the shiny on her finger, and points to the man.

Grinning and nodding, Anna is proud of her for rousting up the courage to join the game. Anna watches Ellen tentatively walk to John's side, precisely as she had done, glancing back to Anna a few times. She nods, patting her hands together to inspire Ellen's playful streak. A moment later, another belt loop is sporting a lovely trinket. Together, they take turns transforming John into a handsome, if excessively bedecked, sleeping prince. Anna grins at Ellen who smiles and rolls her eyes. They make their escape with the box of decorations and disappear into Ellen's room, shutting the door behind them. With innocent expressions, they continue to rearrange ribbons and baubles on the little tree.

A distant knocking drags John out of a rather pleasant dream. He wipes a bit of drool off the corner of his mouth with his sleeve as he looks 'round the sitting room. The knock comes again, and he gets up from the sofa, stepping on the crumpled pile of newspaper pages in his haste. He walks to the door, wondering what that soft jingling sound is. He yawns and opens the door. A blast of cold air brings him to a chilled state of alertness. In front of him stands Father Horatio Willington.

Father Willington is the rector of the local Anglican parish at St. Nicholas at Greendale church. He is keen to visit members of the community to serve their spiritual needs. He is a dear friend and collaborator with Mrs Clara Dewhurst and, together, he and Mrs Dewhurst make visits throughout the parish. Father Willington tends to the spiritual necessities of aristocrats, and poor alike and Mrs Dewhurst manages any medical requirements of the people they visit. Together, they rally resources that benefit each member of the parish. Father Willington is aware of the situation in the Thorpe household, thanks to a confidential discussion he had with Mrs Dewhurst. The purpose of his visit is to enquire after the health and well-being of the young woman known as Ellen. Upon seeing John in the open doorway, he quells the urge to burst into uproarious laughter. He cannot help but notice the brilliant regalia adorning John's person. Instead, Father Willington clears his throat and greets John.

"Good day to you, John. I trust that the Thorpe family is well?"

"Indeed, we are, Father. Do come in, won't you? It's not decent weather for man or beast out there."

"Nonsense, John. A brisk walk does me good. Clears my mind and allows me to ponder my next sermon."

Father Willington allows himself a chuckle, keeping his gaze on John's face. He does not dare to look down at John's shirt and trousers. He sobers a bit, lowers his voice, and states the exact nature of this visit to John.

"Actually, John, I wanted to ask about the young lady you call Ellen. Mrs Dewhurst has enlightened me on the subject, and I wanted to offer any help I may be able to render."

John is caught a little off-guard by Father Willington's statement. He motions the good Father into the house to explain in detail and in comfort. As he does so, he hears the same tinkling noise he heard before. Wondering what it could be as he glances 'round for a possible source, John then returns his attention to the good Father.

"Please, we'd be more comfortable indoors where I can explain at length."

"No, no. I understand the young woman is unusually fearful, and I wish to cause her no fright if she were to see me. Just tell me how she fares and what I can do, if anything."

"You're right, Father, that might be best. I will make it brief. Ellen is adjusting, although I, we, are concerned that it is taking so long for her to relax, smile and feel at ease. Ellen seems most comfortable and close to Anna. They communicate well with the hand gestures they have devised. Of course, her interaction with me is limited. She will tolerate me in the same room, but at a safe distance and with egress at hand."

Father Willington stifles yet another urge to laugh at the Christmas decorations attached to John's clothing. He displays admirable self-control in maintaining his pastoral demeanour.

"I see. I hope that Ellen makes progress, but it will be slow, I'm sure."

"Yes, Father, we can only be patient. If you could be alert to any talk or rumours, though. You understand that we want as few people as possible to know that Ellen is here. That would be most helpful and appreciated. Thank you."

"Consider it done, John."

Father Willington turns away with a wave to take his leave, then turns back to John with another thought.

"John, you may find that her reserve may melt away in a manner you might not expect. A fine evening to you and your family, John. Please give my best to Anna."

John waves as Father Willington walks away into the heavy snowfall. John hears the sound of a man's enthusiastic guffaws. He raises an eyebrow, unwilling to consider their clergyman capable of such unconventional behaviour. Considering they had been discussing Ellen, the likelihood seems even more improbable. He closes the door, feeling the need for some tea to warm him. As John walks to the kitchen, his senses are assaulted by the unsavoury smell of burning biscuits and smoke. He grabs a tea towel and opens the door of the cooker. Smoke burns his eyes, and he covers his mouth with the tea towel. Without thinking, he reaches in with his bare hand to remove the baking pan. The heat blatantly reminds him to reach for a hot pad instead. With muffled curses, he rescues the pan from the cooker and looks 'round the room, wondering where to put the bloody mess.

Hitting upon the only thing he can do, he dashes down the hall to the rear door. He flings open the door and dumps the biscuits, pan and all, into a pile of snow. He breathes deeply of the clean, cold air. He hears that faint tinkle sound again. As he leans down to pick up the cooled but ruined baking pan from the snow, he notices a sparkle. He looks down at himself. He chuckles and then begins to laugh aloud. What could Father Willington have thought of him? He stood there, telling the good Father how reserved Ellen is. The only one who could have perpetrated such antics is his puckish wife. Anna must have lured Ellen into the merriment, as well. It is no wonder he heard a man's hearty laugh fading into the distance. He is sure that Father Willington found great amusement in seeing his unique regalia. He walks back into the house, closes the door, then into the kitchen to clear the air with an open window. Still laughing to himself, he nibbles a biscuit that had escaped the fiery pit of disaster. He places a kettle of water on the cooker for tea, then walks over to the table, and sits. Out the corner of his eye, he sees a line of white at the base of the kitchen counter. More white is visible on the lower cupboard doors. He shakes his head and turns his attention to the biscuit. He notices the mixing bowl on the table, and he gets up to take the bowl of unidentifiable contents to the counter. There is no reason to tempt Anna's dog to engage in a curious romp upon the table.

Anna gets up from the floor and goes to the door of Ellen's room when she hears a clatter and the rush of heavy footsteps in the hallway.

She looks up and down the hall. The smell of burnt biscuits reaches her nose, and Anna groans, putting her hand to her forehead. She hurries to the kitchen, the smoke wafting out of the window. John turns to Anna as he nibbles his biscuit, and grins at her. Anna's sheepish smile brings his hidden mirth to the fore. With a flourishing gesture of his hand to the ornaments on his clothing, he raises an eyebrow.

"Do you know who might have given me such excellent accoutrements?"

John takes off the baubles and places them on the table as Anna stammers in reply.

"Uh, well, um…"

Anna cannot help herself. She bursts into gales of laughter and raises her hands in mock defeat.

"Yes, it was my idea. BUT! I had help."

"You don't mean…?"

Anna nods, unable to speak from laughter. With a grin, John closes the distance between himself and Anna. He gathers her into his arms and kisses her, snuggling her close. Looking up, he sees Ellen and Rupert in the doorway. Ellen stares at them with her hands folded in front of herself. John notices a streak of white on Ellen's forehead next to her hair and thinks that he might not want to know why. Rupert was also staring at them, his head tilted to the side with his tail wagging. John smiles and kisses Anna's cheek as an excuse to whisper.

"Guess who is staring at us."

Anna turns 'round to see Ellen bow her head and frown. Walking over to her, Anna pats Ellen's shoulder. Ellen looks at her own shoulder and then at Anna. Anna points to John, pats her hands together, and draws a smile on her own face. She wants to let Ellen know that John is not upset by their little lark. She points at John, standing aside so Ellen can see him. Ellen looks up at John who has a big smile on his face.

"Anna, how do I tell her that I'm not angry?"

"Point to yourself, draw a smile on your face, and pick up one of the ornaments. That should make your message clear."

John follows Anna's instructions and is pleased to see Ellen nod. He can see Ellen's shoulders relax, and the faintest hint of a smile plays at the corners of her mouth. Their girl, Ellen, is learning what it is like to have light-hearted amusement. Anna tilts her head to the side, points to herself, places her hand on her chest, points to her own eyes, taps three fingers on her chest, and holds up one hand as she pushes her fist behind her hand upwards and extends her fingers. She is asking Ellen if she may show John the little tree in her room, decorated with such care.

Ellen smiles and nods, backing into the hallway, allowing them to pass. Hand in hand, John and Anna make their way down the hall, proud of Ellen in so many ways.

Chapter Nine
23 February 1926

Bouncing Johanna in her arms, Anna is in the kitchen preparing to make tea. Granny will come to visit in a short time, and she wants everything ready. Johanna laughs, the bouncing causing her inner happiness to bubble forth.

"DA DA DA DA!"

She reaches out with her chubby pink hand and grabs the bright hummingbird patterned tea cloth draped on Anna's arm. Anna shifts her daughter to her hip and bounces Johanna to amuse the baby.

"Give that to me, you silly girl! You miss Daddy, don't you? He would let you have this. What a sweet Daddy's girl you are."

Anna takes the tea towel out of Johanna's grasp. She boops her daughter's nose with it, eliciting a barrage of baby babbling. She laughs as Johanna tries to swat at the tea towel and grab it again.

"No, lovey, that's not for you. Mamma needs to make ready for Granny's arrival. Do you want to help Mamma? Maybe Granny will bring you a little something. Would you like that?"

Anna sits Johanna down on a blanket for her to play on the kitchen floor, then reaches for the tea set from the china cabinet and places it on the table. Anna saves this set for special guests, and Granny is dear. She leans down to ruffle Johanna's golden curls as she walks by. Sarah bustles into the kitchen with a cheerful smile. She is busy, but never too busy to tend to Miss Johanna with an abundance of affection.

"Ma'am, it's time for Miss Johanna to have her nap. I'll take her upstairs to the nursery unless Ma'am would rather?"

"No, Sarah, that's fine. Granny will be here soon. I will manage to serve her so you may carry on with your duties. Thank you."

"Oh, Ma'am, I haven't seen Miss Cup in a good long whilst."

"No, Ellen is in her room, and I'll check on her soon."

Anna scoops Johanna into her arms with many kisses over her cheeks and even her little hands. Sarah takes the baby into her arms and protectively holds her. Sarah feels and behaves like a second mother to Johanna. No one could ask for a more competent and caring woman than Sarah to watch over their precious little one. Sarah has even extended her protective nature towards Ellen. Anna strokes Johanna's blonde ringlets and soft cheek. Johanna leans into her mother's hand

and gives her Mamma a sloppy wet kiss on the wrist.

"Thank you for such lovely kisses, my sweet. Be a good girl for Sarah and take your nap. Off with you now, sweetheart."

She pauses with a smile to watch Sarah carry Johanna into the sitting room and listens to Sarah's familiar footsteps ascend the staircase. All the whilst, Sarah speaks and coos to the baby. 'Tis a shame that Granny will miss seeing Johanna as Granny dotes on her so. Anna returns to the task of setting the table with bright flowered placemats. A porcelain tray sits between the place settings with room for sugar, creamer, and the teapot. Standing back, she looks at the table and wonders what might be missing. Oh, yes! A two-tier cake stand will hold a variety of biscuits. Anna withdraws it from the china cupboard and brings it to the counter. She fills it with her homemade biscuits, leaving room for the treats that Granny will likely bring.

Satisfied, she nods and leaves the kitchen and walks down the hallway to Ellen's room. Perhaps Ellen would like some tea. Knocking on the bedroom door out of habit, she opens it and peers in to see Ellen sitting on her bed. She is showing Rupert what appears to be a photograph. Rupert's head tilts to the side with a small 'woof' as he stares intently at Ellen's hand. Anna approaches in a way that will draw Ellen's attention without startling her. Ellen looks at Rupert with a smile and scratches his ears. Noticing Anna standing there, she looks up at her. Ellen tilts her head to the side and holds out the likeness for Anna to see. Nodding, Anna takes it. The rumpled and creased photograph shows a woman that appears to be in her twenties. She is sitting outdoors with a pretty smile. The woman's hair is coiffed, and she wears a dress in the Victorian style. Anna turns the picture over and is a little surprised to see the name Ellen written on it with a date of 1901. Anna tilts her head to the side, points to Ellen and holds up the picture.

She shrugs her shoulders and frowns. She points to herself, points to her own eyes, holds her hands up, then walks two fingers across the palm of her hand then draws an X on her palm.

Most of what Ellen has told her is confusing. Anna replays the gestures in her head, and the best she can understand is that Ellen saw it at a house with a bad man. Anna can only guess at the meaning. She hands the photograph back to Ellen.

She holds up the picture and points to a picture on the wall as she tilts her head to the side.

Anna looks at what Ellen is showing her and realises that Ellen would like a frame for the picture as the others. It seems to mean something to Ellen even though she does not appear to know who the woman is. Anna nods and wonders how to say 'later'. Then, she pantomimes having tea and points in the direction of the front door. She holds her hands up, palms together and pantomimes a door opening. She walks her fingers across her hand, tugs at her dress and pats her hands together. This is her clumsy way of saying that a good woman is coming for tea, but Anna has done her best. She watches Ellen shake her head with a shrug of her shoulders and then she looks down at the dog, scratching Rupert's ears again. Anna leans down to pat her arm. Ellen looks at her arm and back up to Anna. She smiles, nods, and pats her hands together to tell Ellen that it is all right if she would like to avoid seeing the visitor. She tilts her head to the side, points to Ellen, pantomimes drinking tea, and points down. Ellen shakes her head, declining Anna's offer to bring tea to her room. Anna nods then points to herself and points in the direction of the kitchen. Ellen nods, seeming to understand that Anna will be in the kitchen.

Anna exits Ellen's room and leaves the door ajar should Rupert want to come out or if Ellen needs something. Mystery upon mystery rears a masked face as they grow to know Ellen better. How strange it seems that they are getting to know Ellen as a person, but know so little about her life and circumstances. Anna makes her way to the kitchen and puts the kettle on to heat the water for tea. There is a knock at the door. Anna assumes that must be Granny, and she hurries to the door. Opening it, she greets Granny who is laden with a large basket covered with a chequered cloth.

"Come in, Granny. I am glad to see you, as always."

"Thank you, dear. Treats are in the basket, as usual."

Granny winks and hands Anna the basket as she comes in and closes the door. She doffs her size-too-large brown wool anorak and hangs it in the wardrobe. Anna leads the way to the kitchen, and she follows. Granny has a habit of making herself at ease, regardless of whose home she visits. Everyone who treasures Granny's friendship accepts her habits without judgement or question. Walking into the kitchen, she sees the table set with Anna's fancy tea set.

"My word, Anna. You shouldn't have gone to such trouble. It's only me, you know."

"It's not every day Granny comes to visit, and you give me an excuse to use my favourite tea set."

Anna lifts the corner of the cloth on the basket and winks at Granny who takes her seat at the table.

"May I?"

Granny laughs with a wave of her hand towards the basket.

"Well, of course, dear. I brought that for you."

She watches Anna open the basket as the teakettle begins its merry whistle.

"I'll get the kettle. You just look at the basket."

Anna nods and then shakes her head with a smile. It is delightful to have friends with whom affection is unnecessary. She removes the red and white cloth. Inside are an assortment of biscuits, small cakes, and four plush toys. Anna performs the usual ritual of protesting that Granny's parcel is just too much.

"Nonsense, my dear. Biscuits and cake are always good things to have on hand and Johanna will enjoy something different to chew on."

"That she will, Granny. We will certainly enjoy these treats. Thank you."

Anna takes her seat across from Granny. Pouring the tea for them both, Granny chooses a biscuit and dunks it in her tea to soften it. Granny, who has never been one for small talk gets straight to the point of her visit.

"So, Anna, tell me about your guest. I'm curious as a cat and wish to help if I can."

"It's a long story, Granny. We don't know her name, and she deserves one. We chose Ellen for her. She is unable to hear, speak, read, or write. She has made some small progress in writing a few words that have a direct connection to objects. I don't know how to manage abstract concepts, though. We communicate with crude hand gestures. It seems like she's never been to a school where she would have learnt the sign language deaf children learn, now."

"Anna, this is quite a tale. Go on."

"Well, it seems as though she'd been mistreated beyond the telling of it. This seems like a foreign world to her. She has violent nightmares almost every night, and I stay with her through them. They appear to happen upon waking suddenly when she does not realise where she is or shortly after drifting off to sleep. We have come to share a bedtime routine every night. I sit on the bed and stroke her hair until she falls asleep. That way, I can be present if she has a nightmare soon after. I leave the door open a bit so I can hear her during the night. It seems to me that she's not had much mothering and desperately wants to feel that."

"Bless her soul. Please, continue. This completely intrigues me."

"When she arrived here the evening after Christmas, she was begging for food, filthy, and dressed in rags. I convinced her to have a hot meal, take a bath, and stay the night. During her bath is when I saw fresh whip marks and bruises. Clara Dewhurst came to examine her, which was difficult, to say the least. Ellen did not understand what Clara was going to do or why so Clara examined me first to show her what to expect. Ellen finally agreed. She is afraid of anyone new. At first, she had a terrifying reaction to John, but she can abide him in the same room with her, now, and will eat meals with us on occasion. Let me see...what else...She is desperate to love and be loved and seeks approval. She is fearful of punishment for the smallest fault. She also seems to find it unusual to have choices in even the most trivial things, so we suspect she's never been permitted to make her own."

Anna takes a deep breath, and Granny sits back with a thoughtful look on her face.

"Goodness. And the eve after Christmas. You and John do have your hands full. Have you contacted the police station to see if there is a missing person report on her?"

"That's a problem, Granny. We cannot report that she is here. What if the constable has had a report of her missing and returns her to the person who mistreated her? Not being able to hear, speak, read, or write, she cannot defend herself or ask for help. John and I decided to keep her presence here as quiet as we can. The only people who know she is here are you, Clara Dewhurst, Father Willington, and unfortunately Jane Adderley and that son of hers."

Granny takes a sip of her tea and nods her head.

"You and John are in a spot, aren't you? We can trust Clara, and the good Father, but Jane and Lewis might be trouble. Perhaps supervising her at every turn would keep the Adderley's at bay but you cannot very well keep her cooped up in here. She'll come unhinged, as any sane person would."

"At times, I'm at a loss for what we should do. I take the time to look at books with her and practice writing, but it is a slow process. There is one thing you could do if you would. If you hear rumours of any kind floating about, would you try to quell it as best you can? Something. Anything. We don't want rumours to spread like wildfire."

"Well, dear, one saving grace is that few people take Mrs Adderley seriously. Most people know that she tells half-truths with limited accuracy. I do hope that will work in your favour."

Anna considers the truth of Granny's words and finds them

comforting. As a family, with trusted friends, they will just have to do the best they can.

"Oh! Also, Ellen has a remarkable talent for carving. Let me show you the little hummingbird that she made for me."

She gets up and hurries to the china cabinet from whence she brings out the delicate little bird. Granny holds out her hand to take and examine the bird, gasping at the mesmerising life-like detail.

"See? She wants to be accepted, and she gives from her heart. She is the most honest person I have ever seen. There is no duplicity in her, from what I've observed."

"You're right, Anna, I believe this carving is a demonstration of love. Ellen has talent. Wait, what's that sound?"

Granny returns the little bird to Anna and listens to what sounds like banging. The noise comes from the sitting room. Putting the bird away, Anna hurries to the kitchen door and motions for Granny to join her.

"I hear it too. Come with me. I'm not sure I want to see this alone."

Granny gets up and joins Anna at the doorway. They listen to the repeated dull thud of something against a stone. They make their way in unison to the sitting room entrance where they see Ellen. She is striking something in her hand against the hearth. Rupert is hiding under the sofa, his tail curled firmly underneath him. Granny pats Anna on the shoulder and nods.

"My dear, your Ellen needs you. I will be in the way, so I will just let myself out. Later, if you like, give her a few of these cuddly toys. She might like them if she has been so deprived. Johanna won't mind."

Anna nods her farewell to Granny and walks into the sitting room. She makes sure that Ellen will notice her approach. Sarah bustles down the stairs to see what the racket is. Anna puts a finger to her lips and motions for Sarah to return upstairs. Sarah nods and hastily returns from whence she came. Ellen does not notice Anna and seems oblivious to all but the abuse she gives to what looks like a crude carving of a man. Slowly, Anna kneels in front of Ellen. Tears stream down Ellen's pale face as she breathes heavily, and shakes. She finally looks up at Anna, stopping her repetitive beating of the carving on the hearth. Anna tilts her head to the side, asking Ellen what she is doing.

She looks at the lady and hands her the thing of the bad man. She points to the thing, walks two fingers across her palm and draws an X on her palm, and points to the thing.

She looks at the carving and wonders who he might represent as Ellen's emotions and behaviours become more intense. Ellen describes the figure as a bad man, but who is he? Ellen snatches the carving out of Anna's hand, her face contorted with emotion and bashes it even more brutally on her own hand and continues to smash it upon the hearth. Tears stain Ellen's face, and Anna's empathetic nature brings tears to her own eyes. She wants to snatch the carving from Ellen and throw it into the fire along with Ellen's nightmares, her fears, and her frustration at being in a world she does not understand. Anna wonders if this might portray the man who harmed Ellen. Throughout all this, Anna observes Ellen's hand. A bloody cut is oozing its sanguine colour across Ellen's palm. Before Anna can offer to tend the gash, Ellen starts to beat herself on the injury again, and again. With great force, fuelled by the emotions displayed in her heaving shoulders, she flings the blood-tinged figure of the man deep into the fireplace. The carving is hungrily licked into a hellish ember by the tongues of flame. Ellen stares into the fire, drawing an X on her palm. Her heavy breathing and shaking seem unwilling to subside.

Her hand to her mouth, stifling her own emotions, Anna tries to comprehend this violent outburst. It reveals a small, yet confusing, part of Ellen's story. Anna deduces that a man had most likely abused Ellen, clarifying her fear of men. Mistreatment of an extreme nature explains the nightmares that Ellen suffers every night. The scars on Ellen's back, arms and legs bear silent testimony to something horrible that defies understanding. Stifling her own tears, she holds out her hand to Ellen. Anna pats Ellen's arm to get her attention. Ellen looks down at her arm and then back up to Anna. She traces a frown on her face and an imaginary tear down her own face to show Ellen that she is sad for whatever happened to her. Anna takes a deep breath, attempting to restore her composure. With great care, she takes Ellen's bleeding hand in her own. Anna points to herself, hovers her fist over the hand that is holding Ellen's hand, and points to her, telling Ellen that she shall help repair the wound. Ellen stares at Anna for a few minutes as her breathing slows and the shaking relents. She nods. Ellen turns to take a last look at the remains of the carving, glowing in its fiery hell and wipes her eyes on the sleeve of her sweater. She looks away from the fire and stands, waiting for Anna to rise to her feet.

Anna gets up, her legs and feet having that tingling feeling, that comes with kneeling too long. She motions for Ellen to follow her, leading her to the loo next to Ellen's bedroom. Rupert crawls out from under the sofa and trots behind them. The medicine chest on the wall reveals a myriad of ointments, elixirs, powders, and bandages. Anna chooses the proper items and turns on the water. She tests it on her wrist the way she does for Johanna's bath water. When the water reaches pleasant warmth, Anna dampens a flannel. She turns to Ellen and holds out her hand and points to Ellen's bleeding injury. With a nod, Ellen extends her hand and looks away with a grimace at Rupert who tilts his head, watching their every move. Anna carefully cleans the blood away to reveal the wound itself. She inspects it thoroughly, debating whether to give Clara a bell. No, this is something she can tend on her own. Anna applies proper cream and bandage. When she finishes, she pats Ellen's arm to show her that the dressing is in place. Ellen looks down at her arm and then up to Anna. Anna wonders if Ellen remembers the bandage on John's hand.

She looks at the lady and nods. She points to the lady, places her fist over the palm of her other hand, points to herself, then softly pats her hands together. She traces her finger down her face. She puts her hands together at her chest and moves them towards the lady.

Anna understands by Ellen's gestures that she is grateful to her for tending to her wound and asks for forgiveness. Anna pats her hands together, points to herself, places her hand on her heart and points to Ellen. A tiny nod may indicate an understanding that Anna accepts and loves her, and there is no need to beg forgiveness. Anna fears that Ellen still seems to be stifling her feelings of distress, though. Ellen walks back to the sitting room and sits on the sofa. She stares into the fireplace as Rupert hops up to rest beside his friend, leaning against her. Following Ellen, Anna is loath to leave her girl, so she joins her on the sofa. They stare into the fire, losing track of time. The soft footsteps of Sarah carrying Johanna downstairs cause Anna to turn with a little smile at the two of them. Sarah breathes a sigh of relief that the storm with Ellen has passed for now. Johanna leans forwards as she reaches for her Mamma and Ellen.

"Mama...Dada...Cuppa...Goggy!"

"It's all right, Sarah. Johanna can sit with us, and she might make Ellen happy."

Sarah gives Anna her baby girl, watches them for a moment, then nods with a smile of satisfaction that all is well. Sarah walks to the kitchen to prepare their supper. Johanna squeals and pats her Mamma's face with glee. She reaches over to Ellen and grabs her hair.

"Cuppa! Cuppa!"

Anna smiles at Ellen and tilts her head to the side. She points to Johanna, asking Ellen if she would like to hold the baby. Ellen nods and holds out her hands to take the wee one in her arms. Ellen begins to smile as Johanna reaches up to pat Ellen's face. Her chubby hands must feel warm against Ellen's cheeks. Ellen takes Johanna's hand and kisses it, then strokes Johanna's hair and cheek. Johanna relaxes and babbles at Ellen. The baby reaches over to pat Rupert, but he jumps off the sofa to escape. Ellen looks at Anna and tilts her head. Anna surmises that she wants to know what Johanna is saying. She points to Johanna, puts her hand to her mouth and moves her hand as if talking, cradles her arms as if holding a baby and then brings her hand next to her mouth to pantomime talking. Ellen nods as Anna tells her that Johanna speaks 'baby talk'. Ellen shrugs and tickles Johanna, making the baby laugh. This brings a small smile to Ellen's face as she plays with Johanna for some time. Johanna seems to enjoy pleasant frivolling.

Eventually, Ellen hands Johanna back to her mother. Ellen's face sobers as she folds her hands in her lap and looks at them. Anna is confused. She thought that Ellen enjoys playing with Johanna. She tilts her head to the side and pats Ellen's arm. Ellen looks down at her arm and up at Anna.

She points to herself, holds her arms as if cradling a baby, then with one finger draws down her face from her eye.

Anna's head remains tilted, remembering that Ellen had told her before that she had lost a baby. Perhaps playing with Johanna brought that memory and sadness back to her. Anna recalls how she avoided infants and children for months after she had lost her first child, and again after the second baby. She points to Ellen, cradles her free arm as if holding a baby, and shrugs to ask what happened to Ellen's baby. Tears fall anew down Ellen's cheeks as she takes a deep breath.

She points to herself, cradles her arms as if holding a baby, then takes one hand and flings it away from her. She shrugs and shakes her head.

Horror fills Anna's soul at this revelation. Ellen's baby did not die. The infant was taken from her. What kind of cruelty would cause a person to do such a thing to a new mother? Anna has no answer to this. She leans down to sit Johanna on the floor to crawl about; she turns to Ellen and opens her arms. Ellen looks at Anna, the tears of grief flowing.

Ellen leans into Anna's embrace and weeps as if her heart would break. Anna allows herself to cry for Ellen's heartbreak over the child that was torn from her arms. They sit holding each other, Anna rocking Ellen, rubbing her back, and stroking her hair as she does at bedtime. After a time, their tears subside, and Ellen pulls away from Anna's arms. She stares at Anna for a moment then stares down at Johanna. The baby has crawled over to them and is patting Ellen's knee. She reaches down to caress Johanna's cheek, gets up, and walks out of the sitting room. Anna lifts Johanna into her arms and follows Ellen just far enough to see her and Rupert enter her room. She walks into the kitchen to put Johanna in her high chair. She gives Johanna two of the cuddly toys that Granny brought for her. Johanna pounds them on the tray in front of her, speaking in her own infantile language.

"Sarah, I have a few more things I need to do before supper is ready. I'll leave Johanna here, so she's not underfoot."

"Oh no, Ma'am. Miss Johanna is a good little helper. Aren't you, little one?"

"Thank you, Sarah. If John comes, please tell him I am in Ellen's room."

"Of course, Ma'am. Sir should be here soon."

With a nod, Anna leaves the kitchen and carries the other two fluff toys in her arms. Anna wishes to give Ellen a moment to compose herself, and perhaps the dog will lend some solace. She remembers her promise to Ellen that she would find a frame for that picture. Anna makes her way upstairs to a hallway storage cupboard, where she discovers a few frames of a suitable size. She places them in her arms and walks downstairs to Ellen's room. Knocking, Anna opens the door. Ellen sits on the bed holding Rupert. The dog rests his head on her shoulder, licking away the remains of her tears. Anna hopes that the cuddly toys and frames for the picture will bring Ellen peace and distraction from her distressed state of mind. She lays the toys on a chair and approaches Ellen to pat her arm. Ellen looks at her arm and then up at Anna, staring with red-rimmed eyes. Anna picks up the photograph from the night table and holds it against a frame. She lays them in a row on the bed and points to them, points to Ellen, encouraging her to choose the one she prefers. Ellen nods her head, holding her hand out to take the likeness. Anna steps back so Ellen can see her tap three fingers on her chest to tell Ellen John is home as she hears the door, his voice, and his footsteps walking to the kitchen. She hears their daughter break out into gales of laughter at seeing her daddy. Anna smiles at Ellen and pantomimes eating. Then she points to Ellen and to the kitchen. Next, she points to Ellen and then down. Anna is asking Ellen if she would prefer to eat with them at the table or to eat in her room. Ellen shakes her head and lowers her gaze. She points down to tell Anna that she would rather eat in her room.

Anna understands fully as John will when she explains all that transpired. She leans down and puts her hand on Ellen's arm, then kisses her cheek. She reaches over to the chair, picking up the two cuddly toys from Granny. Anna gives them to Ellen and holds her hand to her chest, then, extends her arm whilst opening her fingers. Finally, she points to Ellen to let her know that these toys are a gift. Ellen looks up at Anna and then stares at the toys in her hands. Her eyes open wide, she tilts her head then looks back up at Anna. She looks back down and gently runs her fingers along the softness of the toy. Ellen lifts one up and rubs it against her cheek as she closes her eyes. She opens her eyes and looks at Anna.

She points to herself and places her hand over her heart, then points to the lady. She points to herself and places her hand over her heart, then points to the soft things.

Anna smiles at Ellen, points to herself, puts her hand over her heart, and then points to Ellen, returning the loving gestures. She turns to leave the room, the scent of supper drawing her. Anna hopes that the aroma emerging from the kitchen will stimulate Ellen's appetite. Leaving Ellen's room, she makes her way to the kitchen. John's smile invites her to go to him. He leans down so Anna may kiss him since his arms are full of their wiggling daughter. John's smile fades as he sees the dark circles under Anna's eyes and the redness of crying.

"What's wrong, Anna? Did something happen?"

"John, I've much to tell you, but later. We need privacy for me to relate everything. Just know that for now, all has settled."

She smiles in spite of her emotional and physical fatigue. Since John is minding Johanna, she joins Sarah in preparation for supper. The only cloud dimming the happiness of a family supper is the absence of their Ellen.

Chapter Ten
6 March 1926

After breakfast, a quiet Saturday morning ensues. The sun is shining through the windows, warming each room. The cold and snow outside fail to diminish the cosiness inside. John brings a bit of chill in with him as he enters through the garden door from the garden. He stomps a bit of snow off his boots and claps his gloved hands together.

"Anna? Anna! I could use some help, here. Anna?"

Anna hears John calling to her from the sitting room where she is sewing. She lays aside her fancywork and hurries out of the sitting room and down the hallway to see what John needs.

"What is it, John? Is something wrong?"

"Oh no, nothing's wrong. I just need a bit of help bringing in something I made for Ellen. I hope she's pleased with it."

Bouncing like an enthusiastic little girl, Anna cannot contain her excitement.

"Tell me, John! Do tell!"

Laughing, John leans over to press his cold lips to Anna's warm cheek.

"Get dressed to go outdoors. I'll show you soon enough."

She hurries down the hall to the wardrobe and takes out a wrap that will not mind a bit more wear and tear. She puts it on and pulls on her gloves as she kicks off her shoes. Finally, stuffing her feet into her boots, she trots down the hallway where John is grinning at her.

"Come with me, M'Lady."

John opens the door with a flourish and allows Anna to exit first. She looks 'round to see leafless trees, mounds of snow, and the door to John's woodworking shop open. She looks back at John who is closing the door and points to the open shop door.

"Is it in here?"

Before John can say yes or no, Anna walks over to the shop and looks inside.

"Ohhhh, John! Is this what you've been keeping a secret? It's...I'm speechless!"

Twinkling eyes and a boyish grin are Anna's answer. Anna looks at the workbench with drawers, open bins, and an adjustable table. It is smooth from hand polishing to a gleaming finish.

"I just need some help getting it into the house and to Ellen's room. It's not heavy, but it is cumbersome."

Anna enters the shop and runs her hand across the smooth wood. She opens and closes the little drawers and pulls out the extension that makes a working surface. Looking at John, she smiles.

"A table where Ellen can carve and keep her tools. Brilliant. It's magnificent, John. I'm sure Ellen will be delighted."

John picks up the end closest to the door and motions for Anna to pick up the other end. Together, they carry the carving bench to the garden door. They set it down for a moment to allow John a free hand to open the door. The two of them carry it just into the hallway, and there is a slam as John kicks the door shut with his foot. Just down the hall a small distance, they carry the bench and place it across the hall from Ellen's room.

"I've an idea, John. Ellen might like a little surprise out of this, don't you agree?"

"You've read my mind, Anna. Give me your coat and boots. I'll put them away. You can put your shoes on later. Besides, you have adorable feet."

Anna winks with a laugh and pats John's chest, kissing him lightly. She treads a small foot on his boot to tease him.

"Ooohhh that's cold! Get on with you, then, Mr Thorpe."

The sound of John's laughter rings through the hallway as he makes his way to the front entryway to put their outerwear in the wardrobe. Shaking her head with a happy smile, she puts her hand on the latch of Ellen's bedroom door. Managing to suppress her delight at this surprise, and is imagining Ellen's reaction. Upon walking into the room, she sees Ellen sitting on the floor carving something. Ellen seems wholly absorbed in her craft. Rupert is lying next to Ellen as usual. Anna crouches down, scratching Rupert's ears, and waits for Ellen to notice her. In the meantime, she looks down at the carved figure in Ellen's hands. The figure is a child crouched with its arms over its head as if cowering and trying to protect itself. A feeling of sadness creeps into Anna's heart, replacing some of her earlier exuberance. She wonders if this carving represents Ellen. If it does, the gross harm done to her might have had an early beginning, ruining her childhood.

Anna shakes her head free of the terrible thought, for now. She leans down to pat Ellen's arm to attract her attention. Ellen looks at her arm and then looks at Anna. She musters a smile and points to Ellen and then to the carving, all the whilst tilting her head. Ellen shrugs and sets it on the seat of a nearby chair. She stares at Anna, her head tilted to the side. Anna points to herself, places her fist on her chest, points to Ellen, places a fist on her palm, and points to herself. She pantomimes lifting something heavy, asking for Ellen's help. Ellen shrugs and gets up to her feet, smoothing the wrinkles out of her dress. She reaches out a hand to Anna, helping her to stand. Motioning for Ellen to follow her, she leads the way out of Ellen's room to the hall. Anna waits for Ellen's reaction. Rupert sits just outside of Ellen's bedroom door, watching them.

Ellen stares at the workbench for a little whilst. She looks at Anna and back to the bench shrugging her shoulders. Smiling and nodding, Anna points to the workbench and points to Ellen. Anna taps three fingers on her chest, puts one fist on top of the other repeatedly, and points to the bench. Last, Anna points to the work table, places her fist on her chest and extends her arm and fingers towards Ellen. Ellen's eyes grow wide that John made this for her as a gift from him and Anna. Her mouth opens as she reaches out to touch the polished wood. Her fingertips grow familiar with the smooth grain. Soon, both of her hands are caressing the wood and exploring every nook and cranny. Anna looks at John who is standing a respectful distance from the unfolding scene. He crosses his arms over his chest as he leans against the wall, a proud smile on his face. Working with wood is something special he and Ellen have in common. Ellen tugs on Anna's sleeve. Anna looks at Ellen, nodding. Without warning, Ellen's face illuminates in a joyful smile.

Ellen points to herself, places her hand over her heart and points to the wood thing.

Ellen bounces lightly from one foot to the other, her eyes sparkling with happiness. She grabs Anna in a firm embrace, resting her head on Anna's shoulder. Anna holds her for as long as Ellen likes. Ellen celebrates her new bench, and Anna celebrates the happiest expression she has ever seen gracing Ellen's face. Finally, she steps back and touches Anna's face. She points to the bench and then to her room, tilting her head to the side to ask if she may have this in her room. Laughing, Anna nods. She stops Ellen for a moment and points to herself, taps three fingers on her chest, places her hand over her heart, and points to Ellen to let Ellen know that she and John love her.

She nods and points to herself, places her hand over her heart and points to the lady. She looks back to the man and looks at the lady. She points to the man, pats her hands together, and nods her head.

Anna is sure John has seen the unmistakable gestures from Ellen that say she thinks he is a good man. That must make him happy, considering her extreme fear of him in the beginning. Returning her attention to the task, Anna points to Ellen and to one end of the worktable and lifts the other end. Together, they move it into her room. They set it against the wall next to the door. Ellen seems to prefer to face doorways, rather than have her back to them. Anna brings a chair over to the desk so Ellen can sit and carve in comfort. As she stands back to admire John's workmanship, she feels a tug at her sleeve. Ellen's head is tilted as she points to the desk. Anna realises that Ellen is asking what the workbench's purpose is. Anna walks over to pick up a couple of carving tools and the figure Ellen had been working on. She places the tools in a drawer and sets the carved figure on top of the flat surface.

Ellen smiles as her tears begin to spill down her cheeks again. She takes Anna in her arms, and the two of them share a joyful embrace. Eventually, Ellen pulls away with a smile. She gathers her carving tools and pieces of wood to put away in her new bench. Anna pats Ellen's arm. Ellen looks down at her arm and then up at Anna. She points to herself and to the general direction of the kitchen and pantomimes eating. It is time for lunch. Ellen pantomimes eating and points down to impart her desire to eat lunch in her room. Anna knows that Ellen is too excited to leave her new bench and the process of organising her tools. Anna takes her leave and walks down the hall to meet John who is still leaning against the wall. She can tell he has had an emotional reaction to Ellen's happiness. She takes John in her arms.

"John, she's happy. This is the happiest I've seen her. You're like a loving father to Ellen."

He kisses the top of Anna's head and rubs her back.

"Anna, you've become her mother. Our little girl loves you. You love her. I haven't seen you fall in love like that since Johanna was born."

Together, they walk hand-in-hand into the kitchen to enjoy a bit of lunch with Sarah and Johanna. There, they watch Sarah fondly fussing over Johanna eating finger foods. Rupert comes running into the kitchen as fast as his legs can take him. He takes advantage of the opportunity to abscond with anything Johanna drops on the floor, as any naughty dog would. He takes what he does not eat back to his friend's room. Anna raises an eyebrow at Rupert's antics and mutters to herself something about that dog of John's.

"Ma'am, is Miss Cup coming to the table? I'll take her lunch to her if she's not if you like."

"Yes, Sarah, please take her a tray. Also, notice how happy she is. It will warm your heart."

With a bob, Sarah quickly makes a tray for Ellen and delivers it to her room. She returns to the kitchen with a surprised expression on her face and her hand on her chest.

"Ma'am, Sir, Miss Cup smiled at me! A real genuine smile! Oh goodness, you were right! She is happy."

Anna and John laugh.

"It's a happy thing to see, isn't it, Sarah?"

"Heavens yes! She is such a sweet little thing when she smiles."

Sarah bustles about the kitchen to serve lunch, whilst humming a happy little tune. John and Anna make Johanna's meal enjoyable whilst they wait for Sarah to serve them. Lunch is a simple affair, and it does not take the family long to make short work of Sarah's culinary expertise. Johanna begins to yawn and fuss. John lifts their daughter from her high chair and cuddles her close to him.

"Sarah, I'll take Johanna upstairs, change her nappy and rock her to sleep."

"As you wish, Sir. I will tidy up the kitchen, then."

John carries Johanna to the sitting room and up the stairs. He begins a fascinating Daddy story that will surely keep Johanna's attention.

Anna gets up to help clear the table, bringing a few dishes to the sink.

"No, no, Ma'am. I will manage. You can take your ease."

She chuckles at the way Sarah shoos her away from household tasks. Turning to walk to the sitting room, Ellen appears in the doorway of the kitchen holding her lunch tray. Anna takes it from her and nods her thanks, then hands it to Sarah. Ellen stands there with her hands folded in front of herself for a few minutes watching the two of them. Rupert sits on the floor next to Ellen with his head against her leg and wags his tail with a thump-thump-thump on the floor. Ellen turns and walks down the hallway to the sitting room. She finds her favourite spot between the fireplace and the shelves of books. Rupert follows her, scooting under the sofa and popping out the other side to hop on the sofa and watch his friend.

Pictures in books are what Ellen enjoys. Anna walks into the sitting room to join Ellen and returns to the intricate hand beading of an exquisite bodice for Lady Ashton's new gown. Ellen looks up, and Anna smiles that Ellen has begun to favour books. Even though she cannot read them, she looks at the pictures. Often, Ellen will ask Anna to write the words that correspond with the images. Ellen is quick to remember the words. She places the paper inside the book to mark where the word matches the picture. Ellen gets up to bring a few of the books to the table in front of the sofa.

She pats the lady's knee. She points to herself, places her fist on her chest, points to the lady, points to her head, points to herself, and pats the things with squiggly lines and pictures.

Anna reviews the gestures in her mind and concludes that Ellen wants to share more of herself through the books. She sets her handiwork aside and gives Ellen her full attention. Kneeling next to Anna, Ellen opens one of the books and flips through the pages until she finds the picture she wants, a cow.

She points to the big animal and makes her hands into fists, moving them up and down, one, then the other. She stops and wipes her forehead, closing her eyes as she tilts her head to the side.

Anna gathers from the gestures that Ellen uses, that she has milked a cow and it is hard work. She remembers milking cows when she was a girl. Mimicking Ellen's gestures, Anna points to herself, saying that she has also milked cows and recalls that it is hard work. Ellen nods with what seems to be comprehension of Anna's gestures. She turns more pages and shakes her head, not finding what she is looking for. Setting the first book aside, Ellen opens the next book, turning it so Anna can see a picture of a chicken.

She points to her nose, then leans down to the table, and touches her nose to the flat thing several times. Then, she takes three fingers of each hand and scratches at the flat thing. She looks up at the lady, tilting her head.

Anna smiles, recognising the actions of a chicken and nods her head. In reply, Anna brings the skirt of her dress up a little, holding it like a pouch, then pantomimes picking things up and putting them in the pouch. She points to the picture and hopes Ellen understands picking up eggs from the chickens. Ellen nods enthusiastically. She flips through a few more pages and finds a picture of a garden growing vegetables and points to the image. Anna is impressed with the skills Ellen possesses and assumes she must have grown up on a farm of some kind. Ellen smiles and pats Anna's knee in approval. She turns back to the book and flips through the pages, and frowns. She takes another book and turns the pages without success. She shrugs and turns to Anna.

She places her finger against the tip of her nose and pushes up, looking at the lady.

Anna grins and nods, putting her own finger against the tip of her nose, pushing up. She places her other hand near her nose and pretends to be a pig rooting 'round on the ground. Out of the corner of her eye, she sees Ellen clasp her hand over her mouth. Ellen's eyes are twinkling, and her shoulders are hunched up. She points to Anna, tears beginning to fall down her cheeks as she laughs. Anna joins Ellen in hearty laughter. For the first time, she sees Ellen laugh. Laugh to the point of tears, no less! The more Anna thinks about her pig pantomime, the more amusing it becomes.

Anna's laughter subsides a little, and she looks at Ellen. Ellen looks confused as she slowly reaches up and touches the tears, stares at her finger, and then tastes it. Anna smiles as Ellen looks at her and tilts her head to the side. She realises that Ellen must never have laughed until tears came. Tears came only from sadness, frustration, and fear is Anna's guess. Pointing to herself, Anna traces a line down her face from her eye with her fingertip and draws a frown on her face. Then, she holds up her finger, traces a path down her face from her eye, and draws a happy smile. In this way, Anna tries to explain that a person can cry for sad things and cry for happy reasons, as well.

Tilting her head to the side, she walks four fingers on the flat thing, pats her heart, and pats her hands together. She walks two fingers on the flat thing and draws an X in the palm of her hand.

Reviewing the motions in her head, Anna nods. Yes, sometimes animals are better than people are. Animals are honest, genuine, and they like you, or they do not because an animal cannot deceive. She smiles at Rupert and scratches behind his ears, knowing that this sweet dog is an excellent example. People can be kind and caring whilst other people can be duplicitous and malicious. Anna has to agree with Ellen. An individual who knows both animals and people can indeed discern the difference between their inherent natures. Anna considers that perhaps their assumption is correct, that Ellen has been isolated for so long that she has never learnt the social rules that govern society. Until now, it is possible that Ellen has only known the comfort of animals and has experienced just the cruelty of people. Slowly, Ellen is learning that not all people are evil.

She watches Ellen walk her fingers across her hand, draw an X in her palm, and then stare ahead. Sighing, Anna pats Ellen's arm and points to herself, taps three fingers on her chest, and pats her hands together to say that she and John, and definitely not all people, are bad. Ellen continues to stare ahead of her, oblivious to what Anna is trying to tell her. Waiting for Ellen to shake her reverie, Anna watches until she shakes her head, looks at her, and pantomimes writing. Anna gets up, walks to the desk, and finds a paper and pencil, bringing it back to Ellen. She sits back down on the sofa and places them on the table in front of Ellen. Taking one of the books, she finds the cow picture and taps on the paper, handing Anna the pencil. With a smile on her face, Anna writes COW on the paper. She points to the word, then to the picture. Ellen smiles and searches for another image with success. This time, the pig. Anna writes in clear letters the word PIG and pushes her nose up with her forefinger and winks. Ellen smiles and covers her mouth, her shoulders shaking in what can only be interpreted as a silent giggle. Ellen points to the paper and to Anna and taps two fingers on her chest, asking Anna to write her name. Anna grins and writes ANNA on the paper. Ellen takes the paper, looks up at Anna, and reaches for the pencil. She writes the three words, COW, PIG, and ANNA, and CUP then sits back to look at the paper. She smiles and claps her hands.

She points to the lady, points to the squiggly lines on the squiggly line thing, then pantomimes picking up each bunch of squiggly lines and placing her thumb and forefinger against her head. Pointing to the lady's squiggly lines, she points to the lady. Pointing to other squiggly lines, she points to herself. She nods and pats her hands together.

Anna smiles even though Ellen's gestures confuse her. Ellen does seem to display enthusiasm for learning. She chuckles that Ellen still thinks her name is Cup. Sarah has been calling Ellen 'Miss Cup' ever since the first time Ellen pointed to that word and then to herself. Mistakes are part of learning, and learning things makes Ellen smile. Anna realises that her gestures mean that these words are going into her head. There is unique happiness in watching someone grow and evolve. She considers for a moment all the things that Johanna will learn, as she becomes older. Yet, the thought strikes her that she and John have learnt much from Ellen in such a short time. Ellen has taught them the value of genuine honesty, seeing things and people with new eyes, and unconditional love. Most people never receive that gift.

Interrupting her thoughts, she sees John carrying a sleepy Johanna down the stairs.

"She fell asleep in my arms, and I didn't have the heart to wake her and lay her down for her nap. I just held her. She's a little angel when she's sleeping."

"Yes, she is. She's adorable when she's waking up, too."

Ellen stands and holds up the paper with a smile. She points to Anna's name and points to Anna, then points to the word CUP and points to herself. Ellen kisses Anna on the head and skips off to her room with Rupert trotting behind. John shakes his head with a chuckle.

"Anna, we're going to have to work on that."

"Yes, we are. A little bit at a time, I reckon. She's happy to learn, and that's what matters right now. For someone who doesn't seem to have been exposed to reading and writing, what Ellen has accomplished is exciting progress."

Anna gets up and walks over to John and Johanna. She kisses Johanna's cheek and ruffles her hair as her sweet baby girl yawns and smiles.

"Ma ma ma ma..."

Holding out her arms, Anna takes Johanna from John. He leans down to kiss Anna, rubbing her back.

"I'm proud of you and your patience. I wish I could boast that quality."

He sniffs the air and grins.

"It seems that my patience won't be tested for too long. I smell something cooking."

Anna grins at John and nods, speaking in a conspiratorial tone.

"Tonight's the night. I do hope Ellen likes the surprise we've arranged for her."

"I do, as well. I'll leave it to you to explain it since the two of you seem to understand each other in ways I couldn't begin to grasp."

Johanna reaches over to pat her Daddy's chest and babbles at him with a frown. John sniffs the air as something other than supper reaches his nose.

"Oh, dear...someone needs a nappy change before we eat. I'll take care of it. Come with Daddy, sweetheart. Daddy will fix your little problem."

John winks at Anna as he takes Johanna back into his arms and makes his way, wrinkling his nose. John quickens his pace out of the sitting room and up the stairs to the nursery as Johanna's little problem grows into a more significant problem along the way. Anna walks into the kitchen to help finish preparing the table for their early supper. As she begins setting a place for each of them, she notices Ellen and Rupert standing in the doorway. Ellen stands there with a smile on her face. Anna returns Ellen's smile and hopes that hers is a sign of happiness. Now would be a good time to attempt an explanation of the happy evening she and John have arranged. Anna moves closer to Ellen and points to herself, to Ellen, and taps three fingers on her chest. Anna pantomimes driving the motor and draws a smile on her face with her finger. Explaining a sleigh ride might be too difficult. Ellen has probably never seen a sleigh.

She tilts her head, shrugs her shoulders, and nods. She points to herself, places a fist on her chest, and draws a smile on her face.

Anna nods, understanding that Ellen wants 'happy'. After her time of thinking about the baby that was taken from her and yet another nightmare last night even after their cherished bedtime routine, Ellen deserves this happy outing even more. A sleigh ride will be exciting. Anna gestures to Ellen's place at the table as Sarah brings the food to the table. Just in time, John returns with a fresh and happy Johanna. Rupert sits between Ellen and Johanna, prepared to catch any stray food that might fall or be given to him. John sits Johanna in her high chair and takes his place after pulling out the chair for Anna to sit. Sarah takes her seat next to Johanna. Supper commences with a relaxed conversation. Knowing that Ellen feels left out and troubled if she is excluded, Anna translates their dialogue to her as best she can. Ellen nods and quietly eats her supper.

Once supper is finished, Sarah waves John, Anna, and Ellen out of the kitchen. John and Anna cover Johanna's face with kisses and promise they will be back soon.

"Now, don't you mind a thing. Miss Johanna and I will have a nice time cleaning up and settling in for the night. I hope you enjoy your evening out."

Anna thanks Sarah and taps Ellen on the arm. She walks her fingers across her hand, and pantomimes driving in the motor to say it is time to go. Ellen nods and follows Anna to the hallway wardrobe where John is waiting for them. He hands Ellen her anorak and hat, then helps Anna with hers. Anna takes her handbag and puts on her hat, securing it with a hatpin.

"Ladies, are we ready?"

"I think so, John. I do hope Ellen enjoys this. I'm looking forwards to it."

John holds the door open for Anna and Ellen to go through, then closes it behind them. Anna takes Ellen's hand to reassure her that all is well. John opens the rear door of the motor to allow Ellen and Anna to get in and sit together. He closes the automobile door and walks 'round the motor to open the driver's door and get in. Shortly, the engine purrs to life, and John points the motor in the familiar direction of Ashton Hall. Lord and Lady Ashton have generously granted the Thorpe family the pleasure of indulging in a sleigh ride this evening. They have given their head groom, Mr Higg, the responsibility of managing the sleigh and horses.

Ellen stares out the window and then turns to Anna, drawing a smile on her face as she nods with enthusiasm. Anna draws a smile on her own face to say that she is also happy about this outing. They pass crossroads punctuating the countryside. Ellen's eyes grow wide, and she moves closer to Anna, clutching her hand. Anna smiles at Ellen, thinking she must be excited and maybe a bit nervous at a surprise outing. Anna's gaze out the window of the motor takes in the new-fallen snow sparkling in the tapestry of the early sunset. Shortly, Anna sees Ellen's expression change to what must be awe at seeing the enormous buildings of Ashton Hall. John brings the motor to the rear of the building complex. The estate is like a self-contained village. The stable is their destination. Waiting for them is the head groom with the sleigh and horses at the ready. Parking the motor, John announces the obvious.

"Well, here we are."

He exits the motor and assists Anna and Ellen out, the evening air refreshing them. John walks over to Mr Higg and extends his hand for a hearty handshake. Their handshake is interrupted by Mr Higg's fit of coughing, barely covered in time by a well-worn glove. John politely ignores it and shakes his hand.

"Mr Higg, this is such a treat. We're glad you've given up your evening for this outing."

"'Tis no problem, Mr Thorpe. Always happy to indulge the friends of Lord and Lady Ashton. I've prepared everything if you are ready?"

"One moment, if you don't mind."

John holds up one finger to Mr Higg and walks back to Ellen and Anna. Ellen is holding back, staring at Mr Higg. John nods towards Mr Higg and raises an eyebrow to Anna. Anna takes John's cue and turns to

Ellen. They hear another series of barking coughs from Mr Higg. She points to Mr Higg and pats her hands together to say that he is a good man. She retakes Ellen's hand, giving it a squeeze and motions to the sleigh. Ellen stares at Anna, at John, and then at Mr Higg, and nods slowly. Mr Higg steps forwards, his hand outstretched.

"I'll be happy to assist the ladies if you would like?"

John shakes his head with a smile and quietly whispers to him that the young woman is unable to hear or speak and is terribly fearful of strangers.

"Oh yes, I understand, Mr Thorpe. I did hear that it was the young woman's first sleigh ride, so I took the liberty of preparing a little gift for her when we get back. If you approve, that is. Please, watch your step. Cover up with the furs so you won't catch the chill like I did."

Anna politely extends her hand to Mr Higg, a gentle meeting of hands, and thanks him for his kindness.

"Tis a pleasure, Mrs Thorpe. A fine evening it is, too. With the full moon shining off the snow, you'll have a grand view of the countryside."

Ellen stands next to the sleigh and takes Anna's hand, shaking her head. Anna smiles, nods, and pats her hands together as best she can. She points to the sledge that is polished to a shining glory and the horses that are perfectly matched and groomed. Ellen finally nods. John assists Anna and Ellen into the sleigh, offering them the furs to cover their legs against the cold. Knowing that the cold will numb Ellen's hands, she takes Ellen's bare hands in her own and points to her own gloves and then tugs on her right glove. Ellen nods and takes hers out of her pocket and puts them on, but not before rubbing her nose that is already numb from the cold. John climbs in and sits next to Anna. Mr Higg climbs up into the sleigh, taking his own seat, and then picks up the reins. Ellen leans to look down over the side of the sledge. She pats Anna's arm and draws a circle in the air. Anna tilts her head, not understanding what Ellen means. Interrupting the silent dialogue between Anna and Ellen, Mr Higg announces the beginning of their adventure.

"Is everyone ready? I'll start off slow so the young lady won't be startled."

Mr Higg's comment is cut short by another violent coughing fit.

Concerned about Mr Higg, Anna shakes her head and wonders if he should be out in the cold with that cough. John reaches over to pat Ellen's hand with a smile. The sleigh begins moving, and Ellen stares at the horses.

She looks at the lady and the man, points to the pulling animals, pats her hands together.

They nod in return, agreeing that the horses are good, and to pull such transport, they must be strong. Ellen looks at the scenery from side to side, smiling.

She turns to the lady, pointing at things 'round them, traces a circle 'round her face, and then pats her hands together.

Anna nods, yes; the scenery is pretty, harsh edges softened by the new-fallen snow, a draped mantle of white. Ellen turns 'round and sees the snow thrown up by the sleigh's runners and the tracks they leave behind. She leans forwards to watch the horses' hooves kick up snow with every step as they pick up speed. Anna tucks the furs 'round them and turns to John with cheeks pink from the cold and her eyes sparkling like the stars overhead.

"What do you think? I believe this is lovely."

"Yes, this is grand. Ellen seems to be enjoying it immensely."

John is surprised when Ellen reaches over to pat his arm.

She pats the man's arm and tilts her head to the side as she points to him and draws a smile on her own face.

John smiles and nods, drawing a smile on his face to say that yes, he is happy. Only the quiet trotting of the horses interrupts the peaceful milieu, the soft swoosh of the runners on the snow, and the occasional spasms of coughing that come from Mr Higg. Anna decides that Mr Higg is a grown man and capable of knowing whether he is well enough to be at the reins. Holding each other's hands, Anna and John watch the magical world fly past. They lose themselves in each other's eyes and smile, remembering their first sleigh ride shortly after they married. Their musings shift towards Ellen who leans forwards, sitting tall, with her hands on the back of the front seat. Her eyes are closed, and a smile illuminates her pretty face.

Anna rubs Ellen's back, her heart filled with happiness that Ellen must feel free, alive, and happy. Time stands still out here in the silent landscape. Anna waves back to people walking near the estate cottages who wave to them as they pass. The sleigh must be a marvellous sight to see! Anna watches Ellen, seeing her eyes are still closed, her head held high. The air is brisk, and the breeze sweeps through Ellen's hair. A single tear rolls down her cheek, and she removes her hat. She hands the hat back to Anna and then wipes away the tear. Ellen shakes her head, freeing her hair, even more, to let the wind play with it as they speed along.

Time stands still for them, and they realise that, already, the buildings in the distance are those of the estate. Mr Higg slows the sleigh and brings it to a halt in front of the stables. Ellen turns to Anna and grasps her arm, nodding her head with a beautiful smile. Anna pats Ellen's hand and nods, happy beyond words that Ellen seems to be filled with joy. John hops down and helps Anna and Ellen to alight from the sleigh.

Anna smiles at Ellen, patting her hands together to convey how enjoyable this evening has been. Anna turns to Mr Higg with a pang of concern nagging at her.

"Mr Higg, this has been such a delight. I thank you. I do hope you're well? I don't mean to pry, but I haven't been able to avoid hearing your cough."

Mr Higg waves his hand dismissively and smiles.

"'Tis nothing, Mrs Thorpe. A wee tickle in the throat. I'll be fine."

"I certainly hope so."

She smiles at Mr Higg who holds up his hand with a grin.

"If you'll be so kind as to wait a moment, I'll be back in a wink of an eye with the young lady's memento."

He trots off to the stable whilst Ellen walks over to the horses. She holds out her hands to them, letting the horses sniff her. She looks into the eyes of the first horse for a little whilst, then smiles and nods, finally kissing its nose. She turns to the second horse and does the same. She stands there, caressing both horses and then returns to Anna's side.

She points to a pulling animal, holds her hands up to her own head, palms facing her, then runs her hands down her body, points to her stomach, and then moves her hands outward from her stomach.

Anna smiles, raising an eyebrow at Ellen's assessment of the horse's pregnancy. She turns to Mr Higg who has returned with a parcel, and he is, once again, overcome by a coughing fit. Anna steps aside and points to one of the horses.

"Mr Higg, I would not be surprised if that horse has fallen pregnant."

"You don't say, Mrs Thorpe. Well, I guess time will tell. I'd almost given up on that one having a foal."

Mr Higg smiles and holds out a brightly wrapped box.

"To remember her first sleigh ride, and I hope it will be the first of many."

Anna reaches out, taking the gift in her hands.

"Thank you, Mr Higg. You're too kind."

Anna smiles at him, still worried that he should go inside where it is warm, which is precisely what they are going to do when they get home. John shakes Mr Higg's hand again, thanking him for his time and for making Ellen a jubilant young woman. Ellen turns to Anna, looks into her eyes, smiles, and then gives her a firm embrace. She turns and walks over to John, her hands folded in front of herself, her head lowered but her eyes looking up at him. She smiles and nods. She turns and looks over at Mr Higg and nods. She walks back to Anna and puts her hat back on. With a wave to Mr Higg, the three of them return to the motor. John gallantly assists the women and then takes his place behind the wheel. Without complaint, the engine starts, and John steers them along a different but scenic route. Soon, they arrive, and John silences the engine. They scurry to rush into the house where Rupert greets them with barks, jumps, and wiggles. Ellen reaches down to stroke the dog. Anna lays Ellen's gift on the entry table and peeks into the sitting room, pleased to see that Sarah built up a fire to welcome them before she retired for the night.

John helps Anna and Ellen with their wraps, putting them away.

"You two go and sit by the fire whilst I make us some tea."

Anna motions for Ellen to come into the sitting room and then pantomimes drinking tea. Ellen smiles and shakes her head.

She puts her hands together and leans her head against them.

Anna nods; appreciating that Ellen has fatigued after all that fresh air and excitement. Ellen walks down the hall to her bedroom, closing the door behind her. Rupert barely gets his tail inside before his friend closes the door. Anna walks into the kitchen to see John making hot chocolate, instead.

"Sarah left everything ready for hot chocolate for us to enjoy. She doesn't leave out any detail, does she, Anna?"

Anna kisses his cheek, rubs his back, and smiles at him.

"To think, at first, you thought we didn't need someone like Sarah."

John laughs and shakes his head.

"The correct answer for any husband to make to his wife's

suggestions is 'Yes, Dear.' I've learnt that. Aren't you proud of me, Mrs Thorpe?"

"I'm exceptionally proud of you, Mr Thorpe. Ellen was tired and wanted to go to bed, so when this is finished, I'll take the gift, her cup, and mine in to her. I'm sure lulling her to sleep will not be difficult tonight."

Shortly, the smell of chocolate and peppermint fills the kitchen. Anna takes the two cups and the wrapped gift on a tray to Ellen's room. She opens the door and walks in. Ellen sits in bed with Rupert next to her legs, and the two cuddly toys from Granny tucked under the blanket with her. Anna sets the tray on the bedside table and offers a cup to Ellen. Anna chuckles at Ellen sipping her hot chocolate with gusto until it is finished. She definitely remembers the scent and flavour of chocolate. She hands Ellen her own handkerchief, points to Ellen and then places her finger across her upper lip to tell Ellen that she has a chocolate froth moustache. Ellen tilts her head to the side, looking at the handkerchief. Anna reaches for the hand looking glass and holds it up so Ellen can see. Ellen begins to grin and nod her head, wiping away all traces of their bedtime treat.

Once both empty cups are on the tray, Anna hands Ellen the wrapped gift from Mr Higg. She is sure that Ellen has never seen or opened such a thing. Ellen's expression of confusion gives credence to Anna's assumption. Anna slips her finger under a corner of the wrapping, tearing it. She points to Ellen to do the same. Ellen rips the paper, looking up at Anna several times. Each time Anna encourages Ellen to continue. Underneath the wrapping is a box and Anna pantomimes opening it. Ellen nods as she opens the box. Her face lights up as she takes out a miniature sleigh and horses. The figurine is almost an exact replica of the sledge that delighted them all this evening. Ellen kisses it and holds it to her cheek. She strokes every line and curve. When she is finished, she hands it to Anna and points to the carving desk John had made for her. Anna takes it and arranges it next to the sad sculpture of the cowering child. Anna cannot help but notice the dichotomy between the two objects.

Smiling, Ellen scoots down under the covers and lays her head on her pillow with her fluff toys held tight in her arms. Sitting on the side of the bed, Anna points to herself, places her hand on her heart, and then points to Ellen. She points to herself, puts her hand over her heart, points to her own eyes, points to Ellen, and then draws a smile on her own face. Ellen smiles and nods, seeming to understand that Anna loves her and loves to see her happy.

She points to herself, places her hand over her heart, and then points to the lady. She points to the lady, taps three fingers on her chest; places one fist on top of the other repeatedly, points to herself, and draws a smile on her face.

Anna is thrilled that Ellen has included John in her expression that she is happy. Seeing Ellen gesture her love never fails to warm her heart to its core. Ellen smiles, takes Anna's hand, and then lays it on her own head. Stroking Ellen's hair is a ritual at bedtime they both enjoy. Her fingers running through Ellen's hair, she watches Ellen's eyes flutter closed, open to look at her, then flutter closed again. Soon, Ellen's form melts into full relaxation. When Anna is satisfied that Ellen is safe from a nightmare, she leans down to kiss Ellen's forehead and swishes away a stubborn strand of hair from her sweet girl's forehead. She stretches as she stands, surprised at how tired she is, as well. She picks up the tray with cups and exits Ellen's room, leaving the door ajar. Anna walks into the kitchen, puts the cups in the sink, filling them with water so they can soak. Yawning, she makes her way through the sitting room and then upstairs. She peeks in on Johanna, smiling with amusement to see that little thumb tucked into her precious baby's mouth. She leans down to kiss Johanna's forehead and whispers to her daughter.

"Sleep sweetly, my love. Happy dreams."

She tiptoes out of the nursery and down the hall to her and John's bedroom. She enters, hearing John snore in that soothing rhythm she has come to know and love over the years. She changes for bed without a sound and slips under the covers. Cuddling up to John, she drapes her arm 'round him and whispers.

"I love you so much, sweet one."

She closes her eyes and drifts off to sleep. One mother's ear remains awake for the sound of her children in need. Her dream of snow, sleighs, and the blur of trees in the moonlight is interrupted by the sound of a crash downstairs. Anna sits up, fully awake, recognising the sound of Ellen's struggle with a nightmare. She flies out of bed, throwing on her dressing gown, prepared to rush to Ellen's aid. In the middle of the hallway, she stops. Ellen stands there with her blanket, a pillow, and a cuddly toy in her arms and Rupert peeks out from behind Ellen's legs. Anna closes the distance between them, takes her darling girl into her arms, and rocks her. Ellen's tears soak the shoulder of Anna's dressing gown and nightdress. When Ellen pulls away, wiping her eyes on her nightdress's sleeve, Anna tilts her head to the side. She points to Ellen, places her fist on her chest, puts her hands together and rests her head on them, and then points to the bedroom she shares with John asking if she would like to sleep with them tonight. Ellen nods and looks down at the floor. Anna guides Ellen into the bedroom and Rupert makes himself comfortable under the bed. Anna points to John, points to herself and the middle of the bed, points to Ellen, and finally to the empty side of the bed. Ellen nods and Anna crawls back into bed with John. She holds the covers up so Ellen can slip in. She wraps her arm 'round Ellen, holding her close as she imagines Johanna doing the same, as she grows a bit older. Sleeping with Mamma and Daddy after a bad dream is what every child does.

Finally, Anna feels Ellen relax, her breathing returning to the deep rhythm of sleep. Anna's soul knows the weight and joy of mothering that rests deep within her. As she holds Ellen, she wonders what memories haunt Ellen's dreams. Her last sigh as she falls asleep reflects a lack of hope that they may never know.

Chapter Eleven
10 March 1926

John and Anna walk down to the kitchen for breakfast, and they are surprised to see a carved owl on the kitchen table. They look at one another, wondering if Ellen might have been up all night crafting it. Anna looks at Sarah to ask her about the owl.

"Sarah, was this here when you came to start breakfast this morning?"

"Yes, Ma'am, it was. It was right there."

Given that Ellen has had such horrific nightmares, she might be afraid to sleep. Anna picks up the carved owl and admires the talent behind the beautiful owl.

Johanna makes her presence known in her own charming idiom.

"Ma ma ma da da da!"

"John, last night I was sure she was asleep when I left her. Do you think she feigned sleep and spent the rest of the night carving this? The other night, she was so frightened that she came to sleep with us."

John takes the owl from Anna and admires the workmanship and detail as he turns it over in his hands. Anna bends down to lift Johanna out of her high chair and into her arms for a good morning snuggle kiss.

"You could be right, Anna. You would have noticed an owl in her room, and I'm sure Sarah would have, as well."

At the sound of her name, Sarah looks up and nods from her efficient breakfast routine.

"Yes, Sir. I'd have seen that when I went to tidy Miss Cup's room. It wasn't there yesterday."

John sets the owl in the middle of the table as a centrepiece.

"It looks nice there, for now. Anna, I'm sure you'll find an attractive way to display it."

Anna nods and reaches out to touch the owl, drawing the baby's attention to it.

"Isn't that pretty, Johanna? Ellen made that! Maybe someday she'll teach you to do things."

Anna sets Johanna back in the high chair and tickles her plump cheeks as the little one babbles and bangs on the tray. John pulls out Anna's chair, and Anna gives him a peck on his cheek before sitting down. He leans down to kiss Anna's ear before sitting at his place at the table. Rupert dashes into the kitchen and tries to stop on the smooth floor. He crashes into Johanna's high chair and then looks up at the baby. With one paw held up, he offers the canine version of an apology to his little friend. Johanna reaches down and tries to stroke him.

"Goggie goggie goggie goggie!"

Ellen walks in and stares at them as they ready for breakfast, her hands folded in front of herself. Ellen looks down at her feet as she walks slowly into the kitchen, and then to her place at the table. She sits next to Johanna who reaches over and pats Ellen's shoulder.

"Cuppa Cup Cup!"

Ellen looks at the baby and smiles a little, and then stares down at her hands, folded in her lap. Anna pats Ellen's arm to get her attention. Ellen looks down at her arm and then at Anna. Gesturing, Anna points to herself, John, Sarah, and Johanna. She draws a smile on her own face, points to her own eyes and then points to Ellen. Anna tries to cheer Ellen by letting her know that they are all happy to see her. Ellen nods and looks back down. John and Anna look at one another, noticing the darkness under Ellen's eyes. They wonder if a lack of sleep might explain why Ellen seems unusually subdued this morning. Sarah brings breakfast to the table and plates filled with food pass 'round from one member of the family to the next. Anna notices that Ellen does not reach for the platters as she normally would. She smiles at Ellen as she takes the liberty of spooning small portions onto her plate, hoping that she will eat something. The first meal of the day progresses with minimal conversation. Ellen sits with her head resting against her hand whilst she pushes her food 'round the plate. Anna watches her then turns to John and Sarah and nods in Ellen's direction.

Shaking her head, Sarah clears the table when everyone is finished eating. She serves them each a warm tea with sweet biscuits to warm the bones on a chilly morning. Even Johanna receives a small cup of warm milk with a hot muffin. Much of the liquid trickles down her chin and soaks her bib in her attempt at independence, but some of it goes down to warm her little stomach. Again, Ellen does not pick up her cup. Anna, John, and Sarah exchange glances and they wonder what brought about this change in her. Soon, Ellen pushes her chair back and stands, looks at each of them, giving them a little smile that quickly fades. Ellen turns and walks out of the kitchen with Rupert following. They hear her footsteps in the hallway with the pitter-patter of Rupert's paws, and the next sound they hear is the closing click of Ellen's bedroom door.

"Is Miss Cup all right? She didn't eat a bite. She usually cleans her plate. Come to think, she didn't eat much yesterday, either."

Anna and John both shake their heads at this change in Ellen's behaviour.

"I don't know, Sarah, but yes, she was quiet yesterday, too. I thought it was from her nightmare. It was dreadful. I'll give her a little time to herself before I check on her. She may wish to be alone for now."

John gets up from the table and walks behind Anna, pulling her chair out for her.

"Thank you, John. I reckon it's right time you were off to the shop."

"You're welcome. If I ever stop being a gentleman, please tread upon my bare toes and remind me, if you would."

"I'll keep that in mind. I don't foresee that happening, though."

John walks over to Johanna, leans down to kiss a clean spot on her rosy cheek and then strokes her hair. He narrowly misses two adoring hands covered with food.

"Be a good girl, sweetheart. Daddy will see you at supper time."

He stands and stretches a bit, as his hands knead his lower back for a moment before he comes to take Anna's hand in his own. Together, they walk out of the kitchen to the front door. A moment is all it takes for John to check his pockets for his wallet and watch, then don his overcoat. Anna holds her arms out to him, and he relishes this opportunity to embrace and kiss her. He stands back with a smile and touches her face before he tugs on his gloves and puts on his hat.

"I'll see you this evening, sweet one. I wish you luck with figuring out what is afflicting our girl."

"I hope so. I worry so about both girls when something is amiss. Have a good day, John."

With a nod and another quick kiss, John opens the door and steps out into the brisk morning air that snaps him to attention. Anna watches him from the doorway as he makes his way to the motor, gets in, and drives away. Her teeth chattering, she closes the door and hurries to the fireplace, eager to warm her hands. The fire returns a feeling of sunshine as it thaws her bones whilst her shivering subsides. Sarah comes through the sitting room carrying Johanna, and the child's singsong babbling lends further cheer to the morning.

"Ma ma ma ma!"

Anna smiles at their baby girl, learning to talk in her own expressive way. Sarah stops, and Anna walks up to them to cover Johanna's cheeks in kisses as she puts her damp hands on her mother's cheeks.

"There's my little sweetheart. Have a nice playtime with Sarah. Good girl!"

Sarah bobs her head and takes Johanna upstairs for a nappy change and playtime. Anna watches Sarah carrying Johanna who is looking over Sarah's shoulder to see her Mamma. Anna smiles, waves, and Johanna returns the wave, expressing a new phrase in her vocabulary.

"Buh-bye."

Sarah shares Anna's delight at Johanna's growing repertoire of verbal interactions. Her chuckle fades as she ascends the stairs, laughing at the baby in her arms. Anna reckons that now is as good a time as any to see what might be bothering Ellen. She walks out of the sitting room and down the hall to Ellen's bedroom. She tentatively opens the door, not wanting to startle her if she is in a fragile state of mind. She is surprised to see Ellen tucked into bed, wearing her nightdress, with her eyes closed. Anna frowns, again, seeing the dark circles under Ellen's eyes and the plush toy from Granny lying on the floor. Rupert peeks out at his mistress from under the bed and then rests his head on his paws. Anna sits on Ellen's bed and pats Ellen's arm. She opens her eyes and stares at Anna.

She points to herself, places her fist on her chest, and then draws an X on her forehead.

Anna tilts her head to the side, asking what this gesture means. Ellen rolls her head to the side and opens her mouth. Her limbs go flaccid. Anna comprehends with a heart-stabbing horror that Ellen has expressed a wish to die. Ellen rolls over on her side, facing the wall. Feeling helpless, Anna reaches out to stroke Ellen's hair, hoping that will lend Ellen some comfort. If only she could convince Ellen that she is not a bad person and she deserves a life filled with happiness. Ellen pulls the blankets over her head, and Anna clearly understands the message. She pats the lump under the covers that is Ellen's shoulder. She stands and walks to the door when she hears a 'woof'. Turning, she looks down at Rupert. She watches him crawl out from under the bed, looking up at his mistress, tilting his head to the side, and then lowering his gaze with a soft whine. Anna crouches down to stroke him and buries her face in his fur. She whispers to him, her voice trembling.

"You're a good boy, Rupert. Stay with Ellen and protect her. You're her best friend."

After scratching his ears, she stands up and walks out of the room, leaving the door ajar. She feels at a loss for what she should do, looking back at Ellen's bedroom door with a sigh. All she can do for now is continue to work on Lady Ashton's gown. She plods through the house and up the stairs, hoping that her sewing room will provide distraction and solace from her worry for Ellen. If Ellen rebuffs her presence, there is no point in forcing her to submit to maternal attention. Yes, Anna would have to admit that this turn hurts her feelings. Yet, her mothering instincts overcome the pain and transform it into serenity. She will continue to be a stable and loving presence for Ellen to seek when she is ready to do so. Before Anna reaches her sewing room, she peeks into the nursery to watch Sarah playing with Johanna on the floor. Johanna laughs at the toys that Sarah seems to bring to life. Neither notices her, so she smiles a little and continues to her sewing room to become engrossed in her work. The hypnotic hum of her sewing machine makes the time pass quickly until her concentration shatters with Sarah's excited entrance.

"Ma'am! It's open. The door to the garden. It's open. Rupert is sitting there whining. Miss Cup's door was open, so I looked in, and she was gone! The dress she wore at breakfast was lying on the floor. What must I do, Ma'am?"

Alarmed, Anna gets up and gives Sarah instructions.

"Stay here with Johanna. I'll try to find Ellen."

Sarah nods as she watches the mistress of the house rush out of the room. She hurries to Johanna's bedroom where the little thing is still sleeping. She is unable to think about the tasks that occupied her before this unseemly turn of events. Sarah sits in the rocking chair and prays whilst she watches Johanna sleep.

Anna is just about to dash out the door to look for any footprints in the snow when the telephone rings. She forgets to close the door and ignores Rupert's whining. Impatient, she runs to the kitchen to answer it. Every moment takes Ellen further away from safety. Breathless, she picks up the receiver.

"Hello?"

"Anna...it's Clara...come at once. Ellen..."

Anna hangs up the receiver and runs out of the kitchen, to the garden door, and outside. She forgets to close the door as she dashes as quickly as she can through the snow to Clara's house.

Clara hangs up the telephone and hastens outside to stay close to Ellen. Her daily stroll has taken a drastic change, and the cause of Clara's alarm is Ellen's current state. She does not respond to Clara's attempts to gain her attention, and she is wearing a nightdress with her feet bare on the icy walkway. Ellen holds her arms crossed in front of her with hands clenched into fists. Her face is void of expression except for the cheerless circles under her eyes. She stands where she is, staring down. Ellen's only communication with the world is the occasional exhale of breath turning into what looks like a cloud of despair. Clara prays that Anna will hurry and be able to guide Ellen inside to warmth and safety. Soon, Clara sees Anna running towards them. She gasps as Anna slips on a patch of ice, but releases her fear in a white puff of relief as Anna regains her balance. Anna takes in the situation instantly, and she looks at Clara who shakes her head at Anna's questioning expression. Anna moves in front of Ellen, gently taking both of Ellen's arms in her hands, noting how cold her skin feels under the fabric. Anna releases Ellen's arms to gesture to her, hoping to cross the chasm from the real world into whatever world has lured her away. She points to Ellen, motions walking, points to herself, and then points to the house in front of them.

"Ellen, you must come inside with me."

Ellen's gaze meets Anna's, and a tear trickles down from her eye. Anna slips her arm 'round Ellen's shoulders and guides her. Clara outpaces them and opens the door to her house wide, allowing Anna and Ellen quick entry.

"Bring her into the sitting room where there's heat. I'll get some tea."

She steps aside as Anna brings Ellen into the house. Clara removes her coat in haste, tosses it over a chair, and then hurries to the kitchen. The warmth of the fireplace ushers Anna and Ellen into the sitting room. Anna pats the sofa seat and sits down, patting the cushion again and pulling slightly on her hand, urging her to sit. Ellen stares at Anna for a moment and then sits next to her. For the first time, Anna begins to shiver from the cold, realising she had run all the way in just her dress. She looks at Ellen, clad only in a nightdress. She rubs her back and watches Ellen stare down at her hands that are folded in her lap. Moreover, Anna wonders that Ellen is not shivering.

She looks at the lady and points to herself.

Clara punctuating entry into the room interrupts Anna's curiosity about what Ellen was about to say before she ceased her gestures.

"Here you go. That cup is for Ellen. It's got a splash of brandy in it."

Clara sits in a chair across from the sofa to observe, the nature of

116

a nurse overshadowing that of a friend. Anna takes her cup in her hand and gives Ellen the one with brandy. Anna sips the tea, grateful for its flowing warmth inside her. Ellen holds her cup and stares into the fireplace, now and then glancing at Clara. Patting her arm to get her attention, Anna waits for Ellen to look at her. Ellen looks down at her arm and then at Anna. She points to the cup of tea and takes a sip, then nods as she points to Ellen. Ellen looks at Anna, nods and takes a sip of her drink. Startled, she grimaces and lowers her cup. Ellen looks down at it, lifts it up to her nose and sniffs the aroma wafting upwards. Looking at Anna who is sipping her tea, she pats Anna's arm. She looks at Ellen and tilts her head to the side.

She points to the liquid in the drinking thing and tilts her head to the side.

Anna knows that Ellen has detected a new flavour, one that is obviously unpleasant to her. Again, Anna points to her own tea and takes a sip. She points to Ellen's cup and nods, telling Ellen that she should drink the rest of it. Ellen wrinkles her nose and drinks the tea in one gulp. Her face contorts in an intense grimace as she shakes her head and then sets her cup on the side table and turns towards Clara.

She points at the strange lady, places her fists one atop the other repeatedly, draws an X on her palm, and then points to the teacup.

Clara raises an eyebrow at Anna.

"It seems the brandy snapped her out of...whatever that was. What did she say, Anna?"

"Well...um, she said that you make bad tea."

Ellen watches the two of them move their mouths at each other, then looks at Anna and tilts her head to the side. Anna nods and points to herself and Clara points to the teacup, nods her head, and then draws an X in the palm of her hand. Ellen nods and then looks into the fireplace. Clara understands Ellen's reaction to brandy in tea. Brandy is not a tasty additive to tea. She holds up her hand and nods.

"Anna, I'm going to go find Ellen a pair of house shoes and coats for the two of you to wear."

"Oh, yes. Thank you, Clara. I appreciate that."

Clara excuses herself and walks to the coat wardrobe in the entry hall to retrieve something warm. She checks the pockets and nods with satisfaction that the necessary gloves are present. On her way through the sitting room, Clara drapes the outerwear over the back of a chair. She comes to a hallway that leads to other parts of the house and chooses the stairway up to her bedroom. After a few moments of rummaging in her armoire, she finds a pair of house shoes with solid leather soles that will be suitable for Ellen. As she returns downstairs where Anna and Ellen sit before the fire, she stops for just a moment, witnessing a tender moment. Ellen's shoulders are enfolded by Anna's arm as she rests her head on Anna's shoulder. Clara clears her throat quietly as she walks 'round the sofa to stand near them.

"I found the house shoes I wanted to give Ellen. They'll protect her feet until you get home. If her feet swell from the cold, they will fit until she can wear her shoes again. Do you think she would mind if I put them on her? I would like to check her feet for injury from the cold."

"Thank you, Clara. I guess you can try. The worst that can happen is that she refuses."

Nodding, Clara moves in front of Ellen, kneels, and holds up the house shoes and pats Ellen's arm, emulating Anna. Ellen looks at her arm, then at Clara, and then at the house shoes. Clara points to herself, holds up the house shoes, points to Ellen, and then points to Ellen's feet. Feeling clumsy at trying these gestures, she hopes Ellen will understand her.

She tilts her head to the side and points to herself, stares at the strange lady, and then nods.

Relief fills Clara, and it shows on her face. Ellen holds out one foot, and then the other. Clara examines both feet, and finding no injury, she places the house shoes on her feet and looks up at Ellen with a smile.

She looks at the lady, points to herself, and then draws an X on the palm of her hand. She points to herself, moves her hands down the front of herself, and then draws a frown on herself. She points to herself and then draws an X on the palm of her hand.

Anna blinks at the speed and complicated content of Ellen's gestures. Clara stares at the two of them in amazement, having picked out the few gestures that she does understand. Anna replays Ellen's gestures in her head and interprets them to mean that Ellen feels sad and feels that she is bad. She looks at Ellen, putting her hand on Ellen's hand with a squeeze. She points to Ellen, draws an X in the palm of her hand, and then draws an X in the palm of her hand, again, trying to tell her that no, she is NOT bad. Anna points to her, puts one fist atop the other several times, points to herself, and then draws a smile on her own face to tell Ellen that she makes her happy. Ellen looks at Anna, a tear trickling down her face, and shakes her head. Anna points to herself, points to Clara, and moves her fingers near her own mouth to tell Ellen that she and Clara are going to talk together. Ellen nods and resumes looking at her hands folded in her lap.

"Clara, this, whatever it is, is new. We took her for a sleigh ride two evenings ago. That night she had a nightmare after I'd gone to bed. When I heard her, I got up, and before I could reach the stairs, there she was. She was holding her blanket, pillow, and cuddly toy. She was crying and wanted to sleep in our bed. Of course, I couldn't say no. Yesterday she seemed a little subdued, reflecting back. This morning, there was a carved owl on the table. I don't believe she slept last night, but I did consider it might be due to her bad dreams. She wouldn't eat breakfast this morning, went back to her room, and changed into her nightdress. She ducked her head under the covers when I tried to stroke her hair."

Anna's voice betrays her desire to cry as much as her desire to maintain composure, her eyes pleading with Clara for an answer.

"Now, this. What is happening to Ellen?"

"I'm not a doctor, but I've seen enough depression to consider that as a serious possibility. Unfortunately, we can't know what Ellen is thinking or feeling unless she tells us or we observe her behaviour. This is a difficult situation. For now, get her home and tuck her into bed. If she didn't sleep last night, she needs the rest. Especially after being out in the cold for who knows how long."

"Well, I guess that's the best we can do for now, isn't it?"

Ellen looks from Anna to Clara as they converse and pats Anna's arm, shaking her head.

She frowns and points to herself, places her hand on her chest and draws an X on her forehead.

Anna feels as though she has sustained another kick to her heart. Her eyes mist over as she shakes her head and points to herself, puts her fist on her chest, points to Ellen, and then draws a smile on her face. Tears begin to fall as she points to herself, draws an X on the palm of her hand, places a fist on her chest, points to Ellen, and then draws an X on her forehead. Anna shakes her head at Ellen. Through her tears, she points to herself, places her hand over her heart, and then points to

Ellen. Clara watches the conversation in gestures unfold and struggles to understand it. She can grasp that whatever Ellen told Anna is a sudden and saddening statement.

"What did she say, Anna?"

Choking on her words as she takes Ellen's hands in her own, she attempts to reply through her tears.

"She...she said...she wants to die. She said it this morning, too. I told her that she makes me happy and I love her and that...I...I don't want her to die. Oh, Clara, I couldn't bear it if she came to any harm."

Clara's elbow rests on the arm of her chair, and she rests the back of her fist against her mouth. She struggles to hide her feelings behind a nurse's façade in the face of such a heart-rending admission and its effect on her friend.

"Anna, all we can do is watch over her. If there is any sign of harming herself, stay with her and ring me. We cannot allow a male physician to assess her, obviously. We can't take her to a psychiatrist, or she may be taken against our will and better judgement to an institution. That could cause grave damage that love alone might not be able to heal. Watch and wait. Anna, I am only a ring away. Ring me up if you need me. I mean that. Day or night. I will apprise Dr Harper of what has happened. I've been updating him all along, and he's well-acquainted with the situation."

Wiping her eyes with her handkerchief, Anna nods.

"I will. I don't want Ellen taken from us and left alone at the mercy of people she doesn't know in a strange place. I hope she'll come out of it on her own. What she said frightens me, though. She is precious to us, and I would do anything to protect her."

Clara nods, seeing how much Anna has grown to love Ellen every bit as much as she loves Johanna. After watching Anna and Clara talk, Ellen tugs on Anna's sleeve and points to the door. Anna nods.

"Ellen wants to go home."

"Yes, you both need to take a good rest. This has been harrowing for both of you."

She gets up and walks over to the chair where the coats awaited their use. She picks them up and walks over to Anna and Ellen, holds them out, and nods to both of them.

"Put these on. I won't have the two of you freezing on the way."

Anna stands up and takes one, puts it on, and buttons it. She finds the gloves and puts them on, as well. The other, she receives from Clara and holds it up to Ellen. She stands and allows Anna to put the coat on her and then button it. She reaches into the pockets and hands

Ellen the gloves.

"Thank you, Clara. I'm grateful..."

"Tut tut. This is what friends who are a family do for one another. Hurry, now, and tuck Ellen into bed. The brandy might make her a bit sleepy by the time you get there."

Nodding, Anna takes Ellen's hand and points to the door, and together they pass an attentive Clara who opens it for them. She watches Anna and Ellen leave, moving further and further away with each step. Staring outside, even after Anna and Ellen are no longer in sight, she says a silent prayer that all will be well in the Thorpe household. Finally, Clara closes her door and retreats to the warmth of the hearth. She is too distracted with worry to do much more than sit there, staring into the flames.

Grateful to be home, Anna leads Ellen to the garden door and opens it, allowing Ellen to enter first. She stands, staring at Anna, and then turns, retreating to her bedroom. Anna hears a soft whine and a woof as she walks to Ellen's door and peeks inside. Rupert is up on the bed, wagging his tail. She walks into Ellen's room and doffs the anorak, laying it on the chair with the anorak Ellen had worn. For a time, Anna watches Ellen whilst she stands in front of the looking glass, staring at herself.

She points to herself in the thing and draws an X in the palm of her hand. She points to herself in the thing, places her fist on her chest, and then draws an X on her forehead.

Tears distort her vision as she feels her heart ripped asunder by Ellen's third expression of the day that she is bad and wants to die. She tries to distract Ellen by placing her hand on Ellen's arm and pointing to the bed. Trying not to show that she wants to weep, Anna walks over to the bed with her. Ellen takes the cuddly toy in her arms, slips under the covers and lays her head down on the pillow. Sitting on the side of the bed, Anna reaches out to stroke Ellen's hair. Ellen's eyes close slowly but then open wide. Ellen sits up and silently coughs with growing intensity. It rattles her body so much that tears spring from her eyes and her visage turns crimson. Anna attends Ellen by rubbing her back, hoping to soothe her breathing. Ellen pushes the blankets away from her as she sits breathless, her hand on her chest. Her breathing slightly improved, Ellen gets out of bed to open a window. She pulls a chair close, filling her lungs with the cold air. Ellen looks at Anna with reddened eyes and with growing anxiousness, Anna touches Ellen's forehead.

She stares at the lady and tilts her head to the side. She takes her hand, places it on the lady's forehead, and shrugs.

There does not seem to be a fever, and Anna wishes she knew how to explain all this to her. She contents herself with stroking Ellen's hair, instead. Soon, Anna holds up a finger, points to herself, and then to the general direction of the kitchen to say that she will be right back.

She races to the kitchen to find a carafe and glass. Filling it with fresh water, she rushes back to Ellen's room. She hopes the cooling liquid will soothe Ellen's throat. Anna pours the water into the glass and walks 'round the bed to give it to her. An ember of awareness sparks and she realises that Ellen's cough was silent. Her laughter is silent. Her weeping is silent. Why? Anna's maternal questions tumble about. Is Ellen coming down with an illness? Her thoughts turn to the night of the sleigh ride. Was it too cold or was Mr Higg's coughing contagious or was walking so exposed in the cold today...Anna shakes the possibilities from her mind and decides to just watch Ellen for more signs of illness and the dreaded expressions of depression. She gives Ellen a smile and points to herself, places her hand over her heart, and then points to Ellen.

She points to herself, places her hand over her heart, and then points to the lady. She puts her hands together and moves them from her chest to the lady.

Anna shakes her head, takes Ellen's hands in her own, and kisses them to say that there is nothing to forgive. She is glad and relieved that Ellen expresses her love, though. Whilst Ellen drinks the water, Anna goes to the bureau to take out an extra quilt. She smooths it on the bed and straightens the covers. Fluffing the pillows is Anna's habit of giving her girl more comfort. She walks back to Ellen who has opened the drawer of her bedside table, reaching inside. Ellen holds out the empty glass and a piece of paper. Anna cannot help but smile with misted eyes as she reads the words 'I LOVE YOU'. She holds the paper over her heart and nods. She points to herself, places her hand on her heart, and then points to Ellen to say 'I love you'.

Anna points to the bed and nods, insisting in a motherly way that Ellen should snuggle back into the bed. Instead of lying down, she sits up and looks at the pillow. Fear is written on her face, and Anna guesses it might be a fear of lying down. Propping the paper with the words written on it against Ellen's lamp, she hopes Ellen will look at it and remember that she is loved. She places a second pillow drawn from the bureau drawer on top of the first, and Ellen nods. She lies down, and Anna pulls up the blankets, tucking her fluff toys under the cover with her. Anna points to the window and pantomimes shivering and closing it to explain that leaving the window open would make the room too chilly. Ellen nods and Anna closes the window. She walks 'round the bed to sit next to Ellen and stroke her hair.

Soon, Ellen's eyes close again, and Anna is convinced that she will fall fast asleep. Attentive to Ellen's need for comfort, Anna slides a cuddly toy under her arm. Even a small thing as this seems to be valuable to Ellen. Her eyes open again, and she grasps Anna's arm. She points to Anna and then drops her arm. A second time, she lifts her arm and rests it back down, sliding it back under the blanket. Anna is curious about what Ellen was going to try to say. Stroking Ellen's hair, Anna finally believes that Ellen is sleeping. She stands, walks towards the bedroom door and then stops. She turns 'round to look at Ellen and smiles at Rupert, lying next to her, with his head resting on her legs.

Walking out of the bedroom, Anna intends to have a chat with Sarah in the kitchen. Sarah will have to know that they need to observe Ellen for signs of illness since Ellen makes no sound when she coughs. Johanna is playing on her blanket and, upon seeing her Mamma, begins a barrage of happy baby-chatter. Anna smiles for her baby, walks over to her and scoops her up in her arms.

"Were you a good girl for Sarah? I'm sure you were! I'm happy to see you, too, little one."

She holds Johanna tightly and ruffles her hair. She strokes Johanna's hair and kisses her cheeks. She turns to Sarah who is smiling fondly at the scene of a mum and her daughter.

"Sarah, I knew I might find you in here. Ellen is safe and is in bed sleeping."

"Thank heavens, Ma'am. I was so worried about her, and nothing could have made me as happy as hearing you come in the door. I made a hearty stew that she likes, and maybe she'll be hungry. Miss Cup hasn't eaten all day."

"Yes, maybe she will, later. I need your help, Sarah. We must watch Ellen for signs of illness. She coughed terribly when I was tucking her into bed. There's another thing, and I feel foolish for not putting it together in my head sooner, but, at any rate, her cough is as silent as her laughter and crying. You will see her move as though she is coughing, but no sound comes."

"Oh! I never thought of that...well; of course, I'll help keep an eye on her. I'll keep Johanna away from her until you're sure that she isn't sick."

"Good thinking, Sarah. Thank you."

She notices the owl carved by Ellen during the night and picks it up. She leaves Sarah to her tasks and walks into the sitting room. Johanna pats her mamma's face, and Anna blows against the little hands to make her baby laugh. She rests the owl on the mantle above the fireplace and then sits down with Johanna on the sofa to read until John comes home. Johanna insists on grabbing the book, so Anna closes it, sets it aside, and begins to conjure a captivating story for Johanna. Soon, she hears the familiar sound of the front door opening and the stomping of snow off feet. She gets up, lifting Johanna into her arms and hurries to greet John.

"Come, Johanna. We must welcome Daddy. He'll be as happy to see us as we will be to see him!"

Anna watches with a small smile as John finishes putting away his coat.

"Well, if it isn't my two favourite ladies! Come to Daddy, my sweet."

Johanna nearly leaps out of Anna's arms with excitement. John catches her in his hands and lifts her high in the air, making Johanna squeal with delight. He brings Johanna back down so he can hold her and kiss her. He turns to Anna with a grin.

"Now, this is how a man likes to come home to his family."

"We're happy to see you too, John. You know we miss you every day that you're at the shop...I missed you."

John's smile fades as he leans down to kiss Anna. She tries to extend her arms 'round her husband and daughter, but her arms just will not reach. She stands back and looks up at John, Johanna, and tries to smile as she whispers.

"I do love you so, John, and our little one. You make me happy."

"What about our Ellen? Is anything wrong?"

John frowns, fears rearing their ugly heads in his psyche. Anna's smile fades, and she shakes her head.

"We had a rather eventful day, I'm afraid. I hope Ellen isn't coming down with something."

"Oh? Well, then, we must do all we can to take care of her. Has she eaten today?"

"No, and she's abed sleeping, now. Supper is ready whenever you are. Sarah made a stew, and she'll save some for Ellen if she wants to eat when she wakes up."

"Good. Well, then, let us see what Sarah's stew is like this time."

Sarah had a 'pinch of this and pinch of that' way with her cooking. Nothing ever turned out the same way twice, but whatever she made was delicious. They walk to the kitchen and all of them, even Sarah laugh at Johanna's new word.

"Hungee hungee da da da!"

Johanna lunges for her high chair so rapidly that John nearly loses his grip on her.

"Slow down, Johanna. Trust Daddy to sit you in your chair."

John shakes his head as he settles Johanna in her high chair. He takes the bib from the table, fastens it 'round her neck, and kisses her head.

"That's my girl. You'll have your supper in a moment."

Anna pats John's shoulder and points in the direction of Ellen's room. She points to herself, points to her eyes, and then smiles.

"I'll be right back."

John nods, watching her walk out of the kitchen and hope he will become as fluent in Ellen's language as Anna has. He waits with Anna's chair pulled out until she returns. Anna sighs, returning to the kitchen, taking her seat before John sits at the head of the table, awaiting Anna's report.

"Yes, she's still asleep. She needs that first, then food."

Sarah brings the crock of stew to the table and nods as she fills bowls, hands one to Anna and then one to John. She fills a small bowl for Johanna and sets it out of the curious child's reach. She fills her own bowl last and sits next to Johanna. Sarah mashes Johanna's food and lets her chew on a salty biscuit between spoons full of stew. Quiet conversation tries to fill the kitchen. Anna and Sarah pointedly avoid the subject of Ellen. John wonders what else transpired to elicit such silence about the day. Sighing, he eats the last bite of his second helping of stew. He reckons that Anna will tell him everything in a more private setting. Soon, they all hear a soft 'woof' coming from Ellen's bedroom.

"John, Rupert is calling me. I should see Ellen. We're keeping a close watch on her to see if she is falling ill and...well, I'll tell you about our visit with Clara later."

His curiosity is piqued, but he nods, gets up and pulls out Anna's chair. He watches her kiss the top of Johanna's head, the only place on their daughter that is not covered in food. Anna looks up at him and squeezes his arm as she walks by, on her way to Ellen's room. Anna peeks in, only to see her just wake up with another coughing fit. Rupert backs up, nearly falling off the bed. He jumps down and crawls under the bed. Anna hurries to Ellen's side and rubs her back. She calls out to Sarah.

"Sarah, please bring in some tea with headache powders, honey, ginger and lemon."

The headache powders should ease any pain Ellen has and might occur with coughing. The honey and lemon should reduce her cough and soothe her throat. Ginger will settle Ellen's stomach if she should develop an upset there.

Sarah stops cleaning Johanna's face and hands, looking up at John.

"Sir, um, would you...ah..."

"It's all right, Sarah. Go fix the tea for Ellen. I'll tend to Johanna."

John turns to clean Johanna's mess whilst Sarah scurries to make the tea. She hurries to Ellen's bedroom as she tries not to spill the tea in her haste.

"As you asked, Ma'am."

Sarah smiles, waves to Ellen, and then points to the tea. She gives the tea to Anna who thanks her. As Sarah takes her leave, Anna checks the temperature of the cup on her wrist to make sure it is warm but not too hot. Satisfied that the temperature is perfect, she hands the cup to Ellen. By now, Ellen's coughing has subsided, and she is sitting up in bed staring at the cup of tea. Anna holds up the cup with one hand and pantomimes drinking it with her other hand. Ellen takes the teacup and sniffs it. She tilts her head to the side and then nods, sipping the warmth nodding her head again. Ellen finishes the tea and hands the cup back to Anna. As she takes the cup, Anna reaches over to feel her forehead once more, but it remains cool to the touch. Anna smiles, points to Ellen, puts her hands together and lays her head on them as if they were a pillow to ask Ellen if she wants to sleep more. Ellen shakes her head and points to the bed. Anna assumes that means Ellen intends to stay in bed. She pantomimes eating food, but Ellen only looks down at the cuddly toy in her hands. Anna nods her head. Fluffing the pillows behind Ellen, Anna leans down to kiss her forehead. She holds up one finger, points to herself, points in the direction of the kitchen, points to Ellen and then pantomimes eating. Ellen nods, and Anna is glad that Ellen seems to want something to eat.

On her way to the kitchen, a smile comes to Anna's face as she remembers her own grandmother caring for her when she was sick as a little girl. Finding herself alone in the kitchen, she notices a large pot on the cooker that had not been there before. She lifts the lid and, inside, there is a bowl of stew sitting in scalding water. The pot is on the burner Sarah had used to cook, so that was still warm. Sarah is creative and thoughtful to keep Ellen's food warm in this way, and Anna is impressed. Taking a tea cloth from the counter, she spreads it out next to the cooker. Taking large hot pads, she reaches in to retrieve the bowl and places it on the protected countertop. Setting the hot pads aside to dry, she wipes the outside of the container. She finds the tray and puts the bowl on it, adds a spoon and serviette, then fills a glass with milk from the cold box. Balancing the tray, she makes her way back to Ellen's room. She walks in to see Ellen looking down at her hands, folded in her lap. Anna sets the tray on a nearby chair and sits on the bed next to Ellen. She looks at Anna with tears in her eyes.

She points to herself, points to her head, points to herself, draws an X in the palm of her hand.

Anna shakes her head to disagree with the idea that Ellen thinks she is bad, but Ellen shakes her head and looks down.

She points to herself, moves her hands down the front of herself, points to herself, draws an X on the palm of her hand.

Anna is confused, now. She knows that Ellen feels poorly, expressed that she is a bad person, and wants to die. Maybe Ellen is expressing herself out of exhaustion. Anna reaches for the tray and places it on Ellen's lap. She looks at the plate of food, closing her eyes, and she inhales deeply. With that deep breath, another coughing jag seizes Ellen. Anna barely rescues the tray in time and sets it back on the chair. She returns her attention to Ellen, rubbing her back in gentle circles. Whether Ellen is suffering from depression or illness, she is inclined to insist that Ellen keeps to her bed. When the fit of coughing subsides, Anna fluffs the pillows behind her, and Ellen pushes herself back to sit a little more upright in the bed. Once again, the tray is placed on Ellen's lap. She stares at her food and reaches for the glass of milk. She takes a sip and returns the glass to the tray. Ellen scoops up a portion of stew in her spoon and tastes it before eating it. She glances at Anna who is hovering to ensure that Ellen consumes a reasonable amount. Ellen takes several more spoonsful of stew, consuming it slowly. She drinks a little more milk and then wipes her mouth with the serviette. Without looking at Anna, she pushes the tray away from herself and shakes her head.

Sighing, Anna takes the tray away and returns it to the chair nearby. She pats Ellen's arm and waits for her to look down at her arm and then up. She holds up one finger and points to herself, points at the tray, points in the general direction of the kitchen, points to herself, and then points down. In this way, Anna's gestures communicate her intention to return shortly, from taking the tray to the kitchen. Ellen nods and turns to arrange her pillows, allowing her to lie down. Anna watches her for a moment and then walks out of Ellen's bedroom to the kitchen. She places the milk and stew in the cold box and leaves the tray as it is on the counter. John walks into the kitchen, startling Anna who is deep in thought.

"What's wrong, sweetheart? Is Ellen all right?"

"I don't know what's wrong with her, but something isn't right. I think I need to sit with her tonight, John. Do you mind, terribly?"

"Of course not! Anna, she's our girl. She's like a daughter to us. Whatever she needs, she needs from you."

Anna nods, feeling fatigue setting upon her in anticipation of a night without sleep. If Ellen needs a guardian angel in addition to Rupert, then it falls upon her shoulders to be just that.

"Thank you, John. I worry that you and Johanna suffer for all the attention Ellen requires."

Taking Anna in his arms, he kisses her and then kisses her forehead. He holds her close to him and rubs her back.

"Anna, when we were blessed with Johanna, we knew that she would need us. There are two of us. I can dote on Johanna whilst you tend to Ellen, now that she is like a daughter to us. We have Sarah to help. As for me, I couldn't ask for a more attentive mother to our girls. I love you, I admire you, and we make small sacrifices for the commitment and joys of being Mamma and Daddy. We'll make time for us one of these days. Trust me, we'll make the most of our 'us' time. All right, sweetheart?"

Anna nods, holding him tight.

"I love you, John. So, so much."

She looks up at him, smiles, and touches his sweet face with her fingertips. She caresses the crinkles at the corners of his eyes that speak of sharp and frequent good humour.

"I love you, too, Anna. With everything I am, I love you. Now, Mamma, if you're going to spend the night watching over our girl, you're going to need a comfortable chair. I'll bring one in for you."

He kisses her nose and smiles at how pretty Anna is when she smiles at him. He watches her walk to the kitchen door, turn back towards him, and blow him a kiss. He stands there, listening to the sound of her footsteps moving down the hallway. Smiling at how much he loves Anna and is proud of her, he walks to the sitting room. He pulls out Anna's favourite chair, hefting it into his arms. He makes his way to Ellen's bedroom with his light but clumsy burden.

"Anna, is it all right for me to bring in this chair for you?"

"Yes, John, she's asleep, for now."

Anna moves a few items out of the way so John can position the chair in a convenient place. She intends to keep her hand on Ellen's arm whilst she sleeps. Even if she falls asleep, she hopes that any movement will wake her up straight away.

"I'll get the footstool and a shawl for you."

Anna nods and prepares to settle herself in for the night, smiling at John who returns with the footstool and shawl, placing them where Anna can reach them. He takes Anna by the shoulders, turns her to face him, then cups her cheek with his hand and gently lifts her face towards him to receive his tender kiss.

"Wear the shawl 'round your shoulders and feel me holding you throughout the night. Good night, sweet one."

"Thank you, John; I will feel you with me. I always do. Good night, sweetheart."

John and Anna clasp hands for a moment, and then John turns to leave the room. He stops to smile once more at Anna and then blows her a kiss. As worried as she is about Ellen, John's sweet ways never fail to warm her spirit. She settles herself into the familiar chair and rests her hand on the lump under the blanket that is Ellen's arm. She does not want Ellen to feel afraid or alone. Ellen deserves to feel loved. Tugging the shawl about her shoulders a bit tighter, she smiles to imagine that she is in John's arms even when they are not together.

Chapter Twelve
11 March 1926

Anna awakens in her chair thanks to the bright sunlight that dares intrude into Ellen's room. For a moment, she startles, wondering where Johanna and Sarah are. Her memory comes back to her, as her senses grow more acute. She is grateful that John asked that she not be disturbed. Encouraging Rupert to get off her lap, she rubs her eyes, and then stretches the stiffness from her body. She stands up and walks 'round the bed and closes curtains to dim the room. Opening the window just a crack will allow some fresh air to come in without too much cold. She turns to look at Ellen and sees that she is sleeping. The night was involved with Ellen waking up several times to cough vigorously. The effort left Ellen breathless with each spasm from deep in her chest. Anna tended every episode with care and old remedies in the occasional cup of tea. Finally, both of them fell into a deep sleep. Touching Ellen's hair, she finds it saturated with perspiration. She lightly touches Ellen's forehead with the back of her hand. Ellen's body is radiating a heat that demands fewer blankets. Anna rolls them to the foot of the bed, readily available if Ellen becomes chilled. The dark circles under her eyes are more prominent with her fevered flush. She considers rolling down the third to leave only a sheet, but Anna does not want her to cool too quickly. Rupert stands on his hind legs with his front paws on the bed and then whines. She reaches down to stroke Rupert's head, whispering to him.

"I know you're worried about Ellen. We are, too. Good boy. Keep watch, will you? I know you will."

Rupert hops up on the bed, turns 'round three times, and plops himself at the foot of the bed with his chin on his paws. Anna turns to leave the room and leaves the door open to allow clean air to circulate. She walks down the hallway, through the sitting room, and up the stairs to a storage cupboard near the loo. From inside, she withdraws a metal basin, some flannels, two towels, and clean sheets. Anna hears Sarah in the loo cleaning whilst Johanna plays on a nearby blanket.

"Sarah, Ellen has a fever, and I'll be tending her. If you could care for Johanna and keep yourself and her away from Ellen's room, that would be helpful. I don't want anyone else to fall ill."

"Of course, Ma'am. I'll take care of everything. As soon as Sir comes, I'll inform him. I can put a chair outside of Miss Cup's door, so I can leave you trays of food if you like?"

"Thank you. That's a good idea. If you brought me some pinnies and a bell to signal for help, I would appreciate it."

"Yes, Ma'am. Right away, Ma'am."

Sarah leaves her cleaning and picks up Johanna. Johanna reaches out and frowns.

"Mama!"

"Hush, Miss Johanna. Your Mamma is busy. She'll tend to you when she can."

Sarah hastens to find the items that Anna requested and makes her way downstairs to the kitchen where she sets Johanna on her blanket with toys. She collects the clean pinnies and bell on the table. Sarah lifts a kitchen chair and carries it to Ellen's bedroom door, leaving it in the hallway. Returning to the kitchen, Sarah picks up the pinnies and hurries to place them on the chair's seat. Collecting Johanna and her toys, Sarah takes her back upstairs to the playroom for a romp before her nap, avoiding Anna.

Anna's arms are encumbered with all she needs to care for Ellen as she makes her way downstairs to the loo next to Ellen's room. Rupert comes out of Ellen's bedroom to see what his mistress is doing and sits next to her, wagging his tail. She fills the basin with warm water and then bundles up the rest of the items in a towel to carry everything. On her way to Ellen's room, she is pleased to see the chair, bell, and pinnies that Sarah has already assembled for her. Carrying the basin, towels, and sheets, Anna is careful that she does not spill the water. Rupert runs into his friend's room and dives under the bed, peeking out. Entering Ellen's room, she looks 'round to find a place to set things down. A chair will do for now. Anna chooses the table upon which Ellen has her little evergreen tree and moves it aside to make room for the basin, cloths, and towels. She brings the table close to Ellen's bed and arranges the necessary items upon it. The sheets can wait on the seat of the first chair until later.

She leans down to touch Ellen's forehead and finds that the fever has not abated in the least. Before she begins tending to Ellen in earnest, she dons a pinny. Rupert crawls under the bed to peek out at his mistress's feet as she walks about the sick room. Restlessness descends upon Ellen, her head turning side to side, her mouth opens in what could only be described as a silent moan. Dipping a cloth in the warm water, Anna squeezes out the excess and wipes glistening moisture from Ellen's face. This is enough to cause Ellen to move about more before opening her eyes. She stares up at the ceiling with an expression of confusion before lifting her head to look 'round the room. Her eyes finally rest on Anna who places a cloth on Ellen's forehead. Her eyes close briefly and then open again.

She looks at the lady, points to the lady and then to herself.

She smiles at Ellen and moistens another cloth to wipe away traces of illness from her skin. Thinking and gesturing must be taxing for Ellen, as she seems to be unable to finish what she was trying to say. Frustration must be a part of the reason Ellen turns her head away and lets her arm fall limp against herself. Anna continues to soothe away the dampness from Ellen's exposed skin. These are all things that Anna learnt from her grandmother. She was a woman who could bring anyone back to health. She hopes her grandmother's methods shall help Ellen recover quickly. She turns her head again, and her eyes meet Anna's.

She looks at the lady, points to herself, moves her hands down the front of her, and then draws an X in the palm of her hand.

Poor thing, Anna sympathises. Ellen feels wretched. She wishes she could take this illness away from Ellen and spare her this suffering. Ellen puts her hand to her chest and suddenly raises herself on one elbow, coughing with every ounce of strength she has left. Sitting on the edge of the bed, Anna strokes the moist cloth against the back of Ellen's neck and then holds the fabric there. A back rub seems to be the most effective way to calm Ellen's cough. In due time, the coughing subsides, and Ellen sits up in bed, hugging her drawn-up knees until she can catch her breath. She rests her forehead on her knees and shakes her head slowly. Anna walks to the wardrobe and takes out a new nightdress of a summer weight. She pats Ellen on the arm and waits for Ellen to look at her arm and then back up. Ellen nods her head when Anna shows her the dry nightdress. Anna points to herself, places a fist on top of her palm, and then points to Ellen, saying that she shall help Ellen change into the dry nightdress. She holds up one finger for Ellen to wait a moment. She walks over to the chair full of fresh linens and lays them on the end of the bed. She brings the chair close to the bed so Ellen will not have far to go in her weakened state. Looking at the chair, Ellen nods and swings her legs over the edge of the bed. She sways slightly and puts her hand to her head. Anna steadies her, ready to catch her if she falls. Ellen nods and points to the chair, reaches for it, thereby indicating her readiness to shift to the chair. She stands, and Anna catches her as

Ellen's legs rebel against holding her full weight. Together, they successfully reach the seat. Allowing Ellen's pace to guide her, Anna helps Ellen disrobe.

She points to the thing with water and the wet cloth, holds out her hand, and then points to herself.

Anna gives Ellen a freshly moistened flannel to wipe herself. She keeps a watchful eye on Ellen and then takes the flannel, dampens it again, and rubs Ellen's back. She holds up one finger to Ellen as a way of telling her to sit right there on the chair. Removing the soiled bedclothes from the bed with a swift tug and allowing them to land in a heap on the floor, she immediately applies the fresh ones with a speed she had never before accomplished. Returning to Ellen's side, she holds up the nightdress for her to slip on, but observes that she is too weak to hold up her arms. She rubs Ellen's back to let her know that it is all right. She puts her own hand through the armhole of the nightdress, picks up Ellen's hand, and then draws it through. Anna repeats the process with Ellen's other hand, and then brings the nightdress over Ellen's head.

Ellen bows her head for a moment and then, looking up at Anna, she begins to cry and gesture.

She points to the lady, places her fist on her hand, and then points to herself as she tilts her head to the side.

Anna wonders at Ellen's question asking why she is taking care of her. She wonders if Ellen has never had anyone care for her when she has taken ill. Anna points to herself, places her hand over her heart, and then points to Ellen. As Anna finishes her own gestures that say 'I love you', to explain why she tends to her needs, another fit of coughing seizes Ellen with its stormy ferocity. Anna moves in front of Ellen to prevent her from falling forwards off the chair. She holds Ellen's shoulders, crouching down in front of her. When the coughing subsides, Anna stands, holding Ellen close to her as Ellen's arms slip 'round Anna's waist. She rubs Ellen's back until her breathing slows down to a more normal rhythm. A quick thought comes to Anna, and she grabs a towel with one hand and manages to flick it on the stacked pillows. Lifting Ellen's chin, she motions to the bed with a tilt of her head to ask Ellen if she is ready to go back to bed. Ellen nods her consent, and with some difficulty, as Ellen is weak and dizzy, Anna manages to get her back to bed. Drained by the effort, Ellen slumps against the freshened pillows. Anna pulls the dry top sheet over her and then reaches for the blanket. Beads of sweat already return to Ellen's forehead and trickle down her face. She lifts up her hand and shakes her head, refusing the blanket. Nodding, Anna folds the blanket to the side, ready to pull it over Ellen if needed. She sits on the edge of the bed and places one of Ellen's cuddly toys next to her, and soon, she closes her eyes.

A soft knock at the door draws Anna's attention.

"How is Miss Cup, Ma'am?"

"She isn't feeling well at all. Would you mind ringing Mrs Dewhurst for me? I think it would be prudent to ask her to give an opinion."

"Yes, Ma'am."

Anna hears Sarah's footsteps fading down the hallway to the kitchen. Distantly, she hears Sarah's voice asking Clara to come as soon as she is able. In a few moments, she hears Sarah returning.

"Ma'am, Mrs Dewhurst will be here soon. She wants to talk to Dr Harper first."

"Thank you, Sarah. Will you take these wet things and put them in the laundry when they're dry?"

"I'll hang them outside in the sun, if you don't mind, Ma'am. They'll freeze, but the sun should kill any sickness on them."

Sarah hurries off, and Anna sits on the side of the bed, stroking her hair. Hearing the front door open and close, she wonders if Clara has come so soon or if John is back early. She gets up and peers out of the doorway. Yes, that is John taking off his coat and hat. He notices her and walks down the hall towards Anna who is looking out from Ellen's room.

"Sweetheart, how's our girl? I've been worried about her."

"She's taken ill with the same horrible cough that Mr Higg had. She has a fever, and she's weak. Clara will be here soon. I can't leave her in this condition. And why are you home so early? You look pale. Are you all right?"

He waves his hand in a dismissive gesture.

"I was just tired and thought I'd make an early day of it. The shop is well-managed, and the fellows urged me to go."

"Well, if you're sure that's all it is. Why don't you go upstairs and take a nap? You should indulge yourself."

"Yes, I believe I will. I'd kiss you, Anna, but I have a feeling you'd tell me to keep my distance."

"You know I would. I won't have the rest of the house indisposed."

"Yes, you're right. If Johanna is napping, I'd best leave her sleep."

"Yes. Rest well, sweet one."

Anna blows John a kiss, and he returns the same with a smile. She watches him walk down the hallway and disappear into the sitting room. Shortly, she hears his footsteps on the staircase. She frowns. It is unlike John to come home early just to take a nap. He is pale, too. She hopes that he is not going to begin coughing, also. Anna's attention hastens her to Ellen's bedside as she suddenly jolts up in bed, clutched by another exhausting battle with a malevolent cough. As the wave of distress ebbs, she helps Ellen lay back, two pillows supporting her shoulders and head. Ellen closes her eyes and shakes her head as the fever rages against her will. Anna hopes that Clara comes soon and will bring some medicine from the doctor some remedy to recommend.

Lost in her worry as she strokes Ellen's hair and holds her hand, she finally hears the front door open and close. Anna hopes this is Clara, as she never knocks, but always walks right in, as dearest friends may do. Quiet words exchange between Clara and Sarah and soon Anna hears Clara's footsteps stride towards Ellen's room. She peeks in the door and sets her bag on the floor in the doorway. Rupert scoots further under the bed.

"Well, what have we here?"

"Thank goodness. Clara, she has no appetite, I can barely get her to drink, she's weak, coughing as though her lungs are on fire, and she's got a terrible fever."

"I was afraid of that. This same illness has struck many families in town. Granny, Father Willington, and I have been making extra visits to help. May I borrow one of your pinnies on the chair out here?"

Before Anna can say yay or nay, Clara is donning a pinny and opening her bag. Clara takes out a stethoscope and a thermometer.

"I think the first thing we need to do is have Ellen drink as much water as we can get her to take. Can you manage that?"

"I think so. I'm not sure if she's sleeping, but I'll try."

She pours a glass of water from the carafe on the bedside table. Rubbing Ellen's arm, she hopes Ellen will wake up enough to notice that she is trying to get her attention. Opening her eyes, Ellen looks down at her arm and then up at Anna. She holds up the glass of water and points to Ellen. She nods and tries to sit up, but with the effort, she convulses in another coughing fit. Anna soothes Ellen until her breathing calms down. Ellen sits up in the bed, drawing her knees up and wrapping one arm 'round them. She reaches for the water and sips it, looking at Anna who motions for Ellen to drink all of it if she can. She looks at the glass for a moment and then swallows the rest of the water. She hands the glass back to Anna and looks at Clara.

She points to the strange lady, points to her own eyes, and then points to herself with a tilt of her head.

Clara nods, confirming that she is here to see her. Anna attracts Ellen's attention, points to Clara, places one fist on the palm of her other hand, points to Ellen, moves her hands down the front of herself, then pats her hands together to tell Ellen that Clara is here to help her feel better. Reaching back into her bag, Clara pulls forth a mask to wear, covering her own mouth and nose.

"Dr Harper says that this illness travels through the air in the presence of coughing. That's why I'm wearing a mask. He says that if you block your nose and mouth from someone who is coughing, you might not get sick."

"I wasn't aware of that. Do I need a mask? Am I caring for her correctly? I don't know what else to do."

"At this point, if you've caught it, you've caught it, although some have been 'round the coughing and showed no ill effects. It's hard to say. As to your care, you're nursing her well. I'd like to listen to her lungs and take her temperature if I could."

With a nod, Anna pats Ellen's arm and waits for her to look down at her arm and then look up at her. She points to Clara, places a fist on her chest, points to her ear, and then points to Ellen's chest, holds up one finger, and touches Ellen's forehead, hoping Ellen understands her gestures. All Ellen does is shrug and rest her head back down on her drawn-up knees. Anna nods, and she slips the thermometer under Ellen's arm where it will be the warmest and least invasive. After listening to Ellen's lungs, she removes the thermometer and nods at its reading.

"It's as I expected. Her fever is high enough to make her feel dreadful, but not high enough to be dangerous. Her lungs sound tight and dry. If they sounded wet and I couldn't hear air moving deep down, I'd worry about pneumonia, but that isn't the case."

Clara wraps her stethoscope, mask, and thermometer in a thick cloth, and then places them back in her bag. She extracts a bottle of medicine and a spoon.

"This sounds exactly like the other cases as Dr Harper suspected. He gave me some medicine for her, just in case. Let's try to get a spoon full into her. This should stop her cough, relieve the pain from coughing, and help her sleep. She's young, otherwise healthy, and should recover quickly if she is able to sleep."

Anna pats Ellen's arm and waits for her to look down at her arm and then up at her. Anna points to the bottle of medicine Clara holds in her hand, points to Ellen, and pantomimes taking the medication from a spoon. Ellen shrugs and looks at Clara as Anna pours the dose into the spoon. Ellen opens her mouth, holds on to the spoon as well and takes every drop. Anna rubs Ellen's back and points to the medicine bottle, puts her fist on the palm of her hand, points to Ellen, moves her hands down the front of herself, and then pats her hands together. She smiles as Ellen nods her understanding that the medicine shall help her feel better. Ellen rests her head on her knees again.

"This shouldn't take too long to show its effect. You should give this to her, one spoon full, every four hours, or so. This illness does run its own course, but if she gets some sleep and relief from coughing, she will be well soon."

"Thank you. I understand. I'll offer her more to drink whenever she's awake."

"Absolutely. When she's had some sleep, offer her some soup. Nothing substantial. Then, work your way up to stew or a small sandwich."

"We can do that. Thank you, Clara."

"I'm glad to come. Is anyone else in the house sick?"

"No, John came early from the shop, tired, but he's taking a nap. I think he's been working too hard."

"All right. Keep watch on everyone and seclude him or her at the first sign of coughing. I'll just step into the loo and wash my hands, and then I'll be on my way."

Anna nods and turns back to Ellen, fluffing her pillows and replacing the first towel with a dry one. As she hears the front door open and close at Clara's leave-taking, she helps Ellen lie down and turn to her side, curled up. Sitting with Ellen, she strokes her damp hair until her breathing is even and without labour. Taking this opportunity to leave the room, she takes off her pinny and leaves it folded on the floor by the door. Rupert comes out from under the bed, sniffs the pinny, and then sticks his head out to look up and down the hallway. He wags his tail and trots over to the bed, hops up, and then turns 'round three times. Finally, he plops himself at the foot of the bed. Anna goes to the loo and thoroughly washes her hands as she had heard Clara do. Listening to Sarah in the kitchen with Johanna, she smiles as she walks down the hallway and peeks into the kitchen. Johanna is wholly absorbed by the meal Sarah has made, and Anna is glad she does not notice her mamma, for now.

Anna walks to the sitting room entrance and realises that she feels contaminated. She goes up the stairs to the loo and runs water in the tub. She disrobes with the eagerness of someone who has just been covered with something you might find in a barnyard. Scrubbing herself from head to toe gives her the same satisfaction as knowing she is caring for Ellen. Her dressing gown waits for her on a nearby hook whilst she dries herself. She wraps up her dirty clothes in the wet towel, ready for Sarah to launder. Creeping into their bedroom so she will not awaken John, she puts on a fresh dress. She watches him for a little whilst to make sure that he has no cough and his breathing is normal. Satisfied that John is just weary, as he had said, she walks back downstairs.

She realises that John had not mentioned anything about today's post. She walks to the entryway with the intention of opening the door to look into their post box. Before she gets to the door, she notices several envelopes on the hall table. Picking them up, she sees that one of them has Sarah's name on it. She walks back down the hallway to the kitchen to where Sarah is washing Johanna's hands and face.

"Sarah, John must have been so exhausted that he forgot to say anything about the post. A letter came for you."

Sarah puts the flannel on the table where Johanna reaches for it and waves it 'round. Wiping her hands on her pinny, Sarah takes the letter and looks at the return address. She opens it, reading it once, then again. Her hand covers her mouth, and she sits down at the table. Tugging at the cloth that Johanna holds, Anna lifts her laughing daughter from the high chair. She notices that Sarah has gone quiet and sees Sarah's expression is grim upon reading this letter.

"Sarah, what's wrong? Is it bad news?"

"Ma'am, I don't know what to do. My sister has taken ill with cancer, and my mum has been doing all she can to do for her and the rest of the family. Mum is asking me to come for a little time to give her some relief. Ma'am, I can't leave you and Sir. Not with Miss Cup sick. Oh, gracious, what shall I do? And I've no way to get there."

Sarah begins to cry, her tears smudging her mother's handwriting. Anna walks over to Sarah and slips her arm about her shoulders with a reassuring squeeze.

"Now, don't you worry. We'll find a way. If not tomorrow, the day after. John and I will get you there somehow."

"Oh Ma'am, I can't tell you...my little sister...she's only twenty, you see...Thank you..."

Sarah wipes her eyes on her pinny. She turns to run out of the kitchen, down the hallway, through the sitting room, and then upstairs to her bedroom. Anna wonders how they will manage to get Sarah to her family.

"Well, Johanna, don't you think Daddy has slept long enough? You do? Well, then, let's go wake him up. It's almost time for supper, and you know how Daddy loves his supper."

Johanna claps her hands as Anna walks out of the kitchen, down the hallway, and peeks in at Ellen. Thankfully, she remains asleep. With a sigh of relief, she carries Johanna upstairs towards the bedroom she shares with John, her heart goes out to hear Sarah praying as she tries to decide what to pack. Reaching their destination, Anna pushes open the bedroom door. She smiles as she watches John sleeping as he had been before, atop the quilt, still wearing his shoes and tie. The familiar manly snore elicits a chuckle. Johanna cannot contain herself, and she greets her daddy.

"Daddy! Daddy!"

John awakens to his daughter who is reaching for him. She sets the baby on their bed to crawl over to her father.

"Come here, my big girl! What a happy surprise to wake me up. Is it supper time, Anna?"

"Yes, soon. John, Sarah received a letter, and she's upset. Her younger sister is terribly ill. Cancer, they think. Her mother needs help for a whilst as she's been run ragged. The problem is Sarah has no way to get there."

John rights himself on the side of the bed, scoops Johanna up in his arms, and stands.

"Well, I recall that the village where she grew up isn't far from where I buy fabric and other things for the shop. Make me a list of anything you might need, and I'll drive Sarah directly. I'll find lodging there for a few days and get whatever we need, and then I'll come back or bring Sarah home, whatever is necessary. I might even be able to help there. I shouldn't be more than a week, I should think. Will you manage all right for that long?"

"Oh...a week...well, Clara said that Ellen should be fine in a day or so, and I believe the worst of it is over. Yes, we'll manage, the three of us."

"It's settled, then. Sarah will have only her family to worry over. I'll get her there and back."

Anna ruffles Johanna's curls and kisses John's cheek. She feels at peace with their arrangements for Sarah. Now, supper waits.

Chapter Thirteen
13 March 1926

Anna sits with Ellen in the sitting room and tries to explain, again, why John and Sarah are leaving. Ellen still does not seem to understand why they are going away. Anna's gestures only brought about a shrug. Ellen even reaches over to feel Anna's forehead. Defeat comes with a sigh as she watches Ellen stare at John carrying suitcases from upstairs and taking them outside. Anna thinks to herself that it must seem strange to Ellen that John and Sarah are leaving at this hour. John prefers to drive long distances at night to avoid other motors on the roadways, but explaining that to Ellen would be impossible. Rupert runs back and forth wagging his tail as Ellen walks to the window, moving a curtain aside. She watches John put the bags into the boot of the motor.

She turns to the lady, taps three fingers on her chest, points to the kind lady, points down and then tilts her head to the side.

Anna nods and joins Ellen at the window. She taps three fingers on her chest, points to the kitchen, and then points down to confirm that John and Sarah will return. Perhaps Ellen's fondness has grown towards John and Sarah, naturally causing worry that they are leaving and might not come back. Ellen shrugs with a frown and walks to the kitchen door. She stands, her hands folded in front of herself, and stares at Sarah. She does not notice Ellen at first with her myopic bustle about the kitchen. Sarah knows that hunger will strike them during such a long drive and has prepared a basket of food. She tucks a cloth over the contents and pats it with satisfaction then notices, with a startle, Ellen standing in the kitchen doorway. Without thinking, She approaches Ellen and embraces her. Tears spring to Sarah's eyes as she realises how much she will miss her second family in this house. Ellen remains stiff but puts her arms 'round Sarah for a moment and then drops them to her side, waiting for Sarah to move away. Sarah steps back, chiding herself for being so forwards. Reaching into her pocket to take out her Sunday best handkerchief, she feels the letter from her mother that changed the direction of her days with such drastic suddenness. She feels shame for letting anyone see her so emotional and dabs at her eyes. Looking at Ellen, but not gesturing in Ellen's language, she smiles and nods. John comes back into the house and stands in the entry hall, eager for Sarah to come along so they might reach their destination as quickly as possible. Turning to the table and lifting the basket on her arm, she meets John at the door where he is waiting.

"Is that everything, Sarah? We'd best be on our way."

"Yes, Sir, the basket is the last thing. There's plenty of food if we feel peckish on the way."

"Thank you, Sarah. I'll put this in the motor."

John takes the basket and walks back outside, Sarah closing the door behind him. He notices his breath in the cold evening air, puffs of wishing for home before they have even left. Adding the basket to the back floor of the motor, he closes the door and the boot. He returns to the house, into the warmth of the entry hall, closing out the cold behind him. Anna waits, a longing smile on her face, memorising his sweet face as she does each time he has to leave. She repeats the words that she has spoken a hundred times, reassuring John as much as herself.

"We'll miss you, John. Don't worry about us. We'll manage."

John gathers Anna into his arms, and they share a kiss that does not want to end. He steps back to look into the most beautiful eyes he has ever seen.

"I'm going to miss you too, sweetheart. Give Johanna kisses from me. I have no doubt that you'll have everything well in hand, but it's my job to worry, as I know you worry for me. We'll be fine, and I promise I'll drive safely. I'll telephone when we arrive so you know we're settled."

"Thank you. I was just going to ask that you do that."

Anna takes John's hands in her own, stands as tall as she can, kisses John's cheek, and then steps back. Ellen stands in the hallway with her hands folded in front of herself, staring at John and Anna. John takes a deep breath, hoping to gesture his farewell to Ellen in a meaningful way. He points to himself, places his hand over his heart, and then points to Ellen. He holds up his hand and waves in a similar fashion to Johanna's 'bye bye'. He exhales relief as he sees Ellen nod in what he hopes is her comprehension of his expression of love. He nods to Ellen with a smile and then looks at Sarah who has donned her coat. Standing, Sarah looks at her feet during John and Anna's affectionate farewell. Rupert stands next to his master's legs, looking up with a wagging tail. John reaches down to stroke the little fellow.

"Be good, Rupert, and take care of our girls, all right? That's my boy."

Rupert wags his tail even more as he runs to his friend and stands next to her, leaning against Ellen's legs.

Anna turns to Sarah, embraces her, and then steps back.

"I do hope all will be well with your family, no matter what happens. They will be relieved to see you. Please give them our greetings and wishes for comfort."

"Yes, Ma'am. Thank you for helping me go home...before..."

Sarah dabs at her eyes again as John speaks softly.

"Sarah, it's time."

She nods and follows John out of the door to the motor. John opens the door for her to get in and sit beside him. He closes the door, walks 'round the motor to get in and coaxes the engine to life. They pull away from the house and down the road to begin a journey that will last through the night. Anna watches from the open door until she can no longer see them. Shivering, she closes the door and coughs, trying to suppress its intensity as she covers her mouth with a handkerchief. She watches Ellen return to the sitting room to sit by the fireplace, Rupert by her side. Ellen reaches for a picture book on the table in front of the sofa. Observing Ellen's slouching shoulders, Anna also sees that she is looking at the fire instead of the open book in her lap. She does not look at the pages she turns, twists her hair 'round her finger, and seems to ignore Rupert's presence.

Sighing, she allows herself the full force of another cough, stifled before John and Sarah had left. Supper with Sarah and John had been an effort since her appetite had waned to nothing. She shakes her head, dreading the thought succumbing to the same illness Ellen had suffered. Anna makes her way down the hall to the kitchen and puts a kettle of water on the cooker to heat. She leans back, changing her mind about making tea, not caring to take the trouble. Another fit of coughing reprimands Anna for trying to stifle the tightness in her chest throughout the afternoon. Convenient excuses and steps out of rooms where John and Sarah were making ready, saved her from answering the inevitable questions. She did not want them to worry about her whilst they were away.

Anna is pleased that Ellen's health has improved rapidly. She finds it a dramatic contrast to the poor sick girl with a raging fever. Administration of the medicine worked wonders, with only a drop or two remaining in the bottle. Clara was right. Sleep was just the ticket to help her girl get well. Although Ellen's appetite has improved, she appears downcast and brooding. Ellen has not even bathed since her mood took a downturn. She does not smile and gesturing to ask if John and Sarah will come back was Ellen's first spontaneous communication since she had been sick in bed. Ellen has not lifted a finger to carve, either. It seems, to Anna, that Ellen has lost interest in everything 'round her.

For the first time, Anna is relieved that Ellen cannot hear the coughs that rattle her bones and cause a pounding in her head. She joins Ellen in the sitting room and covers her legs with a blanket. The fire feels good, but chills begin to accompany her coughing, and the warmth cannot banish them. Ellen looks away from the fire and closes the book she is holding. She gets up and returns it to its place on a shelf. Without looking at Anna, she walks out of the sitting room and down the hallway to her room, Rupert following her. With a sigh that stimulates another brutal coughing spell, Anna waits for her breathing to return to normal. Once the wheezing and shortness of breath have subsided, she puts her fingers to her temples, trying to ease her headache.

Anna gets up and walks out of the sitting room to stand for a moment at Ellen's closed door. She pushes the door open and sees Ellen clad in her nightdress. She is sitting on her bed and staring out the window into the darkness. Anna approaches in her usual manner and pats her arm. Ellen looks down at her arm and then up at her. Anna places her hands together and lays her head on them as if they were a pillow and then tilts her head to the side, asking Ellen if she is ready to go to bed. Their bedtime routine is a tender time for both of them as Ellen holds her cuddly toy whilst Anna strokes her hair. Every night, Anna mothers Ellen in ways that Ellen seems to have missed throughout her life.

Looking back to the window, Ellen shakes her head. Stung by this second rebuff, Anna backs away, still looking at Ellen. Sadness fills her heart as she watches her girl pull away into darkness. Ellen gets up, turns down her blankets, and then crawls into bed. Her cuddly toy lies on the floor, unnoticed. Rupert jumps off the bed to retrieve it and then leaps back up on the bed. Ellen turns on her side, away from Anna. Rupert turns 'round three times to plop against Ellen's back, closing his eyes as he rests his head on the fluff toy. Anna leaves the room, closing the door part way. She walks down the hallway, turning out lights as she goes. She enters the sitting room and walks to the staircase. She turns back before going upstairs, listening for any sound coming from Ellen's bedroom. Silence is all she hears, and she wonders what Ellen's silent world is like. With a heavy heart, Anna walks up the staircase. The effort causes another bout of coughing which nearly throws her down the stairs. Clutching the railing, she heaves herself up the rest of the way in spite of the spasms coming from deep in her chest.

Johanna is sound asleep, and Anna dares not go any closer with this coughing. It seems to be contagious, and she does not want her baby girl to get sick. Convincing herself that she will be fine by morning, she walks the rest of the way to the bedroom she shares with John. She leaves the door open so she can listen for Ellen. Ready to change into her nightdress, she notes that her underthings are a bit damp. After another spasm of coughing that leaves her exhausted, she hangs them on the armoire door to dry. She sneaks into the loo to freshen herself with a wet flannel. When she is finished, she looks out of the loo door, as if anyone would see her, and then hurries back into the bedroom to don her nightdress. Turning down the blankets, she looks at the empty place where John should be. She frowns, slips into bed, missing him. She curls up 'round his pillow, drinking in his scent as she relaxes in spite of the pain in her head, and begins to drift off to sleep.

The sound of footsteps interrupts her drifting, and she awakens with a start. She gets out of bed and hurries to the bedroom door, hoping it is Ellen and not an intruder. There, in the hallway, stands Ellen, holding her blanket and pillow. Rupert sits next to his friend and stares at his mistress, almost mirroring Ellen's facial expression.

She tilts her head to the side, points to herself, puts her hands together and lays her head on them as if they were a pillow, and then points to the man and lady's room. She taps three fingers on her chest and waves her hand like the man did.

Anna nods, glad to comfort Ellen as only a mother can. She seems to feel insecure with John away and wants to sleep in the bed with her. She motions for Ellen to come along, and turns down the bedclothes on John's side of the bed. Ellen crawls under the covers and turns away from Anna, clutching her blanket. Rupert hops up on the bed to lies between his mistress and his friend. Another of Anna's sighs allows her lungs to be seized by more coughing. Again, she regains her breath and lays down to settle for the night. The night is punctuated by hacking and painful coughs that wake Anna. Near morning, with the vague thought that John and Sarah must be close to their destination, she falls into a fitful sleep.

Morning pours into the window and Rupert whimpers as he sniffs his mistress. He walks across the bed to his friend and tugs at her sleeve. Ellen opens her eyes and looks 'round her and then looks at Rupert's insistent tugging. She strokes Rupert and then watches him bounce across the bed to Anna. He nudges Anna with his nose and then comes back to Ellen and tugs at her sleeve. Her forehead furrowed with a frown, she gets out of bed and walks 'round to look at what Rupert is showing her. Anna's face is flushed with abundant beads of sweat on her face and body, soaking her nightdress. Ellen's eyes grow wide as she touches Anna's forehead, feeling the heat rising from her wet skin. Ellen looks 'round her, picking up Rupert and holding him close to herself, and then puts him down on the floor. Tears forming in her eyes as she looks at Anna.

She holds up one finger to the lady, points to herself, places one fist on the palm of her other hand, and then points to the lady. She points to herself, puts her hand over her heart, and points to the lady.

Running out of the room with a glance into the nursery, Ellen runs down the stairs with Rupert keeping up with her. She runs through the sitting room and down the hall to the kitchen where the bottle that held medicine remains. She holds the brown glass bottle up to the light from the window and sees that it is empty. She leaves it in the sink and then runs through the house, back upstairs to the bedroom where she looks at Anna. Ellen looks 'round the room, then puts her hand on Anna's forehead again. Rupert hops up on the bed and lies down, staring at his mistress. She holds up one finger and begins to cry as she rushes to the loo next to the bedroom where Anna lies. She grabs a flannel, wets it, and then looks up to see her own face staring back at her from the looking glass. She stares at herself for a moment, then reaches up to touch her reflection. Shaking her head, she hurries back to Anna's side and washes her face. Ellen's tears fall as Anna's eyes open, a wan smile making an appearance. The cloth feels good against Anna's skin, and she looks at Ellen's worried and tearful visage. A rogue fit of coughing ends any thought of trying to communicate. Sitting up in bed, Anna brings her knees up, hugs them, and rests her head down as Ellen had done. She finds that it does provide some relief from the aftermath of the coughing storm. Ellen takes advantage of Anna's position and reaches over to turn and fluff the pillows. She rubs Anna's back in a circular motion. With her breath caught in a tenuous hold, Anna rests back on the pillows with a soft moan, turns on her side as the cacophony of pain in her head reminds her that she is not well.

Ellen reaches out to stroke Anna's hair and face, holds up one finger and nods. She walks to the bedroom door, turns to look at Anna, and then runs down the hallway. She stops to peek into the nursery and sees that Johanna is still asleep. Dashing down the stairs to the front hall wardrobe, she swings open the door, grabs a warm shawl, and then stuffs her bare feet into a pair of boots. She rushes down the hallway to the door leading to the garden. She opens it, allowing Rupert to come outside with her, and then closes the door. She stops, looks 'round her, and sets off in a familiar direction as rapidly as her legs will carry her. Rupert's bark follows her as fast his legs do.

Anna realises that her body hurts in places she did not know she had. Wriggling to find a comfortable position is an exercise in futility. She tries to sit back up, but the roaring in her head, dizziness, and more coughing make this endeavour impossible. Sinking back into the pillows, she turns on her other side, closing her eyes with a groan. Hearing the jangle of the telephone in the kitchen brings frustrated tears, knowing she cannot get out of bed to answer. John will worry. Panic sets in, like a flash, as she wonders how she will take care of Johanna. How will Ellen manage to hear Johanna cry? A cloud of despair falls over her, as she knows she is too weak to get out of this damnable bed to do anything.

Rounding the last corner to Clara's house, Ellen's breath comes in terrified staccato puffs. She continues running, up the walkway, up the front steps, and straight through the front door, leaving it open. She and Rupert rush through one room after another. Rupert barks as Ellen searches for Clara. Hearing footsteps, barking and feeling a draught, Clara walks into the hallway from the library and nearly collides with Ellen. Ellen's face is flushed with an expression of panic, out of breath, and Clara wonders what could be so dire, to warrant such urgency, and to bring Ellen this far without Anna by her side.

She looks at the helping lady, taps two fingers on her chest, and then points to home. She points to the helping lady, places a fist in the palm of her hand. She pantomimes holding a spoon and pouring into the spoon.

Clara looks at Ellen, dumbfounded. If only she had a better grasp of Ellen's language. John and Anna's dog, Rupert, is jumping up on her and tugging on her skirt. She does understand that Ellen wants her to come with her and it is critical enough for her to run out wearing only a nightdress and heavy shawl. Wait. Ellen is pantomiming pouring something into a spoon, and Anna must be the one who needs help. She nods her lean understanding then hurries to get her coat and a medical kit containing another bottle of medicine. She will have enough to give Anna if she has taken ill. Ellen is tugging on her sleeve whilst Rupert is barking as he runs in and out of the open door in circles. Clara shrugs on one sleeve of her coat and hurries out the door after them, barely closing the door behind her. As fast as her middle-aged legs can carry her, she runs with Ellen and Rupert all the way.

Ellen opens the door and rushes in with Rupert. Clara hastens into the house and closes the door behind her. Ellen has already dashed down the hallway and into the sitting room where she tosses her wool wrap over a chair and kicks off her boots. Rupert runs as fast as he is able, leading the way up the staircase. Heading upstairs and running down the hallway to John and Anna's room, Ellen waits with a frightened countenance. Close behind, Clara also tosses her coat over the chair and runs up the stairs, bag in hand. She hears Johanna crying in the nursery, and when she catches up to Ellen in the hallway, she points to Johanna's room. Ellen looks at Anna's room and then to Clara and where she is pointing. Ellen nods and hurries to the nursery to tend to Johanna. Rupert is waiting in the nursery, watching Johanna, and wagging his tail.

Clara catches her breath and walks into Anna's room. She shakes her head, unhappy that her concern was well founded. She puts on her facemask and takes out her thermometer and stethoscope. She tries not to wake Anna, but the cold stethoscope bell on Anna's skin awakens her, and a violent cough rips through her raw throat. She sits up and struggles to breathe until the spasm eases its grip. Clara takes advantage of this opportunity to reposition the pillows against Anna's back. Anna looks up at Clara and struggles to speak before she fully catches her breath.

"Ellen...where is...oh god...Johanna...How did you...?"

"Shhhh...it's all right, Anna. Ellen came to my house. She insisted that I come to help. Ellen is tending to Johanna right now. Where are John and Sarah?"

Anna begins to cry and cough. Anna sits up with the force of coughing through her tears, and Clara rubs Anna's back. This method worked in Ellen's case, and she hopes it will work for Anna as well. The coughing relents, and Clara pours Anna a glass of water from the carafe kept at the bedside to quench night-time thirst. The coughing and wheezing subside along with Anna's tears.

"Drink this, Anna. It will bring down your fever and prevent dehydration. I don't want to drag you to hospital to get fluids. Drink water as frequently and as much as you can."

At the threat of going to hospital, Anna obediently drinks the glass dry. The fresh water soothes her throat and calms her breathing. Her weeping settles into a dull pain in her chest, and Anna does not know whether it is from wishing John and Sarah were there or from her ribs feeling mangled with each rasping cough.

"John drove Sarah to her family...her sister..."

Anna slumps back against the pillows, exhausted and weak. Clara reaches into her bag and pulls out a bottle of medicine.

"Anna, I want you to take this every four hours without fail. I can see how much it helped Ellen, and I know it shall help you."

Clara pours a dose into the spoon she has brought and gives it to Anna.

"Oh, Clara...what to do about Johanna? She can't get sick. She can't."

"Leave her to me. I'll take her home and tend her. I'll send another nurse along with Father Willington and Granny to make pastoral rounds. They won't mind. Will you and Ellen be all right? Shall I have one of the nurses check in with you, perhaps, tomorrow?"

"No...no..."

Anna lapses into another horrid fit that sets her lungs afire.

"Anna, if you need help, I have no doubt that Ellen will come to get me. That's how I knew you needed me. You need to get some rest, dear. Don't let anything prey on your mind. Worry will do you no good."

Anna nods as tears roll down her cheeks again, mixing with the beads of sweat covering her face. Clara wraps the thermometer, stethoscope, and mask before tucking them into her bag. She walks to the loo to find a dry flannel and brings it back to Anna to wipe her face as she needs. Clara straightens the covers on the bed, removing all but the light sheet.

"Rest, Anna. That's an order. You can trust Ellen to manage."

Clara smiles at Anna and leaves the room with her medical kit, walking to the loo next to the bedroom to wash her hands with vigorous friction. She dries them on a clean towel and then walks down the hallway to the playroom. Recognising Clara, Johanna reaches up her arms with a smiling flow of happy babbling. Clara puts down her bag and scoops the baby up into her arms, smiling at Ellen. Picking up her bag, Clara motions for Ellen to follow. Together, they walk to the nursery and Clara hands Johanna over to Ellen. Clara holds up her finger and begins to put necessary items for Johanna into a satchel she finds in the armoire. Rupert trots 'round the room, jumping and wagging his tail. When she is finished, she looks at Ellen, points to Johanna, points to herself, and then points in the general direction of her house. She hopes Ellen understands that she is taking Johanna to prevent the child from further exposure to the contagion and she is glad when Ellen nods, picks up a pink fluffy toy and gives it to her. Ellen reaches down to pick up Clara's bag and the satchel for Johanna and then walks out of the nursery.

They descend the stairs into the sitting room. Ellen puts the bags on the floor and takes Johanna for a moment whilst Clara puts on her coat. Whilst Clara is bundling herself against the cold, the telephone rings in the kitchen. Clara holds up a finger and trots to the kitchen to answer.

"Hello, Thorpe residence."

"Anna? Is that you? This is John..."

"Oh, John, no. This is Clara."

"Clara? Is everything all right? I was just ringing Anna to let her know we've arrived safely."

"Well, I hate to bear bad news, but Anna's taken ill."

"Oh no! The same sickness as Ellen had? Shall I come back straight away?"

"Yes, it's the same illness, but I don't believe it's necessary for you to abort your trip, John. Of course, Anna misses you, but Ellen is the one who came to get me for help, and I'm going to take Johanna to my house so she won't fall ill, too."

"Ellen did? Are you sure you can manage Johanna? If you don't mind, that is?"

"John, have I ever minded? Now go get some rest after that drive. Everything here is going to be fine. I promise."

John gives Clara a number where he can be reached if necessary. Thanking John and reassuring him one last time, she hangs up the telephone. Clara writes it down and stuffs it in her pocket as well as leaving a copy by the telephone. She tugs her gloves onto her hands and makes her way back to the sitting room. Holding Johanna, Ellen looks at Clara with a tilt of her head. Clara assumes that Ellen wonders what caused her to trot off to the kitchen. Trying to remember the gesture for John, it finally comes to mind, and she taps three fingers on her chest, smiles and nods in the hope that Ellen will know that John is all right.

She taps three fingers on her chest and then pats her hands together.

Ellen nods and then gives Johanna back to Clara, tugging a blanket 'round the baby tighter. Clara smiles as Ellen picks up the satchel and bag, handing them to her. Nodding, Ellen walks out of the sitting room and down the hall to the door that leads to the garden. She turns 'round to see Clara coming right behind. Ellen opens the door and waves to Johanna and the baby waves back to Ellen and says 'bye bye'. Clara walks out the door with her precious bundle and their bags.

Closing the door, Ellen and Rupert walk back down the hall. Together they walk into the sitting room where Ellen stops, crouches down, and takes Rupert's face in her hands.

She looks into the dog's eyes, points to the dog, places her fist on the palm of her other hand, points to herself, places her fist on the palm of her other hand, then taps two fingers on her chest.

Rupert turns and runs up the stairs to the room where his mistress is. He hops up on the bed and plops down with his chin on Anna's ankle. Following Rupert, Ellen walks into the bedroom and pours a glass of water for Anna to drink. She taps her on the shoulder and holds out the glass of water. Anna looks up at Ellen, smiles, takes the glass, and then drinks all the water in the glass. She hands Ellen the glass, and she returns it to its place on the bedside table. Reaching for the bottle of medicine and spoon, she pours it, opens her mouth, points to her mouth, and then points to Anna. Anna closes her eyes with a faint smile and opens her mouth to retake the medicine. The first dose has already made her sleepy, so she rests back on the pillows and passively allows Ellen to tug the sheet up to cover her. Ellen looks 'round the room and finds a straight-back chair to bring next to Anna's bedside. She sits down and then holds Anna's hand and strokes her hair. Tears fall down her cheeks as she stares at Anna. When Anna is sound asleep, Ellen puts her hand on Anna's forehead.

She points to herself, draws an X in the palm of her hand, places her fist on her chest, points to the lady, moves her hands in front of herself and draws an X in her hand. She points to herself, places her hand on her heart, and points to the lady.

Ellen stares at Anna before turning to walk out of the room, and she is oblivious to Ellen's expression that she does not want her to be sick and that she loves Anna. Rupert remains on the bed, his gaze fixed on his mistress. Ellen walks downstairs to her own bedroom. She looks down at her nightdress and sniffs under her arms. Wrinkling her nose, she takes off her nightdress and folds it. She leaves it on a chair and puts on her dressing gown. Walking to the loo next to her bedroom, she draws a bath. Ellen makes quick work of bathing herself and scrubbing her hair. She dries herself, wipes out the tub, and then puts her dressing gown back on. Hurrying back to her bedroom, she puts on clean clothes, ties her hair back with a ribbon, and slips into her shoes. She picks up her cuddly toy and tucks it under her arm before leaving her room. Hurrying to the kitchen, she takes a jug from the cupboard and fills it with water. She carries it upstairs to Anna and fills the carafe with water. Sitting down next to her, Ellen tucks the cuddly toy under the sheet, strokes Anna's hair, and takes her hand whilst she watches her sleep. The passage of time, now, is irrelevant.

Slowly, Anna awakens to the gentle dabbing of wet cloth on her face. Rupert's ears perk up as his mistress opens her eyes. Anna smiles her gratitude that Ellen is tending to her when she cannot manage herself. Ellen returns Anna's smile and plucks at the wet nightdress that Anna is wearing, shaking her head. She gets up and searches through Anna's bureau until she finds a clean one. Bringing it over to Anna, Ellen holds it up and nods her head. Agreeing that a fresh nightdress would feel so much better, and knowing that Ellen would not take 'no' for an answer, Anna swings her legs over the side of the bed and tries to sit up. A wave of dizziness threatens to topple her, and she feels Ellen's steadying hands. Vertigo passes, and Anna sits up a little straighter, the stiffness from lying in bed adding to her aches. Ellen pulls the chair closer to the bed, pats the seat, and then points to Anna. Anna cannot help but chuckle as she nods her head; too ill to do anything but put herself in Ellen's hands. The two of them manage to get Anna seated on the chair where she helps her take off the wet nightdress and slip into a dry one. Feeling a bit steadier, Anna sits in the chair whilst Ellen flips the pillows over so the dry side will be up. Ellen looks at Anna and holds up one finger. She fills a glass with water and hands it to Anna to drink. The spoon full of medicine is next, and Anna raises her empty glass to ask for more, shuddering at the foul taste left by the elixir. Ellen smiles and nods, filling the glass and watches Anna drink to the last drop.

Anna nods and pats the bed to show her readiness to return. Ellen helps her move from the chair to the bed and then lifts Anna's legs into the bed. Energy sapped from her body with such simple tasks accomplished, Anna relaxes against the pillows.

She points to the lady, puts her hands together and lays her head down on them as if they were pillows.

Anna smiles and nods, ready to take Ellen's suggestion to sleep. Before she relaxes enough to sleep, she tugs on Ellen's sleeve. Ellen looks down at her arm and then to Anna. Anna points to herself, places her hand over her heart, and then points to Ellen to say, 'I love you'. Ellen smiles, nods, and then points to herself and then to her own head.

Falling asleep, the thought occurs to Anna that her coughing has ceased its constant intrusion. Ellen leans down to stroke Anna's hair and kisses her forehead. She turns to pick up the nightdress, walks to the door, turns 'round, and then nods. She makes her way downstairs to her bedroom where she places Anna's nightdress with her own.

A tug at her skirt surprises Ellen. Rupert is pulling her out of her room, runs down the hallway to the front door and barks. Ellen walks to a nearby window to peek out and sees a smiling old lady standing there with a basket. Ellen looks 'round her, looks at Rupert, and then takes a deep breath. Ellen's hand shakes as she opens the door wide enough to see her. Granny knew, thanks to Clara, that the coughing illness had come to the Thorpe household. She wants to help, and Granny is one to believe that good food is always needed. She smiles at Ellen who looks a bit like a frightened rabbit. Not wanting to push Ellen into a panic, Granny places the basket of food on the stoop, points to Ellen with a nod, and picks her way back down the steps. Turning to walk down the pavement, she stops, turns, and shares a friendly wave of her hand. Ellen stares as Granny walks away and then opens the door wide enough to retrieve the basket and close the door in one motion. Rupert sits with his tail wagging, looking up at his friend.

Carrying the basket to the kitchen, she lifts it onto the table, lifts the covering, and sees bread, cheese, smoked meat, potatoes, and a tin of biscuits. She looks 'round the kitchen and shrugs. She takes the basket to the counter and puts everything from the basket into the cool box. Folding the cloth, she lays it in the basket and rests the basket in a corner, out of the way. Looking at Rupert, she raises her eyebrows and holds up a finger. Rupert looks at his friend, tilts his head, and then wags his tail with a thumpity thump on the floor. Ellen retraces her steps to the cool box and opens it, rummaging 'round inside. She takes out the meat, cheese, bread, and finds a glass of milk. She takes out a plate and makes herself a little meal. Rupert even enjoys a treat or two. Finished with her own meal, she takes her dishes to the sink and cleans them. She returns to the cool box and moves things 'round until she finds what she wants. She takes out a bowl containing leftover stew and puts it on the counter next to the cooker. Opening cupboards, she finds a saucepan and a spoon in a drawer. She places a few spoons full of the stew in the pan and adds a little water. She looks at the cooker, touching the valves that she has seen Anna and Sarah use. She turns one on the far-right side and jumps a little when a blue flame appears in a perfect circle. She twists the valve to and fro, making the fire small and then puts the pan on the burner. Intently watching the pot, she stirs the thinned stew until it bubbles. The aroma is tantalising as she turns off the cooker and finds a bowl in the cupboard. The contents of the cold box are her next idea, and there, she finds a slice of bread and sliver of cheese to add to a plate. She fills the glass with milk and pours the stew into a bowl. Finding a clean spoon and the tray that Anna uses, she arranges things.

Rupert is looking up at Ellen with large eyes, shivering with his tail wagging. Ellen taps two fingers on her chest and points towards the sitting room. Rupert runs off towards the sitting room and up the stairs. Carrying the tray so nothing will spill, she makes her way to the staircase. She brings it upstairs, to John and Anna's bedroom without incident. Rupert jumps up on the bed with Anna and nuzzles her neck with his wet nose. She awakens and smiles to see Rupert staring right into her eyes. Hearing another sound, she turns to see Ellen setting a tray of food on the seat of the chair beside the bed. Anna groans to herself and thinks that the last thing she wants right now is food. Ellen steps closer to Anna and motions for Anna to sit up a little straighter. Resigning herself to the idea that she must do as she is told, Anna feels the pillows behind her fluffed and repositioned. Feeling Ellen's hand on her shoulder, Anna relaxes back to a comfortable sitting position. She finds her lap commandeered by a tray full of divine things. She picks up the spoon, and Ellen gently takes it out of Anna's hand.

She raises a finger, points to herself, points to the spoon, and then points to the lady.

Anna nods with a chuckle and accepts the fact that Ellen is determined to feed her. Spoon by spoon, Ellen encourages Anna to eat the thinned stew and eat the bread dipped in the stew. The milk is refreshing, and Ellen saves the cheese for last, breaking off pieces and popping them into Anna's mouth, one at a time. Anna feels full and satisfied with the clever meal that Ellen made. She relaxes back with her eyes closed, every ounce of strength gone. Who would know that eating could be such a taxing activity? Ellen takes the tray, setting it aside, and then takes the medicine bottle, filling the spoon with its contents. She pats Anna's shoulder, and the first thing Anna sees is the spoon hovering in front of her. It is all she can do to stifle a cough-inducing laugh as she opens her mouth for 'pudding'. Soon, she will be asleep, glad for Ellen's competent care, grateful for Clara's generosity, and hopeful for a recovery that might be as rapid as Ellen's had been.

Chapter Fourteen
20 March 1926

For Anna, a cup of tea begins the day that will bring John home. The house seems too quiet over the past week without John's reassuring presence, and Sarah's busy cheerfulness. Even the sleepy sunshine finding its way indoors appears to be happy for this day. Finally awake, Ellen rubs her eyes as she walks downstairs from John and Anna's bedroom to the kitchen. It was a long night for both of them with the ravenous nightmares eating away at Ellen's peace with a ferocious appetite. The intensity makes the coughing illness seem like a mere tickle in the throat. Rupert was awake and hiding under the bed for much of the night. He follows Ellen to the kitchen, ever her constant companion. Anna is glad that Ellen wanted to sleep with her upstairs whilst John has been away. Anna is able to do double-duty, mothering Ellen through her nightmares and tending to Johanna if she wakes during the night.

Johanna sits in her high chair babbling her happy chatter, reaching down towards Rupert. She bangs her pink fluffy toy on the tray, eager for her breakfast.

"One moment, sweetheart. Your porridge is almost ready."

She sets the bowl on the table to cool with a cup of juice, bib, and a wet cloth, just out of Johanna's reach. Anna smiles at Ellen, who is still rubbing the sleep from her eyes. She turns to take another cup and saucer out of the cupboard. She holds it up to Ellen who stares at it for a moment and then nods her head. Anna pours Ellen tea as well, stirring the milk and sugar to blend the mix before bringing them to the table. Ellen takes her usual seat and looks at Johanna.

She waves to the lady, points to herself, points to the food, points to the baby, and then tilts her head to the side.

Noticing Ellen's wave and question, she nods her assent to Ellen's request to feed Johanna. Anna walks across the kitchen to fill Rupert's bowl with fresh food and water. He trots over to his dishes, wagging his tail, and tucks into his food as though he had not eaten in a month. Anna turns to watch Ellen tickle Johanna's neck and touch her nose to Johanna's before putting on the bib to cover Johanna's nightdress. Ellen pats her arm and Johanna looks down at her arm, up at Ellen, and then releases a storm of babbling that Anna wishes Ellen could hear. Ellen pulls the dish and cup of juice towards herself and smiles at Johanna.

She looks at the baby, points to herself, holds up the spoon, and then points to the baby, tilting her head.

Anna chuckles at Johanna's enthusiastic reply to Ellen's question to her, asking if Johanna would like Ellen to feed her. Johanna pats herself on the chest and speaks.

"Cuppa Cuppa Cuppa!"

With a smile, Ellen brings the spoon to Johanna's mouth, opened like the beak of a baby bird. Johanna tries to talk with her mouth full, spewing porridge that Ellen wipes away, booping Johanna's nose with the wet cloth. Between spoons full of porridge, Ellen sips her tea. Rupert has returned to the table between Johanna and Ellen, looking up at the spoon as it moves. Ellen looks down at him, holds up one finger, and then shakes her head. Rupert lowers his head and walks away to a corner of the kitchen to watch them. Raising an eyebrow, Anna thinks back to the way Ellen had of 'talking' to the horses after their sleigh ride. Ellen seems to have the same ability to communicate with Rupert.

Anna's thoughts turn to Ellen's own baby, cruelly taken from her. The way Ellen interacts with and treats Johanna, she is convinced that Ellen would have been a tender mother in spite of her inability to hear or speak. Ellen proved her resourcefulness whilst John was away. She would have found a way to care for her baby. Shaking her sadness for Ellen away, for now, she takes a sip of her tea, replaces it on its saucer and takes two eggs from the basket on the counter. She takes out her frying pan, places it on a burner and slices a pat of butter from the stick that sits on a plate near the cooker. Tapping the knife against the side of the pan, she waits for the familiar sizzle and cracks eggs into the pan, making herself and Ellen an egg each. A few sliced potatoes left over from last evening's supper fry to complete their simple breakfast. She takes two plates from the cupboard, cutlery from the drawer, and scoops the food onto the plates. She brings them to the table and then walks over to get glasses, filling them with milk from the cold box.

Looking at the plate of food before her, Ellen nods with a smile. She alternates bites of food for herself and spoons full of porridge for Johanna. Johanna reaches for Ellen's plate but to no avail. Ellen mashes a potato and holds it up to cool. Watching this, Anna smiles as Johanna's face lights up when Ellen puts it in her mouth.

"Mmmmmmmmmm Cuppa Cuppa foo!"

"Yes, sweetheart! Ellen gave you a potato! You're a big girl, now!"

Johanna claps her hands and laughs, causing Ellen to smile. The three of them finish breakfast and Anna gets up to clear the table, taking the evidence of their morning meal to the sink. Ellen wipes Johanna's face, removes the soiled bib, and then lifts Johanna out of her high chair. Ellen approaches Anna, patting her on the arm. Anna looks at Ellen, tilting her head to the side to ask Ellen to communicate whatever is on her mind.

She points to the baby, places her two fingers against the side of her nose and then points up. She points to the baby and wrinkles her nose.

Anna laughs and nods. Johanna does need her nappy changed and a new dress to wear. The 'name' Ellen has just given Johanna, placing two fingers against the nose, is fitting. Whilst Ellen walks out of the kitchen to change and dress Johanna, Anna fills the sink to wash the dishes. She makes short work of it, puts the last of the dishes away, and then folds the tea towel on the counter. Hearing Rupert's tail thumping on the floor, Anna grins at him as he trots over to her. He follows his mistress out of the kitchen, to the sitting room where she makes herself comfortable on the sofa. Rupert hops up to lean against his mistress. Soon, they hear Ellen's footsteps on the staircase and Johanna's chatter. Ellen brings Johanna to her mother and then spreads a blanket on the floor with some toys.

She points to herself, tugs at her sleeping dress, and draws a frown on her face. She points to herself and points towards her sleeping place.

Anna nods, understanding that Ellen wants to get dressed. As Ellen leaves the sitting room to go to her bedroom, she leans down to retrieve one of Johanna's toys. Anna plays with Johanna whilst they wait for Ellen to come back. Rupert hops down from the sofa, grabs one of Johanna's toys in his mouth, and then scoots under the sofa, unnoticed.

"You were such a good girl for Ellen! Yes, you were. I can't wait to tell Daddy that you're a big girl, now, eating big girl food."

Johanna reaches up to pat her mamma's face, and Anna catches her hands to blow noisy kisses into them. Johanna squeals with delight as Anna continues the noisy kisses on Johanna's neck and chubby cheeks. In a short time, Ellen reappears to stand in the doorway to the sitting room with her hands folded in front of herself and stares at Anna and Johanna. With her head down, she walks to the sofa and sits down. Anna notices that Ellen's mood seems to have changed in such a short time. She gets up, sets Johanna on the blanket, gives her a plaything, and then returns to the sofa to face Ellen. She pats Ellen's arm to gain her attention and waits for Ellen to look down at her arm and then up at her. She tilts her head, draws a frown on her own face, and then points to Ellen and shrugs, asking why Ellen seems sad. Ellen shakes her head with a shrug of her shoulders and stares down at her hands. Patiently, Anna waits for Ellen to be ready to gesture a response. Ellen's shoulders move as if she exhales a sigh, and turns to Anna.

She points to Anna, taps two fingers on her chest. She taps three fingers on her chest. She points to Johanna and places her forefinger against her nose. She points to herself and shrugs.

Pondering what Ellen means, the thought finally occurs her that Ellen is wondering what her own name is in gestures. Johanna has earned her name, two fingers against the nose, by the odour that issues forth from her nappy. Anna's name is two fingers tapped on the chest, and John's is three fingers tapped on the chest. Thinking of a gesture that might fit Ellen, Anna hits upon an answer. Since Ellen is pretty, Anna puts two fingers against her cheek and then points to Ellen. This is a gesture they have never used before so it will be as unique as Ellen is. She looks at Anna and nods, a smile growing on her face. Johanna crawls over to them, pulling herself up to stand, her little legs wobbly with their task. Rupert scoots out from under the sofa, puts his front paws on the sofa cushion, and then licks his little friend's face. Giggling, Johanna pats her mother's lap and lays her head down. Anna smiles, scratches Rupert's ears, and then picks Johanna up to cuddle her. She rocks Johanna, caressing her hair, lulling the little one to sleep.

Johanna's eyes close, her mouth slack, her body limp with sleep. Anna smiles at Ellen who is watching with rapt attention and points to herself, places her forefinger on the side of her nose, lays her head on one hand as if on a pillow, and then points upstairs. Ellen nods; folding her hands in front of herself, she turns to watch the flames in the fireplace. Anna takes Johanna up to the nursery to lay her down for her morning nap. When she returns, she sees Ellen sitting with Rupert leaning against her, his chin on her shoulder. As she crosses to the sofa, she hears a sound at the door. She waves to Ellen and motions for her to come. She taps three fingers on her chest and runs to the door.

A mild breeze ushers John into the house as he sets his suitcase on the floor and shuts the front door. Removing his hat and shrugging off his parka, Rupert's jumping and barking greet him. Ellen stands in the doorway of the sitting room with her hands folded in front of her as a jubilant Anna bounces past her and into John's arms. He laughs and holds Anna close to him. He kisses her in that silent communication between two united hearts that tells her how much he missed her. John leans back and looks into her eyes with a smile of his own.

"Well, then, I take it you're happy to see me?"

"Of course, I'm happy to see you. I missed you terribly. Come along and get comfortable."

John picks up his suitcase, scratches Rupert's ears, and then allows Anna to lead him into the sitting room, followed by Ellen and Rupert. He places his bag on the table in front of the sofa, eliciting a raised eyebrow from Anna. What an odd place to put a suitcase.

"I'd like to greet Ellen and tell her that I'm happy to see her. How do I do that?"

Anna looks back to see Ellen standing by a chair in the sitting room. She looks back at John and speaks softly, although it is unnecessary.

"First, John, point to yourself, draw a smile on your face, point to your eyes, and finally, point to Ellen."

"I'll give that a go, then."

Anna watches John smile at Ellen and repeats the hand gestures that Anna explained. Ellen nods in return.

She points to herself, draws a smile on her face, points to her own eyes, points to the man. She taps two fingers on her chest, holds out her hand palm-up, pulls her hand and arm close to herself as she closes her fist, points to herself, places two fingers against her cheek.

"Uh, Anna, help me, here...I have no idea what she said beyond that she's happy to see me, as well."

"Well, by the last gesture, she's telling you that I figured out a 'name' for her. Just as she has with Johanna and us, she wanted a name. Placing two fingers against your cheek is her name because she's pretty."

"Brilliant, Anna. I must say. Let me try."

Feeling confident in his efforts, he points to himself, places his hand over his heart, points to Ellen, and then puts two fingers against his cheek. Anna pats John's arm in approval and turns to see Ellen's response to John using her name to say that he loves her.

She nods, stares at the man and lady, points to herself, moves her hands down the front of herself, and then draws a smile on her face.

Anna and John feel a mutual warmth as Ellen expresses that she feels happy, although her face does not mirror those feelings. 'Tis no small thing for them to learn and adjust to a new language and improvise gestures as needed. Anna is grateful that Ellen is patient with them as they learn together.

"John, our daughter has a new name, as well. In caring for Johanna, Ellen decided to make this gesture special for her."

She places two fingers on the side of her nose and laughs. She points to Ellen, moving her fingers next to her mouth, and then tells Ellen, in gestures, that she is telling John how Johanna earned her name. Ellen nods, smiles, and repeats the gesture of two fingers against her nose. John cannot help but burst into laughter.

"I know good and well what Johanna's name means. She'll never live it down, either, I'll wager."

"No, she won't. She's even starting to mimic simple gestures. Our daughter will grow up knowing Ellen's language."

"That is something. Ellen has no idea how much she is teaching us. Now, if you ladies will have a seat, I have brought the most wondrous things to dazzle Ellen's eyes."

Anna walks over to Ellen and takes her hand, leading her to the sofa to sit beside her. He chuckles at Rupert's hop up to the cushion to relax next to Ellen. John makes an ostentatious flourish and opens his suitcase. He wiggles his eyebrows at Anna and Ellen, then brings forth a bright red and gold box. The rectangular box is the size of a biscuit tin. Adorning the box are all colours of sparkling glass beads that catch the light as if they were gems. The lid shows a miniature oval painting depicting a young girl dressed in a Victorian gown. She reclines under a tree, a yellow bird perched on her finger. The gift garners the response John was hoping to elicit. Both Anna's and Ellen's eyes grow wide. John smiles at them both.

"If you will allow me."

John turns a golden key hidden on the back and then bows slightly as he opens the box. A pink ballerina with golden hair dances in circles upon a larger reflective circle. The interior boasts a lining of red velvet with silk-covered partitions for jewellery. He hands the music box to Ellen, and she gingerly takes it in her hands. She strokes the smooth finish and runs her fingers over the glass beads that catch the light, watching the tiny figure move as if by magic. Rupert's tail wags as he strains to look at this shiny thing. Although Ellen cannot hear the music, her wide eyes can see the beauty and movement. Anna looks at John, smiles, and nods her approval. They watch until the ballerina stops. Ellen tilts her head and looks at John. Chuckling, he turns the box to the side where the key lays folded against the box. He shows Ellen how to wind the music box to make the ballerina move. When the music box finishes for the second time, Ellen smiles and hands it back to John.

Anna pats Ellen on the arm and waits for Ellen to look down at her arm and then up at her. She points to John, points to the music box, places her fist against her chest and then extends her arm as she opens her hand. This is how Anna tells Ellen that this music box is a gift from John. Ellen's eyes begin to fill with tears, and she wipes them away with her hand as she smiles. She rests it on her lap, stroking the raised beads and velvet interior. Reaching into his suitcase, again, John pulls out a small package wrapped in paper and ribbon. Anna pats Ellen's knee to gain her attention and John holds the parcel up to his nose to sniff it. He hands it to Ellen; she looks at him for a moment and then smells it as well. Her eyes grow wide, and a smile glows upon her face. Rupert leans in to sniff at the treat in Ellen's hand. She holds the wrapped chocolate up where Rupert cannot reach and holds up one finger, then shakes her head.

She looks at the man and the lady, points to the thing with the tiny lady, and then the treat, points to herself, and tilts her head.

Anna and John both nod their heads, confirming that these gifts are for Ellen to keep and enjoy. The chocolate is not going to last long since Ellen loves it so much and Rupert will not have a single bite. They look at each other with gladness that Ellen has a happy smile on her face.

She looks at the man and the lady, points to the thing with the tiny lady, and draws a circle 'round her own face. She points to the treat and nods, patting her hands together. She points to herself and then to her room, tilting her head.

Nodding to Ellen with a chuckle, she translates for John, telling him that Ellen thinks the music box is pretty. Of course, Ellen may take her treats and gift back to her room. She should enjoy them as she pleases! John grins at Anna as they watch Ellen almost skip through the room and down the hall to her room, Rupert chasing after her. John smiles as he sighs and closes the latches on his suitcase. Anna laughs as she takes John's hand, leads him to sit in his favourite chair and prop his feet on the footstool.

"Much better. After this past week and the exhausting drive, you're entitled to sit in comfort."

"Anna, you make me feel like the Raj himself. I'm comfortable, and you shouldn't be surprised if I nod off and begin drooling on myself, as you say I do."

She chuckles and points at John, places her hands together and leans her head on them as if on a pillow, and then draws a smile on her face. John reaches out for Anna's hand and pulls her down for a kiss, his other hand cupping her cheek. He stops and looks into her eyes.

"My love, did you just tell me to sleep happy?"

"Yes, John, I did."

"Then, I will. I'm happy to be home, glad to be with my family and eager to catch up on everything that's happened whilst I was away."

Anna stands and strokes John's hair before pointing to herself and then pointing to Ellen's room. John nods, chuckling to himself that he and Anna are practising Ellen's language even when Ellen is not there. John points to Anna, points to his own eyes, places two fingers against his cheek, and then points towards Ellen's room. Anna smiles as he has told her to go to see Ellen.

"Excellent, John. I'm proud of us. I think we've come a great distance in our mutual understanding between Ellen and us. Now, close your eyes. Not a peep from you until you wish to peep. But, first, I'll check on Johanna."

John laughs and closes one eye as he watches Anna walk to the staircase and then up. He closes his open eye and falls asleep. Soon, his manly snoring fills the sitting room as his head rests against the wingback chair in which he sits. Anna walks into Johanna's nursery to find her little darling awake and playing. Anna rubs Johanna's tummy, and a happy giggle delights Anna's ears. Johanna's new 'name' comes to mind with the attendant odour, so she does quick work of changing Johanna's nappy. With that task finished, Anna scoops the little one up in her arms and kisses her cheek.

"We'll have to be quiet, sweetheart. Daddy is sleeping. Shhhhhhh."

Johanna laughs and gives her mamma a sloppy kiss. Anna finds her handkerchief and wipes her mouth with a chuckle.

"Mamma isn't cleaning your kiss away, sweet one. Mamma is rubbing it in and tucking it in her pocket!"

Patting her mother's face, Anna carries her out of the nursery. As they go downstairs, she tries to make as little noise as possible. Anna whispers in Johanna's ear to be hushed, and the baby is quiet, although she is reaching out and smiling at her daddy. Thinking that Johanna would find Ellen's new music box fascinating, she carries her to Ellen's room. Anna opens Ellen's door and sees her sitting on the bed. Rupert lies on the bed, his chin on his paws, staring at his friend's back. Ellen is holding her music box, open, watching the ballerina spinning 'round in circles. Tears flow down her face. Curious, Anna approaches and sits next to her on the bed with the baby on her lap. Johanna looks at Ellen and tilts her head, reaching out to touch her but not able to reach. Anna begins to rub Ellen's back, and she closes the lid to her music box. She reaches over to put it on her bedside table and looks at Anna who is tilting her head, waiting for Ellen to tell her why she is crying. Ellen digs into her pocket to find her handkerchief and then wipes her eyes and face, blowing her nose.

She looks at the lady, points to the thing with the tiny lady, and then pats her hands together. She points to herself and draws an X on the palm of her hand.

Anna points to the music box, pats her hands together, and then draws a circle 'round her face to agree that it is good and pretty. She points to Ellen and pats her hands together to disagree with Ellen's assertion that she is bad, but instead, is a good person. Ellen shakes her head and looks down at her hands, fiddling with the handkerchief she holds.

She looks at the lady, makes an X in the palm of her hand, walks two fingers across the palm of her hand, points to her head, points to herself, and then draws an X in the palm of her hand.

Thinking about the gestures in her mind, Anna can only assume that someone bad thinks Ellen is bad. She shakes her head, points to Ellen, and then pats her hands together to reaffirm that Ellen really is a good person.

She looks at the lady and shakes her head. She points to herself and points to her head and then points to herself and then draws an X in her hand.

Sighing, Anna fears that she is not making progress with Ellen in this conversation. She responds one more time in gestures that Ellen is good, not bad and she and John do not think she is bad. Ellen just shrugs and looks back down at her hands. Anna pats Ellen's arm and waits for her to look down at her arm and then back up at her. Anna points to herself, taps three fingers on her chest, puts her forefinger against her nose, places her hand over her heart, and then points to Ellen. Anna wants to make sure that Ellen understands that all of them love her. Ellen shrugs her shoulders. Wondering if a change of subject might bring Ellen out of this cycle of thinking, she pantomimes eating with a tilt of her head to ask Ellen if she is hungry. Ellen nods and stands. Relieved, Anna stands with her, Johanna taking this opportunity to reach out to Ellen. Anna walks towards the door and steps aside to allow Rupert to pass through the entrance to the kitchen as if he knows there will be food.

They walk to the kitchen where Rupert awaits them, his tail wagging. He looks at his friend, and she shakes her head at him. He obediently trots over to 'his corner' and lays down, his tail wagging. Anna helps Johanna wriggle into her high chair so that she may watch them prepare an early lunch since John must be famished. Anna walks over to the peg holding the pinnies and puts one on, tying it in the back. She takes out the remnants of bread, smoked meat, and cheese from Granny, and a knife; she turns her head and looks at Ellen who is staring at her. Anna smiles at her, makes a slicing motion with the knife, points to her, and then to the cold food. Ellen nods, walks over to the counter, and opens a cupboard to take out a plate for the slices of bread and cheese. Anna hands the knife to Ellen who begins slicing and arranging the food to her liking.

Anna fills a pot with water and sets it on the cooker, waiting for a familiar bubble and steam. She returns to the cold box to retrieve her soup stock and then to the basket with vegetables to make a light but nourishing soup that will serve as lunch. When Anna is finished adding the ingredients to the boiling water, she turns down the heat to gently heat through. The familiar aromas exude from the pot, pervading the kitchen and beyond with the scent of comfort and satisfaction. She looks over to Ellen and is pleased to see that Ellen has covered the plate of bread and cheese with a slightly damp cloth to prevent them from drying out. Anna takes a few spices from their place near the cooker and holds them out to Ellen. She points to the spices, points to the soup pot, and holds her fingers together to show a tiny amount. She points to Ellen and tilts her head, asking if Ellen would like to add the spices. Ellen nods and walks closer to the cooker, opening the first bottle of spice and sniffing it. She shakes a tiny bit in the lid of the jar and sprinkles it into the soup. She does the same with the other spices Anna had chosen. Impressed, Anna pats Ellen's arm, waits for Ellen to look down at her arm, and then up at her. She nods her head, patting her hands together to compliment Ellen. She smiles and points to the pot of soup that is already smelling delicious and then waves her hand as if bringing the aroma closer to her nose and pats her hands together to tell Ellen that the soup smells good. Ellen smiles and lowers her head.

The increasing volume of Johanna calling to Rupert draws Anna's attention.

"Goggie! Goggie!"

Rupert looks at his friend and then at Johanna. Ellen looks at Johanna reaching for the dog and nods her head at Rupert. With a wag of his tail and a little hop, he trots over to his small friend. Standing with his paws up on the high chair so she can pat his head, his tail wags faster. Amazed at how obedient Rupert is with Ellen, she begins to think that he is becoming more Ellen's dog than theirs. Ellen is a part of their family, now, and the thought makes her smile. Stretching with a yawn, John walks into the kitchen, awakened and drawn by the tantalising smell of cooking food, one of his favourite scents.

"Something delicious woke me up. What are you cooking?"

He walks over to the cooker and lifts the lid of the pot, taking the wooden spoon on the counter and dipping it in the soup for a taste.

"Mmmm...hot, but superb. When do we eat?"

"Right now, if you set the table."

Anna playfully smacks his hand holding the spoon and laughs at his appetite. She is sure he has had little to eat in his haste to return home. Pretending to frown and look put-upon, he gives in to Anna, walks over to the cupboard to take out the place settings they will need. Once the table is set, he walks 'round the table to scoop Johanna out of her high chair and hold her close with kisses.

"Daddy missed you, little one. Are you happy to see me? I thought of you every moment whilst I was away."

Delighted babbling is his answer as Johanna pats his face and plants a sloppy kiss on his mouth before he can duck away. John chuckles and returns her to her seat, wiping his face. He walks back to the cupboard, takes out a tin of biscuits, and walks back to the table with them. Taking his seat, John sets the biscuits right in the middle of the table to make it seem that he brought them out for them all to eat. His smile greets the tureen of soup that Anna brings to the table. The plate with bread and cheese that Ellen carries looks like the perfect pairing with his hungry palate. Anna spoons soup in a bowl to cool, next to it, a slice of the bread, just out of Johanna's reach. She places a bib on Johanna and nods approvingly that Ellen sits next to Johanna, ready to feed the little girl. Reaching for each bowl, Anna fills them with the soup and passes one to John, places one by Ellen, and finally, one for herself. John picks up the plate of bread and cheese, taking one of each, then passes it to Ellen who does the same, and then to Anna. Rupert continues to sit next to Johanna, his nose in the air, twitching.

"This is just what I was hoping for, Anna. It smells delicious."

"Thank you, John. You can also thank Ellen since had as much part in making it as I did."

Feeling Ellen's gaze upon them as they talk, Anna turns to Ellen. She taps three fingers on her chest, draws a smile on her face, points to the food, and then pats her hands together. Ellen nods, looks at John, and turns to spoon the warm soup to Johanna, dipping a bit of bread in the soup for her to chew on, as well. John raises an eyebrow at the natural way Ellen tends to Johanna whilst eating her own meal.

"With Sarah away, Ellen has become rather proficient in caring for Johanna. She should be proud of herself."

"Yes, she has, and I wonder if she misses her own baby so much, that tending to Johanna makes her feel better. I hope so, at any rate."

Small conversation peppers their lunch as Anna translates for Ellen, including her in the dialogue. John and Anna notice that Ellen's movements have become slower, and a stoic appearance affects her expression as she finishes feeding Johanna. Standing to wipe away Johanna's mess and removing the bib, Ellen leans down to kiss Johanna's head and caresses her cheek. She lifts Johanna out of her high chair and holds her close as she nods at John and Anna. She lowers her head to nuzzle Johanna's hair. Ellen carries her out of the kitchen to her room, followed by Rupert at a trot to keep up with her.

Looking at each other, their faces register surprise and Anna breaks the momentary silence.

"Well, that's the first time Ellen has taken Johanna into her room. She might enjoy playing with Ellen in there for a change."

"Yes, I'm sure she will since they get on so well together."

She leans over to kiss John's cheek, gets up from her chair, and begins to clear the table. John gets up to help Anna, first, sneaking a biscuit out of the tin, biting it in half so it will fit in his mouth. Eager to hear how things are with Sarah's family, she asks John to speak of his time away as they wash dishes together and put things away. He relates the family's difficulty in caring for Sarah's sister whilst trying to manage the grandchildren as well. Of course, her father is working as hard as he can to support such a large family. Sarah, as the eldest, feels a heavy responsibility to her kin in shouldering some of their burdens. The younger sister's needs come first, of course. Each member of the family does what they can to care for her in their own way. The unspoken assumption in that household was that the sister did not have much time left in this life.

"I assured Sarah that she may stay as long as she's needed. She will not have to fear that she will be replaced in her absence. I even gave her a generous sum of money for her to use as she pleases whilst she's with her family. The less Sarah has to worry about here, the better."

"We miss Sarah, but it's only right that she be with her family, now. I'm glad you helped her join them and reassured her. You're right, John, the fewer worries she has, the better able she will be able to give her fullest attention to her current priorities."

"I'm so glad you fully recovered from being so sick whilst I was gone. Clara told me how you were coming along and how Ellen jumped in to manage. We should be grateful that Clara took Johanna with her. Hearing your voice when you were well enough to come down to answer the telephone was a great relief. I understand that coughing illness was exceptionally dire for the elderly and the very young. She said she'd seen nothing like it since the Spanish flu in 1918. I'm sure you also remember, as I do, how it spread like wildfire."

"Yes, I do. I'm glad to be well again. I am grateful that Clara was here to help, and Ellen kept giving me the medicine even after I no longer needed it. I felt her love in that, but I finally had to pour the rest of the medicine in another bottle and hide it! I missed you so, but I knew you were where you needed to be. I'm so happy you're here, now, and we'll manage along without Sarah until she returns."

"Anna, I love you. I will always worry. You worry about me. It's what we do because we love one another."

John smiles and takes Anna in his arms, kisses her, and then strokes her cheek. Anna smiles up at him.

"I missed you, too, sweetheart."

"I'd be hurt if you didn't, my sweet Anna."

With a smile and a touch of her fingertips to his cheek, she then reaches behind her to untie her pinny. John smiles at her and turns her 'round to face away from him.

"Let me get that for you. It seems to have worked itself into a knot."

"Thank you, John. Now that my hero has freed me, I'm going to see what our girls are up to."

Anna reaches for her pinny, but John holds it up and out of reach.

"I will put this away, and you will go and mother our girls. I've a few more things in the motor that I need to bring in, so I'll do that and unpack my suitcase."

Shaking her head with a grin, she walks out of the kitchen, to Ellen's room. Pausing at the door, the only sound she hears is Johanna's soft voice. Anna pushes open the door to see Ellen sitting on the bed, holding Johanna, rocking her, looking into her eyes. Tears flow down Ellen's face as she takes one of Johanna's hands and kisses it. She strokes Johanna's hair whilst the baby reaches up to grab a handful of Ellen's hair. Anna watches them and wonders what could have caused Ellen to become tearful. Could Ellen be even more heartsick over her own baby than they imagined? Crouching down so that Ellen will notice her, Anna looks up at her, a troubled expression on her face, and a tilt of her head that asks Ellen what is wrong. Ellen looks at Anna and then back down at Johanna. She kisses the baby's forehead and disengages her hair from Johanna's fist. Ellen sits Johanna upright in her lap and bounces her a few times to make Johanna's face light up with a smile. She hands Johanna to her mother who helps the baby stand up, her little hands full of blanket to steady herself. Anna keeps Johanna close with one hand to steady her, then looks up at Ellen whose breathing has become laboured and faster. She tilts her head to the side, points to Ellen, and then draws a tear down her cheek to ask her why she is sad.

She looks at the lady and points to herself, draws a tear down her cheek, draws a frown on her own face, points to herself, cradles her arms as if holding a baby, and then shrugs her shoulders.

Sympathy filling her, she nods, comprehending with an aching heart that Ellen is sad and unhappy that she does not know what happened to her own baby. Fear that the child suffers in some way must be a stabbing part of her agony. Not knowing the fate of her baby must be unbearable pain. When was the infant born? Where is it now? How does the child fare, wherever he or she might be? Is the child still living? Anna fears that all these thoughts must pass through Ellen's mind and even reside in the darkness of her nightmares. Ellen still has little grasp of time passing, and although they have worked out a simple gesture for it, the concept remains nebulous. Putting a hand on Ellen's knee, Anna looks up at her, tilts her head to the side, points to herself, places a fist against her chest, puts one fist on the palm of her other hand, and then points to Ellen. In this way, she asks Ellen how she can help. Ellen wipes the tears away with the handkerchief from her pocket and shrugs as she shakes her head.

With little to no information that would lead them to an answer, she decides to ask Clara for help. The thread of hope is thin, but it is the only possible solution. She pats Ellen's knee, again, points to herself, points to her head, and then holds up one finger. Anna has an idea. She points towards the kitchen and nods. Standing, she picks up Johanna, settling the baby on her hip. Rupert moves closer to Ellen and rests his head on her lap. Anna turns and walks out of Ellen's bedroom to the kitchen to ring Clara. Taking a deep breath, she says a silent prayer before lifting the receiver and ringing Clara. Relief mixed with trepidation flows from her exhaled breath when she hears her friend's voice.

"Dewhurst residence, this is Clara."

"Clara, this is Anna. I've a favour to ask of you, and it's going to be daunting at best, perhaps impossible, I fear."

"Do tell? Is something wrong?"

"Not wrong, exactly, but something is plaguing Ellen. She misses her baby terribly, more each day, it seems. She told me that she wonders whatever happened to him or her. She never even held the infant in her arms. Clara, if this were either of us, the torture of not knowing would be unbearable."

"I agree, Anna. How can I help, though?"

"You've access to so many records. I only have a name and a date from a picture Ellen showed me. Oddly, the name is Ellen and the date 1901. Ellen doesn't know who the woman is, but there is a faint resemblance between the two unless it's my imagination. It's all I've got, but if we find something, anything, a clue that might lead us to the baby, Ellen would have that answer."

"You're right. This is going to be daunting. I have several volunteers at the hospital who are eager and competent. They can help me retrieve records and sift through them with what little information we have. I'll ask Father Willington if we might work our way through church records for whatever crumbs we might find."

"Thank you, Clara. At least I can tell Ellen you're helping and we'll try. It's all we can do."

"Yes, we've not much to go on, but we'll jolly well give it our best."

"I'll tell Ellen, then, what is happening on her behalf. Thank you."

Ringing off, she turns to go back to Ellen's room and startles to find Ellen standing directly behind her. Anna points to herself, moves her fingers near her mouth to pantomime talking, walks two fingers across her hand, pantomimes pouring medicine in a spoon, places her fist on the palm of her other hand, points to herself and Ellen, points to her own eyes, and holds her free arm as if holding a baby. It is a clumsy way to tell Ellen that the woman who brought medicine shall help them look for Ellen's baby. Ellen nods her head and wipes at her eyes, again. Anna watches Ellen's eyes look down, and her shoulders begin to shake. She looks up at Anna, once more, shaking her head.

She tilts her head to the side, points to herself, and then shrugs her shoulders.

Tears spring to Anna's eyes and she wonders the same thing. Why did this happen to Ellen? Why? Inviting Ellen into a comforting embrace, she holds out her free arm towards Ellen. Even Johanna has been quiet but is now extending her own little arm towards Ellen. Nodding, Ellen moves into the comfort of those who love her, arms that support her, arms that desperately want to help her. Anna hopes in the face of hopeless odds that an answer will come.

Chapter Fifteen
15 April 1926

Anna drops her reticule on the floor with a leathery splat on the entryway floor by accident as she was checking to verify there are enough funds to take Ellen shopping for new dresses. Rupert takes this opportunity to nick the tasty leather item and dash off with it. Anna trots after him into the sitting room, rolling her eyes at John's dog.

"Come here with that, you rascal. I say..."

Rupert stops, turns 'round to face his mistress, his head and tail down. Anna picks up her handbag and wipes dog spittle from the handle.

"What am I going to do with you, you scamp?"

Anna reaches down and scratches Rupert's ears with a chuckle of affection. Returning to the entry hall, she cannot help but feel a flutter of excitement. Ellen even smiled at the prospect of buying new dresses. Both of them endured a hellish nightmare the night before, and this will be a welcome contrast. Ellen has not been out for anything fun since the sleigh ride, and she hopes Ellen will enjoy choosing some frocks that will belong to her. Explaining this outing to Ellen was daunting, but Anna thinks they managed to reach an understanding. Johanna relaxes in her pushchair, bundled against the approaching spring breeze. A light wrap is all Anna needs, and she puts the pale green jacket on along with the matching hat. She chooses a similar coat for Ellen and drapes it over her arm. She tucks Johanna's crochet blanket even more snugly 'round the baby's slight form. Smiling, she strokes Johanna's hair and then caresses her little girl's cheek.

"Yes, sweetheart! We're going to take Ellen shopping for new dresses. Are you going to help? Good girl. You point to the prettiest dresses, all right?"

"Mmmmmmmm dama, Cuppa, Cuppa!"

Anna laughs and kisses Johanna in response to the baby's soft voice. She does not notice Ellen's approach and is startled to see Ellen standing in the hallway with her hands folded in front of her. A smile warms Anna's face, seeing that Ellen has chosen her favourite dress to wear on this excursion. She reckons that Ellen has never been to a dress shop. Ellen looks lovely in soft floral prints, and Anna makes a mental note to seek out something equally becoming. Shaking her dressmaker's habits out of her head, she hands Ellen her jacket and hat. Ellen slips into it and then puts her hat on, fastening it with a hatpin in the same way Anna does. The crook of Anna's arm holds the well-worn strap of her handbag that bumps against her hip as she positions the pushchair to leave the house. Opening the door and pulling it out backwards, she waves at Ellen to hold the front of the buggy as they guide it down the steps. Together they accomplish a task that would have been too much for just one person. Ellen walks back to the door and holds up her finger to Rupert, shaking her head. Rupert's tail stops wagging, and he slowly backs away from the door. Ellen closes it and then pushes against it. She nods and walks back down the steps to join Anna and Johanna.

Smiling at Ellen, Anna points down the street and nods to show the direction in which they will walk. It is a beautiful day to be outside, for shopping, for being alive. Breathing in the fresh air, Anna can hardly believe that it was not so long ago that snow covered the ground. Admiring the buds and new life sprouting all about them, she decides that it must have been the crocuses bursting through the snow that frightened the unexpected snow away. She looks at Ellen who is watching 'round from one side to the other, holding Anna's sleeve. To Anna, Ellen seems tense, but her expression is unreadable. Sighing, Anna wheels the pushchair and wonders, as always, what thoughts tumble about in Ellen's head. She turns to Anna and taps her arm. Anna, unconsciously adopting Ellen's habits, looks down at her arm and then up at Ellen, tilting her head.

She points to the lady, points to herself, points to the baby, points down the road, and tilts her head. She points to her dress, points down the road, and then tilts her head.

Anna can only decipher that Ellen is asking if this is where they go to buy dresses. She nods with a smile at Ellen and then points to the left that takes them down a street where small shops congregate. A little whilst longer and they arrive at a quaint shop with dresses on forms gracing the window display. A couple of women are standing in front of the shop window, and Ellen moves behind Anna, clutching the back of Anna's coat. Anna turns and puts her arm 'round Ellen's shoulders to shield her from these strangers. She smiles and nods at Ellen, unable to pat her hands together to tell Ellen that everything is all right. Ellen lets go her grasp on Anna's coat and gestures.

She points 'round them, then walks two fingers across her palm, and then draws an X on her palm.

Anna shakes her head to tell Ellen that no; the bad man is not here. She pushes her curiosity about the 'bad man' away, determined to make this shopping trip a pleasant one for Ellen. She points to the door, asking Ellen to open it, allowing her to enter with Johanna's pushchair. A merry jingle from a bell that dangles in mid-air announces their entrance. A peal of laughter erupts from Johanna as she points to it. With a relieved sigh, Anna sees that they are the only customers in the shop. A young woman approaches them with an engaging smile. She is pretty, close to Anna in age, wearing a conservative dress in the latest style that Anna recognises is from Paris.

"May I be of assistance?"

Anna pats Ellen's clutching hand reassuringly and lowers her voice as she speaks to the sales clerk.

"I've brought my daughter here to find some new dresses. She can neither hear nor speak, but we can communicate. She's rather afraid of new places and new people, understandably."

The young woman nods with a smile of compassionate understanding.

"Of course. I'm at your disposal for anything you might require. Perhaps you'd like to make some selections, and then I can find the dresses in suitable sizes if you like."

"Yes, thank you. Oh! Would you mind picking out some pretty underthings? She might feel awkward with something like that."

"Of course, that's no problem, Ma'am."

Grateful that the young woman is so accommodating, Anna turns her thoughts to dresses for her girl. She steers the pushchair out of the way, preventing Johanna from helping herself to things hanging nearby. Anna glances at Ellen who is taking in the whole of the shop with wide eyes and slack jaw. Smiling, Anna pats Ellen's hand for attention and waits for Ellen to look down at her hand and then back up at her. She points to Ellen, points to her own eyes, points to the dresses, points to Ellen, and then pats her hands together. She is asking Ellen to look 'round and find something she likes.

She points to herself and tilts her head to the side.

Anna nods, realising that so many choices might be overwhelming for Ellen. Knowing Ellen's tastes, Anna searches the myriad of dresses until she finds several that might suit Ellen's fancy. She glances down at Johanna, asleep in her pushchair, and with relief, she turns to their purpose. A slightly shorter hemline on a bright yellow frock catches

173

Anna's eye. Another dress in pale ivory displays embroidery in a rose design. Simple to fancy, plain to lace, dresses accumulate on a nearby rack. Anna feels a pat on her arm, looks down at her arm, then back up at Ellen.

She tilts her head to the side, points to the pretty things to wear, and then shrugs her shoulders.

Anna chuckles and points to the dresses, points to Ellen, points to her own eyes, points to the frocks, and then pats her hands together. She wants to make it clear to Ellen that she may choose what dresses she likes most. Ellen's eyes grow wide as she touches the fabrics, then pulling her hand away quickly, and then looking at Anna. She nods to Ellen, encouraging her to feel the material as she looks at each one. Wholly absorbed in comparing one dress to another and admiring the selections, they fail to notice the jingle of the bell on the door as it opens. Jane Adderley strides into the store and begins to sift through the racks of dresses, first holding up one and then another. She holds one of them up to herself and shakes her head. She walks over to the counter, still holding the dress up to herself.

"How does this look on me, miss? I fancy a new dress, and I want it to be flattering, you know."

Smiling, the sales clerk steers Mrs Adderley to a looking glass so she can admire her reflection. Anna hears a familiar voice, stops, and then cringes, hoping with every ounce of her will that Jane Adderley will remain oblivious to their presence. Unfortunately, Anna's hope comes too late. Jane unceremoniously shoves her chosen dress at the clerk.

"Here, take this, tally it up."

Jane accosts them in clumsy strides, waving at Anna, bumping into racks, and then almost knocks over a display of hair ornaments.

"Mrs Thorpe! It's nice to see you. What brings you here, this fine day?"

Gritting her teeth, Anna puts on the best social smile she can muster. Of all the times, all the places, why her, why now?

"Mrs Adderley, it is a lovely day. Shopping seemed to be a nice way to occupy the day. And you?"

"Oh, yes, yes. I see your cousin is still visiting. How do? Are you finding any dresses you like?"

Anna looks at Ellen, thankful that she cannot hear this woman's grating voice. Of course, Ellen does not respond to Jane's greeting and continues looking at the dresses.

"Well, I never. She's just as rude as the first time I laid eyes on her. A rude little thing, Mrs Thorpe. Why don't you teach her some manners?"

Ellen turns 'round holding up the pale-yellow dress and the one with the rose embroidery. Seeing Jane, her eyes grow wide, and her shaking hands drop the clothes, a puddle of fabric lying on the floor. Ellen moves to put Anna between herself and the woman. Ignoring Jane, Anna turns towards Ellen, points to Jane, points to her own eyes, points to herself and points to Ellen. She points to herself, draws an X on her palm, places her fist on her chest, points back to Jane, points to her own eyes, and then points to herself and Ellen. Finally, Anna points to Jane, places her fist on the palm of her hand, points to herself, and then draws a frown on her face. Anna communicates to Ellen that Jane saw them, unfortunately, and how this encounter makes Anna unhappy. Ellen is still shaking, and her eyes are enormous.

She nods, points to herself and then crosses her arms over her chest, fists clenched, and then points to the frown lady.

Anna nods and moves to shield Ellen from Jane. Again, the grating voice...

"What was all that? Is she one of those unteachable simple-minded folks? Does she know why you're here with her? They don't know much, you know. Sometimes you've got to feed 'em, I hear."

Anna clings to whatever composure and decorum she can scrounge from deep within herself and speaks through clenched teeth.

"Well, Jane, since you are not acquainted with this young lady, you are not qualified to make an educated guess on the matter. Thank you for stopping to greet us. I wish you a good day."

Turning away from Jane and back to Ellen, she stoops to pick up the dresses that Ellen seems to have liked the most. Hoping that Jane takes the hint to leave, disappointment crashes in on Anna. Jane gestures to Ellen, speaking with an air of self-declared authority.

"I say, there's a madhouse up in Yorkshire with a prominent doctor who does wonders with her kind. I'd be more than happy to get the address and telephone number for you to ring them. You'll be glad to get this one off your hands. I daresay, she's got to be an unwelcome burden to your family, being daft and whatnot."

Anna stands, leaving the dresses where they lay and walks closer to Jane and hisses quietly to her.

"I'll have you know, MRS Adderley that what goes on in my

household is MY business, not yours, and you may keep your advice to yourself. I do not need or want your so-called help. DO YOU COMPREHEND?"

Each word, held by a thin thread of restraint, issues forth like maternal venom from a vicious cobra. As if slapped, Jane takes a step backwards and, again, bumps into a rack. This time, a display of jewellery topples to the floor. She turns and rushes out of the shop, looking back at Anna and Ellen with a look of indignant horror as she mutters to herself.

"Well, I never. Not in my life. And from Mrs Thorpe. I try to be helpful, and this is the thanks I get. Why that ungrateful...."

Anna turns to Ellen and pats her hands together to assure Ellen that everything is fine, now. Ellen looks from Anna to the door and back to Anna.

She points to herself, draws an X in the palm of her hand, places a fist on her chest, points to her eyes, and then points at the door.

Anna nods in complete agreement. Neither of them wants to see Jane Adderley again. She bends down to pick up the dresses that fell to the floor and holds them up for Ellen to see. Anna points to Ellen, places her fist on her chest, and then points to the two dresses. Ellen lets out a deep breath, nodding her head slowly. Anna pats the two dresses and hands them to Ellen. She takes the handle of the pushchair and wheels Johanna in it to the side of the shop as she motions for Ellen to follow. Anna looks at Ellen, points to the dresses, and then pats the counter. Ellen lays down the dresses and moves behind Anna as the saleswoman comes to finalise the transaction.

"Are these the correct size, Ma'am? I can find another size if you need."

"No, we're the same size, so these will be fine. Thank you."

The clerk folds the dresses and wraps them in paper along with the lacy underthings she has chosen for the young woman. She prepares to calculate the price and then hesitates.

"Ma'am, uh, Mrs Thorpe, if I may be so bold, I couldn't help but overhear everything that...happened. I'm so sorry. No, not that it happened here, but that it happened at all. It wasn't right."

"No, I'm the one who should apologise for such an unseemly scene in public. I am protective of my daughter, though, and that woman did push me to the edge. I'm sorry that I wasn't able to hold my tongue properly."

The saleswoman smiles, chuckles, and pats the packages.

"No, not at all. Your decorum and restraint were admirable. Had it been me, I'd have only...well; my reaction wouldn't have been as civil as yours. At any rate, I would like to pay for the dresses, myself, as a small gift. If you wouldn't be offended?"

"Oh, my word, miss, I couldn't ask you to do that. No offence is taken, but I'm able to afford..."

"Ma'am, you didn't ask. I offered. Your daughter seems like such a sweet girl, and I'd like to show her that there are people in the world who are kind. It would make me proud to be one of those people."

Anna feels a pat on her arm and looks at Ellen.

She points to the lady and then to the woman, moves her fingers by her mouth to pantomime talking, tilts her head to the side.

Turning to the woman behind the counter, Anna explains.

"She's wondering what we're saying, and it makes her feel as if she's not included. If you give me a moment, I'll translate for her."

As best she can, she relates to Ellen what she and the saleswoman had said to one another. Ellen tilts her head to the side and nods, shrugging her shoulders. Anna turns to gather the parcels and pays for the under things. She thanks the young woman for her kindness and generosity. She takes Ellen's hand, gives a reassuring squeeze, and then hands them to Ellen to carry, nodding towards the door. Taking hold of the handle, Anna manoeuvres the pushchair through the shop to the door. Ellen hurries ahead to open the door for them. Once outside, Ellen looks up and down the street, taking hold of Anna's sleeve. A brisk pace spurs them on their way, as Anna understands Ellen's desire to return to, what Ellen seems to feel, is a safe place.

Arriving home, Anna gestures that they should go 'round the house to the garden door. It is more level there and much easier to bring the pushchair indoors. Ellen peeks into the pushchair and smiles as she tucks the packages under her arm.

She points to the baby, puts her hands together and lays her head on them as if sleeping, and draws a circle 'round her face.

Anna chuckles and nods in agreement. Johanna is pretty when she is sleeping. That Johanna is still sleeping, in spite of a bumpy ride, amazes Anna and she shakes her head. She imagines telling John, who will not believe it. Ellen tucks her parcels into the pushchair so she can use both hands to pull it through the soft grass, whilst Anna pushes. It will not do to have the wheels mire into the spring soil. The gate to the garden opens at Ellen's touch, and they make their way to the rear of the house. Again, Ellen minds the door, and they enter without waking Johanna. Rupert jumps and wiggles with enthusiasm as he watches them walk inside. Hesitating and taking a deep breath, Ellen walks outside to close the garden gate, followed by Rupert. She looks all 'round her, motions to Rupert and then hurries back into the house, closing the door behind them. Ellen catches up with Anna in the kitchen and watches her clean the wheels of the pushchair, Rupert sniffing each one. Johanna awakens and stretches with a yawn, rubbing her eyes. Ellen walks over to the buggy, takes out the package containing her garments and lays them on the table. She picks up the baby, swaying with her, snuggling her with kisses. Patting Ellen's face, Johanna repeats the words 'Cuppa Cuppa' as she plants a sloppy kiss on Ellen's cheek. Anna looks up at her girls and smiles to see them sharing genuine affection.

The pushchair wheels clean, Anna pushes it into a corner of the kitchen, out of the way. She reaches for Johanna who holds out her arms, wanting her mother's attention, as well. Anna bounces her on her hip and then looks at Ellen with a grin, putting her finger against her nose, the gesture designating Johanna's 'name' in Ellen's language. Wrinkling her nose and smiling, Ellen nods, points to her new dresses and then points to her bedroom. Nodding, Anna walks out of the kitchen with Johanna, and up to the nursery. Ellen looks 'round, smiles, and holds the parcels close to her, skipping out of the kitchen to her bedroom with Rupert trotting along.

John looks about and is disappointed that his usual greeting from Anna is missing. John takes off his jacket and tie as he walks into the sitting room. He drapes them over the back of a chair, promising himself that he will take them upstairs when they retire for the night. Looking 'round, he feels a bit lost in the silence. Some tea seems appealing, so he trudges, with the day's weariness in his limbs, to the kitchen. Disappointment taps his shoulder at Anna's absence in the kitchen, as well, but he busies himself and fills the kettle with water to heat on the cooker. With today's newspaper and a biscuit tin from the cupboard, he sits at the kitchen table. He has barely read the headlines when he hears Anna's familiar footsteps. Getting up from his chair, he smiles and opens his arms wide to greet Anna who is holding Johanna.

"Come to daddy, little one. I'm so happy to see you."

He takes Johanna in his arms and covers her face with kisses that interrupt her babbling laughter. Anna laughs at the two of them and is full of pride that her husband and daughter share a special bond that seems to be missing in so many families, as she has observed.

John brings Johanna to her high chair and settles her into it, the baby banging the tray and chattering. John walks over to Anna and takes her in his arms for a kiss that makes up for the one that didn't greet him at the door. Leaning back, Anna's eyes sparkle as she smiles at him.

"Well, I'm happy to see you, too, John. The teakettle is even happy, now. So, tell me, how was your day?"

John laughs as he hurries to take the kettle off the burner to interrupt its steamy song.

"The shop was busy. Several weddings are in the planning, and nervous grooms are in dire need of appropriate attire, or so say their mothers and brides-to-be."

Anna chuckles, at the visual of nerve-wracked youths who are bracing themselves for a lifetime of marriage. John walks over to the counter and makes the two of them tea to go with the biscuits. When finished, he brings both cups to the table and pulls out Anna's chair for her to sit, then takes his own seat.

"Well, good wishes to them, then. If they can make it through planning a wedding, the marriage is certain to last."

"True, Anna. I'll have to mention that if one of the young men admits that their last nerve is frayed. Did you and Ellen shop for dresses today? You'd talked about that this morning."

"Yes, we did. Ellen has two of them. Unfortunately, we saw Mrs Adderley there, and everything went well once I put Jane in her place. I'll tell you about it later when I'm not fuming about it. She has some gall."

"Anna, I can see you're still upset about it. How did Ellen fare through this?"

"She's fine, now. I think it unnerved her, but she calmed quickly. I'd say that's progress."

"Yes, it is. I hope to see her new dresses as much as I hope to have supper tonight."

Anna and John laugh, realising that time has flown away from the supper hour. Tonight's supper will have to be simple.

"John, I'm sorry, I haven't started...time just passed so quickly..."

"Don't worry, Anna. I was a bachelor for a good long time before we met. I can be useful in the kitchen. Why don't you see if Ellen will put on her dresses so we can admire them properly? I'll make something for us to eat. It won't be fancy, mind you, but I'm sure it will be edible."

Anna gets up from the table and walks 'round to wrap her arms 'round John from the back and kiss his cheek.

"Thank you, sweet one. I'll see what Ellen is doing."

John turns to watch Anna walk out of the kitchen and smiles. He gets up and offers Johanna a biscuit to occupy her busy hands and mouth. He walks over to the cold box and tries to remember how to sustain the body with edible food that is cooked rather than burnt to bachelor standards.

Walking down the hallway to Ellen's room, Anna pauses at Ellen's door and hears Rupert's tail thumping against the floor. Pushing open the door, she sees Ellen wearing one of her new dresses, sitting in the corner of the room, on the floor, holding her hands cupped together. Rupert looks up at Anna, stands, and wags his tail. He walks over to Ellen, nudges her arm with his nose and looks back at his mistress. Ellen looks at Rupert, up to where he is looking and sees Anna standing there. She smiles at Anna and nods her head in the direction of the bed. Curious, she sits on the bed as asked and chuckles to see Ellen wiggle with excitement as she stands up and walks over to sit next to her. Her hands cupped to her chest, Ellen shakes her head at Rupert who is poised to jump up on the bed. Obediently, he walks to the corner where his friend had been sitting and curls up on the floor.

Ellen looks at Anna and nods, slowly bringing her hands towards Anna and opening them. A brownish-grey animal rests calmly in Ellen's hand. Leaning closer to see, Anna's eyes meet those of a field mouse. Nose-twitches greet Anna as she moves her finger to touch the soft creature, although her natural reaction would be completely different. She looks up at Ellen and points to herself, draws a smile on her face, points to her own eyes, and then points to the mouse to reassure Ellen that she is happy to see the mouse. Ellen smiles and nods then looks down to stroke the mouse's fur. Its tail curls 'round its feet and the relaxed appearance seems to be genuine. Anna pats Ellen's arm to get her attention and waits for Ellen to look at her arm and then back up at her. Tapping three fingers on her chest, pointing to her own eyes, pointing to the mouse, and tilting her head to the side is how Anna asks Ellen if they could show the little twitch-nose to John. Ellen smiles and nods, standing up and walking to the door. Anna chuckles as Ellen stops at the door, looks back at her, and nods as if to encourage her to come along. Rupert takes the hint, gets up from his corner, and dashes past Ellen's legs.

The first room into which Ellen looks is the kitchen where John and Johanna are discussing plans for their supper. Ellen stands in the doorway, a smile on her face, with her hands cupped protectively 'round her little treasure. Walking up beside Ellen, Anna clears her throat to catch John's attention. He is busily making the bachelor's standby, hearty sandwiches. Johanna's high chair tray is littered with bits of bread, sliced meat, and sliced cheese. Rupert takes up his post by Johanna to catch any bits that might fall to the floor. Johanna leans down, trying to reach the dog.

"Goggy goggy!"

She drops a piece of bread and Rupert catches it in mid-air, his tail wagging. Together, they play their game of drop and snatch, ignoring all but their amusement.

"John, Ellen's wearing one of her new dresses, and she has something special to show you."

Startled from his intent focus on his masterpiece sandwiches, he looks up at Anna and Ellen, lays the knife on the counter, and then wipes his hands on the pink pinny he has donned for this foray into the culinary abyss.

"There's our girl! Well, aren't you pretty!"

John points to Ellen and draws a circle 'round his face to express his

that she looks pretty. He is not surprised when Ellen looks down at her feet upon seeing the compliment. She usually does, causing John and Anna to wonder at times like these if she is just unaccustomed to hearing that she is pretty and it makes her feel self-conscious. John notices that Ellen has her hands cupped together.

"Anna, what's that? It must be delicate, the way she's holding it."

"You'll see, John."

Anna rubs Ellen's arm with a smile, and a nod and Ellen looks at her. Anna points to John, points to her own eyes, and points to Ellen's hands to say that John wants to see what she is holding. Nodding, Ellen walks over to John and opens her hands to reveal the mouse. The little fellow looks up at John and twitches his whiskers, the only response he gives to being near such large people-creatures. John smiles and nods at Ellen, patting his hands together to lend his approval of this new addition to Ellen's world. He walks close to Anna and leans down to kiss her cheek and whisper.

"Anna, it's...a mouse. Did she find it in her room? What if there are more? I should set some traps."

Anna turns with a grin and strokes John's cheek with her hand.

"Calm yourself. It's a mouse, John. It makes Ellen happy. This one is hers."

John smiles at Ellen and considers himself dim for agreeing to keep a field mouse as a pet, but two against one assures his defeat. He walks closer to Ellen and reaches out to touch it, surprised at how soft it is and how calm it seems. He steps back a pace and points to himself, places one fist on top of the other several times, points to the mouse, and then pantomimes the shape of a box. Since the mouse is officially a member of the family, it needs a place to call home. Ellen nods and bounces on the balls of her feet, happiness lighting up her face. His heart melting at Ellen's reaction, he walks over to Anna and takes off the pinny, handing it to her.

"I guess it's only right that the little fellow has a proper home. There's an aquarium we used some years ago that's still 'round somewhere."

"That will be perfect, John. Thank you. In the meantime, Mr Mouse seems to be happy right where he is."

Laughing and shaking his head, he begins to walk out of the kitchen. Anna catches his sleeve, and he hesitates, looking at her. She desperately tries to stifle her laughter.

"John, a pink pinny is rather becoming on you. I thought you should know that."

Laughing at the image Anna and Ellen must have enjoyed when they came into the kitchen, he walks to the storage cupboard upstairs. Anna turns to Ellen and pats her hands together to convey that their bid to keep the mouse was successful. Ellen holds the mouse up to her face, nose-to-nose and tilts her head. Her eyes open wide and she looks at Anna, one finger held up. She walks over to the counter and finds a sliver of cheese no bigger than Johanna's fingernail.

She walks over to the lady, points to her own eyes, and then to the little furry. She puts the food in the palm of her hand and holds up one finger in front of the little furry. She looks at the lady, nods, and then holds up her finger in front of the small furry and then nods her head.

Anna's eyes grow wide to see the mouse refrain from eating at Ellen's gesture and then gobble the cheese when Ellen seems to give her permission. She has never seen the like, and John is not going to believe this. Anna looks at Ellen and smiles, her eyes wide with admiration for such a unique skill. Ellen smiles back at Anna and then turns her attention to the mouse with a fingertip tickle to its little head.

John's footsteps coming down the stairs draw Anna's attention.

"Did you find it, John? I forgot to mention..."

He walks into the kitchen and sets the aquarium on the table.

"I remembered what you forgot to mention, never fear."

John holds up the screened lid for the aquarium and then pulls out a black and red board with alternating squares and the corresponding pieces for playing draughts.

"This was in the storage cupboard, as well, and I thought it might be fun to play draughts, Anna. I haven't had the pleasure of winning a game in some time."

"Splendid, John. This will be fun."

He kisses Anna's cheek and then turns to Ellen. He points to the mouse, points to the aquarium with its glass sides. He holds up a finger to say he will be right back. He walks out of the kitchen, down the hallway, and they hear the door to the garden open and close. Ellen tilts her head at Anna who shrugs in reply. Anna peeks out of the kitchen doorway towards the garden door. Soon, John's form fills the door's window, and he comes back into the house with something in his hands. Grinning, he makes his way into the kitchen with his handful of an idea. He dumps wood shavings wrapped in a cloth into the aquarium and then a half-round of wood, hollowed out. Finally, he takes the fabric and tears it into strips that he lays 'round the enclosure. He looks at Ellen, hoping his efforts at making a mouse-house into a mouse home meet with her approval. Ellen's tearful smile and a nod are thanks enough.

Anna moves close to John, slipping her arm 'round his waist, resting her head against his shoulder.

"That was sweet, John. You've made Ellen and Mr Mouse exceedingly happy."

They watch Ellen place the mouse in its new abode and dangle a piece of bedding in front of him. He takes the cloth in his mouth and scampers into his hiding place to make a nest. Ellen stands up and puts the cover on the aquarium.

She looks at the man and the lady, points to the little furry's place, and then points to her sleeping place.

Anna nods and holds up a finger for Ellen to wait just a moment before taking her new pet to her room. Anna finds two tiny bowls in the china cabinet and fills one with water, the other with a mixture of nuts and dried lentils from the cupboard. She walks back to the table with the mouse-feast and nods at Ellen who removes the screened cover. Anna places the food and water into the mouse's enclosure and steps aside for Ellen to replace the lid. Ellen tilts her head to the side, and Anna nods to say that it is all right to take Mr Mouse back to her bedroom. Nodding,

Ellen picks up the aquarium and walks past John and Anna, into her room where they hear the door softly kicked shut.

Rupert looks at the kitchen door and whines as he looks up at his master and mistress. John walks over and scratches the dog's ears.

"I tell you what, little fellow. You can join Anna when she takes Ellen her supper."

He looks up at Anna with a sheepish grin.

"You will take her supper in to her, won't you?"

Anna laughs and shakes her head as she walks over to the counter and lays the pinny aside to finish the sandwiches.

"Of course, I will. She isn't going to leave Mr Whiskers, I'm sure. I'll even finish making these sandwiches if you hang up the pinny right where you found it."

"Anything you say, ma'am."

Obediently, John picks up the pinny and hangs it on its peg, shaking his head with a laugh and thinking that next time, he should choose the green one. It is a manlier colour. He walks over to the table to sit next to Johanna, giving her another biscuit, knowing Anna will fuss at him for it. Fortunate for him, Anna does not notice the biscuit and walks out of the kitchen with a glass of milk and the plate holding a sandwich. He hears Anna walk down the hallway to Ellen's room, Rupert close on her heels.

"Well, my little princess, Sarah would have my head for this meal, but we won't tell her, will we?"

Johanna shakes her head, her curls swishing this way and that.

"Da da noooo nodada."

Chapter Sixteen
19 April 1926

Lewis Adderley trudges through Chelsey's Market looking for the items on his mother's list. He looks at it and takes off his cap, slapping it against his thigh before returning it to his head at a jaunty angle. Marketing is a dreaded chore, and it is his two penn'orths that this is a woman's task. Grumbling under his breath, he tosses things in the shopping basket, not caring if cans are dented or if vegetables are fresh. He takes more care in selecting meat, realising that even if his mother's cooking leaves much to be desired, he has to eat it. Rounding a corner, he almost bumps a basket out of a young man's hands. It is the market's deliveryman, William Tenney. Lewis takes a step back, ready to apologise. William is a decent sort and is the kind of fellow who keeps his tongue even when a customer fusses and refuses to tip. Lewis had always been envious of the fact that everyone seems to like William. Lewis, though, had to admit, he likes William, too.

"Sorry about that, mate. Got a delivery to make?"

"Yes, the Thorpe housekeeper gave me an endless list."

"Blimey, it won't do to have that Sarah nag you. She runs the house, ya know. Say, have you met the girl living with 'em?"

"Girl? What girl? I never heard of a girl there besides the daughter."

"She's a right skittish little thing, I tell you. Scared of everything. She's not puttin' on, either. Not a sound from her. I think she's completely mutton. Mum thinks she's barmy, but I don't trust Mum's two penneth on much. That girl's good looking!"

"Well, maybe I'll see for myself. I'd best get this done, or I'll only get a biscuit for a tip. Cheerio, mate."

William returns to his selections for Sarah. He knows the housekeeper would not hesitate to send something back for a replacement if it was not suitable. He checks the list one more time and walks over to the owner of the market to tell him where he will go on his delivery. The grocer waves his hand without a word, not even looking up from balancing his accounts. Trying to be polite, William takes a step back.

"Yes, Mr Chelsey."

William walks out of his employer's office and winds his way through the aisles to the back room. He takes off his stained pinny and hangs it on its peg. The cap he puts on is a dull brown plaid thing with a well-worn spot where he grabs it to put it on and take it off. He picks up the basket and eagerly goes outside. It is a gorgeous day, and he rather enjoys his deliveries. As he walks along and whistles a tune he just made up in his head, he starts to muse about how he gets out, talks to people, and how each day is different. His mum always wished he had gone on to school, but his dad died in the Great War. He felt a responsibility to help his mum until she died, but now that she is gone, he is just glad to have a job when so many people cannot find work. William is happy enough with his bedsit, a one-room flat, above the market. Life, as a whole, is good. His thoughts carry him all the way to the Thorpe house, sweeping away the time. The Thorpe's housekeeper, Sarah, likes him to deliver goods to the garden door, so he walks 'round the house and opens the garden gate. His eyes focus on the door, oblivious to the girl standing near some shrubbery. Her movement to the side of him catches his eye. Stopping to turn his head, he sees a pretty girl who seems about his age. He wonders if this is the girl Lewis mentioned. Rupert, the Thorpe's dog, runs towards him, tail wagging, but barking at him, as he has never done before.

"Hey there, old boy. Calm down. It's just your old chum William."

He strokes Rupert's head and then smiles and waves to the girl. Her reaction to his friendly greeting surprises him. He sees her eyes grow wide, and she moves towards the door. He thinks to himself that Lewis was telling the truth for a change. He notices her hands shaking, and he feels sorry for her and sorry that he seems to have frightened her. It does not appear to take much to alarm her, so William musters his best smile but does not approach closer. He points to himself, holds up the basket of food, and then points to the door.

"I'm here to deliver food from the market. My name's William."

If she is deaf, as Lewis described, he hopes she will at least understand he is not here to hurt anyone. With surprising speed, she makes a dash for the door, opens it, and runs inside. Rupert follows behind Ellen, barking. William takes off his cap and scratches his head, figuring he has never seen a girl so scared of a fellow delivering goods from the market. He walks over to the open door and knocks to make his presence known as if Rupert had not already done so. It would not do for him, a delivery boy, to just walk in. Mr Chelsey would give him a good bit of advice about keeping his job if he did. He sees Sarah poke her head out of the kitchen.

"There you are. You must be the cause of Rupert's excitement and

Miss Cup's flight into the kitchen. Come in, William. And shut the door behind you."

He follows Sarah's simple instructions and brings the basket laden with foodstuffs into the kitchen for Sarah to inspect. The girl is there in the kitchen, standing in a corner, breathing heavily, staring at him with her arms clasped in front of herself. Her knuckles are white, and he reckons she is trying to keep them from shaking.

"William, are you listening to me? Come, now."

"I'm sorry, ma'am. Is there something you want me to return? I don't mind."

"No, William. I was going to give you a tip and a biscuit. Mrs Thorpe left a generous tip for you."

Taking the money in his hand, his eyes grow wide as he notes the amount.

"Thank you and my thanks to Mrs Thorpe. Thank you."

"You're welcome, William. Now, don't you worry about Miss Cup. Ma'am will be here to see to her in a moment, and in the meantime, she knows she's safe with me."

Sarah just smiles at him and turns her attention to putting the food away. Hearing the voice of young William, Anna walks into the kitchen. Knowing Ellen had been outside; her first worry is where Ellen is now. If she saw William when he arrived and became frightened by an unknown man walking up to their door, Anna worries about her reaction to him. After last night's nightmare, she hopes Ellen's terror during the night will not resurface most unpleasantly. Her answer is standing in a corner with wide eyes, heavy breathing, and arms crossed in front of her with her fists clenched. Rupert sits next to Ellen and leans against her legs, staring at William. Anna walks over to stand in front of Ellen and rubs her arms, tilting her head to the side, silently asking Ellen to tell her what might be wrong.

She points to the young man, crosses her arms tight over her chest and then points to herself. She tilts her head to the side, points to the young man, and then draws an X on her palm.

Anna shakes her head. No, William is not bad. Anna points to William and pats her hands together to say that he is a good fellow and did not mean to frighten her. Fascinated, William watches the girl and Mrs Thorpe move their hands to 'talk' to each other. Convinced, he believes what Lewis told him, that the girl cannot hear or speak.

"Mrs Thorpe, if you don't mind my asking, she can't hear, can

187

she?"

"No, William, she can't hear, and she can't speak."

"Uh, may I ask what were you saying to each other? I couldn't help but notice that you both pointed at me. I think I scared her when I came, and I'm awfully sorry about that."

Anna appreciates that he is expressing himself kindly about Ellen.

"William, she told me that you frightened her and asked if you were a bad man. I told her that you were a good person. I'm going to walk over to you and shake your hand so she can see that I'm not afraid of you."

"Yes, Mrs Thorpe. I don't want her to be scared of me. I feel terrible about upsetting her. I didn't know."

She walks over to William and extends her hand with a smile. William takes Anna's hand and feels a wave of awkwardness filling him. He takes a slow breath to quell his trepidation as Anna pats his hand and they both look at Ellen. She releases his hand, looks at Ellen, and pats her hands together again as she points to William, reaffirming that William is a person worthy of trust. Her gaze returns to William, and she smiles at him, trying to reassure him that he is in no trouble from this incident.

"Don't worry, William. As you said, you didn't know, and it's evident that you feel bad about it. As you come 'round more often, she'll likely see you and become accustomed to your deliveries."

"Thank you, Mrs Thorpe. I'm grateful that you're not angry with me. I'd best go, now, and thank you for the tip, also. Thank you."

William backs towards the doorway, watching Ellen with a smile, his cap in his hands. In doing so, thanks to his inattention, he smacks his left shoulder on the doorjamb. More startled by the sound than the pain in his shoulder, he steps sideways to back through the door without further injuring himself. He smiles, waves at Ellen, and then finds his way out through the garden door, into the sunshine, taking a deep breath of belated courage. Relief pours out of him on the exhale as he closes the door. William never has in his life...and that girl fills his mind on his way back to the market. He mutters to himself as he walks.

"What was her name? Oh, yes. Ellen."

Anna's inner mirth subsides at the thought of William's mishap at the doorway. She turns back to Ellen who seems to be less afraid, now. Anna opens her arms to gather her into an embrace, and Ellen walks into her arms. She wraps her arms 'round Anna tightly, resting her head against Anna's shoulder. She can feel Ellen relax and her breathing return to normal rhythm as she strokes her girl's hair. Today was unusual. Sarah's order is usually not this large, and William typically comes to the door, delivers the goods to Sarah, and then leaves. Ellen has missed his deliveries until today. Ellen pulls back from Anna's embrace and nods.

She points to herself and pats her hands together.

Anna pats Ellen's arm with a reassuring squeeze, letting Ellen know that she understands Ellen's return to calmness. Ellen nods, looks down at Rupert, motions for him to come along, and the two of them walk out of the kitchen, to the sitting room. Anna looks at Sarah, then the table, and opens her eyes wide at the amount of food left to put away.

"Is there anything I can do to help, Sarah?"

"No, Ma'am. I will take care of it. It feels good to keep myself busy after my sister..."

"I understand. We've said this before, but if you or your family need anything, please tell us. You're family, here. Your family is dear to us. I hope you know that."

"Yes, Ma'am. You and Sir have been kind to us, and we're ever so grateful. I missed all of you whilst I was away. Thinking about you, Sir, Miss Johanna, and Miss Cup helped me keep my chin up for the rest of the family."

"I'm glad, Sarah. I'll be in the sitting room if you change your mind about me lending you a hand in here."

Giving Sarah's wrist an affectionate squeeze, Anna leaves Sarah to her task. Sarah nods and turns back to the basket of produce, not wanting Anna to see the emotion filling her. It threatens to spill from her eyes; grief at her sister's passing still fresh in her heart. Anna walks out of the kitchen to join Ellen in the sitting room where she is sitting in front of the bookcase looking at pictures in books. Rupert has his head on Ellen's arm as if trying to see the pictures, too. Anna settles into her favourite chair to work on some intricate stitching on a bridal gown. She feels immense relief that Lady Ashton and the Dowager Countess Ashton were pleased with the dresses she created for them. Hearing that her most particular clients are happy to give Anna the impetus to design more frocks. This time of year, she works long hours to make bridal gowns for young women who will, soon, be walking down the aisle to say, 'I do'.

Lost in her work, Anna does not see Ellen until she senses a presence beside her. Startled, she looks up at Ellen and tilts her head to ask Ellen what she might want. Ellen holds out a book and points to a picture, tilting her head. Anna takes the book in her hands in this everyday occurrence. Frequently, Ellen brings books to Anna, asking for explanations about things she has never seen before. This time, the picture in the book shows a young girl on a swing. Smiling at her own memories of happy hours spent swinging, the sunshine on her face, the breeze in her hair, Anna points to the tree, the rope, and the seat of the swing. Then, she holds her hand horizontally as if it were the seat of the swing and moves it back and forth, pointing to the swing at the same time. She hopes Ellen does not find this explanation confusing. Ellen takes the book back into her hands and stares at the picture. She walks over to the sofa, holds the book on her lap, and holds her hands up as if clasping swing ropes, holds her legs out, and then looks up at the ceiling just like the girl in the picture. Rupert hops up on the sofa and watches Ellen, his tail thumping against the cushion. Ellen returns to a proper sitting posture and touches the image with her fingertips. Anna wonders if Ellen has ever had the pleasure of swinging. She will ask John if he can make one for Ellen. A tree in the garden with an overhanging limb that is sturdy enough to hang a swing will suit. When Johanna is a bit older, she will enjoy the swing, as well.

As she thinks of Johanna, Anna hears her baby girl up in the nursery, awake from her nap. She waves to attract Ellen's attention, and when Ellen looks at her, she points to herself, points upstairs, and then places her finger against the side of her nose to tell Ellen that she is going upstairs to tend to Johanna.

She tilts her head to the side, points to herself, places her fist against her chest, points upstairs, puts one fist in the palm of her other hand, and then places her finger against the side of her nose.

Anna nods, giving Ellen permission to go upstairs to care for Johanna. Ellen seems to enjoy looking after their little one as much as Johanna seems to adore Ellen. Ellen glances at the picture in the book one more time and then gets up to hand it to Anna. She climbs the staircase, followed by Rupert who makes his presence known by vocalising the occasional 'woof'. Looking at the picture of the swing, Anna feels sure that John can make one for Ellen. She lays the book on the table next to the sofa and closes the book on a bit of lace doily between the leaves to mark Ellen's place. She returns to her stitching on the sheer over-dress of the wedding gown, finding these new fashions fascinating. Imagine a bride getting married wearing a knee-length dress. Ten years ago, such a thing would have been scandalous. Anna reminds herself that it is her business to accommodate the changing fashions and tastes of her clients. She has seen hemlines rise, necklines dip and skirts flare and then shrink to fit the feminine form. Seamstress work is never dull.

Ellen carries Johanna down the stairs to the sitting room in time for Anna to hear John walk into the house. Rupert tears through the sitting room to greet his master with barks and jumps. Anna sets her sewing aside and motions for Ellen and Johanna to come along, tapping three fingers on her chest to say that John is home. Ellen sets Johanna on the floor, and the little one pats her chest as she toddles to see her father.

"Daddy home! Daddy!"

John hears Johanna's voice, and he crouches down, covering his eyes. Johanna comes 'round the corner and sees him. Her laughter fills the house as she pulls at John's wrists to uncover his eyes, supporting herself with one hand upon his knee. Feigning an expression of surprise and delight, he uncovers his eyes.

"You found me! You're such a big girl!"

John scoops his daughter up into his arms and lifts her high, drawing out more peals of laughter. Anna and Ellen watch father and daughter have their moment, smiling at the two of them having a right grand time greeting one another. A few minutes of merriment end with John's kiss to Johanna's cheek. He sets her down, holding her hand, steadying her whilst she walks over to Ellen. He smiles at Ellen to greet her, pointing to himself, drawing a smile on his face, pointing to his eyes, and then pointing to Ellen, saying that he is happy to see her.

She smiles, points to herself, draws a smile on her face, points to her eyes, and then points to the man.

John turns to Anna, taking her in his arms for an 'I missed you' kiss. Anna steps back a pace and looks up at John with the warmth of his kiss filling her. Ellen stands nearby, staring at them, her hands folded in front of herself, tilting her head to the side.

"Well, you're early, sweetheart. Did those grooms finally make you crack?"

"No...well, yes. The men can manage the shop and a few simple alterations, so I thought I'd spend a little extra time with my girls."

"Splendid! I want to show you something, John."

Anna turns to Ellen and points to herself, John, and then to the sitting room to tell Ellen that this is where they are going. Ellen's smile is her reply and indicates her understanding. John and Anna look at each other as their hands slip together. For Ellen to say that she is happy to see John is such a monumental step from where she began some months ago in the dead of winter. Johanna looks up at Ellen, points to herself, pats her chest with her hand, and then points to the kitchen.

"Cuppa, Cuppa! Bikit. Me bikit."

Ellen smiles at Johanna and then looks up at John and Anna.

She tilts her head to the side, points at herself, places her finger against her nose, and then points to the food place.

Anna chuckles and nods her head. Yes, Ellen may take Johanna to the kitchen, and Sarah can help Ellen sort out what Johanna wants. Anna turns to John and pulls him into the sitting room whilst Ellen, Johanna, and Rupert walk to the kitchen.

"I'm so happy that Ellen and Johanna get on so well. Johanna is learning Ellen's language so easily, just as her vocabulary has grown. I'm so pleased."

"Yes, Anna, I'm happy that Johanna is growing up with two languages. They couldn't be better together. Ellen takes good care of Johanna."

"John, there's something I want to show you that I think will make you smile."

She walks over to the side table next to the sofa and picks up the book, nearly upending the items sitting on the makeshift bookmark.

"Oh dear...that was a close one. At any rate, John, Ellen seemed to favour this picture."

John takes the book and looks at the picture of the young girl on a swing. He grins and looks at Anna.

"You're right, Anna, this makes me smile. Are you thinking what I'm thinking?"

"Oh yes, would you, John? I think Ellen would be so happy! I don't believe she's ever seen one."

"Of course! Let me change, and I'll set to work straight away. Ellen will have her swing."

John kisses Anna and holds her close, oblivious to the two pairs of eyes watching from the doorway. John steps back and turns to hurry up the stairs, taking them two at a time. Johanna toddles over to her mother and pats Anna's dress.

"Oh, my goodness, Johanna! What do you have? A biscuit! Did Ellen get that for you? That was so sweet!"

Johanna smiles, nods, and then speaks incoherently with her mouth full of biscuit. Anna laughs, crouches down to kiss Johanna's crumb-flecked cheek, and then reaches for one of Johanna's picture books on the floor.

"There you go, sweet one. Sit over here and practice the animal sounds from the pictures. Good girl!"

Johanna steps over to the sofa, holding her animal book high. Clumsily, she sits on the floor near Rupert. She opens the book and with each animal picture, makes the noises she has learnt. The biscuit muffles her imitations, but the little one is trying. Anna smiles at Ellen, points to Johanna, pantomimes eating a biscuit, and then pats her hands together to say that Johanna enjoys her biscuit. Ellen smiles and nods.

She points to herself, places her hand over her heart, and then points to the baby.

Anna nods, glad that Ellen loves Johanna so much. She points to Johanna, places her hand over her heart, and then points to Ellen, telling her that she loves Ellen, too. Nodding, she walks over to the sofa and sits, looking at Anna, and patting the cushion next to her. Wondering what Ellen has in mind, she gets up, steps over to the sofa, and sits down. She looks at Ellen with a tilt of her head, asking Ellen to share her thoughts. She pauses for a moment, looking at her hands folded in her lap, and then looks up at Anna.

She points to the lady, taps three fingers on her chest, and then touches her lips. She tilts her head to the side.

Anna does not understand, at first, what Ellen means by pointing to her lips. Then, she realises that Ellen was watching her and John kissing. Ellen has seen them kiss and show affection towards each other before, but this is the first time she has asked about it. The only way to explain is to tell Ellen that people kiss when they love each other and that she and John are married. Kissing is one thing that people who love each other do. To begin, Anna wants to establish the idea that she and John love each other. Anna points to herself, places her hand over her heart, and then taps three fingers on her chest. She taps three fingers on her chest, puts her hand over her heart, and then points to herself. She points to herself, taps three fingers on her chest, and then places her hand over her heart and then places her finger on her lips. Ellen's head-tilt elicits a sigh from Anna, her explanation fumbled at best.

John walks down the staircase to the sitting room and waves to Anna and Ellen. Anna smiles at John and mouths the words 'good luck' to him whilst Ellen stares at him.

"Here I go. I'll be back when I'm finished."

He winks and makes his outside, closing the door behind him. He is eager to begin the project that he hopes will make Ellen happy.

Returning her attention to Ellen, Anna contemplates for a moment, wondering if Ellen has ever seen a married couple show affection towards one another. Perhaps, this is the first time that Ellen has been able to muster the courage to ask such a question. With everything else Ellen has never experienced, the relationship between a husband and wife might be entirely new to her. Acting upon an idea, Anna holds up one finger to ask Ellen to wait for a moment. She gets up from the sofa and retrieves a photograph album from the bookcase. Opening it, Anna finds several family pictures to show her. Anna points to one that shows the bride and groom dressed in their wedding attire. She looks at the picture and tilts her head to the side. Anna points to the wedding rings that the couple wears, points to the bride and groom, puts her hand over her heart, and then places her finger on her lips in a bid to succeed in setting forth the notion that people dress up, exchange rings, and then kiss. Anna points to herself, taps three fingers on her chest, places her hand over her heart, and then points to Johanna. The more gestures she makes, the more Anna is convinced that Ellen will think she is daft, but she hopes that Ellen will understand when people love each other, marry, and kiss, a baby eventually comes into the world. Ellen's response is shaking her head and tilting her head to the side. Anna points to her wedding ring, a simple gold band symbolising John's undying love for her, taps three fingers on her chest, and then holds out her hand with an open palm, and then draws her hand to her chest as she closes her hand into a fist. She points to her wedding band, points to herself, and then holds her fist to her chest, extends her arm as she opens her hand, and then taps three fingers on her chest to attempt a description that she gave a ring like this to John just as he had given one to her. Ellen looks down at her hands, looks at the photograph, and then reaches out to touch it, the wedding bands seemingly of particular interest. She reaches over to take Anna's hand and touch the gold circlet.

She points to the shiny circle on the lady's finger, points to the lady, taps three fingers on her chest, and then places her hand over her heart. She touches a finger to her lips and then points to the baby. She points to the lady, taps three fingers on her chest, and interlocks her forefingers, and thumbs together.

Nodding with relief, Anna comprehends the meaning of the interlocking fingers. They must mean two rings joining two people who love each other. She hopes that Ellen will understand it is good for a man and woman who love each other to marry and have a family. This must be completely different from what she imagines Ellen experienced in the past. Before Anna can finish her train of thought, she hears John come back into the house. He walks into the sitting room brushing the imaginary dust from his hands as he grins at Anna. Ellen noticed Anna turning 'round and smiles as she turns to see John. Johanna sees her daddy and waves her hand at him.

"Daddy! Daddy! Daddydaddydaddy!"

"Have you made some progress, John?"

John cannot restrain a chuckle at his daughter's greeting before returning his attention to Anna who is waiting for an answer.

"Progress? M'Lady, I have completed the task you set before me. Do I at least get a kiss for my labours?"

Laughing, Anna gets up from the sofa and walks over to John, stands on her tiptoes, and kisses his cheek.

"Let's take our girl outside and show her, John."

Nodding, he looks at Ellen who is staring at the two of them. John points to himself, puts his fist on his chest, points to Ellen, points to his own eyes, points to himself, puts one fist on top of the other several times, holds his fist to his chest and then extends his arm whilst opening his hand, and then points to Ellen. He wants to show Ellen the gift that he made for her. Ellen nods and stands, tilting her head to the side. Anna picks up Johanna and carries her to the kitchen to let Sarah mind their little princess for a whilst. John and Anna lead the way down to the garden where Rupert is already waiting for them, jumping up at the door. John opens the door with a flourish to usher his ladies outside into the deepening shadows attempting to dim the latest of the afternoon. He shuts the door and watches Rupert dash 'round the corner of the house to do whatever it is that dogs do. They watch Ellen, waiting for her to notice the swing. A simple but smooth wooden seat held aloft by two sturdy ropes that clasp a sturdy overhanging branch of the largest tree in the garden attracts her gaze. Ellen's eyes open wide, staring at the swing.

She looks from the hanging thing to the man and the lady. She points to the hanging thing, points to herself, moves her hand back and forth, and then tilts her head.

They nod in reply that yes; this swing is for her. Standing closer to each other, with John's arm 'round Anna's shoulders, they watch Ellen approach the swing. She touches the rope, runs her hand over the smooth wood of the seat, and then walks 'round to sit on it. The seat bumps against the back of her legs, and she turns 'round to look at what bumped into her. With wide eyes, she holds on to the ropes and sits down on the seat. Her mouth opens when the swing moves with the motion and weight of her body. Ellen sits for a moment and then pushes with her feet, causing the swing to go back and forth. A smile growing on her face, she pushes harder, swinging higher. Her dress flutters in the breeze as she kicks her legs in rhythm with her movements. Leaning her head back, she lets her hair flutter 'round her. Eyes closed, she continues to swing, kicking off her shoes. Her whole body adapts to the motion and sensation of this new amusement, with her toes wiggling free in the refreshing air. Her face flushed and happy, with merriment sparkling in her eyes, she let the swing slowly come to a stop. Delighted with Ellen's enjoyment of the swing, they laugh as Ellen skips over to them and grabs Anna's hand, fairly dragging her to the swing.

"Oh my! I guess it's my turn now!"

She points to the lady, points to the thing that moves, and then moves her hands like the thing that moves. She nods her head, pointing to the lady, and then points to the hanging thing.

With a good-hearted laugh, John watches Anna sit down and begin to push with her feet, higher and higher. Anna shakes her hair free of its pins and allows it to flow behind her, flaxen silk in the late afternoon sun. Following Ellen's example, Anna kicks off her shoes and wiggles her toes in the air, marvelling at how good this feels. Laughing, she decides she does not care that her dress has blown above her knees.

"John, I haven't felt this carefree since I was a little girl!"

His arms crossed, leaning against the house, he grins as he watches Anna swing. Ellen claps her hands and bounces on the balls of her feet. Breathless and flushed with elation, Anna brings the swing to a stop. She looks at Ellen with a conspiratorial grin, and the two of them walk over to John.

"Now wait, just hold on a minute...I don't know if the swing..."

Without further ado, Ellen and Anna take John's hands and shepherd him to the swing in spite of his impotent protests. Realising that he is vastly outnumbered, he sits down, looking up at the tree limb. Slowly, he begins to swing, hoping that he will not hear a crack and feel an undignified thump to the ground. Satisfied that the swing will bear his weight, he swings higher, and his soul fills with fun he has not known in many years.

"I'm not going to kick off my shoes, mind you!"

Anna laughs and turns to Ellen to tell her what John said. Ellen grins, turns to John, and frowns at him, with her hands on her hips. With high spirits, John returns the swing to a stop. He gets up, walking over to Ellen and Anna.

"You were both right. That was a great deal of fun. I would imagine that Sarah has our supper ready and we shouldn't delay her. I should clean up a bit before we eat, though."

"Yes, John, you should. I should put away my sewing before Rupert tries to 'help'."

He opens the door for Ellen and Anna to go indoors. Hearing the door, Rupert makes a mad dash towards it and into the house, barking all the way to the kitchen. Anna pats Ellen's arm and waits for Ellen to look down at her arm and then back up at her. She points to John and pantomimes washing, points to the kitchen, and then mimes eating. Ellen nods and walks over to John.

She points to the man, puts one fist on top of the other several times, points to herself, and then draws a smile on her face.

Ellen takes John's hand and squeezes it before she skips to her room.

"Anna, that makes me happier than any swing ever could."

"I feel the same way, John. She trusts you more each day. I'm proud of her and proud of your patience."

Together, they walk to the sitting room, followed by the enticing smell of Sarah's cooking that lures them back to the kitchen. John holds up one finger to tell Anna that he will be back in a moment. Anna watches him disappear up the staircase to wash and change into clean clothes before supper. Anna returns to her chair, folds the fabric upon which she had been working, and then drapes it over the back of it. She gathers up the thread, needles, and scissors, putting the implements of her trade into their box. Anna hears Sarah setting the table and walks over to the staircase to call out to John.

"Sarah is setting the table. Hurry."

Hearing John's muffled reply from upstairs; she walks out of the sitting room and down the hallway to Ellen's room to let her know that supper is ready. Opening Ellen's door, she looks 'round the room. It is empty. Anna feels a desperate urge to find Ellen, remembering her fear when she first laid eyes upon William.

"Sarah! John! Ellen's not in her room."

John comes running down the rest of the staircase and meets Anna in the hallway.

"We saw her go into her room, and I didn't see her upstairs, Anna."

"After seeing William earlier, she was so frightened, and I don't want to leave her alone."

"What? William...?"

Sarah looks out the kitchen windows to see if Ellen is anywhere about. She smiles with relief and calls out.

"Ma'am? Sir? Miss Cup is outside. I can see her!"

Anna and John dash to the garden door and run outside as quickly as they can. A breathtaking sight greets them as thoughts of supper flee. They look at each other in wonder, sharing this moment in silence. Ellen, in the growing shadows, swings with grace. Every detail of her is highlighted by the glow of a sleepy sun, as the pure amusement carries her. Ellen's feet are bare, her skirt, a fluttering butterfly in the breeze, and her hair a mass of gold in the last blazes of glory before night fills the garden.

Chapter Seventeen
23 April 1926

Anna's mind whirls with thoughts of all she must do in preparation for Lady Ashton's visit. To speed things along, Anna helps Sarah clear away the final reminders of their breakfast whilst John spends a few minutes in the sitting room, reading newspaper headlines before he leaves for the shop. Music comes from the wireless, soothing Anna's nerves as it wafts through the house. Ellen sits with Johanna, helping the baby finish her breakfast as Rupert sits nearby, ready to lick away stray crumbs that fall to the floor. Finally, kitchen chores are completed, Johanna is clean, and Sarah is instructed to focus on upstairs tasks as well as minding Johanna for most of the day. Ellen stares at Anna and Sarah from time to time, tilting her head. She removes Johanna's bib and hands the flannel to Sarah. She wanders to the sitting room where John is folding up the newspaper. Ellen stares at John and then sits on the floor next to the bookcase. Rupert turns 'round a few times and lies down next to his friend. She watches John with the newspaper as he stands from his chair. Anna enters and walks over to John to kiss his cheek. Johanna waves to her mum and daddy, carried by Sarah as she walks with her to the staircase. John and Anna wave and blow kisses to Johanna as she looks back over Sarah's shoulder, carried, now, to prevent a tumble. Turning back to John, Anna prods him to be prompt.

"Sweetheart, you'll be late to open the shop."

"I'll be right on time, Anna. Don't worry. I don't expect a queue pressing against the door."

John holds up the newspaper, tilting his head to the side.

"Would you mind if I take this with me? There are a few things I'd like to read if I have time."

"Of course, John. I won't have the time to read any of it today. I'll be busy preparing for Lady Ashton's visit, showing her fabric."

"All right, Anna. Good luck. The whole family can be terribly particular. Every last one of them."

Anna laughs and nods as she pats his chest.

"That's why I'm so nervous, each time."

"It will be all right, Anna. The Wardley family is just like us. They put on one sock at a time."

With a chuckle, John waves to Ellen and nods, acknowledging

Ellen's wave in return. Rupert sits up and wags his tail, watching his master and mistress. Holding hands, John and Anna walk to the entryway. He places his bowler correctly on his head, tucks the newspaper under his arm, and then kisses Anna farewell for the day.

"I'll see you soon, sweet one. I love you."

Anna touches his face and smiles up at him.

"I love you too, John, and I'll miss you."

With that, John opens the front door and exits, leaving the door open for Anna. He walks out to the motor and with a final wave, he gets in, spurring the engine to life. Watching him drive away, Anna sighs when she can no longer see him. She closes the door and returns to the sitting room. Surveying the room and appraising the tidying she would like to accomplish, she strides to the kitchen. The utility cupboard is large, housing the washing machine, the Hoover and miscellaneous cleaning items. Anna chooses a dusting rag, the Hoover, and a yellow pinny, carrying them to their destination. The Dowager Countess of Ashton, her daughter-in-law Lady Ashton, and their children have been a faithful clientele for Anna since the early days of her business as a seamstress. The Dowager Countess will arrive soon after lunch, giving Anna the full morning to release her nervous energy through cleaning. Meeting with aristocratic families has always unnerved Anna.

She begins to dust under Ellen's watchful eye. She gets up from the floor where she has been sitting and stands with her hands folded in front of her, watching Anna. Oblivious to her audience, Anna shudders, finding the music from the wireless grating on her nerves, now. She puts down her dusting rag, walks over to the wireless, and turns it off. Noticing Ellen staring at her, she smiles and returns to pick up her dust cloth to continue. As the faint traces of dirt disappear from surfaces that might be noticeable to someone who has an army of servants to maintain an immaculate mansion, Anna sees Ellen out of the corner of her eye. She is walking across the sitting room to the Hoover. Stopping, Anna watches Ellen approach it.

Taking the handle, Ellen begins to move the device back and forth over the carpet. She has, no doubt, watched Sarah doing the same, and seems to want to help. Anna smiles and shakes her head that Ellen is so sweet to help, but Ellen cannot hear that the Hoover is not turned on, nor is it plugged into a socket. Putting down her dust cloth, Anna walks over Ellen and touches her arm. She waits for Ellen to look down at her arm and then back up at her. Smiling at Ellen to show her that she has not done anything bad or wrong, Anna touches the body of the Hoover where the motor is. She takes Ellen's hand and places it in the same location on the contraption. Ellen looks at Anna with a tilt of her head, pulling her hand away. Anna holds up a finger, unwinds the cord and holds it up for Ellen to see. Anna plugs the cord into the wall outlet and then points to a switch on the side of the machine, turning the Hoover on. Taking Ellen's hand, she places it on the body of the Hoover and watches Ellen's eyes grow wide as she feels the vibration of the gizmo coming to useful life. Smiling, Ellen nods and begins the back and forth motion that Sarah uses with this item. Her eyes grow wider as she sees the nap of the carpet move and bits of this or that disappear with each pass. Each new day brings some novel discovery or insight.

Ellen cleans the rug with the Hoover twice, turns it off, holding her hand to the casing over the motor to feel for vibration. She pulls her hand away quickly from the warmth from the motor. It is not hot, but it is surprising to someone who has never used such a machine before. She walks over to Anna who is fluffing curtains and dusting windowsills. Ellen taps her on the arm and waits for Anna to look down and then look at her.

She points to the floor thing, tilts her head to the side, and pats her hands together.

Anna has to admit that Ellen has done an excellent job of cleaning the area rug. She smiles at Ellen and pats her hands together, saying that Ellen did well. Since the Hoover cleaner is not upright, but a long canister with a hose and wand, Anna has an idea. She holds up her finger to tell Ellen to wait. She watches Anna hurry out of the sitting room, and she stands with her head tilted to the side. Shortly, Anna returns with a small tool for cleaning upholstery. Anna holds up the attachment and walks over to the Hoover. She changes the attachments, affixing the small one. Anna brings the Hoover over to the seating area and takes the cushion off a chair. She holds up the brush tool on the hose, turns on the Hoover, and shows Ellen how to clean Rupert's fur off the furniture. It wouldn't do at all for Lady Ashton's fancy dress to be covered in dog hair. Smiling and nodding her head, Ellen moves closer and takes the upholstery tool in her hand. She stoops down to feel for vibration, turns it on, and nods. She Hoovers the chair, mindful of every nook and cranny. In this way, she cleans each piece of upholstered furniture in the sitting room.

Her dusting and straightening completed at about the same time Ellen finishes with the Hoover, Anna looks at the time. There is just enough time for lunch and donning a clean dress. Removing her pinny, she looks up the staircase, watching Sarah bring Johanna downstairs.

"Sarah, if you'd prepare a light lunch for us, I'd appreciate it. I'm going to change my dress whilst you do that."

"Yes, Ma'am, that was my intention. I'll put away the Hoover."

Looking over at Ellen, Sarah is surprised to see her holding the hose with the upholstery brush in her hand, smiling.

"Ma'am, did Miss Cup use the Hoover? My goodness, she's done a fine job! Would you tell her for me, please? I'm so, so proud of her if I may say."

"I'm proud of her as well. Of course, Sarah. I will tell her."

To relieve Sarah of her angelic burden, Anna scoops Johanna out of Sarah's arms, kissing her baby girl to make her laugh. Handing her pinny to Sarah, she watches their housekeeper and nanny bustle off to the kitchen. Anna steadies the child on her feet and points to Ellen.

"Go to Ellen, sweetheart. She'll take you to the kitchen for lunch."

"Mamma, Cuppa Cuppa, yummmmmmmmm!"

Ellen watches Johanna, crouches down and then opens her arms. A huge smile welcomes her as she toddles into Ellen's arms. Ellen stands, holding Johanna's hand and she looks at Anna, tilting her head. Anna points to Johanna and to the kitchen, asking Ellen to take Johanna to the kitchen. Anna holds up one finger, almost forgetting to give Ellen the message from Sarah. Anna points to the kitchen, points to her own head, points to Ellen, gestures 'round the room, pantomimes using the Hoover, and then pats her hands together. Ellen nods, seeming to understand that Sarah thought she did a good job cleaning. Anna flares her dress out slightly, frowning, brushing off imaginary dirt, pointing upstairs, pointing to her dress, and then patting her hands together, she tells Ellen that she will go upstairs to change her dress. It would not do for her to look shabby for Lady Ashton's visit. Ellen nods and crouches down to kiss Johanna's head. Johanna puts her fist on her chest, points to Ellen, and then points to the kitchen whilst speaking.

"Janna wanna go chen."

Ellen walks with Johanna to the kitchen where Sarah is busy making lunch. Ellen lifts Johanna into her high chair and holds one finger up to the baby. Seemingly, the child understands, quieting, and laying her hands on the tray. Ellen walks over to Sarah, pats her shoulder, causing Sarah to jump slightly, surprised by this interruption. Ellen steps back a pace and tilts her head to the side.

She points to the baby and pats her hands together. She points to herself, pulls at the flower dress, moves her hand against it, and then points to her room.

Sarah looks at Johanna, nods and smiles, hoping that this is the appropriate response to Miss Cup. She watches Ellen walk out of the kitchen and then turns back to the makings of a meal. Reaching her room, Ellen finds Rupert peeking out from under the bed. Crouching, she reaches out her hand, coaxing him out. Ellen pats the bed, and Rupert jumps up, wagging his tail before he lies down with a plop. She closes her bedroom door and opens her armoire. She selects a yellow dress and lays it over the back of a chair. Removing the flowered dress, she folds it and puts it on her bed. She slips into the yellow dress and turns to look at herself in the full-length looking glass. Ellen stares at herself, smoothing down her skirt. Sighing, she turns and motions to Rupert, telling him to follow her. Obediently, Rupert hops off the bed and follows Ellen to the sitting room. She watches Anna come down the last few steps and stands with her hands folded in front of herself.

Anna suppresses a chuckle that Ellen has also changed her dress. There was no need, but Anna guesses that since she went upstairs to change hers that Ellen assumes she should change her dress, as well. Ellen does look nice, though, so Anna points to Ellen's dress and then draws a circle 'round her face to tell Ellen that her dress looks pretty. Anna is sensitive to the fact that Ellen reacts with discomfort when she is told she is pretty. As a result, she and John have learnt to focus their compliments on individual aspects of her appearance that are pretty. Ellen seems to be more at ease with this approach. Pointing to Ellen and herself, she points to the kitchen and pantomimes eating. Ellen nods and follows Anna to the kitchen. The table set with simple fare, place settings, and beverages, Sarah has settled in to supervise Johanna's meal. Rupert dashes to sit next to Johanna, looking up at his little friend. Sarah looks down at Rupert and shakes her finger at him.

"Master Rupert, you know better than to beg at the table. Off with you, now."

Rupert continues to sit, staring, first from Sarah, then to Johanna. Ellen sees Rupert's disobedience and walks 'round the table to hold up one finger to him. The dog hangs his head and skulks off to his corner to lie down, his chin resting on his paws.

"Ma'am, I don't know how Miss Cup does that, but I wish I had that gift."

"I know what you mean, Sarah. She has a way with animals that I couldn't begin to understand."

Ellen and Anna take their seats at the table, and everyone finishes lunch in short order, thanks to its simplicity. Anna motions for Ellen to follow her into the sitting room. She has an idea that might help Ellen understand more clearly that someone influential is coming. Anna pats the cushion on the sofa, and Ellen sits, watching Anna walk over to the bookcase and pulls out a photograph album. Returning to the sofa, Anna sits next to her and flips through the pages until she finds one that will suit. She shows Ellen a photograph of an older, dignified, and aristocratic woman staring back at them from the page. The photographer, no doubt, asked her to smile, and she did not acquiesce to his request. Her hair is full and dressed to accommodate a tiara and what little can be seen of her gown displays light playing off silk with lace and a cameo brooch gracing a pearl choker. Lady Ashton, The Dowager Countess, gave this photograph to Anna as a token of gratitude for creating this gown.

Ellen stares at the picture and tilts her head as she looks at Anna. Anna points to the image, points to the front door, and points to the floor, points to her own eyes, and then points to the fabric assembled nearby. All this to help Ellen understand that this woman is coming to look at the fabric.

Her eyes grow wide, and she draws an X in her hand, tilting her head to the side. She points to herself and then points to her sleeping place.

Anna shakes her head. There is no need for Ellen to leave the room. She points to the picture of Lady Ashton and then pats her hands together to say that she is a good woman. Ellen continues to stare at Anna and moves to the furthest place on the sofa with her hands folded in front of her. Getting up to put the photograph album away, Anna stops to reach down, patting Ellen's hands in a reassuring gesture. She returns the album to its place on the shelf and looks about the room, nervous that everything should be perfect. This is not Ashton Hall, but it is as presentable as she can make it. Sarah walks through the sitting room, having finished in the kitchen, holding Johanna's hand. Johanna waves and tries to keep up with Sarah. Sarah stops to watch Johanna point to herself, point to her mother, point to Ellen, and then point upstairs.

"Mamma...Cuppa...nappy."

"Yes, darling, it's time for your nap. Mamma and Ellen will stay here. Be a good girl for Sarah! I love you, my sweet."

"Lovva Mamma Cuppy!"

Anna watches Johanna pat her chest as she talks. Sarah lifts Johanna and takes her upstairs as Ellen attracts Rupert's attention and points upstairs. He obediently follows Sarah and his little friend. Hearing a knock at the door, or rather, a sharp rapping sound, Anna hurries to the front door and opens it. There stands Lady Ashton, cane in hand, dressed to perfection. The sound Anna heard was Lady Ashton's cane against the door.

"M'Lady. Please come in."

"Always a pleasure, Anna. I don't expect this will take long. I've told the chauffeur to wait."

"Of course, M'Lady. I have the fabrics out and ready for your inspection."

With an imperious nod of her head and a genuine smile, Lady Ashton walks to the sitting room and stands, waiting for Anna to close the door and join her. She cannot help but notice the young woman sitting on the sofa, turned to stare at her. Anna returns to the sitting room and sees Ellen staring at the titled lady.

"Anna, this must be the young woman about whom I've heard? The one who can't hear or speak?"

"Yes, M'Lady. We named her Ellen. Please don't be offended by her timidity. She is fearful of strangers at first. How...how did you hear...?"

Lady Ashton chuckles, waves her hand in a dismissive gesture, and walks through the sitting room to a chair near the fabric display.

"Anna, it would take far more than the fear of an innocent girl to offend me. And hearing of her? I have my eyes and ears everywhere."

"Thank you. I didn't think of...pardon me, M'Lady, I translate for Ellen in gestures, so she doesn't feel isolated with people speaking all 'round her."

"By all means, Anna. Do what you must for the poor child."

She watches in fascination with the gestures between Anna and this girl they call Ellen. Such a novel yet effective means of communication. The explanation to Ellen complete, Anna turns to Lady Ashton.

"Please, sit wherever you like, M'Lady. I fear I've forgotten to make tea, and I hope you'll forgive me for neglecting my manners."

"No, no, dear Anna. The greatest houses in England could learn a thing or two from you about genuine hospitality. I rather enjoy the change from boring social obligations."

"Thank you, M'Lady. You're very kind. Now, the fabrics..."

Lady Ashton takes her seat whilst Anna holds out the first of many samples of material for Her Ladyship to see, bringing them close to touch and examine. Pictures of conservatively modern gowns are offered for Lady Ashton to consider, and she chooses two that appeal to her.

"Goodness. I'm becoming rather modern and almost racy in my dotage."

Anna stifles a chuckle, thinking that a woman in her sixtieth year is hardly in her twilight years. She sobers, though, remembering why Lady Ashton is now the Dowager Countess. Her husband, the fifth Earl of Ashton, died far sooner than he should have during a foxhunt, leaving Lady Ashton, a widow. His horse stumbled, and he met his untimely end from the fall, resulting in a broken neck. His death brought her son and daughter-in-law, Charles and Amelia Wardley, hereditary titles, making them the sixth Earl and Countess of Ashton. Anna wonders for a flash of a moment how she could ever explain to Ellen the class structure that is slowly dying in England.

"M'Lady, you've the right to wear what you please, if I may say. Further, your tastes have always set your features to the greatest advantage. I'm honoured that you entrust your wardrobe to me."

"My dear, I wouldn't have another pair of hands..."

Their conversation interrupted, they see Ellen standing next to them, staring from Lady Ashton to Anna, and then back again. Anna tilts her head to the side, asking Ellen what is on her mind.

She points to the old lady, points to her own nose, and holds one hand up with the other hand pushing up from behind, her fingers extending outward like a flower pushing out of the ground.

"Wha...what did she say, Anna? I rather feel quite the foreigner here."

Lady Ashton chuckles as she compares this to a foreign language, and it is, to her. Anna smiles with slight embarrassment.

"Ellen said...well...she told me you smell like flowers."

"Oh! My goodness. Why, yes, I am wearing an eau de toilette with a faint note of roses. She does make keen observations. I'm impressed."

Anna feels a patting on her arm and looks down at her arm, and then at Ellen.

She points to herself, places her fist on her chest, points to her own eyes, points to the old lady, and then points outside.

With an inward groan covered by a smile, Anna holds up one finger to Ellen. Ellen steps straight past Anna without looking at her gesture to wait a moment. Ellen stands in front of Her Ladyship and takes her hand. She motions for The Dowager Countess to come with her.

"Anna? Do help me, here. What is she doing?"

"I'm terribly sorry, M'Lady. She wants to show you something outside in the garden. She doesn't understand..."

Taking Ellen's hand, she uses her help and that of her cane to rise from Anna Thorpe's impossibly comfortable chair.

"Tut, tut, Anna. I'm determined to enjoy every moment away from the estate. If the girl wishes to show me something, I'll be glad to see it. She's a sweet child. What harm could there be in it?"

Both Ellen and Lady Ashton ignore Anna's futile protests and apologies, as she follows them out the door to the garden. In her nervous state of mind, Anna forgets to close the door, more concerned that Lady Ashton should not fall.

"Please be careful, M'Lady. The ground is uneven in places..."

"Nonsense. I have a skilled guiding hand here."

Anna stays as close to Lady Ashton as she can, cringing inside that this sort of thing is just not proper. Ellen urges Her Ladyship towards the swing and Anna's eyes grow wide. Oh, no...not that...not Lady Ashton of all people...

"I'm so sorry, M'Lady, I'm not so sure this is a good idea..."

Anna wonders how she would ever explain to Lord and Lady Ashton that The Dowager Countess came to injury by a swing in a garden of all things. Ellen leads the matriarch of the Wardley family to the swing. She pats the seat and moves her hand in a back and forth motion to explain how the swing works. A benevolent chuckle escapes Lady Ashton's lips as she gives Anna her cane. She turns to sit carefully on the swing, glad that her feet firmly make contact with the ground beneath her.

"My goodness. This is an adventure. Nothing ventured, nothing gained, as they say."

Smiling, she slowly begins to move the swing, watching Ellen smile and make gestures that apparently tell her to swing higher. Pushing her feet a bit harder, she does reach a height and rhythm of that elates her. The smile on Ellen's face, the precise meaning of Ellen's pointing to her and drawing a smile on her own face is something she understands instinctively. Lady Ashton has not felt this happy since she was in the care of an affectionate nanny. The world and all its concerns fade away to the breeze on her, her dress lifting slightly like a flower in bloom. Her hair escapes from their pins when her hat flies off her head, to Anna's horror as she dashes to pick it up before it becomes soiled. Anna is convinced that the lady's maid who tends to Lady Ashton's every need and want would come to throttle her if the hat came to ruin. Breathless and exhilarated, Lady Ashton brings the swing to a stop, amazed and dazed with wonder that such a simple contraption could make her feel so young and free. Patting her chest to coax her breath back, Lady Ashton makes a motion for Anna to bring her cane.

"Anna, I'm well over fifty years out of practice, but the joy is the same as it was when I was a small girl. I wish I knew how to thank Ellen for giving me the joy and fun of my childhood that I had all but forgotten."

Unseen by the three women in the garden, William remains 'round the corner of the house, wishing to avoid intrusion. He is familiar with Lady Ashton by reputation, having delivered goods from the market to the servants' entrance of Ashton Hall. He would rather not incur her wrath by interrupting her visit with Mrs Thorpe. He can hear their voices, but frustration pokes at him because he is unable to hear what the women are saying. He waits, holding the box of chocolates he brought for Ellen. Smiling, he traces his finger on the raised design on the lid, hoping that she will like them. He also hopes that she will not be afraid of him and will accept this as the best apology he can give since she cannot hear him. The thought occurs to him that Mrs Thorpe may not be pleased that he comes without notice or invitation. A closing door snaps him out of his reverie, and he peeks 'round the corner of the house. He grins with relief as he sees that Mrs Thorpe has taken Old Lady Ashton back inside. As he watches Ellen walk 'round the garden, he takes off his hat and enters the garden. William is careful that he does not approach too closely, so he stands, waiting for Ellen to notice him. He watches her walk from one flowering shrub to the next, then stopping. She holds out her hand, and his mouth drops as a butterfly alights on her finger. He sees the smile on her face from the profile view he has of her as she touches her finger to the delicate wings. William almost drops the box of boiled and chocolate sweets thanks to the distraction of such a pretty vision. She lifts her finger, and the butterfly takes its leave from her finger, alighting on a flower nearby.

William stares at the butterfly opening and closing its wings that look like peacock feathers. Intently watching the trusting insect, he does not notice Ellen turned towards him, staring, her hands folded in front of herself. When he does notice, with a start, he smiles, nods, and holds the tin out for Ellen to see it.

"Hello...I reckon you remember me. I'm still awfully sorry I scared you the way I did last time I was here. I'm not making a real delivery, I just wanted to deliver somethin' special to you, you know, to make up for..."

Mentally, he kicks himself for flapping his gob like the village idiot since Ellen cannot hear him anyway. What she must think of him! He smiles and nods, walks a pace closer, holds up the tin of chocolates, points to himself, and then holds it out towards Ellen.

"This is from me to you. I brought this for you."

He sees Ellen tilt her head, her eyes wide, looking at the door to the house and then back to him. She points to herself, and he figures that she is wondering if this really is for her. He takes a leap of faith and moves closer to Ellen, making sure she can run inside if she wishes. He holds out the tin, again, nodding, hoping that she will take it. He watches her reach out her hand to take the tin box. He grins as she opens the box and sniffs it, a smile teasing the corners of her mouth, making her pretty face even prettier. She takes a piece of chocolate, closes the lid of the box, and hands the tin back to him. She nods whilst she nibbles the treat. He does not know what to say to help Ellen understand he wants her to have the whole box, not just one piece. He holds it out to her, again, this time pointing to himself, gesturing to the entire box, and pointing at Ellen.

"No, I mean, I want you to have the whole thing. It's for you."

She tilts her head and takes the tin back in her hands, staring at the box. She opens the lid, holds it out to William, and he assumes that she is offering him a piece. As he takes one, nodding his thanks, he pops it in his mouth and nearly chokes on it when Mrs Thorpe comes out of the house.

"Good afternoon, William. We weren't expecting a market delivery today, were we?"

He gulps the chocolate down and stands up straight, his cap dampening in his sweaty hands.

"Uh, no, Ma'am. I was just making a special delivery to, uh, Ellen to make up for scaring her. I hope you don't mind. I reckon I should have asked permission. Golly, I'm sorry for being a dope, Mrs Thorpe. I wouldn't blame you if you were angry with me. I'll go if you want me to."

Anna smiles at William's thoughtful gesture and turns to Ellen to translate. She points to William, holds her fist to her chest and then extends her arm outwards with her fingers opening, points to Ellen, points to the box of chocolates, puts her hands together at her chest and moves them towards Ellen, crossing her arms in front of herself, and then points to Ellen. William's eyes grow wide, the flurry of gestures making a whooshing sound as they fly straight over his head.

"Gosh, Mrs Thorpe. I'm sorry, I didn't understand any of what you said. I've never seen anything like it."

"It's all right, William. It's not the usual sort of sign language taught in a special school. These are just our gestures that we've invented along the way. I told Ellen that the chocolate is a gift from you which is your way of asking forgiveness for frightening her."

"Well, yes, that's the sum of it, Ma'am. I'll be going now. I didn't mean to intrude."

Ellen tilts her head to the side, watching the exchange between William and Anna. She holds out the box of sweets to Anna, opening the lid. With a smile, she nods at Ellen and takes a piece, nibbling it before it melts in her hand.

"Those are delicious chocolates, William. I'm sure Ellen appreciates them. If Ellen is comfortable with you staying, you may. That choice is hers to make."

William watches Mrs Thorpe gesture to Ellen and holds his breath to see if Ellen wants him to stay or go. His question is answered when Ellen looks at him for a moment and then nods her head before walking into the house.

"Uh, Mrs Thorpe? I might be wrong for asking this, but I have to. May I come 'round to see Ellen from time to time? I don't want to be a bother, but maybe now and then. She's really nice and...well...I'd like to see her...be a friend."

"It's all right, William. Just know that Mr Thorpe and I will be close in case Ellen needs us. I'm surprised she didn't run inside when she realised she was alone with you. That's good, though. Maybe she realises that more people are good than bad and trusting me when I say someone is a good person."

William's stammering is suffocated by his boyish grin.

"Thank you, Mrs Thorpe. I won't be a nuisance, I promise, and I won't do anything to scare Ellen. In fact, I'd like to learn how to talk to her, so I don't feel so...well...you know...dumb."

"William, all in due time. Thank you for bringing Ellen chocolate. That is her favourite treat. It was the right choice. I'm going inside, and I think you have other places to be and other things to do, am I right?"

Eyes wide, nodding his head, he begins to back away at Mrs Thorpe's raised eyebrow and not-so-subtle hint, he takes his leave. With that grin still on his face, whistling and humming, he slaps his cap to his head. He stuffs one hand in the pocket of his trousers that he had put on just for this occasion. He muses to himself as he walks back to his bedsit above the market, that he will have to save his pennies to improve his Sunday best if he is going to be out visiting a really nice girl.

Hearing William's whistle fade into the distance, Anna smiles to herself as she goes back into the house. Could it be possible that Ellen has made a friend? A friend of her own age? That would be something uniquely special for Ellen. A friend of her own that is hers, not someone who is a friend of the family. Ellen has gone into her room, by the looks of the closed door, so she walks to the kitchen to join the happy voices of Sarah, Johanna, and Rupert's barking.

Ellen circles 'round her bedroom, setting down the box of chocolate sweets, then picking it up, then placing it in another spot, and then finally sitting down on a chair. She holds it in her lap, staring at it. With one finger, she traces 'round the raised picture on the lid. The palm of her hand smooths over the textured tin as she closes her eyes. Opening her eyes, she looks up to see herself in the full-length looking glass. She sits, staring at her reflection.

Chapter Eighteen
30 April 1926

Ellen crouches down, careful to keep her favourite dress clean as she tugs at weeds reaching through the soil to find sunlight. The flowers in the little garden patch are full of promise, but the green interlopers are threatening to overgrow them. She spies a nightcrawler squirming about in the open and looks up 'round her, then back to the nightcrawler. She pokes a finger deep into the soil, wiggles it 'round, and picks up the nightcrawler, stroking its length with her dirty finger. Guiding its head into the safety of the hole, the nightcrawler wriggles off her hand, making its way deep into the moist darkness. She smiles, covering up the hole when it has gone deep enough to escape a bird's appetite. In no time at all, Ellen has plucked every weed out of the garden. She stands, stretches, and gathers the weeds to toss them over the fence, sending them to certain doom in a shaded hollow. She walks 'round the garden to examine the flowering bushes whilst Rupert romps about, jumping at every twittering bird he sees. A stick lying on the ground near her swing catches her eye, and she picks it up. Looking 'round, she sees a patch of dirt next to the garden bench and walks over to it. Crouching, one arm 'round her knees to keep her dress out of the way, she stares at the dirt for a moment. She sticks her tongue out the corner of her mouth slightly, the stick is poised in her hand. Rupert trots over to sit next to Ellen and leans his head against her arm, wagging his tail. She lays the stick down, scratches his ears, and then watches the dog run off to play. Picking up the stick, again, she traces words in the dirt. DOG, GIRL, BOY, ELLEN, ANNA, and CUP. She lays the stick down, sits back on her heels, and looks at what she has written. Nodding her head, she stands, sits on the garden bench with her hands folded in her lap, and looks 'round her. Her gaze falls upon the two colourful rocks resting between the bench and her writing. A panting Rupert walks to his friend and lies on her feet with his head on his paws.

Walking up the lane towards the Thorpe house, William whistles a jaunty tune. He hopes, with a little more money saved, he will be able to buy something nice for himself. Looking down, he makes a face at the trousers that have seen better days. Lewis even teased William about saving his wage packet. As if Lewis had ever planned ahead or used money wisely. William wishes he had never said anything to him. True to form, Lewis launched into a taunting litany of jibes about the evils of hoarding money and greed. William finally set the matter to rest with a final comment that would have set his late mother's teeth on edge. William considers that whilst he is no aristocrat, he should be a decent man with decent manners, the way his mother raised him. Arriving, William finds that he has walked more quickly than he expected. Smiling, he walks 'round to the garden gate. He stops when he sees Ellen sitting on the bench, and he watches her. He wonders why she stares at a couple of pretty rocks. They are unusual and beautiful, but they are rocks.

Pushing the gate open, William walks through, and then closes the gate behind him. Stopping to take off his cap, he folds it, and stuffs the old thing in his back pocket, making a mental note to add a new cap to the list of items he wants to purchase. He looks at Ellen and wonders how to move closer without startling her. He decides to come slowly and from in front of her so she will spot him. Rupert sees William first, gets up, and runs towards him to welcome the familiar chap. He bends down to give the dog some attention since Rupert is one of the few dogs that are friendly when he makes deliveries. Ellen raises her head, her eyes following Rupert, and she stares at William whilst he plays with the dog. Smiling, William waves to Ellen and walks closer as soon as he notices that she is looking at him.

"Good evening, Ellen. I came by to see you. I thought it may be nice to visit for a whilst if you don't mind."

William wishes he knew Ellen's language so he could 'talk' with her. Speaking when he knows she cannot hear makes him feel stupid and inadequate. He wonders if he asked Mrs Thorpe, she might teach him a little of Ellen's language. He is eager to learn, and he is sincere in his willingness to try. Slowly, he walks closer towards Ellen and is glad that she does not appear afraid. A little wary, perhaps, but she is not getting up to move away from him. He sits on the ground near her, but not too close. Rupert scoots under the bench and peeks out at William from behind his friend's legs. The silence makes the rustling leaves, and singing birds seem louder than usual by comparison. He glimpses a few long blades of grass next to the bench, so he plucks them, holding them up to show Ellen. She tilts her head, and William is happy to see that she seems to relax a little bit. He plaits the grass together into what looks like a chain of squares. He holds it up for Ellen to see, smiles and then holds it out to her. A heartbeat of angst seizes him as Ellen continues to stare at him. Then, slowly, she takes the woven grass from him, placing it in her hand to examine it. She nods and hands it back to William.

She points to the grass thing and draws a circle 'round her face.

William knows that Ellen said something about what he had made, but he does not understand her. Sighing, he stretches out his legs, leans back on his elbows, and looks up into a tree. His eyes catch the shape of a nest cradling baby birds who are poking up their heads, clamouring for their mother to bring them food. With Ellen still staring at him, he is grateful that he can draw her attention to this confirmation of spring. He smiles, using the best and only form of communication he has, as he points up to the tree. Ellen tilts her head to the side and then looks up where William is pointing. He watches her stare and nod, satisfied that she sees the nest, too. After they look at the mother bird arrive, feed her young, and fly away, Ellen turns to him and nods.

She links her thumbs together, moves her hands like a bird, cradles her arms as if holding a baby, tilts her head back, opens her mouth, and pantomimes dropping food in her mouth.

William feels a rush of encouragement. He understood what she told him! He knows that she was talking about the mother bird feeding her babies. He nods enthusiastically with a grin on his face.

She nods, points up at the birds, looks back to the young man, and then draws a circle 'round her face.

Seeing her draw the circle 'round her face, again, he wonders what that means. This is the second time she has used that gesture, and it puzzles him.

She points up to the birds, points to herself, cradles her arms as if holding a baby, points to herself, and then draws an X on the palm of her hand.

William is taken aback by what he is able to understand. Ellen has a baby? The X in Ellen's hand confuses him, though. He watches Ellen, her blue eyes watering, bowing her head, and then staring at her hands. Taking in this surprising news, all he can do is sit quietly next to her. He hears the door to the house open and turns to see who it is as Mrs Thorpe is closing the door behind her and walks over to them.

"I saw you sitting with Ellen, William. Is anything wrong?"

Anna turns to Ellen, tilts her head to the side, and pats her hands

215

together to ask if everything is all right. Ellen continues to sit there, looking at her hands. Ellen's posture tells her that Ellen must be sad about something. William stands and nods still perplexed at what Ellen said to him.

"Yes, it is, I guess. At least, I think so. Ellen said something that puzzles me and, I think it makes her sad."

"Oh? What did she say?"

William describes the gestures Ellen used, and Anna sighs with a nod of her head.

"I'm pretty sure that she told me she has a baby, but I don't know what the X in her hand means."

"Yes, she did say she had a baby. She must trust you to tell you that. Pointing to herself and drawing an X in her hand is her way of saying that she thinks she is bad."

"I'm sorry, Mrs Thorpe....she looks so sad, and all I could think of to do was sit here with her. May I ask what happened...and to the baby?"

"William, let's walk a little way towards the swing."

Anna turns to Ellen who is staring at them moving their mouths, and she smiles at Ellen. Anna points to herself and William, points over to the tree holding the swing, and then places her fingers near her mouth, moving them as if talking. Ellen nods, looking back down at her hands. Anna and William walk to the tree, and Anna turns to William.

"You see, we've pieced together that Ellen had a baby. Everything she's said about the baby tells us that he or she was taken from her at birth. We're trying to find the child. We assume that something terrible happened to her over time as her fear of people in general and of men, in particular, shows. We don't know what, exactly, but we've put two and two together to guess."

William looks down at his feet, trying to comprehend.

"No wonder she's sad. I'm sorry for what happened to her. I don't know what to say."

"Just be her friend, William. She must trust you, or she wouldn't have told you that. I believe that it means a great deal to her to have a friend who is HER friend. She knows the people in our circle, but it's not the same. Let's go back to her, now."

William nods, his imagination whirling with this revelation of Ellen's horrible experiences. As Anna and William return to Ellen, they hear the garden gate open and close. They turn to see Clara coming towards them, accosted by Rupert's greeting.

"Down boy. I'm happy to see you too!"

Clara reaches down to scratch the dog's ears and then walks over to Anna, Ellen, and William.

"It's a lovely evening, isn't it?"

"Yes, it is, Clara. This is William, Ellen's new friend that I mentioned when you rang to ask if you could come."

"Oh yes. I'm glad Ellen has a friend her own age. It can't be easy for her."

Clara turns to greet William, and he reaches to take off his hat, realising that he has already stuck it in his pocket. With a sheepish grin, he nods at Mrs Dewhurst.

"Yes, Ma'am, it's good to see you, Ma'am."

Ellen stares at the three of them moving their mouths and looks down at her hands. Anna holds up a finger.

"Ellen is probably wondering what we're saying to each other. I'll tell her."

Anna crouches down to Ellen's level, points to herself, William, Ellen, and Clara, draws a smile on her face, points to her own eyes, and then points to all of them again. She wants Ellen to know that the subject of conversation is greetings that mean they are happy to see each other and Ellen. Ellen looks at each of them and nods.

"Anna, as we spoke on the telephone, I wanted to come sooner rather than later. May we go inside?"

"Of course, Clara. I'll make some tea."

Anna looks at Ellen who is staring at them, points to herself and Clara, and then points to the house. Clara and Anna begin to walk towards the door when Ellen rises from her seat and hurries to catch up to the two women. William watches, curious to see what Ellen is doing. Ellen tugs on Clara's sleeve, and Clara stops to look at Ellen, tilting her head. She pulls Clara by the sleeve back to the patch of dirt next to the bench where she had written some of the words she knows. William follows just close enough to be able to see what Ellen is doing. She points to the word DOG and points to Rupert who is sniffing William's pant leg. She points to the word GIRL and points to herself. She points to the word BOY, hesitates, and then points to William. She points to the word ELLEN and points to herself. She points to the word ANNA, and taps two fingers on her chest whilst pointing to Anna. She points to the word CUP, looks 'round, and then looks up at Clara with one finger raised. She gets up and hurries into the house as the three of them look at each other, wondering what Ellen is going to do. Rupert trots behind Ellen into the house, his paws making an audible rhythm on the hardwood floor inside. They watch through the open door, and in a moment, Ellen returns with a teacup. She places the teacup next to the word CUP, points to the name, and then to the cup. She points to the word CUP, points to herself, shakes her head and then draws an X in her hand. With a chuckle, Clara points to the words, pats her hands together, points to the name ELLEN, and then points to Ellen. Ellen nods her head and looks at William. Fascinated, he looks at the words in the dirt, at Ellen, at Anna, and then at Clara.

"Um, may I ask what these words mean? Well, I know what they mean, but...Oh, golly, I don't know how to say it."

Anna gives William a kind smile.

"It's all right, William. You see, when Ellen first came here, she was not only unable to hear or speak, she couldn't read or write, either. I have been able to teach her a little and Ellen is quick to learn. For a little whilst, in her excitement, she confused the words ELLEN and CUP. In other words, she thought her name was Cup. Johanna and Sarah still call her Cup, each in their own way."

"Oh, I see. She does seem smart, just a feeling I get. If I were Ellen, I'd be really proud of that."

"She is, William. She does not show many people her accomplishments. Apparently, you can count yourself amongst those she trusts enough to share these parts of herself. Now, Mrs Dewhurst and I need to go inside and have our chat. If you'll excuse us."

Clara turns to Ellen and points to herself, points to the door, moves her fingers by her mouth as if talking, and then taps two fingers on her chest.

Ellen nods, points to herself, draws a smile on her face, points to her own eyes, and then points to the helping lady.

Clara returns the gesture to confirm that she is happy to see Ellen, as well. Clara and Anna walk into the house, leaving William and Ellen. She walks back to the bench to sit down with her hands folded in her lap. William sits back down on the ground near her, growing accustomed to the quiet. He is hearing sounds he had hardly noticed before with people 'round him talking. He looks up at Ellen who is staring at him, now. She leans down to pick up the stick that was lying on the ground next to the bench.

She points to the lady's name, taps two fingers on her chest. She points to her name and points to herself. She points to the shiny thing on the young man's arm, points to the young man, and then taps two fingers on her wrist. She points to the young man and taps two fingers on her wrist.

He watches Ellen and puzzles together what she is telling him. Names. His eyes grow wide as he realises that Ellen gave him a name in her language. He smiles, nods, points to himself, and then taps two fingers on his wrist, understanding that Ellen must have noticed his wristwatch. A mixture of feelings rumbles through his chest. He feels honoured that Ellen has given him his own name, yet he feels sorry for Ellen, having been through a lifetime of horrible ordeals. Ellen nods at him and then looks down at her hands. They sit together for a little whilst until the shadows lengthen and William's sense of propriety tell him that it is time to go. He waves to get Ellen's attention, and when she looks at him, he points to himself, points to the rising moon, points to himself, and points to the gate. He feels clumsy in how he tries to tell Ellen that he should leave because it is getting late. She looks up, nods at him, and then stands with her hands folded in front of her. He backs away towards the gate, waving, and then stops to smile at Ellen and wave to her again. He leaves the garden and disappears 'round the corner of the house. Ellen's measured paces carry her to the gate, and she peers 'round the corner. She watches him walk away with his hands in his pockets, looking down at his feet. Her eyes follow until he is no longer in sight. Turning to look at the swing, she walks over to it, sits, and moves it slightly with her feet whilst looking down at her hands that are folded in her lap.

In the kitchen, Clara's mood and expression turn sombre as Anna finishes making their tea. Together, they walk into the sitting room where they settle on the sofa for a serious chat. Clara clears her throat and looks into her teacup, summoning what strength might flow from the amber liquid. She is filled with sadness, failure, and dread at her role as the bearer of bad news. Taking a sip of her tea, Anna leans forwards and sets her cup aside.

"What is it, Clara? What was so urgent that you couldn't explain over the telephone?"

"I...I'm afraid I have bad news, Anna. Father Willington and I exhausted all avenues in our search for Ellen's baby. We found hospital, church, and municipal records between the years 1900 and 1925. We searched for someone who might be her mother, who might be Ellen and the baby. We sifted through marriage, death, and birth entries. We found nothing. There was so little information, but we did try. I'm so sorry, Anna."

The assault of such news feels like a kick to her chest and Anna's eyes fill with tears. Her voice quavers with misery for her sweet daughter as she looks ahead of her at nothing in particular and tries to speak.

"We knew there was little chance, but we still hoped…"

"I know, Anna. We all held on to a small flame of hope. I wish I could have brought you happy news."

"You and Father Willington did the best you could on Ellen's behalf, but how do I tell her this? How?"

Clara aches at Anna's earnest plea and for Ellen, knowing this will be especially heartbreaking for her. Clara sets down her teacup, wraps her arm 'round her friend's shoulders and pulls Anna close. She fears that her words will fall flat, impotent to comfort in the face of resurfacing grief.

"I don't know, dear, but somehow, I know your love for her will find a way."

Clara places her hand over Anna's hand and squeezes it fondly.

"Anna, I need to go, now, but I wish I could stay. Are you and Ellen going to be all right?"

Anna nods, desperately trying to maintain her composure and failing.

"John…John will be home soon from his meeting…I'll tell Ellen when she comes inside…I guess we'll be…"

"All right, Anna, I'll leave through the front door. She'll come inside when she's ready. Perhaps that will give you time to collect your thoughts and consider the best way to tell her. I…"

At a loss for words, Clara gives Anna's shoulders another gentle caress and kisses her friend's hair. She stands, stoops to pick up her handbag, then sees herself to the front door, and then opens it, pausing. Taking a deep and ragged breath, she walks through. Closing the door, Clara feels as if she is closing the door on faith. A reunion between Ellen and her baby would have been…Clara shakes her head and walks away, staving off her own tears with a determination she prayed would not fail her, now.

Sitting alone, Anna breaks down in tears. Sobbing into her handkerchief, her whole body gives way to grief on behalf of Ellen and the dashed hope of her baby's return. Anna does not hear Ellen come into the house and then to the sitting room. She stands in the doorway, stares at Anna, and then hurries across the room to crouch down in front of her. She pats Anna's arm with her head tilted to the side. Anna looks at her arm and then at Ellen, trying to dry her eyes on the wet and useless handkerchief. She tosses the soggy thing aside, using her sleeve instead. Anna tries to calm herself, but pressing the back of her hand to her face is not enough to cool the redness of her eyes or cheeks from the storm of tears. Anna pats the cushion of the sofa next to her, inviting Ellen to sit next to her and Ellen does as Anna requests.

She looks at the lady, tilts her head to the side, points to the lady, draws a frown on her face, and draws a line on her face downwards from her eye.

She looks into Ellen's eyes, wishing she had a better way to explain why she is weeping. Anna had hoped this moment would never come, no matter how inevitable it was. She breathes deeply and composes herself to tell Ellen the truth as she and John have always done. Ellen deserves the truth, but she does not deserve these tidings. Looking at Ellen, she draws an X in her hand, points to her own eyes, and then cradles her arms as if holding a baby to tell Ellen that they could not find her baby. Ellen clenches her hands together in her lap, her knuckles turning white. Her breathing quickens and deepens as she begins to shake. Tears spill down her cheeks, her shoulders start to heave with sobs, and she covers her mouth with her hand. She rests her elbows on her knees, burying her face in her hands. The tears of a mother cut away from her child whose fate will remain a mystery, misery flowing from deep within Ellen's soul. Anna joins her in the brutal truth, pulling Ellen closer. Throwing herself into Anna's arms, her emotion pours forth uncontrollably. Anna is sure that she can hear the sound of a heart shattering, thrown from the heights of hope to crash upon the stones of despair. Suddenly, Ellen pulls back, gets up and runs out of the sitting room, to her bedroom, slamming the door. At the harsh noise, Anna jumps, sensing the same knife that thrusts through Ellen's heart, is cutting hers asunder as well. New tears flow for her daughter's loss and the unknown fate of the baby Ellen loves. Anna shakes her head against the unthinkable and cruel reality that someone would tear Ellen's infant from her arms.

John returns home to the sound of convulsive weeping that echoes from the sitting room. Alarmed, he takes off his hat, tosses it to the entry table, and does not notice or care that it falls to the floor. He rushes into the sitting room to find Anna in an inconsolable state. He sits on the sofa next to her, gathers her into his arms, stroking and kissing her hair, wondering what could have sent Anna into hysterical sobbing.

"Anna, Anna...shhhh...I'm here...shhhh..."

Gulping, her face buried in John's shoulder, Anna tries to catch her breath long enough to tell John something, anything.

"Clara...the baby...they couldn't...I had to tell her...she ran...Oh, John..."

With the flowing of fresh tears from Anna's eyes, John's eyes mist, a mixture of sadness and anger for this new injury to the heart of a girl he has come to love as his own child. They hold each other, John trying to be strong and hide his own urge to weep with Anna who is in breathless misery for Ellen's pain. Anna looks up at John with aching eyes that reflect a mother's troubled soul.

"John, I feel that I need to sleep down here, tonight. I'm certain that Ellen will have..."

He strokes Anna's hair and cheek, aching to fix all that hurts those he loves most in this world.

"Yes, I agree. Ellen needs you tonight. I'll fetch a pillow and blanket for you."

John lifts Anna's chin to look at him, a thought popping into his head.

"Sweetheart, we have the guest bedroom upstairs. Why don't we bring Ellen up there and she can have that room for her own? She'll be between our room and Sarah's room. Maybe she'll feel safer, more a part of the family, and we'll hear her when she needs us. Tomorrow is Saturday so we could explain it then, and I can move whatever she wants upstairs."

Anna nods, too numb to comprehend what John is suggesting.

"I...I have to go to Ellen...she needs..."

John kisses Anna's forehead and strokes her tear-stained cheek.

"Yes, she needs you. Go."

He watches Anna get up and steady herself with a deep breath that crumbles to a sigh as she walks away from him. He rests his face in his hands, allowing his empathy to flow. Upon reaching Ellen's door, Anna opens it just enough to see Ellen lying on the bed, holding Rupert who rests his head on Ellen's arm. Ellen stares at the far wall, silent tears wetting the pillow. Unwilling to leave but unable to interfere with Ellen's grief, Anna walks over to the bureau, opens the bottom drawer, and takes out a quilt. She walks over to the bed and covers her baby girl, the only maternal gesture Anna can give, for now. She turns off the light on the bedside table and then sits on the edge of Ellen's bed. Anna reaches out to stroke Ellen's hair, hoping that she can feel how the family who love her, hurt for her and she is not alone in this. Determined to stay with her daughter, Anna leans over, kisses Ellen's head, and then whispers.

"I love you."

Chapter Nineteen
12 May 1926

After their supper, Anna, John, and Ellen bid Johanna an affectionate good night with many kisses, snuggles, and laughter. Johanna waves to her parents and 'big sister' as Rupert barks once.

"Nite nite Mamma! Nite nite Daddy! Nite nite Cuppa! Roop nite nite!"

Sarah chuckles and picks up Johanna to carry her upstairs since the little one's legs are still too short and unsteady to manage the climb. Ellen follows them up the stairs, smiling and wiggling her fingers at Johanna who is looking back and waving to Ellen in return.

"Nite nite Cuppa! Nite nite!"

Sarah smiles at Ellen when they reach the top of the stairs and walks with Johanna to the loo for the usual bedtime ritual of a bath, followed by stories, singing, and laying a sleepy cherub in her little bed. Ellen enters her new bedroom upstairs and stares 'round the room. Rupert dashes in after her and leaps onto the bed, plopping down to watch his friend. She walks over to a chair near her dressing table where her nightclothes lay folded, drapes them over her arm, walks over to the bed, and spreads them out. She touches the embroidery that Anna worked to make the plain satin dressing gown and nightdress pretty, expressing Ellen's love of flowers. Rupert sniffs the fabric and then lays his chin on his paws. Ellen changes from her dress into her nightdress, dons her dressing gown and ties the belt snugly. She carries the dress over to the armoire and hangs it up. Passing the looking glass on the dressing table, she picks up a strand of hair, wrinkles her nose, and picks up a hairbrush. Without bothering to sit down, she pulls the brush through her thick hair in a similar fashion to Anna's vigorous grooming. Soon, her long golden locks are smooth and gleaming.

She holds up her hair, taps two fingers on her chest, drops the hair, and then pats her hands together.

Ellen returns the brush to her dressing table and stares at herself. She shakes her head and walks over to the low, long dresser where she keeps her mouse. Rupert raises his head and ears, scoots to the edge of the bed and hops off. He trots over to see what his friend is doing. She lifts the screen, smiles, and then puts her hand into the re-purposed aquarium. The little fellow scurries towards her hand and hops into it as he always does. Lifting the mouse to her eye level, she brings the little fellow close and touches her nose to his twitching mouse nose. She smiles, rubs her nose, tucks her furry little friend into the pocket of her dressing gown, pulling the pocket open to look at him staring back at her with his beady little eyes. Ellen bends down to scratch Rupert's ears and walks to the door. Looking 'round the room once more, she leaves the new place that she can call her own and makes her way to the sitting room. Rupert brushes past Ellen's legs as they descend, and she stops on the bottom step, staring at John and Anna.

Anna has cleared the table in the sitting room and is raising the drop leaf. Holding the draughts game board and game pieces, John waits until Anna is ready for him to set up the game. Rupert plants himself in front of the fireplace, chewing on an old toy that belongs to Johanna. Soon, he falls asleep on his side, his legs stretched out, twitching slightly. Whilst they wait for the tea kettle in the kitchen to sing, Anna pulls up three chairs 'round the table. She makes a silent observation that Ellen seems to enjoy a game of draughts now and then. Hopefully, this will take Ellen's mind off William for the evening. He has not been by to visit her in a few days, and Ellen has been staring out the window. When Ellen is outside in the garden, she looks 'round the corner of the house. Today, Ellen sat on the front steps looking to the right and then to the left. Anna and John look at each other, hoping that playing draughts will be a diversion for all of them in the face of unsettling times in the past week, or so.

"I wonder why William hasn't come 'round to see Ellen? Could he have been put off by the talk of Ellen's baby? Oh, John, I hope not."

"I hope not, as well, Anna. William made such a favourable impression on us, and it would be a shame for him to change that."

Turning their attention away from gloomy thoughts, they focus on their amazement that Ellen is learning how to play draughts quickly and adeptly. It requires no reading or arithmetic, and all it needs is a strategy. Ellen has proven that she is cunning with her approach but has not yet won a game against either John or Anna. As the teakettle steams its readiness, Anna walks to the kitchen to make them all some tea. John remains in the sitting room to place the pieces on the board and notices Ellen standing on the bottom step with one hand in a pocket of her dressing gown. He points to Ellen, points to the draught board, taps two fingers on his chest, and then points to himself as he tilts his head, inviting Ellen to play the game with them. Ellen nods and comes further into the sitting room and watches John walk over to the wireless to turn it on. He sees Ellen staring at him and motions for her to come over. Putting his hand on the wireless, John feels a vibration from the music coming from it and sways to the music. He looks at Ellen, nods, points to her, and places his hand on the wireless again. Ellen walks over to John and the wireless, reaches out to touch it and pulls her hand back quickly. She reaches over to touch it again and this time, leaves her hand there, staring at John and nodding her head in time to the music, or rather, the vibration. Taking her hand off the wireless, she looks up at John, stares at him, then reaches into the pocket of her dressing gown, and brings out the mouse, nestled in her hand. She holds him up for John to see and then holds him close to the wireless. He pokes his nose towards it and wiggles his whiskers. John chuckles to himself at the small things that seem to make an impression on Ellen. With a little smile, Ellen rubs the mouse's fur and turns to look at Anna walking back into the room. Holding a tray with teacups for three, Anna sets it down on the table.

"Are you two ready to play? Oh...were you showing Ellen something?"

"Yes, I showed her the wireless. I say, she seems interested. She even showed it to her pet mouse. I coaxed her to place her hand on it so she can feel the vibration in a similar way that you showed her the Hoover."

"Splendid, John. Every little thing she learns should make us proud of her."

John and Ellen walk back to the table, Ellen looking back at the wireless several times. They take their seats, and Anna hands them each a teacup. Ellen slides her chair closer to Anna, pitching their mutual skills against John.

"Last time, you went first, Anna. I believe it's my turn to move the first piece."

Anna laughs and takes a sip of her tea, a lovely mixture of lemon and black tea with sugar and milk. She reaches over to the creature in Ellen's hand to stroke his head, and he stares at Anna, not moving even a whisker.

"I don't remember, John, but I'll take your word for it."

Anna turns to Ellen and points to John and then points to the board, feeling that Ellen understands that John will play his piece first. Ellen nods and holds the mouse closer, facing him towards the board. It is covered in alternating squares of black and red with round playing pieces in the same colours. His whiskers twitch, and he looks back at Ellen with his unblinking black eyes. Holding him up to her nose, she touches her nose to his, again. Smiling, she strokes him and tucks him back into her pocket, pulls the pocket open to look at him, and then turns her attention to John and Anna. She pats Anna's arm and waits for Anna, who has unconsciously assimilated Ellen's habits. She looks down at her arm and then to Ellen.

She taps two fingers on her chest and points to the lady. She points to the man and taps three fingers on her chest. She points to herself and rests two fingers against her cheek. She points to the little furry and puts two fingers under her nose and wiggles her fingers.

"John, look! She has given the mouse a name. She is moving her fingers like the mouse moves his whiskers. I think she's named him Whiskers?"

"By Jove, I believe you're right, Anna. It's a perfect name for the little fellow."

John and Anna pat their hands together to gesture that they not only think it is an excellent idea to give the mouse a name, but that the name is fitting, as well.

Game after game, cup after cup of tea, John wins, Anna wins, and Ellen wins her first effort against John, without help from Anna. The music playing in the background gives toes a reason to tap, unbeknownst to the owners of said toes. They agree that Ellen is growing more proficient at this pastime with each attempt. They both point at Ellen and pat their hands together, bursting into laughter that they gestured at the same time, how well Ellen is learning this amusement.

She points to herself, points to the thing with little things that move, and then pats her hands together. She tilts her head, taps two fingers on her wrist, points at the thing with little things that move, and then points to herself.

Anna sees that Ellen is saying that she enjoys the game, then sighs, musters a smile, and nods, in response to Ellen's question asking if William might enjoy playing draughts with her. John sees the gestures, too, and believes they have failed to distract Ellen as thoroughly as they had hoped. Ellen is still thinking about William, and they assume, missing him. Anna and John look at each other, trying to hide their disappointment at William's absence. Ellen gets up to gather the pieces into their box and fold the board. She puts the game where it belongs, in the cupboard beneath the bookcase. Noticing that Anna begins to clear away cups and saucers, Ellen walks close to her, reaches down to stay Anna's hand, and gestures her intentions when Anna looks up at her.

She points to herself, places her fist on the palm of her hand, points to the lady, points to the drinking things, and then points to the food place.

Anna nods, musing how different it must be for Ellen to help because she wants to help. She imagines that might not have been the case before Ellen's life here, perhaps an existence of a dreadful duty to perform tasks by force. Holding the tray of cups and saucers, Ellen stops to stare at John turning off the wireless for the night, and then she continues on her way to the kitchen. Anna hears water running from the tap in the kitchen as she puts the table leaf down to make the table thin, again.

"John, she's rinsing the cups and saucers. She doesn't have to do that."

"She knows, that, Anna. It's sweet of her to want to, though. I believe that it means that she feels like a contributing member of the family."

"You may be right. I'm certain that she grows to feel more a part of our family with each passing day, and I'm grateful."

Ellen comes out of the kitchen and walks over to the front door. She opens it, walks outside, and closes the door behind her. Alerted by a simple click, Rupert awakens and runs into the entry hall, scratching at the door, and whining. The front stoop, middle step, is her seat of choice. Reaching into her pocket, she takes out her twitchy-whiskered friend and cups him in her lap. As she strokes his fur, she looks up the road in one direction and then the other. In the growing darkness, she glances 'round her more quickly and then returns to staring, her head turning from one side to the other.

"There she goes, again, Anna. I do wish William would come 'round to see her. Even to just tell her that he doesn't want to see her anymore. If he doesn't, she's always going to wonder."

"Yes. A straight-forwards good-bye is better than nothing at all. John, why don't you settle things down here for the night and go up to bed. I'll go outside and coax Ellen indoors."

John takes Anna in his arms and kisses her, holding her close to himself. They both lean back to smile at each other and gaze into each other's eyes. John boops Anna's nose with his finger and then bestows that lucky nose with a kiss. Laughing softly, Anna pats John's chest.

"I'll join you after I tuck Ellen into bed. Would you find Rupert and shoo him into Ellen's room? He's going to end up there anyway."

John nods and kisses Anna's cheek one more time.

"Rupert! C'mhere, old chap. Let's go up to Ellen's room. She'll be along in a moment."

As Anna walks out to the front door, the dog comes running to his master, tail wagging, jumping up with a wiggle. Laughing, he watches Rupert's antics with one canine ear perked to attention and the other flapping with each jump. John walks out of the sitting room, checking the doors and windows for secure closure against any rain that might begin during the night. As he does so, he turns out the lights except for a small table lamp in the sitting room. He has stubbed his toe on the furniture more than once on his way to the kitchen for something refreshing to drink with a midnight snack, and he appreciates a bit of illumination. Rupert follows John and sniffs as far as his nose can reach.

"Duties done, my boy. That's a good fellow. Let's up to bed, shall we?"

Wagging his tail and the back half of his Terrier body, he trots along beside his master, then speeds ahead of John to wait at the top of the stairs. John makes his way down the hallway, stopping to peek in at Johanna. He quietly walks over to her and kisses her forehead, whisking away a stray curl on her forehead. With one last lingering glance at his daughter, he goes to Ellen's room where Rupert awaits. He pushes the door open, walks to the bed, and pats it, whilst he turns on a small lamp.

"There you go, my boy. Ellen will be along soon."

Rupert hops up on the bed, sniffs about to find his favourite spot, turns 'round three times in the familiar dent, and then plops himself down to watch the door. John smiles at Rupert, chuckling to himself that Anna's dog is a little character. He walks out of Ellen's room to the bedroom he and Anna share and closes the door behind him, careful to not make a sound so he will not disturb Johanna or Sarah.

Outside, Anna has joined Ellen on the front steps. Time passes with the stillness of gestures as Ellen's hands hold her pet and Anna's hands lay folded in her lap. Darkness overtakes them with the only light coming from a flickering street lamp. Finally, Anna pats Ellen's arm, and she looks down at her arm, and then over to Anna. Anna tilts her head to the side, places her hands together as if they were a pillow, and rests her head on them to ask Ellen if she is ready to go to bed. Ellen nods her head and stands, tucking the mouse in her pocket. She reaches for the handle of the door, opens it, and holds it for Anna to pass through. Ellen closes the door, pulls it firmly again, and then pats the door. Anna stands aside to make room for Ellen to lead the way and then follows her up the stairs into her room.

Anna turns down the flowered patchwork quilt that cheers Ellen's bed and fluffs the pillows into acceptable softness whilst Ellen unties the belt of her dressing gown. She walks over to the mouse's lair, lifts him from her pocket, kisses his furry head, and then places him inside. She closes the mesh covering over the little creature's abode as he dashes into his hiding place. Patting the top of the glass container that serves as a mouse house, she walks over to a chair, takes off her dressing gown, and drapes it over the back. Anna waits for Ellen at the dressing table with a hairbrush and a ribbon. As always, Ellen faces away from the looking glass whilst Anna plaits her hair. Brushing and plaiting Ellen's thick hair seems to soothe her, Anna treasures it as a part of their bedtime ritual. She hopes Ellen enjoys having her hair tended in this way as much as she enjoys making her daughter's hair tangle-resistant for the night.

Finished all too soon, Anna walks over to Ellen's bed and pats it. She gets up, walks over to her bed and slides in, pulling her cuddly toy next to her. Rupert scoots closer to his friend and lays his head on her legs. Anna tugs the sheet and quilt closer to Ellen's chin and then sits on the bed. Ellen stares at her, and Anna wonders what she is thinking. Ellen pulls her hands out from under the covers, and Anna tilts her head to the side, asking Ellen to speak her mind, as it were.

She points to herself, rubs her fist in circles on her chest, taps two fingers on her wrist, points to her own eyes, and then points to herself.

Ellen tucks her arms back under the blankets and continues to stare at Anna. Anna gestures in reply to Ellen that she also wishes William would come to see her. Ellen tilts her head to the side, asking Anna if William will visit again, and Anna must shrug in reply to say that she does not know. Ellen always deserves an honest response. Ellen nods, pulling her plush toy closer to her and takes Anna's hand, placing it on her own hair. Her eyes close as Anna begins to stroke Ellen's hair, only stopping to brush away that one stubborn strand that insists on lying on Ellen's forehead. Ellen slips out one arm from under the quilt and gropes about until she finds Anna's hand. She pulls Anna's hand close to rest it against her cheek, holding Anna's thumb. Anna sings to Ellen, more for herself as a mother than for Ellen's benefit as she strokes her hair.

"Hush little baby, don't say a word…"

The lids that cover Ellen's blue eyes flutter with sleep, and her body relaxes enough to release her grip on Anna's thumb. Anna gently tucks Ellen's arm under the blanket and stands up. She reaches over to dim the lamplight so Ellen will still be able to find her way in the dark. Stepping back, Anna watches Ellen sleeping, smiles, and whispers.

"I love you."

Anna walks out of Ellen's room, leaving the door ajar so they will be able to hear the first sound of a nightmare. She walks down the hallway, peeking into the nursery to check on Johanna. The baby is asleep, sucking her thumb, holding the ear of her cuddly pink bunny. Smiling at her little girl's sweetness, she tiptoes to her bedside and leans down to kiss Johanna's forehead. To not awaken her, Anna points to herself, places her hand over her heart, and then points to Johanna to tell her sweet child that her mother loves her. She walks out of the nursery, into the hallway, leaving Johanna's door ajar, as well. Making her way down the corridor, she stops at the loo to freshen up before going to bed. Anna's reflection reveals that the dark circles under her eyes have faded since bringing Ellen upstairs. Nodding, she leaves the loo, walks to the door of the bedroom she shares with her husband and opens the door. Unwilling to awaken her love, she tries to be as quiet as she can. Slipping out of her daytime garb, she drapes the garments on her dressing table's stool and then wriggles into her nightdress. Gingerly, she walks to her side of the bed, turns down the coverlet, and slides in next to John.

"I was hoping you'd be along soon before I fell asleep."

Startled out of her skin by John's whisper, she rolls over with a chuckle to snuggle against him. She drapes her arm 'round his waist and looks up at his silhouette in the moonlight.

"You, you, scamp, you. Why I should..."

"You should kiss your beloved husband, Mrs Thorpe. I think that's more than fair."

John pulls Anna closer, tucks his finger under her chin, and tilts her head as he lowers his lips to hers, the two of them savouring a moment of tenderness, alone.

"You're right, Mr Thorpe, that was fair. I love you, John."

"I know you do, Anna. As much as I love you."

He strokes her cheek as she rests her hand against his chest, both musing how they fit together perfectly in each other's arms after all these years, cradling each other until they fall asleep.

Hours and dreams go by until an insanely jarring din wrenches them from sleep into fully attentive alarm. John looks at the clock on his bedside table and wonders why the wireless is blaring at two o'clock in the morning. Flying out of bed, housecoats donned, John and Anna bolt out of their bedroom and down the hallway, oblivious to Sarah's flight into the nursery, closing the door behind her. At the top of the stairs, Anna puts her hand on John's arm to watch the unfolding scene lit only by the glow of a lamp and whispers.

"Look..."

John puts his arm 'round Anna's shoulders as he takes in the same sight gracing the sitting room. Ellen, swaying, her arms held up and eyes closed, she moves as if she could hear the music coming from the wireless.

"John, she's dancing. How would she know how to do that to music?"

"She can feel it, sweetheart. She can feel it even though she can't hear it."

They make their way down the staircase, and John walks over to the wireless to turn it down to a volume that will not wake the neighbours. Rupert cowers under the sofa, still and quiet, not taking his eyes off his friend. Anna walks over to rest her hand on the back of a chair near the wireless. She watches their daughter feel the music, and John joins Anna, his arm resting 'round Anna's waist. Stopping, Ellen opens her eyes and sees them. She takes a step back and lowers her head.

She puts her hands together near her chest and moves them outward towards the man and lady.

They look at each other and Anna steps forwards, towards Ellen. She smiles at Ellen and nods, drawing an X in her own hand to tell Ellen that there is nothing to forgive. Ellen stares at Anna and then at John, folding her hands in front of her. Anna points to the wireless and then begins to waltz, holding out her hand to John.

"Join me for a dance, sweetheart?"

"With pleasure, my dear."

John steps close to Anna, taking her hand in his, resting his hand on her waist, they engage in a waltz to music better suited for a tango. Oblivious to the music playing, John and Anna lose themselves in each other's eyes, feeling only touch, and movement. For a whilst in their dance, they both realise they have not gone out to dance in months. Smiling into each other's eyes, they step back from each other, and Anna turns to Ellen who continues to stare at them. Anna approaches Ellen and points to her and then points to herself, holding up one hand and swaying back and forth. Looking at Anna and then at John, Ellen returns her gaze to Anna and nods. She walks towards Anna, lifts her hand to meet Anna's, and Anna holds out her other hand so Ellen can take that hand as well. Slowly, they begin to sway together, turning as they feel each other's movements. Ellen closes her eyes, following Anna with her remaining senses. Watching his daughter and his wife dance together makes the hour of the night irrelevant. He leans on the back of a chair, watching the beautiful sight before him as time melts away for all of them. Rupert comes 'round to sit next to his master's legs, leaning against John.

With natural ease, Ellen and Anna bring their dance to a feminine close. Chuckling, Anna curtsies to Ellen, thanking her for the dance in the time-honoured fashion of bye-gone eras. Smiling, Ellen imitates Anna's posturing and then closes the distance between them to walk into Anna's waiting embrace. John watches them hold each other, swaying slightly as if still feeling the music in their souls, not the music from the wireless. Stepping back, Anna puts her hands together and rests her head on them as if they were a pillow to ask Ellen if she would like to go back to bed. She nods and takes Anna's hand, leading her to the staircase as Anna whispers to John as they pass.

"You'll turn off...?"

John nods, still smiling and filled with a father's warmth and pride. He reaches over to the wireless, turns it off, and then watches Anna ascend the staircase behind Ellen. As they disappear 'round the corner, John makes his way with Rupert upstairs, as well, and once they arrive at Ellen's door, John urges the dog inside to give Ellen comfort through the remainder of the night. Rupert disappears into Ellen's room with a trotting gait, and John returns to their bedroom. He walks into their room, takes off his dressing gown and hangs it on a hook behind the door. Smiling, he walks over to Anna's side of the bed to turn and fluff her pillow as he has seen Anna do for Ellen every night over the past months. Patting Anna's pillow one more time, he walks 'round the bed to slip under the covers, awaiting Anna's return.

Still smiling, Ellen moves under the blankets on her bed, and Anna sits on the bed. She reaches over to take the soft toy in her hand, bounces the furry animal upwards on the quilt towards Ellen, and then boops her nose with it. Grinning, Ellen takes the toy in her hands and tucks it between her arm and her body, then covering it with the blanket. Anna reaches out to stroke Ellen's hair as she had done before, watching her slip into a deep sleep with a faint smile playing at the corners of Ellen's mouth. Assured that her girl is asleep, again, she gets up from the bed and stands near, watching Ellen sleep in peace for the first time in weeks. Knowing that the nightmares will return, Anna prays that Ellen's demons will restrain their torment for just this one night. She leans down to kiss Ellen's forehead, swiping back that one stubborn strand of hair on Ellen's forehead. Leaving the room, she sets the door ajar. She returns to their bedroom and peers in, looking to see if John is asleep yet. Taking off her dressing gown, she hangs it on the hook behind the door next to John's. She smiles, touching the fabric of John's dressing gown, leaning in to smell his familiar scent. Turning, she walks to her side of the bed and carefully slips under the covers, trying to leave John undisturbed.

Again, John rolls over with a smile and takes Anna in his arms. This time, Anna is not surprised that John is as awake as she is. Tilting her face upwards to share a kiss, his hand travels from her shoulder down to her waist, pulling her close to him. Together, they create the script for the happiest of dreams. Once John's breathing and manly snore announce his depth of sleep, Anna slides out of bed, walks back to Ellen's room to check on her. Smiling at her girl in the moonlight, she whispers.

"I love you."

Chapter Twenty
31 May 1926

William works as quickly as he can to finish his list of duties at Chelsey's Market. His thoughts are concentrated on what he wants to do and places he wants to go when his work is done. An unexpected interruption taps him on the shoulder, causing him to scramble, rescuing a load of cucumbers from an unfortunate fate on the floor just in time. Wheeling 'round, still supporting the display with his hands and hip, he sees Lewis leaning on another display stand trying to suppress laughter.

"You're jumpy, old boy, aren't you? It's just me."

William sighs with an inner groan at seeing his lifelong acquaintance.

"Having my work end on the floor would make me a bit on edge, yes. What brings you here, Lewis? More women's work for your mum?"

William regrets the dig, although he does feel somewhat justified in giving a response in kind to the jabs that Lewis has thrown his way over the past weeks.

"No, no, I told Mum that I'd go with her to the market, but I'm not going alone anymore. I told her that exercise is the best thing for her aches and pains."

"You're such a considerate fellow, Lewis."

"Why, yes, I am, William. I was wondering if you'd fancy a pint and visit the pub with me one evening. I haven't seen you in a whilst. What do you say?"

"Um, Lewis, I've been rather busy lately, and I haven't the time or the interest to visit a pub. Sorry to disappoint you."

"I was figuring you'd say that. Say, have you seen that girl who lives with the Thorpe family? Was I right about her?"

William remembers what Lewis had said about Ellen and the opinion Lewis' mum held.

"Well, yes, I've seen her, and for once, you were right, and as usual, your mother was wrong. She's a sweet girl. And...she has a name, I'll have you know. Ellen. She's not just 'that girl'."

"Touchy, touchy. Well, that explains a few things."

Lewis walks away laughing, slapping his limp cap on his thigh. Glaring at the lean young man sauntering away and flaunting his smug arrogance, William grits his teeth against a retort that would cause him to lose his job. He turns back to his work, hoping that his employer did not see him dilly-dallying with someone who did not intend to make a purchase.

Anna sits at the kitchen table writing out her market list of items she will need to order. It consists of fabric, thread, fastenings, trim, and a new pair of fabric shears. She chuckles that, perhaps, she can beg, borrow, or steal one from John's shop. He must have an extra pair that he will not miss. Johanna sits in her high chair, babbles at her mother, reaches over to the table, and bangs her favourite cuddly toy.

"Are you trying to help, little one? What else should Mamma put on the list? A new toy for Rupert? Maybe a new toy for...let me see...a little girl named Johanna?"

"Toy! Toy! Me! Me! GoggieRoop!"

Anna laughs and tries to coax Johanna to be a little quieter for Sarah, who is preparing supper. Rupert sits next to Johanna's high chair; his ears perked and tail wagging. Johanna tosses her toy as far as she can throw it, and Rupert trots across the kitchen floor to retrieve it. He brings it back to Johanna who squeals with delight. Again, Johanna throws the toy and Rupert retrieves it for his little friend. Grinning and shaking her head, Anna stands, leans over to lift Johanna from her high chair and covers her little girl's face with kisses. As Johanna laughs, pats her mum's face and gives her own sloppy kisses, Anna walks with her to the blanket on the floor. She reaches for the cuddly toy and gives it to Johanna.

"Now, we must be quiet for Sarah. She's making our supper! Your picture book is here, and you can make animal noises if you like. Rupert can help you."

Standing back up, Anna looks towards the kitchen door and wonders why Rupert is not with Ellen. Anna considers going upstairs to see if Ellen is all right, but before Anna can finish her thought, Ellen walks through the doorway and stands near the table. Rupert gets up trots over and sits next to Ellen, looking up at her. Ellen's hands cup her mouse close, her head lowered, blue eyes peeking up at Anna. Curious why Ellen's demeanour has changed so much from this morning, Anna tries to think of anything through the day that may have triggered such a difference. This morning, Ellen looked up at the sky from the hammock John had set up in the garden. After lunch, she planted the flowers from Clara's greenhouse. Ellen's mood, now, is grey and subdued. Anna walks over to her, reaches out to caress her sweet girl's face with her hand, and tilts her head to the side. Ellen tucks the little creature they've named Mr Whiskers into her pocket and begins to gesture.

She taps two fingers on her wrist, draws an X in the palm of her hand, places her fist on her chest, points to her own eyes, and then points to herself. She taps two fingers on her wrist, points to her head, points to herself, places her index fingers together, lowering one of them, she points to herself, points to her ears, points to her mouth, cradles her arms as if holding a baby, places her index fingers together, and then lowers one of her fingers down from the other. She points to herself, moves her hands down the front of herself, draws a frown on her face, and then draws a line down from her eye. She points to herself and draws an X in her palm.

Anna is saddened for Ellen that she thinks William does not want to see her because she cannot hear, or speak, and has had a baby. How could William dare to make Ellen feel sad and broken when she has waited at the window, sat outside looking up and down the road, waiting for her friend to come. Anna wants to find William and tell him that he is her only friend, and this friendship means so much to Ellen's fragile spirit. Anna points to Ellen, draws an X in her hand, holds her index fingers together, and then pulls one down from the other to tell Ellen that she is not broken. She points to Ellen, points to her own ears, points to her own mouth, cradles her arms as if holding a baby, points to herself, places her hand over her heart, and then points to Ellen. Anna hopes that Ellen will understand she does not think that Ellen is bad or broken. In spite of all that makes Ellen feel 'broken' and 'bad', Anna and John still love her.

She tilts her head to the side, taps two fingers on her wrist, draws an X in the palm of her hand, places her fist on her chest, points to her own eyes, and then points to herself.

Anna had hoped that William would come 'round, thus allowing her to avoid answering the question that Ellen poses, now. A shake of Anna's head and a shrug are the only replies to her question that asks why William has not come to see her. She and John do not know, and William has not been here to explain himself. Anna opens her arms, hoping to give her daughter comfort and Ellen walks into Anna's embrace for only a moment. Disappointed in the minimal duration of their embrace, Anna watches Ellen step back with a nod, take her pet out of her pocket, turn, and then walk out of the kitchen. She hears Ellen's footsteps take her into the sitting room, with Rupert trotting behind. Anna turns to check on Johanna and then turns to Sarah. Sarah looks at Anna and shakes her head as she beats some dough a little more roughly than usual.

"I hate seeing Miss Cup so sad, Ma'am, if I may say. That William had best not hurt her, if you don't mind my saying, Ma'am."

"I feel the same way, Sarah. I'll give her some time alone. I hope she realises that we love her unconditionally."

"Yes, Ma'am. She's family, now, and nobody hurts this family if I've anything to say about it, Ma'am, if you'll pardon my saying."

Anna pats Sarah's arm in reassuring agreement. Walking back to the table and taking her seat, she returns to her list with the idea that she will give Ellen some time alone, and then spend some time with her girl. She looks down at Johanna with a maternal smile from time to time, finding the animal noises that Johanna makes as she points to pictures in her book, comical. When Johanna has made the last animal sound in the book, she closes it with a thud and lays it on the blanket next to her. Johanna gets up and toddles over to Sarah, pulling on Sarah's dress.

"Janna wanna bikit!"

Looking over to Anna who nods her approval, Sarah opens the cupboard and brings down the tin to give the little one a biscuit. A knock at the front door startles Anna, and she gets up from the table and peeks into the sitting room to see Ellen and Rupert sitting by the fireplace on her way to the front door. She opens it and can hardly believe her eyes. William stands there, holding flowers, and wearing a new suit. His sheepish expression does not match the brown wool suit, starched white shirt, and shiny new shoes. His cap is a crisp and smart thing that matches his suit.

"Well, William, you look very smart today. Won't you come in?"

William removes his new cap and stops himself from stuffing it in his pocket.

"Thank you, Mrs Thorpe. I...I'm terribly sorry I haven't come by of late. I hope I haven't made anyone cross with me. I would have explained sooner, but, um, I wanted it to be...well...a surprise."

"Well, if those flowers are for Ellen, she will be surprised, and I'm sure she would appreciate an explanation. She's been looking and waiting for you. She thought you didn't want to see her, again."

"I hope she forgives me for not coming 'round. I was, well, I was working extra to make money for this suit. I wanted to...well, look nice for Ellen."

With one eyebrow raised, Anna waits for William to go on with what he is about to say, watching him fidget with his hat.

"Um, before I see Ellen, can I ask you a question, if you don't mind, Mrs Thorpe?"

"Of course, William."

"Well, I know you and Ellen use gestures with your hands to talk with each other, and, well, I'd like to learn so Ellen and I can understand each other better. I want to talk with her the way you do."

"Of course, William. If you're serious about learning, I'd be happy to teach you another time, though. Ellen is in the sitting room. Why don't you go in?"

"Thanks, an awful lot, Mrs Thorpe."

With a smile and a nod of his head, William makes his way to the sitting room doorway, just watching Ellen sit on the floor, looking at a book. He thinks she is even prettier than the flowers he has picked out for her. For the first time, his appearance, giving a girl flowers, and making a good impression on his friends' parents matter to him. William wonders if this is how it feels to grow up rather than relying on age to determine adulthood. He walks into the room and sees Rupert lift his head from Ellen's lap to look at him. Rupert's movement alerts Ellen to the presence of someone in the room. Ellen looks 'round as Anna takes her leave from the entry hall and walks back to the kitchen. Anna returns to her place at the kitchen table and listens for anything that might be amiss. This visit is between Ellen and William, and she trusts Ellen to make sensible choices as the two of them sort things out between them. Ellen's gaze comes to rest on William. In her scramble to stand up, she catches her foot in the hem of her dress and nearly falls, catching herself by grabbing the arm of the sofa. She stands straight, puts her hand in her pocket, and then smooths her dress. William's instinctive urge to help Ellen turns to relief as he watches her walk 'round the sofa, folding her hands in front of her, lowering her head, but peeking up at him. William feels himself holding his breath until he sees Ellen smile, realising that Ellen's smile matters to him, too.

He turns his thoughts to the flowers in his hand that he could not name to save himself. The myriad of dancing colours remind him of how honest, fragile, complicated, and special his Ellen is. Their delicate fragrance reminds him of Ellen's sweet spirit. William walks closer to Ellen and holds the flowers out to her with a smile and a nod, wishing he could tell her more clearly that he brought them for her. He watches Ellen tilt her head to the side, point to the flowers, and then point to herself. All he can understand is that she is probably asking if the flowers are for her. He nods, hoping that is the correct answer, and Ellen takes them from his hand. Lifting them to her nose, she closes her eyes and then peeks at William over the top of the flowers. Ellen smiles when she sees his smile and nods as she points to him and then to a chair. Taking the obvious hint to sit in that particular chair, William nods and stands in front of it, waiting for Ellen to take her seat, as a gentleman should. Ellen nods her head, holds up one finger, and hurries out of the room.

Scratching his head, William sits down and puts his cap over his knee to keep it new for as long as he can. He wonders why Ellen left the room, and he hopes she returns. He and Rupert sit, staring at each other, causing William to compare the dog's stare with that of a protective elder brother. Hearing soft footsteps, he stands up and turns to see that Ellen has placed the flowers in a vase. She sets it on the table in front of the sofa, points to William, and then makes a gesture that William recognises as 'sit'. He sits, and Ellen sits across from him. The lengthening silence seems thick to William as the moments tick by. Not the lack of speech, but the lack of communication of any kind bothers him. His attention belongs to Ellen when she smiles, points to the flowers, and then draws a circle 'round her face. He knows she is talking about the flowers, and he has seen the gesture of a circle 'round the face before, but he has not the foggiest idea what it means. All he can manage is a stupid smile and nod, hoping he is not making a fool of himself.

Awkwardness envelops William until Ellen reaches into her pocket. His curiosity grows to see what she might be holding in her hand. He watches her hold her hand up to her face, her finger touching something of a greyish-brown colour. He tilts his head, trying to get a better look at whatever she is holding. Ellen smiles at William and gets up from her seat on the sofa. Crouching next to William's chair, she lifts up the mouse in her hand for him to see. He pauses and wonders what Ellen could find so special about a mouse. Looking at Ellen's face, he realises that this is much more than a mouse; it is a dear pet. William reaches a finger out and waits for Ellen's permission to touch it. He had never felt a mouse before, except the tail of a dead one that was thrown into the alley for a cat to finish. At her permissive nod, he touches the mouse's head with his finger, careful to not hurt the little thing. Surprise covers his face along with a grin at the softness under his fingertip. He nods as he pulls his hand away, wishing that he could somehow thank her for sharing her pet with him. William has to admit that the little fellow is cute in a mousey kind of way with its soft fur and twitching whiskers.

Ellen stands, holds the mouse's nose to her own nose, smiles, and then rubs her nose, tucks her pet in her pocket, and then holds the pocket open.

She taps two fingers on her wrist, points to the young man, points to the furry thing, puts two fingers under her nose and wiggles them.

William remembers that the first gesture is his name in her language, and the second gesture must be the mouse's name. The little fellow's name must have something to do with whiskers, based on her previous interaction with the mouse. He smiles, nods, and copies the gesture for the name of the mouse.

She smiles, pats her hands together, and then holds up one finger.

Finally, understanding what it means to hold up one finger, he nods, knowing he will have to wait for her to leave and then come back. Ellen turns away and walks to the staircase, then turns back to glance at William before ascending the stairs to her room. Walking directly to the old aquarium, she lowers him down and watches him scurry into his hiding place. She tucks a few seeds close to his bed made from scraps of cloth, sets the screen lid over the container, and then walks over to her armoire. Opening it, she pushes aside each dress, one at a time. With a nod, she takes out a green dress that she has never worn before. As quickly as she can, she changes from her everyday dress into her favourite dress. Smoothing down the skirt, she walks over to the dressing table's looking glass and looks at herself. Picking up a lock of her hair, she wrinkles her nose and frowns. She takes the hairbrush in her hand and makes short work of brushing her hair to a glossy shine. Putting down the brush, she steps back, holds up a lock of her hair, taps two fingers on her chest, and then pats her hands together.

She walks downstairs, unable to hear her shoes on the wooden flooring beneath her. William turns to see Ellen descending the stairs and catches his breath. Never in his life has he seen such a beautiful vision. Blinking his eyes, he tries to convince himself that this beautiful girl standing, now, in the sitting room, with her hands folded in front of her, is the same girl he came to see. She is, though, and even prettier than he could have imagined as she lowers her head, peeking at him with a smile. Kicking himself for forgetting his manners, he stands up and smiles at her with a nod, wishing he knew how to tell her that words to describe her beauty do not exist. William gestures to Ellen that she should come and sit, so she does so, smoothing the fabric of her dress. An idea pops into his head that shall help him try to tell her that she is pretty. He points to the flowers and then points to Ellen, and she nods.

241

She points to the flowers and then draws a circle 'round her face.

A flash of insight strikes William. The circle drawn 'round the face means 'pretty'. Ellen just told him that the flowers are pretty, but it seems that Ellen still thinks he is telling her that the flowers are hers. He is not sure how to tell her that she is the pretty one. Whilst he mulls this communication dilemma, Ellen holds up a finger and gets up. She walks over to Anna's writing desk, opens a drawer, and then pulls out a sheet of paper and a pencil. She closes the drawer, walks back to the sofa, and then sits down. Ellen reaches out and takes the paper and pencil as William watches her draw a window with a girl's face inside of it.

She points to herself, points to her own eyes, and points to the young man. She points to herself, places her fist on her chest, points to her own eyes, and points to the young man. She points to herself, points to her head, points to the young man, draws an X on the palm of her hand, places her fist against her chest, points to her own eyes, and points to herself.

With a sinking spirit, he hears Mrs Thorpe's voice in his head telling him that Ellen had waited and watched for him, wanting to see him and she was afraid he did not want to see her. His heart tells him that this is what she is trying to say, and he does not know how to tell her how sorry he is for causing her even a moment of worry. He motions for the paper and pencil, taking up the pencil when the items are pushed across the table towards him. He sets his mouth in concentration, drawing a line of what he hopes look like suits. He finishes, looks at his efforts, and then turns the drawing so Ellen can see. He points to one, shakes his head and then draws an X on it. He points to the next one, drawing an X on it also until he comes to the last one. He traces a circle 'round it, nods, smiles, and pulls at the lapel of his suit jacket. A breath of relief comes when he sees Ellen smile and nod.

She points to the young man, and then draws a circle 'round her face.

Grinning, he thinks it is rather spiffy for a girl to call him, of all people, 'pretty'. He returns the compliment by pointing to Ellen and drawing a circle 'round his face, telling Ellen that she is pretty, too. Ellen's smile fades, and she shakes her head, looking down at her hands.

Soon, though, she looks up at William, gives him a soft smile, picks up the vase of flowers, and then smells their sweet aroma before setting them back on the table. Lost in the quiet happiness of Ellen's presence, William does not hear rapid footsteps towards the front door and hushed whispers. Anna wants to intercept John before he comes in and walks into the sitting room. Ellen and William are getting on just fine, and there is no reason to disturb them. Anna opens the front door as John reaches the door handle. She reaches out to take John's hand as he enters the house and whispers to him whilst closing the door as quietly as she can.

"Come with me. Quickly. Now."

Wondering what could be wrong, possibilities run through his head. Fire? Accident? Illness? Bad news? Confused concern growing, he allows Anna to drag him down the hallway and into the kitchen.

"Hold on, Anna. What's wrong? I haven't even hung up my hat. And why all this whispering? Tell me."

"I'm going to kiss you, first."

Anna slips her arms 'round John's neck and kisses him firmly. Sarah discreetly keeps her back turned, and Johanna laughs as she points.

"Mamma! Daddy! Kissy!"

Anna and John turn towards their daughter and chuckle.

"Now, Anna, tell me what's going on?"

"William came to see Ellen. They're in the sitting room right now."

"Alone? Is that wise? After being away for so...wait...a fellow at the shop said that William came in to buy a suit off the peg and everything that goes along with it. Do you think...?"

Anna grins at John and explains.

"Yes, I do. William apologised for his absence and told me he had been working hard to save enough money to buy a suit to wear when he comes to see Ellen."

"But wouldn't Ellen still be upset with him? She waited, watched, and blamed herself for his absence..."

"Apparently not, John. I've been peeking in on them from time to time, and I have to admit, things seem to be coming along splendidly."

"Hmmm...I'd like to see this for myself."

John turns to walk out of the kitchen, but Anna catches his sleeve.

"Now, don't you go in there and make a fuss. Leave them alone to sort this out for themselves."

"I'm only going to put my hat where it belongs. Don't worry. I won't intrude."

John smiles and walks out of the kitchen, slowing his pace as he walks past the sitting room, glances in, and then continue into the entry hall to hang up his hat. Returning to the kitchen, he slows his pace, again, taking a second peek into the sitting room, satisfied that Anna's assessment of the situation was accurate.

"Well, you were right. They're getting on famously, from what I see. William is even sitting on the sofa near Ellen. She must be trusting and taken with him. Come to think of it, I don't recall Ellen wearing that particular dress, before."

"Sitting on the sofa with Ellen? Let me see. He was seated in a chair across from her, earlier."

Before John can stop her or say another word, Anna hurries out of the kitchen to casually walk past the sitting room, have a look, and then to the entry hall. She picks up her handbag for no reason at all and carries it back to the kitchen with another glance into the sitting room. Ellen and William look at each other, their eyes twinkling, sharing suppressed mirth.

She taps two fingers on her chest, taps three fingers on her chest, points to her own eyes, points to the young man and then to herself.

Fully understanding THIS set of gestures, that Mr and Mrs Thorpe are keeping an eye on them, he nods with a conspiratorial grin. Ellen stands up and points towards the door to the garden. William nods and begins to follow her. He mimics Ellen's sneaking walk past the kitchen door to avoid the keen eyes of Mr and Mrs Thorpe. He hopes that he will not get into trouble with this caper, but he is sure that Ellen will vouch for him. Outside, Ellen closes the door with care, leaving Rupert indoors, and then motions for him to follow her. She takes him over to the swing.

She points to the young man and then points to the moving thing.

William looks 'round, points to himself, and then to the swing. He has not been on one of these since he was but a lad on the schoolyard with his chums. He points to Ellen and then to the swing, thinking it is only right for ladies to go first. At Ellen's insistence, he admits defeat and sits down on it, and then feels Ellen's hands on his back. She is pushing him, higher and higher, and he cannot imagine anything grander! Exhilaration filling him, he holds up his hand to signal Ellen to stop pushing. He brings the swing to a stop, gets off, and then invites Ellen to sit on the swing with a flourish of his cap and a courtly bow. Grinning, Ellen comes 'round and sits down.

She points to the young man, makes her hands move like pushing the moving thing, and then points to herself.

Pausing for a moment, he considers how tentative Ellen has been, being too close to him. Any close proximity has been Ellen's choice, and he would never violate her decision to maintain a safe distance. Pushing her on the swing would mean touching her. Yet, she asked him to do so, and he will not refuse her request, although he steadies himself for her to change her mind if she wishes. Giving Ellen a gentle push, he slowly increases the height of her swing. Touching her back, he can feel how petite and fragile she is. He feels the delicate beauty within her blossom like a flower in human form. As Ellen's head tilts back with her enjoyment of this pastime, her hair flows aside, revealing a scar on her neck. Shocked, William narrowly misses a painful hit by the swing as he realises that Ellen has genuinely been hurt, yet, she blooms. The words Mrs Thorpe had told him had fallen on ignorant ears, until now, he hears them with understanding. He sees, now, from his soul, that Ellen is not her past or her horrible treatment or her scars. Ellen is Ellen, pure and straight-forwards, beautiful, inside and out.

The swing slows to a stop, and Ellen hops off to stand there, looking at William. She points to the garden bench, and he nods, happy for the chance to just be near her. They sit down, William taking care to not sit too close, out of respect for Ellen's comfort. He looks 'round the garden, admiring the beauty surrounding them. He feels a rustle next to him and smiles. Ellen has slid herself just a bit closer to him. With her by his side, he imagines he could conquer the world with his happiness.

Chapter Twenty-One
20 June 1926

Lewis Adderley rolls his eyes, lagging behind his mother as they move through each aisle and display in Chelsey's Market. Jane Adderley is badgering her son to fetch this or that, and he grudgingly does so. All the whilst, Lewis looks 'round for his only friend, William Tenney. For once, relief surges through him that William is nowhere in sight. His mother and her festering gob are enough to embarrass anyone.

"LewwwwIS!"

Cringing, Lewis quickens his pace to catch up to his mother. He does not want her shrill voice ringing through the market calling out his name, again.

"You say you'll come to the market with me to carry the baskets, and then you act like you don't want to be seen with me. You do hurt a mother's heart, you know. But...you're all I've got."

Jane is not even looking at Lewis during her little speech. She picks at vegetables and slaps a handful of rocket against his chest.

"Put that in the basket. Say, bring me two aubergines. That will be tasty with lamb."

Lewis mutters to himself that these baskets are bloody heavy. For a tick, he wishes he had come to the market alone so he could conveniently forget half the items on the shopping list. His mother's impressive inventory of expletives uttered during one of her diatribes would be worth it. Anything to unburden his arms of hampers full of food that will rot before his mother cooks them. Jane dodders to the stall where payment is taken. She goes on about her rheumy joints and listing every ache and pain. Lewis feels a twinge of sympathy for the poor fellow taking their money. None too soon, Lewis and his burden are following behind his mother. A motor would have been nice, but Jane would not hear of it. They cost too much. The petrol stinks. They go too fast. Her hair would be disarranged. Nine hundred reasons to afflict her son with Jane's version of sensibility. With his mother's meagre pension and his lack of contribution to their funds, a motor would be out of their reach, anyway. In the growing shadows of the evening, they arrive at their cottage. Adjusting the weight of four baskets on his arms, he is thankful that they were two of the last customers at the market before it closed. He resents his mother crowing with pride and angst that she must carry the bread, or it will be good for only a pudding.

"Mother, if you don't mind, I'd like to get inside and put these away. My arms are falling off."

"Don't be a git. They are not. I had to carry the bread, you know. If you're in such a hurry to get inside, why don't YOU open the door?"

An annoyed grunt escapes his lips, and he wonders how he is going to manage that feat. Approaching from across the road, a voice can be heard as a man comes towards them.

"Oh, Ma'am? Sir? I'm so terribly sorry to intrude. I've been going 'round making inquiries, and I wondered if you could help me. I do hope that you can."

Jane and Lewis turn 'round at the sound of the man's voice. A tall, bearded man is removing his wide-brimmed hat and bobbing his head like a junior servant as he approaches. Jane looks him up and down, appreciating his rugged appearance and the scent of hard work that wafts through the air in her direction. Rare sentimentality rises in her breast at the presence of this fellow who reminds her so much of her late husband, mayherestinpeace. Jane clears her throat and steps forwards with a smile, ready to help a stranger in need.

"Inquiries? What sort of inquiries?"

Unlike his mother, Lewis does not appreciate the smell of the pastoral life radiating from this man like petrol fumes from a motor. Perhaps his mother was not so wrong about motors and the stink of fuel, after all.

"Well, Ma'am, I'm looking for my daughter. She went missing some months ago, and I've been searching as best as I can, you know, with farm work and the joints, you see."

The man holds up a cane upon which he has been leaning. Curiosity drives Lewis forwards.

"Your daughter, you say? Have you asked the police to help?"

"Oh yes, but they've given up. They think she's been taken to London and, well, they were no help. I'll not give up, though. She's my girl, and she needs to be with the only family she has. Is there anything you can tell me? Anything?"

Lewis's eyes narrow, trying to get a better look at the fellow in the shadows thrown by the house. The man wipes his eye with his sleeve and sighs, drawing forth curiosity-driven pity from Jane.

"Well, a description would help...Mr...?"

"Of course, of course. She's just a little thing, hair like wheat; eyes like the sky...just like her mother's, God rest her soul. She's all I have left of her precious mother. What frightens me most, for her safety, is that she's different. You see, she can't hear, and she can't speak. The thought of her falling into the hands of some..."

Lewis, again, adjusts the baskets on his arms, painful from the weight. Lewis pauses for a moment at hearing the description given by the old man.

"I'm sorry, sir, haven't seen nor heard of a girl like that 'round here. Terribly sorry. Must be the worst worry in the world for a father to miss his daughter. Mum, I'm going to take this inside and put things away."

"You're about as helpful as a maggot's eye, Lewis. Here, take the bread with you."

Jane tosses the bread on top of an over-filled basket as Lewis struggles and then triumphs over the stubborn door. It gives way, he turns sideways to get himself and his parcels inside, and then kicks the door closed behind him. Cursing under his breath, he brings their purchases into the kitchen and begins to put them away.

"Ma'am, I'd be ever so grateful for any help. If even a hair on her head...oh, Ma'am, I can't...just can't..."

Jane motions the man closer to her and drops her voice.

"I'm so, so sorry for your loss. I can't imagine how I would feel about losing my son. I might be able to help you."

Chapter Twenty-Two
21 June 1926

John bounces Johanna on his knee, making his baby girl's effervescent laughter and squeals. She pats her father's face with both hands and leans forwards to kiss him and talk at the same time.

"Daddy! Horsie! Phhhhhhhhhh"

John laughs, discreetly wipes his mouth on his sleeve and then gathers the baby snugly into his arms. Sitting on the sofa next to John, Anna laughs at his attempt to wipe away baby drool from such a messy show of affection.

"You're such a bright little thing. Making horse noises! What will my little princess do next?"

Anna reaches over to rub Johanna's back; leaning over to receive her share of Johanna's evening kisses. John helps Johanna scramble over to her mother's lap where Anna and Johanna kiss and cuddle. Stroking Johanna's hair calms the little one, as does hearing her mother hum softly as she rocks her. Sarah walks into the sitting room, drying her hands on her pinny. She stands next to the sofa and waits for a moment before clearing her throat and speaking.

"Well, it's Miss Johanna's bedtime, if that's all right."

"Yes, of course. We need to keep our little one on her timetable, don't we?"

Anna cuddles Johanna closer to her one more time and kisses the curls on the baby's forehead.

"There you go, sweetheart. Be good for Sarah. Mamma and Daddy and Sarah and Ellen love you."

Sarah leans down to take Johanna into her arms and waves her own hand in a good night gesture. The wee one copies her nanny and waves, pats her chest, points to her mother, points to her daddy, and then looks 'round.

"Nite nite! Janna love! Cuppa?"

Sarah strokes Johanna's hair and then points outside.

"Miss Cup is outside with Mr William. Miss Cup loves you, too."

"Cuppa 'side."

Johanna nods, rests her head on Sarah's shoulder, and she waves again as Sarah carries her to the staircase. John and Anna wave to their child and together, they chuckle at the sweet growth of their baby girl, who is less and less a baby, each day.

Anna and John wave as Johanna waves, yawns, and waves again. They watch whilst Sarah takes Johanna upstairs until they disappear at the top. Relaxing back on the sofa, Anna slips her hand into John's hand.

"We do have precious children, don't we?"

"Yes, we do, Anna. You're a devoted mother to them."

"John, I couldn't be a good mother without you as their attentive father."

He slips his arm 'round Anna and pulls her close, kissing the top of Anna's head.

"Speaking of our beautiful children, Ellen and William have been outside for some time, haven't they?"

"Shhh, John. William and Ellen have been making up for lost time. You have to give William credit for visiting Ellen every day for the last few days. They enjoy each other's company, and there's no harm in that."

Closing the topic, Anna leans over to kiss John and then caresses his cheek with her hand as she smiles into his eyes. John pulls her closer, feeling the truth of Anna's words and the warmth of her love.

William and Ellen return from the brook in the field near the house with Rupert trotting ahead of them and back again. William did not even know the stream was there, hidden behind trees and shrubs. He thought it was a shame that Ellen could not hear the water trickling over the stones, but she looked happy, though. He is convinced she could listen to it in her heart as she looked at it. Ellen glances up at William as they walk, and he can feel her gaze without looking at her. She took his hand to help her across the stepping-stones in the brook, and he wishes he could feel the delicate grasp of her hand in his, now. Grasping her hand out of necessity is one thing, but holding her hand out of affection is quite another. He is afraid that Ellen might not want him to express the growth of his feelings by holding her hand, and kissing her would be out of the question. He would sever his own arm before he would cause her distress. William looks at her with a smile as they approach the house. He harbours no doubt that knowing Ellen and being with her touches him in places he did not even know existed within his own soul.

Reaching the garden gate behind the Thorpe house, he turns to Ellen, points to himself, draws a frown on his face and points down the road to tell her that he is unhappy that he has to leave. Immediately, he follows those gestures with those that tell Ellen of his happiness to see her. Smiling, Ellen nods and opens the gate, gesturing for William to come into the garden. He tilts his head, grinning, wondering what Ellen has in mind, yet is grateful for a few more moments with her. She leads William to the swing.

She points to herself, places her fist on her chest, points to the young man, and points to the thing that moves.

Nodding with a chuckle and unwilling to deny Ellen anything she asks of him, he sits on the swing. She holds up one finger, nods, and then runs to the house, Rupert following her. She slips inside and dashes down the hallway to the sitting room. With a breathless smile, she walks in and over to Anna.

She tilts her head to the side, points to herself, places her fist on her chest, draws a circle 'round her face, and holds out her hand and makes squiggly lines on it with her other hand's finger.

Nodding, yet wondering what Ellen might want with a piece of pretty paper and a pencil, she gets up, walks over to her writing desk, and finds her fancy stationery. Flowers, birds, and a lace border should appeal to Ellen. Anna hands the paper, pencil, and a matching envelope to Ellen. She holds the items close to her chest and smiles at Anna. Ellen turns and runs into the kitchen. She lays the paper on the table and writes ELLEN on it. She holds it up to look at it and then folds it to fit into the envelope as she has seen Anna do many times. Leaving the pencil on the table, Ellen dashes out of the kitchen to the garden door and stops. She smooths her dress and opens the door with the envelope hidden behind her back in one hand. She walks outside, towards William, with both hands behind her back. With her head lowered, she peers over to him.

Curious, William gets up from the swing and walks towards Ellen to meet her halfway, his head tilted to the side. He stops, close enough to draw Ellen into his arms and kiss her, yet too far away by circumstance to make that possible.

She points to herself, points to her head, points to the young man, points away, places one fist on top of the other over and over, points to herself, and draws a frown on her face. She points to herself, draws a smile on her face, points to her own eyes, and points to the young man.

William nods, glad that Ellen is as happy to see him as he is to see her and shares his disappointment each time he must leave. He feels the cooling blanket of grey that fuses shadows together as evening transitions into night, granting them a moment of privacy. He smiles at Ellen as he turns to walk away, as much as he hates to depart. Feeling a tug on his sleeve, he looks down at his arm and then to Ellen as she tucks an envelope into the pocket of his jacket. She raises her face to look into William's eyes. Unwilling to let his eyes part from her gaze, he moves his hand to take the envelope out of his pocket. Stepping closer to him, she places her hand on his to stay his curiosity.

She smiles and shakes her head, raises one finger, and tilts her head towards the direction the young man walks.

Her touch lingers upon his hand a moment longer than it ever has. He desperately wants to reach out and touch her face, settle that stray lock of hair off her forehead, and take her in his arms. As Ellen pulls her hand away from his, he steps back from her, smiles, nods, and waves his good night to her. He walks over to the garden gate and steps through, making sure the latch is firmly closed. This unnecessary action is but one more excuse to look at her. He waves, withdraws his cap from his back pocket, and pops it back on his head.

He looks back every few paces to see if Ellen is watching him, but she is not there. Looking down and patting his jacket, he smiles to feel the crisp envelope that she had tucked there. He draws it out, turns it over, withdraws the paper, and then unfolds it. One word. One name. He leans against a nearby tree, staring at what Ellen had written. ELLEN. His heart melts. His hand holds the most heartfelt gift he has ever received in his entire life from the most enchanting young woman. He traces the letters with his finger, remembering the first time he saw ELLEN written in the dirt. He recalls how proud she was of the words she had learnt. Smiling, he carefully refolds the paper to fit into his wallet. He wants to keep it with him. Somehow, he senses that Ellen is always with him in one way or another, whether they are together or apart. Walking the rest of the way back to his bedsit above the market, he feels warmth enfolding him the way he imagines Ellen's arms would hold him...if she could.

Walking into the kitchen to retrieve the pencil she had left on the table in her haste, Ellen picks it up. Rupert trots into the kitchen and raises his paws to her, and she bends down to stroke the fur on his head. Standing, she takes the pencil with her to the sitting room where she makes her way to Anna's desk. Ellen looks at John and Anna who are flipping through pages of a photograph album, pointing at pictures, and talking with one another. Ellen puts the pencil away and walks over to the sofa, sits down, and then leans her chin on Anna's shoulder to see better. Rupert hops up to the sofa and leans his chin on Ellen's shoulder. Anna chuckles and leans back a little so Ellen can see that she was pointing to a picture of John when he was a much younger man. Anna taps three fingers on her chest, points to the picture, points to John, and then draws a circle 'round her face to tell Ellen that John is pretty. John laughs to see Ellen covering her mouth and her shoulders shaking with silent laughter. He tilts his head to the side, points to himself, draws an X on the palm of his hand and then draws a circle 'round his face to ask Ellen if she disagrees that he is pretty. Ellen's eyes twinkle as she shakes her head.

She points to herself, points to her head, the face thing, points to the man, and draws a circle 'round her face.

John gives an exaggerated expression of relief with laughter to see Ellen confirm that he is pretty, after all.

"Anna, I was worried for a moment."

Anna leans over to kiss John's cheek.

"I've always thought you were pretty, and you'll always be pretty to me, John."

Now, it was John's turn to find a likeness of Anna when she was young to show Ellen. Finding a page of Anna's photographs, he moves the album so Ellen can see. He points to himself, points to his head, points to each photograph of Anna and then draws a circle 'round his face to tell Ellen that he thinks Anna is pretty.

She pulls the thing with faces closer, points to the face of the lady, and then draws a circle 'round her face.

Ellen touches the border of each photograph. She looks up at John and Anna with her finger against one in particular.

She tilts her head to the side, points at the man and the lady, extends her arm with her hand open and draws her arm back as she closes her fist, points to the face thing of the lady, and points to herself.

Anna looks at John and nods, John nodding in return, agreeing that they should give Ellen a photograph if she so desires. Anna slips her fingers under the picture that Ellen wants and frees it from the sticky corners holding it in place. Anna holds the photograph in her hand, points to herself, points to John, holds her fist to her chest, extends her hand with the picture, and then points to Ellen. Taking the photograph in her hand, Ellen looks at it, touching the likeness. She looks up at Anna.

She tilts her head to the side, points to the lady, wiggles her finger on the face thing, making squiggly lines, and then taps two fingers on her chest.

Getting up from the sofa, Anna walks to her writing desk and finds an elegant pen. Ellen has asked her to write her name on the photograph, and Anna does not question why Ellen would want her to do this. She returns to the sofa, sits, takes the picture from Ellen's hand, leans over to the table in front of her, and then writes ANNA across the corner of it. She hands it back to Ellen who stares at it, tucks it in her pocket, and then smiles. Standing up, Ellen holds out her arms to Anna, and with misting eyes, Anna stands and walks into Ellen's embrace. They hold each other tightly, both of them stroking each other's hair. John's eyes show his emotion as he watches his wife and his daughter share this tenderness between them.

Anna and Ellen step back from one another, and Ellen takes Anna's hands in her own. She presses them between hers and then holds them against her cheek. She releases Anna's hands as mother and daughter smile at each other with smiles that rise from deep in their souls. Ellen walks 'round the table to stand near John. She opens her arms to John, tears finally making their way down her cheeks. A tear escapes John's eye as he stands, and walks into his daughter's embrace for the first time, Ellen's head resting on his shoulder. His daughter. He whispers into Ellen's hair as he strokes it softly.

"I love you, my sweet daughter. I couldn't be prouder to be a father to you. I'll do everything I can to be a good father and make you proud of me."

Ellen steps back to look at John and Anna.

She points to the lady, points to the man, puts one fist on top of the other, alternating, points to herself, and then draws a smile on her face. She places her hands together, leaning her head against them, and points to the things that take her up to her sleeping place.

Anna moves closer to John, slipping her arm 'round John's waist, both of them deeply touched to know how completely they make Ellen happy. Nodding to her, Anna acknowledges that Ellen is sleepy, now, and wishes to go up to bed. She points to Ellen, points to the staircase, holds up one finger, and points to herself, letting Ellen know that she can go up to her room and will be up soon to tuck her into bed. They watch Ellen make her way to the staircase and ascend, stopping halfway to turn back, giving them her most beautiful smile. Looking down at Anna, John takes Anna in his arms and wipes away a tear that strays down his cheek, his voice filled with emotion as he whispers.

"She embraced me, Anna. She's accepted my love for her. Our daughter."

Anna holds John tight to herself, her eyes closed against the happy tears that eagerly wish to express how she feels. She looks up at John and whispers, as well.

"Yes, our daughter."

Both of them wipe away each other's tears and share a smile as they take a step apart. Anna points to herself, upstairs, places her fist on her palm, places two fingers on the side of her cheek, and then puts her hands together as if they were a pillow and rests her head on them. John chuckles as he nods, moves his fingers next to his mouth as if talking, places two fingers against the side of his cheek, points to himself, places his hand over his heart, and then places two fingers against the side of his cheek. As Anna nods and turns to go upstairs to help Ellen to bed, as she told him in gestures, John knows that Anna will tell Ellen that he loves her. He watches Anna walk to the staircase, look back at him with a happy smile, and then walk up the stairs until he can no longer see her.

Reaching the top of the stairs, Anna walks down the hallway to Ellen's room. The door is open, so she walks in and finds Ellen sitting at the foot of her bed, dressed in her nightdress. Walking over to the bed, Anna turns down the blankets, fluffs the pillow, and pulls Ellen's plush toy next to the pillow. Standing back, Anna gives Ellen space to come to the head of the bed and slip under the covers. Anna stifles a chuckle to see Ellen wiggle a bit, making herself comfortable, pressing her head deeper into her pillow. Ellen takes her toy in her hands and holds it on her chest as Anna tugs the blankets up, praying for an intense moment that Ellen's tormenting nightmares will keep their distance tonight. Her daughter is so happy now, and she deserves a pleasant night.

Anna sits on the edge of the bed and strokes Ellen's hair, smoothing away the stubborn strand that insists on curling itself on her forehead. Smiling at Anna, she moves her cuddly toy in a bouncing fashion towards Anna. She lifts the toy and boops Anna's nose with it, and they both laugh, Anna softly and Ellen silently. Ellen pulls the cuddly toy back under the blankets with her and snuggles it close.

She points to the lady, points to herself, places her fist on her chest and covers it with her other hand, taps two fingers on her chest.

Anna smiles, her heart filled with joy that Ellen has said that she is her mother. Anna points to Ellen, points to herself, and then cradles her arms as if holding a baby to tell Ellen that she is her baby. Ellen nods, smiling and staring up at Anna. She takes Anna's thumb in her hand, and Anna resumes stroking Ellen's hair with her free hand. Ellen's eyes flutter closed, her body relaxing with a smile still gracing her pretty face. When Anna is satisfied that Ellen is asleep, she stands, leans over to kiss her daughter's forehead, takes a step back, points to herself, taps three fingers on her chest, places her hand over her heart, and then points to Ellen. She keeps her promise to John to tell Ellen that he loves her, although she is asleep, now. Anna is sure, though, that Ellen feels their love and sees it in all they do as a family. Anna walks out of Ellen's room and closes the door part of the way, committed to coming to Ellen's aid whenever she needs them, day or night.

Chapter Twenty-Three
22 June 1926

"Ma'am, it's such a lovely day, I thought I'd take Miss Johanna out for a walk in her pushchair if you approve. The fresh air and sunshine will do her a world of good."

Preparing tea in the kitchen, Anna stops, turns and nods to Sarah who is holding Johanna's hand in her own. Anna leans down and scoops Johanna up in her arms.

"Yes! You're going outside with Sarah! A nice long walk. Maybe Sarah will take you to the park and let you run about with Rupert. Would you like that?"

"'Side! Pak pak! Pert run!"

Rupert runs in circles and woofs. Anna and Sarah laugh whilst Anna snuggles Johanna, covering her face with kisses.

"I believe it's unanimous, Sarah. Let me get you a little extra something to buy all of you a treat."

Sarah takes Johanna from her mother's arms and sets the little one on the floor to stand. Anna hurries out of the kitchen, down the hall, and to the front entryway, retrieving a pound from her handbag. She rushes back to the kitchen and gives Sarah the money. Crouching down to kiss Johanna again, she strokes her sweet little face.

"Be good for Sarah, all right? That's my big girl. Bye bye, sweetheart!"

Anna waves bye-bye to Johanna and Sarah's wave bye-bye encourages Johanna to do the same. Sarah guides Johanna out of the kitchen, with Rupert following them. They make their way down the hallway and outside to the garden where the pushchair waits, ready for their outing. Rupert stands on his hind legs, resting his front paws against it whilst Sarah settles Johanna. She ties the wee one's bonnet under her chin, and the baby will ride in comfort.

"There you go, Miss Johanna. We don't want your beautiful face to have too much sun."

Rupert licks Johanna's face, making her squeal and laugh.

"Sayah! Goggie kissy!"

"Of course, Miss Johanna, Rupert loves you. Now, Rupert, get down. Lead the way, little fellow. There's a good dog."

Together, they begin their adventure. Sarah opens the gate, manoeuvres the pushchair through it, and they proceed down the path to the road. They walk along the side to avoid motors, taking the most prolonged and sunniest route. Rupert trots beside them until he feels the urge to run ahead, turning to look back at his humans. Watching out the window, Anna is pleased that they are getting out for a long walk, today. Playing with Johanna outside is lovely, but outings like this are a healthy and welcome change for Johanna and Sarah. With tea concocted, she places the kettle on a cold burner and then puts the cups on a tray. Anna walks out of the kitchen to the sitting room, where she waits whilst Ellen finishes setting up the draught board. Anna puts the tray of teacups to one side of the playing board and smiles at Ellen's eagerness since she has already placed the red and black pieces.

She looks at the lady, points to herself, points to the thing with pieces that they move, and then pats her hands together. She points to the lady, draws an X in the palm of her hand, and then points to the thing with pieces that they move.

Anna laughs, and Ellen covers her mouth with a twinkle in her eyes. They have become competitive opponents in the game and victory is never certain at the outset. Ellen seems to assume she will win and Anna will lose. Anna considers that the match itself will put the proof in the pudding. The two of them sit down, and since Ellen arranged the board for Anna to play the first piece, Ellen sits back to take a sip of her tea. Piece after piece is moved, a sip of tea after sip of tea is enjoyed. Anna wins the first game, a triple jump to her credit. Ellen sits back in her chair and smiles.

She points to the lady, nods, and pats her hands together. She points to herself, points to the thing with pieces they move, holds up one finger, and pats her hands together.

Nodding with a chuckle, she has to admit that Ellen is probably right, that she will win the next game. Three moves into the next game, she sees Ellen wiggle in her chair, a grin on her face. Anna sighs as she realises that she has made a move that will cost her the game and Ellen knows it. She reaches over to pat Anna's hand, shaking her head, showing Anna sympathy for her loss before they have finished. They play out the game with the inevitable outcome, and Ellen leans back to clap her hands together, a look of triumphant glee on her face. Pointing to Ellen, Anna pats her hands together, congratulating Ellen on her win. Anna points to their empty teacups, stands, picks up the tray, and then points to the kitchen. Ellen comes to her feet and shakes her head.

She holds up her hand, points to the things that hold drink, points to herself, and then points to the food place.

Anna smiles and gives Ellen the tray, anticipating the tea that Ellen makes. Tea is always better when someone else makes it. She watches Ellen walk out of the sitting room to the kitchen, and then hears her fill the kettle with water and set it to heat on the cooker. She hums a soft song as she sets up the board for one more game, the tiebreaker. The cloth on the table needs to be straightened because of their enthusiastic play, so Anna does just that.

A bearded man with long grey hair, wearing a faded plaid shirt with the sleeves rolled up, and worn braces that hold up his filthy trousers, walks along the road, looking 'round him. His feet encased in large brown boots that have seen better days carry him towards a house where he stops. He stands to the side and looks from the house to the piece of paper in his hand. He taps the paper, stuffs it back in his pocket, and then hawks before spitting on the ground. Looking 'round him, he takes a deep breath, walks up the stairs, and knocks on the door.

Anna looks up when she hears a knock at the door. She walks out of the sitting room, meeting Ellen in the hallway. Anna holds up one finger, points to the front door, shrugs, as Ellen stands aside with the tray of fresh tea, her head tilted to the side, looking past Anna to the door. Anna opens the door partway and sees an unkempt man she does not recognise. To make it easier to speak with him, she opens the door further.

"Hello, can I help you?"

Seeing the man, Ellen's eyes grow wide, her mouth opens, and with shaking hands, she throws the tray of cups containing hot tea at the man's head. His face, covered in recently boiling water, reddens and he utters a bellow of fury mingled with pain. Incensed that his daughter should be so insubordinate, he shoulders the door wide open and charges through it. He elbows Anna out of his way, violating the Thorpe home with his uninvited presence. Anna loses her balance and stumbles back against the side table near the door. Stunned, shocked, and frightened, she regains her footing and runs after the stranger who thunders after Ellen into the sitting room. Tranquillity dies with the guttural howl of one word from this vile man's mouth that spews the flames of hell from his soul.

"SIGNE!"

With dogged determination, he ploughs forwards to get his hands on that dim-witted tramp. Ellen's foot catches on the edge of the carpet, she falls, looks back at the man, and her face flushes with terror, her body quaking. She scrambles towards the stairway whilst Anna rushes behind the man and shrieks at him with a ferocity no one could have guessed possible.

"LEAVE MY DAUGHTER ALONE! GET OUT OF MY HOUSE!"

Blindly enraged by his demon-spawn daughter's blatant attempt to evade his justifiable anger, he lunges at Signe. He gropes, unyielding in his pursuit to grasp a wrist, an ankle, a bit of fabric, her hair, anything at all that brings her closer to him so she can taste the fullness of his wrath. Through gritted teeth, he snarls at her.

"When I get hold of you, you'll feel the bite of my belt, my simple-minded goat."

Trying to get up from the floor, Ellen turns to see the man reaching for her. She crawls as fast as she can to the staircase, her hands grasping one stair after the next, hauling herself up, her fingernails digging into the wood. Her nails tear, bloodying her fingertips; she tries to pull herself up to what might be safety. She feels his heavy boots pounding the floor as he comes close to her with alarming speed.

Oblivious to everything but the imminent peril to Ellen, Anna instinctively runs to the fireplace and grasps the iron fireplace poker in her hand. She raises it with both hands, charges at the beast, and then strikes the brute with all her strength. The blow connects between his shoulder blades, and the force throws her off balance. She falls, landing hard on her left arm, her head bouncing off the floor, the poker clattering away in defeat. Dazed and feeling pain sear down her arm, she watches with wavering vision, Ellen's terrifying attempt to crawl up the stairs. Ellen's eyes are wide open, and she is by now, hyperventilating as she quickly turns her head to see where the man is.

She sees the lady on the floor and taps two fingers over her heart over and over.

Ignoring the blow to his back and seizing the moment of Signe's pause, he lunges, his arm lashing out to tangle his fingers into her hair. Tearing her down the stairs, he roughly shakes her head, as he would a helpless animal, by the scruff of its neck. Signe raises her hands, attempting to beg him to stop but to no avail.

"I'LL TEACH YOU TO RUN AWAY FROM ME, YOU DISGUSTING

HELL-SPAWN!"

Shaking the fog from her head, Anna's maternal fury overwhelms her pain and fear. Anna reaches for the iron poker again, leaning against it to help her stand. With the poker held in both hands, she aims at the man's head, shouting at him.

"YOU BASTARD! I'LL KILL YOU!"

She strikes as hard as she can, missing his head but catching the rear collar of his shirt with the sharp hook. Hearing the fabric rip, she expects and hopes to see blood and flesh torn from this devil's body.

Fuelled by rage that this insignificant shrew is trying to stop him from taking this thing that rightfully belongs to him, he releases his hold on Signe. Raising his arm, he whirls about, striking Anna full to the side of her head with his forearm. She staggers backwards and falls against the sofa, shoving it against the side table. The crashing sound of fragile sit-abouts drowns in a sea of violence. The man's fist clenches, poised to smite Anna's bloody mouth, again.

Collapsing to the floor when the man releases his grip on her hair, Ellen turns to see Anna, hurled backwards by the man's blow. Ellen pulls herself up with inhuman strength and leaps onto the man's back. Her arm holds him 'round his neck as she pummels his head with her fist and gropes to reach his eyes to gouge them with her bloody fingers. With a demonic howl, he reaches 'round, peels Signe off his back, and throws her to the floor like a tattered rag.

"Lay there and bleed, you stinking pigs."

Ellen's head thumps on the floor, and she lay there, stupefied, blood seeping into her hair like lies contaminating truth. She slowly lifts her head looking 'round, and her eyes find Anna. The man also turns to see where that damnable woman is now, the fiendish gutter-whore who stole his property.

Anna's vision slightly blurred from the blow and her right eye already swelling, her terror and maternal outrage drive her onward with an urgent need to save her daughter. Anna heaves herself up with a groan, lunging wildly for the beast, intent on killing, maiming, hurting, or exorcising him from their home in any way she can. She grabs a lamp as she lurches forwards and hurls it at him with all the strength she has in her uninjured arm, smashing it into unrecognisable pieces against him. He wheels 'round, shouting.

"BEGONE YOU STINKING ROT!"

He bashes the woman in the face with a closed fist, sending Anna reeling across the room, her upper back striking against a protruding table leaf with a sickening thud. The same table where she and Ellen had played draughts and sipped tea, it seems, an eternity ago. The force of the impact tips the table, cracks the mahogany, turning amusement to ashes with sparks of playing pieces raining down upon her. Her breath driven from her body, he watches the woman crumple to the floor like some filthy dead thing, its eyes still open, staring at him open-mouthed. His chest heaves with fury and exertion whilst he watches with narrowed eyes and cold satisfaction.

"Bloody scum whore."

He coughs, spits on the floor, aiming for the woman, and laughs when she flinches away from his noxious spittle.

Ellen's eyes open wide, her small form consumed with spasms of panic. Shaking her head, she reaches towards Anna, her mouth open in a silent scream, at witnessing the man hit Anna with grotesque force. She winces with pain as she drags herself to Anna's side as quickly as she is able. The man's maniacal laughter rings through the room and painfully stabs into Anna's head. Ellen rises to her knees in front of Anna and gently strokes her hair and swelling cheek, wiping away a trickle of blood with her thumb. She rests her hands on Anna's shoulders, preventing her from getting up. Holding her hand up to Anna, she motions for her to stay down, shaking her head, looking at Anna with tears in her eyes.

She points to the lady, points to herself, taps two fingers on her chest, places her fist on her chest, patting it with her other hand. She points to herself, places her hand over her heart and points to the lady.

Anna sees only Ellen's eyes, her daughter's tears, and feels Ellen kiss her forehead. Stinging wetness falls from Anna's eyes into bloody streams from her marred face as she watches Ellen's blurry visage through her one open eye. Ellen holds up a finger and then holds up her hand, a gesture that Anna recognises as a sign that she should not get up. The sight of Ellen telling her that she is her mother, and she loves her is a knife twisting in her heart, filling her with fear. Ellen sits back on her heels, stares at Anna, tilts her head, and then slowly lifts her hand to wave. Turning away from Anna, she stands with a stagger and sways with dizziness. Ellen turns to look at the man and wipes her eyes on the back of her hand. She walks closer to him as her breathing quickens with sobbing that refuses to abate. She clenches her fists in front of herself, lowers her head, and then nods.

Leaning forwards with a shroud of deathly comprehension descending and smothering her, Anna crawls towards them, looking at

Ellen, her arm stretched out to her daughter. Anna's broken voice screams through her tears. She understands, now, that Ellen is saying good-bye, sacrificing herself to that creature.

"NOOOOOOOOOOO...NOT MY BABY....Ellen..."

He moves swiftly to grab Signe, pulling her against him and nearing the door so Signe can see the pathetic wretch creep towards them. He produces a knife from its sheath on his belt and holds it against Signe's throat as he kicks at that stupid woman with a gravelly snarl.

"Come any closer, and I'll cut her like a pig."

Desperately failing to quell her tremors, with tears rolling down her cheeks, Ellen closes her eyes and holds a hand up to Anna, motioning for her to stop. Watching Ellen telling her to stay back and seeing a drop of blood glisten on the blade from Ellen's throat, she realises that this monster would have no qualms carrying out his threat. Anna slumps back, overwhelmed with panic for the child of her heart. She watches helplessly with sobs wracking her body, her heart cruelly snatched from her breast by the sight of the grim reaper at Ellen's throat. The man's demonic laughter cuts through the pained sound of grief.

"Oh cry, cry, cry, you bloody wench. I should kill you for keeping what's mine. Mine. MINE I TELL YOU, YOU DISGUSTING BITCH!"

Jabbing the knife back in its sheath, he weaves his fingers into Signe's hair, steps forwards, kicks Anna's ribs, and then drags Signe by her hair out of the sitting room, and through the still-open front door. Signe stumbles as he pulls her to his lorry parked nearby. He opens the door, throwing her in like a sack of grain and slams the door on her ankle. Signe's mouth opens in a silent scream as her face contorts in pain.

"Get IN there you pile of shit!"

He opens the lorry door far enough to grab her ankle and give it a savage squeeze where the door had crushed against it. He shoves Signe with a violent thrust the rest of the way into the lorry and slams the door shut, again. He runs 'round the vehicle, gets in, starts it, then drives away in a billowing storm of dust. He looks down at Signe, cursing her for being so damn much trouble.

With every fibre of her body wracked with pain, reaching down to touch her ankle, Ellen turns her head to look back through the grimy window, tears making it difficult for her to see what had become home.

Anna drags herself out of the sitting room to the front door, to look outside. Her eyes see the lorry pulling away and the sweet face of her girl looking back at her through the grimy window. Dust hangs between mother and daughter like a malevolent phantom. As the lorry moves further away and she loses sight of it, she slumps to the floor, curling into a foetal position with gut-wrenching sobs, seizures of anguish. She pounds the palm of her hand on the floor with impotent fury and despair as she curses herself for failing to protect Ellen.

Chapter Twenty-Four
22 June 1926

John chuckles to himself that Anna will enjoy the anecdote that Lord Ashton's valet related to him this afternoon. The Dowager Countess was delighted at Ellen's insistence that she have a go on Ellen's swing. The happy memories that such an innocent frolic brought back to Lady Ashton inspired her to have a swing put up on the estate. Since then, she has been demonstrating its use to her grandchildren. In fact, the grandchildren grow impatient when she monopolises this grand amusement. The valet even remarked that The Dowager Countess seems more jovial and spirited than anyone in the house has ever seen her. John marvels that Ellen gave Lady Ashton, a woman who could buy anything she could ever want, something that money cannot buy. Ellen touched Lady Ashton with a gift that will gladden the elderly lady's heart for the rest of her life. The astounding thing, to John, is that Ellen is unaware of how unique and genuinely giving she is. She touches everyone she meets and, perhaps, returns to them a bit of their soul that disappeared in the bustle of growing up into daily life. He shakes his head, thinking he is becoming a little too philosophical this close to supper. John rounds the corner, homecoming into view.

"How odd...the front door is open."

Sensing something is out of sorts; John brings the motor to a stop, silences the engine, exits it, and then hurries to the door. A growing sense of fear claws at his gut, every step confirming his dread. Looking through the open doorway, he sees Anna's familiar form heaped on the floor like a broken doll that some ungrateful child has cast aside. Rushing up the steps and into the entryway, he kneels beside Anna. He flicks away broken shards of teacups on the floor. He struggles to believe what he sees. He reaches out to touch Anna's shoulder, fears striking deep into his soul at the sight of blood on Anna's arm, in her hair, and on the floor. Desperate to maintain a sense of control and reason, he tries to reach Anna and find out what he can.

"Anna...it's John...can you hear me? Anna? What happened?"

Curled up on the floor, she stares at the open door, trying to convince herself that the horror was just a figment of her imagination and Ellen will walk back inside at any moment with a handful of flowers. Ellen will breeze into the kitchen, find a vase, fill it with water, and then fluff the flowers into a presentation that pleases her. In a hoarse voice, she sings in a whisper, staring past John at nothing.

"Hush little baby, don't say a word, mamma's going to buy you..."

Painful spasms cause her to whine in pain and curl up tighter into herself with a whimper. Anna's breath comes in soft gulps, the sound of someone who sobs without tears. John slips his hand under Anna's head, cradling her as much as he dares. Shock overtakes him to see her face bruised and bloodied. He grows livid that someone would dare invade their home and wreak such devastation on Anna. Nobody hurts his sweet Anna.

"Anna, love. I'm here. I'm going to help you sit up and lean against me so I can hold you. I'll be gentle."

Tenderly, he lifts Anna to sit, settling himself so she can lean against him. He moves her carefully, whilst observing how and what causes her to grimace in pain. Breathing catches in Anna's chest with movement, and she groans, resting against John's chest. He strokes her hair, wary of touching the areas where blood has tainted its golden beauty and holds her steady in his arms. Not knowing what else to do, he rocks her the way he cradles Johanna. The velvety soothing voice from deep in his chest reaches out to Anna, now.

"Sweet one...speak to me. Can you? Are you all right?"

Fresh tears flow from Anna's eyes, and she lifts her uninjured arm to grasp the lapel of John's jacket with her hand.

"John..."

Her body dissolves into uncontrollable sobs that cause Anna to cry out in fresh agony. The only thing he can do is get Anna away from the sharp reality of broken china and to the sofa where she can be more comfortable.

"Shhhh...Anna...I'm going to lift you and carry you to the sofa. The floor is no place for you. I know this is going to hurt. I promise I'll be gentle and quick. Trust me, sweet one."

Still clutching the lapel of John's suit jacket, she passively sags against him, tears and blood staining his shirt. He cradles her in his arms and rises to his feet. Trying not to jar her with his efforts, he carries her to the sofa. Even with the most humane handling, Anna moans and cries out during the interminable journey from the front door to the sitting room sofa. John rests her down on the cushions, settling a pillow under her head. He reaches for her favourite coverlet that fell to the floor and covers her. Kneeling beside Anna, he reaches out to touch her face, still beautiful, in spite of the crusted blood down her chin from a cut on her swollen lip. Yet lovely in spite of the purple, swollen, and closed eye, from which tears still fall. Always his dear Anna is beautiful in spite of the blood in her hair, the marks on her swollen cheek in the perfect form of a fist. Anna continues to wince and attempt to make her arm comfortable. John places a pillow under the injured limb, the one that is grossly swollen from her fingertips and up under the sleeve of her dress. John wonders whom he should ring first, the constable or Clara.

Deciding to tend to Anna's needs first, John rings Clara's house. A growing sense of urgency fills him when Clara does not pick up. John rings the hospital and the nurse on duty informs him that Mrs Dewhurst has gone from her office early this day. With overwhelming need, he tries one last desperate option. He rings Father Willington at the clergy house.

"Father Willington, here, how may I help you?"

"Father, have you seen Mrs Dewhurst? Anna has been attacked, injured, I'm not sure how severe her injuries are, and I'm afraid to move her any more than I already have. I've called everywhere..."

Without asking questions, Father Willington promptly informs John.

"John, John, calm yourself. She is here. We were about to go on our rounds to make pastoral visits, but they can wait for another day. I will tell her and send her over to your house straight away. Is there anything I can do?"

"Thank you, Father. For now, no, although, when Anna comes 'round and feels like talking, she may need you. Thank you, Father."

Without saying good-bye, John rings off and rushes back to Anna's side. She struggles to regain her senses enough to speak, gulping air into her battered body. She dabs her tears away on the cuff of her dress, not comprehending why there is blood on her sleeve. She looks up at John, trying to focus her eyes on his face, looking with sudden panic for any signs of injury to her husband. Closing her eyes tightly, she takes a deep breath, licks her lips, and tastes blood. She touches her lips and face, flinching. Anna opens her eyes as best she can to look at John, before she lifts her uninjured arm to him, trembling, feeling terribly cold and empty. He kneels by Anna's side, taking her hand in his, kissing her hand.

"It's okay, it's okay, I am here, and you are safe."

Looking 'round the destroyed sitting room, he is concerned that he does not see Ellen, as he knows Ellen would never leave Anna in this state unless she ran to Clara's house. He wonders if Sarah whisked Johanna to safety when this, this, whatever it was, happened. Anna's voice wavers with the effort to speak.

"He came and took her. Ellen is gone. She's gone, John."

She dissolves into quiet weeping, the truth, now spoken, hitting her as squarely as the final blow the man had dealt her. John is startled at her statement, feeling outraged, but he remains calm for Anna's sake.

"I found Clara. Father Willington said she is on her way here. Don't try to move, for now. I'm going to ring the police."

Anna nods dumbly, looks at her swollen arm that is throbbing, now. She tries to move it and gasps at the ache. She cradles it in her other arm, against the pillow. She stares up at nothing, vaguely hearing John's voice in the kitchen. The urgency in John's voice seems out of place in her mind, because the emergency has come and gone, taking with it, her sweet Ellen. She closes her eyes against the shattered peace.

Hanging up the telephone, John finds a clean cloth in the kitchen and wets it with warm, running water. Wringing it out, he hurries back out of the kitchen, down the hallway, and into the sitting room where he goes back to Anna and kneels by her side. He dabs at the cuts on her face, seeing for the first time the extent of the bruising on her face, her swollen-shut eye, her bloody and swollen lip. Fear wells up within him, wondering what happened to Ellen and where Sarah and Johanna are. He looks 'round for Rupert, and their dog is gone, too.

"Anna, Constable Frayser is on his way, now. There. That's the best I can do."

John lays the cloth on Anna's forehead, afraid to ask Anna anything else since the constable is sure to ask the same questions that want to spill out of him. Anna adjusts her arm, turns her head, and then looks at John, whispering.

"A man...he...he came to the door...and...it all happened so fast...I tried...I fought him...but Ellen..."

"Shhhhh...Let's just wait till the constable arrives."

He places his hand gently on her face and then brushes her hair behind her ear. She thinks a man came...who? Why? He wonders what she means 'but Ellen'... could she have been...he immediately shoves the thought away. The front door opens and closes, and the familiar, business-like footsteps of Clara come towards the sitting room.

"Clara, we're in here. Anna's on the sofa."

Medical bag firmly in hand, she strides to Anna's side and sits on the table in front of the sofa, one of the few pieces of furniture that escaped damage during the rape of the Thorpe home. Shocked at the battered form of her friend, she looks at John and lowers her voice as she places her bag next to her on the floor.

"Oh, dear God...John, what happened? Who did this? Did you ring the police?"

"We don't rightly know, Clara, and yes, I did. Constable Frayser should be here soon."

"Good. Good. I spoke with Dr Harper and told him what Father Willington related to me. He doesn't like to go on preliminary third-hand information, but I didn't take no for an answer. If you don't mind, John, I'll take a look at her."

John moves aside and allows Clara to pull the table closer to the sofa. She opens her kit, takes the cloth from Anna's forehead, and then hands it to John.

"Would you mind wetting this again, John? Warming it up?"

Nodding, John takes the cloth and leaves Clara to her work whilst he hurries to the kitchen to fulfil Clara's request.

"Anna, I am sorry we discussed you as if you weren't even here. I'm going to assess your injuries and if I need to notify Dr Harper, I will."

Anna's nod and moan are Clara's first indication that Anna understands what she says to her. John returns with the cloth warmed and dampened. Clara takes it from John's hand, noting that the only other time she has seen John's hand shake as it is now, was during Anna's labour and birthing of Johanna. Anna nearly died that day. John, acting as Clara's assistant for the moment, nods and hurries off to fetch a dry tea cloth and put ice in a bag for placement on Anna's eye. Clara sifts through her valise and finds the procaine ordered by the physician. Dabbing it on the cloth, Clara proceeds to examine and numb each laceration and contusion. Finally, the cold compress is positioned, and the bag of ice is gingerly placed over Anna's eye and that side of her face which has swollen into grotesque deformity.

A rapping at the front door stirs John from his readiness to be Clara's loyal minion on behalf of his injured wife. He holds up a finger to Clara who nods, turning her attention back to Anna. John's long paces take him through the sitting room, and a quick left brings him to the front door. He opens the door to see Constable Harrison Frayser standing there, notebook and pen already in hand.

"Please, come in, constable. Please do."

John holds the door open for the resolute young constable who walks in, doffs his kit's helmet, tucks it under his arm, and waits for John to shut the door behind them.

"Mr Thorpe, I'll get right to it, if you don't mind. Mrs Thorpe is the only witness, is that correct?"

"Yes, she is. She's injured and laying on the sofa in there. Mrs Dewhurst is tending to her, now."

"I'm sorry. Of course, I'll have to speak with Mrs Thorpe, but if you don't mind, I'll speak with you, first. Is there somewhere private where we might be able to talk?"

Nodding, John gestures for the constable to follow him down the hallway and into the kitchen. Constable Frayser glances into the sitting room, disarray and devastation meeting his gaze as they pass by. Entering the kitchen, John gestures to a seat at the table, and the two men sit down.

"Now, Mr Thorpe, tell me what you know. Don't assume that any detail is insignificant."

"Yes, I understand, constable. I returned from work, saw that the front door was open and immediately grew concerned since that was grossly out of the ordinary. The closer I came to the door, I saw Anna lying there in the entry hall. Oh...that reminds me...I should clean up the blood."

John looks towards the kitchen door, shock beginning to take hold. A sympathetic tone draws Constable Frayser's line of questioning further.

"That can wait, Mr Thorpe. I need to hear everything you can tell me so I can move this investigation forwards as quickly as possible."

"Yes, yes, of course. Where was I...Oh yes. I knelt by her side, and she was crying and moaning in pain. She tried to talk. A couple of times, she said something about a man and that Ellen, our daughter, is gone. I lifted Anna from the floor, carried her to the sofa, tried to make her comfortable, and then discouraged her from talking. I thought it best for her to save her strength since you'd be coming to ask questions."

Writing in his notebook, Constable Frayser nods.

"Do you think Mrs Thorpe is ready for me to have a chat with her? I'll not press her for more than she's able to divulge. I see that Mrs Dewhurst is with her, and I know that she'll wave me away if I'm causing your wife too much distress."

"Yes, there's no time like now, I reckon. I'll show you into the sitting room. At least, what's left of it."

John and Constable Frayser stand and John leads the way out of the kitchen, down the hallway, and into the sitting room. Finished with the examination, Clara sits to the side of Anna, stroking her hair and speaking softly to her. Clara looks up at the constable and nods.

"She's awake, and she's ready to speak to you. Be patient. She has a great deal of pain."

"Of course, Mrs Dewhurst. May I?"

Constable Frayser gestures towards the table upon which Clara sits, asking to join her so he can be at eye-level with Mrs Thorpe. A permissive nod from Clara brings him closer to the victim who appears so changed from the woman with whom he had previously been acquainted.

"Mrs Thorpe, I don't know if you remember me. Harrison Frayser. Constable. I need to ask a few questions."

John's attention turns to the back-door opening, and he dashes out of the sitting room and into the hallway, prepared to fend off whatever evil might dare return to his house. Stopping short, he sees Sarah holding Johanna's hand and Rupert running up to him with a wag of his tail to greet his master. Unspeakable relief expresses itself in his haste to hurry to his baby girl, gather her into his arms, and hold her tight; his eyes squeezed shut in a silent prayer of thanksgiving that Johanna, Sarah, and Rupert are all right. Rupert trots to the sitting room door looks inside and then runs back to John and Sarah, jumping and barking.

"Daddy! Saya Jana goggy 'side n pay!"

Sarah chides Rupert's disturbing behaviour.

"Rupert, whatever is the matter, boy? Hush, now. We're inside."

John holds Johanna against him, stroking her hair, feeling his daughter's arms 'round his neck, her head against his shoulder.

"That's a good girl. Shhh...No, Sarah, he's right. He's telling us something is wrong, and there is...where have you been?"

"Well, Sir, I had Miss Johanna out for an afternoon stroll and romp in the park, we had a lovely treat, and, Sir, I'm confused. What's wrong? Should I not have taken Miss Johanna out? Ma'am told me it was all right."

John looks back to the sitting room door, wondering how he will explain that which he does not comprehend.

"No, no, Sarah, that's fine. Johanna enjoyed that. Didn't you, Princess? Yes. I know you were a good girl for Sarah, too."

John pats Johanna's back and lowers his voice.

"Trust me, Sarah. Don't ask questions right now. I want you to take Johanna and Rupert upstairs as quickly as you can. I'll explain to you later. To the nursery and close the door. Do you understand?"

"Y-yes, Sir. Miss Johanna, let's go upstairs and play before your nap, all right? Rupert, come along."

Confused yet following instructions, Sarah takes Johanna from John's arms and walks down the hallway to the sitting room. John follows closely with the intention of moving in such a way as to prevent Johanna from seeing her battered mother. His plan failing, Johanna looks at Anna with Clara and a man next to her. Johanna frowns, reaches out to her mother and wiggles in Sarah's arms.

"Mamma, Jana wan kissy...Mamma...Mamma..."

Hastening towards the staircase, Sarah stifles her shock at what she sees, and revulsion for the sort of ne'er do well who would perpetrate such an invasion. A shudder races down her spine to think that, but for the grace of God, Johanna could have been hurt in all of this...

"Shhhh...it's all right, Miss Johanna. Grown people are talking. This is no place for a wee one. We'll go upstairs to play."

Johanna looks back over Sarah's shoulder as Sarah tries to hurry up the stairs with her wiggling charge. Rupert barks and Johanna begins to cry, reaching back towards her parents.

"MAMMA OWIE!! DADDY!! DADDY!!! CUPPA CUPPA!"

John, at the bottom of the stairs, wishes he could wipe away his daughter's distress. He pats Rupert's hindquarters to encourage their dog to go on up as he watches Sarah take his little girl up to the nursery. As a father, he regrets that he could not give his daughter the happy homecoming she deserves from what was likely a pleasant outing. Constable Frayser's heart goes out to the distress overflowing from this family. The sympathy expressed in the constable's voice brings John's attention back to Anna and Ellen at the centre of this adversity.

"It's all right, Mrs Thorpe. Take all the time you need. Don't apologise for not recalling my question. You're in pain. I understand. When you're ready, try again from the beginning."

Constable Frayser looks from Anna to Clara to John, and then back to Anna.

"Unhh...let me see...Ellen and I over there playing draughts. Ellen went to...oh, more tea. A knock at the door. A man I didn't recognise. Next thing I knew, a tray of hot tea flew past my head and splashed all over the man."

Anna puts her functioning hand to her forehead, pushes away the ice from her eye and takes the damp cloth in her hand. She moves it to cover her eyes, trying to block what she cannot stop seeing in her mind. She licks her lips.

"So thirsty..."

Clara raises a hand, gets up from her seat on the low table in front of Anna, and then hurries out of the sitting room, down the hallway to the kitchen. She looks through the cupboard to find one of Johanna's unbreakable cups and fills it with water. She makes her way back to the sitting room and sits back on the table, leaning close enough to assist Anna to sip a bit of water. Anna sips the soothing fluid and sighs.

"Thank you. Let's see...the man came in, thrust his way in. Actually, the door opened with such force it pushed me aside, and I lost my balance for a moment. He yelled a name...what was it..."

Anna removes the cloth from her eyes and looks at the blood stains.

"He shouted...oh yes...Signe. I don't know that name. He ran into the sitting room, here, after our daughter, catching Ellen by the hair and...and...he shook her head like an animal...John, please...tell how Ellen...forgive me, constable, I forget your name."

"It's all right, Mrs Thorpe. I understand. Mr Thorpe?"

Nodding and taking a deep breath, John relates their history with Ellen.

"Ellen, that's what we named her, arrived at our door the evening after Christmas. She was at the door and made gestures that indicated she was hungry. She was dressed in rags that were unfit to wear outdoors. Anna had given her a bundle of food but felt guilty for turning her out into the night. She ran outside to coax Ellen indoors where she could have a hot meal. Anna took her in, drew a bath for her, gave her some clean clothing, and a place to sleep for the night. Now, when Anna went into the loo to bring in the new clothing, she saw red welts, new cuts, and bruises on her back, arms, and legs. We decided to allow her to stay here for as long as she wished. We've come to love her like a daughter. She's a part of our family. Oh! Yes, we discovered that Ellen could not hear, speak, read, or write. She was terrified of men in particular and is still wary of strangers. I wonder if that man who did this to Anna and took Ellen away from us is the one who had abused Ellen so horribly."

Constable Frayser takes notes as quickly as he can, documenting the conversation.

"Mrs Dewhurst, are you familiar with this girl?"

"Yes, constable, I am. At first, she did not trust me, but in time, she came to know me as a friend of the family and by extension of that, her friend as well. I think she trusts me more than other...'outsiders' if that makes sense. Oh! And she's a pretty girl, late teens or early twenties. She's about the same size as Anna with long blonde hair and bright blue eyes. She's intelligent, quick-witted, and devoted to her family here."

"Thank you, Mrs Dewhurst. Mrs Thorpe, I know you're weary, but can you give any more descriptions of what happened, of the man, anything else you can think of?"

Clara gives Anna another sip of water, and Anna nods, her head pounding fiercely.

"Yes, that bastard, forgive me, was tall...as tall as John. He wore dirty clothing, had long grey hair and a beard. I couldn't guess his age, but not a young man. His voice was gruff like gravel. Oh, and he stank of farm animals, strong drink, and the odour of someone who hasn't bathed for some time. He, he…chased after Ellen and I fought to get him away from her. I wanted to hurt him. Kill him if I had to. He was hurting my daughter. As we fought, the sitting room fell to shambles. He did this to me, and as I lay there, he grabbed Ellen when he had the chance, held a knife to her throat and made threats. He dragged her out by her hair and threw her in a lorry. I saw it. Dirty brown thing. He drived that way, and I saw…saw…Ellen looking back."

Anna pointed in the direction of the lorry's egress and began to weep, the emptiness in her heart as painful as her physical injuries. Looking at his notes, Constable Frayser clears his throat.

"I'm so sorry, Mrs Thorpe. That must have been heartbreaking. So, we have the name 'Signe', a description of the man and his lorry. Did you see the number plate? Is there anything else? The name of the man? Where he lives? Anything at all?"

John hangs his head, shaking it in a silent 'No'.

Constable Frayser pauses, trying to formulate a compassionate way to express the difficulties that abound in this case.

"We shall investigate, be sure of that. We will do so, quietly, so anyone who knows anything about this man will not alert him and move Signe. Now, please understand, I use the name 'Signe' because that's what the man called her. That may be her given name. We don't know her specific age, we don't know anything about the man or where he lives. The description of him could fit any number of men in the area. This is going to be difficult if not impossible, but we WILL do everything in our power to find her. If we find a trace of her or the man who did this, we will let you know. Should we discover Signe and take this man into custody, we would need to take her to hospital as we can assume she will be injured. I'm sorry to say that, but we have to consider everything."

Clara pats the constable's arm, and he turns to look at her.

"If you find her and bring her to hospital, please notify me first. I'm the matron of the nursing staff there, and as we said, she is terrified of men. I can work with the physicians to assure she receives the care she needs without having to come into contact with a male."

"Yes, Mrs Dewhurst. That would be wise. I will make a note of that and communicate this to the other constables here. I will also notify surrounding villages about this situation and our agreed-upon approach. We'll need all the help we can muster. I am sorry, Mr and Mrs Thorpe. I will be in contact with you as any developments arise. Please, don't get up. I'll see myself out. Mrs Thorpe, I hope your recovery is swift. Mr Thorpe, Mrs Dewhurst, thank you. If any of you recall anything else, you know where to reach me."

With his final words, Constable Frayser walks to the sitting room door, looks about the room, fixing the scene of battle firmly in his mind. He mentally shakes his head that such violence could invade what appears to be a peaceful place as he walks to the front door. He dons his custodian helmet, opens the door and out into the maddening dichotomy of the cheerful afternoon sun against the heart-breaking interior of the Thorpe home. He walks to his motor, gets in, and then starts the determined thing. He drives to the Police station to enter his report, notify other authorities, and attempt to sort an investigation.

John sits next to Clara, taking Anna's hand in his own.

"I know that was difficult, sweetheart. I'm proud of you."

Clara rubs John's back and lowers her voice to speak.

"John, I'm going to have to get Anna upstairs to bed to examine her more thoroughly. Anna? Do you feel that anything is broken? Can we help you upstairs to bed? We'll take our time and if you need to rest or stop at any point on the way, just say the word."

"Yes, I think so, and nothing feels broken. My arm hurts and my head..."

Clara and John aid Anna's effort to sit up on the sofa. Her swaying steadies as her swirling vision settles and Anna leans against John who sits next to her on the sofa.

"You're dizzy, aren't you, sweetheart?"

"Yes. It's passed, for now. I can make it if you help me. Just give me a moment to regain my sea legs."

Clara and John look at one another and nod.

"All right, Anna, John and I shall help you stand. We'll get you to the staircase and see how you're feeling."

Nodding, Anna rises to her feet, John and Clara both supporting her. A moment of swaying passes and with one foot in front of the other, they guide Anna to the staircase. John sits on the stairs, holding out his hands, poised to catch her if she falls. Anna grasps the railing, and Clara keeps her hands on Anna's waist. They slowly make their way up the steps amid Anna's groans, gasps, and tears expressed through the clenched teeth of determination. At the top of the stairs, John scrambles to his feet to slip his arm 'round Anna's waist, Clara trotting ahead to open their bedroom door, hurry inside, and turn down the bedding. John helps Anna into the room, walks with her to the bed, and turns her so she can feel it against the back of her legs.

"You can sit down, Anna. The bed is behind you. Easy, now. I shall help you lay down."

Satisfied that John is helping Anna properly, Clara bustles downstairs to retrieve her bag. She rushes back up the stairs, stopping only to nod at Sarah who is peeking out of the nursery door. Walking into the bedroom Anna and John share, she places her bag on a nearby chair and nods to John, silently asking him to leave whilst she examines Anna. The thought does cross Clara's mind that it is a ridiculous request since he is her husband, yet she does not wish to shock him with what he might see with Anna's garments removed. John nods and exits the bedroom, closing the door without a sound and makes his way down the hallway, down the staircase, into the ruined sitting room. His footsteps echo as if he were walking through a mausoleum.

Turning her full attention to Anna, Clara wipes away Anna's hair from her forehead, mentally noting each contusion, abrasion, and laceration. Turning back to her bag, she produces a pair of bandage scissors.

"Anna, I hope you weren't fond of this dress. I'm going to have to cut it off you. I won't be able to get the sleeve off of your swollen arm, and I don't want to move you any more than we already have."

She nods to Clara, giving her consent for Clara to do what she must. Deftly, Anna's clothing is removed, exposing Anna. Contusions of varying severity to the ribs, both hips, both legs, and the left arm, useless with oedema, are observed and noted.

"Anna, wiggle your fingers and toes for me. Rotate your legs with your feet pointing out and then pointing in. Lift your right arm as high as you can. Now, your left. I'm going to touch your left arm, and it's going to be painful, but I'll be quick about it."

She nods, closing her eyes against the anticipation of more pain, no matter how gently intended. Wincing and moaning with pain, Clara draws a pillow close and rests Anna's arm upon it. She covers Anna with a sheet to preserve modesty. Turning to the bureau, Clara rummages about until she finds an old and threadbare nightdress. Without asking, she cuts the fabric all the way up the backside.

"Excellent. Nothing seems to be broken. I'm sorry that I hurt you, but I needed to know. If there had been anything more serious, I would have asked Dr Harper to come here and verify my findings. Here, let's pull down this sheet and give you a proper nightdress. If you were especially fond of it, I apologise, and I'll buy you a new one. Now, I've got a cocktail to prepare for you. I'll warn you, it's not going to taste good. It will ease your pain, though, and help you sleep. First, I'm going to raise your shoulders to have you take a sip of water."

Clara slips her arm under Anna's shoulders and raises her to take a drink from the glass next to the carafe on the bedside table. Anna can only manage a sip before she shakes her head slightly, indicating that she has had enough. Clara relaxes Anna back into her pillows, sets aside the glass, and then, takes a phial and a packet of powder from her bag. She opens them, emptying them into the glass, swirling the cloudy liquid 'round. Clara slips her arm underneath Anna's shoulders one more time, to drink the noxious mixture.

"You need to drink all of this, Anna. It's foul, but it shall help."

Making a face at the taste of the medicine, Anna manages to drink the contents of the glass. Setting aside the empty glass, Clara eases Anna back down, straightens Anna's nightdress, and then pulls up the sheet. The voice of the friend replaces the tone of the nurse, now.

"Are you warm enough, dear? Is there anything else you need?"

"John...I want John...and...and...I want Ellen..."

"I know, Anna. I know. I'll go downstairs right now to fetch him. I need to tell him about the medicine I've given you, what I saw on my examination and things like that. He'll be up shortly. You know that I love you like a sister, Anna. We'll take good care of you and do the best we can...in all ways."

Nodding and already beginning to feel the effects of the medication, she whispers her husband's name as she closes her eyes, one tear squeezing out to fall down her cheek.

As quietly as she can, Clara packs up her bag and walks to the bedroom door and turns to look at her friend. Anna is broken and broken-hearted. Clara has never seen Anna so hurt in so many ways. Lowering her head, she opens the bedroom door, exits the room, and then closes it behind her. She makes her way down to the sitting room. She sets her bag on a chair and takes out the medicines for Anna. Clara watches as John picks up pieces of furniture as if they were shattered dreams. He makes a pile of broken items and pushes some undamaged furniture into their former positions. It seems to Clara that he tries to lose himself in some kind of work to stifle his feelings. She walks up to John and puts her hand on his arm to draw his attention. He looks at her with reddened eyes, the only evidence of a man's weeping for his family having to endure such a violation and father's fear for his daughter's life. Clara's voice is barely a whisper and it finally waivers with the emotion she has kept in check until now.

"John, Anna's injuries are superficial, as horrid as they look, now. She is sleeping, and I gave her something to ease her pain and to help her sleep. She's asking for you. Here is what I gave her, it tastes horrid, but give it to her every four hours in water whether she likes it or not. If she's sleeping when it's time, don't wake her."

He takes the phials and packets from Clara, putting them in his trouser pocket.

"I understand, Clara. And I know, I'll ring you if we need..."

His voice breaks and Clara draws John into her arms, the old friends comforting one another as Anna lays upstairs, broken. All of them fearing the worst.

Chapter Twenty-Five
22 June 1926

Cyrus pulls up to the farmhouse in a cloud of dust, grinding the lorry to a jolted stop as he kills the engine. He gets out and stomps 'round to the other side. Opening the door, he grabs Signe's arm in one hand and a handful of her hair in his other beefy paw. He drags her out of the lorry and over to the door of the ramshackle excuse of a house. The rusted hinges whine their complaint as he kicks it open, throwing Signe into the house, sprawling with a sickening thud on the dirty plank floor. He stands in the doorway, daring this misbegotten creature to defy him again.

"You disgusting cow. I'll teach you to run away from YOUR FATHER!"

Signe raises herself on her forearms and looks back at him, shaking, her eyes wide, and tears coursing down her cheeks. She crawls to a corner of the room, shaking her head.

She puts her hands together on her chest and then moves them towards the bad man.

"I keep my word, bitch."

His feet pound across the room to the wall where a belt hangs stained with blood, ready for its evil purpose. He takes it in his hands, caresses the leather, folds it in half, and snaps the two halves together in a crisp and sinister promise. Laughing, he covers the distance between himself and Signe in long, malevolent strides. Trapped, Signe has nowhere to go like a chicken facing its fate as the fox moves in for the kill. He bellows at Signe.

"Turn your back to me, you bint. I SAID TURN YOUR BACK!"

He grips Signe's arm, twists her 'round, facing away from him, her knees grinding into nasty splinters. Her arm is held high behind her as he raises the belt to deliver the blow he has been aching to give her for months, now. Signe lowers her head, grits her teeth, and then closes her eyes. Her body shakes as tears roll down her cheeks. Cyrus sets his jaw, raises his arm, and then brings the belt down with a raw SNAP. He raises his arm again, the belt eager to do its master's bidding as he brings it down again and again. Fury within him builds with each blow as she gets the beating she needs. He laughs to see Signe's glad rags turn to rags fit for the wretch before him. Her hand against the wall, she arches her back at the belt's bitter kiss. With her eyes tightly closed, her mouth opens wide in a silent scream as tears rush down her face. She slumps her forehead against the dirty wall, freeing her unencumbered hand.

She taps two fingers over her heart, over and over again.

Breathing heavily, he throws the belt to the floor, jerking Signe to her feet by her hair and turning her to face him. He forces her to look at the belt, points to the belt, and then to the wall where it belongs. He gives her head a rabid shake by her hair as he shoves her towards a physical tool of Cyrus' cruelty.

"Pick it up and hang it, pig. DO IT!"

Signe falls down from his shove, shaking, her knees, elbows, and palms are scraped raw. She wipes her tears with the palm of her hand, the saltiness stinging as she reaches out to pick up the belt. She struggles to her feet and limps over to the nail, looking back at Cyrus several times on her way. Her hands shake as she hangs it up and stands with her back to him, drawing her arms up against herself, shaking, and eyes closed. Frustrated that this she-thing seems to have forgotten her place, he stomps his foot, walks up behind Signe, grips her shoulders with his fingers digging into her flesh, turning her 'round, and then pointing at the stove.

"I'm hungry, and it's your fault I've had to do for myself. You've got work to do, you stinking sow."

He drives her hard towards the stove, debating with himself whether 'fixing' this broken bag of bones is going to be a constantly irritating process or if it will be somewhat entertaining. Watching Signe's every move, Cyrus deposits his rear on an ill-prepared chair. He opens his bottle of cheap scotch and drinks deeply of the amber poison, wiping the drips from his beard on his shirtsleeve. He glares at Signe, waiting for her to fail to meet his standards. Breathing in ragged gasps, Signe wipes her eyes on the back of her hand, hobbles to the stove, and then turns to open the cupboard next to it. Amongst the dust and cobwebs, she finds some salted meat and a couple of potatoes with sprouts growing from them. Placing them on the counter, she picks up a knife, looks at it for a moment, looks back at that man, and then starts cutting the meat into pieces.

In the midst of her task, she stops, arches her back, and reaches behind herself to touch her back. She brings her hand 'round and sees blood, again. Tears fog her sight as she returns to her task, placing the meat into a pan, cutting the potatoes into smaller bits, and placing them in the skillet with the meat. She opens the stove door and walks over to the small woodpile by the door. A few pieces are all she can carry back to the stove and chucks them inside the cavernous opening. Standing up, she opens a drawer, looking at Cyrus at intervals whilst she does his bidding. She strikes a match, pauses, looks at Cyrus and then lights the wood. Dry kindling brings the cooking fire to life, and the stove heats to a useful temperature. As the food cooks, she takes a fork and picks up a piece of meat to see if it is cooked enough, bringing it to her mouth for a taste. Seeing Signe tasting HIS food, he springs from his chair, slaps the fork and meat out of her hand, causing the utensil to clatter to the floor and the gristled meat to bounce away. He swings the back of his hand across her face and shoves her away from the stove. He scrapes some of the food on a plate, takes the knife from the counter, and then walks back to the table to sit. He looks at Signe watching him, gets up, and rumbles towards her, cursing. He grabs her by her hair and drags her to the table, pointing at the floor.

"You're going to stand there and WATCH ME EAT, you stupid filthy animal. YOU don't deserve food!"

He stabs each piece on his plate with the knife, chewing the tough meat, washing it down with scotch, as his narrowed eyes mock Signe. She stands still, her hands folded in front of herself, watching him eat, and then arches her back again, closing her eyes, her face contorting. Laughing, he finishes what is on his plate. He shoves the dirty thing into her hands and walks over to the stove, picking up the pan with what little food is left. He carries the skillet over to Signe and touches the hot thing to her arm. A cruel laugh erupts when she flinches and draws away, looking at him with wide eyes, covering her arm with her hand.

"You don't need any of this, dim-wit."

He takes the pan outside and throws its contents over the fence to the hogs that gather to devour the scraps. Signe watches him walk out, walks over to the window to look out at him. She hurries to the plate she left on the counter and starts licking it before he returns. With every bit licked clean, she goes to the washbasin and scrubs it with soap that burns her abraded hands. Peering over her shoulder to see if he is there yet, she arches her back again, dropping the plate in the washbasin with a clatter. Reaching her hand 'round her back, again, she looks at the still oozing blood on her hand, covers her face with both of her hands, weeping. Walking back into the house, her father bangs the pan into the washbasin. He grabs Signe's wrist, pulling her hand away from her face. Pushing his crumb and scotch bearded face up to hers, he barks at her.

"Crying? CRYING? You're HOME, you filthy bitch! YOU should be THANKING me, and all I see are TEARS? You ungrateful bag of shit."

A slap to her face once, twice, and backhanded for a third strike sends Signe back against the counter, where the belt had left its lasting impression. His yellow teeth clench in a riled-up snarl as his fingers bite into her wrist, and then he releases her roughly.

"Does that hurt? DOES IT? You little divvy. You don't know how good you have it."

Fingers splayed apart, rigid, her muscles tense, her mouth and eyes wide open, her body shaking violently, she drops to the floor and wraps her arms 'round his legs.
Kicking her away, he grabs Signe by her hair and jerks her up, dragging to the place where he keeps her. Throwing her into the room, sprawling her face down on the dirty blankets, he looks at Signe in disgust.

"I've had enough of you, you disgusting thing."

Spitting on Signe, her father kicks her, walks over to the door, and then looks back at her curling up, staring at him. Shaking his head, he walks through the door, closes it behind him, and takes the key from above the door frame, locking it. He returns the key to its place, makes his way to his chair by the table, thumping himself on it with a petulant creak from the dry wood. Narrowing his eyes as he reaches for his amber comfort, he stares at the door, cursing the piece of hell God gave him for a daughter.

"She's useless. Mindless. Can't teach her a goddamn thing. Disobedient scum."

She rolls on her side to face the cracked plaster with bits of wallpaper flaking away. Fresh blood stains the blanket as she arches her back, a grimace distorting her face. Shivering, she pulls the dirty thing over herself. Shaking, she draws the picture of Anna out of her pocket.

She taps two fingers on her chest, points to herself, places her hand over her heart, and then points to the lady's face.

Closing her eyes against the tears that roll down her cheeks, she tucks the photograph of Anna back into her pocket and then she begins to stroke her own hair.

Chapter Twenty-Six
24 June 1926

"It was sweet of Sarah to make a breakfast that we could share whilst you're still in bed. Anna, you're not eating much. You know what Clara and Dr Harper said..."

"Yes, I know what they said."

She looks at her plate of food and lays her fork down, closing her eyes, thinking of the last time she had breakfast in bed. She was sick and Ellen... John reaches out to stroke Anna's hair, feeling for Anna's emptiness and helpless to change it.

"I wish I could say that it never happened. I woke up this morning, and suddenly it came to me what happened. It was a kick to my chest, as it is to yours. We will find her, Anna."

Anna picks up her fork, eats a few more bites of the fruit-filled crepe, and sips a bit more of her favourite tea, avoiding John's gaze or acknowledging his words. With a sigh, she sets her fork across her plate, folds her serviette, and then rests back on her pillows. She looks at him, the one who has been so gentle, tending to her every need and smiles, more to placate him than to give him an honest view of her feelings

"I can't eat another bite, John. I haven't got an appetite, I guess. Perhaps, for lunch, I'll feel hungry."

"All right, sweetheart. I'll hold you to that."

He gets up from the side of the bed and kisses Anna's forehead. Picking the tray up from Anna's lap, he sets it aside on a nearby chair and then strokes her hair.

"I love you. You know that, right?"

Mutely, Anna nods her head, tugging the blanket up over her sore arm.

"I'll take this down to Sarah. She'll be glad you ate something. You need to get your strength back."

Nodding her head, she looks past John to the wall across from her and begins to feel the hatred for the four walls. John picks up the tray and walks to the bedroom door, turning back to look at Anna.

"John, wait. I love you. And...I'd be lost without you."

Mustering a smile, he nods and looks at his precious Anna. She looks miserable. Not just physically, but there is something in her eyes that seems so far away. He walks out of the door, down the hall, takes the stairs down to the sitting room, and tries to ignore the mess that still dares him to make things right. He quickens his pace through the sitting room that is too quiet, now, making his way to the hallway and into the kitchen. Rupert has eaten only a few bites of his own food and is lying in his corner, his chin on his paws, watching everyone 'round him.

"Sarah, we've finished breakfast. It was delicious. Thank you. Anna appreciated your efforts, too. It was kind of you."

"Oh, Sir, it was no trouble at all. I'm glad that you and Ma'am enjoyed it."

"Daddy! Daddy! Mamma owie? Mamma kissy?"

John walks over to Johanna and kisses her forehead before lifting her from her high chair. He holds her close to him, thanking the heavens that she and Sarah had not witnessed the violence. At the same time, he curses himself for not knowing, not coming home earlier, not protecting his family.

"Yes, little one, Mamma is still owie. She's still in bed. You can see her after a whilst, all right? Then you can blow kisses to Mamma like this."

He puts the palm of his hand to his mouth, kisses it, holds it under his chin, and then blows the kiss to Johanna.

"Then, Mamma will catch your kiss like this."

He moves his hand as if to snatch the kiss in mid-air.

"Now, you try it."

Johanna copies John's example and smiles as she tilts her head to the side and places her hand on her chest.

"Janna make Mamma kissy. Mamma love Janna?"

"Yes, sweetheart. Mamma loves you. She's just...sick right now."

"Daddy, Janna wan Cuppa. Cuppa!"

John's heart sinks as he watches Johanna place her fist on her chest, having learnt many of Ellen's gestures. How does he promise his daughter something he is not sure will happen?

"Cuppa went away for a whilst, but she will come back to us. I promise, little one."

Johanna claps her hands and smiles.

"Cuppa come back a Janna n Saya n Mamma, n Daddy!"

John holds Johanna close, not trusting himself to let her see the expression on his face. Mustering a smile, he sits Johanna back in her high chair and boops her nose with a smile.

"You mind Sarah, now, sweetheart. Daddy has busy things to do. All right?"

Nodding her head, her face serious, Johanna waves to her daddy.

John walks back out of the kitchen, down the hall, and into the sitting room to survey the damage. Not knowing where to begin, he sits down in a chair, looks at the broken furniture, and then leans his head against his hand. Determination finally overcomes confusion and grief. He gets up and begins to gather the pieces of wood that had been furniture and decides to carry it all outside so, at least, they will not have to look at it. After several trips from the sitting room to his workshop in the garden, he returns to the sitting room to check the rest of the furniture. If he cannot repair the safety of their home and his family, at least he can mend the damage to inanimate objects.

Anxious and unable to endure another moment in bed, Anna raises herself up slowly and painfully, hurting in places she did not even know she had. Anna allows the pain to dim the intrusive thoughts of what might be happening to Ellen. She swings her legs over the side of the bed and steadies herself against the sweat that comes with an engulfing wave of dizziness. She braces her hands to steady herself, wondering if this was such a good idea, after all. Putting her hand over her eyes, she ponders for a moment about what she does want, aside from not wanting to stay in that infernal bed. She whispers to herself with painful determination.

"I don't know what I want...No, I do know. I want someone to tell me that Ellen wasn't taken from us. I want someone to tell me that the constable was wrong. I want to know that there is hope that maybe Ellen is safe."

Reaching for her dressing gown, she slips it on, wondering how she will manage to stand. She promises herself that she will move slowly, not that she has a choice, with the pain stabbing her here and there. It is best to be careful, so she does not add insult to injury. She scoots herself to the foot of the bed, holds the bedpost, and slides her feet to the floor to stand. Steadying herself, she praises herself for getting this far and is encouraged that she can make it to the sitting room. Leaning on the bedpost, she pulls the belt of the dressing gown snug and ties it 'round her waist. Anna focuses on taking one step at a time, relying on objects that do not move for support. Successfully, she navigates her way out of the bedroom and into the hallway. Short of breath, she leans against the wall to rest for just a moment. She groans to herself as she hears Sarah bringing Johanna upstairs. Sarah sets the little girl on her feet, holding out her hand to guide Johanna to the playroom. Standing as straight as she can, she braces herself to greet her daughter.

"Mamma! Mamma!"

Sarah's attention moves to Anna and a wave of concern clouds over her, and she hurries to Anna's side.

"Ma'am, should you be out of bed? Shall I call for Sir to help you?"

Anna holds up a hand, trying to smile through her pain.

"No, no, I'll be fine. I just needed to look at something different, that's all. Johanna! That's my pretty baby. Mamma can't pick you up right now, but I wish I could."

"Mamma, kissy!"

Johanna blows her mother a kiss just as her father had taught her. A genuine smile that defies pain crosses Anna's face as she catches Johanna's kiss and blows a kiss back to her. Johanna takes Sarah's hand and smiles up at her nanny. Johanna pats her chest points to Anna, and then to herself.

"Mamma kissy me! Mamma love Janna. Mamma sick n Mamma love Janna. Cuppa love Janna? Cuppa 'side?"

Sarah and Anna smile sadly at each other, and Sarah gives Johanna's hand a little squeeze. To answer Johanna's question requires gentle honesty.

"Yes, your Mamma loves her little Miss Johanna. We all love Miss Cup. We hope Miss Cup will come home soon to see her Miss Johanna. Miss Cup loves Johanna, too."

Johanna nods waves to her mother and then toddles into the playroom. Sarah looks at Anna, tilts her head, and then holds out her hand. Anna shakes her head and resumes her walk down the hallway past Sarah, leaning against the wall for support. Sarah peeks in at Johanna who is playing with her dolls and turns to watch the lady of the house make her way to the staircase. Sarah prays that Anna will not fall, and she considers calling out to John, but she knows that Anna would be upset with her. Trying to be unobtrusive and circumspect as she can, Sarah divides her attention between her young charge and Anna. Sarah holds her breath as she watches Anna take a few steps at a time down the stairs. Her hand to her chest, Sarah breathes a sigh of relief to see that Anna has made her way to the sitting room. Returning to Johanna, they begin to set a child-sized table for tea with Johanna's dolls.

With measured steps, Anna crosses the sitting room, resting against the supportive furniture along the way until she reaches her favourite chair. She turns, carefully sits, as the soft cushion sends a wave of pain through her body. Stifling her moan, she takes a deep breath and lets it out slowly. Reaching for her coverlet and pulling it over her legs, she looks out the window and remembers the night Ellen came to their door. Rupert's whine plucks Anna out of her reverie.

"I know, boy. You miss Ellen. You've been sleeping on Ellen's bed, haven't you? That's a good boy. Keep her bed warm for when...when she comes home."

She scratches the dog's ears and pats his head. He lies down on the floor, his chin on his paws. Walking into the house, John closes the door to the garden behind him. His strides down the familiar corridor echo with too much quiet. Entering the sitting room, he stands, looking 'round the room for anything else that he might set straight. Sarah has out-done herself with cleaning, and the room looks almost...

"Anna, what in God's name are you doing down here? You should be in bed. How did you..."

Anna raises a hand, still looking out the window.

"If...when she comes home, she'll need me straight away. I need to be here. Who knows? She might have become distracted and wandered too far. Picking flowers, you know. She loves flowers."

Alarmed, John hurries to Anna's side and kneels beside her, taking her hand in his.

"Anna, Ellen...the constable said they'd look for her...we won't give up hope. And, you're right. If...I mean, when Ellen comes back, she'll need you most of all."

"John, I have a funny taste in my mouth. Like licking a rusty kettle or something. I can't get rid of it."

Looking askance at her, John pats Anna's uninjured arm.

"I'll get you some water or would you prefer tea? I'll bring you anything you want."

Anna looks at John with a pained expression on her face marred by cruelty. To John, a visage and soul that will always be beautiful to him.

"I want...yes, tea would be lovely. A bit of lemon..."

Patting Anna's hand and bringing it to his lips for a kiss, he nods, gets up, and walks through the sitting room, back through the hallway to the kitchen where he begins to prepare Anna's tea.

William walks to the Thorpe home with a small box, hoping that Ellen might like to sit outside near the swing or perhaps, take a short walk. He walks up to the door, feeling a little nervous as he always does, at the prospect of seeing her. Not fear, but a nervousness that comes from a heart beating a little too quickly, a spirit full of hopeful optimism. He knocks on the door, looking at the small box in his hand, hoping that Ellen will like it. Hearing the knock at the door, John turns off the heat beneath the kettle, walks out of the kitchen, and covers the short distance to the front door. Rupert meets John there at the door, his fuzzy head tilted to the side. John cannot help himself from hoping that it might be Constable Frayser with news. Any news at all. Opening the door, John is taken aback by the sight of William.

"Oh...William. What brings you here?"

"Ahh, well, to see Ellen, and I brought her a little gift if that's all right?"

"Oh, oh...yes...I'm sorry, William. So much has happened. Forgive me if I'm a little...Come in...come in."

Holding open the door, John stands back to allow William to enter.

"Is Ellen upstairs? I'd be happy to wait for her anywhere you like. I don't want to be in the way."

"William, you're not in the way. Anna and I need to talk with you. Please. Come into the sitting room."

Confused, his cap tucked under his arm, he follows John into the sitting room. Rupert trots ahead of them, back to his place near Anna's chair. William sees the room arranged much differently than he had seen it last. 'Tis more than a little confusing to William. To see Anna sitting by the window, wearing but a dressing gown.

"Hello, Mrs Thorpe. I hope you don't mind if I..."

William's eyes grow wide as Anna turns her head to look at him. He looks from Anna to John and then back to Anna.

"Um, I don't mean to...but has there been a motor accident? I'm so sorry...is Ellen...?"

John places his hand on William's shoulder.

"Come. Sit. We'll tell you what happened."

John and William sit down, and William cannot begin to imagine why Anna's visage is so distorted and bruised. Anna tries to smile and puts forth some kind of polite façade.

"It's so sweet of you to come, William. Ellen will be...would be..."

"William, it's a long story, but the short of it is that Ellen was taken from us. A man came and did this to Anna, to our home, and dragged Ellen away from all of us."

Suddenly remembering what she looks like, Anna turns her attention to the window. She does not want the physical evidence on her face to shock William. Her voice, barely a whisper, comes from a place far away in her mind. A lone tear courses its way down her cheek as she looks through the starched, white, lace curtains at the window.

"There was no motor accident, William. There was a man. Then there was no Ellen. She's gone. Just gone."

William stares at Anna for a moment and then looks at John, a pleading look on his face as he shakes his head.

"What? Gone? Why?"

Not expecting an answer, William sets the box he had brought for Ellen on the table in front of him. He rests his elbows on his knees, his face in his hands. All he can see is the stationery with her name that Ellen had given him. That piece of paper is more precious to him than gold. John places his hand on William's arm.

"I'm sorry, Mr and Mrs Thorpe. I don't understand..."

"I know, William. We're still trying to understand it. It was a horrible and violent thing that happened here. There was a fight. Anna tried to protect Ellen. The police station and Mrs Dewhurst were here shortly after it happened. You see, William, the police station has nothing to go on. No real name, no surname, nothing. All we have is hope."

Anger that anyone would dare hurt Ellen or anyone in Ellen's family rises in his throat as bitter bile. His hands begin to shake, and he wishes that he had been here. Here to protect Ellen. To defend Mrs Thorpe. Who was that man? William wants to thrash him within an inch of his life if he hurts a hair on Ellen's head. He struggles to stay calm as he folds his hands in his lap.

"I want to help find her. I mean, she is my friend, and I can't sit by and let someone...and her family...I can't just sit and do nothing."

Looking away from the window at William, Anna shakes her head.

"No, William, look at me. This man is a monster. It's best to let the constables do their jobs. You CAN keep your eyes and ears open and if you hear or see anything that might give a clue, take it to the police station. Don't try to do this yourself. Ellen, John, and I couldn't bear to see you hurt."

She lowers her voice to a soft but urgent whisper.

"William, don't be a hero. Be Ellen's friend."

William sits back in his chair, feeling defeated. Of course, Mrs Thorpe is right. It would serve no purpose for him to charge in blindly even if he did know where Ellen might be. He looks at Anna, then John, an earnest tone to his voice that surprised all of them.

"I would do anything for her. Mrs Thorpe, you've come to know me. You've seen the friendship that Ellen and I have. Ellen has brought something out in me. She's made me see life differently, to see what truly matters. She made me feel excited about things that I'd forgotten since I was a child. She is special. It kills me to sit by and not do anything, but you're right when she comes home, and, she WILL come back, we'll all be here for her. Like you, I won't give up hope."

William's thigh takes a gentle blow from his fist to punctuate his expression of friendship towards Ellen. As Anna and John look at each other, they appreciate the steadfastness of William's friendship and loyalty to Ellen. William holds up one finger, his jaw set with determination, his lips quivering with emotion, and a single tear trying to escape. He points to himself, places a fist on his chest, places his fist on his chest again and slowly extends his arm whilst opening his fingers, places two fingers on the side of his cheek, and then points to the box on the table. As John and Anna look at one another, neither can respond without the threat of tears, as well. William reaches for the box on the table in front of him, puts it on his lap, opens it, and then takes out a figurine. He holds it out to Anna. A figurine of a boy pushing a girl on a swing.

"You see, Ellen is special to me. See, the girl on the swing, that's Ellen. The boy, well, that's me...I wanted to give her something special to remind her how it made me feel the first time she took me to the swing. I felt like a kid again..."

His voice trails off as Anna takes the figurine in her hands, looks at John, and then touches the faces of the girl and boy, and then whispers in a broken voice.

"William, I'm going to make sure this has a place in Ellen's room where she can see it when she comes home. She will know we thought of her every moment. She'll see that we never gave up hope. She'll see that we all love her very much. Thank you, William."

John wipes away a tear, William's touching gesture showing him what a true friend William is to their daughter. He takes the figurine from Anna when she hands it to him, looking at it more closely. The boy is wearing a suit. The girl wears a flowery dress and has long blonde hair. John sets it on the table and looks at William.

"Yes, thank you. We're happy that Ellen has your friendship. She will treasure this gift."

Not trusting himself to not break down, William stands.

"I'd best go, now. I'm going to pray...for Ellen and for you."

William turns to walk through the sitting room to the front door, and John gets up to follow him, Anna watching. As the two men stand in the entry hall, they look at one another. John extends his hand to William, William extending his own hand to take that of John. They share a firm handshake.

"William, I'm proud of you. You're a good man."

Nodding, William lowers his head.

"Thank you, Mr Thorpe. I want to be a good man. Ellen deserves the best of friends."

John nods and opens the door for William to take his leave. He walks out the door, hearing John close the door behind him. Anna looks down at the figurine that William brought for Ellen. Reaching out, she gently pushes the swing, held by string and watches as the figure of the happy girl swinging back and forth till it slowly comes to a stop. Anna covers her face in her hands, fresh tears falling.

Outside, William walks a distance before remembering to put on his cap. He stuffs his hands in his pockets until he comes to the tree that he leant against on the evening that Ellen gave him the paper. Once again, he leans on the tree, takes out his wallet, withdraws the paper, and opens it. Not caring who might see his tears, he traces the letters written there. One word. One name. ELLEN.

Chapter Twenty-Seven
24 June 1926

Irritated beyond words with the demented cow, he realises she is even more stupid than before she ran away. Throwing the key to the room where Signe is locked up for the night on the bedside table, he sits on the creaking bed. The stench of unwashed feet in woollen socks fills the room when he kicks off his boots. The door to the place where Signe is kept mirrors the agony within its walls, paint peeling, hinges rusting, and door latch loosened by neglect. Cyrus stares at it through the doorway of his bedroom and curses the creature behind it. A guzzle of his scotch marks the end of his day, and he slams the bottle on the surface next to him, sending the key clattering to the floor. He lays down fully dressed on top of the fully made bed and stares up at the ceiling until the liquor closes his eyes and he exhales a guttural snore.

Signe lies down on the fouled blanket, taking the photograph out of her pocket. In the darkness, even though Anna's face is barely visible, she strokes Anna's likeness with her finger. Bringing it to her lips, she kisses the image and tucks it back in her pocket. She rests her head down, lifts her head up again, reaches up to bunch the blanket into a lump, and then pats it. A silent sigh escapes her lips as one hand takes a handful of her hair as her other hand strokes it. Darkness claims her, causing her hand to fall away from the bedtime ritual.

During the night, Cyrus awakens to the sound of rain on the roof. Cursing and another swallow of scotch lull him back to sleep.

Signe's head starts turning from side to side, leg twitching, and she begins to sweat. Her arms strike out; a fist clenches and flails at the air. Still asleep, caught in the nightly demonic web of terror, she sits up, her arms protecting herself, shaking her head, her mouth wide open in a silent scream. She rolls back onto the blanket, scooting over to the corner where she kicks the wall, her hands braced with fingers rigid.

Grunting out of sleep, Cyrus rolls over, wiping the drool off his beard and lifts his head to sort the source of that damnable noise. Ire raises him to a sitting position, his legs swinging over the side of the bed. Those sounds are coming from the room she wastes. He stands and storms out of his bedroom, reaches the door, and roars a curse as his groping hand fails to find the key. Remembering that he placed the key on his bedside table, his heavy footfalls carry him back to his room. His groping hand fails to locate the key on his bedside table, but it does manage to knock his beloved bottle to the floor. Roaring with new rage, he picks the bottle off the floor, hefts it, and slams it back down on the bedside table. One hand on his bed supports him as he lowers himself to one knee, searching for the cold metal thing. Fingers and key meet and Cyrus rises to his feet with a groan. Returning to that room, fit only for a semi-useful animal, he unlocks the door and opens it. The shafts of rain-soaked moonlight sneaking in through the boarded window and tattered curtain reveal the source of his sleepless anger.

Still asleep, kicking the wall, her arms held up in front of herself, flailing with her fists, she rolls onto her side to face the wall. Signe's hands reach, meet the wall, and her shredded fingernails dig in. She gouges the once-pretty wallpaper that has faded and peeled from the wooden slats beneath it, adding her own bloody fingerprints to its pattern.

Furious at this crazed lunatic for waking him, he stomps over to her, the floor quaking, even without his boots on. He reaches down, grabs her ankle, and then drags her to the middle of the room. Hauling Signe up by her arm, he intends to knock some sense into her daft and empty head.

"WAKE UP, YOU LUNATIC!"

Thrashing her head and arms, her hands hit his face in the depths of her nightmare. Further enraged, he twists Signe's arms behind her back, shoving her face against the wall. Adjusting his grip on her wrists, he fumbles with his belt, ripping it out of its loops. He kicks Signe's feet apart, raising the belt and bringing it down with one shattering blow after another, grunting with each lash.

Her mouth opens wide, her eyes squint shut with each ripping pain applied to her back and legs. Tears course down her cheeks and neck when her knees buckle, but she is forcibly held upright, her wrists attached to the wall in a burning grip.

Winded from the effort wasted on this worthless piece of rubbish, he releases her wrists, allowing her to fall in a heap on the floor. After one more solid kick to Signe, he puts his belt back on, cinching it tight. He reaches down grabbing a handful of Signe's hair, jerking her up to her feet and dragging her out of the room, and through the kitchen. The front door is no match for his foot, and it slams open with a crash. What he needs is a chain, he thinks, and he will find one in the shed. Still holding Signe's hair in his beefy paw, he drags her through the mud like a sack of grain, to the shed. Pulling down a length of chain, he drapes it over his shoulder and then snatches a padlock from the wall. He drags Signe out of the shed, over to the hog pen, cursing the rain, cursing his wet socks, and most of all cursing Signe. He opens the gate to the pen, shoves her into the muck and chains her to a post by her ankle, ignoring the rusty metal cutting into her flesh.

"There, spend the night with your own kind."

He spits on her and walks back to the house. Sitting in the rain, her hands clutching a splintered post, her body jerks with each breath as tears run down her cheeks. The rain runs down her back, mixing with her blood, causing more pain. A sow makes its way out from the shed, through the mud, and lies down next to her. Signe lowers her head, crying.

She taps two fingers over her heart, then places her fist on the palm of her other hand, and points to herself.

A second, and then a third sow come, the three settling 'round her. She leans across one, embracing its warmth, and shivers.

Chapter Twenty-Eight
15 July 1926

He stands in the doorway to Ellen's bedroom, where Anna sleeps, now, watching her. She is blind to his presence. Anna is laying on Ellen's bed, holding a cuddly animal, staring at all the books and mementoes that Ellen has collected over time. Rupert scoots his head out from under Ellen's bed to look at his master and whines softly. John sighs, mourning the slow loss of his wife. Her charming smile, lilting laughter, and soul dim with each passing hour. Johanna misses her mother's natural affection and care, as well. Deeply affected, Sarah fusses over every meal with tender concern for Anna's health. Giving her utmost, Sarah lavishes Johanna with the attention and endearment that Anna is unable to provide. Now, suppertime is at hand, and John wishes to coax Anna out of Ellen's room, back into the world of her family. He walks into their room and over to the bed, sitting down next to Anna. He rubs her hair, her back, and then speaks to her with tenderness.

"Anna, Sarah has made your favourite roast from your own recipe, with chocolate pudding. Johanna is asking for you, too. Come down and eat with us, sweetheart."

She looks at John with a vacant expression, holding the cuddly animal tighter.

"Chocolate pudding. Ellen will like that. Chocolate is her favourite, you know."

Anna returns her attention to looking at all of Ellen's belongings, things that are not merely possessions, but are an expression of who Ellen was...IS. She shakes her head into the present, angry with herself for thinking of Ellen in the past tense, even if only for a heartbreaking moment. Fresh anger at the beast that tore Ellen away from everything comforting, everything safe, and everything home rise like putrid bile in her throat. She begins to weep anew, knowing that Ellen does not have even a single cuddly toy to comfort her, now.

With each passing moment, John loses hope that they will find Ellen. His calls to the constable are disheartening, although, he knows they are doing their best to locate their daughter. Constable Frayser, on the telephone, is most sympathetic and apologetic for the dead-ends the investigation finds at every turn with no names of people for which they can search. John detects a personal urgency in Constable Frayser's voice, having seen the devastation on that horrendous day, first hand.

His heart aches when he is forced to tell Anna the truth each time she asks about the search for Ellen. With every answer, she falls deeper into the world where Ellen is safe, loved, and...alive. Yes, John fears the worst, hushing his fears, outwardly expressing hope for the sake of his loved ones. Anna looks up at John, pushing herself up to sit next to him. Her outward injuries are healing; John notes, however, the wound to Anna's heart festers with grief that he can only guess will worsen until they have an answer. Not knowing what might be happening to Ellen is the most slaughtering agony they can feel.

"John, if you don't mind, would you call Ellen in from the garden? I'm sure she's hungry. I'll come down to supper in a few minutes. I'd like to tidy her room. She likes to keep things in good order."

Sighing, John nods, rubs Anna's back, giving into her delusions.

"Yes, sweet one. I'll tell Sarah to hold supper for a little whilst until we're ready."

Wiping away her tears, Anna gives John a vacuous smile, getting up from the edge of the bed. John stands, as well, and watches her straighten the quilt, turn it down, fluff the pillows, and place Ellen's cuddly animal next to the pillow. John walks to the door and sees Anna take a clean nightdress and dressing gown out of a drawer and lays it across the foot of the bed.

"There. Everything is ready for Ellen to prepare for bed so I can tuck her in. That's our favourite time together. Tucking her in. I think I enjoy it as much as she does."

John holds out his hand to Anna.

"That didn't take long, at all. Come. Walk down with me, and we'll have supper together. You should eat something."

"I've one more thing to do, and I'll be along. Don't forget to tell Sarah...what was it? Oh yes...the roast...Ellen enjoys a good roast ever since she made that meal for us, all by herself. She loves to cook, now. We should be so proud of her."

Unable to bear another word, John nods, yet he is inwardly terrified that he will never again see the Anna he married. This departure from the real world is far worse than any melancholy she suffered from the loss of their babies. He turns, walks down the hallway to the staircase and hesitates, listening for sounds of Anna in Ellen's room. Hearing her footsteps, he descends the stairs, walks through the sitting room, down the hallway, and into the kitchen. Johanna's genuine excitement at seeing her daddy extracts what little cheer that remains in John's being. He walks over to his daughter, lifts her out of her chair, into his arms, and holds her. Cooing playfully, he gives Johanna the best of himself that he can provide to her. Johanna is the only child that will ever come into this world as an expression of the love he and Anna share, and he shrouds his own sentiment to their plight for her sake. He owes Johanna a father now that her mother is broken, as Ellen would say. Meeting Sarah's scrutiny, he shakes his head, confirming that Anna continues to wander further into despondency.

"Sarah, no matter how this plays out...at some point, I think taking Anna to our seaside cottage would help her. She needs...time..."

"Sir, whatever you need to do to help Ma'am, you can count on me to do whatever I can."

John cuddles Johanna closer, his voice muffled in Johanna's hair.

"When...if...I take Anna there, could you care for Johanna whilst I tend to Anna?"

"Oh yes, Sir. Anything, Sir."

Nodding his head, he begins to dance with Johanna, remembering the midnight dancing that he, Anna, and Ellen had shared, the deafening volume of the wireless bringing them together for a precious memory. He will tell Johanna of that, when she is older, knowing that she will always remember Cuppa.

Upstairs, Anna walks over to the aquarium where Ellen's mouse, Mr Whiskers, lives when he is not Ellen's pocket companion. Tending to his every need is Anna's labour of love. She scoops out a bit of food and pours it in the mouse's dish, and then checks his water. Anna finds it unusual that the little fellow does not come out of his hiding place to enjoy his usual stroking, so she lifts the wooden house that John fashioned for him. Anna's hand flies to her mouth, choking the sob that punctuates the finality of what lies before her. Mr Whiskers lays amongst the wood shavings, motionless and stiff to her tentative stroke to his fur. She sets aside the hollowed wood and lifts his lifeless body into her hand. Tears fall onto his coat, his dead eyes looking at her with eternal emptiness. Cupping his body with both hands, she holds him close to her heart, wondering how she will ever tell Ellen that her Mr Whiskers is...dead? That seems too harsh. Departed? No, Ellen will think he ran away. Walking back to the bed, she holds Ellen's pet and sobs over the loss of such a small life, a life that was...no, IS...precious to Ellen. Wiping her tears away with her sleeve, a sleeve that has covered her arm for several days, she lays the mouse on her lap. Fresh tears fall as she points to herself, moves her hands down the front of herself, draws an X in the palm of her hand, points to the mouse, and draws an X on her forehead. She places her hands with palms together at her chest, moving them towards the mouse. She points to herself and draws an X in the palm of her hand. Begging forgiveness of this small creature for his death is the only way she can ask Ellen's forgiveness for his loss of life.

Returning the soft remains of what was once Mr Whiskers into the cradle of her hands; she stands up and walks to the door, bringing what is left of him to her chest, close to her still-beating heart. Whining softly, Rupert retreats to his place under Ellen's bed. Anna walks out to the hallway and over to the stairs, making her way down to the sitting room.

"John? Come."

Hearing Anna's voice coming from the sitting room, he sets Johanna back in her chair and kisses the golden curls that he loves so much. John hurries out of the kitchen, down the hallway, and through the doorway into the sitting room. He walks over to Anna, reaching out to caress her face, wiping away a tear with his thumb.

"What is it, sweetheart?"

Anna holds out her hands to show John the subject of the wretched news that they must break to Ellen.

"Mr Whiskers...help me tell her...I can't tell her alone. I just..."

With a sombre nod, knowing what this mouse meant to Ellen and the hope it symbolised to Anna, he slips his arm 'round Anna's shoulders.

"I think Ellen would be too upset to give Mr Whiskers the proper... remembrance he deserves. Shall we go out to the garden and spare her the shock of seeing him like this? We can sit down with her and explain...later."

"Yes...before she goes up to see him."

She walks out of the sitting room, holding the furry creature in one hand, stroking his fur with the forefinger of her other hand. Down the hallway, she walks, seeing only the lifeless love in her hand. She is deaf to Johanna's pleas to her mother for attention, blind to the sad shake of Sarah's head. John follows Anna, pushing away the fleeting thought that intrudes. Is this an omen? No. It cannot be. Mice die. They do not have long lives. Mr Whiskers lived far longer in Ellen's care than if he had been put out to fend for himself. Ellen will be upset, yes, but she will feel their comfort at the news. Together, they walk out of the door to the garden, John closing the door behind them.

"Anna, where do you think we should...a special place that Ellen would...I mean, will want?"

Sharply, Anna looks at John for daring to speak of their sweet girl in the past tense, but her attention moves away from the flutter of anger to a cluster of pink flowers in Ellen's garden. Pointing to them, she whispers.

"There. Ellen likes pink, you know. It's her favourite colour. I'm sure she will like...approve..."

Putting his arm 'round Anna's shoulders and then rubbing her back, he turns to walk to the shed. He opens the door, and in the semi-darkness, he finds a garden trowel that should serve their unhappy task. John walks out of the shed, tool in hand, and closes the door behind him. He walks over to the flowers that Anna indicated, and points, looking to Anna for confirmation. She nods, so John kneels to dig. Deeper he breaks into the earth, willing his fears and despair to lay at rest with Mr Whiskers. When the pit is deep enough for Ellen's mouse, John reaches out to take him from Anna's hands. She relinquishes him to John and then touches his arm.

"Wait..."

Anna pulls her handkerchief out of her pocket, stained with countless tears, and kneels beside John. Tenderly, as if wrapping a baby in a blanket, she gives Mr Whiskers a proper covering in which to rest in peace that eludes the rest of them. She returns him to John, too filled with emptiness to display further emotion.

"There...I don't know what to say..."

With gentle hands, John takes the field mouse that became a member of the family and lowers him into his grave. A single tear clouds John's vision, and he dashes it away on his sleeve. Each scoop of dirt that covers the mouse is a bit of hopelessness that shrouds their household, a dirty cloud of waiting for answers to their hopes and fears. Finished with the unhappy burial, John's final act is to take a stone from the garden and place it on the freshly turned earth. He stands, holding out his hand to help Anna rise to her feet. He draws her into his arms holding her, the first time she has allowed him to do so in days. Feeling her in his arms allows him to imagine that his sweet Anna has come back to him. Anna breaks away from their embrace, her face a blank canvas, devoid of expression. She takes his hand and walks towards the house.

"We shouldn't keep Sarah waiting any longer. Ellen and Johanna are hungry, and it's best we eat together as a family."

Looking down at his feet, John walks with Anna, the illusion of the Anna he wanted to come back to him, shattered.

Chapter Twenty-Nine
17 July 1926

Cyrus gulps down his morning dose of medicinal scotch, sets the bottle on the table with a thud, and hauls himself from his chair. He tramples across the decrepit floor to the room where he keeps Signe. He curses the fat thing he is forced to call his daughter, and it is time the lazy thing got to work. He gropes above the doorframe for the key and unlocks the door. Pushing it open, his nose wrinkles in disgust at the foul smells and filth. The evidence of his expertise in the encouragement of obedience greets his vision and meets with his approval. The grimy window is nailed shut, with boards nailed across the frame to prevent the filthy urchin from escaping. A tattered curtain enhances the gloomy interior so the disgusting idiot will not get any ideas. His gaze rests on the sleeping form of Signe, lying on a colourless and rotten blanket in a corner. Deciding on the most effective way to wake the lazy whore, he grabs a handful of Signe's hair as the toe of his boot makes brutal contact with her hip.

"Rise and shine, bitch. My goddamn breakfast isn't going to cook itself."

Signe's eyes fly open, and her mouth opens in a silent scream as she scrambles away from the one who awakened her with evil and fearful intent. Cyrus laughs and points in the direction of the chicken coop and then walks out of the room. Heavy footsteps carry him through the kitchen to his chair at the table. It complains under his weight as he sits at the table to drink his appetiser whilst he waits for breakfast. Wry amusement crosses his face as he watches Signe emerge from that room, looking at him with her arms crossed over her chest, fists clenched, shaking with those damn tears, again. Sarcasm drips from his lips, watching Signe use her hands to stifle her weeping.

"Tears. How quaint."

To reinforce his demand, he points to the door and in the direction of the chicken coop and then to the stove. Signe moves towards the wood stove, and Cyrus leaps out of his chair, covering the distance between him and Signe more quickly than one might expect. He seizes her arm, squeezes and turns his hand to leave a handprint on her skin, and then pushes her towards the door. Raising her hands in a self-protective posture, her shaking increases, and her eyes remain wide. Driving her closer towards the door, he delivers a sharp kick to Signe's ankle.

"You're not going to find eggs in here, you dolt."

Signe limps to the door, her arms crossed in front of her, held tight to herself, watching Cyrus. She looks away from him long enough to open the door, slip outside, and close the door behind her. Not trusting this little slip of a snake, Cyrus leans against the wall to watch Signe from the window, his arms folded across his ample chest. He talks to the empty room as his narrowed eyes follow her every move.

"She'd bloody well not bugger this. It's a simple task for a simpleton. I'm hungry, and I want my breakfast."

Signe's bare feet, tender from wearing shoes, cause her to pick her way across the farmyard, hopping away from stones. She reaches the coop, ducks to enter the structure, and is greeted by squawks and flapping. Dodging the infuriated hens, she gathers her tattered dress in her hands as a means by which she can carry the eggs. She reaches into the nests, collects the eggs, and then places them in her dress.

Already annoyed with her, Cyrus hisses through his clenched teeth.

"It's going to take some time to fix this broken piece of meat."

Yelling out to her, he shakes his fist.

"Break one egg, you stinking rot, and I'll break your arm."

Finished collecting the eggs and holding them in her skirt, she ducks to exit the chicken coop. Turning, she sees him at the window, and then quickly looks down and walks towards the door with shaking hands. She cannot hear the soft thud of the eggs rustling in her skirt. Feeling his glare, her hands shake even more, and she does not notice a hollow in the ground that was not there last fall. His snarl displays his displeasure mixed with perverse anticipation as he imagines his breakfast laying in the dirt and a suitable punishment if she fails to please him.

"Ha...that stupid thing isn't going to see that rut, and she'll fall and ruin my breakfast."

He takes another swig of his liquid comfort and watches with a mix of amusement and annoyance. Signe's vision, clouded by tears, prevents her from seeing this obstacle, and she stumbles. Eggs crash to the ground as she lands in the dirt next to them. Every limb shaking, she curls up, closes her eyes, and holds her arms up next to her head. Cyrus rushes out the door to Signe, not even closing the door behind him, and grabs her by her hair and arm, bellowing at her.

"THIS IS THE LAST TIME YOU RUIN MY BREAKFAST, PIG!"

He shoves her face into the egg-slimed dirt, rubbing it roughly into the egg-mud until he thinks she has learnt her lesson. A boot lands heavily on Signe's back, forcing her to lay in the muck with much of his weight behind his foul mood. Then, kicking her several times, disregarding where his boot lands, he steps back. Shaking, and crying uncontrollably, Signe curls up tighter into herself. She gags, coughs, and then spits out dirt, yolk, and shells. He stands there with a sneer, walks back into the house, slams the door shut, and then sits down to grumble to the amber liquid in his bottle.

"I'm not going to wait all day. She'd better get her fat, lazy arse back in here and do as she's told."

When she lifts and turns her head, she sees that he is not there. Pushing herself up to a sitting position, she closes her eyes, opens her mouth, and holds her side, gasping. Wiping her eyes, she reaches into her skirt pocket, pulls out the photograph of the lady, and looks at it with tears falling again. Putting the picture back in her pocket, she slowly gets up, reacting to the pain in each place where his anger hit her. She walks towards the house, stopping at the door.

She taps two fingers on her chest, points to herself, holds her fist to her chest and then pats it with her other hand.

Looking down, Signe walks into the house and over to the stove, staring at it. Hatred gleaming in his eyes, Cyrus gets up, tromps over to the door, slamming it shut.

"Were you born in a barn, you filthy thing? Look at you. You're disgusting."

Watching him with sidelong glances, she walks to the stove, brushing dirt, slime, and eggshells off her dress. Her hands shake as she reaches to pick up the frying pan, but Cyrus crosses the room faster, grabbing it. Acting as though he would hit her with it, he pushes his face in front of Signe's and grins, showing his yellowed teeth and spewing his fetid breath. His coarse laugh mixes with the din of the pan landing on the stove where he drops it. He thinks that might have been loud enough for her dim-witted deaf ears to hear. Smacking Signe's shoulder with the back of his hand to get her attention, he jabs his finger at the frying pan and then returns to his chair, glaring at this idiot demon child. Holding her arms up against herself, crying, and shaking, she picks up some wood from the pile next to the stove and puts it inside, starting the fire. She finds dried meat in the cupboard, slices it, and then puts it in the pan. Discovering a few stray beans in a cup, she takes them out of the cabinet and adds them to the spitting grease from the meat. Picking up a potato, she takes up the knife, again, looks down at it, her eyes peering 'round to see if Cyrus is watching her. Shuddering and wiping away tears with the back of her hopelessly soiled wrist, she cuts the potato. Looking at him again, she sees him gulp that vile elixir and then wipe his mouth on his sleeve. Cutting the potato, Signe takes a piece of the skin, peers 'round the stovepipe again, and sneaks it in her mouth, adding the rest to the pan. When the meagre meal is cooked, she scoops the contents of the skillet onto a tin plate and picks it up at the edges. Her head lowered, shaking, she peers up at Cyrus. She walks over to the table and sets the plate in front of him, then recoils. He jabs his finger at the floor and snarls.

"Scared, are you? You bloody well should be. Stand there and watch me eat. It's the closest thing to a meal you'll get."

Her shaking hands clenched in front of her and her head lowered, she stares at him stuffing his mouth with food that he stabs with his pocketknife, one piece at a time. He barely chews the food before he gobbles another bite. Looking up at Signe from time to time, he waves a piece of bread on the knife tip, mocking her before popping it into his mouth with an expression of cruel satisfaction. When he finishes his meal, he washes it down with his scotch and wipes his mouth on the dirty sleeve covering his arm. He glares at Signe, throwing the dirty plate at her, hitting her with it as she raises her arms to cover and protect herself. A venomous laugh of amusement slithers out of him.

"You're a scared, empty-headed rabbit with a fox eyeing you for a scrawny meal! Good. Maybe you're learning something. Well? What are you waiting for, imbecile? You wash a dirty plate."

Picking up the plate from the floor, her hands shake, and her fresh tears mix with the grease on it. Her grasp falters, the plate clattering to the floor. She holds her breath and picks it up as quickly as she can and runs to the washbasin. She sees him staring at her as she washes it with a dirty rag, in a fouled bucket, in murky water, and then her shaking hands prop it up to dry. Slamming the bottle down on the table, he heaves himself up from his chair and stomps to the corner of the room where Signe's next task awaits. He kicks a broom and dustpan towards Signe, catching her ankle with the edge of the dustpan. He will teach this ungrateful wretch to take a breath between chores.

"Have you forgotten, swine? You clean up in here after breakfast. It better be good, too. You're the only dirt that's going to be in here."

Crying and shaking harder, Signe bends down to look at her ankle, blood trickling down like a crimson tear. Gloating that he has not lost his touch, he returns to the table where his bottle waits for him. She reaches for the broom and dustpan, beginning to sweep, a hopeless endeavour. Looking up at Cyrus as she cleans, her weeping intensifies.

He glares at her and his eyes narrow as a piece of paper slips out of Signe's pocket and flutters to the floor. It looks like a photograph of a woman. He slams his bottle down on the table, not caring that the bottle tipped over in his haste. He springs up and hulks over to pick it up to see it more closely. Continuing her sweeping, his movement causes her to turn her head, and she sees the photograph of Anna lying on the floor. Her eyes grow wide, and she dives for the picture as the broom thuds to the floor. Stomping his foot on the photograph, he reaches down to pick it up and looks at it.

"Oh! So, you're carrying 'round a photograph of that witch who kept you from me. Ha! I showed her what happens when a woman crosses me."

Her eyes wide open, shaking her head, she quickly gets up and grabs his wrist, her other hand trying to get the photograph away from him. Enraged that Signe would DARE defy him this way, he backhands her across the face, sending her sprawling backwards. He opens the door to the stove and tosses the photograph of that bitch into the fire, spitting curses. Mouth open, shaking her head, she crawls to the stove, reaching out to the photograph of Anna, curling and blackening in the flames of hell itself.

"What? You're willing to burn for a picture of that thieving wench who stole you from me and made you fat and lazy? WELL BURN, THEN."

He grabs Signe's wrist, jerks her to her feet, and then slams her palm hard on the hot stove and holds it there. Her eyes open wide at the pain, tears running down her cheeks, her mouth wide open in a silent scream. She stares at her hand on the stove and then looks up at his face. Satisfied that he has succeeded in showing this animal who is the master in this house, he pulls her hand away from the stove and shoves her to the floor.

"What have you got to say, bitch? Oh, that's right...cat's got your tongue."

Crying, Signe watches the photograph waft into white ash, carried upwards in the tiny hands of flame. He picks up the broom from where it had landed and strikes her with it before dashing it to the floor. Disgusted and cursing, he comes 'round to kick the small of her back before shaking the floor with his riled steps. He glares at her laying there, arching her back with her mouth open, tears spurting from her eyes squinted shut. He watches her struggle to sit up on the floor, rocking back and forth, cradling her burnt hand as she weeps. Holding out her hand to stare at it, she taps two fingers on her chest, places her hand over her heart, and points to herself. Bellowing from his throne, Cyrus jabs his finger in Signe's direction.

"STOP IT! That's what people who've lost their minds do. I'll take you to a place where crazy people live, and then you'll wish you were here with your rightful father."

Grunting with flatulent relief, he kicks his feet up on the table; embracing his bottle and patting it as if were his most prized possession. Signe curls up on the floor, shaking, crying, and holding her injured hand. Feeling the floor tremble under the force of his footsteps, she looks up to see him standing next to her with the broom. Before she can raise her arms to fend him off, he swats her with it and holds it out to her, a dark cloud of fury storming his face. Wincing with every movement of her hand and a grimace on her face, Signe struggles to her feet. She takes the broom in her unburnt hand and begins to sweep the tear-blurred floor as best she can. Proof that this wretched child of his will not disobey him, even with a burnt hand, gives him reason to belch his approval. As he leans against the doorframe to his bedroom, he watches with small amusement that the animal manoeuvres the dustpan with her feet to sweep the dirt into the pan without using her lame hand. He watches her put the broom in a corner by the door and come back to lift up the dustpan, and he glowers at Signe when she dares to look up at him. A disgruntled sound comes from his belly, and he turns to walk into his bedroom, the sight of his bed a welcome idea to his hazy head.

"That'll teach her to carry on with her chores. Bit by bit, I'm beating those highfalutin ideas out of her head."

He sets the precious bottle on his night table and then swings himself onto the bed with a massive flop. An instantaneous snore comes as his head hits the pillow, a pillow still under the quilt upon which he lays. Moving the dustpan with her foot towards the door, she reaches out to open the door, picks up the pan of dirt, and sets it on the porch. She closes the door and then sits on the step next to the filth in the pan. Tears abating, she looks at her burnt hand, red, blistered, weeping, skin peeling away. She closes her eyes, bows her head, and shakes her head. Startling, she looks 'round her, touches the porch floor with her uninjured hand, and takes a deep breath. She picks up the dustpan and adds its contents to the filth at the side of the steps. Noticing a stick, she stares at it and wipes her eyes with the back of her unhurt wrist. She gets up, walks down the two last steps, and crouches down to stare at the stick. Holding her abused hand to her chest, she picks up the stick with her other hand and stares at the dirt.

Fresh tears fall to the ground as she writes in the dirt. CUP. She stares at it. Crouching with one knee ground into the soil, she reaches out to touch the letters, tracing each with her finger. Still staring at what she wrote, she cradles her wounded arm, throbbing, now, from hand to shoulder.

She taps two fingers on her chest, points to the squiggly lines, and then taps her head.

Standing, she tucks her hand into her pocket, feeling the absence of Anna's photograph. Bowing her head, still crying, she turns away from the house and begins to walk. The ground beneath her is a fog of brown with tufts of green desperately trying to survive. The mid-morning sunshine makes no impression as she finds herself at the door to the shed. Pushing the door open, it swings to her touch on the one hinge left that qualifies it as a door. Stepping into the cool and dim interior, her nostrils fill with dust and mites that dance upon the shafts of sunlight that peek through the rotted boards. The inevitable sneeze stabs pain through her arm, and the grimace on her face shows that she keeps to her feet through sheer strength of will. When the pain subsides to a dull roar, she sits on the floor. Looking 'round her, everything slips into a surreal fog, and she looks up to see Anna.

She points to herself, draws a smile on her face, and points to the lady. She tilts her head to the side, nods her head, points to herself, places her hand over her heart, and points to the lady. She holds out her hurt hand to the lady, draws a line down from her eye, and draws a frown on her face. She looks at her feet and looks up at the lady. She nods and smiles. She points to the lady, places her hand over her heart, and points to herself. She stares at the lady, places her hand next to her head and lays her head down on her hand. She nods, tilts her head to the side, points to the lady, and touches her hair. She smiles at the lady and nods.

Signe picks up her cuddly toys, lies down in her bed, closes her eyes, and smiles, feeling Anna stroking her hair. She drifts off to sleep, curled up under her blanket. Minutes later, she awakens with a startle and looks 'round her to see the rusted cans in her arms, the dirt floor, and the rotted boards of the shed. Even the sunlight is dirty as it tries to find a way inside. Another jab of pain from her hand stabs its way through her whole body. Sobbing uncontrollably, she sees, through her tears, a coiled rope hanging on the wall. Breathing heavily, she walks over to the rope and takes it down, a puff of dust rising when it hits the floor. She kneels, trying to tie a knot, hampered by the hand she can no longer use. Sobbing her way through the task, she finally finishes her intended loop. Taking the other end of the rope, she looks up at a beam that seems to be the only thing keeping the shed from falling in upon itself. Holding her breath, she throws the rope as hard as she can and then sobbing harder as the rope falls back to her feet. Gulping deep breaths, she tries again, her teeth clenched. This time, the rope drapes itself over the beam, enough of it hanging down to allow a small desperate hand to grasp it. She ties the end to a hook on the wall, tugging on the knot she closes her eyes and slowly shakes her head. Amongst the waste, she finds a milking stool and drags it under the beam where the rope hangs. She climbs up on the stool, and she slips the loop 'round her neck with fresh tears wetting the rope as they fall.

She points to herself, places her fist on her chest, and places her hand over her heart.

Closing her eyes, she kicks the stool out from under her.

"Where in the devil's hell is that bloody shit? When I get my hands on her..."

Having heard no sound from the kitchen, even in his sleep, Cyrus knows that Signe is not in the house. His first thought is that she dared to run away again, and he swears he will kill her with his bare hands when he catches her if she did run. She could not get far. He would hunt her down. As the myriad of thoughts race through his head, he bursts into the kitchen, runs across the groaning floor, and out of the open front door. A cursory glance shows that the only difference in the dingy farmyard is the shed. The door is open.

"Why that lazy..."

Tearing across the uneven dirt and weeds, he charges into the shed and unleashes a string of curses at seeing Signe hanging by a rope. Grabbing her by the legs, he lifts her weight as he cuts the rope threatening to take her away from him. He eases her down to the dirt floor and listens for a heartbeat, listens for her breath. Enraged cursing spits through clenched teeth as he picks her up and dumps her over his shoulder with the dignity given a sack of flour. He carries her into the house and into the room where he keeps her. An unceremonious thud on a filthy blanket is all one can hear until a shrug, and a sadistic laugh erupts from this volcano of a man.

"Don't you dare move, bitch. It's not likely you could, anyway."

His wry sneer turns to blackened thunder.

"Don't you die on me. You OWE me."

He rolls Signe over with his foot, looking at her. Rage filling him further, he spits on her and then leans down to slap her face, but her head lolls to the side, with no resistance or sound. Disgusted, he walks out of the room, locking the door behind him, cursing this thing for doing this to him, forcing him, now, to do for himself. He slams a pan on the stovetop as he walks by, returning to the bedroom to retrieve his bottle of calm.

Chapter Thirty
17 July 1926

Disgusted, he walks out of the room, locking the door behind him, cursing this unconscious and useless pile of disobedience for daring to run away in the only way she could actually escape his discipline. Now, he is forced to do for himself. He takes a pan and slams it on the stove top with a clang as he mutters vile epithets and rummages 'round for whatever food there is that might make a meal.

Father Willington drives along, Clara Dewhurst checking their list of homes to visit. The good minister is ready to lend spiritual comfort, guidance, and encouragement, whilst Mrs Dewhurst readies herself to tend to the physical needs of the people they visit. Together, they have resources that can benefit the increasing number of disadvantaged people in the county who have fallen upon hard times. They drive past an old farm, and Clara looks down at her list and then puts her hand on Father Willington's arm.

"Horatio, that farm we just passed isn't on our list. Perhaps we should go back?"

Nodding, he turns the motor about and begins to drive back to the farm they had just passed.

"We've had a busy morning, Clara; perhaps we should make this our last visit? You've got work at the hospital to tend, and I've got Sunday's sermon to prepare. What say we have lunch when we return to town and then call it a good day?"

"That would be fine, Horatio. I say we've visited three families already. This makes the fourth."

The motor turns onto the rutted path leading up to the farm. He pulls it near a structure that might pass for a house, noting that the buildings have gone past the sight of better days. He parks, turns off the engine, looks 'round, and then nods to Clara with a smile. She looks about, feeling a pang of sadness for people who are living in abject poverty, and is ready to do anything in her power to bring some relief to their station.

"Yes, I'm ready. Let's see if anyone is here."

They get out of the motor, Clara opening the rear motor door to take her medical bag in hand. Father Willington walks up to the door and waits a moment for Clara, then knocks firmly. His experience has given him that habit, as many who are so poor are often elderly, infirm, and hard of hearing. Looking about them, Clara cannot help but think that the farmstead has a dreary sadness about it. She stands next to Father Willington, her friendliest nurse-smile at the ready, wondering what this visit might bring, as each home they enter is unique.

Cursing at the unwanted intrusion, he stomps to the door and opens it just wide enough to see a man and woman out there. They are too well dressed and must be selling something or want something. He has nothing he wishes to buy and nothing he wants to give. With a low growl, he speaks.

"What are you doing here? Who are you, people?"

Somewhat taken aback by the man's grossly unfriendly demeanour, Father Willington clears his throat softly.

"I'm Father Willington from St. Nicholas at Grindale Church, and this is Mrs Dewhurst. We go 'round visiting people so that we may minister to their spiritual and physical needs. Mrs Dewhurst, here, is a nurse."

He smiles benevolently at the man, unwilling to let himself judge the outward dishevelled appearance, smell of strong drink, and the odour of an unwashed body. Feeling increasingly uncomfortable, but refusing to dismiss her professional air, Clara glances about her, taking in every sad detail. A few pigs wallowing in their pen, a chicken pecking the ground nearby and her disquiet only grows. Her compassion and sympathy fade as her eyes fall upon something distressingly familiar. She returns her gaze to the man with whom Father Willington is conversing, and stifles the rising panic within her. The grizzled farmer snarls at the two dandified strangers.

"Nobody here needs help from a preacher or a nurse. I'm no charity case, and I'm not giving anything to anybody who is."

He glares at the two of them with pointed hostility. Clara looks at Father Willington with a professional smile and pats Father Willington's arm.

"Father, it's obvious that this gentleman has better things to do right now and our intrusion would only delay his work. We should leave him to it."

She smiles and nods to the man at the door and then looks up to Father Willington with one eyebrow raised. He glances down at Clara, sensing something, but does not know what. He looks back to the man, smiles, nodding his head.

"Of course, yes. Mrs Dewhurst is right. Please pardon our intrusion. We'll be on our way."

He takes Clara's elbow and walks with her to the motor, opening the door for her to get in, feeling the man's eyes on them. Cyrus spits on the porch as he watches those two highfalutin' fools drive away slowly. Too slowly for his liking. He slams the door shut and curses at the irony of a preacher at his door. Where has God been for the last 20 years? Sitting on his dark throne and ignoring the likes of him, that's what.

Clara grabs Father Willington's sleeve with an outpouring of urgency.

"Horatio, Ellen is in that house, I am certain. We need to get to the police station as quickly as we can."

Eyes widened in surprise, his foot presses the accelerator, making the motor tear down the dirt road, leaving an air of necessity hanging in the breeze behind them.

"What on earth, Clara...what makes you think...?"

"I saw something. Trust me. Can't you make this thing go faster?"

Father Willington, believing Clara's instincts implicitly, takes in the grave potential of her words, a genuinely frightening situation at hand. He drives at break-neck speed towards town, slowing only upon entering as he watches for other motors and pedestrians. Before long, he is trotting to keep up with Clara as she swings open the motor door, dashes out, and begins to run to the door where she hopes Constable Frayser is on duty. The two of them enter the imposing stone building, breathless, the heavy wooden door closing with a loud finality.

John and Anna walk past a row of houses, and he holds her hand as he tries to point out the colours and cheerful flowers. This is their first outing since...and John is determined to guide Anna back to the real world as best he can. She was silent in the motor and only looked at her hands, folded in her lap. Now, as they walk, Anna tries to admire what John shows her, but the beauty does not cheer her. She sees things without feeling them. She looks down at her feet, holding John's hand a little more tightly. He looks down at her, considering the thinness of her hand, and hopes that she will agree to his suggestion, intended to distract her from her withdrawn thoughts.

"Anna, why don't we stop for tea and a little something to eat? As long as we're out, it might be a nice change, and Sarah won't mind if we're gone for as long as we like."

Still looking at the ground directly in front of her feet as they walk, she shakes her head and speaks softly.

"That's all right, John. We have tea at home."

She pulls her hat down a bit over her forehead, keenly aware of the bruises that are still colouring her face. Their healing, however, is not as simple as the injuries to her heart.

"Yes, certainly, if that's what you wish, we will have tea at home."

John continues walking with her, wishing he could take away her pain, but also feeling his own anxiety, not knowing what Ellen might be going through. As they approach the police station, where he had parked the motor just a short distance away, he wonders if they have any more information. John toys with the idea of stopping in to ask, but he does not want to upset Anna. Seeing Clara and Father Willington walk out of the building, John raises an eyebrow.

"Anna, look...."

She looks up, not realising that they had walked this far, and sees Clara and Father Willington. She puts her hand on John's arm, taking an interest in the happenings 'round her for the first time in many days.

"John, whatever do you think? Why would they be...?"

Crossing the street, John calls out to them and leads Anna along to talk to Clara and Father Willington.

"Is everything all right? It's odd to see you walking out of here in a rush."

Father Willington looks over to see Anna and John approach. He pats Clara's arm and whispers.

"Clara, look..."

Father Willington raises his hand in greeting, steering Clara along with him to meet the couple and calls out to them.

"Uh, well, Clara and I might have found a clue that may lead to Ellen. I don't know, but the police are going to investigate it."

He feels apprehension at giving too much information, getting their hopes up. Father Willington believes that blame would be his to shoulder, should this turn out badly, or at least unfruitful. Clara becomes excited to see John and Anna, quickening her pace towards her friends.

"John, Anna...We were doing our visits together 'round the county, and at one farmstead, the man we talked to was unpleasantly gruff and didn't want to speak with us at all, and I looked down to the ground and in the dirt was written 'CUP'."

Anna gasps, her heart skipping a beat as she takes Clara's hands in her own and looks at John, then back to Clara.

"Oh, Clara, did you see her? Is she all right? Oh, please tell me she's all..."

Anna stifles a sob with her hand as a mixture of emotions pours out of her in the form of tears. John puts his arm 'round Anna and draws her closer to him, as much to comfort her as it is to calm and steady himself.

"Clara that must be Ellen. Who else would write 'CUP' in dirt but her?"

Genuinely afraid of the consequences to Anna and John if the constables investigate and find...he shakes the thought from his head, hoping and praying that Clara's discovery will lead to a happy reunion. Father Willington attempts to be the calming voice of reason.

"Now, the police said they'd go straight away to investigate. We need to let them do their jobs and remain calm. They know what they're doing. All we can do now is wait and pray."

Clara's heart breaks for Anna, and she grasps Anna's hand tightly in her own, making eye contact with Anna.

"Anna, I didn't see Ellen, so I don't know. She may have just been indoors. As Father Willington said, the constables are going out there now to investigate. They'll telephone you to let you know as soon as there's anything to tell, you know that."

John reaches down and grasps Anna's hand, squeezing it with gentle optimism.

"Thank you so much. This is good news. You're right, it's best to wait should one of the constables ring us with some information. Come, Anna, let's go."

John nods his thanks and begins to lead the way over to their motor, quickening their pace. Confused that John is steering her away from the police station, she pulls away from him, tears flowing in earnest.

"John, we can't. We have to go there. Ellen needs me. She needs her mother."

He leans down, speaking in hushed tones.

"I have no intention of taking us home. You're right. Ellen is our family, and she needs you. We will sit in the motor and wait until we see them leave the station. We will follow them at a safe distance."

Wondering if he is doing the right thing, not knowing what the constables might find, he knows that Anna will not rest until they see for themselves. He decides it is better to face the truth face-to-face rather than wait to hear it second-hand. At least he is with Anna and can help her through whatever discoveries might come. John's own desperate hope is that their daughter is all right, yet his fears fight his hopes. Silently he prays, God, the only one hearing his soul's cry for Ellen's safe return to the ones who love her. Thankful that John sees the situation as she does, Anna runs the rest of the way to their motor, opens her own door, gets in, and then turns to watch for the black motors that will leave the station. John opens his door and gets in, ready to roar the engine to life, willing to pursue the truth, whatever it may be. He reaches over to hold Anna's hand, feeling a riot of emotions filling him. He struggles to remain calm for Anna's sake. If this goes horribly wrong, he will have to gather the pieces of the woman he loves more than life. Soon, they see three constables leave the building and pull away in two separate motors.

"And this is it, Anna."

John starts the motor and slowly pulls onto the street, following at a cautious distance. She leans forwards, her hand on the dashboard, willing them all to go faster...anxious to find out if her girl is all right, fearing the worst, hoping...

"John, can't we go faster? I'm sure they won't notice us."

Watching and following each turn of the black motors, he shakes his head.

"We can't take the chance that they'll stop and turn us back. They'll want to handle this in their own way, without interference. We're still following them. We'll get there."

Afraid to put into words her hopes and fears, but needing to share them with John, she whispers, staring ahead at the cloud of dust ahead of them.

"John, do you...."

"I don't know, sweetheart. I honestly don't know. Anna, right now, we're sharing the same hopes, fears, and feelings. We love her. We want her back, safe, with us."

Finally, they see them pull off the road and up to a farm. John pulls the motor to the side of the road, far enough away to not bring notice to them, yet close enough that they might observe the goings-on. He turns off the motor and turns to Anna, taking her hands in his, whilst Anna peers 'round him, staring at the constables walking up to the door.

"Anna, this must be it. We can't just go running out. We need to let them do their jobs. Keep in mind that what Clara saw might be a clue, but it doesn't necessarily mean she's there."

Barely hearing him, she holds his hand tightly and nods, staring intently at the farmhouse with an intensity that could burn down the walls. She waits, afraid to breathe, for any sign...of anything...thinking only of their sweet girl looking back at her from the window of a dirty old lorry as it took Ellen away...John rolls down his window and hears only the sound of a songbird that seems oddly out of place. He is keenly aware of their nervous breathing as they wait, watch, and wonder what might go on inside that farmhouse. John cannot help himself, thinking that if this is where Ellen lived, where she was brought up, they might be the birthplace of her fears and nightmares. Minutes pass, torturing them as though their fingernails are pulled from screaming fingers. Anna's eyes dart about, taking in every detail of the dingy farmstead, looking for any sign of movement or sound that might give evidence to what might be happening behind those walls. She speaks quietly but with urgency.

"John, what's taking them so long? I can't stand this...I need to know..."

He catches Anna's arm to prevent her from getting out of the motor.

"No, not yet, Anna. We don't know...I wish we knew, but we don't. You can't just barge in there...Wait...look..."

Craning their necks to see, two of the constables bring out a man, secured in handcuffs, and they can hear him cursing the air blue. Anna's eyes open wide, and she sits bolt upright, jabbing her finger in that man's direction. Her blood runs cold at the memory of the horrors he wrought and imagining what might have become of Ellen.

"Oh my God, John. That's him! That man took Ellen. He's the one..."

Anna stifles a cry with a bite to her knuckle, anger mixed with terror as they watch the constables force the uncooperative man into one of the black motors. The constables drive away, intent on their destination and passenger. They pass by John and Anna without a glance. Her eyes dart back to the house, staring at the door.

"Where's the third constable? What's happening? Where's Ellen? I want to go...."

She moves to open the door of the motor, struggling with the handle in her frantic attempt to open it. Again, John must physically hold Anna back from her impulse to run to their daughter. John does not want Anna to see what he fears most. Is Ellen dead? Injured? They must wait for the constable to come out.

"Please, Anna, wait. You can't just charge in there. We don't know. We'll go together when he comes out...I promise."

Constable Frayser kicks the door of the house open with his foot, carrying the limp form of a young female in his arms and walks towards the remaining black motor. Without a second thought, recognising Ellen in the constable's arms, she gets out of the motor and runs as fast as she can to the officer. She speaks breathlessly.

"Wait...wait...is she all right? That's my daughter...Ellen? Ellen? Sweetheart? Mamma's here."

Her heart gives a lurch of panic as she sees Ellen's condition. She has dirty and matted hair, bruises, cuts, and the dress she wore that day in shreds. The scene playing out before him, John revs the engine to life and drives up to the farm, turns it off, and bolts to Anna's side. His shock now outweighs his fears, looking at Ellen's unresponsive face from a distance, unsure how involved he should become. He has no desire to be in the way. The constable's words are urgent, unwilling to tolerate any barrier preventing his fragile charge from going to hospital for the help she desperately needs.

"Mrs Thorpe, she's unconscious and is in critical condition. I need to take her to hospital right away. Please, go home. I promise that I will ring you once they can check her condition."

Anna looks up at the constable as if seeing him for the first time.

"I'm NOT going to leave her. I'm her mother!"

Her expression dares him to defy her maternal ferocity as she reaches out to stroke her girl's hair, seeing blood in her hair, now.

"Mrs Thorpe, I don't have time to argue. If you wish to get in the back seat, it shall help if you could hold her whilst I drive, but we need to leave this minute."

Nodding, she opens the rear door of the constable's motor, sliding onto the seat, and then reaching her arms out to receive her baby. Carefully, Constable Frayser slides the girl into the back of the motor, resting her head on Mrs Thorpe's lap. Then, he stands, closes the motor's rear door, opens the drivers' door, hops in, and then starts the engine. As they drive away, John's emotions stand behind, left in the cloud of urgency coming from the motor's departure. Lowering his head and pushing aside his own sorrow and lingering fears, he walks to his motor, gets in, and follows along to the hospital.

Cradling Ellen's head on her lap with one, Anna holds her at the waist with her other hand as the motor lurches over ruts in the farmyard and then speeds down the road towards the merciful help to be found at the hospital. She fights the impending flood of tears as she looks at the cuts, bruises, and welts on her poor girl's body. A sob catches in her throat as she sees the scarlet scrapes 'round her neck. She strokes Ellen's hair, points to herself, places her hand over her heart, and then points to Ellen. She whispers a song to her sweetheart as she tries not to cry.

"Hush little baby, don't say a word..."

Chapter Thirty-One
17 July 1926

She follows closely behind the officer as they rush down the hospital corridor. Carrying Ellen, Constable Frayser is led into an examining room where he lays her on the slab of steel covered with a sheet. Anna's gaze is numb as she fixes her gaze on Ellen, the rest of the room fading away. Suddenly, she is pushed aside by an influx of people in white surrounding Ellen's motionless form, shouting orders and hurrying to carry out orders. A nurse takes her by the arm and proceeds to escort Anna out of the examining room, through the sterile white doors.

"Wait, no... I have to...she needs...you don't understand..."

"Ma'am, you'll have to wait in the waiting area. Someone will come out to see you when we've finished assessing her condition."

She backs away, shaking her head in defeat as she watches the nurse bustle back into the examining room. She turns to look about her, for John, Clara, anyone familiar. She sees the constable who brought Ellen out of the house and approaches him. The man who carried Ellen out of hell, Constable Frayser, had also been pushed out of the examining room after relinquishing his fragile charge. He stands, staring at the double doors. Anna clears her throat and nods when the good constable looks at her, concern and sympathy clouding his professional bearing. She places her hand on his arm and speaks quietly.

"Thank...thank you..."

Not knowing what else to say, she turns away from him and walks over to a waiting area, hoping John arrives soon or that she sees Clara. Taking out her handkerchief, she strives to maintain her composure, but the effort is a struggle. Constable Frayser takes one last glance at the doorway between striving and anxiety, bows his head and prays as his footsteps lead him down the hallway from which he had come, the smell of antiseptic mercy filling his nostrils. Walking outside, the sunshine blinds him for a moment. He gathers himself, takes a deep breath, and once again, dons the façade of a constable on duty, serving this town and its populace. His shoulders squared, he sets himself to return to his work.

John parks the motor haphazardly and hurries into the hospital's front entrance, down the institutional hallway, looking for Anna. He finds a nurse who points and tells him where the waiting area is, without giving further information in response to his many questions. He walks in and quickly goes to Anna's side and sits next to her, the chairs as unwelcoming as the situation in which they find themselves. Seeing Anna's nervousness and welling tears, he takes her hand.

"Anna, what are they saying? How is she?"

She squeezes John's hand and looks into his eyes, pleadingly, and whispers in a trembling voice.

"There's no word yet, John. The officer carried her into a room, and then a nurse made us come out here...and...I just don't...know."

Holding her hand, he pats it with his other hand and looks down at their joined hands, unified in love, concern, purpose, and questions.

"I will see what I can find out. I asked questions when I came in, but the nurse at the desk had no answers."

One more pat to Anna's hand and a gentle caress to her cheek, he gets up to seek out a nurse who might know something about Ellen. He finds a matronly woman in white with a clipboard walking by him, so he politely gains her attention.

"Excuse me, my wife and I are here for the young girl who was just brought in. The one carried in by Constable Frayser. Can you tell me anything? How is she? Is she conscious?"

"Sir, as soon as we've ascertained her condition and the doctor has determined the appropriate course of treatment; we will advise you of such. Please, be patient. I know you and your wife are filled with the utmost concern, but this takes time."

"Yes, of course. We are worried. She has been missing for...I apologise, yes; please let us know right away, please."

John returns to the waiting area and Anna, taking his place next to her.

"The nurse would only tell me that they are examining her, and they'll let us know anything as soon as they are able. I'm sure they are doing all they can, and they're busy, but they do understand we want to be informed the moment they can tell us anything."

She nods, looks down at her hands, and slumps back in her chair, trying not to fidget with her handkerchief. She speaks so quietly that John can barely hear her.

"Yes, I reckon they will. The waiting again..."

She looks at John with fresh tears blurring his sweet face.

"After the waiting before..."

Her words are punctuated by a soft sob as she brings her handkerchief up to her face to stifle the indignity of such a profound show of emotion. John slips his arm 'round her shoulders and lets his inadequate words attempt to reassure her, in spite of his lack of certainty.

"Yes, more waiting, but we have her back with us now. She's safe. Ellen is safe. I know everything will be all right, Anna."

She takes John's hand and squeezes it with surprising strength and resolve. She stares ahead of her, at a wrinkle in the wall's plaster, willing Ellen to heal, be whole, and come back to them from the dark place where she is now.

"Yes, we have her back with us where she belongs and where she'll stay."

A strange doctor that they do not recognise enters the waiting area and sees the only two people there who must be waiting for news of his most recent patient. He approaches the couple and pulls up a chair near them.

"Mr and Mrs Thorpe? I am Doctor Aldrich, Dr Harper's colleague. I know that you're concerned for your daughter, and rightly so. The young woman remains unconscious, as she was when she arrived. As you know, her injuries were cruelly dealt, but they were not life-threatening except for the red marks on the neck. Right now, she is breathing adequately without assistance, and we can only wait for her to regain consciousness to determine what if any, damage exists that only a conscious patient can display."

Doctor Aldrich sits back, waiting to let Mr and Mrs Thorpe digest his words and to see if the couple fully understands what he is saying. John looks down at Anna's hand, held in his, and feels the gall of anger rising in his throat towards the monster that did this to their sweet girl. Gritting his teeth, he musters a question directed at the physician.

"What about her organs and bones?"

"Mr Thorpe, we've conducted a thorough examination with all the technology and skills we have. We found no internal damage or broken bones. Her trauma, so far, is limited to what one can see with the naked eye. Thankfully, it appears that she was healthy before these assaults on her person, which will make her body heal more quickly. Once she regains consciousness, we will be able to determine if she suffers any mental deficiency due to a lack of oxygen, given the marks about her neck. We don't know the cause of the red marks, so we can only guess with caution that they may be the reason for her unconscious state. The nurses are moving her to a bed, now, and when they have her settled, they will allow you to see her for a brief time."

A shaking hand rubbing Anna's back is the best reassurance John can give her as he watches how she is taking the news.

"See? She's in good hands. She'll be settled in her bed, soon, and then we can see her for ourselves. Ellen will be all right, Anna, you'll see."

Dazed, she nods, trying to grasp the idea that Ellen might wake up to silence and a terrifying and confusing world. She sighs, wondering how much more her sweet girl must endure on this earth. Seeing a figure in white, John and Anna focus on the nurse standing in the doorway.

"Mr and Mrs Thorpe, you may come with me to see the patient, but only for a few minutes."

As one, John and Anna stand and follow the nurse, eager to set eyes on their precious girl. They make their way through a maze of corridors to a large room called 'Women's Ward' according to a sign on the double doors. Anna gasps as they enter, seeing row upon row of beds, each holding a female patient. Frantically, she searches from one face to the next as they pass each bed. John, also searching for the familiar face of their daughter, he feels daunted by the anonymity and warehouse feeling that comes over him. These are not women, they are patients. They are just charts. They are merely a number. A chill runs down his spine at the thought that Ellen has been reduced to a diagnosis without having a name. The nurse stops at a bed and gestures to the girl lying there.

"Here she is. Please. Only a moment."

She steps away, looking at her watch, giving the couple privacy, as much as the environment allows. Spotting a chair nearby, Anna pulls it over, next to Ellen's bed, and sits. She takes Ellen's hand, the one that is not bandaged. She strokes Ellen's bruised arm with a mother's touch and whispers to her sweet girl.

"Mamma is here, and I won't leave you."

Her voice breaks as new tears course down her cheeks, and she points to herself, places her hand on her heart, and points to Ellen. Standing behind Anna, John's hand on her shoulder, he looks down at the precious soul who has been tortured, probably for her whole life and whispers as he squeezes Anna's shoulder.

"You are home, sweet Cup. We're here with you, sweetheart. You're safe and never need to worry again."

The nurse, looking at her watch, walks over to the couple by the girl's bed, her footsteps giving an air of authority.

"Mr and Mrs Thorpe, you'll have to leave now. She needs her rest. There are other patients here, as well, who shouldn't be disturbed."

Anna turns to the nurse, her eyes opening wide.

"I can't...no, I won't leave her."

She looks 'round at the other patients lying there, neatly in a row, some looking at them, and then turns back to the nurse, lowering her voice.

"I want her in a private room. I don't care what it takes or how much it costs. I will stay with her in a private room so the other patients won't have to be disturbed. A private room. That's what we need."

"I can understand why you feel this way, Mrs Thorpe, but we can't just give private rooms without a good reason. I assure you, every patient is important, just as your daughter is."

Anger welling up within her, she stands up from her chair and approaches the nurse a little more closely than the nurse expects and speaks quietly but firmly.

"I asked for a private room for her so that I can stay with her day and night. I will not leave her. I want her in a private room, now. Do you understand?"

Clara strides into the women's ward where Ellen is, according to the nurses on duty. She sees Anna standing close to the attending nurse, sensing a battle of wills is at hand. Clara quickens her pace to stave off certain bloodshed, should Anna's will be thwarted in this instance. She reaches them and places her hand on Anna's arm, giving a reassuring squeeze.

"Anna, allow me."

She turns to the nurse, and in a quiet yet authoritative tone speaks to her.

"Nurse, I'm confident that whatever Mrs Thorpe has requested is not unreasonable, is it?"

Stepping back and standing up straight, the nurse faces her director.

"Mrs Dewhurst, Mrs Thorpe has asked for a private room for this patient so that she can stay with her and not leave, but we don't just...Not without a doctor's..."

Clara raises an eyebrow at the nurse.

"I know this girl and the care she's received from Mr and Mrs Thorpe. Her needs are unique, and the situation does require special handling due to this young woman's requirements for care. You will move her to a private room immediately, you will allow Mrs Thorpe to stay, and you will afford her every courtesy. Do I make myself clear?"

The nurse nods and hustles away to carry out her superior's orders. John greets Clara with an expression of gratitude."

"Clara, thank you, we both thank you. You know what this means to us."

John turns to Anna, reaching out to rub her arm, hoping to lend her some of his strength for the agonising wait ahead of them.

"Anna, I will go, explain everything to Sarah, give Johanna your love and try to help her understand why you aren't there. I'll pack a bag for you and will return with it soon."

He leans down to kiss her cheek and whisper in her ear.

"I love you, Johanna loves you, and Ellen loves you."

John straightens up, looks at Clara with a thankful nod, and then walks through the ward, averting his eyes from the stares of women following him as he departs.

Clara nods her understanding and watches John take his leave. She turns to Anna, gathering her in her arms for a gentle embrace.

"Now, Anna, leave it all to me. If there is any problem in the slightest, let me know, and I will see to it personally that it is made right."

Anna nods, wiping away tears of relief. Clara massages Anna's back and gives her a reassuring smile. Clara turns, taking one last look at Ellen as she walks away with a prayer that Ellen will recover...begging God silently. Anna watches Clara walk away and feels sure that she and Ellen will have the privacy they need to ensure that Ellen will see her mother first if...no, when she wakes up. She sits back down in the chair next to Ellen and takes her hand, again, reaching up to stroke Ellen's fouled hair. Her heart breaks as she watches Ellen just lay there, motionless, helpless, bruises in all colours covering her visible body. This is so different from her sweet girl drifting off to sleep in her own bed, surrounded by her cuddly animals, and the love of her own dear family.

"Mamma is here, Ellen. I won't leave you."

She points to herself and points to her own eyes, giving a gesture that encompasses Ellen from head to toe and then points to Ellen, telling her sweet girl that she will watch over her in gestures that Ellen could 'hear' if only she were awake.

Chapter Thirty-Two
18 July 1926

Constable Frayser shakes his head in disbelief at Mr Holmes and his behaviours, not the least of which is his declaration of innocence. He refuses legal counsel, he refuses to believe he will go to trial, and he does not want to go to London whilst he awaits trial. The man even waives his rights, as he'd been cautioned. He sighs at the prospect of questioning Mr Holmes, an unpleasant task delegated to him by his superiors. Saving for last, the supper intended for Mr Holmes, he carries it to the iron door, holding the tray in one hand and fumbling with the keys on his belt with the other until he finds the correct one. The town does not have a large gaol, but it does serve its purpose in holding up to six prisoners.

"Mr Holmes, I have your supper."

He slides the tray through the slot between the bars, waiting for Cyrus to get up from his cot and take his tray. Cyrus looks at the plate of food, grabs it, sets it aside on the bed, and stands there glaring at the constable.

"You've got no right to keep me here. I've done nothing wrong."

Taking a chair from the wall nearby, Constable Frayser pulls it close to the cell and sits.

"Calm down, Mr Holmes. Just accept the fact that you're here and have your supper. You need your nourishment."

Still glaring at the officer, Cyrus sits down on the cot and begins eating, the best food he has tasted since... He coughs a bit at the thought of his wife's cooking and grimaces, setting the tray aside, staring at a spot on the wall.

"I've lost my appetite."

"I can understand, Mr Holmes. You don't need to eat if you don't feel up to it. I won't take it away until you're sure you don't want it. Maybe you'll change your mind. You may find the food more than palatable, actually."

Pausing to take a deep breath, Constable Frayser attempts to gain the prisoner's confidence by speaking kindly; the intent is to learn some information that might be used by either the defence or the prosecution. A timeline of events is what he would like to construct. He relaxes his face into a more casual expression and continues.

"I am sorry for the events that brought you here."

Cyrus looks up at the constable and mimics him.

"The events that brought me here. Care to enlighten me on that? Because, from where I'm sitting, I didn't do a damn thing wrong."

"Well, that isn't for me to determine. I am just doing what my work requires of me. We can talk about that later if you would like, but for now, I'd like to get to know you, if I may. So...I've been wondering. Tell me, is there a Mrs Holmes?"

Surprised and wary at the change in subject and the friendliness coming from the other side of the bars, Cyrus narrows his eyes and looks at the constable, cautious of potential motives behind the friendly exterior.

"There was. She was the sweetest woman on earth. Why do you care?"

"I'm curious, that's all...I'm sure she must have been an exceptional woman. What was her name? How did you meet?"

He feels as though he might be getting Mr Holmes to talk about himself, which might lead up to the grisly scene he witnessed at the farmhouse. Cyrus sighs heavily and looks down at his folded hands.

"Her name was Ellen."

He sits back, looking up at the constable.

"We met when she was just eighteen. I was twenty-two, working on her father's farm to make some money to buy a bit of land from my dad to start my own farm. She'd bring me lunch every day, out there in the field, and no matter how hot it was or how rainy it was, she always came. It got so that I didn't care what she brought me for food, I just wanted to see her."

"That's a special beginning. She sounds like such a sweet woman. Love is a grand thing, isn't it, Cyrus? Apparently, the two of you married?"

In his attempt to establish a more personal rapport with Mr Holmes, he takes the risk of using the prisoner's first name. Cyrus nods, still looking at his hands, fiddling with the wedding ring that he still wears.

"Yes, we got married. Her father, you see, wanted her to marry someone who could give her a proper house and a good life. He saw how hard I worked and told me that if I felt the same when his daughter was twenty-one, I could ask for her hand. He talked to my father, and I believe he helped to see my way to buying that piece of land from my father long before I thought I ever could."

"Her father sounds like he was a good man and a good father. Is that the land you own, now?"

Cyrus nods and looks up to the man on the other side of the bars.

"He was. Ellen was the only child he and his wife ever had, and I admired the way they looked out for her. I was proud that they approved of our courtship. I tell you, Ellen was the prettiest bride I'd ever imagined. It was for her that I built the house and every building on that farm. I tilled that soil. I raised that livestock. I wanted Ellen to have a good life like her mother and father wanted her to have. Of course, Ellen wanted children. A whole house full, she said. I remember we laughed about having enough children to run the farm whilst we lazed about in our rocking chairs, playing with our grandchildren. Times are tougher, now, and have been getting worse for years, you know, and I've had to sell some land to pay debts. You know how that goes."

"I'm sorry. You're right, the world has become more complicated, and people are having trouble managing. Selling that land had to be difficult for you. In the beginning, though, it sounds like the perfect life, Cyrus. You've been a lucky man. From the sounds of it, your wife was eager to start your family straight away."

Looking at the slant of sunlight reaching through the bars, Cyrus hears birds, motors, and the occasional passers-by. He chuckles at the memories and then sobers, shaking his head as if seeing his wife, fresh, again, in his mind.

"With all the deaths from the flu that went 'round, including Ellen's parents, my father, and some neighbours, Ellen wanted to bring some joy into the world. We tried every chance...well, you know how new brides are...before long, Ellen told me she was with child and that I was going to be a father. I had to sit down and catch my breath because I remember how Ellen became more beautiful to me than I'd ever seen her. She was the vision of an angel."

Genuinely interested in the story behind this man, Constable Frayser slides his chair closer and leans forwards, his elbows resting on his knees, his hands clasped.

"That must have been exciting. Knowing at that moment that you and your wife were living your dream of starting your family together."

"Oh yes, we told everyone and his brother that we were going to have a child. I was convinced it would be a boy. Ellen was convinced it would be a girl. She fussed over that nursery, wanting everything perfect. She even talked me into putting an extra little bed in there so she could tend the baby during the night and not disturb my sleep. Finally, Ellen told me it was time to call over the neighbour woman. She'd brought damn near every baby into this world from miles 'round, as her mother had before her. We were nervous, of course, but that woman knew babies, and she'd brought my wife into the world, so we trusted her. The midwife swatted me out of the room even though my sweet wife wanted me to stay. The midwife said it wasn't proper for a man to be in with a woman giving birth."

Piqued curiosity goads Constable Frayser's questioning, more personal than professional, now, although he kept his kit's inspiration at the fore.

"Tell me, then, how did things go?"

Cyrus sighs and looks back down at his hands.

"It took forever, it seemed. I could hear my wife screaming and the midwife talking to her. I'd go to the door and lean against it, hoping the agony would be over soon, and I could see my wife and son. Then the screaming stopped...everything stopped. I paced back and forth in front of the door, wanting to go in but afraid to. Eventually, the midwife came out holding this bloody thing and told me my wife was dead. I asked if the baby was dead too, and she said no, but there was something wrong with it. It wouldn't cry. It just stared and didn't cry. Damn thing didn't even blink."

Shaking his head, Cyrus looks up at Constable Frayser and whispers in a broken voice.

"I died that day. Almost twenty-three years ago. I died."

Sighing and shaking his head, he can relate to the loss of a beloved wife. In genuine sympathy, he speaks to Cyrus, man-to-man, human being-to-human being.

"I am so very, very sorry, Cyrus. Your heartbreak must have been overwhelming."

He clears his throat and continues.

"The baby, I'm sorry, what was its name?"

Bitter resentment colours his face as his eyes glint, hard, cold, and full of something that stood the hairs on the back of Constable Frayser's neck to attention.

"That wasn't a baby. That was some hellspawn thing that killed my wife. We'd chosen a name for a girl and a boy, and since this creature wasn't a boy, I gave it the girl's name, Signe. I couldn't bear to look at it. I told the midwife to take it out of my sight. What good is a thing like that to me? I had to bury my wife, keep the farm going alone; I couldn't be saddled with something like that. My father passed, leaving the rest of his farm to my brother who sold it right off, and my wife's parents were dead from the Spanish flu."

Shocked by his description of a helpless and innocent baby, Constable Frayser sits back in his chair, determined to keep Cyrus talking. After all, he had a job to do.

"I am sure you must have been grieving terribly. That's an unbearable burden for a man to shoulder alone. Later, you must have reconsidered and taken Signe back to live with you?"

A snort punctuates the laugh that erupts from Cyrus.

"Yes, I took her back when she was old enough to be useful. Four years old, maybe five, I think? The midwife woman had kept her all this time and told me the girl was deaf, couldn't utter a sound, and you could barely get her to do anything. She was glad I took that leech off her hands. I was almost sorry she'd kept a feeble-minded thing like that alive. First thing I did when I got her back was beat some sense into her empty head. She'd do what she was told, dammit, or there'd be consequences."

Feeling the blood rush from his head at what Cyrus is telling him, Constable Frayser struggles to remain calm.

"I reckon she DID help on the farm, and that must have made life easier for you, didn't it?"

Cyrus spits towards the commode in the corner of his cell.

"She was a clumsy animal. Dropped things, spilt things, dumber than a dead cow, she was. I had to keep beating her to get her attention. I locked her in the shed or in the room where I kept her. She was more damn trouble than she was worth. When she actually did something right, I tell you, I was the first one to be surprised. She couldn't cook, she couldn't clean, and you had to slap her 'round some to get her attention."

Disgust filling him like sewage seeping up and into pristine fixtures, Constable Frayser still manages to remain calm in the face of this young girl's treatment at the hands of her own father. He forces himself to continue to encourage Cyrus to relate his story.

"It sounds like you had your hands full. Why did you keep her 'round?"

Cyrus sits back with a smug smile, he taps his head, and a grating chuckle rises out of his throat.

"Well, you see, I was thinking. She wasn't much good for anything, so about the time she started looking more like something a man might find appealing, I asked 'round if there were any fellas interested in paying me for a little time spent with her. She couldn't hear, she couldn't scream, and it was money in my pocket. I made more money off her back than I could pull in with crops. It was a perfect idea, really."

Feeling as though he needs to get out, away from this disgusting excuse for a human and relieve the filth swirling in his belly, Constable Frayser feels himself start to sweat in attempts to subdue his real feelings about what he is hearing. He feels trapped by the situation.

Having begun this encounter, he feels that he must carry it through to its conclusion.

"Cyrus...may...I ask...how you felt about all this? She is your own flesh and blood? Your own daughter?"

He shoots the constable a hostile glare.

"HA! My own blood? My daughter? No child of mine would have killed its own mother. No child of mine would be born into this world useless. That's no child of this world. She's something lower than animals. Dim-witted, slow, lazy, the only thing she was good for was men making her spread her legs and pay me for it. I didn't care what they did to her. She couldn't scream, she couldn't do anything about it, being all tied up, but even then, she had the NERVE to spawn a thing of her own. I kept her in the room where she killed her mother the day she was born. When she spat out the little pig, I was hoping it would kill her the way she'd killed her own mother...would have served her right."

He stares at Cyrus in disbelief, trying to comprehend his words.

"A baby? She had a baby? Where is the baby now?"

Laughing and spitting into the corner, again, Cyrus explains.

"That bitch lost me a lot of money for that, so I made it up and then some by selling the little bastard. I don't know or care what they did with it. We took it before Signe could even get a good look at it. What's a dumb animal like her going to do with a baby, anyway?"

Feeling as though he is about to lose control and shake this vile creature till his teeth rattled in his head, Constable Frayser pushes the memory of his own wife who died in the same flu outbreak and the children they never had. He takes a deep breath to maintain his composure, so close to the line between professionalism and rage.

"Tell me. Where does that take us now? What did she do that was so wrong that you tried to strangle her? Those red marks on her neck didn't just appear from nowhere."

Cyrus raises his wildly disarrayed eyebrows.

"Strangled? You think I choked her? Hell no. The daft fleabag tried to hang herself and would have succeeded if I hadn't caught up to her in time. I figured I'd put her back in the room where she'd killed her own mother, and I was going to beat the daylights out of her once she woke up. Damn spittle of the devil himself...kills its own mother...can't learn, can't talk, can't hear, belongs in hell. HELL, I SAY!"

Jabbing his finger at the constable, he strives to make his point clear. Clearing his throat, constable Frayser feels as though he needs to go out for a stiff drink to drive the images from his mind and then home to offer up tearful prayers for the young woman who was so brutally abused. He stands up and turns to slide the chair back against the wall, his hands shaking with disgust and fury. He holds out his hands for the supper tray, resting his hands on the bars to still their trembling.

"Well, Cyrus, I have to do my paperwork. I'll take that tray if you aren't going to finish it."

Cyrus picks up the tray and slides it back to the constable.

"I got no appetite for this slop."

Constable Frayser takes the tray, turns, and then walks back down the hallway, his footsteps echo in the grey emptiness. He unlocks the door and walks out, the door clanging shut behind him. Slumping against the door, he hears a voice.

"Hey! You never told me why I'm in here! I didn't do a DAMN THING WRONG! YOU took my property from me! You STOLE her. You bastards should be in here, NOT ME!"

Constable Harrison Frayser walks over to the nearest flat surface, puts down the tray of food, and runs to the rear entrance of the station. There, in the alley, he loses both his composure and the contents of his stomach. Sweating, he rests his forehead against the cold brick of the building, finding no relief from his sorrow, disgust, anger, and the assault on human decency. All he can feel is the frail form of Ellen in his arms as he carried her out of hell and into her mother's arms. He slams his fist against the brick.

Chapter Thirty-Three
19 July 1926

Working as quickly as he can, William is placing assorted vegetables in their stands, both hands scooping them out of their crates. The boxes are perched against his hip to save him time running back and forth to retrieve them from the delivery room. Determination and urgency colour the speed at which he performs his duties. He is thankful that Mr Chelsey is allowing him to leave as soon as he is finished and has assigned deliveries to another fellow. Once William explained about Ellen's presence at the hospital, the usually distracted and gruff employer softened, seeing how much it meant to William that he be able to visit his friend. William stacks the empty crates aside as he empties them, his endeavours paying off. Lewis saunters up to William and watches with a curious expression on his face.

"Mate, your hands are flying. I can barely see 'em. What's got you moving today?"

William's focus on his task does not waver as he answers Lewis.

"That girl I've been visiting, Ellen, I told you about her missing. She's back and in hospital. Mr Chelsey says I can leave work when I'm finished with this. I want to see her."

"Blimey, hospital? She must be...come, now. Let me help. We'll get you out of here."

Lewis picks up a couple of crates, perching them against his hip, and follows William's example as he helps his friend stock the displays. In half the time, the vegetables are stocked, the crates returned to the delivery room, and William tells his employer that his work is finished.

"Already? Well, boy, then, off with you. And, well-done."

Surprised by the rare smile from Mr Chelsey, William returns the smile, bobs his head, and then backs out of the office. Lewis is waiting and offers encouragement as the two of them hurry through the market together.

"Say, mate, let me know if there's anything...I mean...good luck...you know what I'm trying to spit out of my ignorant gob. Go on."

Clapping William on the back, Lewis watches him sprint away, behind the market, and hears his footsteps on the wooden stairs leading to the room William rents. Lewis shakes his head, sorry to hear that the girl that William is sweet on has been hurt. He thinks it just ain't right, a nice girl like her...

Anna watches as the doctor assesses Ellen's burnt hand whilst the nurse changes the dressing. She recoils, seeing the blistering, redness, swelling, and peeling skin. She fights to maintain her composure, filled with a mixture of maternal heartbreak and anger at the monster that did this to their Ellen. John sits next to Anna, his hand rubbing her back, feeling her body tense with worry and anger.

"Doctor, why hasn't she regained consciousness?"

Dr Harper comes 'round the foot of the bed to stand closer to Mr and Mrs Thorpe.

"I understand your concern, and when there is an injury to the head or a lack of oxygen to the brain, the brain needs to rest and heal. The patient remains unconscious during that time which is the body's way of preventing further damage with too much activity. We only begin to worry when the patient does not wake up at all, or the muscles begin to stiffen, causing the limbs to settle into an unnatural position. For now, that's not a concern, so we haven't given up hope. She was brought in the day before yesterday, she's sedated and given medication for pain, so part of her current state is the brain's healing process and partly, the medication she's been given."

Before John or Anna can ask any further questions, Clara knocks on the door and walks in. She greets the doctor and nods to the nurse, and then comes over to John and Anna, joining them in their vigil over Ellen. The doctor seizes this opportunity to take his leave and the assisting nurse with him.

"How's our girl, today? And, how are you? I'll stay with you a whilst if you like."

Clara looks at Ellen's still form and reaches out her hand to rub Ellen's foot, neatly tucked under the bedclothes.

John stands and offers his chair to Clara.

"Clara, thank you. There's been no change, and she hasn't come out of it yet. All that we know is that we won't know of any brain damage until she wakes up."

Anna looks up at her friend and tries to smile.

"We haven't given up hope. See? The nurses and I gave her a bed bath and even washed her hair. Even though she hasn't awakened, yet, she does look a little better."

Clara smiles as she looks at Anna, waving at John to take his seat, again.

"Yes, she does look better after a good fluffing. Waiting is the most frustrating part of this, but that's all we can do right now. Keep touching her, talking to her, and yes, I know she can't hear you, but she'll feel you

338

with her, I'm certain of that."

A nurse knocks at the door that was left ajar, peeking inside from the hallway, and then fully entering the room. She clears her throat before speaking.

"Mr and Mrs Thorpe, I'm sorry to disturb you. There is a Constable Frayser here, and he is asking to speak with you. He told me he'd understand if you'd rather not leave Miss Thorpe's side."

Anna and John look at each other and then look at Clara, not knowing what to do. They are loath to leave Ellen's side, but they reckon whatever brought Constable Frayser here must be. Clara makes the decision for them.

"Why don't the two of you go, speak with the constable, and I'll stay with Ellen. Nurse, you may lead them to my office if they would like privacy."

Anna stands, kisses Ellen's forehead and strokes her clean, golden hair.

"We'll be back soon, sweetheart. Clara will stay with you."

Anna points to herself, places her hand over her heart, and then points to Ellen. She looks up at John and nods, taking his hand. Clara stands aside to allow them room to make their way to the doorway where the nurse waits. With one last glance at Ellen, John and Anna follow the nurse out of the room.

Seeing Constable Frayser out of his kit and wearing 'regular' clothing is a surprise to Anna and John, yet his expression is that of the constable they have come to know. They look at each other, wondering what he has to say, curious, yet fearful. What could be so critical that he comes here on what is obviously his day of relief from his job? The nurse gestures to the three of them and leads them to Clara's office to talk.

Sitting down next to Ellen, Clara rubs Ellen's arm and speaks softly to her.

"Ellen, it's me, Clara. Your parents were called away for a short time, but whilst they're out, I will stay with you. My dear, do you remember coming to my house with your mamma? We looked at all the flowers, and you walked 'round my gardens, touching each bloom. I still have the spoon you carved for me after you and Anna recovered from your illnesses. I'm still proud of you for how you took care of Anna, and we did an excellent job of keeping Johanna from falling ill. You know, Johanna adores you. Each time I go to check on her and Sarah, and each time she sees me, she asks about you. You're truly family, sweetheart. We're with you and waiting..."

A knock at the door startles Clara out of her monologue with

Ellen. William is visible through the partially open doorway.

"May I come in, Mrs Dewhurst? I...I...Mr Thorpe told me that Ellen was here and...well, Mr Chelsey let me go early so that I could come...if that's all right...I just want to see her. I won't stay long, I promise."

Clara stands, her heart warmed that Ellen's best and only friend cares enough to visit her.

"If John called you, then I'm sure it's all right that you visit. I'll be just outside the door if you need anything."

William nods, not taking his eyes away from Ellen. Clara walks past him, pressing her hand to his shoulder as she exits the room, remaining in the hallway. Slowly, he walks towards the bed and sees past the bandaged hand, the bruises, and the cuts. All he can see is his friend, looking as though she is asleep. Standing next to her, he places one hand on her arm, the other reaching out to touch Ellen's flaxen hair. Her skin is warm, her hair is soft, her eyes are closed, and he realises that she is not asleep, but unconscious. She is far away from him, from them all. Staring at her, she is as beautiful to him as she ever was. A myriad of thoughts and memories come to his mind as he looks at her. He can see her smile, her energy, the way her face illuminates from within when she sees him, just as his heart becomes happier whenever he sees her. He recalls the moment when she gave him the paper with her name written on it. He carries it always to keep her with him, even when they're apart. He looks at Ellen, tilting his head to the side, wanting to reach her.

"Ellen, it's William. I know it's silly of me to talk, but...I want you to know...I miss you. I miss calling on you. I miss our walks. I miss taking turns pushing each other on the swing. I miss...you."

Struggling to hold back his tears to keep his dignity intact for Ellen's sake, he watches her. He begins to stroke her hair and his hand slips down from her hair to caress her cheek.

"Come back, Cup. Please, come back."

He feels the warmth of her face, the sweetness of her countenance, the beauty he knows is in her soul. Not wanting to overstay his visit, he steps back, points to himself, places his fist on his chest, points to Ellen, moves his hands down the front of himself, and then pats his hands together. He points to himself, places his fist on his chest, points to his eyes, points to Ellen, and then draws a smile on his face. William turns, hating to show his back to someone who means so much to him, but he promised to keep his visit brief. Walking out of the room, he resists the urge to turn back for one last look. He hates what has happened to her. He feels saddened beyond words to see her like this. He wishes he could stay. Coming face to face with Clara, he hopes that if she overheard what he said to Ellen would not cause offence.

"Mrs Dewhurst, thank you. Would you mind telling Mr and Mrs Thorpe that I came? I…"

"It's all right, William. I think they, and Ellen, will appreciate that you care enough to come."

"Thank you…I…I'd best go, now."

Clara watches the young man walk away, his footsteps slow, his head lowered. She smiles fondly at his retreating form, seeing his cap tucked in his back pocket, causing the back of his suit jacket to rumple. Hearing footsteps coming towards her from the direction of her office, she looks over to see Anna and John. Anna's face is pale, John's flushed, and their hands are clasped together.

"What did Constable Frayser…?"

John holds up his hand and shakes his head.

"Not now…we…can't."

Anna walks into Ellen's room and sits back down next to her bed. Knowing better than to press them for details, she can only imagine the worst, her imagination limited by the injuries to Ellen's body that she could see. Clara, nodding her head, she and John walk into Ellen's room, Clara moving to Anna's side. She puts her arm 'round Anna's shoulder, receiving Anna's spontaneous embrace as her shoulders begin to shake. Sobbing from the horrible things Constable Frayser related, she cannot shake the images conjured in her mind. When her tears are spent, she wipes her eyes with the proffered handkerchief produced from Clara's pocket. Anna looks at John who is fighting his own emotions, stroking Ellen's hair.

"John, I want…no…I need to see Johanna. Could you bring her to me? I've been gone too long. I want to hold her. I want to be grateful…"

Clara steps out of the way as John comes 'round to crouch next to Anna's chair. He strokes her tear stained cheek, rubbing away a stray tear with his thumb.

"I know she misses you. It will be good for both of you."

"Yes, John. It's been too long."

Nodding, John gets up and kisses the top of Anna's head, his hand stroking the back of her neck.

"As you wish, sweet one. When I return with some fresh things for you, I will bring Johanna so you can see each other."

Nodding, Anna looks at Clara, reaching out to take Clara's hand as she and John exchange places at Anna's side.

"Clara, we can't thank you…"

"Don't thank just me, dear, thank everyone who cares for Ellen and has prayed for her return and are still praying for her recovery. And, thank William for coming to see his friend. He didn't stay long, but he asked me to tell you he'd been here."

John and Anna look at one another, surprised, yet not surprised that William would come.

He walks to the head of Ellen's bed and with the last stroke of his hand to Ellen's hair, he nods to Anna and Clara, turns, and leaves the room. Clara sighs that duty calls, and she must also go, for now.

"Anna, I need to leave for a whilst. Are you going to be all right? You really should get some rest. Why don't you at least lay your head down until John comes back? Here, put on the quilted jacket that Granny made. It's not going to do you any good just sitting on the back of the chair. You know, she made one for each patient and asked that you have one, as well. Don't disappoint us all by getting sick from the chill. If you need anything, call for the nurse."

Nodding, Anna allows Clara to help her put on the jacket. The warmth does feel soothing to her, and she looks up at her friend.

"Yes, I'll be all right. And yes, I will lay my head down for just a moment. I want to be right here when Ellen..."

Clara nods and rubs Anna's back, rubs Ellen's foot under the blanket, then walks to the door, slipping out, and closing it part way. Vaguely, Anna can hear Clara speaking with the nurse outside as she tucks Ellen's arms under the blankets and tugs them up higher. She slips her arm under Ellen's shoulders, cradling Ellen's head in her hand, and lifts to turn her pillow over to the fresh side. She strokes Ellen's hair to soothe her the way she does for their bedtime routine. The quiet of the room overcomes Anna with fatigue. How long has it been since she has slept? She cannot remember. She sits down and rests one hand on the lump under the blanket that is Ellen's arm, and then she lays her head on the bed using her other arm as a pillow. The moment she closes her eyes, Anna falls into the waiting arms of Morpheus.

William roams, his hands stuffed into his pockets, watching his feet. From the corner of his eye, he sees a tree with overhanging branches that seem to want to enfold him in their green embrace. He leans against it, takes out his wallet, and finds the paper Ellen had given him. He unfolds it and looks at what she had written. ELLEN. Feeling terribly alone, he refolds the paper, returns it to his wallet, and replaces the wallet into his pocket. He walks, again, no destination in mind. Seeing the church come into view, he quickens his pace, reaching the door of the church. Placing his hand on the brass handle of the door, he pulls the door open and walks inside. Father Willington hears the entrance of someone into the church and steps out of his office to see who it might be. William meets Father Willington's gaze, and in a shaking voice, he asks a favour of him.

"Father, there is no one I...may I talk to you?"

Chapter Thirty-Four
20 July 1926

One of the younger nurses walks into the room with a cup of tea for Mrs Thorpe and sees that she is sleeping. Knowing that this dear woman has not slept since her daughter arrived, she places the cup on the table next to the bed, checks the bag of intravenous fluids that hydrate the patient, then leaves the room. Startled, Anna awakens, looks 'round her, and sees the cup of tea on the table. Reaching out to touch it, the aroma draws her to take it into her hands, letting the warmth seep into her as she sips it. She sits by the bed, holding Ellen's hand, fighting sleep. She tries to keep her mind active by peeking out into the hallway where she sees the nurse sitting at her desk. She wonders what is in Ellen's chart. Anna's mind wandering, she looks 'round the private room that is compassionately decorated to make it feel much like a room at a modest hotel, except for the faint smell of bleach and antiseptic.

At Clara's urging, Father Willington feels compelled to visit Ellen and Anna. His prayers go up for the Thorpe family, knowing how their daughter has suffered. Having her back with them brings with it the uncertainty of Ellen's delicate condition. He softly knocks on the doorframe, seeing Anna staring far away as she sips tea from a white institutionally correct cup. Hearing the knock, Anna is jolted back to her senses, realising that she had nearly fallen asleep, still holding the cup of tea in her hands. She sees Father Willington standing there, and she wonders how long he has been waiting. She smiles, deepening the lines of weariness on her face and accentuating the circles of sleeplessness under her eyes.

"Father Willington. Please come in."

She gestures to a chair nearby that he can use. He smiles at Anna, her devotion to Ellen, physically manifest. He brings the chair closer so they can speak in low tones.

"How is Ellen? And...How are you, John, Johanna, and Sarah? This must be exhausting for all of you."

She looks at Ellen's still form and sighs.

"There is nothing, yet. I don't dare fall asleep and miss anything. I want her to know that her mother is here with her the moment she wakes up."

He nods, and looks at Ellen, pitying the dear child for her journey through hell itself. There is a special place in heaven for such souls. He shakes his head at the continuing tribulations of the Thorpe family, now.

"Yes, she won't want to see anyone else. Anna, you are eating what Clara has sent up for you, aren't you? I imagine that food is the last thing on your mind, but you have to maintain your own health to care for Ellen and the rest of your family. I'm sure Clara has given you the same advice."

Anna smiles and reaches over to pat Father Willington's hand.

"Yes, I've heard the same sermon from Clara, Father, and I have done my best to avoid becoming another patient, I promise. I'll admit, I have no appetite, but I eat because I must."

Nodding, he takes Anna's hand, giving it a reassuring squeeze.

"I know you're doing your best. Just know that we're concerned for you and your family, as well. This is a trying time for you in a different way, now. I don't want to sound like a parrot, but if your family needs anything...anything at all...."

Looking at Anna, he hopes that she knows he means every syllable sincerely. Anna looks into the eyes of kindness and nods.

"Yes, I promise, we will call upon you and Clara for anything that we need. Thank you, for...for... making it possible for Ellen to come home."

He nods; a serious expression veils his face as he bows his head with humility.

"Anna, thank God. Clara and I were mere instruments of His miracle. I'm glad we were able to do what we could. It truly was a miracle from Heaven."

Pausing, worry for the Thorpe family and young William never far from his mind, he adds his own admonition to those, he assumes, have already fallen on unhearing ears.

"I'd say get some rest, but I realise that's a futile request. I'll just ask you and John to care for yourselves. Give John my best, and ask him to relay that to Johanna and Sarah as well. I'll ask Clara to let me know if you need anything."

He stands and pats Anna's shoulder, smiling at the mother keeping vigil who returns his smile, grateful for the caring and concern of their faithful friends. With a nod, Father Willington takes his leave. As she watches Father Willington go, she realises how raw her emotions are with her lack of sleep, the whirlwind of events, and the agonising waiting, once again. Having her girl back is not enough. Ellen needs to be HERE. Anna reaches out her hand and strokes Ellen's hair, much softer and cleaner from the gentle bed baths given to her by the nurses, under her ever-present supervision. Laying her head back down on her arm, just closing her eyes for a moment, she drifts back to sleep, an insistent urge that she finds difficult to resist.

Ellen slowly opens her eyes, squinting, a single tear escaping, rolling down into her hair. She looks up and 'round her, squinting and staring, a white patterned ceiling filling her view. She turns her head towards a window, squinting her eyes to slits, again, and then turns her head in the direction of a dresser, and a jug of water that hold her gaze longer than other items in the room. Looking down at herself, she stares at the blankets covering her. The resulting effort of sliding her arm out from under the blanket raises it, and then her arm drops back down onto the bed. Turning her head, she sees and stares at the lady's head lying on the bed next to her. Blinking her eyes, she moves her hand over, touches the lady's hair, and then closes her eyes, her hand relaxing away as she falls insentient, again.

Instantly awakened by a touch on her head, Anna raises her head and looks 'round her. She looks at Ellen and covers her mouth to stifle a cry of joy that Ellen's arm is out from under the blanket, and her head is turned towards her. It must have been Ellen who moved. No one else would have moved her arm or head. Anna notices the tear staining Ellen's temple and leans over to kiss it as she strokes her baby girl's hair. Ellen would not reach out to anyone else, would she? She stands up and leans over Ellen, kissing her forehead, her tears falling on Ellen's sweet face.

"Mamma is here, sweet one. I'm here. I love you. We all love you."

Burying her face in Ellen's hair, she softly weeps for joy at this hint that perhaps Ellen will come back to them completely. Does she dare call the nurse? Was this just an accidental movement? As Anna strokes Ellen's face, she imagines the healing bruises fading even more at her touch. With another gasp, she looks down and sees Ellen's eyes open. Looking at her, Ellen drags her arm towards Anna. She watches Ellen attempt to make signs that not only indicate understanding but recognition of her as well. Anna smiles and nods through her happy tears as she points to herself and places her fist on her chest, patting it with her other hand and pointing to Ellen, saying, 'I'm your mother'. Then she points to herself, places her hand over her heart, and points to Ellen, signalling, 'I love you'.

She taps two fingers on her chest, places her fist on her chest, tries to move her other hand out from under the blanket, stops, grimaces, and tilts her head.

Tears flowing freely, now, Anna nods.

"Yes, Mamma is here, sweetheart. I'm here. You're safe. Your hand is hurt and bandaged."

Anna begins to gesture to Ellen to explain about her injured hand, but Ellen's eyes close, and then open again. Ellen reaches her arm up towards Anna, stopping to look at the tube fastened to her arm. Knowing she should call for the nurse, in fact, should have called immediately, Anna feels selfish that she does not want to let these first moments break by the flurry of activity that will ensue. Easing her arm under Ellen's pillow and putting her other arm 'round Ellen, fresh tears fall with the joy of having her baby girl want to be in her mother's arms. Tears follow Ellen's unmistakable embrace as their eyes meet with sweet recognition, lost in this happiness, as hopes become reality.

She looks down at the blanket and tries to wriggle her sore arm out from under the blanket, again, and then stops. She looks back at the lady, places her hand on her chest, thumb touching, her palm facing the direction of her trapped hand. She moves her hand towards the lady.

Anna shakes her head as she draws an X in her own hand and then places her hands against her chest, palms together, and moves them towards Ellen. In this way, she tells Ellen that there is nothing for which she needs to ask forgiveness.

She nods, taps three fingers on her chest and then places a finger on the side of her nose, tilting her head to the side.

Nodding, Anna makes the gestures for John and Johanna, draws a smile on her own face, points to her own eyes, and then points to Ellen, letting her know that the rest of her family will be happy to see her. Anna holds up one finger as Ellen relaxes, closing her eyes, her limbs relaxing as the medication and efforts fade her into sleep, once again. Stroking Ellen's hair, Anna finally calls out for a nurse, feeling the pangs of guilt that she should have done so immediately.

"NURSE! Nurse...please come...she's awake and gesturing to me and makes sense, please, please, come!"

A matronly woman in white rushes into the room and looking, first, at the patient from head to toe, and then at the intravenous bag and tubing that have delivered fluids from the first day of the patient's arrival. All looks as it has before, but anticipating some sort of crisis, she turns to Mrs Thorpe.

"What is wrong, Mrs Thorpe? What's happened?"

The nurse studies her patient for any signs of distress, assessing the young woman, noting that only the bed linens are rumpled, and the patient's arm is out from under the blanket. Otherwise, the patient's eyes are closed. Anna smiles, unable to contain her excitement through her tears.

"She woke up...she gestured to me and made sense and...she embraced me. Ellen is with us! She's come back to us. Please, can you ring Mr Thorpe at home? Tell him to hurry, please. Ring Mrs Dewhurst...the doctor...Please, anyone you can reach!"

Anna weeps tears of joy, uncaring that she might look a dishevelled mess, only caring that their sweet girl is going to be all right. Her weariness replaced by happy anticipation. The nurse, feeling her own joy for this family, nods and smiles.

"Of course, Mrs Thorpe. I'll notify the doctor immediately and bring in Mrs Dewhurst to assess her further since she knows Miss Thorpe's language."

Rushing out of the room, she runs to her desk to begin her task of telephoning everyone who needs to know this promising change in the patient's condition. Clara drops what she had been working on at the nurse's urgent call telling her of Ellen's awakening. Stopping to speak with the nurse, she asks if Mr Thorpe has been notified and the nurse informs her that their housekeeper says he has already left and is on his way back here. Clara runs into Ellen's room, glancing at Anna, hoping this is not a hallucination brought on by sleep deprivation. Arriving the bedside, Clara looks her over from head to toe, takes Ellen's bandaged hand to see that the bandage remains intact. She strokes Ellen's hair and cheek, then rubs Ellen's chest firmly to wake her up. Slowly, Ellen's eyes open to the stimulation Clara provides. She holds up her bandaged hand, a grimace of pain crossing her face as she looks at it.

Arriving at the nurse's desk, John stops to enquire of Ellen's condition during his absence. Overjoyed by the nurse's news, he rushes into the private room, dropping the bag with Anna's necessities on the floor, and rushes to Anna's side.

"Is it true? Did she...Is she...?"

She sees the helping lady and smiles, tears pouring down her face, points to herself, draws a smile on her face, points to her own eyes, and then points to the helping lady. She sees the man, taps three fingers on her chest and then holds out her arms to him.

Moving past Clara, John slips his arm 'round Ellen's head, his other hand under Ellen's opposite shoulder, returning Ellen's embrace, stronger than he could imagine from a girl so frail and battered.

"Welcome home, sweetheart. Mamma and I will look after you. You're safe, now. You're going to be all right."

Fresh, happy tears fill Anna's eyes as she witnesses the second embrace Ellen has ever given John. Watching their reunion, convinced that Ellen is cognizant of the people 'round her, and is communicating appropriately, Clara smiles, fighting her own tears.

"I'm sure the nurse has reached Dr Harper by now, and I'll speak with him about Ellen coming 'round. From this point on, no other male should enter this room. He knows that, but I'll remind him."

Turning on her heel, Clara hurries out of the room with business-like strides, the nurse taking precedence over her role as a family friend. Encountering Dr Harper in the hallway, she reaches for Ellen's chart and hands it to the doctor, a fresh nurse's note written. He peruses the notes and nods, looking up at Clara.

"So, you've assessed her? What are your thoughts? Do you concur with what Mrs Thorpe has described?"

"I have, and I do, Doctor. She is awake, weak, but she is able to correctly identify Mr and Mrs Thorpe and communicate sensibly, although, I'm uncertain that she knows where she is. I doubt that she has ever been in hospital before this. She is aware that her hand is painful and bandaged."

"Good, good. I'll have to ask you to be my go-between, as I recall, as of now, no males other than her father may enter the room."

"Yes, Dr Harper, I was going to remind you. I'll be happy to serve in that capacity."

Dr Harper turns to the nurse on duty who is watching the exchange, eager to carry out any orders. The doctor writes in the chart, gives the nurse instructions to reduce the sedatives and maintain the pain medications for the patient's injured hand.

"There, that does it. I'm pleased, yes, quite pleased. Let her family know that I am hopeful that she may be discharged when she is stronger. I think she will fare better in familiar surroundings, than here. Mrs Dewhurst, I can count on you to follow the progress of healing to the injured hand and report to me regularly."

"Yes, Dr Harper. I'll be glad to do that. She trusts me."

Nodding, the doctor hands the chart back to the nurse and walks away. Clara re-enters Ellen's room with a smile, seeing a reunited family, minus one charming little girl. Observing that Ellen has closed her eyes and is likely asleep, again, and seeing the intent conversation whispered between Anna and John, Clara slips back out of the room, unwilling to disturb their happiness. Stopping to speak with the nurse who is smiling and staring at the door to Ellen's room, Clara chuckles and waves her hand in front of the nurse's face to get her attention.

"Ring me if you need me. Let the other nurses know that I am available day or night."

The nurse nods, flushing red, caught inattentive to her duties by her highest-ranking superior. She turns to scribble the note and fasten it to the desk, ensuring that she will not fail to pass on this vital piece of information to the following shifts.

Sitting together, now, John rubs Anna's back with one hand, holding Anna's hand with his other hand. They watch Ellen sleep, waves of relief and hope washing over them like refreshing breezes at the seashore.

"Anna, her bruises and her hand...I wish they'd heal faster."

"I worry more for the wounds to her soul, John. Remember how she came to us? No one could go through that again and come away unscathed."

Shaking his head, a sad pall comes over him.

"From what Constable Frayser told us, it is a wonder that she survived at all. The hell she endured and to think that she wanted to end..."

Reaching over to take John's hand, Anna nods, the silence between them thick as honey, sharing the same grim thoughts. Walking through the details of the constable's tale that was off the record, giving them information he felt they had a right to know, they try to shake away the morbid truth. To do just that, John holds Anna closer and manages to smile for her.

"Anna, I brought something for Ellen."

She watches John get up and walk over to the valise he had brought with him. He brings it back and sets it on the chair, opening it, and delving inside, searching for a particular item.

"Johanna was napping, so I thought it best to not bring her today. Tomorrow, I will time things better so that she may come to see you. But, for Ellen, I brought..."

He holds up Ellen's cuddly animal as though it were a trophy. Her favourite bedtime companion, the soft animal she sleeps with every night. Happiness creeps into her soul and sparkles from Anna's eyes to see the furry toy, and nods, grateful that John has remembered such a precious piece of Ellen's comfort. Having overheard the conversations between Clara, Dr Harper, and the nurse in the hallway, John and Anna nod with satisfaction. John tucks the plush toy in the crook of Ellen's arm in such a way as to not wake her. He takes the valise from the chair and sets it on the floor next to Anna's chair. He pulls his seat closer, settling his arm 'round Anna, as they watch Ellen sleep.

"It sounds as if the doctor is pleased and Clara was delighted, too. It's a miracle, Anna. A miracle."

"Yes, that's what Father Willington said whilst you were gone and before Ellen awakened from her unconsciousness. He came to see us, but he didn't stay long."

"I'm glad he did. We will always be grateful to Clara and him for what they did... Anna, it surprised me that Ellen held out her arms to me. I was fearful that she would recoil at my presence as she had before."

"I agree, John. I'm also happy that she wanted to embrace you. We're the closest thing to family and parents that she's ever known. The thought makes me sad, yet I'm so grateful she came to our door that night and became such a precious part of our family. Sarah and Johanna love her so much, as we do."

Falling into silence, they watch Ellen rest, a more natural expression of sleep on her face that is different from the blank visage of a comatose state. As the sun lowers in the sky, John pats Anna's shoulder.

"Will you be all right? I should go and avoid Sarah's fussing over supper and play with Johanna before she goes to bed."

Looking at John, she smiles.

"Yes, I have everything I could ever want or need. I have my family. Our family. Give Johanna extra kisses from me and tell her I'm excited to see her tomorrow. And, when you bring her, bring her animal book and a soft doll or two, if you would?"

Chuckling, John stands and kisses the top of Anna's head, stroking her hair and with the back of his hand, stroking her cheek.

"Of course. I will remember. Johanna is excited to see you, too. This evening and tonight, I must insist that you get some sleep. The cot they brought for you hasn't been touched."

"Yes, my sweet one. I promise I will sleep. In fact, as soon as I finish eating the supper the nurse will bring me, I will carry out my assignment to sleep well and soundly."

Anna salutes John and chuckles, lifting her face to receive a kiss from this dear man. Kissing Anna with restrained affection that he has craved more each day, he stands, his eyes twinkling as he takes her hand.

"Until tomorrow, then, sweetheart. When Ellen wakes up again, remind her that I was here and that she is loved."

"I will. Have no doubt of that."

With that, John makes his way 'round the bed, looks back at Anna with raised eyebrows as he pats the cot, smiles, and then opens the door, walks out, and closes it part way. Anna sits, watching Ellen sleep, taking Ellen's hand in her own. Interrupting her daydreaming, a nurse walks in with a tray of food for Anna and sets it on the table near the bureau. Nodding, pointing to the food and then pointing to Anna, the nurse smiles and leaves the room. Anna moves a chair to the table, mindful of unnecessary vibrations that might awaken Ellen; she sits and tucks into the supper, tasting it for the first time with an appetite that surprises her. Setting her teacup down on the tray, Anna is amazed at the speed with which she consumed her meal. She gathers the tray and takes it out of the room, giving it to the nurse who smiles and nods, glad to see that Mrs Thorpe has finally finished a full meal.

Returning to Ellen's room, Anna finds the bag that John brought to her. She opens it and rummages about until she finds a nightdress. She walks to the door, closes it, and then changes into it, realising how good it feels to have something clean and comfortable to wear. One last look at Ellen, blowing her a kiss, pointing to herself, placing her hand over her heart, and then pointing to Ellen, she turns down the coverlet of the cot and sits on the edge. A feeling of guilt stabs her, but she knows that everyone is right and she does need proper sleep. She lies down and is asleep as soon as her head touches the pillow as the last rays of day dip behind the hospital's garden walls, and bids farewell until the morrow.

A crash of metal awakens Anna with disoriented panic. Looking 'round her, she sees Ellen on her bed, legs thrashing under the blankets. Her head turns back and forth, mouth open in a silent scream. Leaping from the cot, Anna rushes to Ellen's side, beginning the process of soothing Ellen out of a devastating nightmare. The night nurse runs into the room, stops, and her eyes wide to see the writhing figure of her patient.

"Mrs Thorpe, I'll get her some sedation."

Anna calls out to the retreating figure in white.

"NO! No sedation. Just leave the room, and I will get her through this. Just go."

Hoping for some explanation later, she returns to her desk and listens intently to the sounds coming from Miss Thorpe's room. She documents the unfolding events as she hears them transpire, wondering why Mrs Thorpe refused to allow her to give the patient a sedative during such a violent episode. In time, the sounds from the room cease, and she gets up, walks to the door, and peeks in to see if she can assist in any way. The patient is sitting up in the bed, blood stains the blanket from whence the intravenous needle must have dislodged during her struggle. Mrs Thorpe sits on the bed, holding the patient, stroking her hair, and rocking her. Miss Thorpe is holding tightly to her mother, her face buried against Mrs Thorpe's neck, her shoulders shaking as if sobbing uncontrollably. Anna notices the nurse and nods her permission for the nurse to enter.

"These nightmares are not unusual for Ellen. I help her through them almost every night. The needle in her arm pulled out, and she could use a bandage on that, although the bleeding has stopped, for the most part. Please don't be offended that I chased you out, but having you here would have only made the situation worse for her."

Shocked by these events and explanation, she only nods, turns, leaves the room, and retrieves a bandage and tape. With trepidation, the woman in white returns to the room to dress the bleeding from Miss Thorpe's arm as the patient stares from the bandage to the nurse and back to the dressing. Unable to ignore the expression on the patient's face and the tears still flowing, she backs away slowly when her task is completed.

"I'll have to notify the doctor that the needle is out of her arm, and she's no longer receiving fluids. We don't want her to become dehydrated."

"Yes, you can notify the doctor all you like, but there will be no more needles. Now that she's coherent, she should be able to drink. If she's not, then we'll consider that other option. She's been through enough pain. Inflicting more would cause more harm than good, in my estimation. You can verify what I'm saying with Mrs Dewhurst if you like."

Feeling thoroughly chastised, intimidated, yet dutiful, the nurse returns to her desk and telephones Mrs Dewhurst who gives verification to Mrs Thorpe's statements. Mrs Dewhurst offers to notify the doctor and intervene on the patient's behalf, leaving the nurse to document the events she witnessed.

Anna holds Ellen close to her, again, rocking her back and forth, singing softly.

"Hush little baby, don't say a word, Mamma's going to buy you a mockingbird..."

Chapter Thirty-Five
24 July 1926

Sitting with Ellen, Anna holds her hand, patting it to distract and reassure her that this dressing change to her burnt hand is necessary and not going to hurt. At least, not as painful as the nightmare Ellen suffered during the night, a painful return to a dark place for both Ellen and Anna. Ellen stares at what the nurse is doing, jerks her hand back and then looks over at Anna. The nurse cleanses the wound, dead skin sloughing off, leaving healthy pink skin underneath. The application of a medicinal ointment and a new bandage completes the process.

"Her hand is healing more quickly than expected, Mrs Thorpe. Dr Harper approves of her progress and is pleased that no infection has set in."

"Thank you. I'm happy, as well. Dr Harper was right that Ellen is young and was healthy...before all of this."

Anna's head fills with a whirl of thoughts. All of this...what? Ordeal? Descent into hell? Just what would one label these events? She shakes her head to clear the cobwebs of debris, repugnant images cast away. Instead, she attempts to focus on the gratitude she harbours in her heart that Ellen is walking, communicating, and alive. As the nurse takes away the items she had utilised to carry out her ordered tasks, Anna looks at Ellen who is staring down at her hand. Anna points to her bandaged hand, moves her own hands down in front of her, and then pats her hands together as she tilts her head to the side, asking Ellen if her hand feels better. Ellen stares at Anna, holds up her hand, looks at it, frowns, then lightly touches it with her other hand.

She looks at the lady, then takes her finger and draws an X on the palm of her injured hand.

Wondering if Ellen's hand is painful, Anna asks for a further explanation from her by tilting her head to the side.

She watches the lady, again, draws an X on her burnt hand, lifts the blanket, covers it, and then looks at the lady.

Taking Ellen's hand from under the sheet, she holds it in hers and kisses it to show Ellen that she does not find her hand repulsive. She points to herself, places her hand over her heart, and then points to Ellen, reaffirming that she loves her unconditionally.

She watches the lady. She lowers her hands and taps the lady's arm. Pointing to the lady, she places her hand over her heart, points to herself, and nods. She points to herself, places a fist on her chest, and draws an X on her forehead. She stares at the lady. Holding her hands together and resting her head on them as though on a pillow, she points to herself, draws a smile on her face, points to her eyes, and points to the lady.

Tears spring to Anna's eyes as Ellen tells her that she knows she is loved. Ellen wanted to die, but when she woke up, Ellen was happy to see her. The simple gestures convey more than spoken words could ever impart. She nods, points to herself, draws a smile on her own face, points to her eyes, and then points to Ellen, telling her that she was happy to see her, too, when she regained consciousness. For the first time, Ellen swings her legs over the side of the bed and tries to stand. Swaying, Anna reaches out to steady Ellen and assist her to sit down. Their eyes meet, and then Ellen looks down, pulling her nightdress up to her knees. She frowns as tears fill her eyes, the bruises on her legs healing, but visible. Ellen points to one after another, shaking her head.

Looking up at the lady, she points to herself, draws a frown on her face, a tear down from her eye, points to herself, and draws an X on the palm of her hand.

Empathising with Ellen over the bruising, Anna tilts her head to the side and looks deep into Ellen's eyes for a moment. She points to the bruises, brushes one palm against the other with a sweeping motion as if to brush them away, telling Ellen that they shall heal and fade. Anna points to Ellen and pats her hands together to disagree with Ellen's expression that she is bad. No, Anna believes that Ellen is good and a far better person than many people she has known, including herself. Ellen watches Anna, looks down at her legs, fluffs her nightdress over her legs, and then holds up her hand, turning it to expose every angle to view. Ellen looks at Anna then stands, again, this time, steady. She reaches for Anna's hand whilst Anna quickly stands at Ellen's side to catch her if her legs should fail to support her. Slipping her arm 'round Ellen's waist, they take three paces together, and Ellen stares at her feet as they move. A smile softens Anna's face to see that their girl's strength is returning.

Ellen and Anna walk to the window, a view of the hospital garden greeting them.

She looks outside, turns to look at the lady, points to herself, places her fist on her chest, and points outside.

Nodding, Anna considers her request to go outside a good sign, the thought never entering her head that Ellen wants to go home, not just outside. Fresh air, the sunshine, and the smell of flowers shall help to heal her body and spirit. A bench under a stately oak looks like the perfect place to soak in this beauty. She and Johanna had discovered this the day before whilst John sat with Ellen, giving Anna and Johanna their much-needed time to be alone together. Johanna enjoyed running 'round the garden, laughing and pulling Anna's hand to show her the flowers and butterflies. She pointed at the birds twittering in the trees, and finally, crawled up in her mother's lap to hear a story. She even wanted to know where Ellen's window was so she could blow kisses to her with an admonition.,

"No Cuppa owies!"

Now, it is time to enjoy the garden with Ellen. She calls for the nurse who comes to the door, asking what they need.

"May we have a wheelchair? Ellen would like to go outside."

"Of course, Mrs Thorpe. I'll bring one, straight away."

The nurse disappears, and Anna taps Ellen's arm to acquire Ellen's attention. She looks down at her arm and then up to Anna, her head tilted to the side. Pointing to herself and then pointing to Ellen, Anna nods her head and then points outside. Ellen nods, turns, and walks towards the door. Stopping Ellen, Anna holds up one finger to tell Ellen to wait a moment. Ellen is gaining strength, but Anna is afraid that Ellen will not be able to walk that far. The door opens fully as the nurse brings in a wheelchair. Ellen stares at it with a look of confusion crossing her face.

She looks at the lady, tilting her head to the side as she points to herself and to the thing.

Realising that, of course, Ellen has never seen such a chair, she asks the nurse to demonstrate that it is only a chair with wheels. The nurse complies with Anna's request and shows that the wheels move and turn in whatever direction is desirable. She stands up, walks behind it, ready to push its passenger to their destination. Ellen stares at the nurse and then at Anna who nods her head, upholding the idea that this is the best way for them to make their way to the garden. She holds out her hand to Ellen and gestures to the chair. Looking from Anna to the chair and back again, she takes Anna's hand and allows her to lead the way. Holding the arm of the chair steady, Anna guides Ellen to sit, concerned for her balance. The wheelchair moves in spite of the nurse's grasp on the handle, and Ellen's face registers surprise as she looks at Anna. Stifling a smile, Anna pats Ellen's arm and then nods, signalling the nurse to begin their outing to the garden.

As the nurse slowly turns the chair about so they can go out of the room, Ellen's eyes open wide and she holds tight onto the arms, then reaches out to grab Anna's arm. She looks down at the wheels moving, looks up at Anna as she puts a reassuring hand on the arm of the wheelchair, so Ellen will know that everything is all right. Ellen's gaze never wavers from Anna until she watches her point to herself, point to Ellen, and then point to the door at the end of the hallway. Ellen looks ahead as they move forwards to the best medicine imaginable. Reaching the door, Anna trots ahead to open it for them and fills her lungs with the scents of the real world, so much better than the cloying smell of antiseptics. The flowers and trees seem to welcome them with their fragrant beauty that is almost a shock to someone coming out of the stark interior of the hospital. Anna looks at Ellen with a smile, hoping she finds this pleasing to her senses. She releases Anna's arm, looks up at the sky, squints her eyes, shields them with her hand, and then looks back at Anna. She pats Ellen's shoulder and asks the nurse to take them to the tree with the bench, the shade, giving Ellen's eyes relief from the sunshine. The bright light of day seems to hurt Ellen's eyes, and it is no wonder, for all the darkness she has endured for far too long. Settling Ellen under the tree, Anna sits next to her on the bench, and the nurse steps away to give mother and daughter privacy, Ellen staring at the nurse's retreating form.

Glancing out of her office window, Clara sees Ellen in a wheelchair with Anna beside her. Excited that Ellen is finally out from those four walls, she rushes out of her office to join them, waving as she approaches. Anna sees Clara rushing out to them and waves in return. She pats Ellen's arm and points to Clara, hoping that Ellen will recognise Clara in this setting, remembering Dr Harper's caution of the possibility that Ellen's ability to identify people could be setting-specific. Looking down at her arm where Anna touched her, she looks at her, turns to where Anna points, and stares at Clara's approach. Ellen folds her hands in her lap and then looks down at them. Nearing, she waves to Ellen and then hides her disappointment when Ellen does not look up at her. She turns her attention to Anna, sitting on the bench as well.

"It's so good to see Ellen outside! The fresh air will do wonders for her, I believe."

Ellen steals a glance at Anna and Clara conversing with one another, turns to look down at the wheel of the chair in which she sits, and then returns her gaze to her lap, where she strokes her bandaged hand with her uninjured hand. Anna looks at Ellen and wishes she would smile, knowing how much Ellen loves flowers, fresh air, and the sunshine. Anna looks at Clara and smiles with a sigh.

"I agree, Clara. Each day her strength grows, her appetite improves, and I can only imagine Ellen as a flower, needing the sunshine and fresh air to grow and heal. This is a start, and I hope each day brings us closer to the happier Ellen that we'd come to know."

Turning to Ellen, Anna pats Ellen's arm and waits for Ellen to look at her arm and then up at her. She tilts her head to the side, points to Ellen, moves her hands down the front of herself, draws a smile on her face, points to her own eyes, and then gestures 'round them. Hoping for a positive response from Ellen to her question if she feels happy to be outdoors, she is disappointed when the only answer she receives is an unreadable stare. Watching Anna and Ellen, Clara's own disappointment rises along with a nurse's gut feeling that depression might follow Ellen's initial happiness at being alive and seeing the people she loves.

"Anna, right now, she seems disinterested in her surroundings. I would have thought an outing like this would have delighted her. I need to ask...does she still seems as though she is completely aware of her surroundings? Has she had any confusion? It's so hard to discern with Ellen since she can't tell us."

"Yes, she is and has shown no sign of being confused which is why her reaction to being outside, now, confuses me. I want to do anything and everything to make this up to her..."

Anna looks at Ellen tenderly, reaching out to rub her arm, glad that her sweet girl is healing and well enough to be out of doors. Ellen looks up, turns her head away from Anna and Clara, stares in the direction of rose bushes, and then back at her hands. Putting her hand on Anna's arm, Clara seeks to set Anna's mind at ease.

"Anna, I know you want to erase Ellen's past and especially recent events, but you know that you can't...none of us can. We can only love Ellen through her pain as she heals."

Tears spring to Anna's eyes and she looks past Clara to the flowers that are obscenely unaware of the pain sitting under a nearby tree. Her trembling voice comes as a whisper as she shakes her head.

"Clara, no...you don't understand...the day Ellen was taken...she...she..."

Anna's eyes meet Clara's, pleading for Clara's comprehension.

"She went willingly with that man."

Incredulous at these words, Clara shakes her head, trying to grasp the unthinkable as she looks over at Ellen who is still looking at her hands.

"Anna, what are you saying? Willingly? Why would Ellen ever willingly go with that man to what she obviously went through at his hands? I can't believe it."

"That man was hurting me and to make it stop, she stopped me from getting up, told me to stay there, and went to him. He...he held a knife to her throat and threatened to kill her if I tried to come closer. Clara, she sacrificed herself to save me. How..."

Anna's tears flow from the weight of her words, not having spoken them aloud until now. Clara sits back against the tree, stunned into silence. She looks over at Ellen, seeing her in a new light as Ellen raises her head and turns to look at Anna and Clara. For the first time, as she looks into Ellen's eyes, Clara feels the true price of love between a daughter and her mother. Anna's trembling voice interrupts Clara's shock.

"How do I live up to that kind of love? How can I make her sacrifice worth the price she paid? Tell me...how?"

"You and John will never give up on Ellen. I can't answer that, Anna, but I do know one thing. Your family has a bond that few could understand and a bond that can't be broken. Your love for Ellen will satisfy your debt. I believe that, Anna."

Anna wipes her eyes on her sleeve, musters a smile, and turns to meet Ellen's gaze. In response to Ellen's head-tilt, Anna points to herself, places her hand over her heart, and then points to Ellen.

Watching the lady, she nods, points to herself, and points to her head. She points to herself, holds her hands in front of herself and lowers them down, points to the lady, places her hand over her heart, and points to herself.

Nodding, her heart soothed that Ellen knows and feels the love Anna gives freely. She rubs Ellen's arm, feeling there might be a glimmer of light in the darkness of memories that refuse to die.

Observing the tenderness between Ellen and Anna, Clara grapples with the new knowledge of how deeply devoted Ellen is to her family, especially Anna. Slowly, recalling recent events, a pattern emerges in her thoughts. Softly, she takes a deep breath, daring to speak what, in her own mind, must be the truth.

"Anna...I...I wonder..."

Looking at Clara, Anna tilts her head to the side, puzzled at Clara's tone.

"Yes? What is it?"

"Ellen willingly went with that man to save you because she loves you. She loves all of you. What if...I don't even want to say it. But, what if, after all he did to her...the bruises, the recent burn to her hand, if she couldn't live with that kind of abuse anymore? She would know that If she stayed, the horrors she endured would only escalate. If she ran away, as she did before, that man knew where you live. She couldn't return to you because, well, you know what he's capable of, and I don't believe that Ellen would want to put all of you in danger. Also, she couldn't just run away and go somewhere else because that monster would pay you a visit thinking that you would be the first place that she would go, or at least know where she was. He would have no problem hurting you as he had before, or worse. Ellen knew how far he would go to get what he wanted. Her only option, as she saw it, I'm guessing, was taking her own life."

Stunned, fighting the torrent of emotion welling up within her, Anna glances at Ellen, turns her gaze back to Clara, and whispers.

"I hadn't thought of that..."

Arriving at the hospital, William hurries up to Ellen's room. Finding that no one is there, he walks over to the window. Seeing Ellen, Anna, Clara, and the nurse in the garden make him feel happy for Ellen. She is outdoors amongst the living things that she loves so much. Turning, he walks out of the room and thinks that this explains why his search for Ellen's nurse was an exercise in futility. A jaunty rhythm to his steps carries him down the hallway to the door leading into the garden. Pushing it open, he stops, met with the scent of Ellen as he sees flowers trying to imitate her radiant soul. Walking towards them, his pace slows, and his smile fades as the expressions affixed to Clara's and Anna's faces make him question the wisdom of his visit. The last thing he would ever want to do is intrude on something, especially if it regards Ellen. Seeing that Anna and Clara have taken note of his presence with welcoming waves, he quickens his pace, relieved that he will see Ellen and she will see him. Anna scoots herself over on the bench to make room for William to sit next to Ellen, causing Clara to lose her seat and the movement catches Ellen's eye, drawing her attention to William. Clara stands, appreciating the serendipitous timing of William's arrival.

"William, I'm glad you're here. I'm sure Ellen will be cheered to see you."

"Thank you, Mrs Dewhurst. I hope so. Mrs Thorpe, I hope you're well. I know this has been...well...difficult isn't the word, I guess."

Anna smiles and pats the bench beside her, Ellen continuing to stare at William.

"It's all right, William. I understand and appreciate what you're trying to say. Knowing that your thoughts and prayers...well, we...anyway, you're here to see Ellen. Clara and I will step away so you two can visit."

Taking a seat next to Ellen, William looks at her and smiles. She might be bruised and bandaged, but she is beautiful in his eyes. Moreover, there she is, sitting up, sitting outside, alive, and here he is sitting next to her. Ellen stares at William, and her lack of response to his presence is deafening. He points to himself, draws a smile on his face, points to his own eyes, and then points to Ellen, letting her know that he is happy to see her. Ellen continues to stare at William, and he nods, accepting her silence. He looks 'round them, impressed with the garden he had never seen behind the hospital walls. A touch to his sleeve springs his attention back to Ellen, ready to do anything Ellen wishes of him.

She looks at the young man, puts her hands together and rests her head on them as if they were a pillow. She points to the big house.

His enthusiasm shot down like a poached pheasant, he nods, sorry that Ellen is so tired and asking to go inside. He wishes...Getting up, he walks over to Anna and Clara, crestfallen.

"Uh, Ellen just told me she's tired and would like to go back inside."

Anna puts her hand on William's shoulder and nods, feeling his emptiness from Ellen's self-imposed isolation. Clara motions for the nurse and points to Ellen.

"Anna, why don't you see to Ellen, and I'll walk in with William."

Both nod agreement to Clara's suggestion, Anna walking towards Ellen and the nurse, William and Clara walking back to the hospital. All are disheartened that this outing did not have the desired outcome. Turning back at the door, William looks at Ellen one more time, remaining with her in spirit even though his feet take him away from her.

They enter the building and walk together down the corridor. Reaching Clara's office, she places her hand on the door handle and turns to William.

"Don't be discouraged, William. Give her time."

"I won't be, Mrs Dewhurst. I'd give Ellen anything."

He smiles at Clara, feeling grateful for her kind words, and then finds the rest of his way through the maze of hallways to the front door of the hospital. He exits into a world that is different from the one Ellen sees, now, and he hopes that he can be part of her journey back into the joy of living.

The nurse pushes Ellen's wheelchair towards the building after Anna's failed attempt to ask Ellen how she feels. Anna feels sad for William who is such a faithful friend to Ellen. She continues to look down at her hands, cradling the bandaged one in her other. Reaching the door, Anna opens it to allow the nurse to manoeuvre the chair through it. They look at each other, look down at Ellen, and then look at each other; again, not knowing what to make of Ellen's withdrawal from human interaction and activities that once pleased her. Arriving at Ellen's room, they enter, and the nurse brings the chair to a halt. Anna crouches down to allow Ellen to see her, and she raises her head without her arm touched. Putting her hands together and laying her head on them, Anna points to Ellen and then to the bed. Ellen shakes her head.

She points to the strange chair on which she sits, points to herself, and then points to the place between the window and table.

Patting Ellen's arm, she nods to the nurse who has come to understand a few gestures. The nurse wheels Ellen to the place to which she pointed, and then walks over to the bedside table where a glass and metal jug sit. Picking them up, she brings them to the table, just in case Ellen becomes thirsty. As the nurse leaves, Anna pulls a chair over to the table to join Ellen who is staring out of the window and wonders what she sees, what thoughts are whirling through her mind. Ellen begins to hyperventilate, her body shaking in waves that match the heaving of her shoulders as tears start to flow from her eyes. Leaning forwards, Anna prepares herself to intervene in whatever way she can to comfort Ellen.

Abruptly, Ellen throws up her hands with rigid and outstretched fingers that form into fists. She looks up at the ceiling, her mouth opens wide, and moves her hands to her head, gritting her teeth as she shifts her gaze downwards. Standing with alarm at the sudden outburst, Anna walks 'round the table towards her as Ellen shakes her head and pulls at her hair, her mouth open in a silent scream. Reaching Ellen's side, a frightened Anna crouches down beside her, opening her arms as she opens her heart, hoping to comfort her girl and bring her peace. Ellen pushes her away, turning to pound both fists on the table, the sound matching the rhythm that threatens to leap from Anna's chest. Standing, Anna begins to cry at the sting to her heart when she most wants to soothe Ellen and hold her, feeling helpless and useless at this moment. Knocking over the glass of water, Ellen picks up the jug, closes her eyes, and throws it across the room where it crashes against the opposite wall, then resumes slamming her fists on the tabletop and hitting herself.

The nurse hears a commotion and bustles into the room, almost stepping on the metal jug that bounced off the wall and spun to the middle of the floor. She picks it up, walks over to the table and sets it back where it belongs, righting the tipped glass, as well. She looks at Ellen with a measure of alarm, seeing such an extreme change in behaviour. Mrs Thorpe's distress is equally alarming.

"Mrs Thorpe, what's wrong? What happened?"

Anna holds up her hand to the nurse, shaking her head, trying to speak through her own tears.

"Please, leave us. I will...handle this...please."

With reluctance, the nurse leaves, and Anna turns back to Ellen, reaching out to her with another attempt to offer a mother's touch. Her weeping intensifies as Ellen ignores her, the sound of enraged fists pounding on the table punch at Anna's gut, making her feel helpless to reach her daughter. Slumping into the chair she had pulled over, she stares at Ellen and wonders what is happening in Ellen's heart with such a violent display of anger, grief and sadness trapped within her. Anna's own emotions that rumbled like a troubled volcano over these past days and weeks grows within her and erupts in the lava of sobbing, gall that wracks her body as she joins Ellen in expressing herself in the only way she can. Anna pounds her fists on the table as if trying to destroy the monster that brutalised Ellen and left her with demons in her dreams that will never go away. She pounds out her grief for all of Ellen's pain that she would gladly take into herself if only it would be gone to allow her to heal and become complete again. Anna lays her head down on the table, breathless, her arm cradling her head, tears soaking the sleeve of her dress.

Amid her throes of emotion, Ellen stops to stare at Anna. She looks down at her hands that have stopped shaking and takes a deep breath. Tasting the saltiness of her own tears, she wipes them from her face with the back of her bandaged hand. Looking back up at Anna, she reaches over to tug on Anna's sleeve. Feeling the fabric against her arm pulled, Anna raises her head, and her eyes meet Ellen's. They stare at one another for a space of time, Anna imagining that her own eyes must be as red-rimmed as Ellen's are. Ellen reaches over, picks up the jug, and hands it to Anna. She looks at it, looks at Ellen, and then back at the jug. Taking it from her hand, Anna feels the weight of it. She draws her arm back and hurls it across the room with all of her strength. It smashes into the wall across the room and clangs to the floor.

Once again, the nurse loses her restraint and runs into Ellen's room, expecting to see someone or something damaged.

"What...are you..."

Before the nurse can finish speaking, a small smile works its way to Anna's mouth.

"It's all right. We're all right. We'll make it through this."

Hoping that Mrs Thorpe is right, the nurse shakes her head and backs out of the room, leaving the door open a crack so she can hear and respond to her patient and the patient's mother. She considers that Dr Harper would want to know about these events, so she sets her nursing notes in front of her and rings the switchboard. Reaching Dr Harper, she explains all that has transpired and writes down his orders regarding his patient.

"Miss Thorpe may be discharged on the morrow, as she will better regain her health in every way under the care of her family in familiar surroundings. Mrs Dewhurst will be asked to make daily visits to change Miss Thorpe's dressing to her hand and monitor healing."

Relieved to give Mrs Thorpe the happy news, the nurse thanks the doctor, hangs up the telephone, gets up and walks to the door of her patient's room. She stops, seeing that Miss Thorpe and Mrs Thorpe are, now, calm, and communicating. Smiling, she turns, closes the door, and returns to her desk, deciding that the news can wait for a little whilst.

Anna turns her smile towards Ellen and nods.

She puts her hands, palms together, at her chest and moves them outward towards the lady.

Shaking her head, Anna gets up and walks over to Ellen, where they reach out to each other. She takes Ellen into her arms, holding her baby girl with all the love and longing she had felt whilst Ellen was parted from them. She rocks Ellen gently, empathic to all the anger and sorrow they share for all that has transpired with Ellen and their family. Her mother's heart determines that she will walk through fire if she has to if it will only help Ellen heal. Whatever journey Ellen's pain takes them on, they will take each step with her, as a family. Pulling back from their embrace, Anna wipes away a stray tear from Ellen's cheek.

She points to herself, places her hands together and lays her head on them as if on a pillow, and points to her sleeping place.

Anna smiles at Ellen, knowing that she must be exhausted beyond words. She holds out her hands, taking Ellen's delicate hands in her own. Standing, Ellen steps away from the wheelchair and walks with Anna to the bed. She waits whilst Anna turns down the blankets, fluffs and turns her pillow, and places Ellen's cuddly toy peeking out from the coverlet. Ellen turns and slides into bed, reaching for her toy and clutching it close. Pulling up a chair next to the bed, Anna strokes Ellen's hair, watching her eyes flutter shut. Ellen's eyelashes are veils that hide the heart-rending storm of emotion that has passed, leaving both of them spent. Feeling Ellen relax into a peaceful sleep, Anna leans forwards to kiss Ellen's forehead. She points to herself, places her hand over her heart, and then points to Ellen. Overcome with fatigue, Anna's arm serves as a pillow to support her head, sleep entering her soul the moment she closes her eyes.

Chapter Thirty-Six
25 July 1926

Wearing her blue dress and matching shoes, Ellen sits on the bed with Anna, waiting for John to arrive. The valise is packed, and whilst Anna is excited to bring Ellen home, Ellen's enthusiasm is subdued. She remembers feeling a similar excitement when she and John brought Johanna home after the difficult birth that nearly cost Anna her life. Gratitude fills her as she thinks of the hardships they have survived and the beauty that permeates their lives. Not possessions, but people. Johanna, Ellen, Sarah...all are precious gifts in their lives. John arrives and peeks into Ellen's room, grinning with a cheery wave. Returning his wave, Ellen stands and looks at Anna. They have tried to explain that they are taking her home, but the explanation draws a shrug and a tilt of Ellen's head. Giving Ellen the dress to put on and pantomiming a drive in the motor seems to register some kind of understanding. In a jiffy, she changes from her hospital-issued nightdress and dons her dress, sitting on the bed with Anna, staring at the door. John walks into the room and over to Anna, giving her a kiss and then looking from Anna to Ellen as he reaches down to pick up their bag.

"Well, are my girls ready to go?"

"More than ready, John. Ellen will thrive there. These four walls are starting to close us both into a corner. It will feel good to be where we belong."

"I agree. Johanna will be so happy. I told her this morning that I was coming to collect you. She clapped her hands and said 'Mamma, Cuppa, home. Daddy go!'"

Laughing, Anna turns to Ellen who is watching them talk with one another. She places her finger against her nose, puts her fist against her chest, points to her own eyes, and then points to herself and Ellen. Then, she places her finger against her nose, draws a smile on her face, points to her own eyes, and points to herself and Ellen. Anna wants to make sure that Ellen knows how happy Johanna will be to see her. Ellen nods before answering.

She points to herself, draws a smile on her face, points to her own eyes, and places her finger against her nose.

John motions for them to come along with him, taking Anna's

hand in his as they walk to the door and out to the nurse's desk where the nurse has the papers ready to sign, releasing Ellen from her medical prison. She hands John an ink pen and points to the lines that require a signature.

"It will just take a moment if you'll sign here...and here..."

Completing the requisite formalities, John thanks the nurse for her work and asks that she convey their thanks to the other nurses who have tended Ellen with care and compassion. He smiles at Ellen and motions for her to come along and together they walk down the corridor to the front door of this institution. Ellen pauses, catching Anna's sleeve. Stopping, John and Anna look at Ellen, their heads tilted, curious why Ellen has stopped them.

She points to herself, draws her arms up and crossed over her chest, walks two fingers across the palm of her bandaged hand, draws an X on her palm, and points outside.

Looking at each other, they silently struggle with the idea of explaining that the bad man is incarcerated and Ellen has no need to be frightened. The only thing they can do is shake their heads whilst Anna points outside, draws an X on her palm, walks two fingers across the palm of her hand and draws an X on her palm, again, telling Ellen that the bad man is not outside. Ellen looks down and then back up at John and Anna, nodding, yet the trepidation remains marked on her face. Anna takes her hand, and they walk through the door together into the bright light of freedom.

She looks at the motor, points to it, tilts her head, and then points to herself, the man, and the lady.

John nods his head, opens the rear door of the motor, and assists them inside. He makes sure they are settled before closing the door and walking 'round to the boot, lifting it and placing the valise inside. With a thunk, the boot lid drops shut, and John walks 'round to open the drivers' side door, and slips behind the wheel. He closes the door, and the engine gives a happy purr as it springs to life. Ellen looks out the window and then turns to face Anna, reaching out to pat her arm. Anna gives Ellen a reassuring smile, hoping that Ellen's fears ease.

She points to herself, points to her head, points to herself, places her hand over her heart, and points to the lady. She points to the lady again, points to herself, puts a fist over her heart and pats it.

Placing her hand on Ellen's, Anna nods, ready to respond to Ellen's gestures. Anna's heart warms to know that Ellen loves her and feels that Anna is her mother. She replies by pointing to herself, pointing to her head, pointing to Ellen, placing her hand over her heart, and then pointing to herself. She points to Ellen, points to herself, and then cradles her arm as if holding a baby. It is true. Anna does feel that Ellen is their own child, as much as Johanna who was lovingly conceived, brought into this world, and placed into her parents' arms just moments after her birth. She loves her daughters, and she knows that John adores them, as well.

Whilst they wind their way through the streets towards their home, William arrives at the hospital after hearing from John that Ellen would leave the hospital today. He wanted to see her and wish her well, even though she had turned him away at his last visit. He rushes to the desk where the nurse sits, and breathless from his eagerness to see Ellen, he smiles politely at her and waits for her to notice him. She turns to look at the young man and smiles at him.

"May I help you?"

"Yes, I've come to see Miss Ellen Thorpe. Her father told me that she would be discharged today and I hoped to see her before her parents took her home."

"Mr and Mrs Thorpe left with Miss Thorpe just a short time ago. I'm sorry you missed them."

Disappointed, William forces himself to smile and nods his thanks to the nurse. He turns to look through the open door and empty room where Ellen had been, then walks back down the hallway to the front door and pushes it open. He steps outside where the sunshine seems to have dimmed for him, the sky is clear, yet a cloud of dismay settles into him. Walking back to his room above Chelsey's Market, he gives his thoughts an about-face to happier themes. Recollections of the past and hopes for the future of the girl whose inner beauty fill his soul, and he grows a genuine smile. He quickens his pace, eager to reach his room, where he will change his clothes to something more suitable for work. His first priority, though, is sitting down to take from his wallet the paper Ellen gave him, tracing the letters ELLEN with his finger as he imagines her writing them.

Anna reaches for Ellen's hand, watching her eyes grow wide as familiar surroundings come into view. Ellen squeezes Anna's hand firmly as John pulls the motor up to the house, stops, and silences the engine.

He turns to Ellen, hoping to gain her attention, but she continues to stare, with Anna looking at Ellen for any outward reaction.

"Anna, I wonder what she's thinking? Do you think she's all right?"

"I haven't the foggiest idea, John. She must have so many thoughts and feelings running through her. I hope she's happy to be home. It was a horrible...."

"Yes, for now, let's try to let go of that and consider how we can help Ellen feel at ease."

He opens the motor's door, steps out, and opens the rear door, ready to assist Anna and Ellen. John walks ahead of them, up the steps, and opens the door. Ellen pauses, staring up at the house, and then at Anna's gentle urging, they ascend the steps and walk inside. Rupert dashes out of the sitting room, tail wagging, and barking his greeting. John walks back out to the motor with Rupert following on his heels, watching him retrieve the valise from the boot. Both walk back to the house and enter, John, closing the door behind them. Putting down her handbag and taking off her hat, Anna studies Ellen out the corner of her eye, seeing her look 'round as if viewing everything for the first time.

The silence and reverie are broken when Sarah and Johanna come spilling out of the kitchen, a riot of greetings and smiles rushing towards them. Rupert runs circles 'round them, runs down the hallway, and skitters on the hardwood floor to make his turn into the kitchen where the sound of an overturned chair causes a flurry of chuckles. Johanna finds her way to her mother and lifts her arms in the universal gesture for 'Pick me up!' Laughing, Anna complies, raising her daughter into her arms and covering her face with kisses as she cuddles Johanna so snugly that Johanna squeals and giggles. Soon, she wriggles, eager to get down, so Anna stands her on the floor, tousling her golden curls. She runs to Ellen and wraps her arms 'round her legs.

"Cuppa, Cuppa, no owie. Cuppa home a Janna."

Holding on to the wall, Ellen crouches down to Johanna, smiles at her, and takes the child in her arms. She leans back to look at her and caresses Johanna's sweet face with her un-bandaged hand.

She points to herself, draws a smile on her face, points to her own eyes, and points to the baby.

Tapping Johanna on the chest as she points, she smiles to see the baby laugh, clap her hands, and then draw a smile on her face. Using the wall for support, Ellen stands, watches Sarah and Anna embrace, whilst standing with her hands folded in front of herself. Breaking away, Sarah turns to Ellen and hurries over to her, tears in her eyes. She sweeps Ellen into her arms and holds her close. Slowly, Ellen returns the embrace.

"Oh, Miss Cup! I'm so happy to see you. I'll fix your favourite supper and give you some real food. I even made a chocolate sandwich cake to celebrate."

Feeling abashed that she may have overstepped the bounds of propriety with her enthusiastic welcome, Sarah breaks away from Ellen, bobs, mumbles, and wipes a tear away. With a smile, she bustles back into the kitchen, followed by a chattering child as Rupert runs out of the kitchen to his friend. Ellen stands in the doorway to the sitting room with her hands folded in front of herself, watching John and Anna embrace with kisses. She lowers her head, turns, and walks through the sitting room to the staircase. Rupert speeds up the stairs and waits at the top, looking at Ellen. With one foot on the bottom step, she turns to stare at the pair still showing each other with affection and talking.

Walking up the stairs, Ellen is careful to hold the railing. At the top, she turns, walks to the familiar door, and stops. Rupert paws at the door and looks up at her. A deep breath fills her as she pushes the door open, left ajar as always. Inside her room, she looks 'round. Rupert follows her as she walks 'round the bedroom. She touches everything, just as it had been the morning when she was taken away. The full-length looking glass reflects the image of a young woman, void of expression, who reaches out to touch it. Tracing the features of the person displayed before her, she shakes her head, frowns, reaches for a dressing gown on a nearby chair, and then drapes it over the looking glass. She walks over to her dressing table, touching the brush, comb, and hand-held looking glass set, looking up to see yet another reflection of herself in that looking glass. Turning away, she takes the nightdress from the same chair that held the dressing gown and drapes that over the dressing table's looking glass.

She walks over to the window, looking outside. Pulling down the shade, the room darkens, and she turns to look at her bed. All her soft toys are in a row against the pillows. She walks over to the bed, caressing the flowered quilt that was stitched together with so many colourful pieces of fabric in a dizzying mix of patterns and textures. As she stares at the quilt, Rupert scoots under the bed, out from the other side, and then hops up on the bed, wagging his tail, tilting his head so that one ear flops in an odd direction. Ellen sits on the bed, reaching over to scratch the dog's ears. He lies down, wagging his tail, watching his friend. Her attention moves to her dresser, bureau, and bookcase. Sitting with her hands folded in her lap, she stares at everything displayed.

When John and Anna finish their affectionate celebration of being together, again, as a family, he picks up the valise and offers to take it upstairs to their bedroom.

"Thank you, John. I'll come up with you and find the cuddly animal you brought to Ellen whilst she was in hospital. I'll take it to her and add it back to her collection."

Nodding, John walks to the staircase, stepping aside, allowing Anna to ascend the stairs first. He follows her up and down the hallway to their bedroom, setting the bag on their bed. Anna opens it, rummaging through the items it contains, then pulls out Ellen's comfort toy. Smiling, she walks over to kiss John.

"Would you mind setting aside what needs to be laundered? I'd like to take this to Ellen and see how she is. I noticed that her door was open, and she was sitting on her bed."

"Yes, of course, I'll do that. I hope Ellen is all right."

Nodding as she strokes the artificial fur on the toy, she walks out of their bedroom, down the hallway, and stops at the door to Ellen's room. She sighs when she sees that the looking glasses are covered, and the blinds are darkening the room. Ellen just sits, staring, and Rupert lies with his chin on his paws, watching Ellen. Anna decides to make her presence known and approaches her from an angle where she is sure to notice that a familiar presence is in the room, and she waits. Turning her head, Ellen looks at Anna and then looks back at the things that belong to her. Anna walks over to Ellen and sits next to her on the bed, looking ahead of her and wondering what Ellen thinks as she sees her room again. She turns to look at Anna, tapping Anna's arm. Looking at Ellen, she tilts her head to the side, points at Ellen, moves her hands down the front of herself, and then pats her hands together to ask if Ellen is feeling all right. Ellen's response is to stare down at her hands, covering her bandaged hand with the other hand. Silently, they sit together, Anna looking about the room, reliving for a moment the hours she spent here worrying, waiting, crying...She shakes the memories of such an unhappy time from her head and turns to Ellen, tapping her arm to garner her attention. Ellen looks down at her arm and then up at Anna, tilting her head to the side. Sweeping her hand to take in all the room and its contents, Anna tilts her head to the side, points to Ellen, and taps her head, asking her what she is thinking. Ellen shrugs and looks 'round the room.

She looks at the lady, points to the place with things to wear, and then wiggles her fingers under her nose.

As Anna had dreaded, she must tell Ellen that her mouse, Mr Whiskers, is dead. She points to where the mouse's home had been, cradles her hands together, pantomimes stroking the mouse, and then draws an X on her own forehead. Looking down at her hands, Ellen nods and tilts her head to the side, looking at Anna, again, with one tear falling. Assuming that Ellen wonders what happened to the mouse after it died, Anna reaches into her pocket and takes out her handkerchief. She spreads it on her hand, drawing the corners together, and then pantomimes digging. She lowers her hand holding the imaginary mouse into the imaginary hole and pantomimes covering the dead pet with dirt. Anna pantomimes once more, taking what she hopes Ellen understands is a rock and pretends to place it on the imaginary grave. Anna points to herself, draws a frown on her face, and then draws a line down from her eye to tell Ellen that the death of her pet made her sad. Ellen nods, looking down at her hands, once more. Again, Ellen raises her head to look at her belongings.

She looks at the strange thing, the boy and girl and swing, points to it, looks at the lady, and tilts her head to the side.

Finally, able to smile at something, Anna taps two fingers on her wrist, taps her fingers on her head, and then points to Ellen. She taps two fingers on her wrist, holds her fist against her chest, and extends her arm as she opens her hand, points to the figurine, and then points to Ellen. She hopes that Ellen will be happy that William had been thinking of her and brought her a gift. Ellen gets up from the bed, walks to the bureau, and touches the boy and girl playing on the swing. She lifts the figurine in her hands, walks back to the bed and sits. Ellen gives the figurine to Anna.

She points to the lady, holds her fist to her chest and extends her arm whilst opening her hand, and then taps two fingers on her wrist.

Surprised that Ellen would want to give this gift back to William, she shakes her head and hands it back to Ellen. She taps two fingers on her wrist, taps her fingers on her head, and then points to Ellen. She taps two fingers on her wrist, holds her fist against her chest, and extends her arm as she opens her fingers. She gives firm affirmation that this was a gift from William and it cannot be returned. Anna taps two fingers on her wrist, holds her fist to her chest, points to the figurine, points to Ellen, puts one fist on top of the other several times, points to Ellen and draws a smile on her own face. In this way, she informs Ellen that William gave her the gift to make her happy. Again, Ellen hands the gift back to Anna, shaking her head. Firmly, Anna gives it back to Ellen, strongly reinforcing that the figurine shall not be returned to the one who gave it. Anna points to Ellen, places her fist on her chest, extending her arm whilst opening her fingers, points to the figurine, taps two fingers on her wrist, and then draws a frown on her own face, tracing a line down from her eye. Anna watches Ellen hold the figurine in her hands, get up, and place it back on the bureau where it was, and then stand, staring at it. Anna rises to her feet, walks over to Ellen and rubs her back. Ellen looks at her as Anna pantomimes that it is time to have supper. She turns back to look at the figurine as Anna turns and leaves the room, giving Ellen time to sort out her thoughts before coming down to eat with the family. Staring at the figurine, Ellen reaches out to touch it, causing the swing to sway slightly. She turns 'round, walks over to her bed, pulls down the blankets, and slides between the sheets, fully clothed. Pulling the blankets up to her chin, Rupert scoots closer, resting his chin on the lump under the blanket that is Ellen's knee. She pulls a cuddly toy close to her and holds it close to her heart, closing her eyes.

Walking down the hallway, down the stairs, making her way through the sitting room, through the corridor to the kitchen, she tells John and Sarah that Ellen should be down soon. Sarah serves them their supper, feeding Johanna and allowing the little one to feed herself, even though it is a messy process. Near the end of a quiet meal, Sarah gets up from the table, walks to the sink to retrieve a clean cloth, wets it, and walks back to clean Johanna's face and hands.

"Ma'am, if I may, could I take a tray up to Miss Cup? I feel sorry that she isn't coming down, and I'd like to take her up a tray if you approve."

"Of course, Sarah. If you would like, that's fine. John, I thought...well...hoped, that Ellen would feel better about coming home, but she seems even more despondent as the day wears on."

Sarah hurries to make a tray for Ellen, rushes out of the kitchen, down the hall, through the sitting room, and up the stairs as quickly as she is able, without spilling anything.

"Yes, she does, and Johanna's greeting seemed to make her happy. That was the first smile I've seen on her face in...how long..."

Anna gets up from her chair and walks over to Johanna's high chair, lifting her baby girl into her arms whilst John clears the table to help Sarah. Anna bounces Johanna on her hip and kisses the top of her head.

"Goodness, you're getting to be such a big girl! I say you get taller every day."

"Janna biiig Mamma 'n' Cuppa."

Johanna holds her arms out as wide as she can, a beautiful grin lighting up her face.

"Yes, you are getting that big, sweetheart!"

John finishes Sarah's tasks for her and looks about the kitchen to make sure everything is up to Sarah's standards. They take Johanna into the sitting room, making themselves comfortable on the sofa.

Trying to coax Ellen to eat something proves fruitless. Sarah stands with the tray in her hands, wishing she had a way to let Ellen know that she needs to eat to keep up her strength. When Ellen shakes her head and rolls over, facing away from Sarah, she swallows her disappointment and makes her way out of Ellen's room, down the hallway, down the stairs, and stops at the bottom to look at John and Anna.

"I'm sorry, but she wouldn't have any of it. I tried..."

"It's all right, Sarah. We had a feeling she might refuse supper. You tried, and that's what matters, for now. Thank you."

"Oh, Sarah? Anna and I want to spend some time with Johanna, so if you like, you can go on up, and we'll take care of her bedtime routine."

"Yes, Ma'am and Sir. I'll put Miss Cup's food away in case she changes her mind. I'll finish in the kitchen and then go to my room. Thank you for understanding..."

John and Anna smile at their devoted housekeeper, and nod hoping that Sarah understands that Ellen would not have taken a tray of food from them, either. Playing a game of patty-cake with Johanna, they pass the time, bidding Sarah a goodnight as she makes her way through the sitting room, upstairs, and to her own bedroom. Again, taking turns making up a story for Johanna who points to one or the other of her parents to pick up the story where the other had left off. It is not long before all three of them are yawning.

"John, I'm exhausted. You look tired, too. And look at our sleepy girl."

They chuckle as Johanna stretches and yawns.

"Janna beddy-bye. Janna seepy."

John takes Johanna from Anna's arms and cuddles her, nuzzling her neck with his nose.

"Well, then, sleepy princess, Mamma and Daddy will take you up to your bed."

Standing, John carrying Johanna, and Anna walk to the staircase, John standing aside to let Anna lead the way. At the top of the stairs, they make their way to Johanna's nursery where John takes a clean, pink nightdress out of the bureau and hands it to Anna. Whilst Anna is changing Johanna into her nightclothes, John walks to the playroom, looking for Johanna's favourite bedtime toy. Successful in his quest, he returns to Johanna's room in time to see Anna tucking her into her bed.

"There you go, sweetheart. Sweet dreams and sleep happy."

John leans over to give Johanna her pink bunny and kisses her forehead.

"Daddy loves you, sweet one. Always remember that."

Johanna reaches up to put her arms 'round her father's neck and holds him tight. When she releases him, she points to herself, pats her chest, and then points to John.

"Nite-nite Daddy. Janna love you."

John and Anna look at each other, melting at the way Johanna has learnt Ellen's language. Standing, John smiles and blows a kiss to his daughter who blows a kiss back to him. Johanna snuggles back under blankets with her toy and smiles at her mother.

"Anna, I'll turn down the bed."

"All right, John, I'll check on Ellen and be along, shortly."

Nodding, John leaves the room and walks down the hall to the bedroom he and Anna share, peeking into Ellen's room, seeing her curled under the covers with Rupert stretched out beside her. Shaking his head and wishing that the happier Ellen would return soon, he walks to the bedroom, opens the door, closes it, and begins to ready himself for bed.

"Mamma sing me?"

"Of course, sweetheart. What song should I sing?"

"Birdie song."

Softly, Anna begins to sing and stroke Johanna's hair, watching her baby girl's eyes struggle to stay open and then flutter shut.

"...Don't say a word...Mamma's going to buy you..."

With Johanna sound asleep, Anna leans down to kiss her forehead, stands and walks out of the room to the hallway. A few paces take her to Ellen's room and stepping inside, she walks over to see if Ellen is sleeping. Her eyes are closed, her breathing is even, and Rupert snores beside her. Feeling cheated out of their bedtime routine, Anna points to herself, places her hand over her heart, and then points to Ellen. She points to herself, puts her fist on her chest, points to Ellen, and then draws a smile on her face. Reluctantly, Anna turns and walks out of Ellen's room, leaving the door open.

Walking down the hallway to their bedroom, fatigue hits her like a gust of snow carried on a biting wind. Shivering, she opens the door and enters their room, a welcoming light from John's night table lamp illuminating the room. She closes the door and dispenses with the idea of plaiting her hair for the night, so she removes the pins, letting her hair cascade over her shoulders. Finding her nightdress hanging on the hook behind the door, she changes into it and thinks how luxuriant it will feel to stretch out in their own bed, sleeping next to John. Sliding into bed, she curls up to John, slips her arm over his chest, and rests her head on a pillow she had forgotten was so soft. John opens his eyes and reaches over to turn out the light, and then he slips his arm 'round Anna, pulling her closer as he kisses her forehead.

"I'm glad you're here. I missed you. It feels good to be a family again."

"I thought you were asleep. Yes, it does feel good to be home, all of us."

Silence and sleep overtake them with John and Anna too exhausted to move, blissfully unaware of the rest of the world. In Ellen's room, she lays there, opening her eyes from time to time, looking 'round the room that has darkened into nighttime shadows shifting with the movement of clouds and shafts of moonlight sneaking 'round the blind covering the window. She strokes Rupert's fur, slipping out of bed, leaving the dog undisturbed. She walks over to her bureau, opens a drawer, and pulls out a nightdress. She changes into it, draping her dress and unmentionables over a chair. Walking to the door of her room, she looks up and down the corridor, steps out and down the hallway to the staircase. Before descending the stairs, she stops.

She points to herself, pulls her arms up, crossed across herself.

Walking down the staircase, in the darkness, she passes through the sitting room and makes her way to the kitchen. Picking up a chair, she carries it out of the kitchen and down the hallway to the door leading to the garden. She rams it under the door handle, tests it with her hand and then nodding, returns to the kitchen to take another chair and do the same with the front door. Looking up and down the hallway, she nods and then makes her way back through the sitting room, up the stairs, and into her room. She closes her door, looks at the chair with her dress hanging over it, and then shakes her head. She opens the door a crack, then walks over to her bed and snuggles into her own bed.

Hearing a noise, Johanna awakens and holds her fuzzy bunny in her hand, climbing out of her bed, the toy dragging on the floor as she walks out of her room and over to Ellen's room. She walks over to the bed and climbs up, pulling the blankets aside, so she is able to crawl in next to Ellen. Turning to see Johanna in bed with her, Ellen moves aside, making room for her. Johanna snuggles up to Ellen, smiling and touching her face. With a tear rolling down her cheek, leaving salty evidence on her pillow, she draws Johanna into her arms and snuggles her close. Both close their eyes and relax with deep sighs.

Chapter Thirty-Seven
10 August 1926

Laundry is a never-ending task in a busy household. Anna helps Sarah put things away, bringing Ellen's clean clothing into her room. Humming to herself as she puts items in drawers and hangs up clothing, she glances about the bedroom. Rupert lies on Ellen's bed, his tail wagging. Her bedroom seems alive again with Ellen in it, even if Ellen is still subdued and ashamed that she and John know every aspect of her past. Hearing Ellen walk into the room, she turns to see her girl come in, freshly bathed and patting her hair dry with a towel. Ellen stares at Anna for a moment, walks over to her dressing table, and looks at her scarred hand without its bandage. Turning, she holds up her hand for Anna to see. She walks over to Ellen and examines it. Pink, healthy skin, blisters gone, any dead skin has sloughed off with Ellen's bath, and Anna is amazed that she is healing so rapidly. At first glance, it does not look as though it needs a dressing on it. Anna tilts her head to the side, points to Ellen's hand, moves her hands down the front of herself, and then pats her hands together to ask Ellen if her hand feels good.

She shakes her head, draws an X in the palm of her hand, and holds up her hand with her fingers open.

Yes, Anna can see the remnants of dead skin, open blisters, and healing that needs to be protected by a bandage. Anna holds up one finger to tell Ellen she will be right back. Anna leans down to grab the laundry basket, and carries it out of Ellen's room, down the hallway to the loo, setting it where it belongs. She turns to the medicine cabinet, opens it, selects the ointment Clara left for them to use on Ellen's hand, a roll of gauze, and tape to re-dress Ellen's hand. Walking back to Ellen's room, Anna is relieved that at least, Ellen is more responsive to questions and the most adequate conversations they can manage with gestures. She enters Ellen's room and joins Ellen at her dressing table, waiting, holding her hand in a position that allows Anna to dress it with ease. Checking to see that the wound is completely dry, Anna sets the items she brought from the loo on the dressing table. Deft motions that Anna has learnt from Clara and years of experience as a wife and mother allow her to complete the task in a jiffy. Ellen stares at her hand, turning it to see the hand in its entirety. Touching the bandage, she shakes her head, lowers her gaze, and tugs the lower part of her nightdress over her hand to cover it.

In an attempt to draw Ellen's attention away from her wound and to something more pleasant, Anna moves behind Ellen and rubs her back until she looks into the looking glass, again, meeting Anna's eyes. Pantomiming plaiting Ellen's hair, her suggestion elicits a nod and Ellen reaches for her hairbrush, handing it to Anna. Happy that Ellen would like her to do this for her, she takes the brush in her hand, and as she carefully detangles Ellen's hair, the memory of doing this for her brings a smile to Anna's lips. She makes quick work of plaiting her hair, reaches over to return the brush to the dressing table and looks at Ellen's reflection in the looking glass. Anna pats Ellen's shoulder and leans over to kiss her cheek.

Anna points to herself, points to her head, points to Ellen, points to herself, draws a circle 'round her own face, cradles her arms as if holding a baby, telling Ellen that she is her pretty baby. Ellen turns to stare at her reflection in the looking glass, pulling the still-damp plait over her shoulder to the front, looking at it. Patting her shoulder, Ellen looks up at her, tilting her head to the side. Anna points downstairs and pantomimes eating since it is time for lunch. Anna also tugs at her own dress's skirt and then points to Ellen, suggesting that she put on a dress instead of her nightdress. Both suggestions are met with a negative shake of Ellen's head. Anna rubs her back with a little sigh and nodding, she accepts Ellen's choice. She hopes that soon, Ellen will feel like dressing, eating, and joining the family for meals as she had done previously. At least, taking the initiative to bathe is a good sign of progress that Anna will accept.

Turning, Anna walks to the door of Ellen's bedroom, turns once more to look at her sweet girl, walks downstairs to the kitchen, where she hears Sarah and Johanna making merry with lunch. Entering the kitchen, she stops to smile at her daughter, wearing some of her food on her face, with what had been a sandwich in one hand and a cup of soup in the other.

"See? I told you your mamma would be here to have lunch with us. And, there she is!"

Johanna's enthusiasm is intercepted by Sarah's accurate aim that takes the food from her hands, preventing a mess that Rupert would be happy to clean.

"Mamma! Luncha Janna! Cuppa?"

Anna sits at the table next to Johanna, tousling her baby's hair, keeping her own food safely away from those curious little hands.

"Yes, Mamma came to have lunch with you. I see you're eating all by yourself! What a good girl. That's what a big girl does! Cuppa is tired, so she's going to rest, sweetheart. She'll eat when she's hungry, all right?"

As Anna speaks to Johanna, she places two fingers against the side of her cheek, puts her hands together, and then leans her head against them as if they were a pillow. Anna and John have decided to help Johanna learn as much of Ellen's language as they can and are proud of the little one for learning quickly. Bobbing her golden curls in a nod, Johanna reaches for the sandwich that Sarah holds in her hand. Together, they eat their lunch, finishing it in short order. When Sarah gets up to clear away the evidence of their meal, Anna tends to Johanna's need for a wet cloth to wash her face and hands. She removes the bib, sets it aside on the table, and reaches out to take Johanna into her arms, lifting her from the high chair.

"Janna nappa-bye! Janna seepy a Cuppa."

Chuckling, Sarah and Anna grin at one another, seeing more evidence that Johanna enjoys copying whatever Ellen does.

"Yes, sweetheart. It's your naptime. Mamma will tell you a story and rock you to sleep, all right?"

"Story! Mamma love Janna."

Anna cuddles Johanna close as she pats her mother's chest and then pats her own chest. She sets the energetic toddler down, and they walk to the kitchen door. Stopping, turning, to give Johanna a lesson in proper manners, Anna bends down and whispers in her ear. Johanna turns to Sarah and waves.

"Tanku food, Saya! Janna love!"

Sarah waves a soapy hand, dripping from the dishwater.

"You're welcome, Miss Johanna. I'm glad you liked your lunch."

Anna and Johanna turn, again, and walk out of the kitchen, to the staircase, and Anna walks behind Johanna as she climbs the stairs, who is determined to accomplish this herself. At the top of the stairs, Johanna runs into the nursery and climbs up on the rocking chair, holding up her arms to her mother. Laughing, Anna scoops her up, settles into the chair with her, and begins to tell Johanna a story as she rocks her sweetheart to sleep. Once Johanna is sound asleep, Anna carries her to her bed and tucks her in, snuggling the pink bunny close to her. In her sleep, Johanna grasps the toy's ear and turns her cheek against its softness. Anna kisses her forehead, smoothing her hair, and then stands, watching Johanna sleep.

Feeling the need to check on Ellen as frequently as she can, she walks over to her door, opens it, and sees her sitting cross-legged on the bed, wearing her nightdress, and stroking Rupert. Anna walks in, approaching from an angle where Ellen will notice her without feeling startled. Looking up at Anna, she tilts her head to the side and continues stroking Rupert. Tilting her head to the side, Anna points to Ellen, moves her hands down the front of herself, and then pats her hands together, asking in their language of gestures if Ellen feels all right. Ellen looks back down at Rupert and shrugs her shoulders, leaving Anna feeling lost. Patience, she reminds herself, and time, are what shall heal Ellen and bring her back to a happier place. Reaching out to rub Ellen's shoulder, hoping for a reaction and getting none, Anna turns, walks to the door and out into the hallway. She walks downstairs, and into the sitting room, picking up her favourite book, in an attempt to relieve her mind of worry. She settles into her favourite chair and manages to read one page before she hears a knock at the door. Setting her book aside, she rises to her feet, walks to the front door, and opens it.

"William. Please, come in."

Anna opens the door wide to allow him entry. Cap in hand, William smiles, nods, and enters the house, standing aside as Anna closes the door.

"Thank you, Mrs Thorpe. It's such a glorious day, I thought I'd go for a walk, and here I am."

"Yes, William, it is a lovely day. I'm glad you came again. Won't you come into the kitchen and have a glass of lemonade? You must be parched after your stroll."

"Thank you, I'd like that. Is Ellen...?"

Anna leads William to the kitchen, gesturing to the table, walking to the cold box to take out a jug of lemonade. With a glass from the cupboard in one hand and the jug in the other, she walks back to the table and fills the glass with the refreshing drink. She sits down, noticing that William has waited for her to sit before taking his own seat.

"Well, William, Ellen is still reserved and there's little change in her mood. I think she's glad to be home, but she seems more fearful than ever. Her nightmares are worse, and she jammed chairs against the doors to prevent anyone from entering. John taught her how the locking mechanism on the door works so she can check them for herself before we all go to bed. It will just take time."

Looking at his glass, he traces the beads of condensation on the outside of the glass with his finger. He looks up at Anna and takes a deep breath.

"May I see her? I wish I could tell her that nothing that has happened to her changes how I feel. She's still Ellen. I'd like to help her see that we can be all right again."

"Of course, William. She's upstairs, so I'll tell her you're here again and want to see her. I can't guarantee that she'll come down, but I will try. I hope that you can lift her spirits."

"Thank you, Mrs Thorpe. I can't tell you..."

Anna smiles at this dear young man, gets up from her chair, and turns, walking out of the kitchen. Hopeful steps take her upstairs to the corridor leading to Ellen's door. Trepidation fills her as she wonders how Ellen will react to her visitor today and hopes that William's visit will brighten her spirits. She walks into the room, and Ellen knows to look up when Rupert moves, seeing his mistress come in. Smiling, Anna sits down on the bed and taps two fingers on her wrist, points downstairs, points to her own eyes, and then points to Ellen. Ellen shakes her head at the news that William is downstairs and has come to see her. Anna sighs and taps two fingers on her wrist, places her fist on her chest, points to her own eyes, and then points to Ellen to say, again, that William wants to see her. Ellen shakes her head and looks down, requiring that Anna taps her arm to gain her attention. Looking up, Ellen sees Anna tap two fingers on her wrist, draw a smile on her face, point to her own eyes, and then point to Ellen. Anna's hope crumbles away when Ellen rejects the idea that William would be happy to see her. Patting Ellen's arm, she gets up, turns, walks out of the room, wishing she did not have to tell William that Ellen still does not want to see him.

Making her way back to the kitchen, she enters, startling William out of what looked to be deep thought. He stands, watching Anna walk to the table, an eager and expectant expression on his face. Anna hates to disappoint William again, but the truth is always best.

"I'm sorry, William. I told her that you are here and want to see her, but she shook her head and doesn't want to come downstairs."

Fighting the dejection that threatens to spread to his face, William sits back down after Anna takes her seat.

"Mrs Thorpe, should I...I mean...am I making things worse for her by coming to visit?"

"No, William, I don't think so. I believe, in time, she'll see that you aren't going to abandon your friendship because of what has happened to her. You're a good and faithful friend. Ellen has never..."

Anna stops when she sees William's eyes grow wide, and a smile spread across his face like the sunrise over a darkened world. Turning, Anna sees what caught William's attention. Ellen is wearing her favourite flowered dress and holding the figurine that William had brought for her shortly after she was dragged away from everything and everyone she holds dear. William stands, smiling at Ellen, thinking that he has never seen her more beautiful than she is at this moment. He points to himself, draws a smile on his face, points to his own eyes, and then points to Ellen, just in case his facial expression is not enough to convey the message that he is happy to see her. Anna looks at the figurine that Ellen carries of the boy pushing the girl on a swing; the one Ellen asked Anna to give back to William. She holds her breath, wondering what Ellen is thinking. Ellen walks over to the table and sets the figurine near William. He looks down at it, remembering how much he wanted her to have this and the circumstances surrounding his delivery of this gift. Ellen points to the boy and then points to William. She points to the girl and then points to herself. She touches the swing to make it move slightly.

She points to the thing, puts one fist on top of the other several times, points to herself, and then draws a smile on her face.

Relieved beyond words that Ellen says the figurine makes her happy and she is not giving it back to William, she relaxes and smiles at the two young people standing before her. William turns to Anna, with hope shining in his eyes.

"May I...I mean, with your permission...go outside with Ellen? Just to the garden."

"Of course, William. If Ellen wishes to go with you, that's fine."

William looks back at Ellen, tilts his head to the side, points to her, points to himself, and then points outside. At William's invitation to go outside with him, Ellen nods her head and turns to walk out of the kitchen, then stops, looking over her shoulder to see if William is coming. He hurries to reach Ellen's side, casting a glance over his shoulder to mouth the words 'thank you' to Anna as the two of them walk out of the kitchen and down the hallway towards the door leading outside. William fumbles with the door handle in his eagerness to open it for Ellen. When it finally yields to his insistence, he opens it wide, watching Ellen walk through, her hands clasped in front of her. Following her to the bench where she has taken a seat, he sits down on the bench, as well, keeping a respectful distance. He does not want to frighten her or chance the ruination of their time together in any way. Watching Ellen out of the corner of his eye, he sees her picking at the bandage on her hand, which is much smaller than the one he had seen when she was in hospital. Ellen looks at him, staring into his eyes. He cannot look away, seeing her eyes, now, even more beautiful in reality than they could ever be in his many thoughts of her. Staring at one another, William feels content that this is a gift...to be able to see her...to be sitting near her...

She points to herself, draws an X on the palm her hand, points to her own eyes, and then points to the young man.

Not understanding why Ellen would say that she is bad and cannot see him, he tilts his head to the side to ask her why.

She looks down at her hands, points to herself, and draws an X on the palm of her hand. She points to herself, holds her index fingers together, and draws one downwards.

William shakes his head. No, she is not bad, and he is saddened that she tells him she cannot see him because she is broken. He taps two fingers on her arm to encourage her to look at him. She looks down at her arm and then up at William. He shakes his head, again, points to himself, holds his two index fingers together, draws one downwards, points to himself, and draws an X on the palm of his hand, points to his own eyes, and then points to Ellen. It is true. He is broken when he does not see her. He feels empty. Incomplete. Ellen stares at him for a moment. She looks down at her hands, covering the bandage with her unblemished hand. Seeing this and taking a chance, William reaches over, gently takes Ellen's injured hand into his own, looks at her, and strokes her hand. He is trying to let her know that her scars, injuries, or past does not change who she is. How can he tell her that he accepts her, that she deserves care and respect, that his feelings for her are not going to change because of what has happened to her?

She looks at him, stands, tilts her head to the side, points to herself, points to the young man, and then walks two fingers across the palm of her hand.

Smiling, he springs to his feet with hope. He reaches for her hand, and she reaches out to take his, and then pulls back. William looks at her, wondering if she has changed her mind about going for a walk. With a little smile, Ellen walks 'round to the other side of William to take his hand with her unblemished hand. His smile softening, he shakes his head as he steps in front of her, reaches for the hand with the bandage, and holds it as part of a rare treasure. Ellen looks down, the smile still gracing her face, and they turn to their walk 'round the garden.

Chapter Thirty-Eight
11 August 1926

William's daily visits have cheered Ellen significantly, and her mood is almost as it was before...The household is returning to some sort of normality. Anna chuckles at the idea of what 'normal' might be, but if it means that their family is returning to a happier state, then she will grasp the concept with enthusiasm. Of course, Ellen's nightmares return with a vengeance each night, and she asks to sleep in their room more often than not. They cannot deny Ellen the comfort of their watchful presence as she sleeps. The house is quiet with John at the shop, Sarah out with Johanna for fresh air and play at a nearby park, and Ellen looking at pictures in books by the fireplace with Rupert. With a few dresses in the queue to sew, and embellish, she takes up her crochet hook to create a bit of lace for a collar. With a sigh of gratitude that these dresses are not the intricate attire worn by the local aristocracy, she sits in her favourite chair and takes up her task.

A curt rapping follows a growl from Rupert as he leaps to his feet, looking towards the front door. Setting aside her crocheting, Anna gets up to answer the door. Opening the front door, her blood runs cold as she sees Jane Adderley standing there. Rupert sits in the doorway of the sitting room, glaring at the woman and emitting a soft growl at the grating voice.

"Mrs Thorpe, I'm glad it was you who answered the door. My visit is two-fold if I may come in?"

"No, Mrs Adderley, you may not come in, but I will allow you to speak your piece right here, and now if you must."

Anna's hand grips the door handle as tightly as she would like to seize the throat of anyone who has caused her family any distress whatsoever.

"Well, fine, then. My Lewis is working, now, at Chelsey's Market. Got the job on his own, he did. I want everyone to know how proud I am of him and that now, he can bring me my list of needs since he's there anyway. He's just a delivery boy, for now, but he'll work his way up, I'm sure."

"Congratulations. I'm sure he'll do well. Now, what else have you got to say before you leave? And please, do be brief."

Eager to have this odious woman away from here before anyone sees Mrs Adderley, Anna grits her teeth and raises an eyebrow, waiting for the next bit of 'news'. Jane takes a deep breath after hesitating at seeing the expression on Anna's face.

"Well, your reputation for hospitality seems to be exaggerated. At any rate, I will get to the point. I just want to say that I heard about that girl. It has been on my mind, and I have to tell you how terrible I feel about it. Mrs Thorpe, Anna, it was my fault. I thought I was doing the right thing. That is all I wanted to do. I thought this man was her right family and I was only thinking of you and Mr Thorpe and where that girl needed to be, and I..."

Jane Adderley reaches into her handbag and pulls out money, handing it to Anna. She takes it, looking at the coins in her hand and then back to that woman.

"This is the money the man gave me for information on where he could find her. Here. This is your money, you deserve it."

Outraged and unwilling to believe what she has just heard with her own ears, she stares at the money in her hand for a moment. Her hand begins to shake as tears spring to her eyes as she looks at Mrs Adderley.

"You...you did that to her...every bit as much as the creature who gave you this money...She was beaten. She was tortured. She was so desperate to get away from that animal that she tried to kill herself. DO YOU HAVE ANY IDEA WHAT HARM YOU'VE DONE?"

Anna pulls her hand back, the door swinging open, wishing she could slap Jane's corpulent head straight off of her hunched shoulders. Instead, she hurls the money at Jane's reddening face.

"Keep your Judas blood money. If Ellen had died because of you, her blood would have been on your hands. As it is, the wounds to her SOUL are on your hands in equal measure as the beast that put her through unspeakable hell."

Looking up from her book, Ellen looks towards the sitting room doorway where Rupert remains, standing, now. She gets to her feet and walks towards the door to stand next to Rupert, her eyes growing wide as she stares at the woman standing outside.

"Anna, Mrs Thorpe, I only wanted to..."

Shocked at Anna's behaviour and her words, Jane's train of thought derails as she looks over Anna's shoulder and sees that girl. Noticing that Jane's gaze runs past her, Anna turns to see that Ellen is standing behind her, in the doorway to the sitting room. Anna turns back to Jane with renewed venom.

"I don't care what you WANTED to do. I see what you've DONE. Go. Just go. You aren't wanted here, and your filthy money is as vile as what you've done. GO! NOW!"

Rupert's barks elicit a wary but contrite expression that spreads over Mrs Adderley's face as she stoops to pick up the money and tuck it back into her handbag.

"Mrs Thorpe, I only want to set things right. If I could have just one moment to talk with that girl..."

Anna takes a protective stance between Ellen and their unwelcome visitor as Rupert comes to stand beside Anna's legs.

"You can't talk with her because you can't hear her. You never will."

Ellen walks closer to Anna, taps her shoulder, and as Anna turns to look at her, she sees Ellen tilt her head and then stare at Jane. Anna slips her arm protectively 'round Ellen's shoulders, tempted to slam the door in this viper's face, but unwilling to mar the door with Jane's blood. For a moment, Anna curses her lady-like upbringing. Confusion crosses Jane's face at Anna's statement that she cannot hear the girl. What of it? The girl cannot speak.

"Please, Anna. I admit I was wrong. If I could just let that girl, Emma, see that I meant no harm, I will be on my way."

Anna rubs Ellen's back as she moves closer to Jane.

"It's Mrs Thorpe to you, and HER NAME IS ELLEN. You did harm. How many times do I have to tell you that you are not welcome here? Are you hard of hearing?"

Feeling Ellen begin to tremble, Anna pulls her closer, reassuring her that everything is under control.

She looks at the frown lady, looks at the lady, and then tilts her head. She looks back at the frown lady, points to her, places her fists one on top of the other several times, points to the lady, holds her hands up in front of herself and moves them down in front of herself, and draws an X in her hand. She points to the frown lady and points to the road.

Mrs Adderley watches the girl making motions with her hands and juts her head forwards at what, to her, is a strange sight.

"What in the world is that girl doing? That sort of thing makes no sense, and she still looks daft to me."

Changing her mind about pushing the busybody down the front steps, Anna folds her arms across herself and taps her foot. She is proud of Ellen for standing up to Jane, a woman who can be intimidating in her bearing. That Ellen told her that she made Anna feel bad and told Jane to leave marks a new and assertive side to Ellen that she has never seen before.

"See? This is why you don't belong here. You can't hear Ellen, but she can hear you. I can hear you, and I don't like anything a base-born witless fool has to say."

Shaking more, Ellen pushes forwards to face Jane.

She points to herself, points to her own ears, and points to the frown lady. She points to the frown lady, draws an X in the palm of her hand, points to her own ears, points to herself, points to the frown lady, draws an X in the palm of her hand, and places her hand over her heart.

Jane holds the railing of the stairs and steps down them to the walkway. Stifling a proud smile, Anna rubs Ellen's back, drawing her away from Jane. Anna is amazed and appreciates Ellen's insight into Jane's personality, telling her that although Ellen can 'hear' Jane, that Jane cannot hear because she has no heart.

"There. Now you've got your dismissal from both of us. Go."

As Anna closes the door on this woman and a part of the hell that invaded their home, she hears Jane protesting with indignation.

"Why, I never...In all my born days...treated this way for trying to help them get rid of that leech...base-born and a fool, indeed..."

The door closed against the coarse voice, Anna whispers to herself.

"Good riddance to bad rubbish."

She turns to Ellen with a smile, noting that her shaking has ceased. Anna points to Ellen, places one fist on top of the other several times, points to herself, moves her hands down the front of herself, and then pats her hands together to tell Ellen that she makes her feel better. Nodding, Ellen turns and walks to the kitchen, disappearing for a moment. She returns to the front door holding a chair. She wedges it under the door handle and turns to Anna.

She points to herself, points to her own eyes, draws a frown on her own face, walks two fingers across the palm of her hand, places one fist on top of the other several times, points to the lady, and draws a frown on her own face. She points to herself, places one fist on top of the other several times, draws a frown on her own face, walks two fingers across her hand, and sweeps one hand across the other. She points to herself, places her hand over her heart, and points to the lady.

Anna draws Ellen into her arms, feeling her trembling subside completely. She cannot help but feel pride and love for Ellen as she defended her against Jane's antagonism. Anna steps back from their embrace and returns Ellen's expressive gestures as she points to herself, places her hand over her heart, points to herself, and then cradles her arms as if holding a baby to tell Ellen that she loves her baby.

She nods, points to the lady, points to herself, taps two fingers on her chest, places her fist on her chest, and then pats it.

Seeing her say that she is Ellen's mother warms Anna's heart as few things could. They smile at one another for a moment, and then Anna bends down to scratch Rupert's ears, his tail wagging against Ellen's legs. Ellen looks down at Rupert, pats her thigh, and walks back into the sitting room, settling herself by the fireplace to look at her book, the faithful dog following his friend. He sniffs, turns 'round three times, and then flops himself down next to Ellen, his chin resting on his crossed paws.

The physical fatigue of an emotionally wrought encounter settles into Anna as she makes her way back to her handiwork. Picking up her crochet hook, she stitches away the time until Sarah returns with Johanna through the garden door. A sleepy little girl runs to the sitting room and crawls up on her mum's lap. Anna listens patiently with delight as her sweet girl tries to find the words to describe her outing with Sarah. Finally, sleep attempts to wind itself 'round Johanna like a warm and fluffy blanket, but Johanna has one more thing she wants to do. She kisses her mother's face, gets down from Anna's lap, and trots over to Ellen who has been sitting there watching. Johanna toddles up next to Ellen and throws her arms 'round Ellen's neck, kissing her face. A pair of smiles match the warmth of an embrace that only sisters understand. She leans back, pointing to herself, patting her chest, and then pointing to Ellen.

"Janna love Cuppa. Janna seepy."

She puts her hands together and lays her head on them as if they were a pillow. Ellen and Anna look at one another with smiles that defy words. Johanna understands how to use Ellen's language of gestures as quickly as she learns the spoken word. Hearing Sarah's busy meal preparations in the kitchen, Anna gets up from her chair and walks behind Johanna. She scoops the child into her arms and kisses her cherubic cheeks.

"Mamma will take you up for a little nap before Daddy comes home, all right? Then we'll have supper."

The reply consists of a yawn as Johanna rests her head on Anna's shoulder. She chuckles as Ellen smiles and waves to Johanna, then turns to go upstairs where Johanna's little bed awaits its drowsy occupant. Before Anna can lay her down, Johanna is limp and asleep. She tucks her precious treasure under a blanket and wraps the baby's hand 'round the ear of her favourite toy, the pink rabbit. Anna kisses Johanna's forehead, smooths away a stubborn curl from her forehead, and then stands, giving one last glance to her daughter. She walks back downstairs, looks at the collar that she has been crocheting, and then decides she would instead join Sarah in the kitchen.

Deep into the preparations for a supper that already smells inviting, the opening and closing of the garden door causes Anna and Sarah to look at one another. They were not expecting anyone...Anna wipes her hands on her pinny and peeks out of the kitchen door, still feeling a jump of nerves whenever she hears one of the doors to the outside open and close unexpectedly. A sigh of relief and a smile meet John as he strides down the hall, a bemused air about him. Anna hurries to him, shares his embrace and matches the intensity of his kiss with her own. Stepping back, John tilts his head to the side.

"Anna, I couldn't get into the front..."

Looking past Anna, he sees a chair wedged against the door, the reason he was unable to come into the house by his entrance of habit.

"What...? Did something happen?"

"It's all right, John. I have a great deal to tell you this evening. It will take far too long to elaborate this close to supper, though. Johanna is sleeping, Ellen is in the sitting room, and I'm helping Sarah."

Playfully, Anna pats John's chest.

"Why don't you go make yourself at home?"

"Well, thank you, Mrs Thorpe. I think I will."

John kisses Anna's forehead before she walks back into the kitchen. He makes his way to the entry hall, hanging up his hat and jacket, and then walks into the sitting room to greet his girl. Ellen looks up at him from where she sits at the hearth and smiles.

She points to herself, draws a smile on her own face, points to her own eyes, and then points to the man. She places her forefinger against her nose, points up, places her hands together, and then rests her head on them as if they were a pillow.

Chuckling, John points to himself, draws a smile on his own face, points to his own eyes, and then points to Ellen, saying that he is happy to see her, too. He points to himself, points to his own head, places his forefinger against his nose, and then points upstairs, telling Ellen that he knows Johanna is upstairs sleeping. Eager to see Johanna, he points to himself, points upstairs, points to his own eyes and then places his finger against his nose to tell Ellen that he is going up to see Johanna. Ellen nods.

She points to herself, moves her fingers next to her mouth as if talking, taps two fingers against her chest, points to her own eyes, and points to the man.

John grins, nods, and begins to head upstairs to see his little poppet, knowing that Ellen will tell Anna where he is, should she come looking for him. A knock at the door stops him, and he looks longingly upstairs, having missed Johanna as he does each day. Sighing, instead, he walks to the front door, setting aside and relieving the chair from its sentry duty. He opens the door, and a minuscule beat of fear makes his heart skip.

"Constable Frayser. Would you like to come in? Is this official business?"

Stepping through the open doorway and into the Thorpe residence, Constable Frayser takes an uneasy stance in the entry hall, looking behind him through the still-open door.

"This is not really what you'd call official, Mr Thorpe. May I speak with both you and Mrs Thorpe? I'll be brief."

"Of course. I'll go and get her."

John walks to the kitchen, looks in, and then walks over to Anna, speaking in hushed tones.

"Anna, Constable Frayser is here, and he'd like to speak with both of us. He said it isn't exactly official business, so..."

Wiping her hands on her pinny and nodding, she hurries out of the kitchen and to the entry hall, followed by John.

"Constable Frayser. It's good to see you"

"Yes, Ma'am. It's...well...this is about Mr Holmes."

John's shoulders square with Anna's audible sharp intake of breath, her hand coming to her throat to quell the upheaval of bile stirred by the sound of that name. John's voice breaks the suspenseful silence.

"What about him? He hasn't...I mean, did he?"

Once again, seeing activity in the entryway, Ellen gets up, followed by Rupert, stands in the doorway to the sitting room, and stares at them. She backs away slowly, her gaze concentrated on the strange man.

393

Constable Frayser raises his hand as he shakes his head.

"No, no, he did not escape, and, if you ask me, he did not escape justice, either."

Noticing Ellen in her peripheral vision, Anna turns to see her backing away from the man who carried her out of hell and into salvation. Anna turns to Constable Frayser, suppressing her trembling as the need to reassure Ellen takes precedence.

"One moment, constable. I need to explain to Ellen who you are."

Nodding and understanding the unique situation at hand, he realises that Signe, or more her more proper name, Ellen, would have no memory of him. The constable looks at his shoes, waiting for Mrs Thorpe to satisfy this young woman's questions about who he is and why he is there. Remaining with Ellen who has her arms drawn up and crossed in front of her, Anna wraps her arm about her daughter's trembling shoulders. Satisfied that they are as ready as they will ever be, John looks back to the constable.

"All right, we're ready to hear what you have to tell us."

John moves closer to Anna, taking her hand and squeezing it.

"This is completely off the record, you understand. I thought, though, given the circumstances, you have every right to know. Mr Holmes...met with a situation whilst in prison. Other inmates heard him bragging about what he had done to Signe, proclaiming his innocence. You see, even hardened criminals don't take kindly to abuses of that nature. Sparing you the unsavoury details, Mr Holmes is dead. No one at the prison will admit to anything, but I wanted you to know that it's over. He's gone. He'll never harm anyone, ever again."

Her hand over her mouth, tears cloud Anna's vision, the second shock in one day causing her to slump against John's sturdy frame. She can scarcely believe that the monster is gone. Dead. The joy rising in her breast shames her for she has never rejoiced in another's death until now. John slips his arm 'round Anna and looks at Ellen who will need an explanation. Constable Frayser nods, acutely feeling the family's emotion at this news.

"Well, I said I'd be brief, so I'll take my leave. I wanted you to...know."

Nodding and showing the constable to the door, emotion chokes John as he watches him walk away to his official motor that carried a man delivering personal news. A shaking hand closes and locks the front door, and John turns to Anna and Ellen. He gestures for them all to go into the sitting room so that Ellen can receive the news and explanation that she deserves to know.

Chapter Thirty-Nine
13 August 1926

Intermittent rain these past few days make today so much more enjoyable with its sunshine and warm breeze. Anna sits at the table in the garden, stitching an embellishment for the hem of a dress she is making, watching Johanna play with Rupert, whilst Ellen relaxes in the hammock that John put up earlier in the season. Sipping her tea, she muses how their lives have changed over time. Johanna has grown in so many incredible ways, Ellen came by chance or miracle and became a part of their family, tragedy has struck joy returned, and yet, she concludes that change is the only thing that remains a constant in their lives. She shakes her head, finding such philosophical musings far too dark on such a peaceful day. Laughing, she watches Johanna attempt to fly like a bird whilst Rupert's efforts to chase birds fail with hilarity. Sarah comes out to the garden, places her hands on her back, and stretches, taking in the essence of summer.

"Ma'am, it's time for Miss Johanna's nap, if you think she's ready?"

"Oh yes, Sarah. She has had her fill with fresh air and sunshine. She'll rest well."

Nodding, Sarah playfully chases Johanna, catches her up in her arms, and brings her to her mother.

"There, now, wee one, give your mum a happy kiss, and we'll be off for a nap, then."

Taking Johanna in her arms, Anna cuddles her baby, covering her face in kisses, and receiving a fair share of them in return.

"That's my girl. Sleep happy with sweet dreams, sweetheart. I love you."

Johanna smiles, points to herself, places her hand over her heart, and then points to her mother.

"Janna lova Mamma."

Anna repeats the gestures that mean 'I love you' in return to Johanna and then waves to her as Sarah helps Johanna off her mother's lap and leads her by the hand into the house. The enticing fragrances and a blurred riot of colour in the garden cause Anna to delay her trip to the kitchen to refill her teacup. The last sip punctuated her dip into the philosophical pool, and another cup of tea with milk and sugar would be nice. Looking over at Ellen, she smiles at her sweet girl's hand grazing the tips of grass beneath her, sleep fluttering her eyelashes the way the petals of a flower wave to its scent as a breeze carries it away. She had intended to ask Ellen if she would like tea, but disturbing such a peaceful sleep would be a shame. Ellen has so few chances to rest, undisturbed, that when benign sleep takes her, 'tis best to let it last.

She gets up from her chair, pats her leg and calls Rupert to her, then chuckles when he scoots under the hammock, evidently preferring to stay with his friend. Anna walks to the door, turns to enjoy one more look at Ellen's peaceful sleep, and then walks inside, to make more tea. As she waits for the water to boil, she watches Ellen from the window, thinking of how peaceful she looks. Ellen's fear of that man returning has subsided after knowing that he died, yet she still locks the doors at night. She looks back at the teakettle, reminded of the saying, 'A watched pot won't boil', so she returns to her vigil at the window. Just as she was wondering when William might arrive, she sees him enter the garden gate and walk over to Ellen. Anna relaxes, just a little, knowing that someone she trusts is with Ellen as she sleeps. Taking this opportunity, she takes her time making more tea and then considers the merits of taking some lemonade out to William and Ellen.

Walking up to Ellen as she lays in the hammock, he sees that she is asleep. Smiling, he sits on the ground next to her and notices that the hand that had been so damaged has healed, although prominent scars remain. Still, her hand is beautiful to him. Her hair falls from the side of the hammock, and he reaches out to touch it, soft, glowing, and delicate, just like Ellen's soul. A natural instinct draws his hand to the hammock itself, pushing it to rock, back and forth, soft as a breeze, the way he would rock her in his arms if he could.

Listening to her breathing and watching her as his thoughts wander, he comes to attention at the sound of Ellen's sharp intake of breath. Her arms draw up to cover her face, as it changes from a peaceful visage to one filled with terror. Her head begins to turn back and forth, her breathing becomes more burdensome, and she starts to shake. Alarmed that he is alone with Ellen, yet not wanting to leave her, he fears that this may be a nightmare. He looks towards the house for a moment as he rises to his knees, stroking Ellen's arm and speaking reassuring words. Ellen's distress does not go unnoticed as Anna walks out with the tray of lemonade and glasses. Rushing to the table, she sets them down, and as she hurries to them, Ellen's eyes open wide as she suddenly sits up, causing the hammock to overturn, and dumping her on the ground. Her mouth opens wide in a silent scream, arms reaching out with stiff fingers, flailing against some invisible attack as she kicks in the air. Taken aback by this turn of events yet wanting to convey Ellen's fear and pain into himself to spare her the horror, William reaches out to Ellen and gathers her in his arms, realising that she is still deeply asleep. Anna puts her hand on William's arm, looking at him with a mother's earnestness as she moves closer to Ellen.

"William, I'll help her through this. Just stay back..."

"No, please...let me..."

William holds Ellen gently to himself, stroking her arms, rocking her.

"Shhhh... Ellen, come back...your mother and I...it's William ...we're here. You're safe. Wake up, Ellen. It's all right. You're safe."

Anna watches William care for Ellen with sympathy and kindness as she, herself, would. Ellen slowly comes 'round, looking about her with, what can only be described, as panic written on her face. William continues to stroke Ellen's hair, soothing her with words she cannot hear, and rocking her in a soothing rhythm. Though his arms are strong, his demeanour is filled with tenderness and compassion. Ellen looks up at William and dissolves into tears, uncontrollable sobs wracking her body. She wraps her arms 'round him, clinging to the only reality she can see through the veil of horror that has finally lifted. Touched to the core, Anna sees William fighting his own tears and failing as they fall, mixing with Ellen's.

"Hush, sweet Cup...you're not alone. You're never alone."

Anna's own tears begin to fall, feeling at the same time proud of William for his caring instincts yet cheated out of a chance to mother Ellen through this darkness. She reaches out and places her hand on William's shoulder and whispers to him.

"Well-done, William. She trusts you as much as she trusts us, and we trust you even more, now."

"I...I was only rocking the hammock a little...it must be my fault...I frightened her...I didn't mean..."

"No, no, William...you didn't frighten her. The past reared its gruesome head and assaulted her. Neither of us could have prevented it, but you brought her safely back as well as I could ever do."

William looks down at the sobbing girl in his arms for whom he has come to care so much. He buries his face in her hair as he strokes it and rubs her back, devoting himself entirely to Ellen's comfort in her time of need. As Ellen's emotional storm subsides, William sees her eyes brighten with right-minded focus. Ellen looks 'round her, seeming to re-establish her place in the real world. Anna sees Ellen stare at William and then at her, pulling away from William's arms and crawling to her.

She looks back at the young man, puts her hands together at her chest and moves them towards him. She turns to the lady, taps two fingers on her wrist, points to her own eyes, and points to herself.

Ellen wraps her arms 'round Anna's waist, lays her head on her mother's lap, and cries anew, cries until there are no more tears.

Feeling empty and helpless, William's heart feels a pain he has never known when he sees Ellen ask him to forgive her for having seen her in the violent throes of a nightmare. As he watches mother and daughter, his gut fills with guilt as though he is an interloper, intruding where he does not belong.

"Mrs Thorpe, if you want me to leave..."

"No, William, I want you to understand something if you truly want to be Ellen's friend. No matter how well she can keep these memories at bay and be happy when she's awake, these demons come with cruel regularity when she sleeps. She will most likely have them for the rest of her life. She'll never fully escape her past."

Looking down, he can yet feel Ellen's troubled warmth in his arms, her terror, her trembling, and her tears. He would do it all again, always willing to do, give, be anything that offers Ellen peace and comfort. He looks up, watching Ellen and Anna holding one another, a mother soothing her child, grateful that he could lend himself in some small way.

"Mrs Thorpe, I had no idea how violent her nightmares could be. Thank you for allowing me to show her that I'm not afraid..."

"Yes, William, you've proven that time and again. I'm glad that you're not afraid. But...Ellen feels shame that you saw her...like this, and afraid that you'll think ill of her."

Wiping her eyes on the back of her hand, Ellen sits up, breathless from the terror that carried her away. She looks at William, looks down, shakes her head, gets up, and runs to the house, Rupert running after her. Ellen enters it with haste and does not look back. William watches Ellen leave, taking the sunshine and fragrance of the flowers with her.

"But...she hasn't done anything to forgive. I don't think less of her for...being who she is. She's at the mercy of something she can't control."

William looks down at his shoes and whispers.

"I should go. I hope I've done nothing wrong, and I hope Ellen will come to see that."

William rises to his feet and lends his hand to Anna to help her stand. She brushes the grass from her dress as she finds her footing and gifts William with a weary smile.

"No, you've done nothing wrong. I'll give her some time to herself, and then she may wish to express herself. Don't worry, William. I think she knows that you don't fear what makes her different. You mean so much to her. That's why she's upset that you saw her have a nightmare."

Nodding, William turns and walks towards the garden gate, reaching for the cap that is not in his back pocket. Anna watches him walk away, sighs, and then walks to the door, entering. William's thoughts flow from sorrow and anger for what Ellen has endured, to an admiration for Ellen's strength, to the insecurity that he could not possibly be good enough for her. No matter how his emotions writhe, one thing remains clear as he stops to lean against a tree. As he pulls out his wallet, tugs out the piece of paper she had given him, he realises that his feelings are more profound than he had ever anticipated. Unfolding it, he stares at the name written on it. ELLEN. He recognises that, to him, she will always be Ellen. All of her. Her past, her fears, her happiness, her playfulness, her sorrows, and her pain. He would not want to know just a part of Ellen. He wants to know who she is with his heart, not only what he sees with his eyes. He wants to hear her with his soul, but he cannot share with her, the feelings growing within him for fear of damaging the heart of one he holds so dear. Folding the paper and returning it to his wallet, he continues on his way, fresh air being his only destination.

Standing for a moment, leaning against the door, Anna braces herself for whatever Ellen's state may be since she expressed shame that William was witness to her nightmare and asked his forgiveness. If only Ellen could see that these visible and invisible scars are not her fault. She walks down the hallway to the sitting room, peeking in rooms as she goes along, looking for Ellen. Her quest takes her upstairs where she can see Ellen sitting on her bed, holding the plaited grass that William had made for her on his first visit. It is brown, now, dry and fragile, but Ellen holds it in her hand, tracing its weave with her fingertip.

Anna pushes the door open and walks into Ellen's room, her movement catching Ellen's eye, causing their eyes to meet. A mother's compassionate gaze meeting that of her haunted daughter. She sits on the bed next to Ellen, tilting her head to the side, encouraging her to communicate her thoughts and feelings. Ellen looks away, stands, walks over to her bureau, and then lays the grassy gift next to the figurine of the girl and boy swinging. She touches it, causing the swing to sway. Anna watches Ellen, wondering what she is feeling, thinking, wanting to express but cannot. Ellen returns to sit next to Anna with her hands folded in her lap, staring at them. Patting Ellen's arm to seek her attention, Anna waits for Ellen to look at her arm and then look up at her. She asks Ellen if she is all right by pointing to Ellen, moving her hands down the front of herself, and then patting her hands together. Ellen stares at her for a little whilst and then shakes her head.

She taps two fingers on her wrist, points to her own eyes, points to herself, draws an X on the palm of her hand, and then points to her head. She taps two fingers on her wrist, points to her head, points to herself, and then draws an X on the palm of her hand.

Shaking her head, Anna places her hand on Ellen's increasingly rapid gesturing. Yes, William saw her nightmare, but no, William does not think Ellen is bad. Pulling her hands away from Anna's touch, Ellen begins to gesture again, as quickly as before.

She points to herself, draws an X on the palm of her hand, places her fist on her chest, taps two fingers on her wrist, points to her head, and points to herself. She points to herself again, draws an X on the palm of her hand, places her fist on her chest, taps two fingers on her wrist, and draws a frown on her own face. She points to herself, draws an X on the palm of her hand, places her fist on her chest, taps two fingers on her wrist, points to her head, and draws an X on the palm of her hand.

Anna mentally deciphers what Ellen is communicating at a dizzying speed. She holds up her hand to stop Ellen's flow of gestures to reply that William is happy to know her, and does not think she is bad. As for not wanting William to know her, Ellen can rest assured that he remains ignorant of the brutal facts surrounding her past, except what he has deduced or what Ellen has told him. She lifts Ellen's chin with her finger so she can see the fullness of a mother's love. Slowly, as best she can within the limits of their gesturing, she tells Ellen that William thinks she is good and she makes William happy. Next, she gestures that she and John know everything about her past and still love her, accept her, and know that she is a good and pure soul. Ellen's eyes open wide as she shakes her head, new tears falling from her eyes.

She points to herself, draws an X on the palm of her hand, places her fist on her chest, points to the lady, taps three fingers on her chest, points to her head, and points to herself. She points to the lady, taps three fingers on her chest, points to her head, points to herself, and draws an X on the palm of her hand. She points to the lady, taps three fingers on her chest, draws an X on the palm of her hand, places her hand over her heart, and points to herself. She holds her forefingers together, drawing one down from the other, and points to herself. She places her hands together at her chest and moves them towards the lady.

Anna's own tears flow to think that Ellen did not want her and John to know everything and she thinks they believe that she is bad and will not love her anymore because they know. The worst pain of all is seeing Ellen's shame, her feeling that she is broken, and the need to ask forgiveness. She gathers Ellen into her arms, a mother hen protecting her chick, and rocks her, pouring out of herself all of the unconditional acceptance that she and John both hold in their hearts for Ellen.

Chapter Forty
14 August 1926

The light of a new day tries to crack through the turmoil of the previous day. Breakfast passes in relative silence, the unique babbling of a toddler subdued by the mood of the adults 'round her. Whilst Sarah and Anna clear the table, John takes Johanna in his arms, holding her with fatherly affection, yet not feeling the usual playfulness that permeates his time with her on a Saturday. Anna tries to engage Ellen in the domestic tasks that the three of them generally enjoy, but to no avail. Ellen stands from her place at the table, picks up and carries her plate to Rupert's dish, and spills the uneaten breakfast to the mercy of an opportunistic dog. Without looking at Anna or Sarah, she settles her plate into the sink with the rest of the dishes.

John, Anna, and Sarah watch Ellen and then look at one another, each wondering what they could do to ease her melancholy. William witnessing her nightmare seemed to be the event that brought out visible signs of distress and disquiet in Ellen. Anna begins to go after Ellen when she leaves the kitchen, but John puts his hand on her arm.

"Let her sort out a few things, Anna. I think she needs time to think. Then, we can see if she'd like to talk to both of us."

"All right, John. You know how I always want to 'fix' things, but you're right. Ellen does need some time to herself."

John kisses Anna's forehead and leans down to Johanna to give her his special Daddy kisses. Standing, again, he caresses Anna's cheek and then takes Johanna out of the kitchen. Hearing the door to the garden open and close, Anna and Sarah look at one another and resume their cleanup. When they are finished, Anna fills the teakettle and turns on the heat.

"Sarah, join me in a cup, would you? I'd like it if you'd keep me company for a little whilst if you could."

"Of course, Ma'am. I'd like that very much."

Sarah walks to the cupboard to gather what they will need for tea, but Anna waves her away with a wan smile, gesturing to the table.

"Sit, Sarah. It's my turn. I...want to do something for someone and since Ellen seems to want to be alone right now, you're the only one left."

Nodding and feeling a bit awkward at this role-reversal, Sarah does as she is asked and sits down at the table, fighting the urge to get up and do her job. Before long, the kettle sings its siren's song to the teacups, and Anna finishes making their tea. She sets it on the table, takes her own seat, and the kitchen fills with the hollow sound of sipping tea, the clink of cups on saucers, and the aromatic tea leaves from India.

"Sarah, I apologise. I'm not much company. It is a comfort, though, to have you with me. Sometimes it's so hard..."

"Ma'am, no need to apologise. 'Tis a pleasure to take tea with you. I wish I could offer help or advice, but now, with Miss Cup, I'm afraid I'm useless."

Anna sighs and reaches over to pat Sarah's hand, offering an empathetic smile.

"Then, I say, we'll be useless together and do a fine job of it, too. I reckon I'll give Ellen a bit more time. When John comes in with Johanna, we'll talk with her together."

"Yes, Ma'am. When you do, be sure that I'll mind Miss Johanna and keep her occupied."

"Thank you, Sarah. We'd be lost..."

A knock at the garden door interrupts them, causing Sarah to rise from her chair with a start.

"Oh dear, I completely forgot...the market delivery. Ma'am, if you'll excuse me..."

Anna watches Sarah bustle away, sorry that their brief interlude to commune as women comes to an abrupt end. She stares at her reflection in the china cupboard until she recognises a familiar voice at the garden door. She gets up and walks out of the kitchen to where Sarah is speaking with Lewis Adderley, of all people. Seeing Anna, Lewis takes a step back and bobs his head slightly, words pouring out of him like a quiet geyser.

"Mrs Thorpe. I'm...delivering from Chelsey's Market, now. I hope that's okay? I could ask one of the others to take this route if you like. You don't have to tip me, or anything. I'd understand. I don't want trouble."

"Lewis...slow down. It's all right. I heard that you had started working there and I'm glad for you. I wish you the best with it."

Lewis stares at Anna, unable to believe that she is so nice to him after what his miserable mum did. Shame fills him, but he refuses to let it spoil the best thing that he has heard yet today.

"Th...thank you, Ma'am. I have William to thank for it. He put in a good word for me, and I think that tipped the scales in my favour. He's a good friend, I say. And, I'm rambling and wasting your time, Mrs Thorpe. I'm sorry. I'll be on my way."

"Lewis, wait just a moment. Sarah, if you'll take the basket, I'll get his tip. Lewis, wait right here if you would."

Taking the basket, Sarah bustles off to the kitchen, keeping her opinions about the Adderley family to herself. Anna walks to the entry hall, rummages through her handbag to find an adequate tip. Returning to the garden door, Anna smiles at Lewis.

"Hold out your hand, Lewis."

Staring at Anna, he does as he is told and then looks down as he hears the clink of coins in his hand. His eyes open wide as he sees the first tip he has received. So far, no one else has bothered to tip him. He suspects that his mother's reputation is to blame, as well as his misspent youth as a rapscallion. Lewis looks down and lowers his voice, the shame he feels overflowing into words.

"Mrs Thorpe, I don't know what to say...Wait, I do. My mum...she...well, she's gone on and on about what happened...you know what I mean...I'm sorry for what she did, all of it. It was all wrong and...I don't know what else to say, Ma'am. I'm sorry."

Anna's heart softens towards this young man who is trying to make something of himself in spite of his mother's shrewish behaviours.

"Lewis, none of it is your fault. You aren't responsible for your mother's deeds. You didn't speak to...that man...did you?"

"Oh no, Ma'am. I had a feeling he was up to no good, and I wasn't about to spill where Ellen is. No, Ma'am. If William is sweet on her, then she has to be a really nice girl, and I'd never do that to her, and I'm really sorry for what...happened...I heard some...I'm sorry."

"There you have it, then, Lewis. You can carry a clean conscience. None of it was your doing. You can always deliver here, and I promise you'll always receive a tip for a job well done. And, Lewis?"

"Yes, Ma'am?"

"I meant what I said, that I wish you the best."

Brightening, the shame falling away from his soul like so much dried cow droppings, he stuffs the tip in his pocket and smiles.

"Thank you, Ma'am. That means more to me...Well, I'd best go. Thank you, again."

He waves his cap as he turns to leave, unwilling to let Mrs Thorpe see how much her kind words touched him. Someone was kind to him for being a decent man. He makes a promise to himself to thank William for that, one day. It is a lesson and experience he will not soon forget. Anna watches Lewis walk away, feeling sorry for the young man, in a way. Returning inside and closing the door, she does give him credit for trying to better himself and is proud of William for giving the lad a hand up with finding gainful employment. She reckons there is hope for most anyone if one looks deeply enough. Two laughing faces bursting through the front door halt her slow steps down the hallway.

"Watch your head, love, Daddy doesn't know how tall he is!"

Johanna's head is bowed next to John's ear as her arms cling 'round his neck, her legs draped over his shoulders.

"Daddy pony! Mamma! Daddy pony!"

Chuckling and shaking her head, she walks to them and reaches up to help Johanna dismount, setting her on the floor so she can stand on her own two feet.

"I see! Daddy gave you a pony ride! You're so big sitting on Daddy's shoulders! My goodness!"

Johanna laughs, holding out her arms as wide as she can.

"Janna BIG!"

John laughs, ruffling Johanna's hair.

"We had a good little trot about the neighbourhood. Perhaps, when she's a bit older, we can find her a pony and stable it at one of the farms and find her a proper riding instructor."

"Aren't we getting a little ahead of ourselves, John? It's a lovely idea, but she's not even three years old, yet. Let's think about it for a whilst. A whilst, being, a few years."

Anna leans up to kiss his cheek, sure that Johanna will have her horse, one day, and her father will make sure she learns how to ride like a proper lady. She crouches down to Johanna, takes her hands in her own, claps Johanna's hands together, and gives her baby girl an excited expression.

"Johanna, why don't you go into the kitchen to find Sarah? I'm sure she'll have something special for you. She might even let you help her. Would you like that?"

Nodding with a sparkling smile that shines through her eyes, she trots off to find Sarah. Anna stands, moves closer to John slips her arm 'round his waist, and they watch Johanna, growing up before their eyes. John looks down at Anna, his face becoming serious.

"How is our girl? Do you think we should go to her together?"

"Well, she's been up in her room, I assume. I believe we should both go to find out if there's anything more bothering her and if there's something we can do about it. Between the two of us, we might be able to help her."

"She's certainly had enough time to think a bit. Let's go on up."

Together, they walk to the staircase, John standing aside for Anna who takes a deep breath of trepidation with her first few steps. Reaching the top of the stairs, they look towards Ellen's room, see her door ajar, and they look at each other, again. With his hand on Anna's lower back, he whispers.

"There's no time like the present, Anna."

Anna takes John's hand, and they walk to Ellen's room, opening the door enough so that she will see both of them standing there. Rupert's wagging tail against Ellen alerts her to their presence, and she looks up at them, then back down at her hands. Anna walks in and sits down on the bed next to her, reaching out to stroke Ellen's hair and rub her back. John pulls up a chair and sits on the other side, leaning forwards, his elbows on his knees, hands clasped. Patiently, they wait, Ellen staring at them, first John, and then Anna. Fresh tears falling from Ellen's eyes join the dry trails of those already shed in private. She wipes them away on the sleeve of her dress and takes a deep breath.

She taps two fingers on her wrist, points to her head, points to herself, and draws an X in the palm of her hand.

John leans further in to pat Ellen's knee and then shakes his head in disagreement with Ellen's expression that William thinks she is bad. He points to Ellen and pats his hands together. He taps two fingers on his wrist, points to his own head, points to Ellen, and then pats his hands together. He wants Ellen to know that she IS good and William knows it. Staring at John, she shakes her head and looks at Anna.

She holds her palm up and makes two fingers walk across it, points to her head, points to herself, and draws an X in her hand.

This time, it is Anna's turn to disagree. How does she explain that just because other people have thought she was bad or unworthy or less of a person does not mean that she IS all of those things? The best she can do is point to Ellen, pat her hands together, and place her hand over her heart. Then, she points to Ellen; puts one fist on top of the other several times, points to herself and John, and then draws a smile on her own face. She sighs with frustration that telling Ellen she has a good heart and she makes them happy is a poor substitute for what she would wholeheartedly like to express. A disheartening shake of Ellen's head causes John and Anna to look at one another, silently wondering how they can get through to Ellen. They know she is kind, honest, generous of heart, sensitive, and brings people joy. She could not be anything else but her own precious self, if she tried. Ellen stands up and turns to face both of them.

She points to the man and the lady, taps two fingers on her wrist, shakes her head, points to her head, and points to herself.

Confused that Ellen would say that they and William do not know her, John and Anna look at one another, sharing the same thought that before they knew ABOUT her, they knew HER. As they look back to Ellen, they wonder, what she means. Anna shakes her head, pointing at her own head to tell Ellen that they do not understand.

She points to herself, points to her own head, points to herself, and draws an X in the palm of her hand.

Before they can protest Ellen's opinion that she knows she is bad, Ellen holds up her hand.

She looks at the lady and the man, points to herself, draws an X in her hand, and holds her arms as though cradling a baby. She points to herself, draws an X in her hand and holds her hand low by her knees. She holds her palm up and makes two fingers walk, then motions as though hitting herself, points to herself, and draws an X in her hand.

John raises his hand, gesturing that he wishes to communicate something on the subject even as his heart cries out for his innocent daughter who thinks she has been bad all of her life thanks to the brutality of a monstrous and twisted creature. He walks two fingers across his hand, pounds his fist into his hand, points to Ellen, and then draws an X on the palm of his hand. He points to Ellen and then pats his hands together. He needs her to understand that the people who hurt her were bad even though she is good. Anna raises her hand to capture Ellen's attention. She points to Ellen, pats her hands together, cradles her arms as if holding a baby, then holds her hand down by her knee and raises it slowly to tell her that she has been good all her life. Fresh insight fills Anna as she grasps that Ellen's opinions of herself are based on the actions of a monster who did not deserve to be her father. She holds up a finger to signal that she wishes to continue. She points to herself and John, points to her own head, points to Ellen, pounds her fist on her hand, draws an X on the palm of her hand, walks two fingers across her palm several times, pounds her fist on her hand, and then points to Ellen. She points to herself, points to John, points to her own head, points to herself and John, places her hand over her heart, and then points to Ellen. John looks at Anna, wondering if it was wise to tell Ellen that they know all the sordid details of her anguished past, including the men her so-called father allowed to abuse her at will. Ellen's reaction to this is answer enough, although the revelation is couched in the reassurance of parental love. She takes a step back, covering her mouth with her hand, shaking her head.

She points to the lady and the man, draws an X in the palm of her hand, places her hand over her heart, and points to herself. She points to herself again, draws an X on the palm of her hand, puts her fist on her chest, taps two fingers on her wrist, and points to her head.

John motions to attract Ellen's attention, desperate to help her understand, even with this dreadful knowledge, they do not hate her, nor does William know anything but the most superficial facts. As parents, they love her. Unconditionally. Nothing has changed. Genuinely, he senses that nothing would change for William, either, even if he did know. John tries to gesture this to her as anger swells in his chest at the beast which caused Ellen to come to this place where she believes no one will love her if they know the full truth about her life. Ellen's breathing quickens and deepens, her hands trembling.

She points to herself, places a fist over her heart, and points to the lady and the man, points to her own head, and points to herself again.

Looking at each other, they wonder what else Ellen could possibly want them to know about her? They can see that Ellen is becoming more agitated as they continue talking about this. Anna reaches out to Ellen and then pats the bed next to her, inviting Ellen to come back and sit. Comforting her will be more comfortable if she sits close to them. Nodding, wiping away her tears, Ellen comes back to the bed and sits down between Anna and John. She looks down at her trembling hands as the silence between them grows like the suspense of an undetonated bomb. Finally, Ellen looks up at them, licking her lips, her eyes darting back and forth between John and Anna.

She points to herself, places a fist over her heart, points to the lady and the man, points to her own eyes, points to the outside, points to herself, holds her hand down near the floor and raises it higher.

"Anna, did she just tell us that she wants us to see where she grew up?"

"I think so...why would she..."

Anna looks at Ellen and tilts her head to the side to ask 'why'? Crumbling into tears, Ellen gives her answer.

She points to herself, places her hand over her heart, points to the lady and the man. She points to herself, places her fist on her chest, points to the lady and the man, points to her head, and points to herself. She points to herself again, places her fist on her chest, points to the lady and the man, places her hand over her heart, and points to herself.

Anna looks at John with pleading eyes, silently mouthing 'John' and gathering Ellen into her arms, wondering how going back to that horrible place will affect Ellen? How will this venture help them know her in ways they do not already? Why does Ellen think that seeing where she spent most of her life in torment would challenge their love for her? The memories...the horror...the abuses...John wonders how it will affect all of them. This is the hell that imprisoned their daughter and nearly cost Ellen her life. Of course, they know that Ellen loves them, as she gestured. Perhaps by wanting them to understand her more deeply...

She points to the lady and the man, extends her arm with her hand open and draws it to herself, closing her fist against her chest, points to herself, holds both hands palm up in front of her and lowers one, then raises the other. She points to herself, places her fist on her chest, places her fist on her chest again and extends her hand outward, points to the man and the lady, holds both hands palms up in front of her and lowers one, then raises the other, points to her head, points to herself, places her hand over her heart, and points to herself.

Affected deeply by Ellen's gestures, Anna and John avoid meeting each other's eyes, afraid that their tenuous grasp on composure will crumble in front of Ellen. Neither of them wants Ellen to misinterpret an emotional display. Anna's voice quavers in a whisper.

"John, she's giving us a choice. She thinks she's taking a gamble that we won't love her once we've walked that path with her. We've always given Ellen choices, and now, she wants us to see, with her, the place where her past happened."

"I don't like it, but that makes sense, Anna. I wish she trusted our love, enough, but we will do as she asks, and soon. It's going to eat at all of us until we do. Most importantly, Ellen needs to understand we love her."

"I hope when she sees that you and I will always love her, that she will see how accepting William has been of what he knows of her past and the scars she bears. I know that William can't go with us, but if he did, I honestly believe that he would only care for her even more."

John nods and clasps his hands, looking down at his feet as if praying for a miracle that shall help Ellen know that she is worthy of love. Anna takes Ellen in her arms and rocks her, Ellen clutching Anna like a drowning child clutches at anything they can grasp. Ellen's desperate yet silent need to be loved screams out in the ocean of uncertainty that surrounds all of them. Anna nods her consent to this unpleasant foray into the dying embers of Hades. Now that...that man...is dead, there are no people to fear, only memories. She and John will be with her, attentive and watchful. If this is what will bring Ellen peace of some sort, then this is what they must do. As John rests his face in his hands, fighting wave after wave of emotion, Anna buries her face in Ellen's hair, holding her close, her feelings crashing against the shore of her heart. Without speaking, soul to soul, John and Anna know that even though this visit to Ellen's past 'home' will be a trial; they will confront the unknown together. No one in this family stands or walks alone.

Chapter Forty-One
15 August 1926

Rain falls from sympathetic clouds in a sombre sky and patter on the roof of the motor like tears. Holding Ellen's hand, Anna cannot suppress the gnawing dread in her gut. When she and John agreed to take Ellen to the farm, today, they thought it best to get it over and done. They did not sleep between Ellen's nightmare and thinking about their destination. Anna looks out the window, partly seeing the countryside and partly seeing her reflection in the rain-speckled window. So many questions had whirled in her head since last night when Ellen challenged their love with this visit to her past. John has not spoken much, but the brooding furrow between his eyes was enough to know that his unsettled spirit matches her own.

"Well, we're almost here. The rain seems to have let up, too."

The clench of Ellen's hand draws Anna's gaze to Ellen who sits there, pale, shaking, staring at the farmstead coming closer like a crazed phantom. John pulls the motor near the house, or what had once been a house. Anna imagines that it was, at one time, painted and clean, with curtains full of breeze at open windows, and flowers sprinkling their aromatic magic like promises made with the touch of a hand. Her domestic imaginings are cut asunder as the acutely real shabbiness accepts its neglect just as Ellen had acquiesced to hers, at one time. Anna watches her staring out the window, and gives her hand a reassuring squeeze, uncertain if Ellen feels it. Suffocating tension fills the motor until John bursts the cloying atmosphere by opening his door. He walks 'round and opens the door for Anna and Ellen, offering his hand to assist them.

She sighs and gathers all the courage she can muster.

"I reckon we're as ready as we'll ever be, John."

Anna steps out of the motor, holding John's hand, and turns to give Ellen her hand to assist her out of the motor as well. Ellen just sits in the motor, staring at her with wide eyes, shaking her head, turns to look at the farmhouse, then back at Anna. Nodding to tell Ellen that she understands, Anna points to herself, places a hand over her heart, and points to Ellen to say, 'I love you'. She turns to John and takes his hand.

"Well, here we are...I think Ellen is nervous, and rightly so. If she feels she can, she'll come when she's ready. For now, though, I think she feels safe in the motor."

"Yes, I reckon you're right. I hate leaving her alone, but if she feels safer there, then, so be it."

John turns to Ellen and gestures the same 'I love you' to her, hoping that she understands that regardless of what happens here, they are by her side and love her. They walk up to the porch and stop at the rusty-hinged door that dares them to open it and hear its whine of protest.

"Anna, I don't know what she expects us to find here. We know what she's been through."

Nodding, Anna steps back a pace whilst John opens the door, revealing an interior that matches the grey exterior. She wrinkles her nose at the musty smell, like socks that have never been laundered. Dust motes float in the air from the small shaft of light coming through the window above the washbasin. A pan of unidentifiable food sits on the stove, and a tin plate is on the floor. She looks 'round the room, shivering, reaches up to open cupboards and drawers, finding little of use and even less food. An overturned chair sits next to a table that displays a half-empty bottle of liquor, an empty glass next to a stain on the ragged cloth covering the surface, and a dead fly floating atop the amber liquid. Their shoes crunch glass and dirt as they move about what had once been a kitchen.

John walks to an open door whilst Anna walks towards a bedroom. He peers into the room, steps in, and gasps at its sparse and cruel atmosphere. A filthy blanket is strewn in the corner of the room, covered in grime and brown...no, wait...bloodstains. Ellen's blood. Tears fill his eyes as he sees the hooks in the wall with ropes still attached, the blood-stained belt hanging on the wall, and worst of all, the gouges in the wall where the paper was partly torn away...four gouges at a time. Fingers...Ellen's fingers. Holding his breath and closing his eyes, he tries to erase the horror before him. He feels a presence next to him, and he turns and sees Ellen who is staring into the room. Her arms crossed over her chest, hands clenched into white-knuckled fists. John moves closer to Ellen, puts his arm 'round her shoulder and pulls her closer to him. He knows it would be pointless to ask Ellen if she was all right.

She turns to the man, points into the room, walks her fingers across her hand, pounds one fist into the palm of the other. She points to the sleeping place on the floor, cradles her arms as if holding a baby, and then puts her hands together as if a pillow, and rests her head on them.

Ellen lowers her head, looking at her feet. John shakes with sorrow and rage, thinking of what their daughter endured at the hands of that bastard. If Ellen thought that seeing this would make them love her less, she was wrong. John just wants to hold Ellen close and help her feel safe. He knows that Anna would feel the same if she saw the room, but he wishes to spare her the stark abomination that screams from it. Reaching out to close the door, a dull click shuts away that part of Ellen's past. John turns to meet Ellen's tear-filled eyes, points to the door, holds out his palm and sweeps his other hand across it as if sweeping something away to tell Ellen that this part of her life is over. She needs never fear this room or the abhorrent abuse within any longer. Ellen squints her eyes and nods, looking back down at her feet. He wishes with all his heart that life could have been different for Ellen, but it was not. The truth shrieks at them from every corner. John vows in his mind, heart, and soul that he will be the father that Ellen deserves. Taking Ellen's hand, he tilts his head and points towards the bedroom where Anna is sifting through drawers, looking for things that would rightfully belong to Ellen.

Anna had walked into the monster's bedroom wondering what they would find since it seems as though no one else has been in the house. The room is dim with the only illumination coming through a tattered curtain on the grimy window. The bed is made, but rumpled, as if someone had slept on top of the covers and never slipped under their warmth. There, a highboy, armoire, mirrored bureau, and a washstand line the walls. Anna finds the overpowering odour of human sweat repulsive. Seeing the stains of wet on the floor, she looks away in disgust from the evidence of rabid spittle from that creature. Taking in the room, she decides there could be no harm in looking through drawers. At first, she only finds a nonsensical jumble of men's clothing. She opens more drawers and is surprised to discover so many pieces of clothing for a woman. The fashions are Victorian and yellowed, but they are preserved as if they had been put away just this morning. Saving the mirrored dresser for last, Anna works her way down, one drawer at a time. In the bottom drawer, she gasps to see an inlaid box with an unusual design on it and a velvet and gold box adorned with glass beads, wrapped in a sheer scarf. Setting the two items on the bed, she first opens the inlaid box, seeing letters. The ones at the bottom of the box are tied with a ribbon, and some are unopened on top.

Raising an eyebrow, she looks at the return address and realises that the letters did not originate from England. Anna returns the correspondence to the box, hoping they will reveal more about Ellen's mother. Carefully, she unwraps the fragile scarf, afraid it will disintegrate at her touch. Opening it almost reverently, Anna removes a tarnished silver brooch, an ivory brooch that looks as if it was painted by hand, a pink crystal necklace, and a set of pearls. These must have belonged to Ellen's mother, and therefore, now, belong to Ellen. With a gentle hand, she wraps the jewellery in the scarf and places them back in their box, closing the lid. She looks 'round the room one more time and turns towards the door, startled to see John and Ellen watching her.

"Goodness, how long have you been standing there?"

"Long enough to see that your curiosity has turned up something."

"Yes, John, letters and some jewellery that must have belonged to her mother. It might mean a great deal to Ellen if these letters could shed some light on her."

Seeing Ellen tilt her head as she looks from Anna to John and back again, Anna gestures that the things she has found belong to her. Ellen's head-tilt as she looks 'round the room implies to Anna that she does not fully understand. Ellen closes her eyes and backs out of the room, standing in the kitchen with her back to the door. Anna watches Ellen's visible reaction to looking into this room and picks up the items to follow John, joining Ellen in the kitchen. Anna puts her arm 'round Ellen, wondering what she might be thinking and feeling. She rubs her back, reassuring Ellen that, now, there is nothing to fear except memories and only the hope of love from her family and friends. Out of the corner of her eye, Anna sees a closed door, taps Ellen's arm, waits for her to look down and then back up at her. She points to the door with a tilt of her head. Ellen shakes her head and shrugs. Walking over to it, Anna turns the latch and jiggles it, but the door denies her attempt to open it and reveal what lurks behind it. Anna looks at the door, up and down, surprised that anything would be secured by lock and key in this hovel.

"John, this door is locked. Whatever could be in there?"

Feeling above the doorframe, knocking down filth in the process, John finds a skeleton key. Taking it in his hand, he blows on it and places it in the keyhole. The lock slides with a stubborn click and the hinges swing the door open with a creaking objection. Sprinkles of dust floating in the air are visible in the shaft of sunlight that has emerged from its dark hiding place. The room is cosy and charming in spite of the shroud of grey covering everything. Curtains match the wallpaper, faded, threadbare, and peeling over time. A fireplace with charred logs, flanked by two chairs invites the observer to recall a happier time. The sofa is big enough for two people, end tables with oil lamps, and a case full of books make this sitting room appear as though it had been well used and enjoyed, long ago. To the side, near the window, a chest, table, rocking chair, and stool occupies the space. Eyeglasses, a cup of what had been tea, a book, and a pen sit next to the empty oil lamp. Anna, John, and Ellen stand transfixed at what lies before them. A room that was perfectly preserved, as if whoever left it had intended to return but never did. John's astonishment registers in his voice.

"By Jove, I don't know what to make of all this."

Anna walks into the room, then turns to John, handing him the boxes of letters and jewellery. He takes them in his arms and follows Anna to what appears to be the favourite nook in this room. Anna holds up the teacup and then looks up at John.

"Look, this cup must have held tea, and it evaporated. See the stain?"

"Yes, I see it. This seems to be a room that a woman would have enjoyed. It's strikingly out of place with the rest of the house we've seen. I wonder..."

Anna feels a tug at her dress and looks at the source. Ellen is staring 'round the room with wide eyes. Anna slips her arm 'round Ellen's shoulder and then taps her arm, asking for her attention. Ellen looks down at her arm and then back up at Anna. She gestures, asking Ellen if she has ever seen this room before. Ellen looks away, shaking her head. Curious about the trunk next to the rocking chair, Anna slips her arm away from Ellen and walks over to it. The lid is closed except for yellowed fabric peeking out from under it. She lifts the lid and gasps, seeing baby things. A christening gown, booties, little nightdress, sweater, a silver cup, spoon, rattle, and baby-sized blankets fill the trunk. Taking each item out and draping the fabric over her arm, Anna turns to Ellen, points at the baby clothes, and then points to her.

She tilts her head to the side, points to the small clothes, and points at herself.

Anna hands them to Ellen, encouraging her to take them. These things are tangible proof that her mother wanted her, loved her, and was prepared to make her entrance into the world an event to celebrate. Sinking to the floor, Ellen holds the tiny garments in her lap, bringing them up to her nose and inhaling, touching them, wetting them with her tears, clutching them to herself. Taking the silver pieces in her hands, tarnished with neglect, Anna rubs the spoon against the fabric of her skirt to reveal the true splendour of a devoted mother's preparations for her child. Glinting in the sparse sunlight, Anna crouches down to join

Ellen, showing her the things a mother would want her baby to have. Ellen reaches out to touch the smooth metal, picking up the spoon to see the bright spot that sparkles through the prism of tears, and she touches it to her cheek. She looks up at Anna, tilting her head to the side. Anna points to Ellen, holds her fist against her chest and pats it with her other hand, places her fist on her chest, points to Ellen, and then points to the baby clothes. Tears pooling in her eyes, she places her fist against her chest and pats it with her other hand, puts her hand over her heart, and then points to Ellen. Last, she points to Ellen, places her fist against her chest and pats it with her other hand, places her fist against her chest, and then points to Ellen. Ellen has the right to know that not only are these clothes that her mother wanted her to have, but her mother also loved and wanted her. Holding the clothes that were meant for her, Ellen weeps harder, her shoulders shaking with silent sobs as she sits on the faded carpet, rocking back and forth, looking at each piece repeatedly. Anna draws her gently into her arms and joins her in absorbing this revelation, sharing Ellen's grief for a life out of which she was cheated. Compassionately, Anna imagines the woman who had carried Ellen in her womb, prepared a nursery for her that would also serve as the place where she would give birth, tended to every detail that would ensure that her child would be happy and loved. From the contents of the trunk, it was evident that she looked forwards to life as a new mother and as a family with her husband.

Unwilling to disturb Ellen and Anna as the confirmation of a mother's love is communicated and absorbed, John quietly walks about the room, taking in the pictures hanging on the walls, the books in the bookcase, the keepsakes on the mantle. Everything is just as it was left, one day. He stops at the table next to the rocking chair and moves the eyeglasses from the open book. Reading only a few lines of the elegant handwriting, he discerns that this is a journal. The last entry dated 24 May 1904 reads, 'It's almost time. I'll be holding my sweet baby in my arms, soon. Cyrus has gone for the midwife, and I will retire to the bed in the nursery where my baby will be born and sleep this very night. Little one, I've been longing to hold you, love you, and nourish you from my own breast. God has been good to us, my child. May God grant you the same blessings in your life that I have known in mine.' John pages through the journal, catching phrases that startle him such as, 'we've prayed so long for a child', 'my dearest husband', and 'our happy life together'. Shaking his head that this woman could have written these words about such a savage beast, he closes the journal and slips it into the box of letters. He watches Anna rubbing Ellen's back and asking her if she would like to take these things with her. Wiping her nose on her sleeve and her eyes with the backs of her hands, Ellen nods, folding each element of her mother's love and placing them back in the trunk, along with the cup, spoon, and rattle. Ellen closes the lid and strokes it, leaving a sweep of handprint in the dust.

She looks up at the man, points to the thing, points to herself, and then points outside, tilting her head to the side.

Nodding with a peaceful expression filling his face, he places the other two boxes on the lid of the trunk and lifts them up. Gently, John speaks, breaking the silence that had filled the room.

"I'll take these out to the motor, Anna. I won't be long."

"Oh, John, there's one more room..."

"No, I looked in there. It's empty."

John hopes his words will prevent her from further curiosity that would devastate her. Looking up at him, Anna nods.

"I reckon, an empty room is best left empty. I'll stay with Ellen."

They are not pressed for time, knowing they will need to give her time to feel what she needs to feel, think what she needs to think and see what she needs to see. Looking 'round the room, Anna feels a woman's touch, the expression of a woman's preferences, the care with which each part of the room is filled with memories. Memories...comprehension hits Anna's chest like a fist. Ellen's...that man...must have locked this door the day her mother died to give her life. Constable Frayser told them that he said, 'I died that day'. He closed the room where the happy memories lived, memories of a wife about to give birth to their first child.

The image of the bed...made but rumpled...the bed he must have shared with his wife. He could not bear to sleep next to the ghost of happiness. The bottle of spirits on the table...another escape from happiness...Anna shakes her head, refusing to allow any spark of sympathy to rise in her, knowing what he became, knowing how he viciously harmed Ellen in so many ways. He was a monster. A brutish beast with no conscience, no morals, no human worth. Interrupting her thoughts, a tap on her arm leads Anna to look at Ellen, instinctively tilting her head to the side to ask Ellen what is on her mind.

She points 'round the room; she points to where the thing with the baby things was, points to herself, and places her fist against her chest, patting it with her other hand. She tilts her head to the side, walks two fingers across the palm of her hand, and draws an X on the palm of her hand.

Her heart cries out with desolation that Ellen has finally asked the question she has dreaded since she was rescued from this hell on earth. 'If this is my mother, who was the bad man'? Anna inhales deeply of the musty memories of happier days that turned to hellish misery. She steels herself to give Ellen the truth. They have never lied to Ellen, and in spite of the agonising temptation to do so, now, Anna resists. She walks two fingers across her hand, draws an X in the palm of her hand, places her fist on her chest, and then pats it with her other hand to tell Ellen that the bad man was her father. Ellen's hand flies to her open mouth, her eyes widening and overflowing with tears. Shaking her head, she gets up from the floor and flees the room. Lowering her head, feeling like an executioner who has beheaded one of his own family, Anna gets to her feet, slowly walking to the door. Looking out through the kitchen, she sees Ellen standing on the porch, the breeze running its invisible fingers through her hair and tugging at her skirt. Ellen begins to walk down the porch steps, and Anna makes her way through the kitchen to see where Ellen goes. Anna stands on the porch and watches Ellen walk over to John who is arranging things in the boot so they will not slide about and suffer damage. Ellen pats his arm and waits, John turning his head to see her standing beside him with reddened eyes, and a quivering lip. He stands up straight, tilts his head to the side, points to Ellen, moves his hands down the front of himself, and then pats his hands together, asking if she is all right. His answer comes in the fresh tears flowing down her face, and his own face registers a slideshow of emotion from concern to worry that this visit had been a grave mistake.

She points to the man, points to herself, places her fist on her chest, and pats it with her other hand.

Opening her arms, Ellen sinks into John's embrace, both of them clinging to each other for the truth that has become known. Walking onto the porch, she watches Ellen and John. Anna's hand covers her mouth, moved to happy tears to see their baby girl tell John that HE is her father. Ellen has chosen her family as they have lovingly embraced her into their family. The day Anna hoped and prayed for has finally come. John is the father that Ellen deserves and has always needed.

Wanting father and daughter to have their moment in privacy, she looks back into the house and shakes her head. They have seen all there is to see, there. She closes the door with what sounds like a grateful latch, memories locked behind those doors forever, Anna hopes. She looks about and sees a shed, curiosity gaining the upper hand. She walks over to the dilapidated thing and touches the rough wood that swings open on the remaining hinge that qualifies these rotted boards as a door. Stepping inside, her eyes adjust to the dim light, more dust and filth assaulting her nose with every breath. She looks at the floor littered with rusty tins, an overturned milk stool, and a pile of rope laying there, part of it fashioned into a noose. She begins to shake as her blood freezes within her, and her gaze is drawn upwards; a length of rope barely clings to a beam overhead. The last splinter holding the rope to the beam gives way, and it falls with a thump on top of the rope already on the floor. Her nerves instantly jarred and overwhelmed with more knowledge than she ever wanted to bear, she turns, leaves the shed, and tries to compose herself upon approaching her husband and their daughter. She resolves to never speak of what she saw in that shed, wanting to spare John, the vision of his daughter's attempt to escape a hell that she did not want to spill into the lives of her family.

"Anna, are you all right? You're pale. Is there something wrong?"

"No, no. I'm fine. This has just been so much to take in. It's...overwhelming."

"Yes, yes, it is. We've seen enough."

"Yes, I believe we have, John."

Anna nods to John and musters a smile for Ellen, who still encircles her father's waist with her dainty arms. She points to herself, Ellen, and John points to the motor and points in the general direction of home. Ellen nods, holding out her arms to Anna, the two joining in an embrace before they lean back, smile at one another, and enter the motor. Whilst John walks 'round to the drivers' side to get in, Anna turns to Ellen, smiles, wipes one stray tear away with her thumb, and caresses their daughter's hair. Yes, it is time.

Chapter Forty-Two
18 August 1926

The letters in the box from the farm are perplexing, and the journal that belonged to Ellen's mother is heartbreaking to read. Clara should be arriving soon to give Anna advice on how to translate these letters. Coming home early from the shop, John walks in and is greeted by Rupert's barking, an announcement of his master's arrival. He leans down to scratch the dog's head and then doffs his hat and jacket. Rupert leads the way to the kitchen where John hears Anna and Sarah talking as they look at the letters.

"Sarah, I don't know where to start. A foreign language is something I've never learnt. I hope Clara can help me."

"Yes, Ma'am, if anyone can, Mrs Dewhurst can. I...My grandmother spoke Swedish, and I see the word 'Sverige', which is Sweden, but it's been years since I heard Swedish or imitated words she used. If I can help in any way, I'd be glad to."

"Thank you, Sarah. Between us, we should be able to come up with something that makes sense."

John walks over to Anna, leaning down to kiss the top of her head, and looks at the daunting task she has set for herself. Johanna sits close to the table in her high chair, working her way through some finger foods and a covered cup of milk. Seeing her daddy, she smiles brightly, lifts her arms up, and greets him.

"Daddy! Janna miss you. Me up? Me up?"

Chuckling, he pulls Johanna's chair back and lifts her into his arms, bouncing her on his hip.

"Goodness, you're sitting at the table just like a grown-up! You're getting to be a big girl. Anna, I see you're going through the letters we found. Have you made any progress with them?"

Anna sits back with a frown and a sigh.

"No, I don't have the faintest idea how to translate this, much less read it. Sarah recognised a word that means 'Sweden', so I'm assuming, based on the postmark, stamp, and return address that these came from someone there. I asked Clara to come, and I hope she has some ideas since I don't have many of my own. I haven't opened the most recent letters yet. At least they're all addressed to Ellen Holmes."

She gestures to the stacks of letters and envelopes, organised into piles according to date, a pen, an empty piece of paper, and the journal sitting on the table.

"Well, Anna, it's not like we're in a hurry. I hope we can learn more about Ellen's mother and that the information will make her happy."

"I do, too, John. Ellen deserves happiness."

Giving up, for now, Anna stands up and stretches, turning to give John and Johanna affectionate kisses. John grows serious for a moment with news he wants to share with Anna.

"I met with a solicitor, today, about Ellen's inheritance of the farm. Apparently, creditors are clamouring for their overdue payments. To prove Ellen's claim to the property, she needs to show that she's the child of the previous owner and that there are no other potential heirs. I related the situation to him, and he agreed to keep the creditors at bay until we figure out how to set things right for Ellen."

"Oh, goodness...I hadn't even considered that. You're right. The farm is hers, although, I doubt she would want it. I reckon we need to find a way to get her birth certificate. Maybe Clara can offer ideas on that, as well, when she comes."

"Yes, between Clara and Father Willington, they would know where to start. Maybe she has one, already. The solicitor also said he would make inquiries into the matter. Once we have her identity established, we can move forwards when we decide what to do. We'll have to tell Ellen, but I'm not sure how much of this she'll understand. It's complicated enough for us."

"I agree, John. Why don't we wait to tell Ellen until she might need to be directly involved or it's settled? We don't want to confuse her."

"Right, then. We have a plan. Now, I'm going to take this young lady up to the playroom for a tea party. Would you like that? A tea party with Daddy?"

Johanna pats John's face and then pats her hands together.

"Party Daddy! We maka tea."

"Well, then, it's settled. A tea party, it is."

John leans over to kiss Anna and then she helps Johanna onto John's back to ride up to the playroom. Anna watches them trot away with a grin, hearing Johanna's squeals as John makes the sounds of a happy horse. The trotting of a happy dog follows them up the stairs. The front door opens, revealing their welcome visitor. Hurrying to the front door, Anna is surprised that Father Willington has come along.

"Clara, Father Willington. I was expecting one and now have two guests. This must be my lucky day. Please, come in."

Clara and Anna give each other their customary embrace, and

then, true to her outspoken nature, Clara comes to the point of their visit.

"So, you have some letters from the farm. I brought Father Willington along to help, as he has a broader range of literacy with foreign languages than I do."

"Clara, you're too kind. Latin and French might not be of much use if these letters are in some other language. I'll give it a go, though."

Father Willington closes the door behind them and nods with a smile, hoping he can help somehow.

"Please, come into the kitchen. I have everything there, at least organised by date. Some of the letters have never been opened. Sarah says they're from Sweden, so that narrows things down a bit."

They follow Anna into the kitchen where Sarah is removing her pinny.

"Ma'am, if you don't need me straight away, I'll go see to Miss Johanna's nap."

Anna nods, giving Sarah leave to interrupt the father and daughter tea party if necessary. Anna sits down and silently encourages them to sit with her, gesturing to the chairs 'round the table.

"All right, here's what I have. Clara, these are the letters that had been opened, and, Father, these are the letters that have not been opened. I feel a little strange about reading someone else's post, even if they are deceased."

"I can understand that Anna, but when you think about it, these letters belong to Ellen, now. Since she's unable to read, you need to read them on her behalf. Speaking of Ellen how is she since the visit there?"

"She seems happier. Now that she knows that her mother loved and wanted her and has the baby things that were intended for her, she smiles and even spends more time with me in my sewing room, helping. The first step was knowing that...that man is gone and will never hurt anyone again. She still has the nightmares almost every night, but I reckon she always will."

Perusing the unopened letters whilst Clara and Anna talk, Father Willington holds up the oldest unopened letter, interrupting them.

"May I?"

Anna nods her assent, gets up, finds her way to the writing desk in the sitting room, and finds their letter opener. She hurries back to the kitchen, handing it to Father Willington. Having turned back to the stack of letters, Clara picks out some words written in English.

"I'm glad to hear that Ellen seems to be improving. And, yes, she will probably have the nightmares for the rest of her life. Thank goodness she can be happy during her waking hours."

Clara returns her attention to the letters that are strewn about the table top.

"Anna, other than organising these by date, have you actually looked at them? I do see some broken English in here, but without knowing the Swedish words 'round them, I can't make out the meaning."

"Honestly, Clara, I hadn't got that far. Sarah is the one who showed me that they came from Sweden. I only saw that they were written in Swedish and became overwhelmed."

Together, they go through each letter, writing a list of dates where English words are included, and then placing them back into their envelopes. Clara looks at the journal laying on the table and reaches over to pat the leather-bound book that has the word 'Journal' worked into the leather in a most intricate pattern.

"What is this, Anna? Did you find it with the letters?"

"Oh...no, we found it in a hidden room..."

Anna goes on to explain in full to Clara and Father Willington their visit to the farmstead and everything they discovered. Opening the journal, she turns it so they can see the last entry as it fits with the scene they uncovered in the room that had been locked away in time.

"See? There, Ellen's mother writes that she's ready to bring Ellen into the world. With the baby things we found, Ellen finally understands that her mother loved and wanted her. Unfortunately, she did ask who 'the bad man' was, and I had to tell her..."

Father Willington pats Anna's hand, reassuring her that she had done the right thing.

"Of course, you did. You've always been honest with Ellen, and she had a right to know. When she was ready to know, she was ready to ask. Trust that, Anna."

Knowing that Father Willington's words are right, she nods and looks down at the pen that she absent-mindedly moves through her fingers.

"Father, she was upset, understandably, but she went to find John. She told him that HE is her father. I have to agree with her. John has been the father to her that she has deserved all along."

"Yes, Anna, as you've been the mother she always needed. This is her home. We're her family. Trust that truth."

Clara pages through the journal as Father Willington and Anna talk with one another. Her eyes open wide at the fond descriptions of the man they had only known in loathing. John enters the kitchen, finding the three of them going over the letters and journal.

"Clara...Father Willington...no, no, don't get up. I'm going to have a seat. Anna, Sarah is settling Johanna for her nap. So, tell me...what did I miss?"

Anna brings John up to the present with what they have discussed regarding the letters, journal, and farmstead visit. Nodding, John adds the results of his first visit with the solicitor into the mix.

"This matter is complicated enough, but after meeting with a solicitor today, there is a swamp of details. We know that Ellen should inherit the farm. We need to prove her identity as the rightful heir before anything can be done with it. Certainly, Ellen won't want to keep it, so selling it and paying off debts against it would be reasonable. We could put the proceeds from the sale in an account for her...I'm not sure she would understand all that, though. The legalities are dizzying."

Clara closes the journal, stares at it, biting her knuckle before she speaks.

"Well, the plot at the cemetery where...that man...was buried was next to the headstone of a woman whose name matches that on these letters. The date of her burial matches the time of the last entry in the journal. Yes, I did some snooping. I still wonder about Ellen's missing baby. I jot down everything I can find."

Reaching over to put her hand on Clara's, Anna reassures Clara that her intentions are honourable, but that cause is lost, according to the story related to them by Constable Frayser. Shocked and shaking their heads in disbelief, silence fills the room as a vapour that renders one incapable of forming thoughts into words. Finally, Father Willington rouses himself out of shock to offer his musings.

"Well, done is done. Moving, now, to Ellen's current situation, it seems that a birth certificate must be found. Clara, it's my turn to ask you for help with finding a record of birth. And, John? Anna? I presume that you would put the property up for sale?"

"Yes, but first things first."

"Of course..."

A knock at the garden door interrupts the strategic discussion about how to best deal with Ellen's inheritance. John lifts his hand, indicating that the rest should sit and he will answer the door. He gets up, walks out of the kitchen to the garden door and sees William standing there, the usual smile on his face. Chuckling, John opens the door to greet him.

"William, it's good to see you. Come in. I presume you've come to see Ellen, haven't you?"

He walks into the house and closes the door behind him.

"Yes, Mr Thorpe, if she's not busy?"

"Well, she's up in her room, so, why don't you go on up and see what she's doing. I'm sure she'll be glad to see you."

William's eyebrows raise, surprise and trepidation filling him.

"Uh, upstairs? In her room? Are you sure that's proper?"

"Trust me, William, when I say that you've proven to Anna and me that you are worthy of our trust. Her door is open but tread lightly. Johanna is sleeping."

"Well, all right, and thank you, Mr Thorpe. Mr Thorpe? I...I want you and Mrs Thorpe to know that I...always want to be worthy of your trust."

John claps his hand on William's shoulder.

"You have it, William. You have it."

With that, William walks through the house to the bottom of the staircase, looking up. He has never been upstairs, and his curiosity overcomes his nerves. Walking up the stairs, he comes to the hallway and looks to his right, and then to his left. There is only one door open, so he assumes that must be Ellen's room. Straightening his shoulders, he walks to the door and raises his knuckles to knock, stops, looks at his hand, and feels foolish. Rupert's leap off the bed to beg attention from William causes Ellen to look up at the direction in which Rupert ran. Seeing William standing there, she smiles and waves at him. He smiles at Ellen, waving back to her. She motions for him to come in, scooting over on the bed where she is sitting to make room for him, and pats the side of the bed where she would like him to sit. Rupert hops up on the bed, settling himself near his friend's pillows, watching them. William, still questioning the propriety of visiting a lady's room without a chaperone, walks over to the bed and sits down. Carefully strewn on the bed is an array of baby things. Wondering what Ellen is doing with these keepsakes of infancy, he points to them and draws a circle 'round his face to tell Ellen that they are pretty.

"They're beautiful, Ellen. Are they yours?"

He points to Ellen with a tilt of his head to ask if they are hers. Ellen's smile brightens as she nods.

She points to the baby things and points to herself. She points to herself again, places her fist against her chest and pats it with her other hand, places her fist on her chest again, extends her arms with fingers open and draws it close to herself as she closes her fist, and points to herself.

Confused, knowing that Ellen has called Anna her mother, he tilts his head to the side and taps two fingers against his chest to ask Ellen if she means that Anna had given her what must be mementoes of infancy. Ellen shakes her head, no, and proceeds to explain as best she can.

She points to herself, places her fist against her chest and pats it with her other hand, and draws an X on her forehead. She holds up one finger. She points to herself, places her fist against her chest and pats it with her other hand, places her hand over her heart, and points to herself. She points to herself, places her fist against her chest and pats it with her other hand, places her fist against her chest, and points to herself.

Astonished, William looks from the layette to Ellen and back again. How has Ellen come to know about the mother she never knew? Where did these items come from? How does she know that her mother wanted and loved her? And how...He pushes away the many questions that rise like cream to the top of his psyche. He points to himself, draws a smile on his face, and then points to Ellen, trying to tell her that he is happy for her. Knowing that she is loved, now, and was loved by the woman who gave her life must give her much comfort, and he has never seen her this happy. He reaches out and touches the gossamer fabric of the christening bonnet that could only be meant for the sweetest baby. Ellen pats his arm with a grin on her face. She picks up the christening gown and holds it up to herself as if asking if it would fit her. William laughs and shakes his head, enjoying this playful side of Ellen's personality. Pretending to appear crestfallen, Ellen lays the dress down on the bed and holds up a little nightdress against her, breaking into a smile as she nods. William laughs and shakes his head, again, delighting in her sense of humour. Feigning a pout, she lays the nightdress back on the bed, smoothing it, and then gives him a sideways glance, that playful grin returning to her face.

He looks at Ellen and grins, then leans over to take her ankle and lift her foot onto his lap. He slides her shoe off, picks up one of the little booties, and holds it up to her foot. He looks at her, tilting his head. Ellen holds her hand over her mouth, starts laughing and pulls her foot away. Unable to cease his laughter, he leans down to untie one of his shoes and lay it on the floor next to hers. He points to the two shoes together, looks at her and smiles. Ellen looks at him, nods, and smiles. Scooting to the side of the bed to sit next to William, she slides her foot into his shoe, gets up and starts walking 'round. Turns and looks at him, her head held up, walking in a circle. Looking down at her shoe, he slides a few toes in, looks up at her, grins and shrugs his shoulders.

Still smiling, Ellen clomphs over to the bed, still wearing one of William's shoes, and carefully folds the only link she has to a mother who loved her until she drew her last breath. She places them in the trunk, closes the lid, picks it up, and puts it near her bureau. William watches Ellen walk towards him, and he cannot stop looking at her eyes and the genuine happiness that illuminates them from within. He points to her, places one fist on top of the other several times, points to himself, and then draws a smile on his face, telling Ellen that she makes him happy. She stares at him, her smile softened gently.

She points to the young man, places one fist over the other a few times then points to herself and draws a smile on her face.

Ellen gets up and walks over to her dresser, the 'clomph-step-clomph-step of her wearing his shoe and one of her own, and causes him to chuckle. She picks up the figurine of the boy pushing the girl on the swing, and brings it back to the bed, sitting next to him.

She points to the boy, points to the young man, points to the girl, and then points to herself.

William nods, looking at the figurine he had given her, feeling happiness well up within him at the memory of the first time they played on her swing together. He looks up at her and then watches as she gets up to restore his gift to its place. Returning to his side, she kneels on the floor, unties his other shoe, takes it off him, then sits on the bed. She kicks off her remaining shoe, slides her foot into William's other shoe, stands and takes his hand. He stands as she pulls him up, then groans when she points downstairs and walks, clomphing her tiny feet in his shoes as she walks to the door. Shaking his head, he picks up Ellen's shoes and follows her, wondering what Mr and Mrs Thorpe would think of this silly turn-about.

Still sitting at the kitchen table, John and Anna continue to discuss the letters and options that lay before them regarding Ellen's inheritance. They concur that confiding in Clara and Father Willington was a wise choice, assured that their friends shall help in any way they can. An odd noise grows louder, seeming to come down the staircase. She and John look up from the letters, at each other.

"John, what is that strange clomphing noise? Heavens..."

Ellen tromps into the kitchen, holding the young man's hand. She stands, before them, smiling. William holds Ellen's shoes in his other hand, a sheepish grin telling John and Anna everything they need to know. His face grows red when John and Anna join in the frivolous moment with cheerful smiles and stifled chuckles. Regaining his composure, but with a merry twinkle in his eyes, John takes note of the difference in size between Ellen's feet and William's shoes.

"Well, that explains that. I'm glad to see that Ellen's feet haven't grown."

Chuckling, William sets Ellen's shoes down next to a chair.

"If you don't mind, I'd like to go on a little walk with Ellen."

Anna's delight at what must have been Ellen's idea comes under parental control, the same dancing happiness sparkling in her eyes.

"Of course, we don't mind, William. I do ask, though, that you both put your own shoes on."

"Yes, yes, of course, Mrs Thorpe."

William gestures for Ellen to sit on an empty chair. When she does, he slips his shoes off her feet and then slips her shoes back on to her feet, tying the delicate laces. The warmth of her feet and how they fit so perfectly in his hand gives him pause. Smiling at John and Anna, he sits on another chair, puts his own shoes on, and ties them. He looks at Ellen, points to her, places his fist on his chest, and walks his fingers across the palm of his other hand, and then points to himself, asking if she would like to go for a walk with him. Nodding her head, Ellen stands, takes his hand, turns to look at John and Anna, and smiles at them with a little wave of her hand. They walk out of the kitchen together, to the garden door, and enter the magic of flowers and sunshine. As if of one mind, they look at one another, smile, kick off their shoes, and hurry off for their walk, the grass tickling their feet, the earth cool beneath them.

Watching the young couple walk away, John and Anna cannot restrain their happiness to see that Ellen's sense of humour has returned, and in rare form.

"John, look."

Anna points in the direction of Ellen's swing where their shoes were left. John shakes his head, chuckling as he draws Anna closer to him.

"We were young and carefree, once, weren't we, Anna?"

"Yes, John, we were. We should find some time to relive those times, don't you agree?"

"Yes, we do. The first thing we'll do is kick off our shoes."

Chapter Forty-Three
19 August 1926

The letters in the box from the farm remain perplexing, and the journal that belonged to Ellen's mother is in the capable hands of Clara and Father Willington. Sarah sits down with Anna, trying to decipher the Swedish 'round the broken English to make sense of the missives. Ellen spends a great deal of time in her room caressing and smelling the baby clothes that she should have worn as an infant.

"Ma'am, these letters that were opened before Miss Cup's mother passed on, are full of responses to what must be the progress towards Miss Cup's birth. See? Here Mrs Mortenson says 'lycklig' and 'födelse'. Those words mean happy and birth."

"Yes, that makes sense. But who is...Ingrid Mortenson? She must be a relative or friend of the family. Let's keep looking until we can determine just who she is."

The two women sit at the kitchen table with Sarah's memory and a dictionary that translates Swedish into English. Anna makes notes on each point that directs them to further truths about Ellen's mother, and by default, Ellen's own history. They continue until Anna can no longer see straight. She lays down her pen and stretches.

"Sarah, we've done enough, for now. I get the impression that this woman, Ingrid, is an aunt to Ellen's mother, don't you think? And the following letters express concern that she hasn't received a letter from Ellen's mother in ages."

"Yes, Ma'am. Her worry would be well founded. As to the relationship, I agree with you, although, they seem to be close in age. I know it seems strange, but large families might have aunts who are close in age to the children of their sisters or brothers. I'm the eldest in my family, and my grandmother has children only a few years older than me. I've more in common with my aunts and uncles than I have with my younger brother and sister. Perhaps the same is true for Mrs Mortenson's family."

Picking up an envelope, Anna studies the handwriting of the return address and then lays it down on the table.

"Oh, yes, that makes sense. Well, I'm going out for a bit of air before I sit down to write a letter to this woman, Ingrid. I hope she still lives at that address and is still living. It's worth trying to ease her worries after all these years that Ellen is alive and safe, now, even though her mother died in childbirth."

"That would be the kind thing to do, Ma'am. This lady deserves to know what became of her kin."

"Sarah, if you would check on Johanna, she might be waking from her nap, soon. I'm stepping outside."

"Yes, Ma'am. I hear her playing with her dolls when she wakes up."

Getting up from the table, Anna stretches again, feeling that her mind has also been pulled to its limits.

"Thank you, Sarah."

She walks out of the kitchen to the garden door, aching for the fragrant air that shall inspire her response to the letters. Meandering outside, Anna walks 'round the perimeter of the garden, smelling the flowers, letting their beauty fill her imagination with the words she needs to write. Her mental composition is interrupted by the sound of the gate opening. She smiles to see William, back for his daily visit with Ellen. Removing his cap from his head, he nods with a smile as he approaches Anna.

"It's a fine day, isn't it, Mrs Thorpe? I wonder if it's all right to invite Ellen for a picnic. There's a place nearby with a stream and trees...I thought she might like to see it."

William holds up a small basket with sandwiches, cheese, a jar of lemonade with glasses and a blanket draped over his arm.

"Yes, this is a lovely day for a picnic. Ellen is up in her room, and I'm sure she's looking forwards to your visit."

Ellen, in her bedroom, gets up from her bed and walks over to the window, opening it. Rupert, her constant companion, scoots over to smell the little clothing of a new-born baby. She looks out of the window, watching William and Anna talking to one another in the garden. She waves to them, but her silent greeting fails to draw their attention. Sighing, she looks about her room, walks over to her bed, and picks up one of her cuddly animals. She walks back over to the window and tosses it at them. It lands between William and Anna with a dull thud on the grass. The conversation between William and Anna stops mid-sentence as they look down at the cuddly toy and then up to the window from whence it came. Erupting laughter responds to Ellen's bid for their attention. William picks up the cuddly animal and brushes it off as Anna and he look at Ellen gesture.

She waves to the lady and the young man. She points to herself and points down to where they are standing.

434

"I guess she'll be right down, William. I'm sure she'll love a change of scenery."

Coming through the door, a smiling Ellen walks to William's side. He hands Ellen her toy and then Ellen gives it to Anna. She peeks into the basket on William's arm and nods at him. William points to Ellen, points to himself, walks two fingers across his palm, and then holds the basket up a little. Ellen nods and waves to Anna as she takes William's hand, leading the way to the garden gate. Grinning, William also waves to Anna as Ellen opens and then holds the gate for William to come through. Shaking her head with a smile, Anna turns, walks back into the house, makes her way to the sitting room writing desk to set herself to write a complicated letter to a woman she does not even know. She hopes that Ingrid Mortenson or someone close to her can read English. Attempting to write the letter in Swedish would not make much sense, with her ignorance of the language.

William points in the direction he has in mind for their outing. Ellen nods and matches his pace, looking 'round her as the familiar surroundings evolve into a landscape that she has never seen before. William looks down at Ellen who is holding his hand tighter, yet keeping up with him. He wonders what she thinks of their walk and is eager to see her reaction to the place where he goes to be alone, hear the birds sing, and listen to the babbling of the brook. Soon, they reach the clearing that William had in mind. Whilst Ellen looks 'round them, walks to a tree, touches the bark, and then draws down a limber branch to smell its leaves, William spreads the blanket in the shade. He places the basket in the middle of the blanket and walks over to her. Standing beside her, he did as she had done, touching the bark and smelling the leaves on the branch, that she still held in her hand. Realising that he had never taken notice of such details before, he silently thanks Ellen for teaching him something new about the world 'round him. Through her, he learns to see the world in new ways. The world is full of wonder and beauty that outweighs the mundane routine of daily life. Ellen looks at him and smiles, letting go of the branch as William watches it spring back to where it had been. He reaches out his hand with a smile, and he nods his head towards the stream he wants to show her. She takes his hand, tilting her head to the side, and walks with him. Through the rushes that part at William's touch, they can see the water sparkling as it dances across the rocks, tiny fish swimming about, and a shallow spot where they can cross. He wishes she could hear the sound of the water flowing between its banks, but he senses that Ellen hears things with her soul in a way that he has yet to learn.

Pointing to an open place where they can sit and remove their shoes, William sits down and begins to untie his shoelaces. He looks up at Ellen, points at her shoes, points to Ellen, points to himself, walks two fingers across his hand, and then points across the stream to let her know that he wants to take her to the other side of the creek, but first, she needs to remove her shoes. Nodding, she sits and removes her shoes, as well. He smiles as he stands up, looks at their shoes placed side by side, and then he offers his hand to help Ellen stand. She takes his hand, and walks to the edge of the stream with him, dipping her foot into the silken water. A small movement causes Ellen to crouch down, holding out her hand. A tiny frog jumps into her hand, and she turns to William, holding it up for him to see. He crouches down beside her, tentatively reaching out a finger to touch it, not wanting to frighten the little creature. It sits, allowing his touch, then turns on Ellen's palm as if waiting for her tender touch. She holds it up at eye-level, caresses the frog from its head and down its back. William watches in amazement at her connection with all living things. Slowly, she lowers her hand for the frog to leap away into its natural place in the world.

William stands, steps into the water on one of the stepping-stones that lead across the stream. He holds out his hand to Ellen, offering to assist her across. She takes his hand, and together they cross the creek. The bank on the side they approach is steeper than the one they had left, so William climbs up and, again, offers his hand in assistance. Ellen takes his hand, smiling up at him and climbs up with ease. She looks 'round them, seeing a stand of trees and beyond that an open field, broad and open. The grass in the field is golden in the sun and waist high, inviting Ellen into its warmth. She releases William's hand and walks into the field, surrounded by treasures of nature, seeming to shimmer in the light breeze. He walks a few paces into the field and stops, watching Ellen. She raises her arms, turns 'round slowly, her face upturned, her eyes closed. As she turns, William is so taken with the vision before him; he stares at Ellen's delicate movements and her hair as golden as the wild grass. He sees nothing else but her mesmerising sway as though she is slowly dancing. She fills the isolation surrounding them with music only she can hear. Slowing, she stops, opens her eyes, and lowers her arms. Smiling at him, and he at her, she walks up to him.

She tilts her head to the side, points to the young man, and draws a smile on her face.

He chuckles and gestures in response that yes, he is happy. She takes a step closer to him and looks into his eyes.

She points to herself and places her fist on her chest.

She stops, folds her hands in front of her, and looks at her feet. Curious that she did not finish what she was about to gesture, William walks close enough to touch Ellen's arm, tilting his head to the side, waiting for her to look at her arm and then back up at him but not making eye contact. Curious at her sudden change in demeanour, he points to her, moves his hands down the front of himself, and then pats his hands together, asking if she feels all right. She nods, meeting his eyes, again, tilting her head to the side. Her gestures are slow as she looks into his eyes.

She points to herself, places her fist on her chest, points to the young man, touches her lips, and points to herself.

William looks at her, completely taken by surprise that she would ask him to kiss her, feeling that he would give anything on this earth to kiss her. He holds back, wondering if a kiss would frighten her, ruin what they have between them, or cause her harm in any way. He sees her watching him, lowers her head to look at her feet, and then closes her eyes. Sensing that Ellen might feel ashamed for asking him to kiss her, he reaches down to take her hand in his. She looks at his hand, looks up at him, and then looks away. Reaching out to cup her cheek in his hand, he gently turns her head to look at him. He stares into her eyes and sees the silence and the desire to love and be loved that she has carried inside of her all her life. He reaches up and brushes her hair from her face with his finger then gently places his hand on her cheek, again, feeling the warmth and softness of her skin. Her face that he has wanted to touch for so long.

Ellen gazes up into his eyes and for just a moment, smiles and looks down at his lips. Slowly he leans forwards, touches her cheek, and stops for a moment before his lips lightly touch hers. Savouring her breath against his lips, he softly feels the tenderness of her lips against his and his senses are filled with her as if he has no control. He opens his eyes, closes them, and leans towards her, a deep kiss pulsing between them, palpable and sweet as honey. Her eyes are closed, she raises her hands onto his shoulders. After an eternity of bliss, William slowly breaks away from the kiss, leaning back to look into her eyes and smile. Ellen's eyes meet his as she moves her hands from his shoulders onto his chest. He sees how her eyes sparkle, the honesty, and a new depth that he has never seen before, shining from her to him. Nothing again will matter as long as he can always remember this kiss. His heart leaps in his chest as she smiles at him.

She lifts a finger to her lips, taps them, and nods her head.

Unspeakable happiness causes his heart to skip a beat that she wants him to kiss her again. He leans down, his lips barely touching hers, feeling her delicate lips and kisses her deeply. He feels their surroundings melt away from them, and he holds her close. Slowly, his lips again barely touch hers as he brushes his lips against hers. He slowly opens his eyes as he takes a deep breath, taking in her scent, her presence filling his arms, feeling her slip her arms 'round him, resting her head against his shoulder. Holding her in his arms, he glides his hand against her hair feeling that he never wants to let go of her. He feels her lean back slightly, looking up at him, raises her finger and barely runs it across his lips. She gazes into his eyes, leans her head back against his shoulder, and holds him.

As of one mind, they separate; look into each other's eyes, smile, and turn to walk back, holding hands with their fingers interlaced. Crossing the stream, again, they find their shoes and carry them back to the blanket where the picnic basket and blanket are waiting for their return. They sit on either side of the basket, Ellen peeks under the green cloth to see what William brought. Chuckling and still feeling the glow of their kiss, the scent of her, and the desire to protect her forever, he unpacks the basket. Bread, cheese, and smoked meat come out of the hamper for them to enjoy, as well as an apple he cuts in half. He hands one-half of it to her, seeing the star of seeds inside that reminds him of the brightness in Ellen's eyes that outshine any star in the sky. He pours them each a glass of lemonade, they share their simple meal, watching each other, and William believes in his soul that they are happy together.

The basket packed with what remains of their little feast, William sets it aside and stretches out on the blanket, looking up at the dappled sunlight peeking through the leaves above them. Without looking, he hears Ellen moving and feels her hand reach for his. Glancing to the side, he sees that she has joined him in admiring the many shades of green waving above them. Warm, well fed, and happy, both of them close their eyes and sleep covers them like a blanket of peace.

Awakened by the clutch of Ellen's hand in his, he looks over at her and sees her head turning from side to side. Her breathing grows heavier and faster, her free arm flailing at something unseen. Recognising the effects of her demons as she sleeps, he gets up to his knees beside her. Both of her arms stretch out, hands open with stiff fingers, and she strikes out, hitting William. Unmindful of the hit to his chest, he leans down, speaks to her, and rubs her arm as she shakes, and writhes. She kicks her legs, her face contorted with terror, and her mouth opens in a silent scream. He slips his arm under her neck and shoulders, holding her gently to himself, rocking her.

"Wake up, my sweet Cup. Wake up. I'm here. Nothing will hurt you as long as I draw breath. Shhhhh...it's William...I'm here."

Slowly, awakening, Ellen looks 'round her, regaining her sense of place and time. Breathing slows and returns to normal, shaking subsides, and tears begin to cascade down her cheeks as she turns to clutch William to herself, soaking his shirt. Holding her, rocking her, and stroking her hair, he murmurs comforting words that she cannot hear. Until she calms, his arms cradle her, his protectiveness towards her rising to an unbearable desire to slay the demons he knows he can never reach. Eventually, her uncontrollable sobs subside, leaving both of them spent. Ellen sits up on her knees, facing William, a single tear rolling down her cheek.

She places her hands together at her chest, moves them towards the young man, and then points to herself.

William shakes his head, draws an X on the palm of his hand, places his hands together with arms outstretched, and then draws them back to his chest to tell Ellen, clearly, that there is nothing to forgive. Watching her nod slowly, she moves closer to him, wraps her arms 'round his waist, curls up with her knees drawn close to him, and rests her head against his thigh. Feeling her relax as he rubs her arm, he strokes her hair and vows to protect her with his life if he can. Not just for now, but forever, if she would allow.

Chapter Forty-Four
4 September 1926

John retrieves Saturday's post and finds that a letter from Sweden has arrived sooner than anyone expected. Eagerly, John opens the missive and gives it a cursory glance as he walks into the sitting room. Sitting in her favourite chair, Anna embroiders an embellishment for a dress she is making.

"Anna, it seems like you just sent that letter to Sweden, but we've received a reply. I looked it over, and it's written in English."

"Oh, goodness, let me see."

She sets aside her needlework and takes the letter from John's hand. Sitting forwards, holding it towards the sunlight from the window, she reads the missive. Again, she reads it, two pages of more than they expected to see.

"Well, we were fortunate that Mrs Mortenson is still living and at the address on the envelopes. Her use of English isn't perfect, but it's good enough. She writes that she is surprised at what has transpired over the years. And...she calls her Signe. I reckon, that's the name for a girl that she's had in her mind all these years, knowing, now, that her niece's baby was a girl."

Taking a seat on the sofa, John removes his shoes before turning to put his legs up, stretching the length of the cushions.

"Yes, hearing Ellen's given name is hard for me to hear. I imagine Mrs Mortenson would be surprised, given the last news she probably heard from Ellen's mother. Does she mention anything about that man?"

"Oh yes, she's shocked at how much he changed. She wants to know more, but I'll have to consider how to word things delicately. I can't just write everything that we've seen and the horrible things Constable Frayser told us. It would just be too much."

"I agree. Until we know more, we should wait to tell Ellen. She's outside with William, anyway, and this isn't urgent."

Nodding her assent, Anna folds the letter and slips it back into its envelope. Hearing the door open and close, Anna lays the missive atop her handiwork and gets up from her chair as John swings his legs over the side of the sofa to sit upright. She waves to John to imply that he should stay right where he is.

"It must be Clara. She rang earlier to say she needed to see us."

Rounding the corner into the sitting room, Clara chuckles, holding something in her hands.

"Speaking of the devil, yes, it's me. I hope you'll be happy to see what I've brought."

Anna gestures to a chair and walks over to the sofa to sit next to John who is tying his shoelaces. Anna chuckles at John and turns to Clara.

"Yes? You've made this all sound so mysterious. You wouldn't tell me when you telephoned, and now you're stringing us along on a suspenseful thread. Our curiosity is piqued if that makes you happy."

"It makes me positively gleeful. Here you go, the diary that Ellen's mother kept. Now, for the meat of my visit."

Clara chuckles as she places the daybook on the low table in front of them. Taking an official-looking envelope from her handbag, she opens it and withdraws crisply folded documents. She lays them on the table, opening them, and smoothing them with her hand. Anna takes the papers, showing them to John as well.

"You found it! This is Ellen's birth certificate and, these are identity papers. How did you...?"

Clara looks at Anna and raises an eyebrow.

"Father Willington and I searched for the name 'Signe Holmes' and found nothing. Legally, Ellen didn't exist. So, we devised another approach. We enlisted Constable Frayser's assistance as he witnessed the statement given by...that man. The official report would be on file if the magistrate wanted to see it. The journal was useful, as well, giving the date of Ellen's birth along with the gravestone that shows her mother's date of death. Putting it all together, we could verify her identity, and procure the proper documents for her. We needed to list her name as 'Signe' since according to that man and the mother's writings; the chosen name for a girl was Signe. We also described her unique circumstances and the magistrate was most understanding. It's official. Ellen legally exists."

John takes the papers and looks them over with a smile on his face.

"Straight away, Monday morning, I will take these to the solicitor, and this will prove that Ellen is the legal heir to the property. He's already drawn up papers. It will be a relief to have it sold, and the creditors paid. Then, Ellen will have her own nest-egg."

Staring at the papers she has taken from John's hand, Anna shakes her head in astonishment.

"I'm sure that we couldn't begin to explain this or its importance to Ellen, but if she could understand, I'm confident that she would be every bit as grateful as we are. Clara, we can't thank you enough for doing all this. We..."

"No, no, no thanks needed. It was necessary, and all is in order. All three of us were happy to help. Constable Frayser, by the way, sends his regards."

Touched that the constable who carried Ellen to safety would still want to help, John and Anna look at one another and then back to Clara.

"I wish we knew of some way..."

Coming into the house from the garden after seeing William off and on his way, Ellen smiles as she walks down the hallway. Rupert dashes ahead of her, skittering on the polished floor as he turns the corner into the sitting room. Ellen follows him and stops as John and Anna look up, and Clara turns, hearing her come in. Clara waves to Ellen, points to herself, draws a smile on her face, points to her own eyes, and then points to Ellen to express that she is happy to see the young woman who has been the topic of their conversation. A bright smile lights up Ellen's face.

She points to herself, draws a smile on her face, points to her own eyes, and points to the helping lady.

Happy to see Ellen has been in such a good mood since their visit to that awful farmstead a fortnight ago. Anna pats her hands together, points to her own eyes, points to Ellen, and then draws a smile on her face. John watches Anna's gestures and agrees that it is nice to see Ellen happy.

She points to herself, draws a smile on her face, taps two fingers on her wrist, touches a finger to her lips, and points to herself. She taps two fingers on her wrist, places one fist on top of the other several times, points to herself, and draws a smile on her face.

Hiding their surprise and gut reaction to this turn of events, John and Anna smile and nod, acknowledging at least, that Ellen is happy. They would not dream of crushing whatever happiness touches her heart, no matter how uneasy they feel with the idea of William kissing her.

She tilts her head to the side, places her forefinger against her nose.

443

Anna points upstairs, where Johanna is playing with Sarah. Ellen nods and walks up the staircase, followed by a dog that is wagging his tail. Looking at Clara with frank consternation in their faces, they wonder how William could ever...how Ellen could be...All three look up the stairs where Ellen has disappeared.

"John, Anna, this is...surprising at the very least. None of us ever expected..."

John leans forwards; restraining his disquiet that William would be so bold and take such a chance of doing something that could distress or even hurt Ellen.

"I don't understand. He, William, kissed her. Maybe I should have a talk with William. This is disturbing."

Anna places her hand on John's arm to calm him as her own unease shows itself fully as she asks her own questions.

"After everything, she's been through...how could she...be happy that William kissed her. I'm confused beyond words."

Clara nods, still looking up the empty staircase.

"Yes, one might think this is impossible. I do have a thought or two, though."

John and Anna wait, wondering what Clara's thoughts could be about this situation. She looks at John and Anna, drawing on everything she has learnt and experienced over the years.

"First, keep in mind that everyone is different. In all my years as a nurse, I've never seen two patients exactly alike, even though they suffer the same illness or injury. Of course, Ellen's experiences left indelible scars inside and out. She will probably be haunted, as her constant nightmares show, for the rest of her life."

"Yes, we understand, but for this situation..."

Clara leans forwards, her hands folded in front of her, the voice of logic and experience speaking.

"John, Anna, consider what we know about her past. What we know about the things that happened to her...Every bit of it was violent. She probably never knew love, understanding or kindness before she came to your door that night. She has chosen to see the two of you as her parents. She sees how you, Johanna, and Sarah live together peacefully, with affection and respect for one another. She's seen the two of you kiss. She knows that you love each other. She's learnt that a man and a woman can have a relationship that doesn't include violence."

John and Anna look at one another, allowing Clara's words to make sense in their minds.

"Remember, Anna, that you told me when Ellen asked if John ever hit you?"

"Oh yes, I remember...I told her that John and I love each other and are married, so we don't want to hurt each other. She seemed confused yet satisfied with that answer."

"And, it was a good answer, Anna. That, along with your day-to-day example, showed her that you live what you speak. Now, going back to the kiss, I can't speak for William, of course, but from Ellen's perspective, I can only imagine the unfathomable difference between the violence done to her and what she and William share. There is no similarity between what happened between Ellen and William and the attacks upon her person. A kiss was never a part of that violence. They are two separate things, the kiss from an emotional bond, and the other was real violence. William has been patient, kind, respectful, and has gone out of his way to learn how to communicate with her. He visits her almost daily, and she looks forwards to his visits."

"But..."

"John, what she and William have together is vastly different from anything else she has ever experienced with a man. I'm firmly convinced that she was never kissed, held, or treated with respectful tenderness. What happened to her was violent. Full stop. What she's experienced with William mirrors what she sees between the two of you."

John sits back, rolling Clara's words 'round in his mind.

"Yes, what you say makes sense, but I'd still like to have a word with William to see what he was thinking. It could have gone badly for both of them, especially Ellen."

"John, don't be too hard on William. Clara is right, she can't speak for William, but she's made Ellen's side clear enough. There are two sides to each story, and we can see that Ellen's side of the story makes her happy."

Clara nods, gathers her handbag, stands, and waves for John and Anna to remain seated.

"I'd best go...Just give yourselves time to think about it, and take it easy on William. Just listen to his side of things before you jump down his throat. It's just me...I know where the door is."

With a reassuring smile at her two confused friends, she turns and walks to the front door, letting herself out. She hopes they are able to handle this diplomatically and give themselves time to consider it all.

Whilst John and Anna sit, looking at each other as they try to absorb the logic presented by Clara, Rupert dashes down the stairs. Ellen walks down the stairs carrying Johanna. Reaching the bottom of the stairs, she lets Johanna get down from her arms to stand. With a bright smile on her face, Johanna nods, making her golden ringlets bob like shining bubbles on a breeze. She points to herself, points outside, and then places two fingers on the side of her face, gesturing in Ellen's language as she speaks.

"Mamma! Daddy! Janna go 'sida Cuppa!"

Unable to resist Johanna's enthusiastic charm, John and Anna nod and chuckle at their daughter who is growing before their eyes.

"Yes, sweetheart. You go outside with Cuppa and have fun!"

Johanna reaches up, grasps two of Ellen's fingers, and drags her along, out of the sitting room, followed by Rupert. John and Anna hear them trotting down the hallway, the door to the garden opening and closing.

"John, I don't know whether to be upset about Ellen and William or not. Should we not leave them alone?"

"I'll have a little talk with William the next time he comes, probably tomorrow. Let's not say anything until then, just so we know his side of things. Clara was right, and so were you, earlier. I won't be hard on him. He knows I'm just concerned about our daughter's safety and welfare."

"All right, John, that's all we can do. I'll start making notes to answer questions that Mrs Mortenson had in her letter, and ask a few of our own."

"Good idea. Notes are the way to go. I'll see if Sarah found the shirts I set out to be ironed. I'm sure she has, but I have to look smart for the upcoming week."

Both of them get up from the sofa to go their separate ways, Anna to the writing desk and John to speak with Sarah. Before they do so, they lean in to embrace and share a tender kiss. With a sigh, Anna leans back and looks up at John.

"You know, Ellen has seen us together like this..."

"Let's hear William's side."

John kisses Anna's forehead and turns to walk upstairs. Anna makes her way to her chair where she left the letter from Mrs Mortenson. She walks over to the writing desk, sits down, and begins to make notes on a blank sheet of paper. The actual letter will be written on her best stationery. Sticking the tip of her tongue out the side of her mouth as she concentrates, she sets to her task.

Outside, Johanna, Ellen, and Rupert chase each other until Johanna hides behind the bench. She peeks out at Ellen, points to herself, points to her own eyes, and points to Ellen to say, 'I see you!'. Rupert's bark fails to give away Johanna's hiding place. Ellen pretends to look for her, lifting limbs of shrubs, looking under rocks, and opening the door to John's workshop, shaking her head. She walks all the way 'round the garden, Rupert running back and forth between his friend and his little friend. Johanna watches their every move, giggling behind her hand. Finally, Ellen comes to the bench, sits down, lowers, and shakes her head. Johanna jumps up and wraps her arms 'round Ellen's waist. Feigning surprise, she turns 'round on the bench and lifts Johanna up to her lap. Smiling, the two of them share kisses and snuggles before Johanna decides to get down and run, again, Rupert and his wagging tail joining in with their frolic. Together, they play, sniffing flowers, looking at birds, and finding insects. As Ellen points to each living thing, Johanna points, nods, and reaches out to touch a spider. Gently, Ellen catches Johanna's hand, brings it to her lips to kiss it. Looking at her, Ellen holds up one finger, shakes her head. Johanna nods, the child pulling her hand away from Ellen and folding her hands in front of herself. Fascinated, though, she turns back to look at the spider that is weaving its intricate web as beautifully as Arachne would, but not touching it.

Finally, Johanna stands up straight, points to the door of the house, places her hands to the side of her head and leans against them as if they were a pillow as she says, 'Janna seepy'. Nodding, Ellen stands, takes Johanna's hand, and they return indoors. Walking into the sitting room, Johanna waves to her mother and announces her intentions, as Anna turns to see her girls come in. As if knowing their destination, Rupert dashes past them and up the stairs.

"Janna seepy. Janna 'stairsa Cuppa."

"Yes, sweetheart. You go take a nap, and Cuppa will tuck you in. I hope you had fun outside?"

"Janna Cuppa run!"

Anna smiles at Ellen, happy that the two of them had some sunshine and exercise. She nods at her two loves, points at Johanna, and puts her hands against her head, leaning her head on them as if they were a pillow.

"Yes, it sounds like you're tired. You and your big sister were busy! Nap happy, sweetheart."

Johanna leads Ellen to the stairs, reaches for the railing, and slowly takes, what to her are the massive steps, one at a time, with Ellen guiding her. At the top of the stairs, Ellen turns Johanna to face her.

She points to the baby, draws an X on the palm of her hand, and points to the way down, holds her hand up high, places her fist on the palm of her hand, and points to the baby.

Johanna tilts her head to the side, understanding only that she should not go downstairs. She nods her head as Ellen smiles at her, takes her hand, and leads the way to the little bed in the nursery. Entering the room, Johanna looks at her bed, made neatly with her favourite pink bunny resting against the lump of pillow. She walks over to her bed, grabs one ear of the toy, and turns to grin at Ellen, gesturing that she wants to nap with Ellen.

"Janna wan seepa Cuppa."

Ellen puts her hand over her mouth, silent laughter bubbling up inside her. She follows her out of the nursery to her own room where Rupert has already made himself comfortable on Ellen's bed. Johanna throws her toy on the bed, sits on the floor, tugs off her shoes, and stands. She pulls down the blanket and grunts as she pulls herself up. She slides in as far as she can move to the other side of the bed, patting Ellen's pillow. Grinning, Ellen kicks off her shoes, slips under the covers next to Johanna and draws the wee one into her arms. Johanna holds up one finger, gropes about on the bed, and finds her pink toy. She cuddles the rabbit between them, pats it, and inches herself closer into Ellen's arms.

Chapter Forty-Five
17 September 1926

Hurrying to finish his work before leaving for the day, William double-checks himself to make sure that he will not have to waste time doing things a second time. Lewis walks up behind him and places his hand on William's shoulder.

"Blimey, mate. You nearly scared me out of my wits. How are you, Lewis? Things going well for you, here?"

"They are, my friend. I haven't thanked you proper for puttin' in a good word for me. I owe you, mate."

"Aww, Lewis, I only did what I thought was right. I hear everyone likes you."

As the two young men chat, Jane Adderley accosts her son.

"Lewis, here's my list. Mind you, I want the best, and bring it home with you."

She waves the list at her cringing son who takes it, stuffs it in his pocket, watches her waddle away, and then turns to William who has tried to look busy during the exchange. He could hear each syllable.

"Lucky for me, I didn't tell mum how much Mr Chelsey pays me. Otherwise, I'd be payin' for the marketing."

"Good thinking. She'd...well, you know."

Nodding, Lewis claps William on the arm.

"Right, then. I'd best let you finish, no doubt you've places to go and a young lady to see."

Smiling, he watches Lewis' lanky frame disappear. William finishes and walks to the back room, removes his pinny, takes his cap, and plops it on his head. He walks out of the market and 'round the corner where he takes the stairs two at a time to reach his bedsit. Freshening up, he looks into the looking glass, hoping he is presentable.

At the Thorpe home, Anna is interrupted by Sarah who brings in the post. Another letter from Sweden. Surprised, she thinks how strange to get two letters before she had answered the last one. She looks at it, reads it over, again, and wonders what John will make of this. Mrs Mortenson has arranged for Ellen to live with them in Sweden, citing their relationship as Ellen's maternal family. Anna pales, and she lays the letter down, gets up from the sofa, and begins to pace, trying to grasp the possibility that Ellen might choose to live there. They have always given Ellen choices, and this situation is no different.

Arriving at his destination, William doffs his cap as John comes walking 'round the house, returning from the shop. With a wave and a smile, John comes to the garden gate and opens it.

"William, it's good to see you. Say, I've wanted to speak with you before you see Ellen. Come along."

"Of course, Mr Thorpe. Ellen isn't expecting me. I came to see you, actually. I have something to ask you."

John casts William a curious glance as he leads the way to the wrought iron table and chairs.

"Have a seat, William. Now, Ellen told us something that upset Mrs Thorpe and I a great deal. She said that you kissed her. William, after what she's been through, why would you do such a thing?"

Shaking his head and raising his hand, William looks at John directly.

"Mr Thorpe, the first kiss was Ellen's request. As have all other kisses we've shared. I would never have taken any chances of ruining what I have with her or to hurt her. Mr Thorpe, this brings me to my question. Keep in mind; I've given this lots of thought. I would like to ask for your blessing. I want to marry Ellen. I want to ask for her hand. I want to ask her to be my wife."

Glad that he is sitting down, John looks down, rubbing his forehead.

"William, first, a few kisses don't make a marriage. Second, I don't think Ellen will ever do well in a marriage, given her past."

"I don't know every detail of her past, but I've loved her since...I can't remember not feeling her in my heart as a part of me. I respect her; accept her past, scars, and fears. I want to spend the rest of my life loving, protecting, and making her happy."

"William, I cannot express how strongly I disapprove of this idea. If, and it's a doubtful 'if' Ellen agrees to marry you, you must realise that it would be a silent and celibate marriage. Do you understand? Have you considered that?"

"As with the kiss, her every wish will be honoured. I never have, and will never coerce Ellen. I don't need children to show her how much she means to me. She has changed me and filled a place in my heart that I never knew existed. I could never find that with anyone else, as long as I live."

"William, I believe that's how you feel, now, but I'm afraid you could be setting yourself and Ellen up for a great deal of pain."

"Mr Thorpe, If Ellen refuses, I couldn't marry another woman. It wouldn't be fair to anyone else to be second when Ellen will always be first in my heart. Love and marriage aren't about perfection. Marriage is about two people caring for one another, making beautiful memories together, and growing old together, come what may. If Ellen doesn't want to marry me, I will honour her decision, and I would spend the rest of my life cherishing her, even if I'm alone, if she even rejected my friendship. As far as silence, words can be meaningless and worthless. Ellen's soul speaks to mine and mine to hers with complete honesty. The soul is what matters. Without words, all that's left is the soul. That is what we have, that is all that I want."

"You plead a compelling case, William, and I sense that your intentions and feelings are genuine. I will discuss this with Anna since she is the one who would pick up the pieces if this goes badly for Ellen. I can't give you our blessing, but it is Ellen's choice. Just consider Ellen's limitations and how you and she might be affected."

"I have tried to consider every possibility. Mr Thorpe, I respect your concerns, and we both put Ellen's best interests first. If I could ask one more favour, could you please tell Ellen that I need to work more and I can't come 'round to see her as often as I would like. I've saved some money for a proper ring, but I've got to save a little more to buy it. It shouldn't take long."

"Yes, I can do that for you. I'm glad to see that you're willing to make sacrifices to do things right, not just in this matter, but all that I've seen since you and Ellen have been keeping company. Just brace yourself for the possibility that she may say no."

Standing, William offers his hand to John for a firm handshake of respect. John stands, shakes William's hand, and inwardly prays that these possibilities are not the most painful things that Ellen and William will ever encounter in matters of the heart. With a nod of farewell, William walks with a purposeful stride to the gate, leaving the garden, and John, who dreads telling Anna about this turn of events. John walks into the house, finding Anna in the sitting room. She is pale, and her hand shakes as she holds out a paper to him.

"John, another letter from Sweden. I think you need to read this."

He takes the letter, sits down next to Anna on the sofa, and reads. His heart aches for Ellen and the choices she will have to make in the imminent future. His heart aches for Anna who will be faced, again, with the possibility of losing their daughter one way, or another.

Chapter Forty-Six
24 September 1926

William dons his best suit, his only suit, actually, looks at himself in the looking glass and combs his hair, making sure that his face is clean-shaven. One last critical glance convinces him that he appears presentable for the occasion. He slips his hand into his pocket, feels the softness of the velvet ring box, hoping that Ellen will accept his desire to marry her. Nervous but happy, he leaves his bedsit, trots down the staircase, and begins his walk into his future. A smile and a merry whistle accompany the spring in his step as he walks towards the belief in a happy future.

Looking at the packed baggage in the entryway, Anna has tried her hardest to refrain from the tears that desperately beg to be shed. Stoutly determined and resigned to this trip, she reminds herself that, ultimately, it will be Ellen's choice to stay in Sweden with her mother's family or not. She sighs, remembering the pang of trying to explain this journey to Ellen after seeing the travel documents John had procured in such haste. John walks to the entryway and sees Anna staring at their suitcases. He takes Anna in his arms, feeling the firm resolve in her posture and the melancholy of leaving Johanna behind.

"I know, Anna. I feel the same. We'll both miss Johanna, too, but this trip is necessary. We owe Ellen this choice. It's her life, her mother's family, and her future. It would be wrong and selfish to deny her that opportunity to meet them, at least. And we'll make it up to Johanna."

She steps back from him, looks up at him, her face and eyes betraying the mother behind the mask of duty.

"Yes, I will miss Johanna so, and you're right, John, we do owe Ellen that much. I just wish William...Knowing he intended to propose to Ellen..."

"I tried, sweetheart. You know that. I kept missing him at the market and left messages, he wasn't home, and I even asked Lewis if he'd seen William. Sarah will be here with Johanna. If he comes by, she will explain. Also, I informed Sarah about the goings-on with Ellen's property if the solicitor tries to contact us here, although I told him where we would be staying and to send us a telegram with any news."

Anna nods as she looks down at the pile of baggage, not actually hearing what John said. She packed only enough for all three of them for this brief trip, including Ellen's toy animals and the list of gestures and their meanings so her relatives will be able to communicate with her. If Ellen chooses to stay in Sweden, they will have the rest of her belongings shipped. Feeling guilty, Anna admits to herself the real reason she did not pack more for Ellen. She hopes that Ellen will want to come back with them. John even purchased return tickets for all three of them.

"I'll take these to the motor. I reckon Ellen will come down when she's ready, but we have a train to catch and then off to the ship. They won't wait for us."

"All right, John. I'll come out with you, for now. I need air. Sarah has Johanna upstairs so she won't become upset with our departure. If Ellen doesn't come down soon, I'll fetch her."

Together they walk outside, John filling the boot with luggage as each one settles with a thud that sounds like the dull beating of his heart. Anna takes a deep breath of sadness for all of them, including William. Absently, she looks 'round them, looking at, yet not seeing the trees, the other houses, and William approaching. His happy whistling announces his nearing, then it stops when Anna's eyes meet his. William waves his greeting and approaches John and Anna. She walks close to John and whispers with a wavering voice.

"William is coming. I'll talk with him."

John nods, hoping the task will not prove too difficult for Anna. She turns away from him, walks 'round the motor, and comes close to William who is now, standing close. As he stares at Anna and John, a cloud of confusion falls upon his countenance, the cloud growing darker as Anna places her hand on his arm.

"William, I need to speak with you."

William looks down at his feet, bracing himself against his fears.

"I see, Ellen doesn't wish to see me, or you feel it best that I do not ask Ellen to marry me."

Anna shakes her head and speaks as gently as she can.

"No, no, nothing like that. You see, the relatives we've been corresponding with in Sweden want to take Ellen in and care for her, as they believe Ellen's...mother would have wanted. You know how we value honesty and how crucial it is for Ellen to make her own choices, and this is no different. We're taking Ellen to meet her relatives, and the rest is up to her. I am so sorry, William, we've been trying to contact you about this. Given your intentions towards Ellen, we felt you have a right to know."

Shocked, William takes a step back.

"Do you...mean...that Ellen might not return?"

"William, that's a very real possibility. I think it would be best if you say goodbye to Ellen. I know it would mean the world to her."

Tears begin to roll down his cheeks, he shakes his head, and his words come as a broken whisper.

"I cannot say goodbye to her. I can't."

Walking 'round the motor, John comes close to William, putting his hand on William's shoulder.

"William, we know this is difficult for you. It is for us as well. We don't want to lose her, either, but sometimes situations arise that we can't ignore or control. Do go to her, tell her what you wish and say goodbye, as one day, you may regret not doing so."

William shakes his head, fighting against the truth that stabs him. Reaching into his pocket, he feels the ring again, his mind flashing to the jewellery store where he was so happy to find a ring so perfect for her. He turns to Anna with pleading eyes that beg for clemency from this torture.

"I can't. I can't do that. Please tell her goodbye for me."

Tears welling up in her eyes, she feels William's heartbreak at the thought of losing the one person he loves more than life. If she ever doubted William's love for Ellen, those doubts are gone, now. She whispers to him, her voice becoming raw with emotion.

"William, it's the right thing to do. She'll always wonder if you don't."

Ellen walks out of the front door, down the steps, and stops. She stares at William as tears begin to well in her eyes. She looks down and folds her hands in front of herself. Seeing Ellen, tears roll down his cheeks. He walks up to her and places a finger under her chin, lifting her face to look at him. As difficult as it is, he smiles when he looks into her eyes. He takes a finger and wipes away her tears. Ellen looks up into his eyes, shakes her head, tears falling without restraint. She puts her arms 'round his neck and clutches him to her. Exhaling a ragged breath, William knows that holding her like this will only become a memory. He kisses her hair and whispers.

"My sweet Ellen, I only wanted to marry you and make you happy for the rest of your life."

She looks up at him, tears continuing to fall, takes his hand and walks with him 'round the house to the garden. They go through the gate together, and she leads him to the swing. She looks up at him with the same intensity as William's gaze upon her. He looks down at her, remembering that this swing is special to them. He gets down on his knees, brushes her hair from her face and gently places his hand on her cheek. Ellen puts her hand on his as he cups her cheek. She closes her eyes and then looks at him again.

She taps her lips with her finger.

Choking back his tears so he can see the face of his love, her request for him to kiss her pleads its way into his soul. He takes her hand and stands with her. Gazing into her eyes, he places his hand against her cheek again and slowly comes closer, feeling her warmth. He softly kisses her lips knowing that soon, the kiss will break and he will walk away, a different man than when he arrived. He feels her cling to him, sharing a deep kiss, their salty and mutual suffering mixing into a bitter elixir. Slowly, his lips part from hers, his heart destroyed at this last kiss. He holds her, rocking her in his arms.

Wishing they did not have to intrude on their private farewell, John whispers to Anna.

"Anna, we have to leave. The timetable..."

Nodding, her heart breaks for William and Ellen, even more so than for herself and John. She walks 'round to the garden gate where William and Ellen are holding each other so tightly. She enters the garden, approaches, and speaks softly.

"It's time..."

Hearing Anna's words, he looks at her and nods. He leans back, removes his handkerchief from his pocket and dries his sweet girl's eyes, then wipes away his own tears. He looks into Ellen's eyes once more. He points to her, places a fist over another a few times, points to himself, and then draws a smile on his face to tell her how happy she makes him. Fresh tears fall from Ellen's eyes as she nods and grabs on to him tightly as wracking sobs convulse her body. Holding her and stroking her hair, his broken voice breaks Anna's heart.

"I love you, Ellen. I love you more than you will ever know. Thank you, my sweet Cup."

Ellen backs away from William and turns to look at Anna. Silent tears falling, Anna reaches out her hand to Ellen, indicating that it is time for them to leave. Anna looks at William, unable to find the words that will make his broken heart hurt less, only able to nod her head in acknowledgement of his pain. She takes Ellen's hand and walks with her to the motor, followed by William. Anna helps Ellen get inside, and then enters the rumbling auto, watching Ellen, and taking her hand. The worst torment a mother can feel courses through Anna; not knowing how to ease Ellen's suffering that must equal the desolation within William. He comes 'round to the side of the motor and stands, looking at Ellen, touching the glass between them. Ignoring the lurch in his gut, he sees

Ellen touch his fingers, separated by glass that might as well be an ocean. John slips the motor into gear and pulls away, as William watches Ellen turn to look at him through the rear window. He sees his world go dark as the motor drives off, watching his world disappear. He reluctantly raises his hand to wave, sees her look at him, and she raises her hand until the motor is out of sight. Dropping his hand to his side, his shoulders slumped, he whispers.

"Goodbye."

He slips his hand inside of his pocket and feels the ring. Ellen's ring.

Chapter Forty-Seven
27 September 1926

Driving the hired motor to the house of Ingrid Mortenson, John and Anna share the same thoughts about Ellen. She has not gestured much, except to express a desire to have a miniature replica of the ship that carried them into the unknown. Reaching out to Ellen was useless on their two-day journey to Sweden as she stared out of the porthole and refused to eat, no matter how much John and Anna tried to coax her interest. One outing to the ship's deck was enough to frighten Ellen back to their stateroom, seeing the vastness of the ocean and the wealthy women with their parasols and debonair men strolling about. All John and Anna wanted, and still want, is to show Ellen that they love her.

Not wanting to stop at the inn for supper or to unload their bags, they choose to spare Ellen the awkwardness of seeing her own bags left in the boot. Ellen is invited to stay with Mrs Mortenson tonight, in her home. A quick ring from the train station confirmed that their room is ready for them whenever they do arrive, as it might be late. A telegram also awaits them, and John hopes that it is news regarding Ellen's inheritance.

Anna looks out the window as Mrs Mortenson's cottage comes into view. Her heart sinks, having hoped that it would be shabby and run-down. On the contrary, it is a charming little house from the outside, at least. She looks at Ellen who is staring out the window, and Anna is unable to read the expression on her face.

Pulling into the lane and up to the cottage, John stops and deadens the engine, gets out and is ready to help the ladies, Anna stepping out first.

"Well, this is it, Anna. I hate to say, but it looks well kept. We'll see what it looks like on the inside."

"Yes, it does, which is comforting and disappointing all at the same time. I dread this more than I can say."

She sighs and gets out of the motor, looking 'round, and she reaches for Ellen's hand. Squeezing Ellen's hand to give her reassurance, Anna savours the physical contact with her daughter for whatever time they have left together. She feels Ellen's hand clutch hers tightly as she moves closer to Anna, all the whilst staring 'round them and then her gaze rests upon the cottage. Before they can make their way to the door for a proper knock, Ingrid comes out of the house, smiling with the most gracious greeting she can possibly give. She walks towards them with a cordial welcome.

"God dag! Välkommen!"

She chuckles and shakes her head, forgetting to speak English for a moment.

"Good day to you and welcome. I am Ingrid. I am glad to meet you."

Ingrid gestures towards the cottage, inviting them to come in. She looks at Signe, marking how much she resembles her late mother, Ellen. John leads the way to Mrs Mortenson, reaches his hand out to shake hers.

"It is nice to meet you, finally. I'm John Thorpe, of course, and I almost feel as though we know you through the exchange of letters."

John turns and gestures to Anna as she smiles at Mrs Mortenson. She wishes she could dislike their hostess but finds that she cannot, right away.

"I'm glad to finally meet you, Mrs Mortenson. I'm Anna Thorpe, and I'm the one who has been writing to you."

Gesturing to Ellen, John feels as though he is betraying her by this introduction. He tries not to choke on the words he is obliged to utter in the politest fashion he can.

"This is our Ellen. As you see, she's shy and reserved in the presence of people she doesn't know."

Anna chides herself for lying for the sake of social graces, but she resigns herself to maintaining decorum for Ellen's sake as they walk into the house behind Mrs Mortenson, Ellen still clutching Anna hand tightly. Ellen turns, as does Anna to make sure John is close behind them. He walks in behind them, removes his hat, glances 'round the room, and turns to smile at Mrs Mortenson.

"This is a charming home, Mrs Mortenson. It has a warm and inviting atmosphere."

Closing the door behind her guests, Ingrid takes their wraps and hangs them in the wardrobe.

"Thank you and please, do call me by my Christian name, Ingrid. We are more than...bekanta...I'm sorry...let me think...oh yes, acquaintances."

She turns to Signe with a warm smile.

"My goodness, Signe, you are the exceptional young lady your mother would have loved so dearly. I know, she would have been proud of you."

Anna feels a wave of maternal protectiveness and affront at the mention of anyone but herself being called Ellen's mother and the name

'Signe' grates on her heart like sandpaper. She squeezes Ellen's hand and smiles at her, pointing to Ingrid, moves her hands by her mouth, points to Ellen, pats her hands together, and releases Ellen's hand to place one fist on her chest, patting it with the other, placing a hand on her heart, and then pointing to Ellen to translate, roughly, that Ingrid said Ellen is good, and her mother loved her. Ellen stares at Anna, nods then looks at Ingrid. She reaches over to take Anna's hand, again. John watches Anna tell Ellen what is happening, turns and looks at Mrs Mortenson.

"Whenever we talk, we always tell Ellen, we named her Ellen, what is being said. Otherwise, we feel it is rude, and it makes her feel uncomfortable and excluded. She needs to feel she is recognised and a part of things happening 'round her, as we all do."

Ingrid nods her head, smiling at Signe.

"I am eager to learn her hand movements, as you mentioned, Mrs Thorpe. I agree that it is sensible and kind to include Signe, as she is a part of our family. Please, come into the salongen. I have made a little lunch for us whilst we grow to know one another a little."

She leads the way into a parlour where a little table is set to the side, filled with refreshments that she and her daughter had worked for days to make in preparation for this momentous visit. She gestures to the table of food.

"Please, help yourselves and make comfortable. I shall return with kaffe."

Ingrid hurries off to the kitchen to retrieve a fresh pot of coffee for her guests. Anna nods with a smile and leads Ellen to a comfortable little sofa, not wanting to seem impolite by partaking of the treats on the table before their hostess returns. She pats the seat next to her for Ellen to sit and gives Ellen a reassuring smile. John sits next to Ellen on her other side to help her feel more secure. Anna whispers so she will not be heard in the kitchen.

"John, she went to a great deal of trouble to welcome us."

"Yes, it appears as though she did. She seems nice enough, but I do wish she would say Ellen's name."

He looks at Ellen, pats her arm and waits for her to look down at her arm and then look back up at him. He points to Ellen, holds his hands up in front of himself and lowers them down, pats his hands then tilts his head, asking Ellen if she feels all right. He sighs as Ellen looks at him and shrugs her shoulders, taking his hand as well, squeezing it tightly. Ingrid bustles in with the fresh coffee and smiles at her guests as she sets the pot on the table next to the food.

461

"I suppose you have tea in England, but here, we enjoy kaffe, what you know as coffee. There is cream and sugar if you like to have it. Please help yourselves to what I have set out for you. This is a tradition, here, to set out seven different cookies for a speciellt tillfälle, or...what are the words...special occasion. Yes, this is a most special occasion."

Once again, she gestures for John, Anna, and Signe to come to the table to follow her example as she helps herself to a cup of coffee, takes a little plate, a cookie, and then picks up a serviette. She walks over to a chair opposite this dear couple who have been so kind to their long-lost Signe. Anna looks at Ellen, tilts her head to the side, points to her, places a fist over his heart then points to the table with food and coffee. Ellen's answer is a negative shake of her head. Anna turns to Ingrid, translating.

"I asked Ellen if she would like some coffee or biscuits."

Anna pats Ellen's hand, points to herself and then points to the table laden with treats. She chooses two biscuits and puts them on her little plate with the serviette tucked underneath the plate, pours herself a cup of coffee and picks it up, following their hostess' example.

"Thank you, Ingrid. This is kind of you."

Wishing for tea as she returns to her seat next to Ellen, Anna stifles a sigh as the thought passes through her mind, 'When in Rome...'. She looks about for somewhere suitable to rest her cup, then notices a small round thing on the table in front of them that seems made for the purpose. She holds her plate towards Ellen, tilting her head to ask, again, if she would like to have a biscuit. Anna completely understands when Ellen shakes her head, refusing. A sense of obligation raises John from his seat, and he makes his way to the table, not wanting to offend their hostess. He goes through the same motions as Ingrid and Anna had, and returns to his seat, speaking directly to Ingrid, determined to use Ellen's name, as she is known by it to everyone who loves her.

"I am sure you have questions about Ellen. She has been a joy to us and has given our family much happiness. She and Anna have become very close from the first moment she entered our lives, and it is rare when they are not together. Ellen depends on her a great deal."

Ingrid sips her coffee and nods.

"Ja...I mean to say, yes, I can see that, and it is good that Signe has had such devoted care. From what you spoke of in your letters, it seems that because of your good will, she is alive. I am prepared to be as devoted to our dear Signe as her own mother would have been, God rest her soul. I do have many questions, but I think that Signe will answer many, as time passes. Your letters have been more than helpful, and I am grateful for them."

John notices Ellen looking back and forth, as they talk to one another, and feels her hand curl into a fist in the palm of his hand like a child hiding behind their father for protection. Anna's back bristles at the words that feel as though they diminish the depth of love they feel for Ellen as their daughter. She struggles to maintain her manners, reminding herself that they are here to allow Ellen to make a choice to stay with a woman who represents Ellen's blood relatives or to return to England with her family. Neither she nor John partake of the lavish culinary efforts that welcomed them, their stomachs turned upside down with uncertainty.

"Excuse me a moment whilst I try to explain to Ellen what we're saying. Ellen feels different from other people and seeing people talk and not being able to hear them only makes her feel more alone."

She turns to Ellen and points to Ingrid, moves her hand by her mouth to represent talking, then draws a smile on her own face, points to herself and taps three fingers on her chest places her hand over her heart, and then points to Ellen, saying that Ingrid is happy that she and John love her. Ingrid nods and, smiles sympathetically at Signe.

"Of course. She does seem timid. I hope she might feel better once she sees her bedroom and her things are 'round her. You spoke of her nightmares, and I will be aware of them and help her if she requires anything."

She looks to both of the people who seem to love Signe and hopes it will not be too difficult for them to have her spend this night in her house. With a silent sigh that resonates deep in her soul, Anna turns to Ellen and points to her, places her hands together as a pillow and rests her head on them and points towards the staircase going up to where she assumes Ellen's room has been prepared. She looks to Ingrid, her heart tearing bit by bit with each word she says each dreaded word.

"I've explained to Ellen that she'll sleep here, tonight."

"Thank you, Mrs Thorpe...Anna, if I may be so familiar with you, considering we have our dear Signe in common."

Ingrid stands with a smile and holds out her hand to Signe, nodding and points up the stairs where Signe's room has been prepared with the greatest of care. Again, she nods, encouraging Signe. Ingrid, Anna, and John watch Ellen as she turns to look at each of them and then stands to take Ingrid's hand. Ellen's gaze turns to rest on Anna, again, and she gives Ellen the best smile she can muster as her heart tears into smaller and smaller pieces. She nods, patting her hands together, telling Ellen that this is good, and it is all right to go with

Ingrid. John rises to his feet and looks at Anna, knowing she is feeling the intense grief and loss as he is.

"I will go out to the motor and get her bag. I won't be but a moment."

Grateful for something, anything, to do that takes him away from watching their daughter walk away to sleep with strangers, he trudges over to the door, and walks into the darkness, to the motor. Opening the boot, he rests his forehead against the metal, closing his eyes against his tears and the memory of Ellen's embrace as she told him that he was her father. Composing himself with difficulty, he reaches for Ellen's valise, silently cursing the letters they found and their obligation to do the 'right thing'. He hefts it out of the rear of the motor, closes the boot, and reluctantly makes his way back to the house that might be Ellen's new home.

Ingrid takes Signe's hand with a reassuring squeeze and a smile as she leads her up the staircase and through the little hallway to Signe's bedroom. She and her daughter had worked diligently to prepare it, beginning as soon as they heard that Signe was alive and well. She opens the door and steps inside, watching Signe, hoping her great-niece will approve, and she says a silent prayer that Signe's mother would agree, as well. She watches Signe standing with her hands folded in front of herself as she stares 'round the room. Reaching over to the hook behind the door, she reaches for a lovely new nightdress, embroidered by her own hand and just finished the day past. She points to Signe and then to the nightdress smiling kindly, nods, walks out of the room, and downstairs where John and Anna Thorpe are waiting.

Back into the cottage, John comes into the sitting room where Anna waits and sees Ingrid walking down the stairs. He places the bag on the floor by the stairs. He looks over to Anna and understands that she feels as grief-stricken as he does and that they need to leave before their emotions can no longer be stifled.

"Ingrid, I hope that you don't mind that we go to the Inn. We are exhausted from the trip, but we will be back tomorrow to see Ellen."

Feeling gutted and close to tears thinking that Ellen's bedtime routine with her will not happen, she suddenly realises that she is carrying the papers she had written on the ship of the gestures they use to communicate, Ellen's bedtime routine, and how they help Ellen through her nightmares. She opens her handbag, takes the papers out, and hands them to Ingrid. Struggling to maintain a clear and steady voice, Anna speaks quietly.

"Yes, we are weary, but I want you to have these. They will help you care for Ellen. And yes, we will be back tomorrow."

Upstairs, in a strange room, with a strange bed, wearing an unfamiliar nightdress, Ellen walks out of the bedroom. Standing halfway down the stairs, she wipes her eyes.

She stares and points at the lady, strokes her own hair, and tilts her head to the side.

Looking up at Ellen's silent request, she looks at Ingrid with pleading eyes in spite of willing herself to be strong.

"I see Ellen up at the top of the stairs, asking if I might go up and tuck her in? Bedtime is special for her. Please."

Ingrid nods understandingly and steps aside. Anna hurries up the stairs to Ellen and lets Ellen lead her to the bedroom prepared for her. Her heart sinks even further that it is pink, floral, exquisite, feminine, and perfect. She pushes these thoughts away as she turns down the covers and lets Ellen slide between the sheets. She tucks her in, realising that her fluffy toys are down in her suitcase. All she has is her handkerchief to give Ellen to hold. Giving her the handkerchief, she sits on the side of the bed, stroking Ellen's hair. She points to herself, taps three fingers on her chest, places her hand over her heart, and then points to Ellen, telling her as she drifts off to sleep, finally, that she and John love Ellen with all their hearts. Once Ellen is asleep, she sits for a few moments longer, brushing away that one stubborn strand of hair away from Ellen's forehead, fiercely fixing that sweet face in her memory. She whispers the words to the song she sings to her babies.

"Hush little baby, don't say a word..."

Finally, she tears herself away from Ellen, closes her door part way, and walks downstairs where John is waiting. They thank their hostess, Anna taking John's hand as they leave the house and their Ellen. Together, they step out into the empty night.

Chapter Forty-Eight
29 September 1926

Spending the day with Ellen and visiting with Ingrid, John and Anna watch how Ellen is reacting to her new surroundings. Anna notices things she had not observed the first evening they were visiting Ingrid. The house itself is small as you look at it from the outside, but it is roomy when you are inside. Each room is spotlessly tidy and full of family heirlooms and pictures. The smell of baking and cooking permeates the atmosphere, even when no meal is taking place. She watches Ellen, thinking that this house is much like her. She may be small when you first see her, but once you know her, you understand there is so much more. The hope John and Anna have felt that Ellen would choose to return with them fades as they watch Ingrid and Ellen gesture to each other. Ingrid is growing proficient in Ellen's language more quickly than they imagined she would. She even managed to comfort Ellen through one of her nightmares last night, from what Ingrid said. This thought saddens Anna the most, who feels guilty that she wants an exclusive privilege in giving Ellen such comfort and love.

From time to time, as he looks intently 'round each room they enter, John glances at pictures of Ingrid's late husband, Rudolph. Ingrid was eager to tell them about him since he was a businessman and John might feel akin to him, given that John owns his own business. Although Rudolph had passed more than fifteen years ago, Ingrid's voice still wavers when she speaks of him. John almost finds him wishing that he could have known the man who inspired such devotion from his wife, even years after his death. Slowly, John feels that he is coming to understand the family that has given much love to a young woman they had only met a few days ago.

Ingrid smiles at John and Anna, who are so attentive to Signe and interested in everything regarding the provisions they have made for her. Ingrid's daughter, Ida, insisted on giving Signe the room she had when she was growing up. Ida was especially eager to make the room fresh and inviting. Ingrid fervently hopes that the couple who have cared for Signe with such faithfulness will finally give their blessing. She only wants everyone to feel at peace with these changes to their lives.

"I hope you find things pleasing here, Signe's home, now. I only want to make her happy."

She reaches over and pats Signe's hand.

"There is something I would like you to see, and it is...well, you will see. Won't you come with me?"

She stands and motions for them to follow her. Startled by Ingrid's comment that it is Signe's home now, John and Anna look at each other, pained by the finality of her statement. John musters a smile as he looks back to Ingrid.

"Of course, we would be happy to see more of the efforts you have made to help Ellen feel wanted."

He stands and reaches his hand out to Anna, knowing how difficult this is for her. Taking John's hand, holding it tightly, Anna forces herself to smile whilst her heart is breaking as she looks at Ellen. She pats Ellen's arm to get her attention, waits for her to look down at her arm and then back up at her. She points to Ingrid, places a fist on her chest, then taps three fingers on her chest and points to herself, then points to her own eyes and points outside, saying that Ingrid wants to show them something outdoors. Ellen nods as she and Anna pull their sweaters a snugly 'round them as they prepare to go out.

"Yes, I'm eager to see as I'm sure Ellen is, as well."

She notices that Anna has told Signe what is happening.

"I hope you'll be proud of me, Anna, that I understood how you told Signe what is happening. This is an adjustment for us all."

Ingrid smiles and leads them outside and to the side of the house where a little shed that matches the house in its tidy appearance, if not size, awaits them. She stands at the door, waits for them all to gather close, and opens the door.

"You told me in your letters how much Signe enjoys gardening and being outdoors and making things. Ida and I thought it would be nice for her to have a place of her own to pursue those things that please her."

Feeling Ellen grasp her hand, Anna watches her look inside the shed and then look back at her. Anna pats Ellen's hand, trying to reassure Ellen as much as she is trying to encourage and comfort herself.

"What a nice thought, Ingrid. This is so kind of you. I am sure that Ellen will enjoy having a place of her own. You have accomplished so much to prepare for her arrival."

Her heart sinks as she remembers the hours she and Ellen spent looking at seed catalogues, planting seeds, watching their garden grow as their family grew closer with each passing day. Anna turns to Ellen, pats her on the arm to get her attention and waits for Ellen to look down at her arm. When Ellen looks back up at Anna, she points to Ingrid, holds her fist close to her chest, extends her arm towards Ellen as she opens her hand and then holds up one hand, pushing her other hand up behind it as she extends her fingers to say that Ingrid is giving this to Ellen as a gift so she can have her own garden. In reply, Ellen nods to Anna and continues to look 'round her. John looks 'round the shed and reluctantly approving, he nods.

"Yes, Ingrid, this is thoughtful. Ellen does love growing things, and she has an intuitive way with animals of every kind, as well."

Ingrid gestures 'round the well-organised interior.

"See? There are pots to grow seedlings, a little stove to stay warm if she is out here in the cold, tools of every kind that she might need, and your mention of animals...there are many animals that wander about here. They may have found a new friend in our Signe."

She smiles at Signe, John, and Anna, hoping they are happy with the care they have given to Signe's interests.

"Have I missed anything? My daughter and I have tried to anticipate her every need and want. Of course, Ida's husband was helpful to build this litet hus, or as you would say in English, little house."

Sensing Ellen is staring at them talking together, Anna feels her cling to her arm. Looking at Ellen, she looks up at what has caught Ellen's attention, as John has also noticed. They understand the expression on Ellen's face. Her demeanour has changed from passively peaceful to one of fear and trembling.

"Ingrid, might I have a word alone with you?"

John takes Anna's hint and comes close to pat Ellen's arm, then waits for her to look down at her arm and back up to him. He points to himself, places his fist on his chest, points to Ellen, to his own eyes, and then points outside, recalling the stream nearby that Ingrid had mentioned. Perhaps a distance from this memory will bring Ellen some calm. John points to Anna and Ingrid, moves his fingers near his mouth as if talking to explain that they should go for a walk so that Anna and Ingrid can chat. Looking up once again, Ellen turns to John, nods, takes his hand, and then looks at Anna. She nods with a smile to Ellen as John explains.

"I would like to show Ellen the stream nearby. I am sure she will love to see it."

"Yes, that would be lovely. I don't believe Signe has been close enough to see it."

He smiles at Ingrid and Anna as he gives Ellen's hand a fatherly squeeze and a pat. He walks out with her to the stream and stands with her, watching the water flow by, dancing over the rocks. He points to the water and pats his hands together to say that it is good that the stream is there. Ellen lowers her head and stands closer to John.

She points to the moving water and pats her hands together.

Putting his arm 'round Ellen, the stream, trees, and everything 'round him fades away. All he knows is that his daughter calls him 'father' which means everything to him.

Ingrid turns to Anna, a cloud of concern clouding her visage, as she fears the worst. The last thing she would ever want to do is offend these good and kind people who have shown such affection and care towards Signe.

"What would you like to speak of? I haven't förolämpade...I mean, offended in any way, have I?"

Anna shakes her head and places a reassuring hand on Ingrid's arm.

"No, no, nothing like that. When I wrote in my letters to you about the horrible things that had been done to Ellen, I didn't give details because I thought they would be too...indelicate to mention. Now, one of those details has become imperative for you to know. You see, that man...Cyrus was so inhumanely cruel to Ellen that she wanted to die. She went to the shed on the farm and tried to hang herself. When she looked up and saw the rafters, she remembered all that and...well, you can understand her reaction to that would be painfully intense. Those memories are what we think come to torment her in her nightmares. This detail is but one of many that would horrify you beyond words, as they did John and me when we found out."

Ingrid's hand flies to her mouth and tears spring to her eyes.

"Oh, Anna...I had no idea...oh that olyckligt flicka...no, I am sorry, poor girl..."

She looks up to the rafters with a shudder, speechless at the horrifying revelation looming above her.

"I shall find some way to remedy this, and Ida's husband may help. My deepest apologies. I will see if she would like to learn sewing or...why don't we go inside now."

Nodding, the two women exit the shed into the lengthening shadows, and Anna calls out to John.

"John, we're going inside now."

Waving, John takes Ellen's hand and points to the house. Nodding, her head lowered, Ellen walks beside him to join Anna and Ingrid. John brings Ellen's hand in front of him, clasping his warm hands 'round her icy fingers. He looks down at her as they stroll, memorising every detail he can find as he looks at her. Soon, they will have to leave, and they must accept and try to understand the loss of their girl to a life none of them anticipated. They enter the warmth of the house behind Anna and Ingrid as the last rays of the sun perish behind the grove of trees to the west. The four of them stand in the room, looking at one another in an awkward silence. Suddenly remembering the model ship that Ellen chose on their voyage here, Anna breaks the silence.

"Oh...I have something of Ellen's out in the motor. I keep forgetting..."

Before her voice betrays her emotions, she tries to smile at Ellen, rubs her arm, and hurries out the door to the motor before she loses her composure. Ellen turns to John and wraps her arms 'round him, clutching him tightly. Wrestling with his own emotions, John holds her, stroking her hair, rocking her back and forth slightly, and fighting the tears that threaten his resolve to be the voice of reason. Ellen leans back, and he looks deep into the soul of the young woman who has changed so many people. Ellen will never know what good she has brought to the world. He does his best to smile, cupping her cheek in his hand, kissing her forehead.

She looks at the man, puts her hands together, and lays her head on them as if they were a pillow. She points to herself and points upstairs.

Through all of this, Ingrid silently looks upon John with a mixture of sadness and compassion for him and his wife. She cannot deny the love they have shown Signe as one of their own, and it is evident that Signe loves them. A prayer for them all to be filled with peace is uplifted from her heart to heaven, knowing that it will take time for adjustment, acceptance, and a return to a new ordinary. Signe nods her head, keeping her gaze lowered, whilst John and Ingrid watch her walk up the stairs to her room, one thinking of her as Ellen, and the other thinking of her as Signe. Anna walks back into the cottage holding the box containing Ellen's model ship.

"Where is Ellen? I wanted to give her..."

"She's gone up to bed. I imagine it will be time to tuck her in, as you say. I will enjoy learning this evening ritual of hers. She is such a dear girl."

Looking at Ingrid, Anna's eyes fill with the tears she has held back since they arrived in Sweden. A ragged whisper is all her grief will allow.

"Please know that the whole purpose of our journey here with

Ellen was to give her a choice of where she wants to be. She's of age. She never had choices all her life, not even having a choice of whether she had food. Since she has been with us, we have given her choices in all things, large and small, talking about choices but letting her make them, herself. If she chooses to stay here, yes, it will break our hearts because we love her as our own child. If she decides to stay here, she will have our blessing and undying love because she made an honest choice based on seeing things for herself. Her future is her choice, and whatever choice she makes, she will know that she will always be loved by two families."

Anna takes a deep breath at the end of what she believes Ingrid needs to hear and cradles the box as if it were an infant. Anna looks at Ingrid with tears in her eyes, begging yet not waiting for permission.

"I'll take this up to Ellen."

She turns away to walk up the stairs to the room Ellen uses. She peers in and sees Ellen wearing her nightdress, walking over to the bed, taking her cuddly from the chair, and placing them on her bed, as they had been arranged at home. Ellen sits on the bed, takes one of the cuddly animals and makes it walk up to her. Holding it in both hands, she pulls it close, stroking it and rocking. Seeing Ellen arranging her furry toys, Anna feels as though her heart has stopped beating. She sees Ellen settling into the room that is now, hers. She thinks of Ellen's room at home that will remain the same as when Ellen left it. All her things...things that no longer have meaning because Ellen won't be there to give them meaning...yet she will treasure each one because that will be all she will have left of Ellen's presence in their lives. She wipes her eyes, willing herself to stop her soul from crashing to the floor and exploding like fine crystal that can never be repaired. Setting the box containing the model ship on the floor next to Ellen's door, a raspy voice she does not recognise as her own comes from her broken heart.

"I can't...I just can't."

She rests her head on the moulding 'round the doorframe for a moment, her hand on the wall. Anna is unaware of Ingrid's approach as she tries to collect her dignity. Ingrid sees the depth of Anna's grief and suddenly fathoms that the grief Anna shows is that of a devoted mother about to lose her child. She puts her hand on Anna's shoulder and speaks softly.

"Why don't you go inside and tell her...? She deserves a proper goodbye. If you don't, she'll always wonder."

She puts her arm 'round Anna's shoulder, appreciating, for the first time, the price Anna and John were willing to pay to allow Signe to choose her own life's direction. They could have withheld the contents of the letters she had sent to Ellen's mother. They were under no obligation to write to her of Signe's life. They love Signe enough to let her go if that is her desire. Feeling as though she had been punched in the stomach, Anna remembers having said those same words to William. She turns to look at Ingrid, shakes her head and whispers, copious tears falling like blood from the depths of a mother's shattered soul.

"I can't right now. I just...can't."

With a heart full of understanding, Ingrid nods as she rubs Anna's arm.

"Yes, I understand. Then, perhaps it is best if you and John come tomorrow morning and say goodbye before you have to arrive at the ship. Signe will want to see you."

Unable to speak, Anna nods, turns away from Ingrid and walks down the stairs to join John. Holding Anna's sweater, he looks up and watches Anna descend the staircase followed by Ingrid. Seeing Anna distraught, he aches to take Anna into his arms and share this loss that they cannot control. John drapes Anna's sweater about her shoulders and turns to Ingrid.

"Thank you, Ingrid."

Choking on the words that would be proper at this time, he cannot bring himself to thank Ingrid for taking care of Ellen. He holds Anna's hand as Ingrid sees them to the door; watching them leave, silence filling the night. They leave the cottage and walk to the motor where he opens the door and looks at Anna once more. Not caring if Ingrid is watching, he pulls her into his arms, holding her tightly, sharing a language that only souls can speak.

Chapter Forty-Nine
30 September 1926

Driving to Ingrid's house where Ellen seems to be settling in, Anna fights her feelings, willing herself to be happy for Ellen, even though Ellen's choice to stay in Sweden breaks her heart. The thumb of her glove withstands the worst of her emotional restraint.

"John, this is one of the hardest things we've ever had to do."

"Yes, it is. We didn't get much sleep."

Paying careful attention to the road, the fog makes it difficult for John to see 'round bends. Even so, his mind fills with a struggling acceptance that this is now Ellen's place in the world and they will return to England without her. The back seat of the motor will never be the same with Anna and Ellen holding hands, looking out the windows, and pointing things out to each other. Anna stares out the window at the fog-shrouded trees that look a little like a skeleton's hands reaching up out of an overgrown and neglected cemetery. She sighs, waiting for those hands to snatch her heart from her and give her peace. Sadly, she looks back down at her gloves, trying not to think of having to say goodbye to Ellen. When shall she see their daughter again? Will Ingrid really stay in touch? Will letters, over time, become less frequent, then stop? She shakes her head, preferring the grim idea of the trees reaching for her through the fog.

"Anna? I don't know...but have you thought that Ellen coming to us might have been meant to be for preparing to bring her here? That she really does belong with her mother's family?"

She looks at John, shrugs her shoulders, and chokes back tears.

"I don't know what 'meant to be' means, John, and it's not a comforting thought."

She stares down at her hands, again and whispers.

"I'm sorry, John, but that's how I feel."

Watching the road, he reaches out one hand and lays it on hers for just a moment.

"What you feel is natural. I don't want you to ever apologise for how you feel. I am proud of you, Anna. You gave birth to Ellen, in a way. She is not the frightened child she once was. She's a grown woman, now, with a mind of her own. We have shown her unconditional love, we gave her hope. We taught her that she has choices and she has the right to make them. Together, our family's love brought to light her beautiful soul."

Anna looks up at John with a tremulous smile.

"Yes, I do feel like a mother to her in that way just as you feel like a father to her. She has grown to be a lovely young woman. For all that you say we've done for her, she's given us more than we could ever have given her. She's touched and changed for the better each person she's met. She'll never know it, though. You're right of course; she'll never know what joy she's brought into our lives. She does have the right to make choices, and we've always given her the chance to do so. I just wish..."

She stares out the window, the road looking terribly unfamiliar with the fog swirling 'round them. Noticing that they are nearing their unhappy destination, John pulls the motor to the side of the road and turns to face her, taking Anna's hand in his.

"I know. I wish the same thing. All the details rumble about in my head. According to the telegram from the solicitor, someone purchased the farm. Ellen's inheritance money is in a bank account at Harald & Howe. We may never know who bought it, but at any rate, we'll need to transfer her funds to a bank here that Ingrid can manage on Ellen's behalf. We'll need to send the rest of her belongings here, help William through this...and he was going to propose to her. I guess this would have been her answer. We will see to it that she hears from us frequently. Ingrid can gesture our letters to her. Perhaps we can visit once a year. We can bring Johanna with us, and Sarah is always welcome to join us."

She looks at John with tears in her eyes that she wipes away on the sleeve of her sweater, remembering that she had given her handkerchief to Ellen before her cuddly toys had been unpacked and she had forgotten to pack another.

"All 'have-to' and 'maybes', John. It's not the same. Perhaps, John...maybe it will all go as it should...whatever that means."

A ragged breath betrays the depth of John's sadness. He looks straight ahead past the bonnet of the motor, but not noting anything in particular. His gaze returns to Anna.

"The way you two teased me. The Christmas decorations that you and Ellen attached to me as I slept on the sofa. Father Willington came to the door, and there I was, unaware and talking with him. You know, he never mentioned that to me. I can only imagine..."

Anna smiles in spite of herself.

"Her smiles, her silent laughter, how she would play with Johanna, and what a draughts champion she became...and...how much Rupert will miss her..."

Her smile fades as more tears spill down her cheeks, and she dashes them away on her sleeve, giving a determined nod.

"John, we're already talking about her in the past tense as if she's gone...and we're on our way to say goodbye to her right now...I don't know how well I'll hold up for this, but for Ellen's sake, I will do my best to make her, and you, proud of me."

He cups her cheek in his hand, wiping away her tears with his thumb.

"You should never question how proud I am of you."

He reaches into his pocket, draws out his pocket watch and looks at the time, goodbye ticking in his heart every bit as intense as his pulse. He hopes Ellen will always remember them. He looks, again, at the time, snaps it shut and whispers.

"It's time."

John looks at Anna, points to himself, places a hand over his heart, and points to her, tears springing to his eyes. She nods, wondering if this is what it feels like to stand before a hangman, knowing that in a short time, life as you knew it would end with a harsh finality. She pauses a moment as she looks up at him, points to herself, places her hand over her heart, and points to him. A shaky smile on his face, to give both of them strength, he whispers.

"I know you do."

He peers into her eyes, then looks ahead and puts the engine into gear and slowly pulls back onto the road. The sounds of the motor break the silence as they come closer to the end of life as they have come to know it. Continuing to stare out into the fog, she can barely make out something that is not a twisted tree. She leans forwards, straining to discern what it is.

"John, be careful. There's something next to the road. It's too foggy. I hope it's not an animal that's going to dart across."

"Yes, I'll be careful."

Seeing the cottage come into form through the fog, John feels sick that this is the last time they may be with their Ellen. As they come closer, a glint of light breaks through the fog, shining on golden hair. It is Ellen, sitting on a suitcase. Feeling as though her heart has stopped beating, she begins to open the door to the motor and speaks softly with the utmost urgency.

"John, stop the motor...please...now..."

Realising that Anna has opened the motor door, he stomps on the brake to prevent her from getting hurt. He recognises Ellen standing up and looking at them with a smile.

She smiles at the lady and the man, places her fist over her heart and pats it.

Anna steps out of the motor and in her haste, she almost trips over a rock and loses her shoe. The cold ground beneath one unclad foot goes unnoticed as she runs towards her sweet Ellen. Her heart races to see that Ellen wants to come home. She reaches Ellen and gathers her into her arms, not caring who might witness her tears and sobs of relief and happiness as she rocks Ellen and strokes her hair. She feels Ellen holding onto her as tight as she is able, tears moistening Anna's shoulder.

"My sweet baby girl...my sweet baby girl..."

John drives the motor close, stops, turns it off, gets out, and walks up to Ellen and Anna, filled with happiness that she is happy to see them, the ones she has chosen as her parents. He takes them both into his arms, holding them as though he would never let them go. When the glorious storm of happiness has dimmed, Ellen leans back from them.

She points to herself, points to her own head, points to the lady, points to the man, draws an X in her hand, places her fist on her chest, and points to herself.

Anna shakes her head no.

"Oh, John, she thought we didn't want her."

She points to herself, to John, and places her hand over her heart and points to Ellen to say that she and John love Ellen. She points to herself, taps three fingers on her chest, places her fist on her chest, points to Ellen, points to her own eyes, gestures 'round them, then puts her two index fingers together side by side, then holds out both hands as if weighing one thing against another. All this to say that she and John wanted Ellen to see for herself the place where her other family is and to make the decision to stay with her Swedish family or to come home with her and John.

Walking towards John, Anna, and Signe, 'Ellen', as they call her, Ingrid pulls her shawl 'round her shoulders, feeling a pang of loss, yet also warmth in her heart at the tender scene that chases the chill of a damp morning. She speaks softly, timidly as if she were the stranger here.

"Anna, John, I made it a point to tell Sig...forgive me...Ellen that you would be here this morning and it was completely her choice whether to stay or to go home with you. I tried as best I could to tell her, but her language is still so new to me. I went to get her for frukost...I mean breakfast and she was already out here, her bag packed and waiting for you. I guess she understood me. I was unable to coax her in for even a little bite to eat, so I brought it out to her whilst she waited for you."

Ingrid smiles gently at them, remarking to herself that they indeed have made a caring family together. Feeling that he is the only one capable of speech at the moment, John smiles at Ingrid.

"I can't tell you how happy Anna and I are at this moment. You truly have been kind to us in so many ways."

The sudden bump against him as Ellen wraps her arms 'round John and rests her head against his shoulder, causes the floodgates that he had held closed so tightly to open, and tears of joy erupt from his soul. As he holds her, he strokes her hair. Smiling through her tears at John and Ellen, feeling wholeness in their family, once again, Anna turns to Ingrid. She comes close to Ingrid and holds out both her hands to take Ingrid's in her own.

"Ingrid, as you have come to know, Ellen is our family. Now that we know you, you are part of our family as well. We mean that. Ellen has two families that love her, and that makes us all family. I will write to you of Ellen's news and please write to us of news from you so that we can tell Ellen. We can't thank you enough for showing us such kindness. You don't know what this has meant to all of us."

She smiles and squeezes Anna's hands.

"Meeting...Ellen...and knowing that my niece's daughter is alive, well, and loved gives me more lycka...I mean to say, happiness, than I had imagined possible. I could not ask for more peace than to know that she is with you and John. Now go, or your ship will sail without you."

She smiles, backing away from them as she watches John lift Ellen's bag into the motor. She must grow accustomed to calling her that, for it fits her better than Signe. She watches them get into the motor, hears the engine sing to life, and waves as they pull away, the fog muting the engine and embracing the motor into the future. She stands for a little time, pulling her shawl close about her, then turns to walk back into her small house, already feeling the emptiness within that Ellen's presence had filled. She understands, now. Ellen has two families who love her, two families to call her own. She wanders into the kitchen to pour another cup of coffee and sit, thinking how grateful she is that families are the greatest gift God can give.

Chapter Fifty
3 October 1926

In their state of mind when packing to come home, things were thrown into suitcases in no particular order. Returning late the previous evening, everyone was just too weary of doing anything but greet Sarah and Johanna with the utmost joy and then settle everyone into bed for a deep and dreamless sleep. Now, Anna sets herself to the task of unpacking, sorting through the jumble and putting things away. Johanna, ever-present and curious, is running back and forth, trying to help her mother and big sister. Finally, she crawls up on her parents' bed by clutching the quilt and climbing against the side of the bed, panting with her success. She plops herself down on the rumpled coverlet next to the suitcases with a triumphant grin as Anna watches with a soft chuckle.

"Janna hepted Cuppa! Janna heps Mamma do?"

"Yes, sweetheart. You can help. Here. You can fold this pretty scarf from the woman we visited. Isn't that nice?"

Johanna holds it up to her face and then drapes the large square over her head. She draws a circle 'round her covered face and laughs.

"Mamma! Janna petty!"

Snatching the scarf off Johanna's head, Anna grins at her baby girl.

"Yes, darling, you're pretty. Why don't you sit there and supervise to make sure I put things away properly? That would be a great help."

"Janna su...su...Janna hep Mamma!"

Anna hands Johanna some small things that she can hold whilst she continues to empty the suitcases, separating what needs laundering from what can be put away, directly. The only clue that someone has entered the bedroom is Johanna's stifled giggle, her hand covering her mouth. John walks into the bedroom with his finger held up to his lips as a signal for Johanna to be quiet. He sneaks up behind Anna, puts his hands on her waist and kisses her neck.

"Are you happy, sweet one?"

Anna turns 'round with a smile and slips her arms 'round his neck, kissing him with lingering tenderness.

"I couldn't be happier than I am right now, John. We're home safely, and our family is together. I couldn't ask for more, could I?"

Wrapping his arms 'round her, he smiles into her eyes.

"No, I don't think we could ask for more. By the way, where is Ellen? She wasn't in her room when I came up."

Johanna takes her hand away from her mouth so she can tell her parents what she knows; nodding with all the seriousness a child her age can muster.

"Cuppa 'side. Janna hep Cuppa a Cuppa 'side. Goggie seep on Cuppa seepybed."

John chuckles as he and Anna part from their embrace and John reaches over to ruffle Johanna's curls.

"Well, I guess that's our answer. I reckon she might be hoping William will walk by. I should try to contact him. He'll be happy to know that Ellen has returned with us."

Anna nods, moving closer to him again.

"Yes, that would be good. William deserves to know how much Ellen wants to see him."

A sly smile curving the corners of her mouth, she points to the side of her neck that John neglected to kiss when he came in.

"Before you try to reach William, with all the travelling we've done, my neck is a bit sore...would you mind...since you've missed a spot...?"

"I have? Well, we can't have that, now, can we?"

He leans down to kiss her neck, then takes her hands and brings them to his lips.

"I'll fix your aches and pains properly, later when we don't have a little girl pointing and giggling at us."

They look at Johanna, looking at her parents and laughing.

"Mamma Daddy kissa! Kissa Janna! Kissa Janna!"

She holds out her arms, and John scoops her up, kissing as much of Johanna's face as he can and then blowing noisily against her neck, eliciting squeals of delight. Shaking her head, Anna walks over to them, kisses Johanna's cheek and ruffles her hair.

"Now, you two scoot along and let me finish. John, if you wouldn't mind peeking out to see if Ellen is all right?"

"Of course, I'll check on her and then I'll try to reach William."

John sings a little nonsense song to Johanna as he carries her out of their bedroom and all the way downstairs. A happy heart brings a happy humming tune from Anna, trying to make sense of what might loosely have been called packing. Downstairs, John carries Johanna to the window near the front door, looking for Ellen. He sees her sitting on the steps, looking up the road one direction, and then down the road the other direction. Carrying Johanna to the kitchen where Sarah is happily humming as she works, he sets his little bundle of joy down to stand on the floor.

"Sarah, would you mind Johanna for a moment? I need to make a telephone call or two."

"Of course, Sir. I'd be glad. Miss Johanna, would you like a biscuit and a glass of milk?"

Leaving Johanna to happily accept Sarah's offer, John makes his way to the sitting room to telephone 'round and try to reach William with their good news.

Driving Mr Chelsey's lorry to the market to deliver a load of produce from a local farmer, William glances at the Thorpe home. To remember being with Ellen, he has walked past the house, stopping to look at it, knowing he would not see her looking out the window for him or throwing a soft animal out from the window to attract his attention. Once more, he cannot resist the urge and turns his gaze to Ellen's window, futility kicking him. Resolutely, he reins in his attention, focusing on his work and the destinations filling his time, but not his heart.

Ellen looks at a lorry approaching. Noticing William inside as it nears, she stands and runs out into the middle of the road. She stops, watching the vehicle grow smaller as it continues on its way. She lowers her head and holds her hands in front of herself. Looking back up, the lorry returning, her breathing quickens, and she smiles. Stepping up to the walkway, she stares as it pulls to a stop. Unable to hurry fast enough, William fumbles with the handle of the door and leaps out, not bothering to close it. He comes 'round and stares at her, wondering if his grief has finally made him go mad. Ellen smiles at him, clasping her hands in front of herself more tightly.

"Ellen?"

William closes the distance between them in a heartbeat, the smile on his face growing along with a spark of life he never thought he would feel again. Ellen's eyes are wide, staring at him, and she smiles, holding her arms out to him. Laughter bubbling up from his soul's joy, William gathers her in his arms and holds her tightly, his hand cradling one side of her head as he kisses her hair, as he whispers.

"I've missed you; I missed you so, so much. I thought I would never see you, again."

Leaning back from their embrace, he meets Ellen's misting eyes.

She smiles at the young man and taps her lips with her fingertip.

He smiles at her request that he kiss her. Happy to fulfil her every wish, William takes Ellen into his arms, again, leans down, and softly touches his lips to hers. His senses overflow with the warmth and tenderness of her lips that he thought would remain only a memory. Their kiss deepens, their lips joined as though they were made for one another. Holding her close, he rubs her back as he drinks in every nuance of this moment, feeling the vacuum within him filling. Ellen's hand slides up to the back of his head, her fingers run through his hair, and he feels her slender form relaxing against him. William's consciousness is consumed by the kiss they share, swept away by a sensation of drifting away into clouds. Coming to its natural close, their lips slowly part. They lean back from one another and William reaches into his pocket, pulling out a handkerchief to blot away Ellen's tears. Her hand cups his wrist as he erases the evidence of her emotion. Smiling at him, she steps back a pace.

She points to herself, points to her head, points to herself again, places a hand over her heart, and points to the young man.

A rush of joy flows through him as thick as the blood in his veins to see her tell him for the first time that she knows, now, that she loves him. He touches her face with his fingertips, his lips trembling with emotion.

"My sweet Ellen, I've loved you for so, so long...I don't know what it's like to not love you."

She looks at the young man and tilts her head to the side.

"Come with me."

He takes her hand, walks with her 'round to the back of the house, and through the garden gate, leading her to the swing. He guides her to sit on the swing and looks down at her as she stares up at him. Hoping that what he is about to do is not a mistake; he decides to trust his gut instincts that this could not be righter. William kneels, facing Ellen, and reaches into his pocket, finding the thing that has kept him clinging to hope in the face of impossibility. The small velvet box that holds the ring he intended to give her the day she went away brushes against his fingers. Before he realises what is happening, Ellen slips off the swing to kneel with him, facing him, her head tilted to the side.

Glancing out of the window, Sarah notices Ellen and William at the swing and calls out for John and Anna to come quickly, excitement filling her, unable to tear her gaze away. Hurrying at Sarah's call, John and Anna arrive in the kitchen and go to the window as Sarah's animated gesturing dictates. Breathless and silent, they watch the most delicate and fragile life emerge from unimaginable circumstances.

Looking into Ellen's eyes as she kneels with him, William chuckles that she kneels as well. He takes a deep breath, points to himself, places a fist on his chest, joins the forefingers and thumbs from both hands, interlocking them together, and points to her. His gestures are precise and out of the ordinary as he speaks aloud, his devotion to her from the depths of his being.

"Ellen, I want to marry you."

Ellen's eyes open wide, and she stares into his eyes, still as the most delicate statue. Hoping that he has not upset her, he reaches into his pocket, again, pulling out the box, and with shaking hands, opens it. He takes the ring in his fingers, marvelling at its delicacy, and holds the ring up to her. Multiplying his anxiety to a fever pitch, he watches her look at the ring, and then back up at him. His heart begins to beat a rhythm of fear that she has not responded as he had hoped she would, praying he has not lost her forever. Ellen's weeping commences as she looks at him, William's own eyes filling with tears. She reaches up to touch his tear with her finger and then takes another finger and touches one of her tears. Bringing her fingers together, she mixes their tears. With a smile, she gestures her reply.

She looks at the young man, points to herself, places a fist on her chest, joins the forefingers and thumbs from both hands, interlocking them together, and points to him.

He looks at her, hearing her silent reply in his heart and soul. He takes her hand, slips the ring on her finger, and then drinks in the glory of her peacefully radiant face. Ellen watches him put the ring on her finger, looks back into his eyes, and then traces her fingers on his cheek and across his lips. Closing his eyes, he revels in her gentle touch. Opening his eyes, he taps his lips with one finger, asking her to kiss him. Ellen rests her hands on his shoulders, leans close to him, and softly touches her lips to his, for the first time, granting his desire for her kiss. Embracing her with all his being his fingers barely touch her cheek as he feels her lips against his, knowing as only love can comprehend, that this moment joins their souls as one. His fingers whisper across her cheek, tracing the curve of her ear, and tenderly explore the curve of her neck. Time becomes the fragrance of eternal flowers, unfading, ever in the fullness of blooming. Finally, he leans back, looks into the eyes that are able to speak more eloquently than the voices of people limited by the spoken word. William opens his jacket, she slides her arms 'round him underneath his coat, and he wraps his coat and arms 'round her. Slowly, kneeling together, they rock each other in time to their heartbeats.

The happiest tears of all fill John and Anna's eyes as they stand witness to shattered impossibilities. No words could describe the expressions of two souls who declare to each other a desire to share their lives, united. Not the cold and contractual question, 'will you marry me', a soulless shard of tradition that forces a 'yes' or 'no' answer. This is as unique as Ellen and William are as they say, 'I want to marry you', words of truth and emotion joining two hearts, two minds, and two souls.

Chapter Fifty-One
11 October 1926

Driving home from Pulborough, John, Anna, William, and Ellen watch the countryside slide by as the motor chariots them to their destination.

"John, I'm so happy that Ellen and I found the perfect fabrics for the wedding dress she asked me to make for her. When we get home, I'll have my work cut out for me."

"Yes, you will. I can't get over the energy you've got, considering how you've been up with Ellen's nightmares for two nights in a row. You amaze me, Anna. And...whilst the two of you were on your quest, William and I managed to have a productive stroll, as well."

Looking at Ellen, the grin on William's face exudes his excitement at the impending marriage between him and the woman he loves.

"Mr Thorpe, you really didn't have to buy me these cufflinks. That's not to say I don't appreciate them, though. They're the nicest ones I've ever seen. But..."

Chuckling, John looks at William in the rear-view mirror.

"I know, I didn't. I'm glad you like them, though. By the way, since you're about to marry our daughter, don't you think it's time you called us 'John' and 'Anna'?"

Laughing, William nods and prepares to tease his future father-in-law.

"Yes, Mr Thorpe. I'll remember to address you and Mrs Thorpe correctly."

As they near Petworth, having taken the scenic route for Ellen's enjoyment, a lorry filled with timber forces them to slow their speed as it waits for a vehicle to leave what had been the Holmes farmstead. As they wait for the lorry to turn into the drive, Ellen pats William's hand and points. Piqued, Anna's curiosity spills forth.

"John, there's activity there. Shall we stop? Maybe we'll find out who purchased the property."

Nodding, John follows the lorry and parks in a grassy area where they will be out of the way. Turning off the motor, John gets out and helps Anna out of the motor whilst William assists Ellen. Staring 'round them, John and Anna cannot believe how different the place looks. The house has been painted, there are curtains on the windows, that horrid shed is gone, and a horde of smiling people whistle as they work. William looks at Ellen who is clutching his hand tightly, and he imagines that the expression on her face is that of wonder. From the roof of the house, a familiar voice calls out to William.

"Hey, mate! Fancy seeing you here! C'mon up and pitch in!"

Lewis waves, taking a moment away from his task. William looks up, smiles, and waves to Lewis with a grin.

"Lewis, old boy, come down. I've got news!"

Whilst Lewis congratulates William on his engagement to Ellen and stands aside to commiserate in jest, Father Willington emerges from the house. Wiping his hands on his trousers, he quickens his pace to meet their visitors.

"Well, what do you think of the place? Tidying up a bit."

John and Anna walk up to greet Father Willington.

"It's good to see you, Father. Anna and I were wondering who the anonymous buyer of this property was, and we're surprised to see you here."

Anna cocks her head to one side.

"Father, don't tell me you bought this?"

Chuckling, Father Willington shakes his head.

"No, not me, personally. I did petition the church to consider purchasing this for the community. Let me show you 'round."

Watching all of the activity 'round them, Ellen walks towards the house, stepping on the new boards of the porch, and peeking into the open door. The essence of delicious food meets Ellen as Clara notices her standing in the doorway, her hands folded in front of herself, looking 'round. Speaking over her shoulder to the other women in the kitchen, Clara's excitement is on full display as she walks towards Ellen to greet her.

"Oh, ladies! This is the young woman I told you about. Ellen."

Clara welcomes Ellen and gestures that she is happy to see her. Warmed by Ellen's smile, Clara takes Ellen's hand and leads her into the kitchen. Smiling women wave to Ellen as they cook a meal in, what is now, a cheerful and modern kitchen. One of the women looks at Clara with a nod that betrays an array of ideas.

"I would love to learn her language, Mrs Dewhurst, could you please teach me? Just in case I meet up with her somewhere, I'd like to greet her properly, at least."

The other women nod and speak at once, at what a splendid idea this is, certain that many people would like to learn as well. Clara promises to find a way to teach them, amazed at the outpouring of kindness and respect for Ellen. She turns to Ellen, points at the women, draws a smile on her face, and then points to Ellen, translating for her that these women are happy to meet her. Nodding with a small smile, her hands folded in front of herself, Ellen looks at each woman. Eager to show Ellen how the house has transformed, Clara takes her hand and shows her each room, explaining the new purpose for which they will be used. One of the women from the kitchen walks up to Clara with a glass of lemonade for Ellen.

"Thank you, Tillie. She'll enjoy this."

Clara pats Ellen's arm and waits for her to look down and then back up at her. She holds up the glass of lemonade with a tilt of her head, and Ellen nods, taking the drink and sipping the refreshment. Hearing the voices of Father Willington, John, Anna, and William as Father Willington gives his own tour, Clara returns her attention to Ellen. Led by Clara, Ellen's eyes are wide as she stares at each corner that greets her with a strange new life. Finally, Ellen stands at the doorway to the last room, staring at the place where she had been kept. The floors are sanded and polished, white curtains catch the breeze and billow their undulating beauty, and the walls are coming to life. A man who is painting the room hears their approach, doffs his hat, and grins at them as Clara introduces him to Ellen.

"Frank, this is the young woman I've been telling everyone about. This is Ellen."

"Nice to meet..."

Remembering that the dear young lass cannot hear, he nods his head and demonstrates his job of painting the walls. He holds out his paintbrush, points to Ellen, and then points to the wall, clumsily asking if she would like to try her hand at this. Ellen looks at Clara who nods and pats her hands together to say it is all right for her to participate if she would like to do so. Ellen hands Clara her glass and walks up to the man. He moves the paint-laden brush in up and down passes, showing Ellen how to apply the colour to the wall, and hands the brush to her. She emulates Frank's technique for several strokes and stops. She returns the paintbrush to Frank, touches the paint, and he chuckles when her eyes widen, and she steps back a pace. Ellen's finger marks clearly show on the wet paint. Ellen holds her fingers to her nose, sniffing, and then looks at the wall where Frank has painted, causing the fingerprints to disappear. Frank looks at Ellen with a nod and a smile, then a chuckle escapes when he spots the smear of paint on her nose. He fishes about in his pocket for a clean rag, hands it to Ellen, and points to his own nose to tell her that she might want to wipe away the yellow dot. She takes the rag, wipes her fingers clean, and dabs away the evidence of her curiosity from her nose. Handing the cloth back to Frank, he nods at Ellen to let her know that the paint is gone.

Joining Clara at the door to the infamous room, Father Willington, John, Anna, and William have watched Ellen join in the jolly activity that is evolving this place from one of horror and gloom to a place of purpose and fellowship. Ellen returns to the proud faces at the doorway and takes the glass of lemonade from Clara, finishing what is left of it, and hands it back to Clara. Clearing his throat, Father Willington gains the attention of their guests, Ellen follows suit as they all turn to look at the kindly shepherd of the church's congregation.

"I'd like to show you what is happening out back in the fields. Come with me."

Father Willington leads the way out of the house, leaving Clara to wave at them and stay behind to work with the women, again, preparing a veritable feast. They walk 'round the house to the rear where men and women, tilling the soil, work fields to prepare it for the following spring's planting. Gesturing to the side, he shows them the livestock gathered to breed and provide meat. He explains that so many people are unable to afford enough food for their families, that a community garden, divided into plots, gives the opportunity to feed, sell extra to markets, and even barter. Murmured comments between them, remarking at what a novel idea this is, turn to a conversation about William and Ellen's wedding.

"Father, Anna and I would like to talk to you at length, another time, about the details of the wedding. We'd like you to perform the ceremony, of course, and bring Ellen to the church so she will feel more at ease since she's never been inside and it could be intimidating. Of course, you'd need to learn Ellen's language, and it would be a small wedding. We think she'd be most comfortable and unafraid with only the people she trusts."

"Why, of course. Yes, I'll have Clara help me, and we'll speak soon of these details. I'd be honoured to officiate."

Whilst they continue talking about the farm's future benefits to the community, Ellen's attention is attracted to a child, a girl about four years of age. The little one grasps a pot of flowers in her arms from a wheelbarrow, holds it tight to her chest and walks towards a flower bed that adds colour and beauty to the exterior of the house. Unable to see her feet, the little girl trips over a clod of grass, falling, the pot spilling its contents on the ground. She sits up, looks at the mess, and begins to cry. Rushing to her, Ellen crouches down next to the child.

She points to the small girl, tilts her head to the side, moves her hands down the front of herself, and then pats her hands together.

Crying turns to hiccups of curious confusion as she looks at this woman moving her hands, not understanding that Ellen is asking her if she is all right. Ellen's smile makes her feel better, though, and she looks down whilst Ellen helps her to her feet, brushing dirt from her knees and dress. She watches Ellen pat her hands together, unaware that she is telling her that she is a good girl and everything is fine.

She points to herself, places her fist on the palm of her hand, points to the small girl, points at the dirt carrier and growing things, and points to the place with more growing things.

The little girl grasps the idea that Ellen is offering to help her, and she nods, holding the empty pot upright whilst Ellen picks up the flowers and scoops the dirt into the plant pot 'round the roots. Ellen takes the little girl's hand, and lifts the container into the child's waiting arms, and keeps a guiding hand on her back as the little one carries it to the flower bed. Ellen helps her set the pot on the ground and motions for her to tilt it slightly. Sliding the flowers into a hole, Ellen observes an earthworm wiggling its way out of the soil. She picks it up, rests it in her hand, and shows the little girl. At first, the child recoils with a look of disgust on her face that changes to curiosity as she watches Ellen stroke it with her fingertip down its length. Ellen holds her hand up for the child to see the creature arch itself and wiggle at her touch.

She points to the small girl and then points to the dirt animal, tilting her head to the side.

Tentatively, the little girl reaches out to touch the worm and pulls her hand back, an expression of surprise mixed with glee that she was brave enough to touch the little creature. She watches Ellen release it in a place where it will not be disturbed and continues to put the flowers and dirt into the hole. Smiling at the child, Ellen moves the pot aside, out of anyone's way.

She pats the dirt 'round the growing thing, points to the small girl, motions for her to come closer, and pats the soil.

Nodding with a big smile, the little girl crouches down and pats the dirt 'round the flowers, just as Ellen showed her. When they finish,

Ellen stands, reaches out to help the child stand, and brushes the bits of dirt that cling to her tiny hands. She stands back, looking up at Ellen and shines her best smile, then runs to her mother who has been watching the scene unfold, realising that this is the sweet young woman Mrs Dewhurst had described. Ellen stands, brushes off her own hands and walks 'round the house. She walks over to a pump outside and works the handle to begin the flow of water, washing her hands.

Captivated by the way Ellen treated the child, William turns to Anna.

"Anna, you saw how Ellen helped that little girl. What if...I know Ellen still grieves the loss of her own baby? What if she wants to have a baby, again?"

"I don't think that situation would arise, but if it did, William, we would work through it together, as a family."

Nodding, gratitude filling him for the blessing of not only Ellen's love but also the kindness and support of Ellen's parents. He knows he could not be a luckier man. Barely hearing the conversation between John, Anna, and Father Willington, William remains distracted, watching his fiancée. Ellen sees a woman come out to the porch with a bell in her hand. The woman notices Ellen looking at the bell with an air of confusion about her, so she motions for her to come. As Ellen approaches, the woman smiles, points into the kitchen where the table is full of food, points to the bell, points 'round to everyone working, and then motions for them to come. The woman realises the tilt of Ellen's head to the side means she would not hear the bell. She points to Ellen and motions for her to place her hand on it with her. Ellen touches the polished metal, and the woman rings the clapper once. She smiles when Ellen's eyes open wide, no doubt sensing the vibration. Pointing to Ellen, she holds up the bell and nods, hoping that she will understand the invitation to ring it. Nodding, Ellen grasps the thin rope hanging from the clapper and moves it back and forth as the woman had done. The woman points to the people who have ceased their labours and are walking towards the house to partake of the feast prepared for them. Smiling at the woman, Ellen nods and turns to walk back down the stairs and over to John, Anna, Father Willington, and William who cannot take his eyes off her. She stands next to William, looks up into his eyes and takes his hand, both watching the others enjoy their conversation.

"Say, John, why don't all of you stay and eat with us? I'm sure there's more than enough. We'd be happy to include you."

Shaking his head, he holds out his hand to shake that of Father Willington.

"Thank you, Father, but we'd best be on our way. Thank you for showing us 'round, and we share your enthusiasm for the potential good this will bring to the parish."

Father Willington shakes John's hand and extends a firm handshake to William.

"Of course. I'm happy we could share this with you and satisfy your curiosity. I'll in touch with you soon about wedding details, and I'll enlist Clara's assistance with learning Ellen's language as quickly as possible."

With a cheery wave to anyone noticing them taking their leave, John and William assist Anna and Ellen into the motor. Settling themselves into their own seats, John persuades the engine to life, and they continue on their way. Holding William's hand, Ellen glances back to the farm once more, then looks at him with the happiest of smiles.

Chapter Fifty-Two
23 October 1926

The second knock on his door this morning surprises William and causes him to look up from polishing his shoes and considering all the things John had discussed with him. The dizzying array of becoming a husband, the suggestion that he use Ellen's inheritance money to purchase the cottage directly behind John and Anna's home, and the offer of employment at John's haberdashery shop set his mind into whirling distraction. Placing the half-buffed shoes on the floor beside his shoeshine kit, he wonders who else might be calling on him as he gets up to answer the door. Filling the opened door, Lewis stands there, his usual jaunty grin replaced by a genuine smile.

"Lewis! What brings you here? Come in."

The lanky fellow walks into William's one-room bedsit and takes a seat on one of the two chairs by a small table under the one window where the morning light dances into the fullness of day. He places a box on the table, looking at William.

"I've brought you and Ellen a wedding gift. It ain't much, but I'm happy for you, mate, and I wanted to show it."

Sitting across from Lewis, William takes the gift that Lewis pushes across to him and stares at this unexpected gesture.

"Gosh, Lewis, I didn't expect...I mean, thank you. Whatever it is, I'm sure Ellen and I will like it very much. Thanks, again, Lewis."

"Well, it's my way of...well...thanking you both for settin' me straight, in a way. You were a friendly fellow before you met Ellen, but after, you just became...I don't know...different. In good ways. Ways that make me want to be better than I was. You're happy, William, about to get married to someone you truly love, a woman who loves you, too. I want to be the kind of man that a woman would want to love. I want to be a good and decent man like you, William. I want to be happy like you are. And...I hope we can be good friends from now on. I'd always hoped we could be friends. I...I know I haven't always been the kind of bloke that a fellow like you would want to gad about with."

Speechless, William sits back in his chair and looks at Lewis. The light on his face does not just come from the sunshine. Lewis exudes hope for his future, regret for his rapscallion ways that he has put behind him, and William cannot deny that Lewis has been making a significant effort to better himself. Who could begrudge a man for wanting to be happy with his life, to have friends, and find love? William smiles at Lewis and finds his words.

"Well, mate, I don't rightly know what to say, but I have glimpsed marked changes in you. I think you're on your way to finding the kind of life you want. I hope we can be friends and that you will find that special woman someday. Then, Ellen and I will be the ones bringing a wedding gift."

Standing, Lewis pats the parcel and takes the few paces closer towards William to clap his shoulder. William stands and offers his hand, which Lewis takes in a firm handshake, and flashes that old, familiar grin.

"Well, I'd best go. Mum wants me to tag along and listen to her complaints from shop to shop. Guess who gets to lug about her hampers. She's likely a bit off the track and tappin' her foot, waitin' for me. Anyway, give my best to Ellen, and I promise I'll cook up something and invite myself over for a meal."

Laughing, William shakes his head.

"Yes, I know your mum. And, I'll hold you to that meal. You'll be welcome. And...Lewis? Thank you for the gift. That was really good of you."

Nodding, Lewis covers the short distance to the door.

"'Till then, mate."

Before William can reply, Lewis lets himself out. Hearing the click of the door latching and the lean young man's fading trot down the stairs, William smiles and walks back to the table to look at the gift. He touches it; thinking whatever is concealed inside is most likely a thoughtful thing that is an expression of the decent fellow Lewis is becoming. He returns to his bed, sits down, and continues to polish his shoes to perfection, unwilling to let his bride-to-be see him on their wedding day wearing scuffed shoes.

Anna fits the silk underdress to Ellen's slender form as she stands still, her arms held out, holding her breath. The fabric of the dress itself is sheer, making the under-dress a necessity. The tulle that will cause the skirt to puff and billow is resting on the sewing machine, waiting for the stitches that will transform it into an elegant slip. Losing interest in her toys, Johanna gets up and walks over to the sewing machine, and her movements interrupt Rupert's nap. The foot pedal under the sewing table attracts her attention since this is the thing her mother pushes with her foot to make the machine hum to life. Crouching down, she reaches out and presses the pedal with both hands. The motor races, the needle stitches at a blinding speed, and the slip is sewn together in disarray. Rupert dashes out of the room, and a startled, Anna turns 'round, pricking Ellen with a pin, by accident. Wincing, Ellen's gaze follows Anna's. Johanna stands up, only to bump her head on the table. Frozen in pins, Ellen stands, watching Johanna with a visage of sympathy. Rushing to Johanna, Anna picks up her little girl and caresses her head to find evidence of injury. Satisfied that only Johanna's pride has fallen victim to this misadventure, Anna chides her baby girl.

"Sweet one, how many times have I told you that you shouldn't touch things in here? You have your toys, and if you want to look at something, you need to ask. Do you understand?"

"Yes, Mamma. Janna sowwy."

Johanna nods her head and then rests it on her mother's shoulder. Anna snuggles her daughter, grateful that her baby sustained no injury in her pursuit of folly. She mutters to herself with a sigh of pique.

"Oh, how I wish Sarah weren't so determined to clean the house from top to bottom. Sewing and minding Johanna is nearly impossible. Well, we'll do the best we can."

After she sets the errant child back on the blanket with her toys and a kiss, she returns to Ellen, still standing statue-like, no doubt remembering that unpleasant pinprick. Anna examines the fitted dress from every angle and nods with satisfaction. She unpins the dress from Ellen, marking where the seam must be, and Ellen's relaxing exhale of breath signals relief at the release from her cocoon. Draping the dress on the dress form, she pins it together so it will not fall off. Smiling at Ellen, she hands her the dress she had been wearing, and Ellen wiggles it back on and buttons it. The sewing machine reveals the disarray of stitches that Johanna caused. Shaking her head, Anna releases the fabric from the machine, cuts the threads, and takes up her seam ripper to free the ruined seam from its messy state. Ellen walks over to watch what Anna is doing. Seeing the slip sewn in such a fashion, with Anna preparing to right the disarray, Ellen taps Anna's shoulder. Anna looks up at Ellen with a quizzical expression.

She points to the baby, places one fist on top of the other several times, points to the lady's work, and then points to herself. She points to herself, places her fist against her chest, and then points to the lady's work. She points to herself, places her hand over her heart, and points to the lady's work.

Reluctant to acquiesce to Ellen's request that she leave the stitching as it is because she loves Johanna's contribution to her dress, Anna smiles, sighs, and nods, thinking that this IS Ellen's dress, and if this is what she wants, then this is what she shall have. She rearranges the fabric to accommodate Johanna's offering, and proceeds to stitch, shaking her head slightly, unaccustomed to incorporating imperfection into a garment. Ellen rubs the spot where the pin pricked as she walks over to Johanna's corner of the room and sits next to her as Johanna looks up at Ellen with a contrite expression clouding her otherwise happy face.

She points to herself, places her hand over her heart, and points to the baby. She points to the baby, draws an X in the palm of her hand, and points to the lady's work thing.

Johanna nods, looks over at her mother, and then places her hands together, moving them towards Ellen to apologise for touching the sewing machine. Smiling, Ellen catches the baby's hands in her own and kisses them. She picks up one of Johanna's dolls and makes it walk towards Johanna and then jump up to kiss her cheek. This elicits a giggle from Johanna, and she picks up a different doll, makes it walk towards Ellen, and bounces it up to kiss her cheek. Smiling, Ellen lifts the little one onto her lap, picks up a book and points to each picture, watching Johanna move her mouth.

Returning earlier than usual from the shop, John takes off his hat and hangs it up, hearing only the racket coming from the Hoover as he assumes Sarah must be cleaning in the sitting room. Sighing, he walks in and moves to a place where she might notice him above the roar of the Hoover. Out the corner of her eye, detecting John's entrance, Sarah jumps slightly and fumbles with the switch to silence the din.

"Oh, Sir, I didn't see you at first. I'm sorry I didn't finish before you..."

John holds up his hand to stop the flow of Sarah's apologies.

"It's all right, Sarah. I'm early. Where is Anna? I need to speak with her straight away."

"Oh, yes, Sir. Thank you, Sir. They're upstairs in the sewing room, all of them, working on Miss Cup's dress."

Oblivious to Sarah's gesture towards the staircase, John walks up, pausing halfway, and then continues to the sewing room. Anna, Ellen, and Johanna look up at him, and Anna smiles, excited to ask him about his chat with William.

"Sweetheart! You're early. Did you talk with William about working at the shop and buying the cottage behind us? It would be so nice to have them close, especially if Ellen..."

Noticing that John's grim face is not his usual 'happy to be home' expression, Anna's face clouds with concern.

"Yes, Anna, I spoke with William about all those things, and he gladly agreed to everything. Anna...I have some bad news. There's been an accident."

Staring at John and Anna, Ellen looks from one to the other, holding Johanna closer. Even Johanna notices her parents' cloudy exchange and sits perfectly still in her older sister's arms, staring. Anna stands, her hand pressed to her throat.

"Oh my God, John...not...no...not William? Please say it isn't William..."

Shaking his head, he motions for Anna to calm herself.

"No, no, it's not William, thank God. I'm sorry to say, though, Jane and Lewis, were crossing the street when a motor came 'round the corner and hit them. Jane is in hospital with severe injuries. Lewis...Lewis didn't make it."

Relief for William's safety mixes with sadness at the death of a young man who was trying to make something of himself.

"That's terrible, John. He and William were friends. I wonder if he knows? And Jane...as much as I've never liked the woman, I wouldn't wish such on anyone."

"I don't know. I heard the talk of it at the shop, and I came straight home."

Leaving Johanna's side, Ellen stands, walks over to John and Anna, and looks at both of them with a tilt of her head, asking in her way what is wrong. Realising that Ellen would have noticed that something distressed them, Anna turns to her to explain. She draws a frown on her face, walks two fingers across the palm of her hand, cradles her arms as if holding a baby, and then draws an X on her own forehead. Then, she draws a frown on her face, walks two fingers across the palm of her hand, draws an X on the palm of her hand, moves her hands down the front of herself, and then pats her hands together, informing Ellen that Lewis is dead, and his mother was hurt, thus clarifying their discussion for her. Stepping back a pace, her eyes wide, Ellen looks at Anna and then at John. She lowers and slowly shakes her head, walking past John to her room. John and Anna look at one another as they hear the bump-click of Ellen's door closing.

Chapter Fifty-Three
24 October 1926

Concern fills the kitchen during a quiet Sunday breakfast, overpowering the aromas of a hearty English breakfast. Ellen remains in her room, the door closed, except for letting Rupert out. Ellen's absence from the table intensifies the melancholy that shadows even the sunlight that is trying its best to fight its way through the curtains.

"Sarah, I'll help clean up. It's too quiet in here."

Nodding, Sarah quietly begins to pick up dishes and scrape scraps into a bowl for Rupert to enjoy. Anna fills the sink and begins to scour things, lost in her thoughts, not paying attention to the items she washes. The clink of dishes and cutlery makes a pitiful dent in the silence. John walks over to Johanna who lifts her arms to her daddy.

"Come, little one. Let's go outside to play, all right?"

He hefts his daughter into his arms and sets her on the floor to walk with him to the door leading to the garden, holding one finger of her father's hand, Rupert following them. Stepping outside and into their private oasis, Johanna runs to the bench and crawls up to sit, patting the place beside her. She tilts her head to the side, waiting for her daddy to join her.

"Daddy, Cuppa has owie?"

"No, sweetheart, I don't know why Ellen is in her room and doesn't want to come out or be disturbed. I hope she's not sad."

A bright smile illuminates Johanna's face from within her.

"Janna maka Cuppa happy!"

In spite of his worry, John smiles at his daughter and ruffles her curls.

"I know you would, little one. Now, let's go look at the flowers."

He takes Johanna's hand and helps her down from the bench, and together they wander about the garden, Rupert running circles 'round them. John asks her the name of each flower, and she replies with the names of people she knows and animals she can name.

The dishes done, the kitchen tidied, Sarah and Anna look at one another, sharing a sigh.

"Ma'am, Miss Cup didn't want her supper, she didn't want her breakfast. I wish I knew what was ailing her."

"I do, too, Sarah. At least, I didn't hear her have a nightmare during the night. I think I'll go up to her room and try to talk with her. I don't believe that it's right for her to be alone with thoughts that bother her for too long. If John comes back, would you tell him where I am?"

"Yes, Ma'am. I'll tell him."

Distracted by her imagination's musings about what might be causing Ellen to retreat to her bedroom, she enters the sitting room. Ellen stands at the bottom of the stairs, holding in her hand, something wrapped in cloth. Surprised, Anna looks at Ellen with a tilt of her head to ask Ellen a myriad of things that are running through her mind. 'Why have you kept to your room and refused meals? Why are you so sad when your wedding is only three days away?' Ellen holds the wrapped object closer to her and gestures.

She points to herself, places her fist on her chest, points to her own eyes, draws a frown on her face, and walks her fingers in mid-air.

Raising her eyebrows, Anna is incredulous that Ellen would want to visit Jane Adderley. Anna tilts her head to ask Ellen why.

She points to herself, places her fist on her chest, and nods.

Taking a deep breath, Anna nods. Apparently, Ellen is determined to see the woman who has not only been intolerably unpleasant, but committed an unforgivable sin with irreparable consequences when she told that man...Cyrus...Anna nods, points towards the front door, and holds up one finger, telling Ellen to wait by the front door. Then, Anna points to herself, moves her fingers beside her mouth to pantomime talking, and taps three fingers against her chest to tell Ellen she is going to speak with John. Nodding, Ellen walks to the entry hall, Anna watching her, shaking her head in disbelief. Anna walks out of the sitting room to the door leading to the garden and steps out, looking for John. Rupert runs to her, tail wagging, and jumping up with a wiggle. Ignoring the dog, she gestures to gain John's attention and motion for him to come close to her.

"John, I need the motor to take Ellen to visit Jane Adderley at the hospital. I know...I don't think she should, but she's determined."

Stupefied, that Ellen would want to visit that woman after everything...

"Well, if she's determined, there's no stopping her."

Kissing John on the cheek and waving to Johanna with a forced smile, she walks back into the house, closing the door behind her. Seeing Ellen at the front door, her hands in front of her holding whatever that is, Anna quickens her pace to join Ellen and pick up her handbag from its place on the entry table. She nods and opens the door for Ellen who walks directly to the motor and gets in, looking out of the window, watching Anna follow close behind. Stifling her misgivings, Anna gets into the drivers' seat, smiles at Ellen, and then chugs the engine to life. Their destination is not far, so they arrive in short order. Exiting the motor first, Ellen stops and looks up at the imposing building, staring at it. Anna catches up to Ellen, only to see Granny exit through the main entrance.

"Granny, I didn't expect to see you. How are you?"

"I'm all right, Anna. I heard you were amid wedding preparations. Congratulations are in order. I was here to visit with Jane Adderley."

"Thank you. I'll let Ellen know that you're happy for her. I...I was sorry to hear about Lewis. And Jane...how severe are her injuries?"

"Well, it seems that Jane will never walk again, at least that's what the doctor said...And, as for Lewis...he saved her life. He pushed his mother out of the way as best he could before taking the full force of the motor that hit them. Right now, I'm not sure if Jane is cursing him for her present condition or thanking him that she's alive. I've been visiting her and preparing her house for her release when she's ready. She'll need help, and I'm all she has."

Stunned, Anna just stares at Granny. Both notice Ellen's firm stance, looking up at the building where she spent too much time recuperating from a horror that should not have happened. Anna turns back to Granny, wondering if Ellen will lose her nerve to enter.

"It's kind of you to help her and, honestly, I wish I shared your ability to appear and help wherever needed. If anyone would have the patience of Job, it's you. Are there any funeral arrangements?"

"No, no...Jane just wants Lewis buried quietly. She wouldn't be able to go to a funeral in her state, as it is, so this is what she decided."

"I understand, yes. Granny, I think I should nudge Ellen out of her trance and ask her if she still wants to visit Jane. I don't have the faintest idea why..."

"Of course. Oh, and she's in a private room not far from the one Ellen had been in. She was...a little...well, you know how she can be at times."

"Yes, thank you for saving us a trip to the women's' ward. I hope everything goes well as you care for Jane. She couldn't ask for a more devoted guardian angel."

"I'm happy to help, Anna. It seems to be my purpose in life."

The two women embrace, and Anna watches Granny turn and

walk away, in the direction of the Adderley home. Returning her attention to Ellen, Anna approaches her at an angle from which she might see her and not be startled. Jumping slightly, shaken from her fixed gaze upon the structure that held her life and healing in the balance, Ellen looks at her. Anna tilts her head and points to the door, asking if Ellen is ready to go inside. Ellen nods and begins to make her way with Anna to and through the doors. At the single room nurses' desk, Anna steps forwards to inquire about the location of Mrs Adderley's room. The nurse gives Anna the room number but warns that the patient is not keen on having visitors. Nodding, Anna assures her that their visit will be brief. She turns to Ellen, moves close to her, and points in the direction of Jane's room. Together, as they walk, Anna notices that Ellen's head is held high, her back straight, the posture of a woman who possesses resolve and purpose. Shortly, they arrive at the private room where the only sound coming from inside is silence. Anna raps on the door and opens it slightly.

"Go away. I don't want visitors. I told that stupid nurse to keep people away."

"Mrs Adderley, it's Anna Thorpe and Ellen. Ellen wanted to visit you."

Anna pushes the door open, allowing Ellen to enter. A cold chill runs down Anna's spine when she looks at the woman who caused her family so much trauma. Ellen walks into the room and stares at Jane.

"What's she doing here? I told you I don't want any..."

Interrupting Jane, Anna sets Jane straight on one key point.

"Ellen wanted to come here. This was not my idea."

Whilst Anna remains at her post by the door, Ellen approaches Jane's bedside and holds out the wrapped object she carries in her hands. She places it in Jane's hand, a way of urging Jane to unwrap it. Jane stares at Ellen as she unfolds the corners of the handkerchief and then looks down at a carving of a woman holding a baby. She looks back up to Ellen and stares at her, slack-jawed.

She points to the carved wood and points to the tall woman and then points to the frown lady. She points to the sculpted baby in the woman's arms, points to the frown lady, and then cradles her arms as though holding a baby. She points to the frown lady, draws a tear down her cheek from her eye, points to the frown lady, cradles her arms as though holding a baby, and then draws an X on her forehead.

"Mrs Thorpe, what on earth is she going on about? What is this?"

Anna takes a deep breath, now understanding why Ellen would not leave her room, and approaches a few paces closer to translate.

"Ellen said...the woman in the carving is you, and the baby in the carving is Lewis. She knows you're grieving that he died. She stayed up all night to make that for you."

Jane stares back down at the carving in her hands, touching it with her fingertips as she fights back the tears with misplaced pride. A voice barely above a whisper escapes her throat as she looks back up at Ellen.

"But...but...I hurt you."

Ellen turns to Anna, tilting her head to the side. Looking at Ellen, Anna explains what Jane said. She points to Jane, moves her fingers by her mouth as if talking, points to Jane, gently makes one fist pound on the palm of her other hand, and then points to Ellen. Ellen looks back to Jane.

She nods, points to herself, and points to her head.

Jane's eyes open wide and she shakes her head.

"You...knew?"

Jane's eyes fill with tears that threaten to spill over and looks at the carving, staring at it. Finally, a broken whisper is all Jane can manage.

"Please. Please go. I need to be alone."

Nodding, Anna pats Ellen's arm, waiting for her to look down and then back up to her. She points to herself, points to Ellen, and then points to the door to show that it is time for them to leave. Ellen nods, takes Anna's hand, and they walk to the door and out into the hallway. Anna turns to close the door, symbolically and physically closing the door on a chapter in their lives that should never have happened, a chapter she will always remember. A chapter that shows her how Ellen is more forgiving, more compassionate, braver, and a finer woman than she will ever be. Together, a humbled mother and subdued daughter make their way to the door where freshness and purity await them. Emerging into another world of sunshine, hope, and promise, they walk to the motor and get into it. Ellen places her hand on Anna's arm before she is able to start the engine. Anna tilts her head to the side, asking in silence why Ellen stays their journey home.

She points to herself, places her fist on her chest, points to her own eyes, and taps two fingers on her wrist.

Anna nods, understanding Ellen's desire to find comfort and reassurance with William. She coaxes the engine to life and directs their route towards his humble bedsit.

William sits on his bed, stunned and saddened that Lewis lost his life when he had only begun to pursue hope for his future. The gift he gave to them rests on his lap. As William's hands move across the paper, he can picture in his mind the care that went into his efforts to wrap this box. He thinks back to how he had so often avoided Lewis and now, they were just starting to become good friends. He finds himself pulling at the folds of paper, sliding the wrapping off, and allowing it to float to the floor. He stares at the box and slowly lifts the lid, laying it aside. Inside, he notices an envelope atop of the paper stuffed 'round its contents. He picks it up and reads, in surprisingly legible handwriting, the words, 'To William and Ellen'. Slipping the letter from the envelope, he reads what might have been the last words Lewis wrote.

Dear William and Ellen,

I'm really happy that the two of you are married, now, and starting your new life together. I know you'll have a lifetime of happiness and that even in hard times, you'll stay strong. I believe now that there truly can be two people meant for each other, because of you. One day, I would be honoured that the two of you be my guests for supper, once I can cook something edible. Thank you for allowing me to know you. I know what real love is, from what I see in you and Ellen.

All my best,
Lewis Adderley

PS: William, I know I've been a lout over the years, but I want those parts of me to fall away. You've known me as a perfect cad, and I don't blame you for not wanting to be my friend. This is a new start for you, with Ellen, and for me, becoming a better man. I've always wished that we could be friends, William, and I really hope we can. Things are looking up for both of us, mate, and we're going to make the best of it. I know you're going to be happy, and I know I'm going to be just as happy, someday.

Hoping to be your friend,
Lewis

With a lump in his throat, he lays aside the letter and reaches into the packing. A pair of pepper and salt shakers in the figures of a bride and a groom look back at him with their painted smiles. Holding them in one hand, his elbow resting on his knee, he covers his eyes, feeling sadness for Lewis that he never thought he would feel until now.

Ellen opens William's door and stands, looking at him with her hands folded in front of herself. Startled by Ellen's unexpected visit, his hands replace the gift into its box, and he sets it aside, standing, his visage changes in an instant from grief to worry. He cannot fathom why his love's face begins to contort with tears flowing from her eyes. Moving closer, she begins to gesture.

She points to herself, draws an X on the palm of her hand, places her fist on her chest, points to the young man, swipes one hand away from herself as it passes over the palm of her other hand, and points to herself.

He watches her tell him, 'I don't want you to leave me'. His heart sinks for what might have caused her to say that. He slowly walks up to her.

"No, no, no..."

He touches her cheek, looks deep into her eyes, then guides her head to rest on his shoulder. As his arms wrap 'round her, he feels her body shake against him as she cries. He gently kisses her head, then strokes her hair, and buries his face in her hair and whispers.

"Oh, My sweet Cup. I will never leave you. I promise that I will never leave you."

Chapter Fifty-Four
15 November 1926

"I've brought the post, Ma'am. There's a telegram for you, as well."

"Thank you, Sarah. Might I have some tea whilst I go through these?"

"Of course, Ma'am."

Sarah places the post on the kitchen table in front of Anna and walks over to the sink, reaching over to the cooker for the kettle. She fills it from the tap, places it on the burner to heat. Bustling about the kitchen, she finds a clean cup and saucer for Anna's tea.

"Oh, I am so disappointed, and John will be, too. Mrs Mortenson cannot come to Ellen's wedding. I'll have to tell Ellen since she knows we invited her. We did give her terribly short notice, I'm afraid, but we've had such a short time to prepare, and the wedding is on Wednesday. Oh, my...that's the day after tomorrow! Goodness. She said a box was to follow with a gift for William and Ellen and a surprise. Hmm...I wonder what that could be. Oh well, it's a shame she can't deliver it in person. It would be good to have her join us."

Anna starts to stack the post that John will need to have when he comes home and notices there is a letter addressed to Miss Sarah Brown.

"Sarah, this letter came for you."

"Thank you, Ma'am."

Sarah reads the return address on the envelope and then slips her finger under the flap to work it open. Scanning the contents of her letter, she fails to hear the teakettle sing its readiness. Unbidden, she sits down at the table, the letter shaking in her hand like a dead leaf on the wind of a changing season. Tears come to her eyes, and her pinny serves as a handkerchief to soak them away. Noticing that Sarah doesn't hear the kettle, Anna looks at her with curious concern as she gets up to pour herself a cup of tea, then goes to the cupboard to collect one more cup and saucer. She makes Sarah tea as well, and brings both cups to the table, setting one in front of Sarah.

"Sarah? What is it? Is it bad news?"

Kicking herself for stating the obvious, Anna waits for Sarah to compose herself enough to explain her reaction to the letter. Her hand to her breast, Sarah takes several deep breaths to find her voice, wavering though it might be.

"Ma'am, it's my papa. He...he had an attack that left him...oh, Ma'am, I can't speak it..."

Sarah hands the letter to Anna. As she takes the letter from Sarah's shaking hand, Anna dreads the news that has caused Sarah such distress. She smooths the crease in the paper with her fingers and begins to read.

My dearest Sarah,
Please, please come as soon as you are able. Your papa has had an attack of apoplexy, according to the doctor. He lies abed, unable to move or speak. I cannot manage alone, even though your brother and sister do what they can whilst still caring for their own little families, I desperately need you here to help me care for him through the nights and, well, he needs every care imaginable. The doctor told me that your papa is in dire condition, and although he could live for some time this way, it is possible that he could have another attack that would end him. Surely, your employers will understand that you are needed here, and I am saddened for you that you must tell them this news. Please, hurry.
Your loving mum

Stunned by the palpable desperation in the penned words, Anna lays down the letter, gets up, and walks 'round to Sarah, putting her arm 'round her shoulders.

"There, now, Sarah, don't you worry. You've no need to give notice, and we will have you there before you know it. You're family to us, too, and family does what they can to help."

Sarah's tears turn to sobs as she looks up at her employer and then stands.

"Ma'am, I know you mean well, but forgive me for saying and I mean no offence, but I've never felt a part of this family. I...I...know you all meant well by what you say and do, but I'm just Sarah, the housekeeper and nanny."

As though she had been slapped, Anna takes a step back and stares at Sarah as she continues to speak.

"Please understand, I love all of you, I truly do, Ma'am. Everything I do is not just because you pay me, it's because I want to take care of the people who mean as much to me as my own kin. When...when you and Miss Cup were sick, I wanted to help in more ways to take care of you both. All I could do was keep busy, so I wouldn't worry. When that man...that evil man came for Miss Cup and took her away and left you broken in body and spirit, Sir devoted his attention to you, as he should have, Ma'am. I could do nothing but my job and be a mother to Miss Johanna because I was so afraid, she was slowly losing her own mother, even though it wasn't my place to show so much love to the little one as I did. My worry for Miss Cup was unbearable. I missed her so, and my imagination ran wild with the horrible ideas of what might have been happening to her. Even when I heard her having her nightmares night after night, right in the room next to mine, I wanted to run in to her and give her comfort, but it wasn't my place. When Miss Cup came home, I wanted to take her in my arms and tell her everything would be all right. But all I could ever do was my job. I worked and worked and worked to keep my mind away from the loneliness of being invisible to the people I loved and to ease my own pain of what was happening 'round me. I was, and am, alone. My whole life, the people I love leave me...long ago, a beau...my sister...Miss Cup...and now my father is more dead than alive. Now, I'm the one who has to leave the family I've come to love. Forgive me, Ma'am, but I needed to speak my heart before I go."

Eyes wide, the truth of Sarah's words squeezing the life out of Anna's heart, she stares at the woman who had become such an integral part of their lives, who they thought of as family but had never actually treated as such. Digesting the bitter outpouring of Sarah's heart, she tries to catch her breath. She sits on the edge of the nearest chair, looking up at Sarah, whispering through tears that express their failure towards someone who has given everything of herself, receiving nothing but wages in return.

"What have we done? Oh, Sarah, all this time. Why didn't you..."

"It. Wasn't. My. Place, Ma'am. That's why. I didn't want to tax you with my petty feelings when you had larger problems to manage. I'm nothing. Invisible. I...I'm sorry, Ma'am. I...I should go pack my things."

Standing, her body feeling numb with failure, Anna reaches a trembling hand to Sarah.

"Can...can you at least stay for Ellen's wedding on Wednesday? It's the day after tomorrow, and it would mean the world to Ellen...and to us...for you to be a part of her special day with William. John and I will drive you to the train station immediately after the ceremony so you won't have to hire a motor."

Looking down at her feet, Sarah nods, wipes her tears on her pinny and then looks up to the mistress of the house.

"Yes, Ma'am. I can't thank you enough for that. Yes, I would like to stay to see Miss Cup and Mr William marry, more than anything. Oh...if you don't mind, Ma'am, I should go to the telegraph office and send a message to my mother to tell her when to expect me and I should purchase a train ticket..."

"Let John do that. I'll ring him at the shop and have him send the telegram and buy your ticket. I'll explain the situation to him when he gets home. I guess I should go up to tell Ellen."

"Thank you, Ma'am, for your help...I...I want to be the one to tell Miss Cup, after all, I'm the one leaving."

"But how? You've never learnt her language..."

Her cheeks turning a slight crimson, Sarah makes her confession.

"I didn't want to learn it, at first. I knew she was a sweet soul and if I could communicate with her, I'd come to love her more than I wanted to...and...I was afraid that if she went away, it would just hurt too much and when she was taken away, I was right. I learnt it...practised it alone in my room...I knew all along. I'm sorry, Ma'am. I'll go tell Miss Cup, now, and then start packing."

Sarah looks into Anna's eyes, both viewing each other through the blur of their own sorrow. Sarah's sadness, born from the leaving people she loves to return home to care for her father and kin who are just as dear to her as her own life. Anna's grief, borne of the loss of a woman who could have been their friend, a member of the family in more than superficial good intentions, a dear woman who did not deserve to be ignored, left to carry the burden of neglect that was heaped upon her shoulders. Anna shakes her head and takes Sarah's hand, looking down at the clasp that should have been commonplace but is now, a useless gesture to amend their sin of omission.

"No, Sarah, there's no need to apologise. You've spoken the truth from your heart as Ellen does. It's me, us, who need to make amends, too little to matter, too late to repair. John and I failed you. We...we can never make that up to you."

Looking back down at her feet, Sarah pulls her hand out of Anna's grasp and whispers.

"I'll go up and talk to Miss Cup, now, Ma'am."

Turning away from Anna, Sarah walks out of the kitchen and Anna can hear her retreating footsteps through the sitting room, fading as Sarah makes her way upstairs. Anna walks over to the telephone, rings John at the shop, and tells him what he needs to say in the telegram to Sarah's mother, promising to explain everything later.

Sarah stands for a moment, taking a deep breath; she gathers her courage to face the most upsetting thing she has ever encountered. Pushing the door open, she watches Ellen for a little whilst, unnoticed, as Ellen folds her things, placing them in piles on her bureau, gathering the memories contained in treasured objects and putting them together.

She sees Ellen's happiness and is overcome by a torrent of guilt flowing through her. She enters the room to a place where Ellen will notice her and waits. Soon, Ellen looks at her and smiles, tilting her head.

Sarah pulls a chair close to the bed, pointing to Ellen and patting the bed, asking her to sit. Ellen leans her head and walks over to the bed, sits down, and stares at Sarah. Meeting Ellen's eyes with bravery she does not feel, she points to herself, places her fist on her chest, moves her fingers near her mouth as though speaking, and then points to Ellen, telling her that she wants to talk with her. Ellen's face registers immediate shock with her eyes widening and jaw dropping slightly.

She points to the kind lady, points to her head, points to herself, and moves her fingers near her mouth.

Nodding, Sarah makes her silent confession that, yes, she knows Ellen's language, and has, in fact, known all along.

Tilting her head to the side, she shrugs her shoulders, points to the kind lady, draws an X in the palm of her hand, moves her fingers near her mouth to pantomime talking, and points to herself.

The tears coming to Ellen's eyes, show Sarah, now, how wrong she was to close her heart to Ellen. It was wrong to withhold the joy of friendship that would have outweighed any pain. She points to herself, pulls her arms crossed tight against her chest, points to Ellen, and then sweeps one hand over the palm of the other away from herself. She wonders if Ellen will understand and forgive her fear of Ellen leaving. She places her palms together near her chest and moves them towards Ellen, asking forgiveness. Sarah watches a solitary tear roll down Ellen's cheek as she continues her explanation. She points to Ellen, sweeps one hand over the palm of the other away from herself, points to herself, places her hand over her own heart, and then places her forefingers together and draws one down from the other. Sarah needs Ellen to know how broken her heartfelt when Ellen was taken away from them. She waits for Ellen to gesture something...anything. Ellen stares at Sarah, both shedding silent tears. She gets up to walk a few paces away and then turns to face Sarah with tears streaming down her face.

She taps two fingers on her chest, taps three fingers on her chest, places her finger against her nose, taps two fingers on her wrist, points to the kind lady, and draws an X on the palm of her hand.

Sarah nods, looking down at her hands. No, she never had a name. Ellen waves her hand to draw Sarah's attention and waits until Sarah looks up at her.

She points to the kind lady, points to her chest, draws a circle on her chest with her forefinger, and points to the kind lady.

Her eyes fill with tears at such a gift. A name. She has a name in Ellen's language. Sarah called Ellen 'Miss Cup' to express her fondness for her, but no one noticed that. She never went further to show her how she loved Ellen as much as she cherished the rest of the family. Regret, on top of regret, atop more regret suffocates the room. Now, Sarah braces herself to deliver the worst tidings. Looking up with vision clouded by tears, she meets Ellen's eyes. She points to herself, sweeps one hand over the palm of the other away from herself to say that she must leave.

Leaning her head to one side, she shrugs.

Owing Ellen a reason for her departure, answering Ellen's question, 'Why?', Sarah points to herself, places her fist against her chest and pats it, draws an X on the palm of her hand, moves her hands down the front of herself, and then pats her hands together. As Anna had come to find out, Ellen knows, now, that Sarah's father does not feel well. There are no gestures to convey just how ill he is, but Ellen must know that it is severe enough that she must leave.

She looks at the kind lady with a tilt of her head to the side, points to the kind lady, places her fist against her chest and pats it, and then draws an X on her forehead.

Sarah's silent tears turn to sobs as she shrugs her shoulders and shakes her head. She does not know. Her mother does not know. The doctor does not know. Shall her father die? Nobody knows...not if, but when. Feeling chastised under Ellen's tearful scrutiny, she watches Ellen ask the question she has not wanted to form into cogent thought.

She points to the kind lady, sweeps one hand over the palm of the other away towards herself, and points down.

Looking back down at her hands, Sarah shakes her head, knowing that she will ever be able to return to this house and the people within who she has come to love with a devotion that rivals that of her kin. The wracking sobs return to Sarah's body as she looks up at Ellen who has come close to her. Ellen's arms are open wide, tears streaming down her face, and Sarah stands, gratefully accepting the embrace that plainly grants absolution for her own sins of omission. She has failed Ellen and at the same time, cheated herself by keeping her distance. She has withheld affection that Ellen deserves and would have wanted. She should have told Ellen and the rest of the family that she loves them deeply long before now. Now, it is too late. Holding on to Ellen, she feels a gentle rocking motion and Ellen's hands rubbing her back. Sarah's guilt reluctantly recedes into thankfulness that Ellen can find it in her heart to forgive and reach out with comfort when Sarah had intended to come with some small consolation for Ellen.

Chapter Fifty-Five
16 November 1926

Clara, Father Willington, John, and Anna sit 'round the kitchen table after a mouth-watering supper prepared by Sarah. They converse whilst Sarah prepares to perform her usual tasks after serving everyone tea. Laughing spontaneously and holding up her hand, Anna cannot resist sharing a little episode of humour with their guests.

"I must tell you something amusing. Ingrid, Ellen's great-aunt in Sweden, sent a rather large box, and we assumed it would be a wedding gift for Ellen and William. John opened the box, and inside were two boxes. One was wrapped like a gift with a card attached for Ellen and William. The other was wrapped in ordinary paper with my name on it. John handed me the box, intended for me, and took the wedding gift to the dining room with the other gifts. At any rate, when I opened the box, I found a note and my shoe! We probably told you about Ellen sitting on her suitcase and John's panic as I dived out of the motor to go to her. In doing so, I lost one shoe. At the time, I didn't notice, of course, but here, Ingrid had sent me my shoe! The note included a postscript. She wrote, 'I thought you might need this. They were much prettier as a pair.' John and I shared a good laugh over it."

Whilst the four of them chuckle at Anna's anecdote, Sarah is lost in her thoughts that this is the last supper she has cooked for the family. Tonight, was the last time she tucked little Johanna into her bed. Tonight is...She shakes her head, plunging her hands into the soapy water, back to her role as housekeeper and nanny. Ellen had taken her leave after the meal to sit with Rupert in the sitting room after Sarah declines her offer to help tidy after their supper. Those who remain, who can hear and speak, continue their conversation without fear of causing Ellen discomfort. Father Willington expresses his thoughts regarding the wedding.

"I think it was wise to choose the mid-week for the wedding. Ellen won't be frightened and overwhelmed by a throng of people, and even Saturday has its bustle in the church with the choir and organist milling about. At first, I was surprised that you specified that there be no music, but after a moment's thought, it made sense."

Chuckling, John replies to Father Willington's appraisal of the wedding plans.

"Well, we don't know a throng of people, so it wouldn't be a large wedding, anyway. It's just us, the two of you, Sarah, and Johanna. You're right, though; Ellen is more comfortable amongst the people she knows and trusts. As for music, this is her wedding, so why include something like music that would make her feel excluded?"

Clara, ever the rebel against tradition speaks her mind.

"It's a shame that William couldn't be here tonight, although it's bad luck for the groom to see the bride before the wedding."

Nodding, John agrees with Clara.

"Yes, we had to urge William to make himself scarce, earlier. He doesn't believe in bad luck, either, yet, it is a tradition. He argued that traditions were made to be broken."

Clara emphatically agrees with William's perspective as her soft chuckle punctuates the moment. Thinking of William's youthful and modern outlook with amusement cannot overshadow the clink and splash of dishes in the sink. Hearing Sarah, he remembers Anna relating the tearful exchange between them. John pauses, turns to look at Sarah and realises that they have already slipped back into their old, negligent ways. If Sarah is family, he and Anna should live up to their apology and make amends, even if both come too little and too late. He looks at Anna, nudging her foot with his, and he gives a subtle nod towards Sarah, silently reminding her of what is right, that Sarah should join them. Taking John's cue, she nods, turning to Sarah.

"Sarah, you made such a lovely meal, why don't you come and sit with us. I'll do the dishes later. They'll be here. You...won't be, soon."

Turning to face Anna, Sarah's expression is one of surprise. Nodding, she wipes her hands on her pinny and approaches the table. John smiles at Sarah, getting up to pull out a chair for her, and holds up one finger.

"Take your pinny off, Sarah. You're joining us as family."

Again, speechless, Sarah nods, removing her pinny and walking over to the wall where she hangs it on a peg. She returns to the table and sits on the chair that John is holding for her, finally finding her voice.

"Thank you, Sir. I mean, John. I'm sorry. It's difficult to call you and Ma'am by your Christian names."

Anna feels the curious glances of their guests and briefly explains.

"Sarah deserves to be treated like family, and we've asked her to call us John and Anna. It's only right, as we've always called her family. As for her leaving, Sarah's own family is in dire need of her help, and she will leave after the wedding tomorrow. John and I are going to take her to the train station directly after the ceremony."

Their confusion fading, Clara and Father Willington smile at Sarah with a welcoming spirit that causes any discomfort to dissipate. Clara is the first to affirm that this new manner of conduct is a welcome change from traditional employer-servant relations.

"Well, Sarah, we'll all miss you terribly, but I'm sure I speak for everyone when I say that we're all glad that your family can depend on you to do the right thing. I, we, hope that whatever the situation, that all will be well in the end."

Unaccustomed to sitting at a table with such esteemed people and treated as an equal, all Sarah can do is nod and whisper her reply to Clara.

"Thank you. I hope...I'll do my best to help."

"So, Sarah, it must be disappointing with a bit of relief that there won't be a reception. I know you'd have outdone yourself with preparations. You have a great many talents if you've not heard that before now."

"Father Willington, I'd have gladly prepared anything at all if...if I didn't have to leave under these circumstances."

Anna reaches for Sarah's hand, giving a reassuring squeeze. John sits back in his chair and realises that Sarah is the only one without a cup of tea. He excuses himself for a moment, gets up, and walks to the cupboard to find a cup and saucer. He pours the tea and adds sugar, just the way he has observed Sarah's preference. He returns to the table, setting the teacup in front of Sarah.

"Here you go. I thought you'd enjoy a fresh cup."

Changing the subject to wedding details to spare Sarah embarrassment at her new treatment as a member of the family, Anna turns to John and speaks for them both.

"We'd discussed how a wedding reception would have been nice since it would have been an intimate gathering to celebrate, but her needs are paramount. We're not certain she'd understand a reception, and it would be difficult to explain. This is her special day, and she should be able to enjoy it to the fullest."

Father Willington lowers his teacup, nodding his agreement all 'round.

"I agree, Anna. I hope you'll be proud that Clara has taught me Ellen's language to her satisfaction. I've written the service to satisfy the legal points that must be covered, but in Ellen's language. Don't laugh, but I've been practising in front of a looking glass to gesture and speak things correctly."

Clara pats Father Willington's hand and chuckles.

"Yes, you've been a diligent student. I'm sure we're all proud of you."

Murmurs of assent go 'round the table when John's eyes open wide. He holds up one finger, smiles, and gets up from the table.

"Since we won't be having a reception with music, dancing, and all of the trimmings, I think I'll go ask my daughter to dance, now."

Those remaining seated exchange glances, watching him walk out of the kitchen. Shortly, the wireless in the sitting room blares music at a deafening volume. Laughter bubbles from Anna and Sarah as Clara and Father Willington nearly jump out of their skin and jumble their questions to them, wondering what is happening. Getting up, Anna motions for them to follow her. They all follow Anna and Sarah out of the kitchen, feeling their bones shake with the intensity of sound. Stopping at the door to the sitting room, they witness John holding out his hand to Ellen, bowing slightly from the waist. Ellen smiles up at him, places her hand in his, and rises to her feet. Father and daughter begin to dance to the rhythm of the music, not the music itself. The tender smile of a wife and mother graces Anna's face as she walks over to the wireless and reduces the volume to something tolerable. Returning to the others at the doorway, she smiles with a wavering voice.

"John is always going to remember this dance."

Speechless at the love flowing between Ellen and John as they move, there is not a dry eye amongst them as they watch. This is not a dance of obligation or one that finishes when the music stops. This is a dance of the heart that will carry on to its natural close. Clara, Father Willington, Anna, and Sarah, as they watch, are all thinking of this new beginning for Ellen and how many 'last times' have happened this day.

Remembering with a painful tug back to reality, Sarah taps Anna's arm and whispers.

"I don't mean to be impolite, Ma'...Anna, but I should finish packing..."

"Yes, yes, of course. If you need help with something or need me, please let me know."

Sarah convinces herself that a smile is appropriate as she nods to Anna, Clara, and Father Willington who silently bid her goodnight. She quietly excuses herself and makes her way inconspicuously towards the staircase. Ascending the steps, she stops, turns 'round, and holds the railing. As she looks down, observing the people she has come to love as family, her hand strokes the smooth wood of the railing, remembering how many times she polished that railing to glossy perfection. With a lump in her throat and a sigh, she witnesses the last time she will be a part of a happy family moment in this house. Humble sadness balanced with gratitude follow her as she turns to walk the rest of the way up the stairs and retreat to her room. Family. Her last night in this house, and they treated her as a part of their family. Her heart is more happy than sad, knowing that John and Anna are not perfect, but they do try to make amends when they feel they have wronged someone. She enters her room, looking at the emptiness that shouts the finality of her last night in this house, in this bed. Her other suitcases sitting by the door, fill her with an ache at leaving this family and fear of what she will find at home. As is her habit, she shakes her head and closes her inner self by immersing herself in practical activities. One by one, she opens each drawer, checking that nothing is left behind. Opening the last drawer, a few items remain that need to fit in a bag. She walks to her bedroom door, hefts the suitcase that still has space within, carries it across the room, and lifts it onto the bed. She piles the remaining items next to her bag on the bed. She leaves out only a few items she will need on the morrow, her best dress, under things, shoes, and toiletries. Satisfied that she has left nothing behind, she changes for bed, folds today's garments neatly, placing them with the other items that require space in her suitcase, and slips into her nightdress. Opening her suitcase to pack the last of her belongings, she looks down into the valise and sees a cuddly toy animal on top of her clothes, looking up at her. Pent-up emotions flow freely as she picks up the toy and sits on the bed, clutching Ellen's gift to her, rocking back and forth, as Ellen had rocked her in their embrace the day before.

Chapter Fifty-Six
17 November 1926

"You look handsome and smart, today, William. I like those cufflinks."

Outside of the church, John cannot resist the urge to tease the groom, smiling, and easing any nervousness that William might feel. William straightens his sleeves repeatedly, looking 'round them with a happy, but nervous smile on his face.

"To tell you the truth, John, I have been up most of the night. I would say that I am more excited for this moment to come than nervous. I can't believe that soon, Ellen and I will be husband and wife. I know that you and Anna have your concerns, but please know that my feelings for Ellen and...about everything, haven't changed."

"I am glad to hear that. We trust what you have said, and we are happy to have you in our family. Do you have the ring with you?"

Clara walks up to the church before William can answer. Her steps are brisk, matching her happy anticipation for Ellen and William's wedding and she approaches John and William, smiling happily at these two fine men.

"Hello, it's a happy day, isn't it, William? I could hardly sleep for excitement and happiness for you and Ellen. John, you and Anna must be so proud."

Whilst Clara, William, and John exchange pleasantries, Anna helps Ellen fasten her gown in the back and then has Ellen sit down on one of the chairs so she can brush Ellen's hair one more time. She walks 'round Ellen, making sure that every detail is perfect. She smiles with a mother's satisfaction and takes a moment to marvel at what a radiant young woman Ellen is, inside and out. Stopping in front of Ellen, she sighs, satisfied that Ellen would approve. She points to Ellen, places her fist on her chest, points to her own eyes, points to the full-length looking glass, points to Ellen again, tilting her head to the side, asking Ellen if she would like to look at herself in it. Raising her gaze up to Anna, Ellen nods, stands and walks to the looking glass. As Anna holds her breath, maternal emotion welling up within her, Ellen moves closer, staring at herself. Ellen is the most breath-taking vision she has ever seen, and hopes, no, prays, that Ellen is not afraid of the beauty she sees in the looking glass, staring at herself from head to toe.

Staring into the looking glass, Ellen steps closer to touch her reflection. Watching Ellen, Anna takes in her gleaming blonde tresses that have a natural wave, extending past her shoulders, and down her back. The gown Ellen asked Anna to make is breathtaking and causes her skin to bloom with youthful anticipation. It is ethereal, diaphanous silk with a lightweight silk undergown in the faintest shade of pink that flows and silently floats about her as if it were a pleasant dream. Accentuating Ellen's form, a fitted bodice, worked into a swirl from top to waist makes her look as if she is standing even straighter, with dignity. The layers of silk petticoat gathered with care, add fullness to the silently drifting cloud that a mother's love stitched together with care. The cloud-like dress floats and swirls at the mere hint of breath. Ellen's bared shoulders gleam in the sunlight that rejoices through the stained-glass window and surrounds Ellen with a glow of joy that pales next to the bride-to-be's beauty. Ellen puts her foot out from under the skirt to look at the pale pink shoes that match her gown, wiggles her foot back and forth, and then tucks her foot away, under the floor-length creation.

Reluctantly tapping Ellen's arm, hating to break Ellen's gaze from her own visage, Anna waits for Ellen to look down at her arm and then back up at her. She points to Ellen, alternates placing one fist on the other several times, points to herself, and then draws a smile on her own face. She needs to tell Ellen that she makes her happy. Smiling, Ellen turns her gaze back to the looking glass, and Anna hopes that Ellen sees a princess. Her little girl is a princess, especially today when she should feel like royalty. Anna pats Ellen's arm to get her attention, and, again, waits for Ellen to look down at her arm and back up at her. She points to Ellen, moves her hands down the front of herself, and pats her hands together to ask Ellen if she feels all right since Ellen is not gesturing.

She looks at the lady, points to herself, and draws a circle 'round her face.

Seeing the tears in Ellen's eyes and the shy smile on her face, Anna's tears break through to watch her daughter say that she is pretty. For the first time in Ellen's life, unafraid of her scars and her past, she expresses acceptance of her beauty. Anna nods, points to Ellen and draws a circle 'round her face as she whispers.

"Oh, baby girl, you've always been pretty."

She holds out her arms to gather Ellen into hers, no longer her little girl, but her princess who's about to become a married woman. With happy tears, Ellen walks into her mother's arms, and they hold one another, one, a young woman about to marry the man she treasures, and an overjoyed mother who is ready to let her daughter dance into the arms of the man who is utterly devoted to her. Stepping back, Anna wipes away a tear from Ellen's cheek with her thumb and kisses her cheek. She holds up one finger and reaches into her pocket. Drawing out the gold filigree brooch with the dark pink stone set in the centre that had belonged to the mother Ellen never knew, Anna holds it up for Ellen to see it. She points to the spot at the waistline where the bodice swirls to meet the skirt and tilts her head to the side. Ellen's smile and a nod are all the encouragement Anna needs to affix this heirloom to Ellen's gown. Stepping back further, Anna studies Ellen, burning this moment into her memory.

Ellen stands with her hands folded in front of herself. Smiling, she walks close to Anna, takes her hand, and draws her to stand in front of the looking glass, mother and daughter standing together. Looking at their reflection, Anna wishes someone were there to take a photograph of them together. It would not just be of two happy women, but of fresh beginnings.

Looking at their reflections, Anna sees Ellen turns to her.

She points to herself, points to her own head, and flutters her hands.

Ellen sits down on the chair nearby, looking down at her dress. Anna crouches down in front of Ellen, realising that Ellen has much to say but no means by which to communicate her thoughts, and she feels Ellen's frustration. She takes Ellen's hands in her own and gives them a reassuring squeeze as she looks into Ellen's eyes. She points to Ellen, points to Ellen's heart, moves her fingers by her mouth to mimic talking, then points to herself, and points to her own heart to say that Ellen's heart speaks to her own heart. Ellen nods and watches Anna point to the door, hold up one finger, tap three fingers on her chest, and then point to the door again to tell her that outside, waiting, John is there, ready to come in to see his little girl. Again, Ellen nods, a smile coaxing the corners of her mouth.

Anna smiles as she takes one last glance at Ellen, slips out of the room, closing the door behind her; pent-up tears flowing freely in spite of the handkerchief's feeble attempt to stem their course. She everyone gathered outside and tries to smile through her tears, hoping she does not look a dreadful sight for being the mother of the bride. John is the first to notice her emerge from the church and a passing shadow of alarm drops over him at Anna's tears. He fears that Ellen has become too anxious to go through with the ceremony, although, she has not shown any signs of such. He walks over to Anna, drawing close and employs a confidential tone.

"Anna, is everything all right?"

She smiles through her tears and nods, struggling to regain her composure.

"Everything is fine, John. She's beautiful. She's so beautiful."

She turns to everyone gathered and smiles at them with tearful laughter.

"She's beautiful!"

The touch of Lady Ashton's gloved hand on her shoulder startles Anna and the rest of the company assembled. In a soft voice, she speaks to Anna.

"I'm sure your daughter is as lovely as you are, Anna."

The grand lady had approached them with the stealth of a shadow. John regains his senses first and formally addresses her.

"M'Lady, this is an unexpected surprise. It's kind of you to be here. To what do we owe the honour?"

The Dowager Countess of Ashton sheds her title and all its grand accoutrements and assumes the humanity of her common Christian name, Emma Wardley.

"You see, I've come to honour the young woman, Ellen. She gave me the gift of viewing the world and myself, again, as I did when I was a young girl. I'm only here to wish Ellen and, of course, William, all the happiness they deserve."

"How kind of you. We appreciate your desire to be with us today. May I escort you to your family's pew at the front?"

John offers his arm, prepared to escort Lady Ashton, but she waves away his formality with a smile and a flick of her hand.

"Thank you, John. That's kind of you, but I prefer to see myself in to sit in the back, unnoticed."

Emma Wardley pats John's arm, turns, and enters the church without pretence or fanfare. Sarah, arriving with Johanna, walks up to Anna who is still speechless at Lady Ashton's presence, notices that Anna has been crying.

"Ma'am...I mean, Anna, what's wrong?"

"Mamma hava owie?"

Anna smiles at Sarah, leans over to kiss her cheek, and crouches down to give Johanna a kiss, as well, caressing her little girl's rosy cheek. Standing, she speaks to Sarah.

"Everything is perfect, Sarah. Ellen is so lovely. I haven't the words…Johanna, Ellen is pretty!"

Smiling, Johanna draws a circle 'round her face and then claps her hands.

"Cuppa petty! Janna petty likka Cuppa?"

"Yes, my love, you're as pretty as Ellen. Now, you're a big girl, and you'll sit nicely with Sarah, won't you, sweetheart?"

Johanna grows solemn and nods her head, looking from her mother to Sarah, and then to her daddy. Sarah smiles and takes Johanna's hand.

"Johanna, let's go inside and sit where your Mamma and Daddy told me we should sit."

Nodding to Anna, then to John, Sarah walks with Johanna into the church. The little girl turns awkwardly, waving, as she keeps up with Sarah.

"Janna be good for Daddy!"

Anna turns to a chuckling John and kisses his cheek.

"John, your daughter is waiting for you."

Smiling, John nods and walks into the church to see his daughter, the bride. As they all watch him disappear into the church, Clara clears her throat.

"Well, I reckon it's time. Shall we go in?"

Nodding, Anna walks over to William, takes his hand, and kisses his cheek.

"Shall the mother of the bride and the groom walk in together?"

Grinning, he cannot help but think of calling Anna 'Mum' as he extends his arm for her to allow him to escort her.

"I'd be honoured, Anna."

They walk into the church, followed by Clara who nods to Father Willington, who is just stepping into his office. In the little room where Anna has helped Ellen dress for the occasion, John's breath catches in his throat, impacted by her radiance. Ellen is a demure young woman, sitting on a chair, her hands folded in her lap. She looks up at him and smiles. John is captivated by his daughter's beauty and whispers through the tears that affect his voice as he gestures.

"My baby."

He points to Ellen, points to himself, and then cradles his arms as if holding a baby to tell her that she is his little girl. He points to Ellen, draws a circle 'round his face to also tell her that she is pretty. He cannot help but smile at Ellen's typical shyness when she receives compliments. She smiles, looks down at her hands in her lap, and her cheeks colour to match the pink of her gown. John walks over to her and extends his hand to help her stand. Ellen takes his hand and stands up, looking into his eyes.

She points to the man, points to herself, places her fist against her chest, and pats it as a parent would pat a baby's back.

John fights the urge to allow his tears free reign when he sees Ellen tell him that he is her father. He opens his arms and Ellen steps into them, the two of them embracing with all the tenderness a father and daughter share. Unwilling to suspend this moment, he rocks her gently, whispering words of affection the father of the bride would utter at such a time. Stepping back from each other, John takes out his pocket watch and taps it, telling Ellen that it is time for them to walk up the aisle. Ellen nods in reply and then tilts her head to the side when John holds up one finger. He slips his pocket watch back in his waistcoat pocket and pulls out a small, silver, filigree watch on a neck chain. Ellen's eyes grow wide, and John fastens the necklace 'round her neck. It drapes perfectly, almost touching the neckline of the dress Anna created for her. She touches it, picks it up to look at it, and then taps it, nodding as she looks up to him. He points to himself, places his hand over his heart, and points to Ellen, telling her that he loves her.

She points to herself, puts her hand over her heart, and points to the man.

A knock at the door interrupts the last private moment of a father with his little girl before she takes her vows to become the wedded wife of a good man. John steps over to the door and opens it a crack, surprised at Father Willington with a perplexed expression on his face.

"John, ahh, we may have a problem. People are filing into the church and filling the pews. John, they've taken leave of their jobs today to come here to honour Ellen. What shall I do? Should I turn them away?"

Considering the situation, John smiles at Father Willington.

"It's not our choice. The decision belongs to Ellen."

John turns towards Ellen who is tilting her head to the side, watching John and Father Willington speak with one another. John points in the general direction of the knave, walks his fingers across the palm of his hand, points to his own eyes, points to Ellen, taps two fingers on his wrist, and then interlocks the forefingers and thumbs of both hands to tell Ellen that many people have come to the church to celebrate her marriage to William. He tilts his head to the side, points to Ellen and then pats his hands together to ask her if this is all right. Ellen pauses, staring at John and Father Willington before she gestures her answer.

She points to the man, taps two fingers on her chest, taps two fingers on her wrist, places one palm against the other and sweeping one away from herself, and then points to herself.

John shakes his head, silently telling Ellen that he, Anna, and William will not leave her. A sigh of relief escapes both men to see Ellen nod her head and step closer to John.

"Well, Father, I guess that's our answer."

Father Willington smiles with relief and nods his head to Ellen.

"Yes, I'm glad. I'll make my way to the front, and the two of you may come out when you're ready."

The door closing behind the good Father, John turns to Ellen, points to the watch hanging from the chain 'round her neck, taps it, and smiles as he offers his arm to escort the bride down the aisle to her future. Ellen smiles, takes John's arm, and they walk out of the little room together and into the knave where a sea of people awaits the service. John and Ellen stand upon the red carpet leading to the altar, keenly aware of William and Anna watching them as they await the signal from Father Willington to approach. Father Willington smiles at the sight of Ellen standing with her happy father, a vision of beauty, waiting to proceed. A nod from the good Father turns John's tender gaze to Ellen as he looks down at his daughter. He straightens his shoulders with pride, and they slowly begin their walk to the altar where William and Anna wait.

A wave of rustling passes through the crowd of people as they stand and turn to watch the simple procession. Ellen stares 'round her, clutching John's arm a little more tightly. As they start walking, the man who showed her how to paint catches Ellen's eye, points to her, points to his own head, and then points to himself, asking the bride if she remembers him. Her eyes misting, Ellen smiles and nods. Amazement overcomes John, seeing first-hand the people in their town who care enough to learn her language. With a few more paces behind them, a woman, the same woman who brought Ellen lemonade at the farmhouse, points to Ellen and then draws a circle 'round her face to tell Ellen she is pretty. Ellen's breathing comes more heavily, and John looks down at her, afraid that all of these people are making Ellen fearful. But, no,

Ellen is smiling and fighting back her tears. He gives her hand a reassuring pat and then looks ahead at William. His mouth agape, showing awe at his bride's beauty, he watches her glide towards him.

Further, down the aisle, a little girl pushes her way to the end of the pew. The child she had helped in the flowerbed at the farm looks up at Ellen and holds out a flower. Smiling, Ellen releases John's arm for a moment, crouches down, takes the flower from the little girl, and caresses her cheek. She looks up at him, smiling, then stands and takes his arm, again, John hearing the little girl's footsteps patter back to her mother's side. Coming to the foremost pew where Sarah, Johanna, and Clara are seated, the three are turned 'round to witness their approach. Ellen looks to Sarah who points to herself, places her hand over her heart, and then points to Ellen to tell her that she loves her.

She smiles at the kind lady, points to herself, and then points to her own head.

That small gesture is a great comfort to Sarah to know that Ellen accepts and understands her deep affection. Even Johanna, standing on the pew with her waist encircled by Sarah's protective arm, waves to Ellen with a wide-eyed smile and Ellen returns the wave with graceful subtlety. William's attention is unwaveringly focused, and he is unaware of the rustling of the congregation sitting down. His eyes open wide with a catch of his breath, stunned by the sight of the most radiant person he has ever seen. The person that he always felt was pretty, but today, right now, Ellen is even more beautiful than he ever imagined. Finally, John and Ellen arrive at the altar with Anna to Ellen's left and John taking his place to William's right, the four of them turning to face the altar. Father Willington smiles down at the bride and groom and then lifts his head to look out over the myriad of faces who are giving their rapt attention. Father Willington begins the service, simple enough to accommodate Ellen's language, yet satisfying the legal necessities.

"Family and friends, we are here to witness the marriage of William and Ellen, today."

He gestures 'round to everyone assembled, points down to the floor, points to his own eyes, the points to William and Ellen, then links together the thumbs and forefingers of his hands.

"I will be using the languages that both Ellen and William understand. This is their wedding, and we honour both of them as we include both languages."

He points to himself, moves his hand near his mouth to signify speaking, points to William and Ellen, points to his own head, and then holds up his hands to display the gesturing language Ellen uses to communicate. He lifts both hands, palms up, and then pats his hands together to say that both languages are good.

He turns to William with a smile.

"William, do you want to marry Ellen?"

He points to William, taps two fingers on his wrist, places a fist on his chest, then links together the thumbs and forefingers of his hands, then points to Ellen, then places two fingers against his own cheek. William turns to look at Ellen.

"I do."

William points to himself, places a fist over his heart, links together the thumbs and forefingers of his hands then points to Ellen, saying that he wants to marry her. His heart melts at Ellen's smile whilst she looks into his eyes. Knowing that Father Willington will address Ellen next, Anna pats Ellen's arm, waits for her to look down and then back up at her. She points at Father Willington to draw her attention to him.

"Ellen, do you want to marry William?"

He points to Ellen, places two fingers against his cheek, places a fist on his chest, then links together the thumbs and forefingers of his hands, then points to William and then taps two fingers on his wrist.

She watches the collar man, turns to the young man, points to herself, places a fist against her chest, links together the thumbs and forefingers of her hands, points to the young man, smiles, and takes his hand, nodding her head.

Continuing, he speaks to William who looks up at him, after reluctantly pulling his gaze away from the woman he adores.

"You may place the ring on Ellen's finger so that everyone can know your love for her."

He points to William and pantomimes putting a ring on the fourth finger of the left hand, points to Ellen, gestures 'round to those assembled, points to his own eyes, points to William, places his hand on his heart, and then points to Ellen. William reaches into his pocket, produces the ring, as she turns to look at him. He takes her hand and slips the symbol of his troth onto her finger. He points to himself, places a hand over his heart and points to her to say 'I love you' whilst he whispers those words. Again, his heart overflows with happiness to make their mutual endearment public, official and real for a lifetime. He is aware of only Ellen's smile that mirrors his own joy as she gazes at him and then looks down to touch the ring that will remind her of William's devotion, each moment, for the rest of her life. Smiling as Anna and Father Willington see that Ellen only has eyes for William and the ring gracing her finger, she leans towards Ellen to gently pat her on the arm to attract her attention, waiting for her to look down at her arm and then back up at her. Anna places the ring for William in Ellen's hand and then Anna points to Father Willington. Nodding, Ellen looks back up at him.

"Ellen, you may place the ring on William's finger so that everyone can see your love for him."

He points to Ellen, pantomimes putting a ring on the fourth finger of the left hand, points to William, gestures 'round to those assembled, points to his own eyes, points to Ellen, places his hand on his heart, and points to William. She turns to face William, smiles, takes his hand, and slips the ring onto William's finger.

She points to herself, places her hand over her heart and points to him.

Father Willington smiles, his heart full of happiness for this dear young couple, hopeful and confident that they will share devoted adoration for all time. Now, Ellen looks back up without prompting, following William's gaze.

"I now pronounce you man and wife. William and Ellen, you may kiss for the first time as a married couple."

He points to himself, moves his hand near his mouth to connote talking, points to William, points to Ellen, and then links together the thumbs and forefingers of his hands. He points to William as he taps two fingers on his wrist, then to Ellen as he places two fingers against his cheek, nods, and taps his lips with his finger. William and Ellen turn to look at one another, and he takes a step closer, tapping his lips with his finger. With wide eyes, she looks at him, then looks at the congregation, and looks back up at him. Recognising her reserve in kissing in front of so many people, he holds his finger and thumb close together, to say 'a small kiss'. Nodding, the young couple leans towards each other, clasping their hands together, and share a brief but tender kiss. Leaning back from their display of shared bliss, William smiles and holds her hand. He guides her to turn, so they are both facing the assembly gathered to honour their union. Father Willington smiles broadly, extends his arms as if embracing every soul gathered and makes his announcement.

"I am honoured to introduce, Mr and Mrs William Tenney."

Under his breath, he whispers.

"God grant you love, prosperity, and peace through all the days God gives you on this earth."

Once again, the assembled members of the local populace rise to their feet and witness a joyous William turning to Ellen, smiling at her, and beginning their walk back down the aisle. Ellen returns William's gaze and smile before casting a glance across the filled church. As of one mind, John and Anna move close to one another, reaching for and grasping hands. Allowing their happy tears to flow freely, their parental fulfilment could not be more apparent as they watch their daughter and her husband make their way towards a new life together. Coming to the back of the church, William reaches out to open the door. Abruptly, Ellen stops, squeezing William's hand tighter. He turns to her, tilting his head to the side, but Ellen's eyes are not on him. John and Anna look at one another and then back to Ellen, dabbing at their tears, wondering if anything is amiss. Together, they look at their daughter and son-in-law, smiling their encouragement and boundless care to them. Ellen stares up to the front of the church at John and Anna, tears making her eyes sparkle as a smile glows upon her lips.

She stares at the man and lady, points to herself, places a hand over her heart, and then points to them.

Ellen looks up at William, smiles, squeezes his hand, and then looks back at John and Anna, lifting her hand, and waves.

The Final Chapter
1987

Elaine Hastings looks out over the well-kept grounds of the cemetery. She begins to walk towards four familiar headstones, lined next to one another. Upon reaching the first, she places her hand atop the deathly cold stone and shivers in the March wind. Crouching, she looks at it, memories coursing through her mind as she traces the inscribed name, John Thorpe.

"Poppy, I love you and miss you. Always."

Rising to her feet with help from her grandfather's headstone, she walks over to the second marker. Stooping, her knees complaining bitterly, she places one hand atop the stone to maintain her balance. With her fingertip guided by the smells, sights, and memories of childhood, she traces the name, Anna Thorpe, engraved upon it.

"Granna, I'll never forget anything about you. I will always keep you in my heart."

Grumbles come from Elaine's back as she rights herself straight and looks at the third stone that calls to her with a familiar voice in her mind. She covers the short distance to it, leans down to kiss the top of it, holds the curved top of the marker, and ignores her knees' protests. Crouching down, she touches the name carved into its cold marble. The inscription blurs, thanks to her misting eyes. With more recent memories in mind, she rests her forehead against the stone, its cool surface mirroring the emptiness in her heart, the wind of sorrow still howling through her emotional abyss. William Tenney.

"Dad, I will forever cherish you and the love you showed Mum and me. You and Mum taught me how to love...and how to live. I'm thankful to God each day that you were...are my daddy."

Her whisper cut short by the all-too-familiar lump in her throat, she points to herself, draws a smile on her face, points to the grave, points to herself, and then places her fist against her chest, patting it with her other hand. Unable to say it, she tells her father in her mother's language of gestures, that she is happy that he was her father. She expresses herself to him by pointing to herself, placing her hand over her heart, and pointing to the mound of dirt under which her father lies. Clearing her throat and finding her voice, again, she continues her one-sided conversation.

"I'm glad you both knew David. He's much like you, Dad. He was more than fond of you, and you held his respect from the first day he met you. He still feels that way. David wanted me to...to say that he wishes he'd known you longer, and he sends his love."

Her joints whining about the deathly chill of a cloudy, English day, she struggles to her feet once more, walks to the last tombstone, and kneels. Tears cloud her vision as she reaches out, placing her palm against the name of her mother, Ellen Tenney.

"Mum...I...This is the last time I can come to visit. I have..."

Choking on her words, as if saying them aloud makes the reality harsher, she stares at the stone, imagining her mum's generous heart and loving face.

"I have cancer, and I haven't long left to live. The doctors have done everything...but it's spread...everywhere. David hasn't left my side through all of this. You'd be proud of him, Mum. I...I don't want to die and leave David, Iris, our grandchildren, Aunt Johanna, Cousin Christianna..."

She thinks of the people who will mourn her death as they had grieved the ends of cherished lives that passed before. Elaine wipes away her tears, and with them, thoughts of her own mortality.

"Mum, I want to tell you how proud I was and am that you are my mum. You were always patient in every way. You taught me so many things I could never have learnt in school. The lessons that I brought from school fascinated you. You encouraged me to learn, as you'd point to the book and paper, and then tap my head. I wanted you to feel proud of me as much as I was, and am proud of you."

Taking a deep breath, her lungs burning with the effort of speaking so much at one time, she swallows and bares her soul.

"I never told you this, Mum, but I'm sure you remember that day I came running home from school, in tears. I ran past you to my bedroom without greeting or cuddling with you as I always did. You came into my room, finding me curled up on my bed, sobbing. You sat down next to me and began to rub my back. Your touch only made me cry harder. I remember how you leant down to kiss my cheek, and I looked up into your eyes. You tilted your head to the side, pointed to me, drew a frown on your face, and then traced a line down from your eye to ask me why I was so upset. I...I couldn't bear to tell you, then. You smiled at me, nodded, and opened your arms to me. I crawled into your lap, you rocked me, and I felt safe. Mum, do you know why I cried that day?"

Closing her eyes, Elaine remembers that day, etched in her mind as indelibly as the names carved on the headstones before her.

"Some children at school were mocking you to my face because you couldn't hear or speak or read or write. They called you...names. Bad names. Even now, I can't say them because they still hurt my heart. I was so furious and hurt that I began to cry. All I could say was 'Leave her alone. SHE'S MY MUM!' and then, I ran all the way home. Mum, I didn't care that you were different. I didn't think you were different. I thought you were special and blessed. I loved our silent home. Mum, you could hear things with your soul that others could never understand. You were always wise and honest with me, and you loved me so much. I never had to question what you meant when you talked to me in our family language. Mummy, you were the most precious mother I could have ever imagined. I wouldn't have wanted anyone else."

Recalling nights that were less than peaceful, she rests her hand upon the prickled turf that blankets her mother.

"Dad knew when I was little, that your nightmares gave me such a fright. He taught me how to help you through them and that made me less afraid. Sometimes, even though Dad was already there, I'd run into your bedroom to help, and all I wanted was for you to wake up and not be in that terrible dream anymore. I wanted you to come back and see that Dad and I were with you. That was our family. We supported and helped each other."

Shortness of breath stops her from further speech, her hand resting against her chest until that moment of breathless panic subsides. Elaine looks over her shoulder at David, standing next to their car, who is watching her. Bowing her head, her voice lowers to a whisper, her breath growing more laboured with each word.

"You and Dad, the way you adored each other, set an example for me. I wanted the kind of marriage you had. When David and I met, to me, it felt as though we were replaying what you and Dad shared. Thank you for teaching me about love. Thank you for teaching me to wait for the precious relationship that David and I have."

Her legs growing numb from kneeling, she shifts to sit on the ground, still hard and cold from winter's choking grip, seated between her parents' final resting places. Resting there, her need to bare her heart in words gives way to memories that belong only to the living, now, her eyes closing as her mind drifts.

...3 March 1986 was a cruel day, yet the suffering was finished. At least it was for Ellen. In the days prior, Elaine and her daughter Iris, Aunt Johanna, and her daughter Christianna relieved one another in shifts, keeping vigil at Ellen's bedside with William. Husbands and sons remained downstairs, ready to fetch anything for those tending to

William and Ellen's every need. The hospice nurse would come into the bedroom, perform her duties, and quietly take her leave. Her body language would silently inform them of Ellen's condition. William rarely left his wife's side. Sometimes she would open her eyes to smile at him, squeeze his hand with the little strength she had left and then close her eyes to sleep the sleep of the living. William would join Ellen in slumber, resting his head on his arms upon the bed, never letting her hand slip away from his. He looked so thin and weary, those last days. Elaine, Iris, Johanna, and Christianna would attempt to coax him away to rest. He would smile at them, shake his head, look back at Ellen, and entwine his fingers with hers.

That last day, Ellen's breathing changed. It was more laborious and shallow, and she was more restless because of it. Not even the application of oxygen calmed her patient. The hospice nurse would assess Ellen more frequently and then give her medication to calm her and make breathing easier. The four women walked into the hallway with the hospice nurse. Again, as they had many times before, they asked her to coax William away to get proper rest, for the sake of his own health. Shaking her head, the nurse spoke gentle words.

'He needs to stay with her, now. You should all remain close. I'll go downstairs and...'

Watching the nurse nod and walk away, four hearts silently shattered. They knew the time was near, but none were ready to hear those words. They walked back into the bedroom that William and Ellen had shared for over sixty years and stood to the side, glances exchanged between them. As one, they felt wrong to intrude on these intimate moments between William and Ellen. Quietly, the four women slipped out of the room and into the hallway to comfort each other. They remained just outside the door to watch, outsiders looking in at the culmination of sixty-one years of two people who lived for each other.

William's warm hands cupped Ellen's cold hands as he looked at the face that would always be young and beautiful to him. Even now, in the end, he beheld a graceful beauty that could only hint at her radiant, honest, and pure soul. Ellen opened her eyes and turned her head to look at William, tears welling up from her soul that was still very much alive. The effort to move caused her breath to come in short puffs that sought life-giving air. She pulled her hand away from William's grasp, took hold of the watch necklace that lay on her chest, and held it up. She tapped it, and held it out to him, telling William that it was time. He unclasped the necklace from 'round her neck, curling his fingers 'round the warm metal that nudges time along, unbearably forwards. William tilted his head to the side, knowing more than that frail body before him, but also knowing the strong spirit within her.

She places her hands together at her chest and moves them towards the young man.

Again, he tilted his head to the side, asking why she would ask him for forgiveness. Reaching out, he wiped away a tear from her cheek with his thumb.

She points to herself, sweeps one palm across the other, away from herself, and points to the young man.

He closed his eyes, shaking his head, remembering his own promise to never leave her. Now, she asks his forgiveness for leaving him. Opening his eyes to peer into hers, he pointed to himself, traced an X in the palm of his hand, swept one palm across the other, away from himself, and then pointed to Ellen, reaffirming his promise that he would never leave her. Tucking the watch necklace in his shirt pocket and taking her hand in his, again, he watched her eyes close, then she opened them to look at him, then they would flutter closed, again. Allowing himself to weep, he took Ellen's hand in his, curled her fingers within his, leaving her forefinger extended. He pointed to himself with her hand held in this way, and then gently opened her fingers and placed her hand over his heart that beat only for her. Again, he took her hand, curling her fingers in his, leaving her forefinger extended, and pointed her finger to herself. It was the only way he could tell her that he loved her.

Ellen's breathing slowed, would stop for a moment, and then begin again with a gasp. Placing his hand over her heart, he could feel the life ticking within her as the watch in his pocket does, slowing, and eventually stopping. Her hand in his, his other hand touching the shell that held her heart, he felt Ellen's last breath sigh away from her. She no longer slept the sleep of the living, but dreamt, now, without nightmares, of eternity. Desperately clutching what strength of will he had in him, he regained his composure enough to bring her hand to his lips, and then rest it across her, his hand unwilling to leave hers. Standing, William leant over, caressed her cheek, kissed her forehead one last time, and whispered.

'Good-bye, for now, my sweet Cup.'

A slap of wind rudely pulls Elaine back to the present, strangely energising in its suddenness.

"Mum, I know, I tell you some of these things every time I visit, but it's good to remember. I hope you know that after you...when you were gone from us, we tried to take care of Dad. He sat in your favourite chair, holding your necklace watch, looking at a worn piece of paper he pulled from his wallet. You'd written your name so long ago on the paper. That was the day he knew you were the one he wanted to have in his life forever. We brought Dad food, tea, anything that was his favourite. He just smiled, shook his head, and whispered, 'Thank you'. He wouldn't eat or drink anything. We would tell him that we loved him. He would smile, nod, point to himself, and then point to his head. Then, he would point to himself, place his hand over his heart, and point to us. Mum, he knew we loved him, and we knew that he loved us. We would ask him if he was all right, and he would shake his head, point to himself, put his fingers together and draw one down from the other to tell us he was broken. Six days after you left us, I wanted Dad to eat something, anything. We knew he was slipping away from us, as you did, and we couldn't bear to lose him, too. I kissed his cheek, patted his arm, and promised to make him his favourite soup, just the way you made it, Mum. He smiled at me, nodded, and turned back to stare at the fireplace. When I returned with the tray of food, he...he'd gone to be with you, Mum. He always said he couldn't live without you, and he kept his word. His eyes were closed; a smile touched the corners of his lips. His hand, gone slack, still held your watch necklace, and the piece of paper with your name on it had drifted to the floor."

Feeling the need to use her inhaler, she reaches into her pocket and produces the hated evidence that her lungs would not sustain her life much longer. Elaine puffs it twice and pauses to let it work before she can utter another word. Tears do not pour down her face; sobs do not wrack her body. A warming peace begins to course through her veins.

"Mum, I've worn your watch necklace every day since and I framed that piece of paper to pass down to your granddaughter. Soon, Iris shall wear this. Very soon."

She holds up the watch necklace, taps it and whispers.

"It's time."

Although peace warms her spirit, her body is frigid with cold and resists multiple attempts to rise to her feet. Unwilling to give up, she reaches out and grasps the gravestones on either side of her. As her parents did in life, their death markers now support and allow their daughter to gain her footing in spite of the dizziness floating about her.

Deep breathing calms her body's stubborn acts of submission to cancer, and she steps back a pace. She tells her parents for the last time that she loves them by pointing to herself, placing her hand over her heart, and pointing to the ones who, not only gave her life but also taught her how to live. Bowing her head, she watches her paces crunch along as she makes her way towards the man standing next to the car.

Elaine walks with a stumble into David's outstretched arms. They hold one another for as long as they need to do so. David speaks softly.

"Sweetheart, are you all right?"

Elaine nodding, backs away a pace, points to herself, places her hand over her heart, and with tears finally breaking free, she points to the man who is the life of her soul. A smile that can only come from devotion to someone who completes you illuminates David's face. He points to himself and then points to his own head to tell Elaine that he knows that she loves him. He points to himself, places his hand over his heart, and then points to Elaine. Through her tears, she smiles, points to herself, and then points to her own head. As if of one mind, they gather each other into another embrace, two souls communicating what no one else can hear.

Thank you for being a part

of Ellen's world.

Ellen's journey isn't finished...
"CUP, The Continuation"

Rob and Rachael

About the Authors

Rachael K. Kasper

Drawing from a diverse set of interests, Rachael brings her nursing skills and knowledge of medical history to the table with this project. Her study and experience as a historical re-enactor and portraying women's roles in living history events give her a first-hand perspective on society's evolution with time. Over the years, she has written in several genres about nursing from the perspectives of the patient, family, and caregiver. Rachael lives with brain damage and the debilitating effects of fibromyalgia, and she works hard to inspire herself to prove that every day can have moments of success in spite of insurmountable odds.

Robert E. Wills

After working at an insurance company's home office, having helped create a successful department, he took a position in Financial Control with a mutual fund firm. In later years, deciding to leave the corporate environment, he accepted a position in journalism with a local, small-town newspaper, where he enjoyed writing human interest articles. He continues to work with the publication in advertising, and graphic design. Robert believes that words and behaviours that we express towards others are of great importance in creating a positive interaction with all people he meets.

As a Team

Robert Wills and Rachael Kasper have collaborated on various creative and entertainment endeavours over the past few years. They have written short stories that were an exercise in collaborative teamwork and shared among a group of like-minded wordsmiths. In addition to their partnership in writing, they form two of a trio that records a weekly syndicated variety radio show that is now, heard 'round the world. The show is unique in that it is ad lib and unedited. They were honoured in a special session of the Vermont State House of Representatives. By a concurrent house resolution (HR 10), Timeless Oldies Variety Show and its hosts Dex Rowe, Robert Wills, and Rachael Kasper were given special recognition. Their innovative utilization of internet technologies, personal expertise and enjoyment of music spanning a century, serves to entertain people around the world. Currently, Timeless Oldies Variety Show is heard in 67 countries and carried on eight radio stations that use traditional broadcasting and internet streaming. The show is offered free of charge to the hosting stations and remains commercial-free and non-profit. The projects that appeal most to Robert and Rachael as a collaborative team are spontaneous, inspiring, and creative ventures that touch the heart.

Made in the USA
Monee, IL
05 October 2020